RANDOM HOUSE

LARGE PRINT

# THE COLLECTED SHORT STORIES OF LOUIS L'AMOUR

Also By Louis L'Amour
Available from Random House Large Print

NOVELS
**High Lonesome**
**Hondo**
**Kiowa Trail**

SHORT STORY COLLECTIONS
**The Collected Short Stories of Louis L'Amour (vols. 1–7)**
**From the Listening Hills**
**May There Be a Road**
**Off the Mangrove Coast**
**With These Hands**

SACKETT TITLES
**To the Far Blue Mountains**
**The Warrior's Path**
**Jubal Sackett**
**Ride the River**
**The Daybreakers**
**Sackett**
**Lando**
**Galloway**

# THE COLLECTED SHORT STORIES OF LOUIS L'AMOUR

THE FRONTIER STORIES:

*Volume 1*

Louis L'Amour

RANDOM HOUSE LARGE PRINT

Published in the United States of America by Random House Large Print in association with Bantam Books, New York.

Distributed by Random House, Inc., New York.



The Library of Congress has established a Cataloging-in-Publication record for this title.

ISBN: 978-0-7393-7746-8

www.randomhouse.com/largeprint

FIRST LARGE PRINT PAPERBACK EDITION

Printed in the United States of America

10 9 8 7 6 5 4 3 2 1

This Large Print edition published in accord with the standards of the N.A.V.H.

# *CONTENTS*

# THE COLLECTED SHORT STORIES OF LOUIS L'AMOUR

# *The Gift of Cochise*

Tense, and white to the lips, Angie Lowe stood in the door of her cabin with a double-barreled shotgun in her hands. Beside the door was a Winchester '73, and on the table inside the house were two Walker Colts.

Facing the cabin were twelve Apaches on ragged calico ponies, and one of the Indians had lifted his hand, palm outward. The Apache sitting the white-splashed bay pony was Cochise.

Beside Angie were her seven-year-old son Jimmy and her five-year-old daughter Jane.

Cochise sat his pony in silence; his black, unreadable eyes studied the woman, the children, the cabin, and the small garden. He looked at the two ponies in the corral and the three cows. His eyes strayed to the small stack of hay cut from the meadow, and to the few steers farther up the canyon.

Three times the warriors of Cochise had attacked this solitary cabin and three times they had been turned back. In all, they had lost seven men, and three had been wounded. Four ponies had been killed. His braves reported that there was no man in the house, only a woman and two children, so Cochise had come to see for himself this woman who was so certain a shot with a rifle and who killed his fighting men.

These were some of the same fighting men who had outfought, outguessed and outrun the finest American army on record, an army outnumbering the Apaches by a hundred to one. Yet a lone woman with two small children had fought them off, and the woman was scarcely more than a girl. And she was prepared to fight now. There was a glint of admiration in the old eyes that appraised her. The Apache was a fighting man, and he respected fighting blood.

"Where is your man?"

"He has gone to El Paso." Angie's voice was steady, but she was frightened as she had never been before. She recognized Cochise from descriptions, and she knew that if he decided to kill or capture her it would be done. Until now, the sporadic attacks she had fought off had been those of casual bands of warriors who raided her in passing.

"He has been gone a long time. How long?"

Angie hesitated, but it was not in her to lie. "He has been gone four months."

Cochise considered that. No one but a fool would leave such a woman, or such fine children. Only one thing could have prevented his return. "Your man is dead," he said.

Angie waited, her heart pounding with heavy, measured beats. She had guessed long ago that Ed had been killed but the way Cochise spoke did not imply that Apaches had killed him, only that he must be dead or he would have returned.

"You fight well," Cochise said. "You have killed my young men."

"Your young men attacked me." She hesitated, then added, "They stole my horses."

"Your man is gone. Why do you not leave?"

Angie looked at him with surprise. "Leave? Why, this is my home. This land is mine. This spring is mine. I shall not leave."

"This was an Apache spring," Cochise reminded her reasonably.

"The Apache lives in the mountains," Angie replied. "He does not need this spring. I have two children, and I do need it."

"But when the Apache comes this way, where shall he drink? His throat is dry and you keep him from water."

The very fact that Cochise was willing to talk raised her hopes. There had been a time when the Apache made no war on the white man. "Cochise speaks with a forked tongue," she said. "There is water yonder." She gestured toward the hills, where Ed had told her there were springs. "But if the people of Cochise come in peace they may drink at this spring."

The Apache leader smiled faintly. Such a woman would rear a nation of warriors. He nodded at Jimmy. "The small one—does he also shoot?"

"He does," Angie said proudly, "and well, too!" She pointed to an upthrust leaf of prickly pear. "Show them, Jimmy."

The prickly pear was an easy two hundred yards away, and the Winchester was long and heavy, but he lifted it eagerly and steadied it against the doorjamb as his father had taught him, held his sight an instant, then fired. The bud on top of the prickly pear disintegrated.

There were grunts of appreciation from the dark-faced warriors. Cochise chuckled. "The little warrior shoots well. It is well you have no man. You might raise an army of little warriors to fight my people."

"I have no wish to fight your people," Angie said quietly. "Your people have your ways, and I have mine. I live in peace when I am left in peace. I did not think," she added with dignity, "that the great Cochise made war on women!"

The Apache looked at her, then turned his pony away. "My people will trouble you no longer," he said. "You are the mother of a strong son."

"What about my two ponies?" she called after him. "Your young men took them from me."

Cochise did not turn or look back, and the little cavalcade of riders followed him away. Angie stepped back into the cabin and closed the door. Then she sat down abruptly, her face white, the muscles in her legs trembling.

When morning came, she went cautiously to the spring for water. Her ponies were back in the corral. They had been returned during the night.

Slowly, the days drew on. Angie broke a small piece of the meadow and planted it. Alone, she cut hay in the meadow and built another stack. She saw Indians several times, but they did not bother her. One morning, when she opened her door, a quarter of antelope lay on the step, but no Indian was in sight. Several times, during the weeks that followed, she saw moccasin tracks near the spring.

Once, going out at daybreak, she saw an Indian girl dipping water from the spring. Angie called to her, and the girl turned quickly, facing her. Angie walked toward her, offering a bright red silk ribbon. Pleased, the Apache girl left.

And the following morning there was another quarter of antelope on her step—but she saw no Indian.

Ed Lowe had built the cabin in West Dog Canyon in the spring of 1871, but it was Angie who chose the spot, not Ed. In Santa Fe they would have told you that Ed Lowe was good-looking, shiftless, and agreeable. He was, also, unfortunately handy with a pistol.

Angie's father had come from County Mayo to New York and from New York to the Mississippi, where he became a tough, brawling river boatman. In New Orleans, he met a beautiful Cajun girl and married her. Together, they started west for Santa Fe, and Angie was born en route. Both parents died of cholera when Angie was fourteen. She lived with an Irish family for the following three years, then married Ed Lowe when she was seventeen.

Santa Fe was not good for Ed, and Angie kept after him until they started south. It was Apache country, but they kept on until they reached the old Spanish ruin in West Dog. Here there were grass, water, and shelter from the wind.

There was fuel, and there were piñons and game. And Angie, with an Irish eye for the land, saw that it would grow crops.

The house itself was built on the ruins of the old Spanish building, using the thick walls and the floor. The location had been admirably chosen for defense. The house was built in a corner of the cliff, under the sheltering overhang, so that approach was possible from only two directions, both covered by an easy field of fire from the door and windows.

For seven months, Ed worked hard and steadily. He put in the first crop, he built the house, and proved himself a handy man with tools. He repaired the old plow they had bought, cleaned out the spring, and paved and walled it with slabs of stone. If he was lonely for the carefree companions of Santa Fe, he gave no indication of it. Provisions were low, and when he finally started off to the south, Angie watched him go with an ache in her heart.

SHE DID NOT know whether she loved Ed. The first flush of enthusiasm had passed, and Ed Lowe had proved something less than she had believed. But he had tried, she admitted. And it had not been easy for him. He was an amiable soul, given to whittling and idle talk, all of which he missed in the loneliness of the Apache country. And when he rode away, she had no idea whether she would ever see him again. She never did.

Santa Fe was far and away to the north, but the growing village of El Paso was less than a hundred miles to the west, and it was there Ed Lowe rode for supplies and seed.

He had several drinks—his first in months—in one of the saloons. As the liquor warmed his stomach, Ed Lowe looked around agreeably. For a moment, his eyes clouded with worry as he thought of his wife and children back in Apache country, but it was not in Ed Lowe to worry for long. He had another drink and leaned on the bar, talking to the bartender. All Ed had ever asked of life was enough to eat, a horse to ride, an occasional drink, and companions to talk with. Not that he had anything important to say. He just liked to talk.

Suddenly a chair grated on the floor, and Ed turned. A lean, powerful man with a shock of uncut black hair and a torn, weather-faded shirt stood at bay. Facing him across the table were three hard-faced young men, obviously brothers.

Ches Lane did not notice Ed Lowe watching from the bar. He had eyes only for the men facing him. "You done that deliberate!" The statement was a challenge.

The broad-chested man on the left grinned through broken teeth. "That's right, Ches. I done it deliberate. You killed Dan Tolliver on the Brazos."

"He made the quarrel." Comprehension came to Ches. He was boxed, and by three of the fighting, blood-hungry Tollivers.

"Don't make no difference," the broad-chested Tolliver said. " 'Who sheds a Tolliver's blood, by a Tolliver's hand must die!' "

Ed Lowe moved suddenly from the bar. "Three to one is long odds," he said, his voice low and friendly. "If the gent in the corner is willin', I'll side him."

Two Tollivers turned toward him. Ed Lowe was smiling easily, his hand hovering near his gun. "You stay out of this!" one of the brothers said harshly.

"I'm in," Ed replied. "Why don't you boys light a shuck?"

"No, by—!" The man's hand dropped for his gun, and the room thundered with sound.

Ed was smiling easily, unworried as always. His gun flashed up. He felt it leap in his hand, saw the nearest Tolliver smashed back, and he shot him again as he dropped. He had only time to see Ches Lane with two guns out and another Tolliver down when something struck him through the stomach and he stepped back against the bar, suddenly sick.

The sound stopped, and the room was quiet, and there was the acrid smell of powder smoke. Three Tollivers were down and dead, and Ed Lowe was dying. Ches Lane crossed to him.

"We got 'em," Ed said, "we sure did. But they got me."

Suddenly his face changed. "Oh, Lord in heaven, what'll Angie do?" And then he crumpled over on the floor and lay still, the blood staining his shirt and mingling with the sawdust.

Stiff-faced, Ches looked up. "Who was Angie?" he asked.

"His wife," the bartender told him. "She's up

northeast somewhere, in Apache country. He was tellin' me about her. Two kids, too."

Ches Lane stared down at the crumpled, used-up body of Ed Lowe. The man had saved his life.

One he could have beaten, two he might have beaten; three would have killed him. Ed Lowe, stepping in when he did, had saved the life of Ches Lane.

"He didn't say where?"

"No."

Ches Lane shoved his hat back on his head. "What's northeast of here?"

The bartender rested his hands on the bar. "Cochise," he said. . .

For more than three months, whenever he could rustle the grub, Ches Lane quartered the country over and back. The trouble was, he had no lead to the location of Ed Lowe's homestead. An examination of Ed's horse revealed nothing. Lowe had bought seed and ammunition, and the seed indicated a good water supply, and the ammunition implied trouble. But in that country there was always trouble.

A man had died to save his life, and Ches Lane had a deep sense of obligation. Somewhere that wife waited, if she was still alive, and it was up to him to find her and look out for her. He rode northeast, cutting for sign, but found none. Sandstorms had wiped out any hope of back-trailing Lowe. Actually, West Dog Canyon was more east than north, but this he had no way of knowing.

North he went, skirting the rugged San Andreas Mountains. Heat baked him hot, dry winds parched his skin. His hair grew dry and stiff and alkali-whitened. He rode north, and soon the Apaches knew of him. He fought them at a lonely water hole, and he fought them on the run. They killed his horse, and he switched his saddle to the spare and rode on. They cornered him in the rocks, and he killed two of them and escaped by night.

THEY TRAILED HIM through the White Sands, and he left two more for dead. He fought fiercely and bitterly, and would not be turned from his quest. He turned east through the lava beds and still more east to the Pecos. He saw only two white men, and neither knew of a white woman.

The bearded man laughed harshly. "A woman alone? She wouldn't last a month! By now the Apaches got her, or she's dead. Don't be a fool! Leave this country before you die here."

Lean, wind-whipped, and savage, Ches Lane pushed on. The Mescaleros cornered him in Rawhide Draw and he fought them to a standstill. Grimly, the Apaches clung to his trail.

The sheer determination of the man fascinated them. Bred and born in a rugged and lonely land, the Apaches knew the difficulties of survival;

they knew how a man could live, how he must live. Even as they tried to kill this man, they loved him, for he was one of their own.

Lane's jeans grew ragged. Two bullet holes were added to the old black hat. The slicker was torn; the saddle, so carefully kept until now, was scratched by gravel and brush. At night he cleaned his guns and by day he scouted the trails. Three times he found lonely ranch houses burned to the ground, the buzzard- and coyote-stripped bones of their owners lying nearby.

Once he found a covered wagon, its canvas flopping in the wind, a man lying sprawled on the seat with a pistol near his hand. He was dead and his wife was dead, and their canteens rattled like empty skulls.

Leaner every day, Ches Lane pushed on. He camped one night in a canyon near some white oaks. He heard a hoof click on stone and he backed away from his tiny fire, gun in hand.

The riders were white men, and there were two of them. Joe Tompkins and Wiley Lynn were headed west, and Ches Lane could have guessed why. They were men he had known before, and he told them what he was doing.

Lynn chuckled. He was a thin-faced man with lank yellow hair and dirty fingers. "Seems a mighty strange way to get a woman. There's some as comes easier."

"This ain't for fun," Ches replied shortly. "I got to find her."

Tompkins stared at him. "Ches, you're crazy! That gent declared himself in of his own wish and desire. Far's that goes, the gal's dead. No woman could last this long in Apache country."

At daylight, the two men headed west, and Ches Lane turned south.

Antelope and deer are curious creatures, often led to their death by curiosity. The longhorn, soon going wild on the plains, acquires the same characteristic. He is essentially curious. Any new thing or strange action will bring his head up and his ears alert. Often a longhorn, like a deer, can be lured within a stone's throw by some queer antic, by a handkerchief waving, by a man under a hide, by a man on foot.

This character of the wild things holds true of the Indian. The lonely rider who fought so desperately and knew the desert so well soon became a subject of gossip among the Apaches. Over the fires of many a rancheria they discussed this strange rider who seemed to be going nowhere, but always riding, like a lean wolf dog on a trail. He rode across the mesas and down the canyons; he studied sign at every water hole; he looked long from every ridge. It was obvious to the Indians that he searched for something—but what?

★ ★ ★

COCHISE HAD COME again to the cabin in West Dog Canyon. "Little warrior too small," he said, "too small for hunt. You join my people. Take Apache for man."

"No." Angie shook her head. "Apache ways are good for the Apache, and the white man's ways are good for white men—and women."

They rode away and said no more, but that night, as she had on many other nights after the children were asleep, Angie cried. She wept silently, her head pillowed on her arms. She was as pretty as ever, but her face was thin, showing the worry and struggle of the months gone by, the weeks and months without hope.

The crops were small but good. Little Jimmy worked beside her. At night, Angie sat alone on the steps and watched the shadows gather down the long canyon, listening to the coyotes yapping from the rim of the Guadalupes, hearing the horses blowing in the corral. She watched, still hopeful, but now she knew that Cochise was right: Ed would not return.

But even if she had been ready to give up this, the first home she had known, there could be no escape. Here she was protected by Cochise. Other Apaches from other tribes would not so willingly grant her peace.

At daylight she was up. The morning air was

bright and balmy, but soon it would be hot again. Jimmy went to the spring for water, and when breakfast was over, the children played while Angie sat in the shade of a huge old cottonwood and sewed. It was a Sunday, warm and lovely. From time to time, she lifted her eyes to look down the canyon, half-smiling at her own foolishness.

The hard-packed earth of the yard was swept clean of dust; the pans hanging on the kitchen wall were neat and shining. The children's hair had been clipped, and there was a small bouquet on the kitchen table.

After a while, Angie put aside her sewing and changed her dress. She did her hair carefully, and then, looking in her mirror, she reflected with sudden pain that she **was** pretty, and that she was only a girl.

Resolutely, she turned from the mirror and, taking up her Bible, went back to the seat under the cottonwood. The children left their playing and came to her, for this was a Sunday ritual, their only one. Opening the Bible, she read slowly,

". . . though I walk through the valley of the shadow of death, I will fear no evil; for thou art with me; thy rod and thy staff, they comfort me. Thou preparest a table before me in the presence of mine enemies: thou . . ."

"Mommy." Jimmy tugged at her sleeve. "Look!"

* * *

CHES LANE HAD REACHED a narrow canyon by midafternoon and decided to make camp. There was small possibility he would find another such spot, and he was dead tired, his muscles sodden with fatigue. The canyon was one of those unexpected gashes in the cap rock that gave no indication of its presence until you came right on it. After some searching, Ches found a route to the bottom and made camp under a wind-hollowed overhang. There was water, and there was a small patch of grass.

After his horse had a drink and a roll on the ground, it began cropping eagerly at the rich, green grass, and Ches built a smokeless fire of ancient driftwood in the canyon bottom. It was his first hot meal in days, and when he had finished he put out his fire, rolled a smoke, and leaned back contentedly.

Before darkness settled, he climbed to the rim and looked over the country. The sun had gone down, and the shadows were growing long. After a half hour of study, he decided there was no living thing within miles, except for the usual desert life. Returning to the bottom, he moved his horse to fresh grass, then rolled in his blanket. For the first time in a month, he slept without fear.

He woke up suddenly in the broad daylight. The horse was listening to something, his head up. Swiftly, Ches went to the horse and led it back under the overhang. Then he drew on his boots, rolled his blankets, and saddled the horse. Still he heard no sound.

Climbing the rim again, he studied the desert and found nothing. Returning to his horse, he mounted up and rode down the canyon toward the flatland beyond. Coming out of the canyon mouth, he rode right into the middle of a war party of more than twenty Apaches—invisible until suddenly they stood up behind rocks, their rifles leveled. And he didn't have a chance.

Swiftly, they bound his wrists to the saddle horn and tied his feet. Only then did he see the man who led the party. It was Cochise.

He was a lean, wiry Indian of past fifty, his black hair streaked with gray, his features strong and clean-cut. He stared at Lane, and there was nothing in his face to reveal what he might be thinking.

Several of the young warriors pushed forward, talking excitedly and waving their arms. Ches Lane understood none of it, but he sat straight in the saddle, his head up, waiting. Then Cochise spoke and the party turned, and, leading his horse, they rode away.

The miles grew long and the sun was hot. He

was offered no water and he asked for none. The Indians ignored him. Once a young brave rode near and struck him viciously. Lane made no sound, gave no indication of pain. When they finally stopped, it was beside a huge anthill swarming with big red desert ants.

Roughly, they untied him and jerked him from his horse. He dug in his heels and shouted at them in Spanish: "The Apaches are women! They tie me to the ants because they are afraid to fight me!"

An Indian struck him, and Ches glared at the man. If he must die, he would show them how it should be done. Yet he knew the unpredictable nature of the Indian, of his great respect for courage.

"Give me a knife, and I'll kill any of your warriors!"

They stared at him, and one powerfully built Apache angrily ordered them to get on with it. Cochise spoke, and the big warrior replied angrily.

Ches Lane nodded at the anthill. "Is this the death for a fighting man? I have fought your strong men and beaten them. I have left no trail for them to follow, and for months I have lived among you, and now only by accident have you captured me. Give me a knife," he added grimly, "and I will fight **him**!" He indicated the big, black-faced Apache.

The warrior's cruel mouth hardened, and he struck Ches across the face.

The white man tasted blood and fury. "Woman!" Ches said. "Coyote! You are afraid!" Ches turned on Cochise, as the Indians stood irresolute. "Free my hands and let me fight!" he demanded. "If I win, let me go free."

Cochise said something to the big Indian. Instantly, there was stillness. Then an Apache sprang forward and, with a slash of his knife, freed Lane's hands. Shaking loose the thongs, Ches Lane chafed his wrists to bring back the circulation. An Indian threw a knife at his feet. It was his own bowie knife.

Ches took off his riding boots. In sock feet, his knife gripped low in his hand, its cutting edge up, he looked at the big warrior.

"I promise you nothing," Cochise said in Spanish, "but an honorable death."

The big warrior came at him on cat feet. Warily, Ches circled. He had not only to defeat this Apache but to escape. He permitted himself a side glance toward his horse. It stood alone. No Indian held it.

The Apache closed swiftly, thrusting wickedly with the knife. Ches, who had learned knife-fighting in the bayou country of Louisiana, turned his hip sharply, and the blade slid past him. He struck swiftly, but the Apache's forward movement deflected the blade, and it failed to penetrate. However, as it swept up between the Indian's body and arm, it cut a deep gash in the warrior's left armpit.

The Indian sprang again, like a clawing cat, streaming blood. Ches moved aside, but a backhand sweep nicked him, and he felt the sharp bite of the blade. Turning, he paused on the balls of his feet.

He had had no water in hours. His lips were cracked. Yet he sweated now, and the salt of it stung his eyes. He stared into the malevolent black eyes of the Apache, then moved to meet him. The Indian lunged, and Ches sidestepped like a boxer and spun on the ball of his foot.

The sudden sidestep threw the Indian past him, but Ches failed to drive the knife into the Apache's kidney when his foot rolled on a stone. The point left a thin red line across the Indian's back. The Indian was quick. Before Ches could recover his balance, he grasped the white man's knife wrist. Desperately, Ches grabbed for the Indian's knife hand and got the wrist, and they stood there straining, chest to chest.

Seeing his chance, Ches suddenly let his knees buckle, then brought up his knee and fell back, throwing the Apache over his head to the sand. Instantly, he whirled and was on his feet, standing over the Apache. The warrior had lost his knife, and he lay there, staring up, his eyes black with hatred.

Coolly, Ches stepped back, picked up the Indian's knife, and tossed it to him contemptuously. There was a grunt from the watching Indians, and then his antagonist rushed. But loss of blood had weakened the warrior, and Ches stepped in swiftly, struck the blade aside, then thrust the point of his blade hard against the Indian's belly.

Black eyes glared into his without yielding. A thrust, and the man would be disemboweled, but Ches stepped back. "He is a strong man," Ches said in Spanish. "It is enough that I have won."

Deliberately, he walked to his horse and swung into the saddle. He looked around, and every rifle covered him.

So he had gained nothing. He had hoped that mercy might lead to mercy, that the Apache's respect for a fighting man would win his freedom. He had failed. Again they bound him to his horse, but they did not take his knife from him.

When they camped at last, he was given food and drink. He was bound again, and a blanket was thrown over him. At daylight they were again in the saddle. In Spanish he asked where they were taking him, but they gave no indication of hearing. When they stopped again, it was beside a pole corral, near a stone cabin.

WHEN JIMMY SPOKE, Angie got quickly to her feet. She recognized Cochise with a start of relief, but she saw instantly that this was a war party. And then she saw the prisoner.

Their eyes met and she felt a distinct shock. He was a white man, a big, unshaven man who badly needed both a bath and a haircut, his clothes ragged and bloody. Cochise gestured at the prisoner.

"No take Apache man, you take white man. This man good for hunt, good for fight. He strong warrior. You take 'em."

Flushed and startled, Angie stared at the prisoner and caught a faint glint of humor in his dark eyes.

"Is this here the fate worse than death I hear tell of?" he inquired gently.

"Who are you?" she asked, and was immediately conscious that it was an extremely silly question.

The Apaches had drawn back and were watching curiously. She could do nothing for the present but accept the situation. Obviously they intended to do her a kindness, and it would not do to offend them. If they had not brought this man to her, he might have been killed.

"Name's Ches Lane, ma'am," he said. "Will you untie me? I'd feel a lot safer."

"Of course." Still flustered, she went to him and untied his hands. One Indian said something, and the others chuckled; then, with a whoop, they swung their horses and galloped off down the canyon.

Their departure left her suddenly helpless, the shadowy globe of her loneliness shattered by this utterly strange man standing before her, this big, bearded man brought to her out of the desert.

She smoothed her apron, suddenly pale as she realized what his delivery to her implied. What must he think of her? She turned away quickly. "There's hot water," she said hastily, to prevent his speaking. "Dinner is almost ready."

SHE WALKED QUICKLY into the house and stopped before the stove, her mind a blank. She looked around her as if she had suddenly waked up in a strange place. She heard water being poured into the basin by the door, and heard him take Ed's razor. She had never moved the box. To have moved it would—

"Sight of work done here, ma'am."

She hesitated, then turned with determination and stepped into the doorway. "Yes, Ed—"

"You're Angie Lowe."

Surprised, she turned toward him, and recognized his own startled awareness of her. As he shaved, he told her about Ed, and what had happened that day in the saloon.

"He—Ed was like that. He never considered consequences until it was too late."

"Lucky for me he didn't."

He was younger-looking with his beard gone. There was a certain quiet dignity in his face. She went back inside and began putting plates on the table. She was conscious that he had moved to the door and was watching her.

"You don't have to stay," she said. "You owe me nothing. Whatever Ed did, he did because he was that kind of person. You aren't responsible."

He did not answer, and when she turned again to the stove, she glanced swiftly at him. He was looking across the valley.

There was a studied deference about him when he moved to a place at the table. The children stared, wide-eyed and silent; it had been so long since a man sat at this table.

Angie could not remember when she had felt like this. She was awkwardly conscious of her hands, which never seemed to be in the right place or doing the right things. She scarcely tasted her food, nor did the children.

Ches Lane had no such inhibitions. For the first time, he realized how hungry he was. After the half-cooked meat of lonely, trailside fires, this was tender and flavored. Hot biscuits, desert honey . . . Suddenly he looked up, embarrassed at his appetite.

"You were really hungry," she said.

"Man can't fix much, out on the trail."

Later, after he'd got his bedroll from his saddle

and unrolled it on the hay in the barn, he walked back to the house and sat on the lowest step. The sun was gone, and they watched the cliffs stretch their red shadows across the valley. A quail called plaintively, a mellow sound of twilight.

"You needn't worry about Cochise," she said. "He'll soon be crossing into Mexico."

"I wasn't thinking about Cochise."

That left her with nothing to say, and she listened again to the quail and watched a lone bright star.

"A man could get to like it here," he said quietly.

## *That Man from the Bitter Sands*

When Speke came at last to water, he was two days beyond death.

His cracked lips rustled like tissue paper when they moved, trying to shape a thought. The skin of his face, long burned to a desert brown, had now taken on a patina of crimson.

Yet his mind was awake, and alive within him was a spirit that even the desert could not defeat. Without doubt Ross and Floren believed him dead, and this pleased him, stirring a wry sense of humor.

The chirping of birds told him of water before he saw it. His stumbling, almost hypnotic walk ceased, and swaying upon his feet, he turned his head slowly upon his stiff neck.

The basin remained unchanged, only now he had reached the very bottom of the vast depression, and a jagged knife's edge of rocks, an upthrust from a not too ancient fracture, loomed off to his right.

He had seen a dozen such along the line of travel, yet there was a difference. The faint, grayish green of the desert vegetation here took on a somewhat deeper green. Yet without the birds he might not have noticed. There was water near.

Through the heat-engendered haze in his skull there flickered grim humor. Floren and Ross thought they had taken from him all that promised survival when they had also taken his gold. They had robbed him of weapons, tools, canteen, food, and water. They had left him nothing.

Better than anyone else he had known what lay before him. After they had gone he had worked to free himself, but when he had succeeded he did not move away. He waited quietly in the shadow of the ledge, gutted of its small hoard of gold. Only when the sun was down did he move, and then he stepped out with a long, space-eating stride, walking away into that vast wasteland, shadowed with evening.

They had left him two things they did not realize would matter. They had seemed but bits of debris in the looted camp: a prospector's gold pan and a storm square from his canvas groundsheet.

Before it grew too dark to travel he had walked eight miles. Stopping then, he scooped a shallow hole in the sand and placed in it the gold pan. Over it he stretched the canvas, and above that he built a small pile of large stones. When his dew trap was complete he lay down to sleep.

Scarcely a spoon of water rewarded the effort, yet he swallowed it and was grateful. Before the sun topped the ridge he had three more miles behind him. Near two boulders he stopped and made a sun shade of a ruined cedar in the space between the boulders. He crawled into this island of coolness and lay down.

Midafternoon of the second day he found a barrel cactus, and cutting off the top he squeezed some water from the whitish green pulp. On the second and third nights he also built his dew traps, and each time got a little water. When he first heard the birds he thought he was losing his reason, yet turning toward the serrated ridge, he stumbled on. At its base, among some desert willows, was a small pool some four feet across . . . but lying in it was a dead coyote.

Swaying drunkenly, he stared hollow-eyed at the dead coyote and the poisoned water. He could go no farther, he knew. He must drink, yet, in his weakened state, a case of dysentery would surely kill him. It was not in him to yield, and too well he knew the ways of the wild country and the lessons it taught.

The will that had carried him more than forty miles across the desert moved him then. He dragged the remains of the dead coyote from the water. Then he gathered sticks and built a fire. When he had a small heap of charcoal, he scooped up some water with the gold pan. He covered the water until it was two inches thick with charcoal. Then he stoked his fire and waited. Soon the water was boiling.

The desert night drew darkness around him. The firelight flickered on the rock wall and upon the fragile boughs of the willow, and the smoke drifted and lost itself in the night. Sparks flew upward and vanished.

With a flat stick, he skimmed off the thick scum of charcoal and coagulated impurities. Then he added more charcoal and the water continued to boil. A second time he skimmed it, and only then did he put some aside to cool.

The very presence of water seemed to help. His brain cleared and he thought. He was now halfway across the vast bowl of desert. He was walking toward a place he knew, a ranch with a well of cool, clear water, and a man who would lend him a horse. A horse and a gun.

Forcing himself to ignore the water, he leaned back against the rocks. His lips rustled together and his tongue felt like a dry stick. He closed his aching eyes and waited out the minutes, listening like a prisoner to the faint trickle of water into the pool.

When an hour had passed, he allowed himself his first drink. Dipping up a little of the water he took some in his mouth and held it there, feeling the coolness bringing life back to the starved, shrunken tissues. Slowly he let the water trickle down his throat, feeling the delightful coolness all through him. Even that tiny swallow seemed to reach into every part of his body.

He bathed his lips and face then, taking his time, and finally allowing himself another swallow of the water. Finding in the rock a natural basin that was almost a foot across he used it as a mold, and with a rounded stone he carefully pounded his prospecting pan down into it, forcing the pan into a shape more like that of a bucket. Returning to the fire he boiled more water with charcoal, then poured it into the basin in the rock, repeating the process with his newly made pail. Adding a few more bits of charcoal, he lay back on the ground and was almost at once asleep, knowing that with the dawn the water would be clear and sweet.

Long ago he had established a pattern of awakening, and despite his exhaustion he was stirring long before dawn. It was cold when he opened his eyes, and his body was chilled with the cold of the desert night. Hurriedly, he built a fire and let its warmth permeate his entire being. Then he drank, and after a while, drank again. Then he turned to the desert.

A fleshy-fruited yucca grew near the water hole and he picked some of the long pods. He ate one of them raw, then roasted the others with some bulbs of the sego lily. When he had eaten these he took a thin, flat sheet of sandstone and began to dip water from the hole. Despite the little water there was, it took him more than an hour to empty the hole.

From time to time he paused to rest. Once, still having his tobacco, he rolled a smoke. He would need no more water than that in his bucket, but if others came along they would not know of the coyote and the poisoned spring. He did not know if his actions would help, but a water hole was a precious thing, to be safeguarded by all who passed.

When the hole was emptied he scraped the bottom with his flat stone, throwing out huge chunks of the mud. He then enlarged the opening through which the water flowed, still only a mere trickle, and finally sat down to eat more of the pods and bulbs, and to drink more water.

Water slowly trickled back into the hole. By night it would be full, and rested, he would start on with the first shadows.

THREE DAYS LATER, he was mounted on a horse. In the scabbard on his borrowed saddle was a Winchester, and thrust into his waistband was a battered but capable Colt.

They had insisted he remain and rest, but Speke would have none of it. Floren and Ross had taken his gold and he had been abandoned to die, yet it was with no thought of actual revenge that he returned to the desert. Nor did he blame his sufferings upon the two thieves whom he had taken into his camp when they had been half dead from thirst. The sufferings he had endured he accepted, as he accepted so much else as a part of life in the desert, yet the gold they had taken was his, and he intended to get it back.

Speke was not a big man but he was tough. The years and the desert had melted away any softness he might have had, and left behind a hard core of that rawhide resilience that the desert demands. Never a gunman, he had used weapons as a soldier in the Apache wars, as a buffalo hunter, and in his own private skirmishes with desert Mohaves or Pimas.

He needed no blueprint to read the plan in the minds of Floren and Ross. They would go first to Tucson.

It was a sufficient distance away. It had whiskey, women, and for a desert town of the era, remarkably good food.

On a sunlit morning not long after daybreak, Tom Speke rode his shambling buckskin into the main street of Tucson. He rode past staked-out pigs, dozens of yapping dogs, a few casual, disinterested burros, and a few naked Mexican youngsters. He was a lean man of less than six feet, not long past thirty but seasoned by the desert, a man with dingy trousers, a buckskin jacket, a battered narrow-brimmed hat, and a lean-jawed look about him.

He swung down at the Shoo Fly, and went into the restaurant. It was a long room of adobe, walls washed with yellow, a stamped earth floor, and tables of pine covered with cheap tablecloths. To Tom Speke, who had sat at a table four times in two years, the Shoo Fly represented the height of culture and gastronomic delight. He did not order—at the Shoo Fly one accepted what the day offered, in this case jerked beef, frijoles, tomatoes, and stewed prunes (there had recently been a series of Apache raids on trains bringing fresh fruit from Hermosillo) and coffee. All but the coffee and the prunes were liberally laced with chile colorados, and there was still some honey that had been brought from the Tia Juana ranch below the border.

Tom Speke devoted himself to eating, but while he ate, he listened. The Shoo Fly was crowded, as always at mealtimes, and there was much talk. Turning to the kid who was clearing tables, he asked if there was any recent news of prospectors striking it rich in the area. The kid didn't know, but a man up the table looked up and put down his fork.

"Feller down to Congress Hall payin' for drinks with dust. Says he made him a pile over on the Gila."

"Big feller? With blond hair?" A man spoke up from the end of the bar. "Seen him. Looks mighty like a feller from Santa Fe I run into once. They were huntin' him for horse stealin'."

Tom Speke forked up the last piece of beef and chewed it thoughtfully. Then he wiped his plate with a slab of bread and disposed of it in the same way. He gulped coffee, then laid out his dollar and pushed back from the table. The description was that of Floren.

The sun stopped him on the step, and he waited until his eyes adjusted themselves to the glare. Then he walked up the street to the Congress.

Pausing on the step he eased the position of the Colt, then stepped inside and moved away from the door. Early as it was, the place was scattered with people. One game gave the appearance of having been on all night. Several men stood at the bar. One of these was a giant of a man in a stovepipe hat and a black coat. Speke knew him for Marcus Duffield, onetime town marshal and now postal inspector, but still the town's leading exponent of gun-throwing.

Speke glanced around. There was no sign of Ross, but Floren's big blond head was visible. He was sitting in the poker game, and from the look of it, he was winning.

Speke moved down the bar to Duffield's side.

He ordered a drink, then jerked his head at Duffield. "An' one for Marcus, here."

Duffield glanced at him. "Goin' to be some shootin' here right sudden," Speke said quietly. "I figured to tell you so's you wouldn't figure it was aimed at you." He indicated Floren by a jerk of his head. "Feller there an' his partner come into my camp half dead. I gave 'em grub an' water. Second day they throwed down on me, tied me up, an' stole my outfit, includin' three pokes of gold."

"Seen the gold," Duffield said. "Didn't figure him for no miner."

He glanced over his shoulder. "Better wait'll he finishes this hand. He's holdin' four of a kind."

Speke lifted his glass and Duffield acknowledged it. They drank, and Tom Speke turned around and then moved down the bar. He waited there, watching the game, his eyes cold and emotionless. Floren raked in the pot on his four queens and started to stack the money.

And then he looked up and saw Speke.

He started to move, then stopped. His eyes stared, his face went sickly yellow.

A card player noticed his face, took a quick look at Speke, then carefully drew back from the table. The others followed suit.

"You won that with my money, Floren," Speke said carefully. "Just leave it lay."

Floren took a quick look around. His big hands rested on the arms of his chair, only inches from his gun. One of the players started to interrupt, but Duffield's bold black eyes pinned the man to the spot. "His show," Duffield said. "That gent's a thief."

Floren touched his lips with his tongue. "Now, look," he said, "I—"

"Ain't aimin' to kill you," Speke said conversationally, "nor Ross. You stole my outfit an' left me for dead, but all I want is my money an' my outfit. Get up easy an' empty your pockets."

Floren looked at the money, and then at Speke. Suddenly his face seemed to set, and an ugly look flared in his eyes. He started to rise. "I'll be double d—!" His hand dropped to his gun.

Nobody had seen Ross come in the door. He took one quick look, drew, and fired. Even as Speke thumbed back the hammer, he was struck from behind. He staggered, then fell forward.

Floren stood, his unfired gun in his hand, and looked down at Speke. Ross held the room covered. Floren lifted the muzzle of his gun toward the fallen man.

"Don't do that," Duffield said, "or you'll have to kill every man in this room."

Floren looked up at him, and hesitated.

"Don't be a fool," Ross said, "pick up your money and let's go."

★ ★ ★

IT WAS TWO WEEKS before Speke could leave his bed, despite excellent care by Semig, a Viennese doctor attached to the Army. It was a month before he could ride.

Duffield watched him mount the buckskin. "Next time don't talk," he advised. "Shoot!"

Tom Speke picked up the trail of Floren and Ross on the Hassayampa and followed them into Camp Date Creek. Captain Dwyer of the Fifth Cavalry listened to Speke's description, then nodded. "They were here. I ordered them out. Ross was known to have sold liquor to the Apaches near Camp Grant. I couldn't have them around."

Swapping the weary buckskin for a zebra dun mustang, Speke returned to the trail.

At Dripping Springs Speke drew up and swung down. Cherokee Townsend came from his cabin with a whoop of pleasure. The two had once traveled together across New Mexico. In reply to his questions, Townsend nodded. " 'Bout two weeks back," he said. "Didn't take to 'em much. Big fellow is ridin' a bay with three white stockings. The other one an appaloosa with a splash of white on his right shoulder. They headed for Prescott."

Townsend was, he said, staying on. "Watch out for 'Paches," he said. "They are out an' about. I've buried twenty-seven of them right on this place."

Speke rode on, sparing his horse but holding to the pace. He saw much Indian sign.

In Prescott the two had remained more than a week. They had left town headed west. Everywhere he was warned of Indians. The Apaches were out, and so were the Hualapais and Mohaves. There were rumors of an impending outbreak at Date Creek, and General Crook was going down to investigate.

Neither Floren nor Ross was a man of long experience in the West. During their time in his camp, before they had robbed him, he had seen that. They were men who had come west from Bald Knob, Missouri. Tough men and dangerous, but not desert-wise.

On the second day out of Prescott, Speke found two Indian ponies. Badly used, they had obviously been released by Indians who had gone on with fresher, stronger horses. Speke caught up the two ponies and led them along with him, an idea forming in his brain.

On the third day he spotted them ahead of him, and he deliberately created dust off to their left and behind. That night he left his own horse and rode one of the others, and took the other unshod horse around their camp. He left four separate sets of tracks across their trail for the following day.

Moving on cat feet, he slipped down to the edge of the camp. A small fire was burning. Floren was asleep, and Ross sat nearby. Waiting for more than an hour with Indian patience, he finally got his chance. He slipped the muzzle of his rifle through the strap of a canteen and withdrew it carefully. He could have stolen the other also, but he did not. He made his way some distance, then deliberately let a small gravel slide start. Glancing back, he saw Ross come to his feet and leap from the firelight.

It was the beginning of his plan. He watched them draw up when they reached the tracks of the unshod ponies the following morning. To anyone, this certainly meant Indians. Indians often rode horses shod at trading posts or stolen from the white settlers, but white men almost never rode an unshod horse for any length of time. The tracks were headed west and south. Floren and Ross pulled off the trail, working north. Remembering the country ahead of them, Speke was satisfied.

In the four nights that followed, he succeeded in alarming their camp with stealthy noises at least twice a night. He left pony tracks ahead of them and near the camp. Steadily, they bore off to the north, trying to avoid the unseen Indians.

They were worried by the Indians they believed were congregating nearby, they had but one canteen between them, and they were getting only disturbed sleep when they slept at all. It was a calculated war of nerves. Twice Speke lay on a bluff or behind a rock near the camp and heard them arguing fiercely.

Ahead of them on the following morning, he built a signal fire. He used a blanket to simulate Indian signals, then went south a few miles and did the same thing. They were now well to the north of Ehrenberg and headed for Hardyville. At dusk he lit two more signal fires and used the smoke, then put them out and worked closer to the camp of the two outlaws.

Floren was thinner, haggard, hollow-eyed. Ross was tighter, snappish, and shifty. They built a tiny fire to make coffee, and Speke waited. When Ross reached for the pot, he fired rapidly—three times.

The first shot struck the fire and threw sparks, the second drilled the coffeepot—Speke could see the sudden puff of steam and smoke when the coffee hit the fire—and the third shot struck a log on which Floren was seated.

Following the shots there was silence. Evidently the firing had caught both men away from their rifles. Moving a little, Speke watched the fire, relaxed and at ease. He had suffered from these men, and now he expected to recover his gold, and to do it, if possible, without killing.

Yet they had planned for him to die, and only the presence of Duffield and the rest had saved him in the saloon. It was not a consideration of mercy that moved him, rather a complete indifference to the fate of the two men. He wanted his gold; this he had worked for, slaved for. Whatever they had won gambling he would consider his—won with his money and payment for this long trek.

Day dawned with low clouds and a hint of rain. He saw them move out slowly, and knew they had spent an uncomfortable and altogether miserable night away from their bedrolls. Twice during the day he sent them into hiding with quick shots from ambush, not aimed to kill.

Twice he heard them bickering over the canteen, and an idea came to him. He knew they kept the gold close to them, so to get at it was scarcely possible, but there was something else he could get. And that night he stole one of their horses.

At dawn, after a quiet sleep on the desert, Tom Speke was awake. Gathering his horses, he left them concealed in the shelter of an upthrust of rock, and then moved closer to watch.

Already an argument was ensuing. One canteen, one horse, thirty pounds of gold, and two men.

Coolly, Speke rolled a smoke. He could have written the story of what was to happen now. Harassed beyond limit, their nerves on edge from constant attack, from sleepless nights, and from uncertainty as to their enemies, the two were now facing each other. In the mind of each was the thought that success and escape could belong to one man, and one only.

Floren was saddling the horse. Then he picked up the gold and tied it behind the saddle. He seemed to be having trouble. Ross dropped his hand to his gun—he failed to calculate on the shadow, and Floren turned and fired.

Ross staggered, took a step back, then yelled something wild and incoherent. He went down to his hands and knees and Floren swung into the saddle and rode away.

Ross remained on his hands and knees. Speke drew deep on his cigarette and watched Floren go. He was heading northwest. Speke smiled and got up, then went back for his own horses. When he had them he walked down to Ross. The man had fallen, and he was breathing hoarsely.

Working with swift sureness, Speke carried the smaller man into the shade of a cedar and, ripping open his shirt, examined the wound. Ross had been struck on the top of the hipbone, knocking him down and temporarily shocking him into a state of partial paralysis. The bullet had torn a hole in his side, a flesh wound, from which blood was flowing.

Heating water, he bathed the wound. Then, making a decoction from the leaves of a creosote bush, he used it as an antiseptic on the wound. Then he bandaged it crudely but effectively. Ross revived while he worked, and stared at him. "You . . . is it?"

"Uh-huh."

"Figured we'd lost you."

"Ain't likely."

"Why you helpin' me?"

Speke sat back on his heels. He nodded at the horse he had stolen. "I'm leavin' you that horse and a canteen. You head out of here. If I ever see you again, I'll kill you."

He got to his feet and started for the horses. Ross stared after him, then tried to lift himself to an elbow, managed it. "You leavin' me a gun?"

"No."

"Then I'm a sittin' duck for Injuns."

Speke smiled a rare smile. "Maybe you'll be lucky."

He walked his horse away on Floren's trail. He was in no hurry. Before them lay the breaks of the Colorado. Soon Floren would be stopped by the canyon itself. Speke had been long in the desert, and the desert teaches patience. There was no escape for Floren.

For days Speke had directed his smoke columns and his actions to cause the two outlaws to pull farther and farther north, until now Floren was in a cul-de-sac from which there was no way out except back the way he had come. But Floren would not know this. He would waste time looking.

It was a hot still day when the search ended. A day of a high sun and the reflecting heat from the face of vast plateaus of rock and the cedar-clad hillsides. Lizards panted even in the shade, their mouths held open, their sides pumping at the hot, thin air.

Floren was hollow-eyed and frightened. Whichever way he went he faced awesome canyons, and the only water was far, far below. Only a few drops slopped lonesomely in his canteen, and the horse he rode was gaunt and beaten. He swung down, and his heels hit hard, and he stared over the brink into the vast canyon below.

Trapped . . . Seven times he had found new routes, and each had ended in a cliff. Seven times he tried and seven times he failed. And now he knew there was no way to turn but back. He turned toward the horse, and as if expecting him, the animal went to its knees, then rolled over on its side. Fiercely, Floren swore. He kicked the horse. It would not rise, it could not rise. Better yet without the horse he could take the gold and find a way down the cliffs. Then a raft . . . feverishly, he rushed at the horse and stripped off the pack of gold. He started to take his rifle, then shrugged. It would only be in the way.

Shouldering the gold, he walked to the cliff's

edge. There was no way over at that point. He turned, then stopped abruptly. One hundred yards away was Speke. The prospector held a Winchester cradled in his arm.

Speke said nothing. He just stood there, silent, still, alone.

Floren touched his lips with his tongue. He held the gold sack in his right hand. Anyway, at that range . . . a pistol . . . he looked toward his rifle. Too far away.

Speke shot from the hip, and the sack jerked in Floren's hand. Another shot. Speke moved a step forward and Floren dropped the sack and drew. He fired quickly, hastily. He missed. . . .

Speke fired again and Floren felt the bullet tug at his shirt. He took a hasty step back, then fired again himself. The bullet struck far to the left. Speke swung his rifle and fired. Rock fragments stung Floren's cheek. He jerked his head back up.

Speke said nothing. He worked the lever on his rifle and waited. Floren started forward, and a bullet kicked up sand ahead of him. He took a hasty step back.

The edge . . . could not be far behind. He glanced back and Speke fired swiftly, three shots. They scattered rock around his feet and a ricochet burned Floren's face. He was no more than six feet from the edge.

"You ain't goin' to make me jump!" he shouted angrily. He threw up his gun and fired.

Speke waited a minute, then walked swiftly forward and picked up the gold. He backed away, then dropped the sack and fired. His Winchester '73 carried eleven bullets and he was counting them.

The shot whipped by Floren's face, so close it drew blood.

Floren was frightened now. His face was drawn and white. He stared with wide eyes and haggard mouth. Speke picked up the gold again and backed to his horse. Lashing it behind the saddle, he swung into the leather.

As he did so, he dropped the lead rope of one of the Indian ponies. "Help yourself," he said, and rode slowly away.

Floren started after him, shouting. Tom Speke did not turn his head or glance back. He merely rode on, remembering Tucson and the Shoo Fly. He would enjoy a meal like that now. Maybe, in a week or so . . .

He had lots of time . . . now.

# *Desperate Men*

They were four desperate men, made hard by life, cruel by nature, and driven to desperation by imprisonment. Yet the walls of Yuma Prison were strong and the rifle skill of the guards unquestioned, so the prison held many desperate men besides these four. And when prison walls and rifles failed, there was the desert, and the desert never failed.

Fate, however, delivered these four a chance to test the desert. In the early dawn the land had rolled and tumbled like an ocean storm. The rocky promontory over the river had shifted and cracked in an earthquake that drove fear into the hearts of the toughest and most wicked men in Arizona. For a minute or two the ground had groaned and roared, dust rained down from cracks in the roofs of the cells, and in one place the perimeter wall had broken and slid off, down the hillside. It was as if God or the Devil had shown them a way.

Two nights later, Otteson leaned his shaven

head closer to the bars. "If you're yellow, say so! I say we can make it! If Isager says we can make it through the desert, I say we go!"

"We'll need money for the boatmen." Rodelo's voice was low. "Without money we will die down there on the shores of the gulf."

All were silent, three awaiting a word from the fourth. Rydberg knew where the army payroll was buried. The government did not know, the guards did not know, only Rydberg. And Otteson, Isager, and Rodelo knew he knew.

He was a thin, scrawny man with a buzzard's neck and a buzzard's beak for a nose. His bright, predatory eyes indicated his hesitation now. "How . . . how much would it take?" he asked.

"A hundred," Otteson suggested, "not more than two. If we had that much we could be free."

Free . . . no walls, no guards, no stinking food. No sweating one's life out with backbreaking labor under the blazing sun. Free . . . women, whiskey, money to spend . . . the click of poker chips, the whir of the wheel, a gun's weight on the hip again. No beatings, no solitary, no lukewarm, brackish drinking water. Free to come and go . . . a horse between the knees . . . women . . .

He said it finally, words they had waited to hear. "There's the army payroll. We could get that."

The taut minds of Otteson, Rodelo, and Isager

relaxed slowly, easing the tension, and within the mind of each was a thought unshared.

Gold . . . fifteen thousand in gold coins for the taking! A little money split four ways, but a lot of money for one!

Otteson leaned his bullet head nearer. "To-morrow night"—his thick lips barely moved as he whispered—"tomorrow night we'll go out. If we wait longer they'll have the wall repaired."

"There's been guards posted ever since the quake," Rodelo protested.

Otteson laughed. "We'll take care of them!" From under the straw mattress he drew a crude, prison-made knife. "Rydberg can take care of the other with his belt."

Cunningly fashioned of braided leather thongs, it concealed a length of piano wire. When the belt was removed and held in the hands it could be bent so the loop of the steel wire projected itself, a loop large enough to encircle a man's head . . . then it could be jerked tight and the man would die.

Rodelo leaned closer. "How far to the gold?"

"Twenty miles east. We'll need horses."

"Good!" Otteson smashed a fist into a palm. "East is good! They'll expect us to go west into California. East after the gold, then south into the desert. They'd never dream we'd try that! It's hot as sin and dry as Hades, but I know where the water holes are!"

Their heads together, glistening with sweat in the hot, sticky confines of their cells, they plotted every move, and within the mind of three of the men was another plot: to kill the others and have the gold for himself.

"We'll need guns." Rydberg expressed their greatest worry. "They'll send Indians after us."

The Indians were paid fifty dollars for each convict returned alive—but they had been paid for dead convicts, too. The Yaquis knew the water holes, and fifty dollars was twice what most of them could make in a month if they could find work at all.

"We'll have the guns of the two guards. When we get to Rocky Bay, we'll hire a fisherman to carry us south to Guaymas."

THE FOLLOWING DAY their work seemed easy. The sun was broiling and the guards unusually brutal. Rydberg was knocked down by a hulking giant named Johnson. Rydberg just brushed himself off and smiled. It worried Johnson more than a threat. "What's got into him?" he demanded of the other guards. "Has he gone crazy?"

Perryman shrugged. "Why worry about it? He's poison mean, an' those others are a bad lot, too. Otteson's worst of all."

"He's the one I aim to get," Johnson said grimly, "but did you ever watch the way he lifts those rocks? Rocks two of us couldn't budge he lifts like they were so many sacks of spuds!"

It was sullen dark that night; no stars. There was thunder in the north and they could hear the river. The heat lingered and the guards were restless from the impending storm. At the gap where the quake had wrecked the wall were Perryman and Johnson. They would be relieved in two hours by other guards.

They had been an hour on the job and only now had seated themselves. Perryman lit a cigarette and leaned back. As he straightened to say something to Johnson he was startled to see kicking feet and clawing hands, but before he could rise, a powerful arm came over his shoulder, closing off his breath. Then four men armed with rifles and pistols went down the side of Prison Hill and walked eastward toward the town.

One hour before discovery. That was the most they could expect, yet in half that time they had stolen horses and headed east. Otteson had been shrewd. He had grabbed Perryman's hat from the ground. Both Isager and Rodelo had hats of a sort. Rydberg was without any covering for his shaven head.

Two hours after their escape they reached the adobe. Rydberg led the way inside the ruin, and they dug up the gold from a far corner. Each man took a sack, and then they turned their horses to the south and the desert.

"Each year," Otteson said, "the fishermen come to Rocky Bay. They live there while they fish, and then return to their homes down the gulf. Pablo told me, and he said to keep Pinacate on my left and head for the coast at Flat Hill. The bay is on a direct line between the hill and the coast."

Pablo had been killed by a blow on the head from a guard's gun, but he had been planning escape with Otteson. Dawn came at last and the clouds slid away leaving the sun behind . . . and the sun was hot.

From the Gila River to the Mexican border there was nothing. Only desert, cacti, rocks, and the sun, always the sun. There was not even water until one almost reached the border. Water was found only in **tinajas,** basins that captured rain and retained it until finally evaporated by the sun. Some of the **tinajas** were shaded and held the water for a long time, and in others there was just sand. Sometimes water impregnated the sand at the bottom. These things a man must know to survive on that devil's trail.

Their route from the Gila to the border was approximately fifty miles as the buzzard flies, but a man does not ride as the buzzard flies, not even in a lonely and empty land. There are clusters of rock, broken lava, upthrust ledges, and clumps of cacti. And there are always, inevitably, arroyos.

Seventy miles would be closer to the truth, seventy miles of desert in midsummer.

The border was a vague line which in theory left them free of pursuit, but in 1878 officers of the law often ignored lines of demarcation—and the Indians did not notice them at all. Actually, the border was their halfway point, for they had a rough distance of one hundred and forty miles to traverse.

Behind them two guards lay dead, and the hostler only lived because Rodelo was not, by nature, a killer. Rodelo had the sleeping man's hands and feet tied before he got his eyes open. Then he gagged and left him. They stole four horses and three canteens and filled the canteens at the pump. Otteson, Rydberg, and Isager took it for granted the hostler had been killed.

They rode hard for twenty miles, and then they had the added weight of the gold. Otteson knew the way from Pablo and he pointed it out occasionally as they rode. But he did not offer his back to his companions.

Four battered and desperate men headed south under the glaring sun. Dust lifted, they sweated, and their lips grew dry. They pushed their horses, for distance was important. Otteson called a halt, finally. He was a heavy man and the hard riding sapped the strength of his horse.

"Where is it we're gonna find water?" Isager

noted the hesitation before Otteson replied. Isager knew the desert, but not this area. Otteson only had the knowledge Pablo had given him and he didn't want to tell too much.

"Near Coyote Peak there's water. Maybe ten miles yet."

Isager tested the weight of his canteen. Rodelo drank several good gulps and returned his canteen to its place behind his saddle. Rydberg, who had brought the guard's water bottle, drank also. Otteson made a motion of drinking, but Isager watched his Adam's apple. It did not move.

Isager was a lean man, not tall, and narrow of jaw and cheekbone. He weighed one hundred and fifty pounds and carried no ounce of fat. He had been sent to Yuma after killing a marshal, which would have been his sixth notch if he had been a man for carving notches. It was noteworthy that in selecting a weapon he had taken a pistol. Isager was nothing if not practical. The pistol was his favorite weapon, and the four would be close together. By the time they had spread out to where a rifle might be useful, he would have a rifle. Of that he was positive.

Rodelo knew nothing of the desert but much of men. When younger he had sailed to the West Coast of Africa and had seen men die of the sun. He had replaced the bandanna that covered his head when working in the prison yard with a hat stolen from the livery, knowing the sun would be vicious on their shaven skulls. They depended upon Otteson, and he was not to be trusted. Isager alone he respected: he liked none of them. Rydberg did not guess what the others knew—that they would soon be minus a man.

They walked their horses now. Behind them was no dust, but pursuit was certain. It was the Indians who worried them, for fifty dollars was a lot of money to an Indian. Two hundred dollars for them all.

The air wavered and changed before them, seeming to flow and billow with heat waves. On their right was the Gila Range, and the desert grew more rugged. Otteson watched when Rydberg drank, when he passed his hand over his bare skull, saw him put water on his head. Otteson was complacent, confident.

Isager's mouth was dry, but he did not touch the canteen. A mere swallow at dusk could do more good than a bucket now. He watched the others with cat eyes. Rydberg took another pull. The heat baked the desert and reflected in their faces like heat from a hot stove. Twice they stopped for rest, and each time it was Otteson and Isager who stopped in what little shade there was. Rydberg swayed as he dismounted.

"Hot!" he gasped. "How much farther to water?"

"Not far." Otteson looked at Rydberg's horse. It was the best.

Isager took water from his canteen and wiped out his horse's mouth and nostrils. Rodelo thought this was a good idea and did likewise.

"Let's wait until dark," Rydberg suggested. "I'm hot. My head aches. That sun is killing me."

"You want to get caught by them Injuns? Or them laws from Yuma?"

They moved on, and Rydberg's skull was pocked with sun blisters. The dust grew thicker, the air was dead, the desert a pink and red reflector for the sun. Rydberg swayed drunkenly, and Rodelo swore mentally and reflected that it must be 120 degrees or more.

Rydberg began to mutter. He pulled at his dry canteen. He tried again, shook it, and there was no sound. Otteson looked straight before him. Isager said nothing, and only Rodelo looked around as the man swayed drunkenly in his saddle.

"I'm out of water," Rydberg said. "How about a drink?"

"On the desert," Otteson said, "each man drinks his own water. You'll have to wait."

The dust and sun and thirst turned their world into a red hell of heat waves and blurred blue mountains. The hooves of their horses dragged. Rydberg muttered, and once he croaked a snatch of song. He mumbled through thin, cracked lips, and the weird face above the scraggly neck became even more buzzardlike. His skull was fiery red now, and it bobbed strangely as he weakened. Suddenly he shouted hoarsely and pointed off across the desert.

"Water!" he gabbled. "Water, over there!"

"Mirage," Rodelo said, and the others were silent, riding.

"Gimme a drink." Rydberg rode at Otteson and grabbed at his canteen.

The big man moved his horse away, striking at the skinny hand. "Go to hell," he said coldly.

Rydberg grabbed at him, lost balance, and fell heavily into the sand. He struggled to get up, then fell again.

Rodelo looked at him. His own canteen was empty. "The damn fool," Isager said, "why didn't he get him a hat?"

Nobody else spoke. Then Otteson reached for the canteen on Rydberg's horse, but Isager was closer and unhurriedly appropriated it. He also took the rifle. "Take the horse if you like," he said, "you're a heavy man."

Otteson glared at Isager, and Rodelo moved in and took the gold. "Are you going to leave him here like that?" he demanded.

Otteson shrugged. "He asked for it."

"He wouldn't live until night," Isager said. "Stay if you want."

Rodelo drew Rydberg into the shade of an ironwood tree. Then he mounted and followed. Why had they grabbed the empty canteen and the rifle when they could have gotten their hands on Rydberg's share of the gold?

A thin shadow of doubt touched him. Then the answer was plain and he cursed himself for a fool. Nearly two hundred gold coins he now carried, and it was considerable weight. They preferred that he carry the extra gold until . . . His jaw set hard, but within him there was a cold shock of fear.

They thought he was going to die! They thought— He'd show them. From deep within him came a hard burning defiance. He'd show them.

It had been midafternoon when they left Rydberg. It was two hours later when they came up to Coyote Peak. Otteson was studying the rocks around and suddenly he turned sharply left and rode into an arroyo. Twenty minutes later they stood beside the **tinaja**.

Despair mounted within Rodelo. It was only a hollow of rock with a few gallons of water in the bottom. They filled their canteens, then watered the horses. When the horses had finished the water was gone.

"We'll rest a few hours," Isager suggested, "then go on after dark."

Isager ignored the shade and lay down on his side with his face toward the two men and his weapons and water close behind him.

Rodelo found a spot in soft sand, well back in

the shadow of the rocks. He stared at the others and thought exhaustion had made them stupid. Both had relaxed upon hard, rocky ground. The least move would awaken them. They would get no rest that way. While this was soft sand. . . . He relaxed luxuriously.

He awakened with a start. It was cold, dark, and silent. With sudden panic, he sprang to his feet. "Isager!" he shouted. "Ott!" And the desert gave back only echoes. He felt for his canteen, and it was gone. He ran to where his horse had been picketed, and it, too, was gone.

He had slept and they had left him. They had taken the gold, the horse, the canteen . . . only his pistol remained. He had that only because they had feared to awaken him.

He rushed to a rise of ground, scrambled, slipped on the rocks, and skinned his knees. Then he got to the top and stared off to the southeast. All he could see was the soft, velvety darkness, the cool of the desert night, and the unspeaking stars.

He was alone.

For the first time he was frightened. He was horribly, unspeakably frightened. Rodelo hated being alone, he feared loneliness, and he knew the power of the desert to kill.

Then his fear left him, his thoughts smoothed out and the panic ended. They could not move fast without knowing the country better than they did. They would travel at a walk, and if they did, he might overtake them. He was younger than either, and he was strong. He had never found a trial that could test his endurance.

A glance at the stars told him they could have no more than an hour's start. How much would that mean at night in unfamiliar desert? Three miles? Five miles?

Doubt came. Could he make up the distance? They would never suspect pursuit. Suppose the day came and he was still without water? But what would waiting gain? This was not a spring, and the **tinaja** was empty.

He could wait for death, or for capture on the verge of death, or he could fight. He returned to the **tinaja** and found perhaps a cup of water in the bottom. He thrust his head into the basin and sucked it up. Then he straightened, glanced at the stars for direction, and struck out for the southeast, walking steadily.

OTTESON AND ISAGER RODE side by side. Each man led a horse, and on those horses were the gold sacks. The issue between them was clear now. Isager knew he was faster with a gun, and Otteson knew it also. Therefore, the big man would wait for a moment when the killing was a sure thing.

Neither man mentioned Rydberg nor Rodelo. It was like Otteson to ignore what was past.

Isager thought of Rodelo with regret—he had liked the younger man, but this was a matter of survival. They walked their horses, careful not to tire them. Once, encountering a nest of boulders, they circled some distance to get past them. Over the next two hours this allowed Rodelo to gain considerable ground.

The first day netted them sixty miles of distance but twenty of it had been up the Gila for the gold, and the next forty angling toward the border. Daylight found them near the border and Otteson looked back. Nothing but heat waves. "They'll be coming," Isager said. "They'll find Rydberg by the buzzards. Then they'll find Rodelo. That gives them a line on us even if they don't find our trail."

Ahead of them on their right was a cluster of mesas, on their left ahead high and blue on the horizon, the bulk of Pinacate, a fifteen-mile-long ridge that towered nearly five thousand feet into the brassy sky.

The coolness left the desert as the sun lifted. Both men knew the folly of haste. Moreover they had each other to watch. Neither wanted to go ahead, and this slowed their pace. Isager wished it had been Otteson back there rather than Rodelo. He had seen the big man get to his feet and had done likewise. Both had chosen stony ground, as a sound sleep might be their last sleep. Otteson had saddled up, glanced at the sleeping man, and then with a shrug had gathered up Rodelo's gear and horse. To stop him would mean a shoot-out, and neither knew which side Rodelo would join if awakened by gunfire. He had mounted up and taken Rydberg's horse. Neither had planned on abandoning the young man when they stopped, but this was a case of survival of the fittest and Rodelo had given them an opportunity to decrease their number by one more.

"You sure the fishermen come there at this time of the year?"

"Pablo said so. He planned to go this way himself. Rocky Bay, they call it. From Flat Hill we go right down to the water. How could a man mistake a bay? And if the fishermen aren't there, we'll wait."

Not long after that they came up to Tinajas Altas where they watered the horses and refilled their canteens. Isager looked over the back trail from beside the tanks. He saw no dust, no movement. Once he believed he saw something stir down there, but it could have been nothing more than a coyote or a mountain sheep. A horse would make dust.

They rested, drank water again, and ate a little of the hardtack and jerky they had smuggled from the prison, food hoarded against this effort. An hour passed, then a second hour. The rest meant much to them and to their horses. Otteson got up carefully, facing Isager. "Reckon we'd better move on. I won't feel safe until we're on that fishin' boat headed south."

Up on the mesa's side among the talus, something moved. Isager's quick eye saw it and recognized it in the same instant with a start of inward surprise. Otteson's back was to the talus, but he saw a flicker of something in Isager's eyes. "What's the matter?" he exclaimed, starting to turn.

He caught himself, his eyes turning ugly. "Figured I'd turn an' you'd shoot me? Don't try nothin' like that."

Rodelo was on the slope behind and slightly above Otteson and about thirty yards back from him. His face was ghastly and red, his prison jeans were torn from cacti and rocks, but he clutched a businesslike .44 in his fist. He lifted it and took careful sight, shifting his feet as he did so. A rock rolled under his foot.

Otteson whipped around, quick as a cat. His rifle blasted from the hip and he missed. He never fired again. He went down, clawing at the rocks and gravel on which he had fallen, blood staining their pink to deep crimson. Isager held his smoking Colt and looked up the slope at Rodelo.

The younger man had recovered his balance and they stared at each other over their guns.

"You might miss," Isager said. "I never do."

"Why don't you shoot, then?"

"I want company. Two can make it easier than one. Much easier than three."

"Then why didn't you let him kill me?"

"Because he wanted to kill me himself. You need me. I know the desert and you don't."

Rodelo came over the rocks, stepping carefully. "All right," he said. "Gimme water."

Isager holstered his gun. "There's the **tinaja**. Drink an' we'll push on." He looked at Rodelo with curious respect. "How'd you catch up so fast?"

"You rode around things. I walked straight to your dust. You rested. I couldn't afford to."

"Good man." Isager mounted up. Nothing was said about what happened. "If we play it smart now, we'll leave each other alone. Together we can make it through."

One thing they had not forgotten. The knowledge of the **tinajas** lay dead in the skull of Otteson.

"We'll have to make our water last. It won't be far now. That's Pinacate."

The mountain bulked before them now, and by the time the stars were out it loomed huge on the horizon. They slept that night and when they awakened, Rodelo looked around at Isager. His cheekbones were slashes of red from the sun, his eyes deep sunken. Stubble of beard covered his cheeks and his shirt was stiff with sweat and dust. "I smell the sea," he said, low-voiced. "I can smell the sea."

When they started on once more, they kept the mountain between them and the sun, saving themselves from the heat. Once they found a water hole but the mud was cracked and dry in the bottom. Isager's brown face was shadowed with red, Otteson's hat pulled low over his cold eyes.

The horses were gaunt and beaten. Several times the men dismounted and led the horses to spare them. Their hunger was a gnawing, living thing within them, and their spare canteens were dry, their own very low. The eyes of the men were never still, searching for water. Yet it was not enough to look. One had to know. In the desert water may be within a few feet and give no indication of its presence. And then, from the top of a rise, they saw the gulf!

"There it is." Rodelo stared, hollow-eyed. "Now for that bay."

A squarish flat hill was before them. They circled and saw the gulf due west of it. "S'pose that's it?" Isager asked doubtfully.

"You can see for yourself that it's a big bay." The tension between them was back: they were watching each other out of the corners of their eyes again.

Isager stood in his stirrups and looked south. Land stretched away until it ended in a point. There was a hint of sea in that direction but he was not sure. "All right," he said, "but I don't see any boats."

The plain sloping down to the bay was white with soda and salt. Long sand spits extended into the milky blue water. Here and there patches showed above the surface. "Looks mighty shallow," Rodelo said doubtfully. "Don't seem likely a boat would come in here."

Isager hefted his canteen, feeling its lightness with fear. "We'd better hunt for water."

South of them, the rocky bluff shouldered against the sky, dark and rugged. North the beach lay flat and empty . . . frightening in its emptiness. The horses stood, heads down and unmoving. The rocky bluff looked promising, but the salt on his lips frightened Isager. Behind them they heard a deep, gasping sigh and they turned. The paint packhorse was down.

It had sunk to the sand and now it lay stretched out, the hide on its flanks hanging like loose cloth in the hollows of its ribs.

Isager removed the gold from the horse, and with the gold off, it struggled to rise. Isager glanced at Rodelo, hesitant to use both hands to help the horse. "Go ahead," Rodelo said, "help him."

Together they got the horse up, and then they turned south. The salty crust crunched and broke beneath their feet. Sometimes they sank to their ankles; the horses broke through at every step.

They often stopped to rest and Isager glanced at Rodelo. "We better have a truce," he said, his eyes shifting away, then back. "You couldn't make it without me."

Rodelo's lips thinned over his white teeth. "Don't need you. You knew the desert. I know the sea."

"The desert's still with us," Isager said. Suddenly the water in Rodelo's canteen was more precious than gold. He was waiting for a chance to go for his gun.

The white glare around them forced their eyes to thin slits, while soda dust settled over them in a thin cloak. They stared at each other, as wild and thin as the gaunt, skeletonlike horses, white and shadowy things that seemed to waver with unreality in the heat. The milky water, undrinkable, and taunting them, whispered secret obscenities along the blue-white beach. "There'll be a fishing boat," Isager said. "No reason to kill each other. Maybe there's water beyond that bluff."

"There'll be no boat." Rodelo stated it flatly. "This is the wrong bay."

Isager stared, blinking slowly. "Wrong bay?" he said stupidly.

"Look!" Rodelo shouted harshly. "It's too shallow! We've come to the wrong place!"

Isager's dry tongue fought for his lips. There was no hope then.

"Give me your gun," Rodelo said, "and I'll take you there."

"So you can kill me?" Isager drew back, his eyes cold and calculating.

"I know where the bay is," Rodelo said. "Give me your gun."

Isager stared. Was it a trick? How could he actually know?

Suddenly, Rodelo shrugged. "Come on, then! I'll take my chances on you!" He pointed toward the dark bluff. "Look! That's a water sky. There's water beyond that point. Another bay!"

He took a step and a bullet kicked dust at his feet. He grabbed for his gun and whirled on Isager, but the gunfighter had already faced the hillside. Four Indians were coming down the hill, riding hard. As Rodelo turned, Isager stepped his feet apart and fired. An Indian's horse stumbled and went down, throwing the rider head over heels.

Rodelo dropped to one knee and shot under the belly of his horse. He saw an Indian drop and he fired again and missed. A bullet hit Isager and turned him half around. He staggered, and the half-dead horse lunged clumsily away. A hoof went through the crust and the horse fell heavily and lay panting, one white sliver of bone showing through the hide of the broken leg.

Isager fell, pulled off balance by the fall of the horse, and Rodelo fired again and again. His gun muzzle wavered and the shots kicked up dust. Isager rolled over behind the downed horse. He knew from harsh experience that accuracy was more essential than speed. He steadied his gun barrel. The Indian who had been thrown was rushing him. The brown body loomed large and he could see sweat streaks on the man's chest. He squeezed off his shot and saw the Indian stumble in midstride and then pitch over on his face.

Isager pushed himself to his knees, then got up. The beach weaved slowly, sickeningly beneath him. He turned his head stiffly and looked toward Rodelo. The fallen man looked like a bundle of old clothes, but as Isager looked, the bundle moved. Rodelo uncoiled himself and got up. Blood covered his face from a cut on his cheek. He stared at his empty gun, then clumsily began feeding shells into the chambers.

Across the wavering sand the two men stared at each other, then Rodelo laughed hoarsely. "You look like hell!" he said, grinning from his heat-blasted face.

Isager's brain seemed to spin queerly and he blinked. What was the matter with him? A pain bit suddenly at his side, and he clasped the pain with his hand. His fingers felt damp and he drew them away, staring stupidly at the blood dripping from his fingers.

"You copped one," Rodelo said. "You're hit."

Isager swayed. Suddenly he knew this was it,

right here on this dead-white beach washed by an ugly weedy sea. It was no way for a cowhand to cash in his chips. "Beat it," he said hoarsely. "There's more coming."

"How do you know that?"

"That's why they rushed. To get us an' claim the reward. If they'd been alone they would have taken their time." His knees felt buttery and queer. "There's one good horse. Take the gold an' beat it. I'm done in, so I'll hold them off."

He went to his knees. "Only . . ." His voice trailed off and he waited, his eyes begging Rodelo to wait a minute longer, then he managed the words, "get some of that money to Tom Hopkins's wife. He . . . he was that marshal. Funny thing, funny . . . Never meant to kill him. He came at me an' it was just reflex . . . jus' . . . just drew an' shot."

"All right," Rodelo said, and he meant it. He turned and disappeared into the blinding light.

Isager lay down behind the fallen horse. He slid the rifle from its scabbard and waited.

SHERIFF BILL GARDEN and two Apache trackers found Isager a few hours later. Gunfire from the advance party of six Yaquis had led them to this desolate beach. The convict was curled up behind a dying horse, surrounded by bright brass shells ejected from his rifle. Two of the Apache horses were gone and only one of the horses ridden by the convicts was alive. He was standing head down on the hillside not far away.

Horse tracks trailed away from the body of Isager, a faint trail toward the bluff to the south. Bill Garden glanced after them. The remaining scouts were still after the last man. He turned and looked down at Isager. "Lord a-mighty," he said. "What a place to die!"

Far off across the water there was a flash of white, a jib shaken out to catch the wind . . . a boat had left the fishing beds at Rocky Bay and was beating its way southward toward Guaymas.

# *Dutchman's Flat*

The dust of Dutchman's Flat had settled in a gray film upon their faces, and Neill could see the streaks made by the sweat on their cheeks and brows and knew his own must be the same. No man of them was smiling and they rode with their rifles in their hands, six grim and purposeful men upon the trail of a single rider.

They were men shaped and tempered to the harsh ways of a harsh land, strong in their sense of justice, ruthless in their demand for punishment, relentless in pursuit. From the desert they had carved their homes, and from the desert they drew their courage and their code, and the desert knows no mercy.

"Where's he headin', you reckon?"

"Home, mostly likely. He'll need grub an' a rifle. He's been livin' on the old Sorenson place."

Kimmel spat. "He's welcome to it. That place starved out four men I know of." He stared at the hoof tracks ahead. "He's got a good horse."

"Big buckskin. Reckon we'll catch him, Hardin?"

"Sure. Not this side of his place, though. There ain't no shortcuts we can take to head him off, and he's pointin' for home straight as a horse can travel."

"Ain't tryin' to cover his trail none."

"No use tryin'." Hardin squinted his eyes against the glare of the sun. "He knows we figure he'll head for his ranch."

"He's no tenderfoot." Kesney expressed the thought that had been dawning upon them all in the last two hours. "He knows how to save a horse, an' he knows a trail."

They rode on in near silence. Hardin scratched his unshaven jaw. The dust lifted from the hooves of the horses as they weaved their way through the catclaw and mesquite. It was a parched and sun-baked land, with only dancing heat waves and the blue distance of the mountains to draw them on. The trail they followed led straight as a man could ride across the country. Only at draws or nests of rocks did it swerve, where they noticed the rider always gave his horse the best of it.

No rider of the desert must see a man to know him, for it is enough to follow his trail. In these things are the ways of a man made plain, his kindness or cruelty, his ignorance or cunning, his strength and his weakness. There are indications that cannot escape a man who has followed trails, and in the two hours since they had ridden out of Freedom the six had already learned much of the man they followed. And they would learn more.

"What started it?"

The words sounded empty and alone in the vast stillness of the basin.

HARDIN TURNED HIS HEAD slightly so the words could drift back. It was the manner of a man who rides much in the wind or rain. He shifted the rifle to his left hand and wiped his sweaty right palm on his coarse pants leg.

"Some loose talk. He was in the Bon Ton buyin' grub an' such. Johnny said somethin' at which he took offense an' they had some words. Johnny was wearin' a gun, but this Lock wasn't, so he gets him a gun an' goes over to the Longhorn.

"He pushes open the door an' shoots Johnny twice through the body. In the back." Hardin spat. "He fired a third shot, but that missed Johnny and busted a bottle of whiskey."

There was a moment's silence while they digested this, and then Neill looked up.

"We lynchin' him for the killin' or bustin' the whiskey?"

It was a good question, but drew no reply. The dignity of the five other riders was not to be touched by humor. They were riders on a mission. Neill let his eyes drift over the dusty copper of the desert. He had no liking for the idea of lynching any man, and he did not know the squatter from the Sorenson place. Living there should be punishment enough for any man. Besides—

"Who saw the shooting?" he asked.

"Nobody seen it, actually. Only he never gave Johnny a fair shake. Sam was behind the bar, but he was down to the other end and it happened too fast."

"What's his name? Somebody call him Lock?" Neill asked. There was something incongruous in lynching a man whose name you did not know. He shifted in the saddle, squinting his eyes toward the distant lakes dancing in the mirage of heat waves.

"What's it matter? Lock, his name is. Chat Lock."

"Funny name."

The comment drew no response. The dust was thicker now and Neill pulled his bandanna over his nose and mouth. His eyes were drawn back to the distant blue of the lakes. They were enticingly cool and beautiful, lying across the way ahead and in the basin off to the right. This was the mirage that lured many a man from his trail to pursue the always retreating shoreline of the lake. It looked like water, it really did.

Maybe there was water in the heat waves. Maybe if a man knew how, he could extract it and drink. The thought drew his hand to his canteen, but he took it away without drinking. The slosh water in the canteen was no longer enticing, for it was warm, brackish, and unsatisfying.

"You know him, Kimmel?" Kesney asked. He was a wiry little man, hard as a whipstock, with bits of sharp steel for eyes and brown muscle-corded hands. "I wouldn't know him if I saw him."

"Sure, I know him. Big feller, strong made, rusty-like hair an' maybe forty year old. Looks plumb salty, too, an' from what I hear he's no friendly sort of man. Squattin' on that Sorenson place looks plumb suspicious, for no man can make him a livin' on that dry-as-a-bone place. No fit place for man nor beast. Ever'body figures no honest man would squat on such a place."

It seemed a strange thing, to be searching out a man whom none of them really knew. Of course, they had all known Johnny Webb. He was a handsome, popular young man, a daredevil and a hellion, but a very attractive one, and a top hand to boot. They had all known him and had all liked him. Then, one of the things that made them so sure that this had been a wrong killing, even aside from the shots in the back, was the fact that Johnny Webb had been the fastest man in the Spring Valley country. Fast, and a dead shot.

Johnny had worked with all these men, and they were good men—hard men, but good. Kimmel, Hardin, and Kesney had all made something of their ranches, as had the others, only somewhat less so. They had come west when the going was rough, fought Indians and rustlers, and then battled drought, dust, and hot, hard winds. It took a strong man to survive in this country, and they had survived. He, Neill, was the youngest of them all and the newest in the country. He was still looked upon with some reserve. He had been here only five years.

Neill could see the tracks of the buckskin, and it gave him a strange feeling to realize that the man who rode that horse would soon be dead, hanging from a noose in one of those ropes attached to a saddle horn of Hardin or Kimmel. Neill had never killed a man or seen one killed by another man, and the thought made him uncomfortable.

Yet Johnny was gone, and his laughter and his jokes were a thing passed. They had brightened more than one roundup, more than one bitter day of heartbreaking labor on the range. Not that he had been an angel. He had been a proper hand with a gun and could throw one. And in his time he had had his troubles.

"He's walkin' his horse," Kesney said, "leadin' him."

"He's a heavy man," Hardin agreed, "an' he figures to give us a long chase."

"Gone lame on him maybe," Kimmel suggested.

"No, that horse isn't limpin'. This Lock is a smart one."

They had walked out of the ankle-deep dust now and were crossing a parched, dry plain of crusted earth. Hardin reined in suddenly and pointed.

"Look there." He indicated a couple of flecks on the face of the earth crust where something had spilled. "Water splashed."

"Careless," Neill said. "He'll need that water."

"No," Kesney said. "He was pourin' water in a cloth to wipe out his horse's nostrils. Bet you a dollar."

"Sure," Hardin agreed, "that's it. Horse breathes a lot better. A man runnin' could kill a good horse on this Flat. He knows that."

THEY RODE ON, and for almost a half hour no one spoke. Neill frowned at the sun. It had been on his left a few minutes ago, and now they rode straight into it.

"What's he doin'?" Kesney said wonderingly. "This ain't the way to his place!" The trail had turned again, and now the sun was on their right.

Then it turned again and was at their backs. Hardin was in the lead, and he drew up and swore wickedly.

They ranged alongside him, and stared down into a draw that cracked the face of the desert alongside the trail they had followed. Below them was a place where a horse had stood, and across the bank something white fluttered from the parched clump of greasewood.

Kesney slid from the saddle and crossed the wash. When he had the slip of white, he stared at it, and then they heard him swear. He walked back and handed it to Hardin. They crowded near.

Neill took the slip from Hardin's fingers after he had read it. It was torn from some sort of book and the words were plain enough, scrawled with a flat rock for a rest.

> That was a fair shutin anyways six aint nowhars enuf, go fetch more men. Man on the gray better titen his girth or heel have him a sorebacked hoss.

"Why that . . . !" Short swore softly. "He was lyin' within fifty yards of us when we come by. Had him a rifle, too. I seen it in a saddle scabbard on that buckskin in town. He could have got one of us, anyway!"

"Two or three most likely," Kimmel commented. The men stared at the paper and then looked back into the wash. The sand showed a trail, but cattle had walked here, too. It would make the going a little slower.

Neill, his face flushed and his ears red, was tightening his saddle girth. The others avoided his eyes. The insult to him, even if the advice was good, was an insult to them all. Their jaws tightened. The squatter was playing Indian with them, and none of them liked it.

"Fair shootin', yeah!" Sutter exploded. "Right in the back!"

The trail led down the wash now, and it was slower going. The occasional puffs of wind they had left on the desert above were gone and the heat in the bottom of the wash was ovenlike. They rode into it, almost seeming to push their way through flames that seared. Sweat dripped into their eyes until they smarted, and trickled in tiny rivulets through their dust-caked beards, making their faces itch maddeningly.

The wash spilled out into a wide, flat bed of sand left by the rains of bygone years, and the tracks were plainer now. Neill tightened his bandanna and rode on, sodden with heat and weariness. The trail seemed deliberately to lead them into the worst regions, for now he was riding straight toward an alkali lake that loomed ahead.

At the edge of the water, the trail vanished.

Lock had ridden right into the lake. They drew up and stared at it, unbelieving.

"He can't cross," Hardin stated flatly. "That's deep out to the middle. Durned treacherous, too. A horse could get bogged down mighty easy."

They skirted the lake, taking it carefully, three going one way, and three the other. Finally, glancing back, Neill caught sight of Kesney's uplifted arm.

"They found it," he said. "Let's go back." Yet as he rode he was thinking what they all knew. This was a delay, for Lock knew they would have to scout the shores both ways to find his trail, and there would be a delay while the last three rejoined the first. A small thing, but in such a chase it was important.

"Why not ride right on to the ranch?" Short suggested.

"We might," Hardin speculated. "On the other hand he might fool us an' never go nigh it. Then we could lose him."

The trail became easier, for now Lock was heading straight into the mountains.

"Where's he goin'?" Kesney demanded irritably. "This don't make sense, nohow!"

There was no reply, the horsemen stretching out in single file, riding up the draw into the mountains. Suddenly Kimmel, who was now in the lead, drew up. Before him a thread of water trickled from the rock and spilled into a basin of stones.

"Huh!" Hardin stared. "I never knowed about this spring afore. Might's well have a drink." He swung down.

They all got down and Neill rolled a smoke.

"Somebody sure fixed her up nice," he said. "That wall of stone makin' that basin ain't so old."

"No, it ain't."

Short watched them drink and grinned.

"He's a fox, right enough. He's an old ladino, this one. A reg'lar mossy horn. It don't take no time for one man to drink, an' one hoss. But here we got six men an' six horses to drink an' we lose more time."

"You really think he planned it that way?" Neill was skeptical.

Hardin looked around at him. "Sure. This Lock knows his way around."

When they were riding on, Neill thought about that. Lock **was** shrewd. He was desert-wise. And he was leading them a chase. If not even Hardin knew of this spring, and he had been twenty years in the Spring Valley country, then Lock must know a good deal about the country. Of course, this range of mountains was singularly desolate, and there was nothing in them to draw a man.

★ ★ ★

SO THEY KNEW this about their quarry. He was a man wise in the ways of desert and trail, and one who knew the country. Also, Neill reflected, it was probable he had built that basin himself. Nobody lived over this way but Lock, for now it was not far to the Sorenson place.

Now they climbed a single horse trail across the starkly eroded foothills, sprinkled with clumps of Joshua and Spanish bayonet. It was a weird and broken land, where long fingers of black lava stretched down the hills and out into the desert as though clawing toward the alkali lake they had left behind. The trail mounted steadily and a little breeze touched their cheeks. Neill lifted his hand and wiped dust from his brow and it came away in flakes, plastered by sweat.

The trail doubled and changed, now across the rock face of the burnt red sandstone, then into the lava itself, skirting hills where the exposed ledges mounted in layers like a vast cake of many colors. Then the way dipped down, and they wound among huge boulders, smooth as so many waterworn pebbles. Neill sagged in the saddle, for the hours were growing long, and the trail showed no sign of ending.

"Lucky he ain't waitin' to shoot," Kimmel

commented, voicing the first remark in over an hour. "He could pick us off like flies."

As if in reply to his comment, there was an angry whine above them and then the crack of a rifle.

As one man they scattered for shelter, whipping rifles from their scabbards, for all but two had replaced them when they reached the lake. Hardin swore, and Kimmel wormed his way to a better view of the country ahead.

Short had left the saddle in his scramble for shelter, and his horse stood in the open, the canteen making a large lump behind the saddle. Suddenly the horse leaped to the solid thud of a striking bullet, and then followed the crack of the rifle, echoing over the mountainside.

Short swore viciously. "If he killed that horse . . . !" But the horse, while shifting nervously, seemed uninjured.

"Hey!" Kesney yelled. "He shot your canteen!"

It was true enough. Water was pouring onto the ground, and swearing, Short started to get up. Sutter grabbed his arm.

"Hold it! If he could get that canteen, he could get you!"

They waited, and the trickle of water slowed, then faded to a drip. All of them stared angrily at the unrewarding rocks ahead of them. One canteen the less. Still they had all filled up at the spring and should have enough. Uncomfortably, however, they realized that the object of their chase, the man called Chat Lock, knew where he was taking them, and he had not emptied that canteen by chance. Now they understood the nature of the man they followed. He did nothing without object.

Lying on the sand or rocks they waited, peering ahead.

"He's probably ridin' off now!" Sutter barked.

Nobody showed any disposition to move. The idea appealed to none of them, for the shot into the canteen showed plainly enough the man they followed was no child with a rifle. Kimmel finally put his hat on a rifle muzzle and lifted it. There was no response. Then he tried sticking it around a corner.

Nothing happened, and he withdrew it. Almost at once, a shot hit the trail not far from where the hat had been. The indication was plain. Lock was warning them not only that he was still there, but that he was not to be fooled by so obvious a trick.

They waited, and Hardin suddenly slid over a rock and began a flanking movement. He crawled, and they waited, watching his progress. The cover he had was good, and he could crawl almost to where the hidden marksman must be. Finally, he disappeared from their sight and they waited. Neill tasted the water in his canteen and dozed.

At last they heard a long yell, and looking up,

they saw Hardin standing on a rock far up the trail, waving them on. Mounting, they led Hardin's horse and rode on up the trail. He met them at the trail side, and his eyes were angry.

"Gone!" he said, thrusting out a hard palm. In it lay three brass cartridge shells. "Found 'em standing up in a line on a rock. An' look here." He pointed, and they stared down at the trail where he indicated. A neat arrow made of stones pointed down the trail ahead of them, and scratched on the face of the sandstone above it were the words: FOLLER THE SIGNS.

Kesney jerked his hat from his head and hurled it to the ground.

"Why, that dirty . . . !" He stopped, beside himself with anger. The contempt of the man they pursued was obvious. He was making fools of them, deliberately teasing them, indicating his trail as to a child or a tenderfoot.

"That ratty back-shootin' killer!" Short said. "I'll take pleasure in usin' a rope on him! Thinks he's smart!"

They started on, and the horse ahead of them left a plain trail, but a quarter of a mile farther along, three dried pieces of mesquite had been laid in the trail to form another arrow.

Neill stared at it. This was becoming a personal matter now. He was deliberately playing with them, and he must know how that would set with men such as Kimmel and Hardin. It was a deliberate challenge; more, it was a sign of the utmost contempt.

The vast emptiness of the basin they skirted now was becoming lost in the misty purple light of late afternoon. On the right, the wall of the mountain grew steeper and turned a deeper red. The burnt red of the earlier hours was now a bright rust red, and here and there long fingers of quartz shot their white arrows down into the face of the cliff.

THEY ALL SAW the next message, but all read and averted their eyes. It was written on a blank face of the cliff. First, there was an arrow, pointing ahead, and then the words: SHADE, SO'S YOU DON'T GIT SUNSTROK.

They rode on, and for several miles as the shadows drew down, they followed the markers their quarry left at intervals along the trail. All six of the men were tired and beaten. Their horses moved slowly, and the desert air was growing chill. It had been a long chase.

Suddenly, Kimmel and Kesney, who rode side by side, reined in. A small wall of rock was across the trail, and an arrow pointed downward into a deep cleft.

"What do you think, Hardin? He could pick us off man by man."

Hardin studied the situation with misgivings and hesitated, lighting a smoke.

"He ain't done it yet."

Neill's remark fell into the still air like a rock into a calm pool of water. As the rings of ripples spread wider into the thoughts of the other five, he waited.

Lock could have killed one or two of them, perhaps all of them by now. Why had he not? Was he waiting for darkness and an easy getaway? Or was he leading them into a trap?

"The devil with it!" Hardin exclaimed impatiently. He wheeled his horse and, pistol in hand, started down into the narrow rift in the dark. One by one, they followed. The darkness closed around them, and the air was damp and chill. They rode on, and then the trail mounted steeply toward a grayness ahead of them, and they came out in a small basin. Ahead of them they heard a trickle of running water and saw the darkness of trees.

Cautiously they approached. Suddenly, they saw the light of a fire. Hardin drew up sharply and slid from his horse. The others followed. In a widening circle, they crept toward the fire. Kesney was the first to reach it, and the sound of his swearing rent the stillness and shattered it like thin glass. They swarmed in around him.

The fire was built close beside a small running stream, and nearby was a neat pile of dry sticks. On a paper, laid out carefully on a rock, was a small mound of coffee, and another of sugar. Nobody said anything for a minute, staring at the fire and the coffee. The taunt was obvious, and they were bitter men. It was bad enough to have a stranger make such fools of them on a trail, to treat them like tenderfeet, but to prepare a camp for them . . .

"I'll be cussed if I will!" Short said violently. "I'll go sleep on the desert first!"

"Well—" Hardin was philosophical. "Might's well make the most of it. We can't trail him at night, no way."

Kimmel had dug a coffeepot out of his pack and was getting water from the stream which flowed from a basin just above their camp. Several of the others began to dig out grub, and Kesney sat down glumly, staring into the fire. He started to pick a stick off the pile left for them and then jerked his hand as though he had seen a snake. Getting up, he stalked back into the trees, and after a minute, he returned.

Sutter was looking around, and suddenly he spoke. "Boys, I know this place! Only I never knew about that crack in the wall. This here's the Mormon Well!"

Hardin sat up and looked around. "Durned if it ain't," he said. "I ain't been in here for six or seven years."

Sutter squatted on his haunches. "Look!" He was excited and eager, sketching with a stick in the sand. "Here's Mormon Well, where we are.

Right over here to the northwest there's an old sawmill an' a tank just above it. I'll bet a side of beef that durned killer is holed up for the night in that sawmill!"

Kesney, who had taken most to heart the taunting of the man they pursued, was on his knees staring at the diagram drawn in the damp sand. He was nodding thoughtfully.

"He's right! He sure is. I remember that old mill! I holed up there one time in a bad storm. Spent two days in it. If that sidewinder stays there tonight, we can get him!"

As they ate, they talked over their plan. Traveling over the rugged mountains ahead of them was almost impossible in the darkness, and besides, even if Lock could go the night without stopping, his horse could not. The buckskin must have a rest. Moreover, with all the time Lock had been losing along the trail, he could not be far ahead. It stood to reason that he must have planned just this, for them to stop here, and to hole up in the sawmill himself.

"We'd better surprise him," Hardin suggested. "That sawmill is heavy timber, an' a man in there with a rifle an' plenty of ammunition could stand us off for a week."

"Has he got plenty?"

"Sure he has," Neill told them. "I was in the Bon Ton when he bought his stuff. He's got grub and he's got plenty of forty-fours. They do for either his Colt or his Winchester."

Unspoken as yet, but present in the mind of each man, was a growing respect for their quarry, a respect and an element of doubt. Would such a man as this shoot another in the back? The evidence against him was plain enough, or seemed plain enough.

YET BEYOND THE RESPECT there was something else, for it was no longer simply a matter of justice to be done, but a personal thing. Each of them felt in some measure that his reputation was at stake. It had not been enough for Lock to leave an obvious trail, but he must leave markers, the sort to be used for any tenderfoot. There were men in this group who could trail a woodtick through a pine forest.

"Well," Kimmel said reluctantly and somewhat grimly, "he left us good coffee, anyway!"

They tried the coffee and agreed. Few things in this world are so comforting and so warming to the heart as hot coffee on a chilly night over a campfire when the day has been long and weary. They drank, and they relaxed. And as they relaxed the seeds of doubt began to sprout and put forth branches of speculation.

"He could have got more'n one of us today," Sutter hazarded. "This one is brush wise."

"I'll pull that rope on him!" Short stated positively. "No man makes a fool out of me!" But in his voice there was something lacking.

"You know," Kesney suggested, "if he knows these hills like he seems to, an' if he really wanted to lose us, we'd have to burn the stump and sift the ashes before we found him!"

There was no reply. Hardin drew back and eased the leg of his pants away from the skin, for the cloth had grown too hot for comfort.

Short tossed a stick from the neat pile into the fire.

"That mill ain't so far away," he suggested, "shall we give her a try?"

"Later." Hardin leaned back against a log and yawned. "She's been a hard day."

"Both them bullets go in Johnny's back?"

The question moved among them like a ghost. Short stirred uneasily, and Kesney looked up and glared around. "Sure they did! Didn't they, Hardin?"

"Sure." He paused thoughtfully. "Well, no. One of them was under his left arm. Right between the ribs. Looked like a heart shot to me. The other one went through near his spine."

"The heck with it!" Kesney declared. "No slick, rustlin' squatter can come into this country and shoot one of our boys! He was shot in the back, an' I seen both holes. Johnny got that one nigh the spine, an' he must have turned and tried to draw, then got that bullet through the heart!"

Nobody had seen it. Neill remembered that, and the thought rankled. Were they doing an injustice? He felt like a traitor at the thought, but secretly he had acquired a strong tinge of respect for the man they followed.

The fire flickered and the shadows danced a slow, rhythmic quadrille against the dark background of trees. He peeled bark from the log beside him and fed it into the fire. It caught, sparked brightly, and popped once or twice. Hardin leaned over and pushed the coffeepot nearer the coals. Kesney checked the loads in his Winchester.

"How far to that sawmill, Hardin?"

"About six miles, the way we go."

"Let's get started." Short got to his feet and brushed off the sand. "I want to get home. Got my boys buildin' fence. You either keep a close watch or they are off gal hootin' over the hills."

They tightened their saddle girths, doused the fire, and mounted up. With Hardin in the lead once more, they moved off into the darkness.

Neill brought up the rear. It was damp and chill among the cliffs and felt like the inside of a cavern. Overhead the stars were very bright. Mary was going to be worried, for he was never home so late. Nor did he like leaving her alone.

He wanted to be home, eating a warm supper and going to bed in the old four-poster with the patchwork quilt Mary's grandmother made, pulled over him. What enthusiasm he had had for the chase was gone. The warm fire, the coffee, his own weariness, and the growing respect for Lock had changed him.

Now they all knew he was not the manner of man they had supposed. Justice can be a harsh taskmaster, but Western men know their kind, and the lines were strongly drawn. When you have slept beside a man on the trail, worked with him and with others like him, you come to know your kind. In the trail of the man Chat Lock, each rider of the posse was seeing the sort of man he knew, the sort he could respect. The thought was nagging and unsubstantial, but each of them felt a growing doubt, even Short and Kesney, who were most obdurate and resentful.

They knew how a backshooter lived and worked. He had his brand on everything he did. The mark of this man was the mark of a man who did things, who stood upon his own two feet, and who if he died, died facing his enemy. To the unknowing, such conclusions might seem doubtful, but the men of the desert knew their kind.

The mill was dark and silent, a great looming bulk beside the stream and the still pool of the millpond. They dismounted and eased close. Then according to a prearranged plan, they scattered and surrounded it. From behind a lodgepole pine, Hardin called out.

"We're comin' in, Lock! We want you!"

THE CHALLENGE WAS HARSH and ringing. Now that the moment had come, something of the old suspense returned. They listened to the water babbling as it trickled over the old dam, and then they moved. At their first step, they heard Lock's voice.

"Don't you come in here, boys! I don't want to kill none of you, but you come an' I will! That was a fair shootin'! You've got no call to come after me!"

Hardin hesitated, chewing his mustache. "You shot him in the back!" he yelled.

"No such thing! He was a-facin' the bar when I come in. He seen I was heeled, an' he drawed as he turned. I beat him to it. My first shot took him in the side an' he was knocked back against the bar. My second hit him in the back an' the third missed as he was a-fallin'. You hombres didn't see that right."

The sound of his voice trailed off, and the water chuckled over the stones and then sighed to a murmur among the trees. The logic of Lock's statement struck them all. It **could** have been that way.

A long moment passed, and then Hardin spoke up again.

"You come in and we'll give you a trial. Fair an' square!"

"How?" Lock's voice was a challenge. "You ain't got no witness. Neither have I. Ain't nobody to say what happened there but me, as Johnny ain't alive."

"Johnny was a mighty good man, an' he was our friend!" Short shouted. "No murderin' squatter is goin' to move into this country an' start shootin' folks up!"

There was no reply to that, and they waited, hesitating a little. Neill leaned disconsolately against the tree where he stood. After all, Lock might be telling the truth. How did they know? There was no use hanging a man unless you were sure.

"Gab!" Short's comment was explosive. "Let's move in, Hardin! Let's get him! He's lyin'! Nobody could beat Johnny, we know that!"

"Webb was a good man in his own country!" Lock shouted in reply. The momentary silence that followed held them, and then, almost as a man they began moving in. Neill did not know exactly when or why he started. Inside he felt sick and empty. He was fed up on the whole business, and every instinct told him this man was no backshooter.

Carefully, they moved, for they knew this man was handy with a gun. Suddenly, Hardin's voice rang out.

"Hold it, men! Stay where you are until daybreak! Keep your eyes open an' your ears. If he gets out of here he'll be lucky, an' in the daylight we can get him, or fire the mill!"

Neill sank to a sitting position behind a log. Relief was a great warmth that swept over him. There wouldn't be any killing tonight. Not tonight, at least.

Yet as the hours passed, his ears grew more and more attuned to the darkness. A rabbit rustled, a pinecone dropped from a tree, the wind stirred high in the pine tops, and the few stars winked through, lonesomely peering down upon the silent men.

With daylight they moved in and they went through the doors and up to the windows of the old mill, and it was empty and still. They stared at each other, and Short swore viciously, the sound booming in the echoing, empty room.

"Let's go down to the Sorenson place," Kimmel said. "He'll be there."

And somehow they were all very sure he would be. They knew he would be because they knew him for their kind of man. He would retreat no farther than his own ranch, his own hearth. There, if they were to have him and hang him, they would have to burn him out, and men would die in the process. Yet with these men there was no fear. They felt the drive of duty, the need for maintaining some law in this lonely desert and mountain land. There was only doubt which had grown until each man was shaken with it. Even Short, whom the markers by the trail had angered, and Kesney, who was the best tracker among them, even better than Hardin, had been irritated by it, too.

The sun was up and warming them when they rode over the brow of the hill and looked down into the parched basin where the Sorenson place lay.

But it was no parched basin. Hardin drew up so suddenly his startled horse almost reared. It was no longer the Sorenson place.

The house had been patched and rebuilt. The roof had spots of new lumber upon it, and the old pole barn had been made watertight and strong. A new corral had been built, and to the right of the house was a fenced-in garden of vegetables, green and pretty after the desert of the day before.

Thoughtfully, and in a tight cavalcade, they rode down the hill. The stock they saw was fat and healthy, and the corral was filled with horses.

"Been a lot of work done here," Kimmel said. And he knew how much work it took to make such a place attractive.

"Don't look like no killer's place!" Neill burst out. Then he flushed and drew back, embarrassed by his statement. He was the youngest of these men and the newest in the country.

No response was forthcoming. He had but stated what they all believed. There was something stable and lasting and something real and genuine, in this place.

"I been waitin' for you."

THE REMARK from behind them stiffened every spine. Chat Lock was here, behind them. And he would have a gun on them, and if one of them moved, he could die.

"My wife's down there fixin' breakfast. I told her I had some friends comin' in. A posse huntin' a killer. I've told her nothin' about this trouble. You ride down there now, you keep your guns. You eat your breakfast and then if you feel bound and determined to get somebody for a fair shootin', I'll come out with any one of you or all of you, but I ain't goin' to hang.

"I ain't namin' no one man because I don't want to force no fight on anybody. You ride down there now."

They rode, and in the dooryard, they dismounted. Neill turned then, and for the first time he saw Chat Lock.

He was a big man, compact and strong. His rusty brown hair topped a brown, sun-hardened face, but with the warmth in his eyes it was a friendly sort of face. Not at all what he expected.

Hardin looked at him. "You made some changes here."

"I reckon." Lock gestured toward the well. "Dug by hand. My wife worked the windlass." He looked around at them, taking them in with one sweep of his eyes. "I've got the grandest woman in the world."

Neill felt hot tears in his eyes suddenly and busied himself loosening his saddle girth to keep the others from seeing. That was the way he felt about Mary.

The door opened suddenly, and they turned. The sight of a woman in this desert country was enough to make any man turn. What they saw was not what they expected. She was young, perhaps in her middle twenties, and she was pretty, with brown wavy hair and gray eyes and a few freckles on her nose. "Won't you come in? Chat told me he had some friends coming for breakfast, and it isn't often we have anybody in."

Heavy-footed and shamefaced they walked up on the porch. Kesney saw the care and neatness with which the hard hewn planks had been fitted. Here, too, was the same evidence of lasting, of permanence, of strength. This was the sort of man a country needed. He thought the thought before he fixed his attention on it, and then he flushed.

Inside, the room was as neat as the girl herself. How did she get the floors so clean? Before he thought, he phrased the question. She smiled.

"Oh, that was Chat's idea! He made a frame

and fastened a piece of pumice stone to a stick. It cuts into all the cracks and keeps them very clean."

The food smelled good, and when Hardin looked at his hands, Chat motioned to the door.

"There's water an' towels if you want to wash up."

Neill rolled up his sleeves and dipped his hands in the basin. The water was soft, and that was rare in this country, and the soap felt good on his hands. When he had dried his hands, he walked in. Hardin and Kesney had already seated themselves, and Lock's wife was pouring coffee.

"Men," Lock said, "this is Mary. You'll have to tell her your names. I reckon I missed them."

Mary. Neill looked up. She was Mary, too. He looked down at his plate again and ate a few bites. When he looked up, she was smiling at him.

"My wife's name is Mary," he said. "She's a fine girl!"

"She would be! But why don't you bring her over? I haven't talked with a woman in so long I wouldn't know how it seemed! Chat, why haven't you invited them over?"

Chat mumbled something, and Neill stared at his coffee. The men ate in uncomfortable silence. Hardin's eyes kept shifting around the room. That pumice stone. He'd have to fix up a deal like that for Jane. She was always fussing about the work of keeping a board floor clean. That washstand inside, too, with pipes made of hollow logs to carry the water out so she wouldn't have to be running back and forth. That was an idea, too.

They finished their meal reluctantly. One by one they trooped outside, avoiding each other's eyes. Chat Lock did not keep them waiting. He walked down among them.

"If there's to be shootin'," he said quietly, "let's get away from the house."

Hardin looked up. "Lock, was that right, what you said in the mill? Was it a fair shootin'?"

Lock nodded. "It was. Johnny Webb prodded me. I didn't want trouble, nor did I want to hide behind the fact I wasn't packin' an iron. I walked over to the saloon not aimin' for trouble. I aimed to give him a chance if he wanted it. He drawed an' I beat him. It was a fair shootin'."

"All right." Hardin nodded. "That's good enough for me. I reckon you're a different sort of man than any of us figured."

"Let's mount up," Short said. "I got fence to build."

Chat Lock put his hand on Hardin's saddle. "You folks come over sometime. She gets right lonesome. I don't mind it so much, but you know how womenfolks are."

"Sure," Hardin said, "sure thing."

"An' you bring your Mary over," he told Neill.

Neill nodded, his throat full. As they mounted the hill, he glanced back. Mary Lock was standing in the doorway, waving to them, and the sunlight was very bright in the clean-swept dooryard.

# *From the Listening Hills*

The hunted man lay behind a crude parapet in a low-roofed, wind-eroded cave on the north slope of Tokewanna Peak. One hundred yards down the slope, at an approximate altitude of eleven thousand feet, just inside a fringe of alpine fir, were scattered the hunting men.

The bare, intervening stretch of rock was flecked here and there with patches of snow. Within the fringe of trees but concealed from his view except for the faint wisps of smoke, were the fires of his pursuers.

Boone Tremayne had no fire, nor at this time dared he make one, for as yet his position was not exactly known to the armed men.

It was very cold and he lay on his stomach, favoring his left side where the first bullet had torn an ugly wound. The second bullet had gone through his thigh, but his crude bandages as well as the cold had caused the bleeding to stop.

A low wind moaned across the rock, stirring the icy bits of snow on the cold flanks of the peak which arose two thousand feet above and behind him. Within the low cave it was still light, and Boone Tremayne clutched the stub of pencil and looked down at the cheap tablet at his elbow.

He must write with care, for what he wrote now would be all his son, as yet unborn, would ever know of his father and uncles. He would hear the stories others would tell, and so it would be important for him to have some word in his father's hand.

The pencil clutched awkwardly in his chilled fingers, he began to write:

It's getting mighty cold up here, Son, and my grub's about gone. My canteen's still half full, but it ain't no use, they've done got me.

Time to time I can hear them down in the brush. There must be a hunert of them. Seems an awful lot of folks to git one lone man. If I only had Johnny here I wouldn't feel so bad. Johnny, he always sort of perked a feller up no matter how bad things got.

Except for you, I'm the last of the Tremaynes. Somehow it ain't so lonely up here knowing there's to be a son of mine somewheres.

Now, Son, your ma is a mighty good woman as well as a pretty one. I never figured, no way you look at it, to get such a girl as Marge. If she'd married up with Burt, or

Elisha, I'd no-ways have blamed her. They were the pick of the lot, they were.

Just had me a look down there an' I reckon they are gitting set to rush me. Wished they wouldn't. I never aimed to kill nobody. They figured to hang me if I'm got alive, and I promised Ma I'd never stretch no rope. Least a man can do is die with his face toward them who aims to kill him.

Boone Tremayne put down the stub of pencil and chafed his cold fingers, peering through the stacked flakes of rock he had heaped into a wall before the opening. The cold was all through him now, and he knew he would never be warm again. That was okay, he had this one last job to do . . . and then he no longer cared. The wind whispered to the snow and then he saw a man, bulky with a heavy coat, lunge from the trees and come forward in a stumbling run.

A second man started as the first dropped behind a shelf of rock, and Boone put his cheek against the cold stock of the Winchester and squeezed off his shot. He put the bullet through the man's leg, saw the leg buckle and saw the man fall. Another started and Boone dropped him with a bullet through the shoulder.

He gnawed at his lip and stared, hollow-eyed and gaunt, at the shelf of rock where the first man had fallen. "Reckon I'd best let you git cold, too, mister," he said, and flicked a glancing shot off the rock over the man's head. That would let him know he had been seen, that it would be dangerous to try moving.

He shifted his position, favoring his wounded side and leg. Nobody moved, and the afternoon was waning. At night they would probably come for him. He glanced at the sullen gray sky. There was still time.

It started over a horse. We Tremaynes always found ourselves good horse flesh. Johnny, he ketched this black colt in the hills near Durango. Little beauty, he was, and Johnny learned him well and entered him in a race we always had down around there.

Dick Watson, him and his brothers, they fancied horses too and one of Dick's horses had won that race four years running. We all bet a sight of money. Not so much, when you figure it, but a mighty lot for us, who never had much cash in hand. Johnny's black just ran off and left Watson's horse, and Watson was mighty put out.

He said no horse like that ever run wild, and that Johnny must of stole him somewheres. Johnny said no he never and that Watson's horse just wasn't all that fast. Watson said that if Johnny wasn't such a boy, him being just sixteen, he'd whup him good.

Then our brother Burt, he stepped up. Burt was a mighty big, fine figure of a man. He stepped up and said he wasn't no boy, if it was a fight Watson wanted.

Well, Burt, he beat the tar out of Dick Watson. There was hard words said, and Ma, she reckoned we all better git for home. We did, an' everything went along for a time. Until that black was found dead. Somebody shot her down in the pasture. Shot her from clost up.

Johnny, he was all for going to town and gitting him a man, but Ma, she said no and Burt and Lisha, they sided with her. But Johnny . . . well, it was some days for he tuned up that mouth organ of his. And when he done it, it was all sad music.

We wasn't cattlemen, Son, not like other folks around. We was farmers and trappers, or bee hunters, anything there was to git the coon. Mostly, them days, we farmed and between crops we went back in the high meadows and rounded us up wild horses.

They was thousands of them, Son. Land sakes, I wished you could of seen them run! It were a sight too beautiful for man to look upon. We rounded up a sight of them, but we never kept but a few. We'd pick the youngest and prettiest. We'd gentle them down with kindness and good grass and carrots, then we'd break them. My Pap, he broke horses for a gent in Kentucky, a long time ago and he knew a goer and a stayer. I guess none of us ever did forgit that little black mare.

Now that horse was shot clost up. It was no accident. And no man would kill a good horse like that. Except for if he done it in pure meanness. And who had him a reason? Dick Watson. That black mare beat Watson's horse once and he would do it again. Johnny, he never said much, but from that day on he packed him a gun, and he never had afore.

Them boys down in the bresh is fixing to move. Gitting cold I reckon.

Boone Tremayne's head throbbed with fever and he stared through the chinks in the flaked rock. The man under the ledge stirred cautiously and Boone put a shot down there to keep him from stretching out too much. He rubbed his hands and blew upon the fingers. A man moved in the brush and Boone laid a bullet in close to the ground.

Bullets hailed around his shelter, most of them glancing off the rocks, but one got inside and ricocheted past his head. A hair closer and he would have been dead.

Flat on his belly he stuffed the tablet and pencil in his pocket and crawled along the bottom of the shallow cave. Painfully, he wormed his way along the cave for thirty yards and found a place where it was a few inches deeper and where some animal or bird had long since gathered sticks for a nest or home. Gathering some of the dead sticks together, Boone built a fire.

The long-dead wood made little smoke and the tiny flame was comforting. Later, when it was dark the reflection would give him away so he tried to shield it with rocks as much as he could. He held his blue and shaking fingers almost in the flame, but it was a long time before any warmth reached him.

They were waiting now, waiting for darkness. He must finish his letter. There would be no time later.

> Mighty cold, Son, I've moved a mite and got me a fire. Well, the black was dead but we had us about forty head of good horses ready to move. Sam and Lisha, they set out for Durango. We figured to buy Ma a new dress for her birthday and to get us some tools we needed and other fixings. Going in the boys had to drive past the DW where the Watsons ranched. They seen Dick a-watching them, but thought nothing of that at the time.
>
> Well, when they got into Durango the sheriff come hightailing it up with five, six men, all armed heavy. They tell the boys

they are under arrest for stealing horses. The boys tell them they trained them horses, that they was wild stock afore. The sheriff and that bunch with him, one of them was a Watson, they just laughed.

Well, the boys was throwed in jail, but the sheriff, he wouldn't let them get word to the rest of us. Only Johnny, he got to thinking and when the boys was slow gitting back, he mounts up and heads for town. But they was ready for him, the Watsons was.

Johnny, he seen the horses in the corral, and he hightails it for the sheriff. The sheriff is out of town, maybe a-purpose, and Johnny, he goes into the T-Diamond Saloon. And there's three Watsons and two brothers-in-law of there's, all setting around.

These brothers-in-law, one named Ebberly, the other Boyd. This Boyd was some gun-slinger or had that reputation. Johnny, he never knowed them at all, but he knowed the Watsons. He asked the barkeep where was his brothers, and Dick Watson speaks up and says they are in jail for stealing horses, where he'll soon be. Johnny, he knows what Ma would say, and remarkable for him, keeps his head. He says nothing and turns to go and Dick Watson says, "Like you stole that black mare."

The three Watsons are spread out and

ready. He seen then it was a trap, but still he never knowed those other two which sat quiet near the door, never saying I, yes, or no. Johnny, he says, "I trained that black mare, Watson, an' you kilt her. You snuck up an' shot that pore little horse dead."

"I never!" Watson says, and folks say he looked mighty red in the face. "You're a liar!"

Watson grabbed iron and so did Johnny. The Watsons, they got three bullets into Johnny, but he still stood, so this Boyd, he shoots him in the back. Johnny went down, but there was two Watsons on the floor, one dead, and Dick badly hurt.

Johnny, they figured for dead, and they was so busy gitting their kin to the doc they never thought of him. He was alive and he crawled out of there. A girl he knowed in town, she got her Pap, who was a vet, and he fixed Johnny up and hid him out.

This here girl, she run down to the jail and told Lisha and Sam through the bars. She said they better get set, there'd be trouble. She had Johnny's gun and she passed it through the bars and along with it a chunk of pipe standing close by.

We heard about it after. The one Watson that was on his feet, him and Ebberly, Boyd and some half dozen others, they got them masks and come down to the jail to lynch the other boys. They got into the jail and the jailor he just stepped aside, easy as you please, and says, "In the second cell."

They rushed up. The boys just stood a-waiting, just like they didn't know what was going to happen. The barred door swung open and then Lisha, he outs with his gun and that bunch scrambled, believe you me. One of them turns to slam shut the door, but Sam, he got his pipe betwixt the door and the jam to keep it from closing. That feller dragged iron, so Sam raised the pipe and shoved it into his throat. That feller went down. The mob beat it, and so the boys, they took out. They told that jailer they would surrender to a U.S. Marshal, but nobody else.

Lisha and Sam, they went to the corral and got their horses, every head, and they started out of town. By that time the story got around that the Tremayne boys had killed two men and wounded a couple of others, then broke jail. So they fetched their guns and come running.

They got Sam right off. Folks said he was shot nine times in that first volley. At that, Lisha rode back to pick him up, but he couldn't get nigh the body, and could see by the way Sam was that he must be dead. So he headed off to home with his horses.

Boone Tremayne put aside his letter and added a few tiny sticks to his little fire. It was so small a man might have held it in his two hands, but the little flame looked good, and it warmed his fingers which were cramped from writing and the cold.

An icy wind blew over the slope of the mountain. Boone looked longingly at the woods below, and the first silver line that was the Middle Fork of the Green, which stretched away almost due north from where he lay. If he could get down there he might still have a chance . . . But there was no chance. The lost blood, the lack of food and the cold had drawn upon his strength until he was only a dank shell of a man, huddled in his worn clothes, shivering and freezing and looking down at the hunters who held him.

Cautiously, the man under the shelf below was moving. He, too, was feeling the cold. "Well, feel it," Boone whispered, "maybe next time you won't be so anxious to go hunting a lone man!" He ricocheted another bullet off the rock shelf.

Several rifles replied, and suddenly angry, Boone fired a careful shot at the flash of one of the guns. He heard a rifle rattle on rocks as it fell, and then a heavy body tumbling into brush. More shots were fired, but now he had turned ugly; the loneliness, the cold, the fear of death, all crowded in upon him and he shot rapidly and frantically, at rifle flashes, and dusting the brush around the smoke of the fires. He fired his rifle empty and reloaded and then with careful shots, proceeded to weed the woods below.

Then he doused his fire and moved farther along the undercut rock and found another place, almost as good as the last. Here he started another tiny blaze, shielding it with a large slab of flat rock.

Finished off telling how Sam was kilt. Johnny, he was shot bad and we didn't know if he was dead for two days, then that girl, Ellie Winters, she come up the mountain with the news. The town was mighty wrought up. Some of them was coming up after us.

We kept watch, Burt, Lisha and me. Meanwhile, we tried figuring what to do. For Ma's sake we would have to pull out, git up into the high meadows or west into the wild country over the Utah line.

Now we knowed they was hunting Johnny, and Ellie's Pa was worried too. So the three of us ups and goes down to Durango. Johnny, he mounted the horse we brought for him, and we dusted out of there.

Slow, and careful not to leave no tracks, we moved out, leaving our cabin, our crop, everything but the horses. We made it west-northwest past Lone Cone and finally crossing the San Miguel into Uncompahgre Plateau country. We found us a little box canyon there with grass and water, and we moved in. By hunting we made out, but Ma was feeling poorly so Burt, he stayed with her while Lisha and me, we mounted up and with five head of horses, we headed for a little town north of us on the river. We sold our horses, bought up supplies and come back.

Ma, she didn't get no better, and finally, she died one morning, just died a-setting in her rocker. We'd brung that rocker along, and it had been a sight of comfort for her. So Ma died and Johnny played his mouth organ, and we buried her. Then there was just the four of us, with Johnny still recuperating from his bullet wounds.

We could move on, but this here was our country and we knowed it. Pa was buried back at Durango. Sam, too, now. And Ma, she was buried there in the lonely Uncompahgres, all because of the orneriness of one man.

Them horses we sold let folks know where we was, and soon there was a posse after us. We were figured to be outlaws, real bad hombres. We'd killed folks and we'd busted jail. That posse cornered us in the mountains and we shot it out and got away.

That began the bad and lonely time, made pleasant only because we were together. We drifted west into the La Balas and sold our horses except for an extry for each of us, and then drifted into the Robber's Roost country. It was there I kilt my first man. It was that there Boyd. The same one who shot Johnny in the back.

He'd kilt a woman in Colorado, and then her man. After that the country got too hot to hold him so he drifted west to the Roost. There was a shack in the Roost them days, a log shack, long and low. The floor was adobe and there was a bar and a few tables. It was low-roofed, dark, and no ways pleasant. It was outside of that place I come up to Boyd.

He seen me and he stopped. "Another one of them miserable Tremaynes!" he sneers.

Men stopped to listen and watch. "You shot Johnny in the back," I tell him, "and I figure you're good for nothing else!" He grabs iron and about that time my gun bucks in my hand and this gent he just curls up and folds over.

The boys come a-running and we look at that passel of rustlers, thieves and no accounts, and a few mighty good men scattered among them. "Anybody got a argyment?" Burt asks.

One gent, his name was Cassidy, he chuckles, and says, "Boyd was no good and we knowed it. Anyway," he grins at us, "the weight o' the artillery is on your side!" Then he bought a round of drinks.

We drifted north through Wyoming, selling a few horses we broke and working time to time on spreads in the Wind River and Powder River countries. We drifted north into Montanny, and finally down to Deadwood. Here and there we heard rumors. Folks said we were robbing banks and trains, which we never done. Folks said we had killed this man or that one, and without ever doing a thing, we got us a name most as bad as the James boys. All on account of how people love to talk and gossip.

The fact that I killed Boyd got back to Colorado. He'd been some shakes as a gunman, so they now had me pegged as one. Boyd, I kilt, but if they figured he was fast, they wasn't figuring right. In Deadwood I heard Ebberly was in town, making his brags what he would do if he ever come up to any of the Tremaynes.

Bullet come nigh me just now. Better I tend to business for a mite.

Boone edged over a little and peered through the chinks in the rocks but could see only the dark line of the forest. The man he had kept under the rock shelf was off to his right now and it was not an easy shot . . . anyway, he had suffered enough.

His mouth felt dry and he rinsed it carefully with water from his canteen, then let the cool water trickle down his parched throat. It was his first drink in many hours. His face felt hot and there was a queer feeling around the wound in his side.

Bullets snarled and snapped, biting at the rocks, near him and farther along. He held his fire, reluctant to give himself away. Boone found no malice in his heart for the officers of the law. This was their job, and not theirs to decide the right and wrong, but to bring him in. He moved, crawling back along the long undercut of the cave. There was a little more to write. Ten . . . maybe twenty minutes more. Then it could be over . . . he could finally let it be over.

> Ebberly, Son, he made his brags, but we kept away from him. Only we shouldn't have. He knowed we was in town and when we kept away he figured we was scared. Then he seen Burt and took a shot at him. Burt shot back. Both of them missed.
>
> Burt, he hunted him and lost him. It was me who run into Ebberly last. I come down the street afore noon, hunting a couple of copper rivets to use in fixing my saddle. He

stepped down into the street and yells at me, "Boone Tremayne!"

He yelled, and he shot. Yet my gun come up so fast the two shots sounded like one. Only he missed . . . I didn't. I stood there, looking around. "Folks," I said, "I'm surely Boone Tremayne. But none of us, my brothers or me, ever stole a thing off any man. Nor we never shot at no man unless he hunted us down. We got us a bad name, but it ain't our doing. You seen this . . . he come at me with a drawn gun."

"You all better ride," a feller says. "This here Seth Bullock, our sheriff, he'd have to take you in." So we rode out. Sam was kilt and Ma was dead and everywhere they was after us.

We headed west, making for the Hole-in-the-Wall where men beyond the law would be let alone. We come down Beaver Crick out of the Black Hills and we rode up Cemetery Ridge and we drawed up there and rested our horses.

After awhile Lisha, he tunes up his old gitar and starts to play a might, and then we saw a feller coming up the slope. He looked a mighty rough customer and when he heerd our music he slowed up and looked us over. Then he come on up clost.

"Howdy!" he says. "Goin' far?"

"To Sundance," Burt says. "How fer is it?"

"Mebbe fifteen mile," this gent says. "Luck!" An' he rides on.

"Didn't like the look o' that hombre," Burt says, "we better ride out o' here, an' not for Sundance!" So we mounted up and took out south, holding east of Bald Mountain right along the Wyoming–South Dakota line.

Sure enough, Son, that gent was no good. He headed hisself right for Sundance, warning folks at ranches as he rode. The Bloody Tremaynes was riding, he said. We seen the first posse when we was heading to Lost Canyon, but there was no fight until they closed in on us from three directions at Stockade Beaver Crick. We fought her out there, kilt four of them and scratched up a few more, but we lost Burt. He had three bullets in him when he went down, kilt two men before he died. We buried Burt there on Stockade Beaver, and we made a marker for him, which you'll see if you ever ride thataway.

We rode south and west with that there posse setting in the brush licking their wounds.

We made the Hole-in-the-Wall and rode

through and no posse would foller us. We'd no money, only the horses we rode. But we run into a short-handed cow outfit driving to the Buffalo Fork. They didn't know who we was and didn't give two boots in a rain barrel. We done our share like always, and we stuck to our ownselves. The hands, they was friendly cusses, and the boss he only asked for a man a day's work. We drove to the Buffalo Fork and then the boss, he come over to us. "I'll be payin' you off in the mornin'. You boys better buy what ca'tridges we got," he says, quiet-like, "you won't find no place clost by to git 'em."

"That's right friendly o' you, Boss," Lisha says, "we take it kindly."

He stands there a mite, and then he says, "Never did b'lieve all I heerd, anyways," he said, and then he smiled. "We'll sure miss that music you boys make. Would you strike us up some singin' afore you leave?"

So we done it. Lisha, he sung "Greensleeves," and "Brennan on the Moor," an' "On Top of Ol' Smoky" and some of the other old songs from the hills back yonder, songs our folks fetched from Scotland and Ireland. We sang for an evening, and then loaded up with grub and bullets, and took off. Southwest across the Blackrock and camped at Lily Lake, and then on to the

Gross Venture and into the Jackson Hole country.

Son, your Pa's hands is mighty cold now. I guess this here letter's got to end up.

Johnny, he wanted to see Ellie Winters, and Lisha, he wanted to eat fresh melons from the patch, and I wanted to see your Ma again. I never knowed she loved me. I never even guessed she cared or thought of me. I just figured I'd like to see her some.

One night we was setting by the fire and Lisha he looked over at me and he says, "Boys, the melons'll be ripe in the bottom land now, an' the horses will be headin' up from the flats for the high meadows." So then we knowed we was heading home.

We rode down the Snake to the Grey and down the Grey to the Bear, and we followed her south to the border, staying clear of ranches and towns. Of a night we built our fires small and covered them well, and then at last we come riding down to the hills near Durango.

Lisha, he chuckles and says to me, "You all sure been a-talkin' a lot in your sleep, boy. If'n you ever said those things to a girl awake she'd sure be bakin' your corn pone from here on out."

Me, I git all redded up. "Don't give me that," I say, "I never talked none. Anyway, it wouldn't matter. What woman would care for me?"

Both Lisha and Johnny looked up sharp. "You damn fool!" they says, "they'd never git a better man, nowheres. An' that Marge, she's been eatin' her heart out for years over you!"

Me, I just stood there . . . I never figured nothing like that. I sure thought they was wrong, but both them boys, they knowed a sight more about women than ever I would.

Lisha, he rides off to town, and he ain't gone an hour afore he comes back and then Ellie, she and Marge comes a-running, and with them is Betts Warner, Lisha's girl. Marge, she just stopped, took one look, and then run to me and went to crying in my arms.

We made her a triple weddin' just two days later, but folks heerd about it, and one morning Lisha come to the door for his horse and Dick Watson, his brother and four-five friends, they shot him down. Shot him down with him only getting one shot off.

Betts, she come a-running to warn us, thinking of us even when her heart was gone within her, her man laying dead back there full of Watson lead.

"Saddle up," I says to Johnny, "I'll be

coming back soon." Me, I buckled on my guns.

"I'm goin' with you," Johnny says, and I told him no. He'd have to git us packed and ready. Marge, she just looked at me strange and soft and proud. She says, "You go along, Boone, I'll saddle up for you, and I'll be a-waiting here when you get back."

Never a mite of complaining, never a word agin it. She was a man's woman, that one, and she knowed my way was to ride for the man who fetched this trouble down upon us.

It was bright noonday when I fetched up to town. I swung down from the saddle and I asked old Jake. "You go along," I said, "and you tell that Dick Watson I'm here to put him down."

Standin' there, I wondered if it was I'd never have me a home, or see the light in my baby's eyes, or see the sunlight on the green corn growing, or smell the hay from my own meadows. Them things was all I ever wanted, all I ever fixed to have, and now it seemed like all my life I toted a gun, shooting and being shot at.

All I ever wanted in this here world was a bit of land and peace, the way man was meant to live. Not with no gun in his hand a-killing folks.

I seen Dick Watson step from a door down the way, and I seen him start, and I pulled down my hat and stepped out, stepped out and started walking to kill a man.

Then Watson stopped and I looked across the forty paces at him and I made my voice strong in the street. "Dick Watson, you brung hell to my family. You was sore because that black mare beat your horse! You lied about us stealing! You made us into outlaws and caused my brothers to be kilt and some other men too. It'll be on your conscience whether you live or die."

He stood there staring at me like he'd looked right in the face of death, and then he slapped leather. His gun came up and I shot him, low down in the belly where they die slow and hard. God forgive me, but I done it with hate in my heart. And then . . . I should have knowed he'd framed it, a half dozen of his friends stepped out and opened up on me.

Son, what come over me then I don't know. I guess I went sort of crazy. When I seen them all around me, I just tore loose and went to shooting. I went up on the porch after them, I followed one up the stairs and into his room. I chased another and shot him running, and then I loaded up and turned my back on both the dead and the living and I walked down that street to my horse. I was halfway home before I knowed I'd a bullet in me.

When I was patched up some we rode on and Betts went back to her folks, a widow almost afore she was a wife. We fetched up, final, in the Blue Mountains of Utah, and there we built us a double cabin and we ketched wild horses and hunted desert honey, just the two boys of us left from the five we'd been. We lived there and for months we was happy.

Your Ma was the finest ever, Son. I never knowed what it could be like to live with no woman, nor to have her there, always knowing how I felt inside when nobody had ever knowed before. We walked together and talked together and day by day the running and shooting seemed farther and farther away.

Johnny was happy, too. Them days his mouth organ laughed and cried and sang sweet songs to the low moon and the high sun, and he played the corn out of the ground and the good sweet melons. We hunted some and we lived quiet-like and happy. How long? Three months, five months . . . and then Marge comes to me and says Ellie's got to go where she can have a doc. She's to have a baby and something, she's sure, ain't right about it.

We knowed what it meant, but life must go on, Son, and you were to be born and I aimed to give you what start I could. The same for Johnny. So we gathered our horses and we rode out to Salt Lake with the girls. We sold our horses for cash money to some Mormons, and then we drifted north. The girls had to stay with the Doc awhile, so we got us a riding job each.

One day a gent comes into a bar where we was with a star on him and he sees me setting by the window. Marge's time is coming nigh and we're all a-waiting like. This man with the star he comes over and drops into a chair near Johnny and me. "Mighty hot day!" he says. "Too hot to hunt outlaws, especially," he says, "when they size up like good, God-fearin' folks.

"Like t'day," he says, "I got me a paper says them Tremaynes is hereabouts. I'm to hunt 'em up an' arrest 'em, what do you boys think about that?"

"We reckon," Johnny says, very quiet, "them Tremaynes never bothered nobody if they was let alone."

He nods his head. "I heard that, too," he says. "Leastways, if they've been in town they sure been mighty quiet an' well-behaved folks. Worst of it is"—he got up, wiping the sweat-band of his hat—"I took an oath to do my duty. Now, the way I figure that doesn't mean I have to go r'arin' out in the heat of the day. But come sundown"—he spoke slow and careful—"I'm gonna hunt them Tremaynes up."

That sheriff, Son, he looked up at Johnny and then over at me. "I got two sons," he said quietly, "and if the Tremaynes left family in this town, they'd be protected as long as me and my sons lived."

We didn't take long about saying goodbye, although we never knowed it was our last. We never guessed we was riding out of town and right to our death.

It was fifty miles east that we passed a gent on the trail. We never knowed him but he turned an' looked after us. And that done, he hightailed it to the nearest town and before day a posse was in the saddle.

At noon, from a high ridge, we drawed up and looked back. We seen four separate dust clouds. Johnny, he looked at me and grinned. "I reckon we ain't in no hurry no more," he said, "they got us agin the mountains." He looked up at them twelve, and thirteen thousand foot peaks. "I wonder if any man ever went through up there?"

"We can give her a try," I said quiet. "Not much else we can do."

"Horses are shot, Boone," he replies, "I ain't goin' to kill no good horse for those lousy coyotes back yonder." So we got down and walked, our saddlebags loose and rifles in our hands.

Then we heard them on the trail behind and we drawed off and slipped our saddles from the horses and cached them in the brush. Cow Hollow, Son, and that's where we made our stand. We had a plenty of ammunition, and we weren't wasteful, making shots count. We hunkered down among the rocks and trees and stood them off.

Morning left us and the noon, and the high hot sun bloomed in the sky, but it was late fall, and as the afternoon drew on, a cold wind began to blow.

They come then, they come like Injuns through the woods after us, and we opened up, and then suddenly Johnny was on his feet, he's got that old Winchester at his hip and he shoots and then he jumps right into them clubbing with his rifle. He went down, and I went over the rocks, both guns going, and that bunch broke and ran.

I fetched Johnny back, and he lay there looking up at me. "Good old Boone!" he said. "Get the girls and get away. Go to Mexico, go somewheres, but get away!"

He died like that, and I sat right there and cried. Then I covered him over gentle and I slipped out of Cow Hollow and started up the trail toward the high peaks.

It was cold, mighty cold. The sun came up and touched those white peaks and ridges ahead of me, then the clouds covered her over and it began to snow. I walked on, and the snow stopped but the wind blew colder and colder. We was getting high up, I passed the timberline here on Tokewanna and crawled into this here place.

Son, I can't see to write no more, and there ain't no more to say. I guess I didn't say it well, but there she is. You can read her and make up your own mind. This here I've addressed to your mother, care of that sheriff down there. I even got a stamp to put on so's it will be U.S. mail and no one'll dare open her up.

Be a good boy, Son, love your Ma and do like she tells you. And carry the name of Tremayne with pride. It was honest blood, no matter what you hear from anyone.

He was stiff from the cold, but he rolled over carefully and folded the letter and tucked it into an envelope. On it he placed his stamp, and then scrawled the name of his wife, in care of the sheriff. From his throat he took a black handkerchief and fastened it to a stick so its flapping would draw attention. Near it, held down by a rock, he left the letter.

Then he crawled out and using his rifle as a crutch, got to his feet. He still had ammunition. He had no food. He discarded the almost empty canteen. For a long time he looked down the cold flank of the mountain into the dark fringe of trees. Far away among those trees flickered the ghostlike fingers of fire, where men warmed themselves and talked, or slept.

Something blurred his eyes. His head throbbed painfully. His side gnawed with pain and his leg was stiff. For how long he stood there he did not know, swaying gently, not quite delirious and yet not quite rational. Then he turned slowly and looked up, two thousand feet, to the cold and icy peak, gleaming, silver and magnificent in solemn grandeur.

He stared for a long time, and then he began to climb. It was very slow, it was very hard. He pulled his old hat down, put the scarf lower around his ears. To the left there was a ridge, and beyond the ridge there would be a valley.

He climbed and then he slipped, lacerating his hands on the icy rocks. He got up, pushing himself on.

"Marge," he whispered, "Son . . ." He continued to move. Crawling . . . falling . . . standing . . . he felt the snow, felt his feet sink. He seemed to have enormously large feet, enormously heavy. "Never aimed to kill nobody," he said. He climbed on . . . wind stirred the icy bits of snow over the harsh flank of the mountain. He bowed his head, and when he turned his face from the wind he looked down and saw the fires below like tiny stars. How far he had come! How very far!

He turned, and looked up. There was the ridge, not far, not too far . . . and what was it he had thought just a moment ago? Beyond the ridge, there is always a valley.

## *Trap of Gold*

Wetherton had been three months out of Horsehead before he found his first color. At first it was a few scattered grains taken from the base of an alluvial fan where millions of tons of sand and silt had washed down from a chain of rugged peaks; yet the gold was ragged under the magnifying glass.

Gold that has carried any distance becomes worn and polished by the abrasive action of the accompanying rocks and sand, so this could not have been carried far. With caution born of harsh experience he seated himself and lighted his pipe, yet excitement was strong within him.

A contemplative man by nature, experience had taught him how a man may be deluded by hope, yet all his instincts told him the source of the gold was somewhere on the mountain above. It could have come down the wash that skirted the base of the mountain, but the ragged condition of the gold made that improbable.

The base of the fan was a half-mile across and hundreds of feet thick, built of silt and sand washed down by centuries of erosion among the higher peaks. The point of the wide V of the fan lay between two towering upthrusts of granite, but from where Wetherton sat he could see that the actual source of the fan lay much higher.

Wetherton made camp near a tiny spring west of the fan, then picketed his burros and began his climb. When he was well over two thousand feet higher he stopped, resting again, and while resting he dry-panned some of the silt. Surprisingly, there were more than a few grains of gold even in that first pan, so he continued his climb, and passed at last between the towering portals of the granite columns.

Above this natural gate were three smaller alluvial fans that joined at the gate to pour into the greater fan below. Dry-panning two of these brought no results, but the third, even by the relatively poor method of dry-panning, showed a dozen colors, all of good size.

The head of this fan lay in a gigantic crack in a granitic upthrust that resembled a fantastic ruin. Pausing to catch his breath, his gaze wandered along the base of this upthrust, and right before him the crumbling granite was slashed with a vein of quartz that was literally laced with gold!

Struggling nearer through the loose sand, his heart pounding more from excitement than from altitude and exertion, he came to an abrupt stop.

The band of quartz was six feet wide and that six feet was cobwebbed with gold.

It was unbelievable, but here it was.

Yet even in this moment of success, something about the beetling cliff stopped him from going forward. His innate caution took hold and he drew back to examine it at greater length. Wary of what he saw, he circled the batholith and then climbed to the ridge behind it from which he could look down upon the roof. What he saw from there left him dry-mouthed and jittery.

The granitic upthrust was obviously a part of a much older range, one that had weathered and worn, suffered from shock and twisting until finally this tower of granite had been violently upthrust, leaving it standing, a shaky ruin among younger and sturdier peaks. In the process the rock had been shattered and riven by mighty forces until it had become a miner's horror. Wetherton stared, fascinated by the prospect. With enormous wealth here for the taking, every ounce must be taken at the risk of life.

One stick of powder might bring the whole crumbling mass down in a heap, and it loomed all of three hundred feet above its base in the fan. The roof of the batholith was riven with gigantic cracks, literally seamed with breaks like the wall of an ancient building that has remained standing after heavy bombing. Walking back to the base of the tower, Wetherton found he could actually break loose chunks of the quartz with his fingers.

The vein itself lay on the downhill side and at the very base. The outer wall of the upthrust was sharply tilted so that a man working at the vein would be cutting his way into the very foundations of the tower, and any single blow of the pick might bring the whole mass down upon him. Furthermore, if the rock did fall, the vein would be hopelessly buried under thousands of tons of rock and lost without the expenditure of much more capital than he could command. And at this moment Wetherton's total of money in hand amounted to slightly less than forty dollars.

Thirty yards from the face he seated himself upon the sand and filled his pipe once more. A man might take tons out of there without trouble, and yet it might collapse at the first blow. Yet he knew he had no choice. He needed money and it lay here before him. Even if he were at first successful there were two things he must avoid. The first was tolerance of danger that might bring carelessness; the second, that urge to go back for that "little bit more" that could kill him.

IT WAS WELL into the afternoon and he had not eaten, yet he was not hungry. He circled the batholith, studying it from every angle only to reach the conclusion that his first estimate had been correct. The only way to get at the gold was to go into the very shadow of the leaning wall and attack it at its base, digging it out by main strength. From where he stood it seemed ridiculous that a mere man with a pick could topple that mass of rock, yet he knew how delicate such a balance could be.

The tower was situated on what might be described as the military crest of the ridge, and the alluvial fan sloped steeply away from its lower side, steeper than a steep stairway. The top of the leaning wall overshadowed the top of the fan, and if it started to crumble and a man had warning, he might run to the north with a bare chance of escape. The soft sand in which he must run would be an impediment, but that could be alleviated by making a walk from flat rocks sunken into the sand.

It was dusk when he returned to his camp. Deliberately, he had not permitted himself to begin work, not by so much as a sample. He must be deliberate in all his actions, and never for a second should he forget the mass that towered above him. A split second of hesitation when the crash came—and he accepted it as inevitable—would mean burial under tons of crumbled rock.

The following morning he picketed his burros on a small meadow near the spring, cleaned the spring itself and prepared a lunch. Then he removed his shirt, drew on a pair of gloves and walked to the face of the cliff. Yet even then he did not begin, knowing that upon this habit of care and deliberation might depend not only his success in the venture, but life itself. He gathered flat stones and began building his walk. "When you start moving," he told himself, "you'll have to be fast."

FINALLY, and with infinite care, he began tapping at the quartz, enlarging cracks with the pick, removing fragments, then prying loose whole chunks. He did not swing the pick, but used it as a lever. The quartz was rotten, and a man might obtain a considerable amount by this method of picking or even pulling with the hands. When he had a sack filled with the richest quartz he carried it over his path to a safe place beyond the shadow of the tower. Returning, he tamped a few more flat rocks into his path, and began on the second sack. He worked with greater care than was, perhaps, essential. He was not and had never been a gambling man.

In the present operation he was taking a careful calculated risk in which every eventuality had been weighed and judged. He needed the money and he intended to have it; he had a good idea of his chances of success, but knew that his gravest danger was to become too greedy, too much engrossed in his task.

Dragging the two sacks down the hill he

found a flat block of stone and with a single jack proceeded to break up the quartz. It was a slow and a hard job but he had no better means of extracting the gold. After breaking or crushing the quartz much of the gold could be separated by a knife blade, for it was amazingly concentrated. With water from the spring Wetherton panned the remainder until it was too dark to see.

Out of his blankets by daybreak he ate breakfast and completed the extraction of the gold. At a rough estimate his first day's work would run to four hundred dollars. He made a cache for the gold sack and took the now empty ore sacks and climbed back to the tower.

The air was clear and fresh, the sun warm after the chill of night, and he liked the feel of the pick in his hands.

Laura and Tommy awaited him back in Horsehead, and if he was killed here, there was small chance they would ever know what had become of him. But he did not intend to be killed. The gold he was extracting from this rock was for them, and not for himself.

It would mean an easier life in a larger town, a home of their own and the things to make the home a woman desires, and it meant an education for Tommy. For himself, all he needed was the thought of that home to return to, his wife and son—and the desert itself. And one was as necessary to him as the other.

The desert would be the death of him. He had been told that many times, and did not need to be told, for few men knew the desert as he did. The desert was to him what an orchestra is to a fine conductor, what the human body is to a surgeon. It was his work, his life, and the thing he knew best. He always smiled when he looked first into the desert as he started a new trip. Would this be it?

The morning drew on and he continued to work with an even-paced swing of the pick, a careful filling of the sack. The gold showed bright and beautiful in the crystalline quartz which was so much more beautiful than the gold itself. From time to time as the morning drew on, he paused to rest and to breathe deeply of the fresh, clear air. Deliberately, he refused to hurry.

For nineteen days he worked tirelessly, eight hours a day at first, then lessening his hours to seven, and then to six. Wetherton did not explain to himself why he did this, but he realized it was becoming increasingly difficult to stay on the job. Again and again he would walk away from the rock face on one excuse or another, and each time he would begin to feel his scalp prickle, his steps grow quicker, and each time he returned more reluctantly.

Three times, beginning on the thirteenth, again on the seventeenth and finally on the nineteenth day, he heard movement within the tower.

Whether that whispering in the rock was normal he did not know. Such a natural movement might have been going on for centuries. He only knew that it happened now, and each time it happened a cold chill went along his spine.

His work had cut a deep notch at the base of the tower, such a notch as a man might make in felling a tree, but wider and deeper. The sacks of gold, too, were increasing. They now numbered seven, and their total would, he believed, amount to more than five thousand dollars—probably nearer to six thousand. As he cut deeper into the rock the vein was growing richer.

HE WORKED on his knees now. The vein had slanted downward as he cut into the base of the tower and he was all of nine feet into the rock with the great mass of it above him. If that rock gave way while he was working he would be crushed in an instant with no chance of escape. Nevertheless, he continued.

The change in the rock tower was not the only change, for he had lost weight and he no longer slept well. On the night of the twentieth day he decided he had six thousand dollars and his goal would be ten thousand. And the following day the rock was the richest ever! As if to tantalize him into working on and on, the deeper he cut the richer the ore became. By nightfall of that day he had taken out more than a thousand dollars.

Now the lust of the gold was getting into him, taking him by the throat. He was fascinated by the danger of the tower as well as the desire for the gold. Three more days to go—could he leave it then? He looked again at the tower and felt a peculiar sense of foreboding, a feeling that here he was to die, that he would never escape. Was it his imagination, or had the outer wall leaned a little more?

On the morning of the twenty-second day he climbed the fan over a path that use had built into a series of continuous steps. He had never counted those steps but there must have been over a thousand of them. Dropping his canteen into a shaded hollow and pick in hand he started for the tower.

The forward tilt **did** seem somewhat more than before. Or was it the light? The crack that ran behind the outer wall seemed to have widened and when he examined it more closely he found a small pile of freshly run silt near the bottom of the crack. So it had moved!

Wetherton hesitated, staring at the rock with wary attention. He was a fool to go back in there again. Seven thousand dollars was more than he had ever had in his life before, yet in the next few hours he could take out at least a thousand dollars more and in the next three days he could easily have the ten thousand he had set for his goal.

He walked to the opening, dropped to his knees and crawled into the narrowing, flat-roofed hole. No sooner was he inside than fear climbed up into his throat. He felt trapped, stifled, but he fought down the mounting panic and began to work. His first blows were so frightened and feeble that nothing came loose. Yet, when he did get started, he began to work with a feverish intensity that was wholly unlike him.

When he slowed and then stopped to fill his sack he was gasping for breath, but despite his hurry the sack was not quite full. Reluctantly, he lifted his pick again, but before he could strike a blow, the gigantic mass above him seemed to creak like something tired and old. A deep shudder went through the colossal pile and then a deep grinding that turned him sick with horror. All his plans for instant flight were frozen and it was not until the groaning ceased that he realized he was lying on his back, breathless with fear and expectancy. Slowly, he edged his way into the air and walked, fighting the desire to run, away from the rock.

When he stopped near his canteen he was wringing with cold sweat and trembling in every muscle. He sat down on the rock and fought for control. It was not until some twenty minutes had passed that he could trust himself to get to his feet.

Despite his experience, he knew that if he did not go back now he would never go. He had out but one sack for the day and wanted another. Circling the batholith he examined the widening crack, endeavoring again, for the third time, to find another means of access to the vein.

The tilt of the outer wall was obvious, and it could stand no more without toppling. It was possible that by cutting into the wall of the column and striking down he might tap the vein at a safer point. Yet this added blow at the foundation would bring the tower nearer to collapse and render his other hole untenable. Even this new attempt would not be safe, although immeasurably more secure than the hole he had left. Hesitating, he looked back at the hole.

ONCE MORE? The ore was now fabulously rich, and the few pounds he needed to complete the sack he could get in just a little while. He stared at the black and undoubtedly narrower hole, then looked up at the leaning wall. He picked up his pick and, his mouth dry, started back, drawn by a fascination that was beyond all reason.

His heart pounding, he dropped to his knees at the tunnel face. The air seemed stifling and he could feel his scalp tingling, but once he started to crawl it was better. The face where he now worked was at least sixteen feet from the tunnel mouth. Pick in hand, he began to wedge chunks from their seat. The going seemed harder now and the chunks did not come loose so easily. Above him the tower made no sound. The crushing weight was now something tangible. He could almost feel it growing, increasing with every move of his. The mountain seemed resting on his shoulder, crushing the air from his lungs.

Suddenly he stopped. His sack almost full, he stopped and lay very still, staring up at the bulk of the rock above him.

No.

He would go no farther. Now he would quit. Not another sackful. Not another pound. He would go out now. He would go down the mountain without a backward look, and he would keep going. His wife waiting at home, little Tommy, who would run gladly to meet him—these were too much to gamble.

WITH THE DECISION came peace, came certainty. He sighed deeply, and relaxed, and then it seemed to him that every muscle in his body had been knotted with strain. He turned on his side and with great deliberation gathered his lantern, his sack, his hand-pick.

He had won. He had defeated the crumbling tower, he had defeated his own greed. He backed easily, without the caution that had marked his earlier movements in the cave. His blind, trusting foot found the projecting rock, a piece of quartz that stuck out from the rough-hewn wall.

The blow was too weak, too feeble to have brought forth the reaction that followed. The rock seemed to quiver like the flesh of a beast when stabbed; a queer vibration went through that ancient rock, then a deep, gasping sigh.

He had waited too long!

Fear came swiftly in upon him, crowding him, while his body twisted, contracting into the smallest possible space. He tried to will his muscles to move beneath the growing sounds that vibrated through the passage. The whispers of the rock grew into a terrifying groan, and there was a rattle of pebbles. Then silence.

The silence was more horrifying than the sound. Somehow he was crawling, even as he expected the avalanche of gold to bury him. Abruptly, his feet were in the open. He was out.

He ran without stopping, but behind him he heard a growing roar that he couldn't outrace. When he knew from the slope of the land that he must be safe from falling rock, he fell to his knees. He turned and looked back. The muted, roaring sound, like thunder beyond mountains, continued, but there was no visible change in the tower. Suddenly, as he watched, the whole rock formation seemed to shift and tip. The movement lasted only seconds, but before the tons of rock had found their new equilibrium, his tunnel and the area around it had utterly vanished from sight.

When he could finally stand Wetherton gathered up his sack of ore and his canteen. The wind was cool upon his face as he walked away; and he did not look back again.

# *Riches Beyond Dream*

It was June when they arrived at the adobe on Pinon Hill. There had been little change since Kirby Ann had last been there . . . the trees Tom Kirby planted the year before he died were taller, and bunchgrass grew where the lawn should be.

Kirby Ann got out of the jeep and looked at Bob. The ride had tired him . . . a serious wound and a year in a Red Chinese prison camp had wrecked his health. He needed the sun, they told him, with rest and quiet. Well, he could get that here. Maybe it was all they could get here.

"It's a roof, honey," Bob said quietly. "We can fix up the place." He took her hand and they walked to the edge of the hill. "I always loved it here," she said.

Before them lay the long valley, dotted now with cloud shadows, and beyond the valley a rugged hill, and beyond more hills, more valleys, more peaks and ridges.

"Tom built for the view," Kirby Ann said, "and would you believe it? When he was declared mentally incompetent, this was one of the reasons. Because he built an expensive house in a lonely place, and then wouldn't allow a road to be built leading to it."

"He was a good old man," Bob said. "I liked him."

Long after Bob was asleep, Kirby lay awake, remembering. This place had been left to her by her great-uncle Tom. It had been written into his will before his grandchildren had him declared incompetent and took over the handling of his affairs.

They had taken his house in town, the orchard he planted with his own hands, the ranch, and the mine. It was the silver they really wanted, and Blake, his eldest grandson, believed it came from the long-unworked Kirby Silver Mine on the edge of town.

There was never any argument about the adobe. Nobody wanted a house in such a lonely place. Yet when she came for her first visit she found they had been there, too, spading up the yard and blasting rock in the hill, feverishly searching for the silver lode. For the source of the fabulous **planchas de plata** he had sold to the bank in Topa.

Blake Bidwell had been coldly furious after the funeral. "The old fool! He should have been declared incompetent years ago!"

"He was always soft in the head," Archie Moulton said sourly, "but I never dreamed he'd die without telling us."

"And not even to tell Kirby!" Esther was aghast. Esther was always aghast. "And she did so much for him!"

Kirby Ann had sat very still, her coffee growing cold. Not a thought for the poor old man who had died in that narrow windowless room that smelled of disinfectant, died still dreaming of the hills he loved so well.

He had given them all so much. Blake his first car. Archie and Esther a restaurant business. Jake a start in the bank.

And that was to say nothing of the other, intangible things he had tried to give them. His love of wild things, of trees, flowers, of the lonely desert and the enchanted hills. Of them all, she alone shared his love for these. He had, because of this, wanted her to have the adobe.

He never tired talking of the desert. Only at the end had his thoughts turned more and more to mining. Again and again he told her how to stake a claim, build the cairn, post the notices, and register it.

"A staked claim is property, Kirby Ann," he said, winking at her. "Lucky I didn't have one or they'd have taken that, too.

"Now don't you forget what I've told you.

Like me, you love the desert. Someday you may find something . . . someday when you need it worse than now."

Had there been a hint in that? There would never be a time when they would need it worse than this very day. The money Bob would get from the government would help only for a while. It would be months and months before he could work. She searched her memory but could find nothing in the old conversations but the nostalgic wanderings of an old man nearing death.

He had loved the desert, and he knew the lines of ancient beaches where seas and lakes had been. He knew where lay the best beds of agate, jasper, or garnet. He had followed the old, mysterious trails of prehistoric Indians marked by forgotten piles of desert-varnished stones. He had known the plants of the desert, the cacti, the flowers, the herbs and grasses.

She remembered the town's excitement when he first brought in the ore, the sheets and balls of almost pure silver. When men failed to track him, and when his own grandchildren failed to probe his secret, they began to believe he had uncovered a rich vein in the long abandoned Kirby Silver Mine . . . and he let them think so. Not long after, the twins, Blake and Jake, working with Esther and Esther's husband, Archie Moulton, began the move to have him declared incompetent.

They took over the mine and they spent thousands on engineers who probed and estimated and explored to no purpose. And the old man would have no more to do with them.

When she had received the deed to the house, there had been a note inside that she was to keep. Remembering it, Kirby Ann got it out of her overnight bag to show to Bob in the morning.

**You been good to me, Kirby Ann, patient with a tired old man. Marry Bob and spend your June honeymoon here—never sell it or give it away. Enjoy the flowers, and remember what I taught you about them. They ask only care, and they give so much in beauty, and in riches beyond dream.**

Sitting before the kitchen window, they ate their first breakfast in the adobe. " 'Mighty purty sight,' Great-uncle Tom used to say," she told Bob. " 'Come June the purtiest I ever did see.' "

"If we only had the money to fix it up," Bob agreed. "I'll work around, but I'll have to take it slow at first."

Bob lifted his coffee cup, nodding toward the far hill. "Honey, what's the yellow over there across the valley?"

Kirby Ann looked. "It's buckwheat. It blooms in late June. . . .

"Bob," Kirby Ann said, her eyes narrowing, "we were never here in **June**! We postponed our wedding, and our honeymoon was in September."

He chuckled. "I know that. I didn't have any money in June, and not much more in September."

She got to her feet. "Bob, get the jeep. We're going over there."

Twenty minutes later they stood in the patch of buckwheat, golden and beautiful in the morning sun. It was all about them, and at their feet, thicker than elsewhere, it cloaked and disguised an old mine working. Bob held in his hand a chunk of ore, seamed with silver.

"When I was only a child he told me," she said. "It's an old prospector's saying: 'Look where the buckwheat grows—it has affinity for silver.' "

# *The Lonesome Gods*

Who can say that the desert does not live? Or that the dark, serrated ridges conceal no spirit? Who can love the lost places, yet believe himself truly alone in the silent hills? How can we be sure the ancient ones were wrong when they believed each rock, each tree, each stream or mountain possessed an active spirit? Are the gods of those vanished peoples truly dead, or do they wait among the shadows for some touch of respect, the ritual or sacrifice that can again give them life?

It is written in the memories of the ancient peoples that one who chooses the desert for his enemy has chosen a bitter foe, but he who accepts it as friend, who will seek to understand its moods and whims, shall feel also its mercy, shall drink deep of its hidden waters, and the treasures of its rocks shall be opened before him. Where one may walk in freedom and find water in the arid places, another may gasp out his last breath under the desert sun and mark the sands with the bones of his ending.

Into the western wastelands, in 1807, a man walked dying. Behind him lay the bodies of his companions and the wreck of their boat on the Colorado River. Before him lay the desert, and somewhere beyond the desert the shores of the Pacific.

Jacob Almayer was a man of Brittany, and the Bretons are an ancient folk with roots among the Druids and those unknown people who vanished long ago, but who lifted the stones of Karnak to their places. He was a man who had walked much alone, a man sensitive to the wilderness and the mores of other peoples and other times, and now he walked into the desert with only the miles before him.

The distance was immeasurable. He was without water, without food, and the vast waste of the desert was the sickly color of dead flesh deepening in places to rusty red or to the hazy purple of distance. Within the limits of his knowledge lay no habitation of men except the drowsy Spanish colonies along the coast. Yet, colonies or not, the sea was there, and the men of Brittany are born to the sea. So he turned his face westward and let the distance unroll behind him.

Now he had not long to live. From the crest of the ridge he stared out across the unbelievable expanse of the desert. The gourd that hung from his shoulder was empty for many hours. His boots were tatters of leather, his cheeks and eyes sunken, his lips gray and cracked.

Morning had come at last, and Jacob Almayer licked the dew from the barrel of his rifle and looked westward. Although due west was the way he had traveled and due west he should continue, off to his right there lay the shadow of an ancient trail, lying like the memory of a dream across the lower slope of the mesa.

The trail was old. So old the rocks had taken the patina of desert time, so old that it skirted the curve of an ancient beach where once lapped the waters of a vanished sea. The old trail led away in a long, graceful sweep, toward the west-northwest, following the high ground toward some destination he could not guess.

West was his logical route. Somewhere out there the road from Mexico to the California missions cut diagonally across the desert. By heading directly west he might last long enough to find that road, yet the water gourd was dry and the vast sun-baked basin before him offered no promise. The ancient folk who made this path must have known where water could be found, yet if the sea had vanished from this basin might not the springs have vanished also?

Jacob Almayer was a big man, powerful in the chest and broad in the shoulders, a fighter by instinct and a man who would, by the nature of him, die hard. He was also a man of ironic, self-deriding humor, and it was like him to have no illusions now. And it was like him to look down the ancient trail with curious eyes. For how many centuries had this trail been used? Walked by how many feet, dust now these hundreds of years? And for how long had it been abandoned?

Such a path is not born in a month, nor are the stones marked in a year. Yet the ages had not erased the marks of their passing, although without this view from the crest it was doubtful if the trail could be seen. But once seen and recognized for what it was, following it should not be hard. Moreover, at intervals the passing men had dropped stones into neat piles.

To mark the miles? The intervals were irregular. To break the monotony? A ritual, perhaps? Like a Tibetan spinning a prayer wheel? Was each stone a prayer? An invocation to the gods of travelers? Gods abandoned for how long?

"I could use their help," Jacob Almayer said aloud, "I could use them now." Either path might lead to death, and either might lead to water and life, but which way?

Curiosity triumphed, or rather, his way of life triumphed. Had it not always been so with him? And those others who preceded him? Was it not curiosity more than desire for gain that led them on? And now, in what might be the waning hours of life, it was no time to change.

Jacob Almayer looked down the shimmering basin and he looked along the faint but easy sweep of the trail. He could, of course, rationalize his choice. The trail led over high ground, along an easier route; trust an Indian to keep his feet out of the heavy sand. Jacob Almayer turned down the trail, and as he did so he stooped and picked up a stone from the ground.

The sun lifted into the wide and brassy sky and the basin swam with heat. The free-swinging stride that had carried him from the Colorado was gone now, but the trail was good and he walked steadily. He began to sweat again, and smelled the odors of his unwashed clothes, his unbathed body; the stale smell of old sweat. Yet the air he breathed, however hot, was like wine—like water, one could almost swallow it. Soon he came to a pile of stones and he dropped the stone he carried and picked up another, then walked on.

Upon his shoulder the gourd flopped loosely, and his dry tongue fumbled at the broken flesh of his lips. After several hours he stopped sweating, and when he inadvertently touched the flesh of his face it felt hot and dry. When he paused at intervals he found it becoming harder and harder to start again but he kept on, unable to rest for long, knowing that safety if it came would be somewhere ahead.

Sometimes his boots rolled on rocks and

twisted his feet painfully, and he could feel that his socks were stuck to his blistered feet with dried blood. Once he stumbled and fell, catching himself on his hands, but clumsily so that the skin was torn and lacerated. For a long minute he held himself on his hands and knees, staring drunkenly at the path beneath him, caught in some trance-like state when he was neither quite conscious nor quite unconscious, but for the moment was just flesh devoid of animation. Finally he got to his feet and, surprised to find himself there, he started on, walking with sudden rapidity as if starting anew. Cicadas hummed in the cacti and greasewood, and once he saw a rattler coil and buzz angrily, but he walked on.

Before him the thread of the trail writhed among the rocks, emerged, and then fell away before him to a lower level, so faint yet beckoning, always promising, drawing him into the distance as a magnet draws filings of iron. He no longer thought, but only walked, hypnotized by his own movement. His mind seemed to fill with the heat haze and he remembered nothing but the rocks, dropping and carrying stones with the deadly persistence of a drunken man.

Now the trail skirted the white line of an ancient beach, where the sand was silver with broken shell and where at times he came upon the remains of ancient fires, blackened stones, charred remains of prehistoric shells and fish bones.

His eyes were bloodshot now, slow to move and hard to focus. Dust devils danced in the desert heat waves. He clung to the thread of the path as to the one thing in this shimmering land of mirages that was real, that was familiar.

Then he tripped.

He fell flat on his face, and he lay still, face against the gravel of the partial slope, the only sound that of his hoarse breathing. Slowly he pushed himself up, got into a sitting position. Drunkenly he stared at his palms, scraped and gouged by the fall. With infinite and childish concentration he began to pick the sand from the wounds, and then he licked at the blood. He got up then, because it was his nature to get up. He got up and he recovered his gun, making an issue of bending without losing balance, and triumphant when he was successful.

He fell twice more in the next half hour, and each time it took him longer to rise. Yet he knew the sun was past its noontime high, and somehow he must last out the day. He started on but his mouth was dry, his tongue musty, and the heat waves seemed all around him. He seemed to have, at last, caught up with the mirage, for it shimmered around him and washed over him like the sea but without freshness, only heat.

A man stood in the trail before him.

An Indian. Jacob Almayer tried to cry out but he could not. He started forward, but the figure of the man seemed to recede as he advanced . . . and then the Indian's arm lifted and pointed.

Almayer turned his head slowly, looking toward the ridge of upthrust rock not far off the trail. Almayer tried to speak, but the Indian merely pointed.

Jacob Almayer leaned back and tried to make out the looks of the Indian, but all he could see was the brown skin, breechclout, and some sort of a band around his head. Around his shoulders was some sort of a fur jacket. A **fur** jacket? In this heat? Almayer looked again at the rocks; when he looked back, the Indian was gone.

The rocks were not far away and Almayer turned toward them, but first he stopped, for where the Indian had been standing there was a pile of stones. He walked toward it and added his stone to the pile. Then he picked up another and turned toward the ridge. There was a trail here, too. Not quite so plain as the other, but nevertheless, a trail.

He walked on, hesitating at times, reluctant to get away from the one possibility of safety, but finally he reached the ridge where the trail rounded it, and he did likewise, and there in a corner of the rocks was white sand overgrown with thin grass, a clump of mesquite, a slim cottonwood tree, and beneath it, a pool of water.

Jacob Almayer tasted the water and it was sweet; he put a little on his lips, and it had the coolness of a benediction. He put some in his mouth and held it there, letting the starved tissues of his mouth absorb the water, and then he let a little trickle down his throat, and felt it, all the way to his stomach. After a while he drank, and over his head the green leaves of the cottonwood brushed their green and silver palms in whispering applause. Jacob Almayer crept into the shade and slept. He awoke to drink, then slept again, and in the paleness of the last hours of night he awakened and heard a faint stir upon the hillside opposite the ridge beside which he lay. He squinted his eyes, then widened them, trying to see, and then he did see.

There were men there, men and women, and even he in his half-delirium and his half-awareness knew these were like no Indians he had seen. Each carried a basket and they were gathering something from among the squat green trees on the hill. He started up and called out, but they neither turned nor spoke, but finally completed their work and walked slowly away.

Daylight came . . . one instant the sky was gray, and then the shadows retreated into the canyons and the dark places among the hills, and the sun crowned the distant ridges with gold, then bathed them in light, and the last faltering battalions of the shadows withered and died among the rocks and morning was there. In the early light Jacob Almayer drank again, drank deep now, and long.

His thirst gone, hunger remained, but he stood up and looked over at the hill. Had he seen anything? Or had it been his imagination? Had it been some fantasy of his half-delirium? Leaving the spring he crossed the small valley toward the hillside and climbed it. As he walked, he searched the ground. No footsteps had left their mark, no stones unturned, no signs of a large body of people moving or working.

The trees . . . he looked at them again, and then he recalled a traveler who had told him once of how the Indians gathered the nuts from these pines . . . from the piñon. He searched for the cones and extracted some of the nuts. And then he gathered more, and more. And that evening he killed a mountain sheep near the spring.

At daylight he resumed his walk, but this time his gourd was filled with water, and he carried fresh meat with him, and several pounds of the nuts. As Jacob Almayer started to walk, he picked up a stone, and then an idea came to him.

How far would an Indian walk in a day? Those who followed this trail would probably have no reason for hurry. Would they walk fifteen miles? Twenty? Or even thirty? Or would distance depend on the water supply? For that was the question that intrigued him. Where they stopped there would be water. The solution was to watch for any dim trail leading away from the main route toward the end of the day.

Soon he found another pile of the stones, and he dropped the one he carried, and picked up another. And at nightfall he found a dim trail that led to a flowing spring, and he camped there, making a fire and roasting some of his meat. As he ate and drank, as he watched his fire burn down, as he thought of the trail behind and the trail ahead, he looked out into the darkness.

Jacob Almayer was a Breton, and the folk of Brittany are sensitive to the spirits of the mountains and forest. He looked out into the darkness beyond the firelight and he said aloud, "To the spirits of this place, my respects, humble as they are, and in my heart there will always be thanks for you, as long as I shall live."

The fire fluttered then, the flames whipping down, then blazing up, brighter than ever. From far off there came the distant sound of voices. Were they chanting, singing? He couldn't tell . . . it might have been the wind.

# *The Skull and the Arrow*

Heavy clouds hung above the iron-colored peaks, and lancets of lightning flashed and probed. Thunder rolled like a distant avalanche in the mountain valleys. . . . The man on the rocky slope was alone.

He stumbled, staggering beneath the driving rain, his face hammered and raw. Upon his skull a wound gaped wide, upon his cheek the white bone showed through. It was the end. He was finished, and so were they all . . . they were through.

Far-off pines made a dark etching along the skyline, and that horizon marked a crossing. Beyond it was security, a life outside the reach of his enemies, who now believed him dead. Yet, in this storm, he knew he could go no farther. Hail laid a volley of musketry against the rock where he leaned, so he started on, falling at times.

He had never been a man to quit, but now he had. They had beaten him, not man to man but a dozen to one. With fists and clubs and gun barrels they had beaten him . . . and now he was through. Yes, he would quit. They had taught him how to quit.

The clouds hung like dark, blowing tapestries in the gaps of the hills. The man went on until he saw the dark opening of a cave. He turned to it for shelter then, as men have always done. Though there are tents and wickiups, halls and palaces, in his direst need man always returns to the cave.

He was out of the rain but it was cold within. Shivering, he gathered sticks and some blown leaves. Among the rags of his wet and muddy clothing, he found a match, and from the match, a flame. The leaves caught, the blaze stretched tentative, exploring fingers and found food to its liking.

He added fuel; the fire took hold, crackled, and gave off heat. The man moved closer, feeling the warmth upon his hands, his body. Firelight played shadow games upon the blackened walls where the smoke from many fires had etched their memories . . . for how many generations of men?

This time he was finished. There was no use going back. His enemies were sure he was dead, and his friends would accept it as true. So he was free. He had done his best, so now a little rest, a little healing, and then over the pine-clad ridge and into the sunlight. Yet in freedom there is not always contentment.

He found fuel again, and came upon a piece of ancient pottery. Dipping water from a pool, he rinsed the pot, then filled it and brought it back to heat. He squeezed rain from the folds of his garments, then huddled between the fire and the cave wall, holding tight against the cold.

There was no end to the rain . . . gusts of wind whipped at the cave mouth and dimmed the fire. It was insanity to think of returning. He had been beaten beyond limit. When he was down they had taken turns kicking him. They had broken ribs . . . he could feel them under the cold, a raw pain in his side.

Long after he had lain inert and helpless, they had bruised and battered and worried at him. Yet he was a tough man, and he could not even find the relief of unconsciousness. He felt every blow, every kick. When they were tired from beating him, they went away.

He had not moved for hours, and only the coming of night and the rain revived him. He moved, agony in every muscle, anguish in his side, a mighty throbbing inside his skull, but somehow he managed distance. He crawled, walked, staggered, fell. He fainted, then revived, lay for a time mouth open to the rain, eyes blank and empty.

By now his friends believed him dead. . . . Well, he was not dead, but he was not going back. After all, it was their fight, had always been their fight. Each of them fought for a home, perhaps for a wife, children, parents. He had fought for a principle, and because it was his nature to fight.

With the hot water he bathed his head and face, eased the pain of his bruises, washed the blood from his hair, bathed possible poison from his cuts. He felt better then, and the cave grew warmer. He leaned against the wall and relaxed. Peace came to his muscles. After a while he heated more water and drank some of it.

Lightning revealed the frayed trees outside the cave, revealed the gray rain before the cave mouth. He would need more fuel. He got up and rummaged in the farther darkness of the cave. He found more sticks and carried them back to his fire. And then he found the skull.

He believed its whiteness to be a stick, imbedded as it was in the sandy floor. He tugged to get it loose, becoming more curious as its enormous size became obvious. It was the skull of a gigantic bear, without doubt from prehistoric times. From the size of the skull, the creature must have weighed well over a ton.

Crouching by the firelight he examined it. Wedged in an eye socket was a bit of flint. He broke it free, needing all his strength. It was a finely chipped arrowhead.

The arrow could not have killed the bear. Blinded him, yes, enraged him, but not killed him. Yet the bear had been killed. Probably by a blow from a stone ax, for there was a crack in the skull, and at another place, a spot near the ear where the bone was crushed.

Using a bit of stick he dug around, finding more bones. One was a shattered foreleg of the monster, the bone fractured by a blow. And then he found the head of a stone ax. But nowhere did he find the bones of the man.

Despite the throbbing in his skull and the raw pain in his side, he was excited. Within the cave, thousands of years ago, a lone man fought a battle to the death against impossible odds . . . and won.

Fought for what? Surely there was easier game? And with the bear half blinded the man could have escaped, for the cave mouth was wide. In the whirling fury of the fight there must have been opportunities. Yet he had not fled. He had fought on against the overwhelming strength of the wounded beast, pitting against it only his lesser strength, his primitive weapons, and his man-cunning.

Venturing outside the cave for more fuel, he dragged a log within, although the effort made him gasp with agony. He drew the log along the back edge of his fire so that it was at once fuel and reflector of heat.

Burrowing a little in the now warm sand of the cave floor, he was soon asleep.

★ ★ ★

FOR THREE WEEKS he lived in the cave, finding berries and nuts, snaring small game, always conscious of the presence of the pine-clad ridge, yet also aware of the skull and the arrowhead. In all that time he saw no man, either near or far . . . there was, then, no search for him.

Finally it was time to move. Now he could go over the ridge to safety. Much of his natural strength had returned; he felt better. It was a relief to know that his fight was over.

AT NOON of the following day he stood in the middle of a heat-baked street and faced his enemies again. Behind him were silent ranks of simple men.

"We've come back," he said quietly. "We're going to stay. You had me beaten a few weeks ago. You may beat us today, but some of you will die. And we'll be back. We'll always be back."

There was silence in the dusty street, and then the line before them wavered, and from behind it a man was walking away, and then another, and their leader looked at him and said, "You're insane. Completely insane!" And then he, too, turned away and the street before them was empty.

And the quiet men stood in the street with the

light of victory in their eyes, and the man with the battered face tossed something and caught it again, something that gleamed for a moment in the sun.

"What was that?" someone asked.

"An arrowhead," the man said. "Only an arrowhead."

## *End of the Drive*

We came up the trail from Texas in the spring of '74, and bedded our herd on the short grass beyond the railroad. We cleaned our guns and washed our necks and dusted our hats for town; we rode fifteen strong to the hitching rail, and fifteen strong to the bar.

We were the Rocking K from the rough country back of the Nueces, up the trail with three thousand head of longhorn steers, the first that spring, although the rivers ran bank full and Comanches rode the war trail.

We buried two hands south of the Red, and two on the plains of the Nation, and a fifth died on Kansas grass, his flesh churned under a thousand hoofs. Four men gone before Indian rifles, but the death-songs of the Comanches were sung in the light of a hollow moon, and the Kiowa mourned in their lodges for warriors lost to the men of the Rocking K.

We were the riders who drove the beef, fighting dust, hail, and lightning, meeting stampedes and Kiowa. And we who drove the herd and fought our nameless, unrecorded battles often rode to our deaths without glory, nor with any memory to leave behind us.

The town was ten buildings long on the north side of the street, and seven long on the south, with stock corrals to the east of town and Boot Hill on the west, and an edging of Hell between.

Back of the street on the south of town were the shacks of the girls who waited for the trail herds, and north of the street were the homes of the businessmen and merchants, where no trail driver was permitted to go.

We were lean and hard young riders, only a few of us nearing thirty, most of us nearer to twenty. We were money to the girls of the line, and whiskey to the tenders of bars, but to the merchants we were lean, brown young savages whose brief assaults on their towns were tolerated for the money we brought.

That was the year I was twenty-four, and only the cook was an older man, yet it was my fifth trip up the trail and I'd seen this town once before, and others before that. And there were a couple I'd seen die, leaving their brief scars on the prairie that new grass would soon erase.

I'd left no love in Texas, but a man at twenty-four is as much a man as he will be, and a girl was what I wanted. A girl to rear strong sons on the high plains of Texas, a girl to ride beside me in the summer twilight, to share the moon with me, and the high stars over the caprock country.

For I had found a ranch, filed my claims, and put my brand on steers, and this drive was my last for another man, the last at a foreman's wages. When I rode my horse up to the rail that day, I saw the girl I dreamed about . . . the girl I wanted.

She stood on the walk outside the store and she lifted a hand to shade her eyes, her hair blowing light in the wind, and her figure was long and slim and the sun caught red lights in her hair. Her eyes caught mine as I rode tall in the leather, the first man to come up the street.

She looked grave and straight and honestly at me, and it seemed no other girl had ever looked so far into my heart. At twenty-four the smile of a woman is a glory to the blood and a spark to the spirit, and carries a richer wine than any sold over a bar in any frontier saloon.

I'd had no shave for days, and the dust of the trail lay on my clothes, and sour I was with the need of bathing and washing. When I swung from my saddle, a tall, lonely man in a dusty black hat with spurs to my heels, she stood where I had seen her and turned slowly away and walked into the store.

WE WENT to the bar and I had a drink, but the thing was turning over within me and thinking of the girl left no rest for me. She was all I could think about and all I could talk about that afternoon.

So when I turned from the bar Red Mike put a hand to my sleeve. "It's trouble you're headed for, Tom Gavagan," he said. "It's been months since you've seen a girl. She's a bonny lass, but you know the rule here. No trail hand can walk north of the street, nor bother any of the citizens."

"I'm not one to be breakin' the law, Mike, but it is a poor man who will stop shy of his destiny."

"This is John Blake's town," he said.

The name had a sound of its own, for John Blake was known wherever the trails ran; wherever they came from and where they ended. He was a hard man accustomed to dealing with hard men, and when he spoke his voice was law. He was a square, powerful man, with a name for fair dealing, but a man who backed his words with a gun.

"It is a time for courting," I said, "although I want trouble with no man. And least of all John Blake."

When I turned to the door I heard Red Mike behind me. "No more drinking this day," he said. "We've a man to stand behind."

WHEN THE DOOR creaked on its spring a man looked around from his buying, and the keeper of the store looked up, but the girl stood straight and tall where she was, and did not turn. For she knew the sound of my heels on the board floor, and the jingle of my Spanish spurs.

"I am selling the herd this night," I said, when I came to stand beside her, "and I shall be riding south with the morning sun. I hope not to ride alone."

She looked at me with straight, measuring eyes. "You are a forward man, Tom Gavagan. You do not know me."

"I know you," I said, "and know what my heart tells me, and I know that if you do not ride with me when I return to Texas, I shall ride with sorrow."

"I saw you when you rode into town last year," she said, "but you did not see me."

"Had I seen you I could not have ridden away. I am a poor hand for courting, knowing little but horses, cattle, and grass, and I have learned nothing that I can say to a girl. I only know that when I saw you there upon the walk it seemed my life would begin and end with you, and there would be no happiness until you rode beside me."

"You are doing well enough with your talk, Tom Gavagan, and it is a fine thing that you do it no better or you'd be turning some poor girl's head."

She put her money on the counter and met the glance of the storekeeper without embarrassment, and then she turned and looked at me in that straight way she had and said, "My uncle is Aaron McDonald, and he looks with no favor upon Texas men."

"It is my wish to call on you this night," I said, "and the choice of whether I come or not belongs to you and no one else."

"The house stands among the cottonwoods at the street's far end." Then she added, "Come if you will . . . but it is north of the street."

"You can expect me," I replied.

And turning upon my heel I walked from the store and heard the storekeeper say, "He is a Texas man, Miss June, and you know about the ordinance as well as anyone!"

Once more in the sunshine I felt a strength within me that was beyond any I had ever known, and an exhilaration. Lined along the street were fourteen riders. They loitered at the street corners and relaxed on the benches on the walk in front of the barber shop. A group of them waited for me before the saloon. They were my army, battle tested and true. With them I could take on this town or any other.

Then I saw John Blake.

He wore a black frock coat and a wide-brimmed black planter's hat. His guns were out of sight, but they were there, I had no doubt.

"Your men aren't drinking?" he commented.

"No."

"Red Mike," Blake said. "I remember him well from Abilene, and Tod Mulloy, Rule Carson, and Delgado. You came ready for trouble, Gavagan."

"The Comanches were riding, and the Kiowa."

"And now?"

"I will be going north of the street tonight, John, but not for trouble. I was invited."

"You know the rule here." He looked at me carefully from his hooded eyes. "It cannot be."

"There are other ways to look, John, and I am not a trouble-hunting man."

"The people who live here have passed an ordinance. This is their town and I am charged with enforcing their laws." He stated this flatly, and then he walked away, and I stood there with a lightness inside me and an awareness of trouble to come.

THE CATTLE were checked and sold to Bob Wells. We rode together to the bank and when we went in John Blake stood square on his two feet, watching.

McDonald was a narrow man, high-shouldered and thin, dry as dust and fleshless. He looked at me and gave a brief nod and counted over the money for the cattle, which was my employer's money, and none of it mine but wages.

He watched me put the gold and greenbacks

in a sack and he said, "Your business here is finished?"

"I've some calls to make."

"You are welcome," he said, "south of the street."

"Tonight I shall come to call on your niece. She has invited me."

"You must be mistaken." He was a cold man with his heart in his ledgers and his dollars. "You are welcome here to do whatever business you have, and beyond that you are not welcome."

"I am not a drunk, wandering the streets and looking for trouble. I am one who has been entrusted with these two thousand cattle and now, like you, with this money. But, unlike you, I will carry this payment across many dangerous miles back to Texas. My honesty and character are not in question there."

"Mr. McDonald," Wells protested, "this is a good man. I know this man."

"We put up with your kind," McDonald said, "south of the street."

I could see my attempt had been wasted on him. The issue was not character but class. McDonald had decided to put himself above me and there was no chance he'd be seeing it differently.

"Five times I have come over the trail," I told him, "and I have seen towns die. Markets and conditions change, and neither of us has been in this country long enough to be putting on airs."

"Young man, let me repeat. South of the street you and your kind are welcome, north of it you become a subject for John Blake. As for this town . . . I am the mayor and it will not die."

"I have spoken with Mr. Blake. He is aware of my plans." I glanced over at the marshal and deep in his eyes something glinted, but whether it was a challenge or amusement I couldn't be sure. "I know him, Mr. McDonald," I said, "and he knows me."

ROCKING K MEN were in the saloons that night, and Rocking K men were south of the street, but I sat at the campfire near the chuck wagon and Red Mike joined me there.

"If you'll be riding, I'll saddle your horse."

"Saddle two, then."

"Ah? It's like that, is it?"

"A man must find out, Mike, one never knows. If she's the girl I want, she will ride with me tonight."

We were young then, and the West was young, with the land broad and bright before us. We knew, whatever the truth was, that every horse could be ridden, every man whipped, every girl loved. We rode with the wind then, and sang in the rain, and when we fought it was with the same savage joy as that of the Comanches who opposed us, these fierce, proud warriors who would ride half a thousand miles to fight a battle or raid a wagon train. And no Bruce ever rode from the Highlands with a finer lot of fighting men than rode this day with the Rocking K.

"And John Blake?"

"Stay out of it, Mike, and keep others out. John Blake is a stubborn man, and if we go against him there will be killing in the town. This is a personal matter and does not concern the brand."

With a mirror nailed to the chuck wagon's side I shaved and combed my hair and made myself ready for courting. It was much to expect of any girl, to ride to Texas with a man she did not know, and yet in those days when men constantly moved such things happened. There were few men from whom to choose in those wild small towns, and the best were often moving and had to be taken on the fly. And to me this was the girl and now was the time.

There was John Blake to consider, a man seasoned in the wars of men and cattle, who knew all the dodges and all the tricks, and whatever a man might invent he had known before. Each herd had a man who wished to prove himself against a trail town marshal, never grasping the difference between the skilled amateur and the hardened professional. John Blake looked upon men with vast patience, vast understanding, and used a gun only when necessary, but when he used it he used it coldly, efficiently, and deliberately.

In a black broadcloth suit with my hat brim down, I rode up the middle of the street with the reins in my left hand, my right resting on my thigh near my gun.

Tonight I was more than a Texas man a-courting, I was a challenge to the rule of John Blake, and it was something I had no liking for. No man from the Texas trails had been north of the street since he had been marshal, and it was assumed that no man would.

Outside the town a Rocking K rider dozed on the ground near his horse, and grazing close by was another horse, saddled and bridled for travel.

John Blake was not in sight, but when I passed the livery stable Tod Mulloy was seated under the light, minding his own business, and on the edge of the walk near the eating house Rule Carson smoked a cigar. Inside, over coffee, were Delgado and Enright. They would not interfere, but would be on hand if needed. Nor did I doubt that the rest of them were scattered about town, just waiting for my call.

At the end of the street when I turned north John Blake was awaiting me. And I drew up.

"I'd hoped it would not come to this, John,

but a man must go a-courting. He must go where his heart would take him, and I think in my place, you would go, no matter what."

He considered that, a square black block of a man looking as solid as rock and as immovable. "It might be," he agreed, after a moment, "but is it courting you are about, or is this a Texas challenge to me?"

"I wouldn't go risking the lady's reputation by asking her to sneak away and meet me after dark. This is no challenge."

He nodded. "If it was," he replied, "I'd stop you, for kill or be killed is my job when it comes to an issue, but I'd stop no decent man from courting . . . although if I were giving advice about the woman in question—"

"Don't," I said. "A man with his heart set isn't one to listen."

"You're not out of the woods," Blake added. "Believe me, I've nothing against you or any decent man making a decent call. It's the drunks and the fighting I want to keep south of the street. However, that is a thing of yesterday for me. I have quit my job."

"Quit!"

"Aye. McDonald told me to keep you south of the street tonight, or lose my job. He has grown arrogant since he took office, and I work for the town, not just the mayor. I was hired to keep the peace, and that only. So I've quit."

The stubborn foolishness of McDonald angered me, yet in a sense I could not blame the man, for generally we were a wild crowd and if a man did not understand us he might easily believe us capable of any evil. At the same time I had pride in my promises, and I had said I would call.

"If you've actually quit, I'd like to take advantage of the fact you're no longer marshal here."

He shot me a quick look. "I want nobody hurt, Gavagan. I've quit, but I've still a feeling for the town."

"It would be like this . . ." and he listened while I explained the idea that had come to me.

"It must be carefully done, no fighting, do you hear?"

Turning my horse I rode back to talk with Carson, Mulloy, Enright, and Delgado. Immediately after I had finished they scattered out to talk to the others and take their positions.

"I saw them going up to the house with their rifles," Carson said. "Carpenter who owns the store is there, with Wilson, Talcott, and some I do not know by name, but all have businesses along the street, so I think it will work."

Circling through the darkness I rode up to the house among the poplars, but stopped across the street. It had been quiet for the boys from the Rocking K and they ached to blow off steam and dearly loved a joke. So this might work.

Leaving my horse I crossed the alley where the shadows were deep and drew near the house. I heard subdued voices beneath the trees.

"I don't like it," Carpenter was saying. "Once that Texas crowd know Blake has quit they will blow the lid off."

"It was a fool idea. John Blake has kept the peace."

"Tell that to McDonald. He would have Blake on some other excuse if not this. The man will have nobody who won't kowtow to him."

Suddenly there was a crashing and splintering of wood from the street, followed by a gunshot and a chorus of Texas yells that split the night wide open, and then there was another outburst of firing and a shattering of glass.

"There they go!" Carpenter stepped out of the shadows into the moonlight. "What did I tell you?"

Down the street charged four Rocking K riders, yelling and shooting. It reminded me of the old days when I was a youngster on my first trip up the trail.

The front door slammed open and McDonald came rushing out, an angry man by the sound of him. "What's that? What's going on?"

The night was stabbed and slashed by the blaze of gunshots, and intermingled with them was the smashing of glass and raucous yells. The boys were having themselves a time.

"You fired Blake," Carpenter said, "and the lid's off."

"We'll see about that!" McDonald said. "Come on!"

They rushed for the street in a mass, and when they did I moved closer, stepped over the fence, and crossed the lawn to the house.

Suddenly as it had started, and just as we had planned, a blanket dropped upon the town. Not a shout, a shot, or a whisper. By the time McDonald got there the hands would be seated around, playing cards and talking, looking upon the world with the wide-eyed innocence of a bunch of two-year-olds.

The door opened under my rap and June stood there in a pale blue dress, even more lovely than I had expected.

"Why, it's you! But—!" She looked beyond me into the night. "Where is Uncle Aaron?"

"May I come in?"

Startled, she looked up at me again, then stepped back and I went in and closed the door behind me. Hat in hand I bowed to Mrs. McDonald, who was behind her.

The room was stiff, cluttered and lacking in comfort, with plush furniture and a false, unused elegance. There was too much bric-a-brac, and not a place where a man could really sit. Suddenly I remembered the spaciousness of the old Spanish-style houses I had known in Texas.

"We heard shooting," June said.

"Oh, that? Some confusion in town. I believe your uncle went down to put a stop to it."

She looked at me carefully, and I seemed to sense a withdrawing, a change that I could not quite grasp.

"You're not dressed for riding," I said.

She flushed. "You surely didn't believe . . . you weren't **serious**?" She looked at me in amazement. "I thought . . . I mean, it was rather fun, but . . . could you imagine, **me** going with **you** . . ."

Something went out of me then and I stood there feeling the fool I undoubtedly was. Some fine, sharp flame flickered within me as though caught in a gust of wind, then snuffed out and left me empty and lost . . . it might have been the last spark of my boyhood. A man must grow up in so many ways.

On the street she had seemed beautiful and strong and possessed of a fine courage, and in the romantic heart of me I had believed she was the one, that she was my dream, that she was the girl who rode in my thoughts in the dust of the drag or the heat of the flank.

She stared at me, half astonished, and within me there was nothing at all, not sorrow, not bitterness, certainly not anger.

"Good night," I said. "I am sorry that I intruded."

She had cost me a dream, but suddenly I was aware that she would have cost me the dream anyway, for that was what I had been in love with . . . a dream.

Opening the door, I was about to leave when Aaron McDonald pushed past me. Anger flashed in his eyes, and his face paled with fury that was in him. "Look here!" he shouted. "You—!"

"Shut up, you arrogant windbag," I said, and walked on out the door leaving him spluttering. And to the others who were outside, I said, "Get out of my way," and they stepped back and the gate creaked on rusty hinges when I stepped out.

A hand on the pommel of my saddle, I stood for a moment under the stars, cursing myself for seven kinds of an idiot. Like any child I had been carried away . . . who did I think I was, anyway?

Yet although the fire was out the smoke lifted, and I hesitated to step into the saddle, knowing the finality of it. The things a man will wish for are harder to leave behind than all his wants, and who, at some time in his life, does not dream of gathering into his arms and carrying away the girl he loves?

The men of the Rocking K came from the saloons and stood around me, and when they looked at my face, something seemed to shadow theirs, for I think my dream was one lived by them all, and had it come true with me then all their lonely dreaming might be true also.

"We'll be going," I said.

Yet there was a thing that remained to be done, for as I had lost something this day, I had gained something, too.

"I'll join you at the wagon," I told them, and turning at right angles I rode between the buildings toward the south of town.

IT WAS a simple room of rough boards with one window, a small stove, and a bed. John Blake had his coat off and he was packing, but he turned to face whoever was at the door.

"John," I said, "she would not come and I was a fool to expect it. I have grown a little tonight, I think."

"You have grown a little," he agreed, "but don't expect too much of it, for there will be other times. Each time one grows, one loses a little, too."

"John," I said, "there are cattle on the plains of Texas and I've land there. When I come north again I'll be driving my own herd. It is a big job for one man."

"So?"

"There will be rivers to cross and the Comanches will be out, but there's a future in it for the men who make the drives.

"I like the way you straddle a town, and I like a man with judgment and principle. It is a rare thing to find a man who will stand square on what he believes, whether it is making a rule or an exception to it. So if you'll ride with me it's a partnership, share and share alike."

A square, solid man in a striped white shirt and black sleeve garters, he looked at me carefully from those cool gray eyes, and then he said, quite seriously, "I've little to pack, for a man who has never had anything but a gun travels light."

## *Caprock Rancher*

When I rode up to the buffalo wallow, Pa was lying there with his leg broke and his horse gone.

Out there on the prairie there wasn't much to make splints with, and Pa was bad hurt. It had seemed to me the most important things for a man to know was how to ride a horse and use a gun, but now neither one was going to do much good.

Earlier in the day Pa and me had had a mean argument, and it wasn't the first. Here I was, man-grown and seventeen, and Pa still after me about the company I kept. He was forever harping on Doc Sites and Kid Reese and their like . . . said they were no-goods. As if he was one to talk, a man who'd never had money nor schooling, nor any better than a worn-out coat on his back. Anyway, Doc and Kid Reese weren't about to be farmers or starving on a short-grass cow ranch.

Pa, he'd been at me again because I'd be

dogged if I was going to waste my life away on what little we could make, and told him so . . . then I rode off to be an outlaw. For the first two miles I was good and mad, and for the third mile I was growling some, but I'd made most of ten miles before my good sense got the better of me and I started back to help Pa. He had a far piece to go, and he was a lone man packing twenty thousand dollars through some mighty rough country.

It was midafternoon of a mighty hot day when I came up to that buffalo wallow, and Pa had been lying there four, five hours. His canteen had been on his saddle and the horse had taken off, so I got down and gave him a swallow or two from mine.

All that argument was forgotten. Times like that a man is best off doing one thing at a time and not worrying around too much.

"Thanks, boy." Pa returned the canteen to me. "Looks like I played hob."

"That gray never did have a lick of sense," I said, and then I told it to him. "You got a busted leg, but your jaw's in good shape. So you set back an' argue with me whilst I set that bone."

"You just forget about me. All that money is in those saddlebags, and less than a third of it ours. You forget me and hunt down that horse."

That twenty thousand dollars was from a steer

herd we'd taken to Kansas and sold, and folks back home were a-sweating until we got back with the money. Cash money was hard to come by those times, and most of this would go to mighty poor folks who hadn't seen a hard dollar since who flung the chunk.

"You got a broke leg. We'll take care of that first."

Nothing was growing around but short grass and some knee-high mesquite, but I got Pa's leg set and cut mesquite with my bowie and splinted up best I knew how. All that time he set there a-looking at me with pain in his eyes and never let out a whimper, but the sweat stood out on both our faces, you can bet.

If you were ever seventeen years old and standing in a buffalo wallow one hundred and fifty miles from home, and your pa with a broke leg, you know how I felt. And only one horse between us.

With my help he got straddle of that horse and we started off with two things in mind. To get to a creek where there was water, and to find that fool horse.

Judging by the tracks, that gray had taken off like wolves was after him, but after half a mile he began to slow up and look back expecting to be chased. Then on, he got the smell of water and just sort of ambled, taking a bite of grass or mesquite beans now and again. Pa, he sat up in the leather and never said I, yes, or no. This time it was up to me and both of us knew it.

The sun was beyond the hill and color was in the evening sky when we saw those other tracks. They came in from the southeast and they were the tracks of three shod horses . . . and they caught Pa's horse.

This was just across the border from Indian Territory and while honest men crossed it, aside from the Indians, few honest men lived there. To be a Deputy U.S. Marshal in Indian Territory was like standing yourself up in the business end of a shooting gallery. Every outlaw in the country spent time there, and we knew if those had been good men who caught up Pa's horse, or even a decent kind of outlaw, they'd backtrack to find the rider. In those years folks were helpful to one another, and to be afoot in a country like that was about the worst that could happen. It left a man with mighty few possibilities.

These men had caught up Pa's horse and checked the saddlebags, and they didn't come looking for Pa.

"Son"—Pa could read those tracks as well as me—"don't you get any notions. You ain't about to go up against three men, not with me in this condition."

"Ain't nothing to worry about. Those boys are friends of mine. One of them is Kid Reese and another is Doc Sites. Why, I'd know those horse tracks if I saw them in Gilead. This time of night they won't go far and we'll have your horse and money in no time."

Pa, he just sat up there on my horse and he said nothing at all for a while, and then he said, "Ed, you reckon those boys would give back twenty thousand dollars?"

It gave me an uneasy feeling, him saying that. Pa set no store by either of them, but they were good boys. Free and easy, that's sure, but they were friends of mine. When Pa and me moved into that Texas country they'd let me take up with them. We-all were usually up to no good, but that was what you'd expect from three youngsters caught somewheres between being boys and being men. It's true we were always talking of standing up a stagecoach or robbing a bank, but that was mostly talk. Taking money from a friend . . . well, they weren't that kind.

It was not much of a creek. Stars were in the sky when we fetched up to it, and it wasn't more than two, three feet wide and maybe four, five inches deep, but it was wet water, lined with willows and cottonwoods and grass aplenty. When I helped Pa off the horse, I bedded him down and filled the canteen for him.

"You set quiet," I said, "I'll go fetch your horse."

"Don't be a fool, Edwin," Pa said. "You say

those boys are your friends, but there's a sight of money in those saddlebags . . . not many who value friendship that high."

Pa never called me Edwin unless he was downright serious. That money was important for reasons beyond what it could buy. Pa was always holding on about the value of a good name, and for the first time I was faced up to what it could mean. Pa was a respected man, but if we showed up without that money a lot of folks were going to remember that I'd been swaggering it around town with Doc Sites, Kid Reese, and that outfit. Some of them were going to say things about us losing the money, and Pa would take the blame as well as me.

We Tuckers never had much but an honest reputation. We were never able to get ahead. A while back we lived in Missouri, and that was the year Pa had his first good crop, and the year the grasshoppers ate him out. Two years of bad drought followed and we lost the place. We settled in Texas then and worked like dogs, and when we got our first trail herd together the Comanches came down and burned us out in the light of the moon. They burned us out, drove off our cows, and killed Uncle Bud.

They killed Uncle Bud and they'd taken his scalp. Pa, he rode after them but he never got back with any cows. Somewhere along the way he found Bud's scalp, which we buried out where the body was.

This herd we had just sold in Kansas was our first since then, and the first thing Pa had to show for twenty years of hard work . . . and the first many of our neighbors had to show. If we'd got through to the ranch with that money we'd have had an edge on the future.

I guess it was my fault. While we were separated that morning the gray shied and threw him, and had I been where I should have been I'd have dropped a loop over that gray's neck and he wouldn't have gone anywhere at all. It was lucky I'd quit sulking and started back; I'd been mad but I wasn't ready to strike on my own yet. I was figuring on hooking up with Kid Reese and Doc before I did anything permanent.

Those boys were friends of mine, but something was gnawing at me. What were they doing away off up here at a time like this?

Leaving Pa alongside the creek with his pistol to hand, I mounted up and started along the creek in the direction those tracks had taken. About a half mile from where I'd left Pa, I smelled smoke.

They were camped on a grassy bench alongside the creek and under some big old cottonwoods. They had a fire going and I could see the firelight on their faces, and hear the murmur of voices. There was a third man at the fire whom

I had never seen before, but I knew who he was from his description. It was Bob Heseltine.

How many stories had they told me about the doings of Bob Heseltine? To those boys he was big as all outdoors, and according to them he was the best rider, the best shot, and the most fearless man who ever came down the pike. Bob Heseltine, they told me confidentially, had held up the Garston Bank . . . he had killed Sheriff Baker in a stand-up gun battle, and he had backed down two—not one but two—Texas Rangers. And all they could talk about was all they were going to do when Bob Heseltine got back. And here he was.

He was a mite shorter than me but wide in the shoulder, the hide of his face like tanned leather. He had deep-set blue eyes and he wore two guns tied down and sized up like a mighty mean man. Why, I'd heard more stories about him than about Clay Allison or Jim Courtright or Wild Bill Hickok.

Pa's horse was there and still saddled, but the saddlebags lay on the ground near the fire and they had the money out on a blanket where they could count it. They were going to be disappointed when they found that was our money, and belonging to folks back home. It isn't often a man finds twenty thousand dollars riding around on a lost horse.

"Hi!"

They were all so set on that money that when I hailed them they came up with their guns drawn. They stood there blinking their eyes at me like owls in a hailstorm.

"It's all right, Bob," Reese said. "This here is Ed Tucker, the one we were tellin' of. Ed, what in blazes are you doin' out here?"

"I see you found Pa's horse," I said, "and our money."

Doc's lips sort of thinned down and Heseltine's head turned real slow to look at me again. Kid Reese, he looked everywhere but at me. Right then I began to wonder about those boys.

Firelight flickered on their faces, on the flanks of the horses, on the gold and silver spread on the blanket, and off their rifle barrels, setting against their saddles. It was so quiet a body could hear the cottonwood leaves brushing their pale green palms one agin the other, and out there beyond the light the creek water chuckled and whispered around rocks or something in the stream.

"I'm afraid you've got this all wrong, boy," Heseltine said. "I don't know you and I don't know whose horse this is. We found this money, and finders is keepers."

"Now wait a minute . . . Doc here, he knows Pa's horse. So does Reese. They saw it many times down Texas way."

Heseltine turned his head to look at them. "Is that true? Do you know this horse?"

Doc Sites looked at the ground and he looked away at the creek and he shook his head. Kid Reese, he said, "It don't look like any horse I ever saw before, Bob. It's just a lost horse, that's all."

Seemed like a long time I sat there, looking at the firelight on that money. I'd never seen that much money before but it didn't look like money to me, it looked like Pa sweating over his fields back in Missouri, and like all the work we'd done, by day and night, rounding up those cattle and putting brands on them. It looked like all those folks around us who shared the drive with us . . . that money was there for them.

"Stop your foolin'," I said, "Pa's back in the brush with a broke leg, broke when this horse throwed him. I got to get back there with this horse and that money."

"You can have the horse. Take it an' welcome," Heseltine said quietly, "but the money stays here, and you're leavin' unless you want to try to do something about it. . . ."

All three of them were facing me now, and Heseltine was all squared around to make his fight. Doc had a rifle in his hand and Kid Reese stood there with his thumbs in his belt, just a-grinning at me. They would do whatever Bob Heseltine had said, and he'd told me what to do.

"I figured we were friends." It sounded

mighty weak and they could see I was backing down. The three of them stood there looking at me and making me feel mighty small.

"We could take him in with us," Sites said, "he's a good kid. He'll do what you tell him, Bob."

That made me kind of mad. Here I'd been ready to ride off and leave Pa, and they expected me to do what somebody told me.

"Half the money is mine," Heseltine said. "If you boys want to split your half with him, to hell with you. He's your friend."

A stick fell into the fire and sparks lifted into the night. Bob Heseltine was looking straight at me, and I knew what he was thinking. He was thinking he could kill me and wondering if he should.

Pa, he used to tell me when a man is holding the wrong cards he shouldn't try to buck the game. It's better to throw in your hand and wait on another deal.

Only thing that had me worried was whether I could get out of there alive.

"Looks like you got me euchred," I said then, and I started backing to my horse. There was a minute or two when it looked like Heseltine might shoot, but he just looked at me and turned away.

Kid Reese whispered, "You ain't gonna let him go? He'll have the law on us."

"For what?" Heseltine asked. "For finding money?"

Time to time, riding alone and thinking like a body does, I'd imagined myself in positions like this, and each time I'd known what to do. Right off I told them, and then I shot it out with them and always came off a winner. It beats all what a man's imagination will do for him, and how different it is when he faces up to something like that. Right then I felt mighty puny . . . backed down by those three, and me in the right.

Going back down the trail I kept telling myself I'd have shot it out if it hadn't been for Pa, but deep down I wasn't so sure. If I was killed, Pa would be left to die. Maybe I was thinking of that and maybe I was just scared.

Yet I couldn't recall being exactly scared . . . only that I was in the middle of something I'd be better out of.

PA WAS SITTING UP with his back to a tree when I rode up. He had the coffeepot on, for that had been among the stuff I left beside him when I shucked my gear at the camp. Pa was sitting up but he looked poorly. His face was gray and tight-drawn.

"Three of them?" He studied the situation awhile. "That's our money, boy. We were trusted with it."

We drank our coffee, and neither of us talked

much, but it gave me time to sort of get things settled down inside me. A man doesn't always know what to do when things happen quick-like and when for the first time he's faced up with gun trouble and no way accustomed to it. But this was showing me a few things and one of them was that Pa had been right about Doc and Reese.

When it came right down to it those two shaped up like a couple of two-by-twice tin-horns. Neither of them had nerve enough to talk up to Bob Heseltine . . . but neither had I.

"I got to go back," I said, "I got to go back and make my fight. Else I'll always think I was scared."

"You and me, Ed," Pa said, "we've had our troubles but you never showed anything but sand. There's scared smart and then there's scared stupid. I think that you did the right thing." Pa reached for a stick lying among the branches of a fallen tree, and he had out his bowie. "We're going back, boy, but we're going together."

We'd taken our time. Pa had a pipe after his coffee and while he smoked he worked on a crutch. My mouth was all dry inside and my stomach was queasy, but once we decided to go back I felt a whole lot better. It was like I'd left something unfinished back there that just had to be done.

And I kept thinking of Sites, not willing to face up to it, and Reese, who was supposed to be my friend, wanting to kill me.

"You did right, Ed," Pa told me, speaking around his pipe stem. "You did the smart thing. They will think you were scared off."

"That Heseltine . . . they say he's killed a dozen men. He's robbed banks and he's got a mean reputation."

"I like to see a mean man," Pa said. "Most of them don't cut much figger."

Pa had finished working out his crutch. It wasn't much, just a forked stick trimmed down a mite so he could use the fork to hold under his armpit. I helped him to the horse, and once he got a foot in the stirrup and a hand on the horn he was in that saddle. Meanwhile I smothered our fire. Nobody wants to turn fire loose in grass or timber unless he's a fool.

"A bank robber don't shape up to me," Pa said. "When he goes into a bank with a gun, he don't figure to get shot at. If he expected it he'd never take the first step. He threatens men with folks depending on them and steals money he's too lazy to work for.

"The James boys swaggered it mighty big until a bunch of home folks up at Northfield shot their ears off, and the Dalton gang got the same thing in Coffeyville. The McCarty boys tried it in Colorado, and all those bold outlaws were shot down by a few quiet men who left their glass-polishing or law books to do it."

Well, all those outlaws had seemed mighty exciting until Pa put it thataway, but what he said was true. Pa was a little man himself, only weighed a hundred and thirty pounds, though he had the strongest hands I ever did see. Strong hands from plowing, shoeing horses, and wrassling steers.

Close to midnight we fetched up to their fire.

"Help me down, Ed," Pa said, whispering. "I want to be on the ground."

We walked up to the fire, our boots making small sounds in the grass. Pa was carrying my Colt in his right hand, and I carried a shell under the hammer of my Henry rifle. Those boys weren't much account at keeping watch; they were setting around a blanket playing cards for our money.

"You boys are wasting time," Pa told them. "You're playing with money that don't belong to you."

Pa had that crutch under his left shoulder, but he held that Colt in one big hand and it pointed like a finger at Heseltine.

"Hear you're a killing man," Pa said to him, "but you size up to me like a no-account, yellow-bellied loafer."

"You got the drop," Heseltine said. "You got a loud mouth when you got the drop."

"The drop? You figure we're in some kind of dime novel? Ed, you keep an eye on those others. If either of them make a move, shoot both of them and after they're laying on the ground, shoot them again!"

Deliberately Pa lowered the muzzle until it pointed into the grass beside his foot. "Now, Ed tells me you're a fast hand with a gun," Pa said, and he limped forward three steps, his eyes locked on Heseltine's, "but I think you're a backshooting tinhorn."

Heseltine looked at Pa standing there on one leg and a crutch, and he looked at that old pistol. He looked at Pa again and he drew a long breath and held it. Then he let his breath go and stood there with his hands hanging.

"Nobody's got the drop now, Heseltine." Pa spoke quietly but his pale eyes blazed in the firelight. "I'm not going back without that money. And if you try to stop me either you're gonna die or both of us are gonna die!"

Sweat was all over Bob Heseltine's face, and it was a cool evening. He wanted to go for his gun the worst way, but he had another want that beat that one all hollow. He wanted to live.

Kid Reese and Doc Sites stood there looking at the big man and they couldn't believe it, and

I'm sure I couldn't. A body didn't need to read minds to guess what they were thinking, because here was a poor old gray-haired caprock rancher on one leg with his gun muzzle down calling the bluff of a gunman said to be among the fastest—although, come to think of it, I never heard it said by anyone but Doc or Reese.

Out of the corner of my eye I could see Pa standing there; for a little man he looked mighty big, and I suddenly found myself thinking about how it was that my pa had come back with Uncle Bud's scalp. No Comanche warrior ever left a trophy like that beside the trail. Surely no Comanche warrior would ever let a trophy like that go without a fight to the death. It seemed all Bob Heseltine had to do to die was lay hand on his guns.

Pa's pistol swung up. "You had your chance. Now unbuckle your gun belt and step back."

Heseltine did what he was told and I went forward and gathered his guns. Then I picked up all that money and stuffed it in the saddlebags, and I went through their pockets checking for more.

"Time you learned a lesson, Edwin," Pa said to me. "Time you learned that it's what's inside a man that matters, not how fast he can draw a gun."

Pa backed off a few careful steps and without looking at me, he said, "Ed, you and him are going to fight. He needs a whoppin' and you're going to give it to him, do you hear?"

Pa gestured with the Colt. "You others stay out of this . . . it's a fair fight, between the two of them."

Well, I looked over at Heseltine; he was six or seven years older than me an' he outweighed me by more than a few pounds. I thought of that story where he killed the sheriff, and then I remembered that he'd just backed down to a crippled-up old man who'd been armed with little more than a fiery force of will and my old Colt.

I put down my gun.

Heseltine took off his calfskin jacket and spat on his hands, looking over at me. "Why, you weak-kneed little whelp, I'll—!"

Another thing Pa taught me: If you're going to fight . . . fight. Talk about it after.

Lifting my left fist I fetched him a clout in the mouth with my right, and right then I saw that a mean man could bleed.

He came at me swinging with both hands. He was strong, and he figured to put the sign on me. He moved well, better than me, but he hadn't put in all those years of hard work that I had.

He walloped me alongside the jaw and it shook me some, but not like I figured it would. He hit me again and I saw a kind of surprised look come into his eyes, and I knew he'd hit me as hard as he could so I fetched him right where he'd been putting all that whiskey. He grunted, and I spread out my legs and began whopping him with both fists . . . and in that regard I take after Pa. I've got big hands.

He went down to his knees and I picked him up by the collar and looked him over to find a place that wasn't bloody where I could fetch him again, but the fight was all out of him and Pa said, "Let him go, Ed. Just drop him."

Seemed like he would go down easier if I fetched him a clout and I did, and then I walked back to get my gun, blowing on my sore fists.

Pa looked over at Doc Sites and Kid Reese who were staring at Heseltine like it was a bad dream. "You two can keep your guns," he said. "This is Indian country, and I just hope you come after us.

"Whatever you do," he added, "don't ever come back home. There will be too many who'd like a shot at you."

Neither of us felt like camping that night with home so far away, so we rode on with the north star behind us. Pa's leg must have been giving him what for, but he was in a good mood, and my fists were sore and my knuckles split, but I felt like riding on through the night.

"You know, Pa, Carlson's been wanting to sell out. He's got water and about three hundred head, and with what we've got we could buy him out and have margin to work on. I figure we could swing it."

"Together, we could," Pa said.

We rode south, taking our time, under a Comanche moon.

# *Dead-End Drift*

The trickle of sand ceased, and there was silence. Then a small rock dropped from overhead into the rubble beneath, and the flat finality of the sound put a period to the moment.

There was a heavy odor of dust, and one of the men coughed, the dry, hacking cough of miner's consumption. Silence hung heavily in the thick, dead air.

"Better sit still." Bert's voice was quiet and unexcited. "I'll make a light." They waited, listening to the miner fumbling with his hand lamp. "We might dislodge something," he added, "and start it again."

They heard his palm strike the lamp, and he struck several times before the flint gave off the spark to light the flame. An arrow of flame leaped from the burner. The sudden change from the impenetrable darkness at the end of the tunnel to the bright glare of the miner's lamp left them blinking. They sat very still, looking slowly around, careful to disturb nothing. The suddenness of the disaster had stunned them into quiet acceptance.

Frank's breathing made a hoarse, ugly sound, and when their eyes found him, they could see the dark, spreading stain on his shirt front and the misshapen look of his broken body. He was a powerful man, with blond, curly hair above a square, hard face. There was blood on the rocks near him and blood on the jagged rock he had rolled from his body after the cave-in.

There was a trickle of blood across Bert's face from a scalp wound but no other injuries to anyone. Their eyes evaded the wall of fallen rock across the drift, their minds filled with awareness.

"Hurt bad?" Bert said to Frank. "Looks like the big one hit you."

"Yeah," Frank's voice was low. "Feels like I'm stove up inside."

"Better leave him alone," Joe said. "The bleeding seems to be letting up, and there's nothing we can do."

Frank stared down at his body curiously. "I guess I'm hurt bad."

He turned his head deliberately and stared at the muck pile. The cave-in had left a slanting pile of broken rock that reached toward them along the drift, cutting them off completely from the outside world, from light and air. Behind them was the face of the drift where Rody had been drilling. From the face of the drift to the muck pile was a matter of a few feet. Frank touched his dry lips with his tongue, remembering what lay beyond the cave-in.

It could scarcely have been the tunnel alone. Beyond it was the Big Stope. He reached over and turned out the light. The flame winked, and darkness was upon them.

"What's the idea?" Joe demanded.

"Air," Frank said. "There's four of us, and there isn't going to be enough air. We may be some time in getting out."

"If we get out," Joe said.

Rody shifted his weight on the rock slab where he was sitting, and they heard the rasp of the coarse denim. "How far do you reckon she caved, Frank?"

"I don't know." Then he said what they all feared. "Maybe the Big Stope went."

"If it did," Rody commented, "we might as well fold our cards and toss in our hands. Nobody can open that stope before the air gives out. There's not much air in here for four men."

"I warned Tom about that stope," Joe said. "He had no right to have men working in here. That stope was too big in the first place. Must be a hundred feet across and no pillars, and down below there was too much weight on the stulls. The posts were countersunk into the laggin' all of two inches, like a knife in butter."

"The point is," Frank said, "that we're here. No use talking about what should have been. If any part of the stope went, it all went. There's a hundred feet of tunnel to drive and timber, and workin' in loose muck isn't going to help."

No one spoke. In the utter blackness and stillness of the drift they waited. There was no light, no sound. All had been cut off from them. Joe wiped the sweat from his brow with the back of his hand.

The blackness of a mine, the complete darkness, had always bothered him. At night in the outer world, no matter how clouded the sky, there is always some light, and in time the eyes will adjust, and a man can see—a little, at any rate. Here there was no light, and a man was completely blind.

And there was no sound. Only two hundred feet to the surface, yet it might as well have been two thousand. Two hundred feet of rock between them and the light, and that was the shortest route. By the drift or tunnel it was a quarter of a mile to the shaft where the cage could take them to the surface.

Above them was the whole weight of the mountain, before them the solid wall where they had been drilling, behind them the mass of the cave-in, thousands of tons of broken rock and broken timbers.

On the surface there would be tense, frightened men, frightened not for themselves but for those entombed below—and they could not know that anyone was alive.

The skip would be coming down now, bringing men to attack that enormous slide. On top men would be girding for the struggle with the mountain. Around the collar of the shaft men and equipment would be gathered to be sent below. Near the warehouse men would be standing, and some women, tense and white, wondering about those below. And the men who were buried alive could only wait and hope.

"Got a chew, Bert?" Joe asked.

"Sure." Bert pushed his hand into the darkness, feeling for Joe's. Their hands were steady. Joe bit off a chew, then passed the plug back, their hands fumbling in the dark again.

"We ain't got a chance!" Rody exclaimed suddenly. "She might have caved clear to the station. Anyway, there's no way they can get through in time. We ain't got the air to last five hours even if they could make it that quick."

"Forget it," Joe said. "You wouldn't do nothing but blow your money on that frowzy blonde in Kingman if you got free."

"I was a sap for ever coming to work in this lousy hole," Rody grumbled. "I was a sap."

"Quit crabbing," Bert said mildly. "We're here now, and we've got to like it."

There was a long silence. Somewhere the mountain creaked, and there was a distant sound of more earth sliding.

"Say"—Frank's voice broke into the silence—"any of you guys work in Thirty-seven?"

"You mean that raise on the Three Hundred?" Bert asked. "Sure, I put in a couple of shifts there."

"Aren't we right over it now?"

"Huh?" Joe moved quickly. "How high up were they?"

"Better than ninety feet." Frank's tone was tight, strained. He held himself, afraid to breathe deep, afraid of the pain that would come. He was not sure what had happened to him. Part of his body was numb, but there was a growing pain in his belly as the shock wore off. He knew he was in deep trouble, and the chances of his getting out alive were small. He dreaded the thought of being moved, doubted if he would survive it.

"If that raise was up ninety feet"—Joe spoke slowly, every word standing alone—"then it ain't more than ten feet below us. If we could dig down—"

"Ten feet? In that kind of rock?" Rody sneered. "You couldn't dig that with a pick. Not in a week. Anyway, Thirty-seven ain't this far along. We're thirty yards beyond at least."

"No," Frank said, "I think we're right over it.

Anyway, it's a chance. It's more than we've got now."

There was a long silence while they turned the idea over in their minds. Then Joe said, "Why a raise here? There's no ore body here. That's supposed to be farther along."

"Air," Bert said. "They wanted some circulation."

He got up, and they heard him fumbling for a pick. They heard the metallic sound as it was dragged toward him over the rock. "Better move back against the muck pile," he said. "I'm digging."

"You're a sap," Rody said. "You've got no chance."

"Shut up!" Joe's tone was ugly. "If you ain't willing to try, you can go to hell. I want out of here."

"Who're you tellin' to shut up?" They heard Rody rise suddenly. "I ain't never had no use for you, you—"

"Rody!" Frank's tone was harsh. "I've got a pick handle, and I know where you are. You go back where you were and keep your mouth shut. This is a hell of a time to start something."

A light flared in Frank's hand, and he hitched himself a little higher to see better. "That's right, Bert. Start right there. Some of that top stuff will just flake off."

Sweat beaded his strained white face. One big

hand clutched a pick handle. Slowly, as if he had difficulty in moving them, his eyes shifted from face to face. He stared at Rody the longest. Rody's stiff black hair curled back from a low forehead. He was almost as broad as Frank but thicker.

The sodden blows of the pick became the ticking clock of the passing time. It was a slow, measured beat, for the air was already thickening, and the blows pounded with the pulse of their blood. The flame of the carbide light ate into their small supply of air, burning steadily.

Bert stopped, mopping his face. "She's damn hard, Frank. It's going to take the point off this pick in a hurry."

"We've got four of them," Frank said. The whole front of him was one dark stain now. "I always carry a pick in a mine."

Bert swung again, and they watched as the point of the pick found a place and broke back a piece of the rock. The surface had been partly shattered by the explosions as the drift was pushed farther into the mountain. It would be harder as they got down farther.

Frank's big hands were relaxed and loose. He watched the swing of the pick, and when Joe got up to spell Bert, he asked him, "Anybody on top waitin' for you?"

"Uh-huh." Joe paused, pick in hand. "A girl."

Rody started to speak but caught Frank's eye

and settled back, trying to move out of reach of the pick handle.

"My wife's up there," Bert said. "And I've got three kids." He took off his shirt and mopped his body with it.

"There's nobody waitin' for me," Frank said. "Nobody anywhere."

"What d'you suppose they're doing out there?" Bert said. "I'd give a lot to know."

"Depends on how far it caved." Joe leaned on the pick handle, gasping for breath. "Probably they are shoring her up with timbers around the station or at the opening into the Big Stope."

He returned to work. He swung the pick, and a fragment broke loose; a second time and another fragment. Bert sat with his elbows on his knees, head hanging, breathing heavily. Frank's head was tipped back against the rock, his white face glistening like wet marble in the faint light that reached him.

It was going to be a long job, a hard job, and the air was growing worse. Being active, they were using it more rapidly, but it was their only chance. Nobody could get through to them in time. As Joe worked, the sweat streamed from his body, running into his eyes and dripping from his chin. Slowly and methodically he swung the pick, deadened to everything but the shock of the blows. He no longer noticed what progress he made; he had become an automaton. Bert started up to relieve him, but Joe shook his head. He was started now, and it was like an infection in his blood. He needed the pick. He clung to it as to a lifeline.

At last he did give way to Bert. He dropped on the rocks, his chest heaving, fighting for air. He tried to keep from remembering Mary, but she was always with him, always just beyond the blows of his pick. Probably she did not yet know what had happened to them, what this sudden thing was that had come into their lives.

She would be at work now, and as the mine was forty miles from town, it might be hours before she knew of the cave-in and even longer before she knew who was trapped below. It would be her tragedy as well as his. Joe cursed. Tomorrow they would have gone to the doctor. He was reliable, Frank had told him, a good man and not a quack.

Big Frank knew about Mary. He knew that with every drive of the pick it would be a closer thing for her. There were but four of them here, underground, but outside were Mary and Bert's wife and kids. It would be a close thing, any way it was looked at. He, Joe, could take it. He had never done anything else, but Mary was in a strange town with no friends, and unless they got to the doctor—

They were fools to have gone ahead when they knew they were taking a chance, but nobody expected anything like this. He had worked in mines most of his life and no trouble until now, and then the roof fell in. The whole damned mountain came down—or so it seemed. When he heard the crash, his first thought was for Mary. He was trapped here, but she was trapped out there, and she was alone.

"Better take a rest," Frank said. "We've got some time."

Joe sat down, and Bert looked across at him. "We could work in the dark," he suggested. "That flame eats up air."

Frank shook his head. "If you can't see, there's too much waste effort. You've got to see where the pick goes. Try it with the light a little longer."

Joe's eyes went to Frank. The big man lay tense and still, gripping the rock under his hand. He was in agony, Joe knew it and hated it. Frank was his friend.

"Will we make it, Frank?" He was thinking of Mary. What would she do? What could she do? How could she handle it alone? It wasn't as if they were married. "Think we'll make it?"

"We'll make it," Frank said. "We'll make it, all right."

"Listen!" Bert sat up eagerly. "I think I hear them! Wasn't that the sound of a pick?"

They listened, every muscle tense. There was no sound. Then, far away, some muck shifted.

Frank doused the light, and darkness closed in, silent and heavy like the dead, dead air. There was no vibrancy here, no sense of living.

They heard Joe get up, heard the heavy blows of the pick. He worked on and on, his muscles aching with weariness. Each blow and each recovery was an effort. Then Bert spoke, and they heard them change places. Standing once more, Bert could feel the difference. It was much harder to breathe; his lungs labored, and his heart struggled against the walls of his chest, as if to break through. Once he stopped and held a hand over it, frightened.

Long since they had thrown the first two picks aside, their points worn away. They might have to return to them, but now they were using another, sharper pick. They were standing in a hole now. Once a flake of rock fell, and Bert held himself, expecting a crash. It did not come.

Rody moved suddenly. Frank lit the light with a brush of his palm. Rody looked at him, then reached for the pick. "Let me have it," Rody said. "Hell, it's better than sittin' there suckin' my thumb. Give me the pick."

Bert passed it to him; then he staggered to the muck pile and fell, full length, gasping with great throat-rasping gasps.

Rody swung the pick, attacking the bottom of the hole savagely. Sweat ran into his eyes, and he swung, attacking the rock as if it were a flesh-and-blood enemy, feeling an exultant fury in his blows.

Once he stopped to take five, and looking over at Frank, he said, "How goes it, big boy?"

"Tolerable," Frank said. "You're a good man, Rody."

Rody swelled his chest, and the pick swung easily in his big hands. All of them were lying down now because the air was better close to the muck.

"Hear anything?" Bert asked. "How long will it take them to reach us, Frank?"

"Depends on how much it caved." They had been over this before, but it was hope they needed, any thread of it. Even talking of rescue seemed to bring it nearer. The numbness was all gone now, and his big body throbbed with pain. He fought it, refusing to surrender to it, trying to deny it. He held the pain as though it were some great beast he must overcome.

Suddenly Joe sat up. "Say! What became of the air line for the machine?"

They stared at each other, shocked at their forgetting. "Maybe it ain't busted," Bert said.

Stumbling in his eagerness, Joe fell across the muck, bumping Frank as he did so, jerking an involuntary grunt from him. Then Joe fell on his knees and began clawing rocks away from where the end of the pipe should be, the pipe that supplied compressed air for drilling. He found the pipe and cleared the vent, unscrewing the broken hose to the machine. Trembling, he turned the valve. Cool air shot into the room, and as they breathed deeply, it slowly died away to nothing.

"It will help," Joe said. "Even if it was a little, it will help."

"Damned little," Rody said, "but you're right, Joe. It'll help."

"How deep are you?" Frank asked. He started to shift his body and caught himself with a sharp gasp.

"Four feet—maybe five. She's tough going."

Joe lay with his face close to the ground. The air was close and hot, every breath a struggle. When he breathed, he seemed to get nothing. It left him gasping, struggling for air. The others were the same. Light and air were only a memory now, a memory of some lost paradise.

How long had they been here? Only Frank had a watch, but it was broken, so there was no way of calculating the time. It seemed hours since that crash. Somehow it had been so different from what he had expected. He had believed it would come with a thundering roar, but there was just a splintering sound, a slide of muck, a puff of wind that put their lights out, then a long slide, a trickling of sand, a falling stone. They had lacked even the consolation of drama.

Whatever was to come of it would not be far

off now. Whatever happened must be soon. There came no sound, no breath of moving air, only the thick, sticky air and the heat. They were all panting now, gasping for each breath.

Rody sat down suddenly, the pick slipping from his fingers.

"Let me," Joe said.

He swung the pick, then swung it again.

When he stopped, Bert said, "Did you hear something?"

They listened, but there was no sound.

"Maybe they ain't tryin'," Rody said. "Maybe they think we're dead.

"Can you imagine Tom Chambers spendin' his good money to get us out of here?" Rody said. "He don't care. He can get a lot of miners."

Joe thought of those huge, weighted timbers in the Big Stope. Nothing could have held that mass when it started to move. Probably the roof of the Big Stope had collapsed. Up on top there would be a small crowd of waiting people now. Men, women, and children. Still, there wouldn't be so many as in Nevada that time. After all, Bert was the only one down here with children.

But suppose others had been trapped? Why were they thinking they were the only ones?

The dull thud of the pick sounded again. That was Rody back at work. He could tell by the power. He listened, his mind lulled into a sort of hypnotic twilight where there was only darkness and the sound of the pick. He heard the blows, but he knew he was dying. It was no use. He couldn't fight it any longer.

Suddenly the dull blows ceased. Rody said, "Hey! Listen!" He struck again, and it was a dull sound, a hollow sound.

"Hell!" Rody said. "That ain't no ten feet!"

"Let's have some light over here," Rody said, "Frank—?"

He took the light from Frank's hand. The light was down to a feeble flicker now, no longer the proud blade of light that had initially stabbed at the darkness.

Rody peered, then passed the lamp back to Frank.

"There should be a staging down there." Frank's voice was clear. "They were running a stopper off it to put in the overhead rounds."

Rody swung, then swung again, and the pick went through. It caught him off balance, and he fell forward, then caught himself. Cool air was rushing into the drift end, and he took the pick and enlarged the hole.

Joe sat up. "God!" he said. "Thank God!"

"Take it easy, you guys, when you go down," Frank said. "That ladder may have been shaken loose by blasting or the cave-in. The top of the ladder is on the left-hand side of the raise. You'll have to drop down to the staging, though, and take the ladder from there. It'll be about an eight- or nine-foot drop."

He tossed a small stone into the hole, and they heard it strike against the boards down below. The flame of the light was bright now as more air came up through the opening. Frank stared at them, sucking air into his lungs.

"Come on, Rody," Joe said. "Lend a hand. We've got to get Frank to a doctor."

"No." Frank's voice was impersonal. "You can't get me down to that platform and then down the ladder. I'd bleed to death before you got me down the raise. You guys go ahead. When they get the drift opened up will be time enough for me. Or maybe when they can come back with a stretcher. I'll just sit here."

"But—" Joe protested.

"Beat it," Frank said.

Bert lowered himself through the opening and dropped. "Come on!" he called. "It's okay!"

Rody followed. Joe hesitated, mopping his face, then looked at Frank, but the big man was staring sullenly at the dark wall.

"Frank—" Joe stopped. "Well, gee—"

He hesitated, then dropped through the hole. From the platform he said, "Frank? I wish—"

His boots made small sounds descending the ladder.

The carbide light burned lower, and the flame

flickered as the fuel ran low. Big Frank's face twisted as he tried to move; then his mouth opened very wide, and he sobbed just once. It was all right now. There was no one to hear. Then he leaned back, staring toward the pile of muck, his big hands relaxed and empty.

"Nobody," he muttered. "There isn't anybody, and there never was."

# *One Night Stand*

Stephen Malone was tall, handsome, immaculate, and broke. He lay on his back, hands clasped behind his head, trying not to think about breakfast. Three weeks ago he had been playing lead roles in **Hearts of Oak, Hamlet,** and **Davy Crockett** on successive nights. Then the bookings ran out, the play closed, and the manager skipped town with the company funds, leaving them stranded.

For some time he had been aware of voices in the next room. A girl was speaking. "He can't! He wouldn't dare!"

The man's tone was touched with despair. "They say he's killed fourteen men. For the kind of money Mason would pay, the Kid wouldn't hesitate to make it fifteen."

There was a pause. "Even before my hand was crippled I couldn't match him. Now I wouldn't stand a chance."

"But Pa, if Hickok comes—?"

"If he can get here in time! He's not the kind

to forget what I did for him, but unless he shows up I'm finished. Else, I'd give a thousand dollars to see Bill Hickok walk through that door right now!"

Stephen Malone knew a cue when he heard one. He stepped into the hall and rapped on the door of their room.

"Who's there?" It was the man's voice.

"Bill Hickok."

The door opened and he was facing a thin old man with gray hair, and a pretty, dark-haired girl. "You aren't Bill Hickok!" The man was disgusted.

"No," Malone said, "but for a thousand dollars I will be."

"You're a gunfighter?" Else demanded.

"I'm an actor. It is my business to make people believe I am somebody else."

"This is different. This isn't playacting."

"He could kill you," Else said. "You wouldn't have a chance."

"Not if I'm a good enough actor. Not many men would try to draw a gun on Wild Bill Hickok."

"It's a fool idea," the man said.

"So there's an element of risk. I've played Hamlet, Macbeth, and Shylock. Why not Wild Bill?"

"Look, son, you've undoubtedly got nerve,

and probably you're a fine actor, but this man is a killer. Oh, I know he's a tinhorn, but you wouldn't have a chance!"

"Not if I'm a good enough actor."

"He's talking nonsense, and you both know it!" Else protested.

"To play Hickok, son, you've got to be able to shoot like Hickok."

"Only if I play it badly. You say the Kid is a tinhorn, I'll trust to your judgment and my skill."

Brady walked to the window. "It might work, you know. It just might."

"It would be suicide!" Else objected.

Brady turned from the window. "I am Emmett Brady. This is my daughter, Else. Frank Mason wants my range, and the Pioche Kid is a friend of his. He was brought here to kill me."

"The pleasure will be mine, sir." Malone bowed.

"Did anyone see you come into the hotel?" Brady asked.

"Only the man at the desk. It was two o'clock in the morning."

"Then it's all right. Jim Cooley is a friend of mine."

"Get him to spread the story that Hickok is in town, and once the story is around, I'll make my play."

"It's ridiculous!" Else declared. "Why should you risk your life for us?"

"Miss Brady, as much as I'd enjoy posing as Sir Galahad, I cannot. I'm no knight in armor, just a stranded actor. But for a thousand dollars? I haven't made that much in a whole season!"

"You've got sand, Malone. Else, fetch Jim Cooley."

"You've still time to back out," Else warned.

"I am grateful for your concern but this will be the first time I have been offered one thousand dollars for a single performance."

Returning to his room, Malone opened his trunk and chose a blond wig with hair to his shoulders. He selected a drooping mustache. ". . . And the buckskin jacket I wore as Davy Crockett. Then I'll remove the plume from this hat I wore in **Shenandoah**—"

THE PIOCHE KID stared complacently into his glass. Brady was an old man with a bad right hand. He was nothing to worry about.

Jim Cooley came through the swinging doors. "Give me a shot, Sam." He glanced around the room. "Wait until you boys hear who is in town! Wild Bill himself! Rode in last night, all the way from Kansas because he heard his old friend Emmett Brady needed help!"

The Pioche Kid went sick with shock. Somebody was asking what Brady had on Hickok. "Nursed him back to health after a gunshot wound. Hickok nearly killed a couple of horses getting here. He's sleeping it off over at the hotel now."

**Wild Bill Hickok!** The Kid hadn't bargained for this. He took up his whiskey and tossed it off, but the shudder that followed was not caused by the whiskey.

"Sam . . . ?" He pushed the empty glass toward him.

He could feel the excitement in the room. They were thinking they'd see the Pioche Kid shoot it out with Wild Bill Hickok, the most famous of them all.

Somebody mentioned the fourteen men the Kid was supposed to have killed, but the Kid himself knew there had been but four, and two of those had been drunken cowhands, and one of them a drunken farmer who had never held a pistol before.

Suddenly, desperately, he wanted out. How had he got into this, anyway? Hickok could **shoot**! He recalled the stories of Hickok's famous target matches with the renowned Major Talbot, at Cheyenne.

"He's the best," Cooley was saying. "Eyes in the back of his head, seems like. Remember the time he killed Phil Coe, then turned and killed a man running up behind him?"

Cooley smiled at the Kid. "Should be something, you and him. You've killed more than he has if you discount those he killed while a sharpshooter in the Army. But I did see him take four at once. Killed two, a third died later, and the fourth was never any good for anything after."

Cooley finished his drink. "I'm gettin' out of here. I've seen too many bystanders get gut-shot. Sorry I can't wish you luck, Kid, but Bill's a friend of mine."

Men moved to the tables, away from the bar. One hastily paid for his drink and left the bar. The Kid was alone, isolated, cut off.

What the hell was happening? This was **Hickok**! If he won they'd all slap him on the back and buy him drinks, but if he lost they'd just stare at the body as they walked by. He mopped his face. He was soaked with sweat, and he knew why. He was scared.

Mason was at the door. "He's comin', Kid. Be something to be known as the man who killed Wild Bill."

Malone paused in the door to wave at someone down the street, then he walked to the bar. All eyes were on him. "Rye, if you please."

Sam put a bottle and a glass before him. The Kid licked dry lips with a fumbling tongue. Desperately he wanted to wipe his palm dry on his pants, but he was afraid Hickok would think he was going for a gun. Now was the time. He should open the ball. Sweat dripped from his face to the bar. He opened his mouth to speak, but Malone spoke first.

"Bartender, I'd like to find two men for a little job. I'll pay a dollar each. It's a digging job."

"You said . . . a **digging** job?"

"That's right. I want two men to dig a hole about"—he turned deliberately and looked right at the Kid—"six feet long, six feet deep, and three wide."

"Whereabouts do you want it dug?"

"On Boot Hill."

"A grave?"

"Exactly."

Sam motioned to two men at a nearby table. "Tom? Joe? Mr. Hickok wants a couple of men." He hesitated ever so slightly. "To dig a grave."

"And to make a slab for a marker," Malone said.

Sam was loving every moment of it. "You want a name on it?"

"Don't bother with the name. Within the week they will have forgotten who he was, anyway. Just carve on it HE SHOULD HAVE LEFT BEFORE THE SUN WENT DOWN."

He finished his drink. "Good afternoon, gentlemen."

He strolled to the door, paused briefly with his hand on the door, then stepped out on the boardwalk and turned toward the hotel.

Within the saloon a chair creaked as someone shifted weight. The Kid lifted a fumbling hand to brush away the sweat from his face and the hand trembled. He tossed off his drink, spilling a little on his chin. Never had death seemed so close.

What kind of a damned fool was he, anyway? What did he have to do with Brady? Let Mason do his own killing. Suddenly all he wanted was to be away, away from those watching eyes, staring at him, so willing to see him die.

What did he owe Mason? All he had to do was cross the street, mount his horse, and ride. Behind his back they would sneer, but what did that matter? He owed these people nothing, and there were a thousand towns like this. Moreover, he'd be alive . . . **alive!**

He wanted to feel the sunshine on his face, the wind in his hair, to drink a long, cold drink of water. He wanted to live!

Abruptly, he walked to the door. He had seen men die, seen them lie tormented in the bloody dust. He did not want to feel the tearing agony of a bullet in his guts.

There was Hickok, his broad back to him, only a few paces away. A quick shot . . . he could always say Hickok had turned.

Sweat dripped into his eyes, dimly he remembered **eyes in the back of his head**. On that other occasion Hickok had turned suddenly and fired . . . dead center.

The Kid let go of his gun as if it were red hot.

Yet he could still make it. He was a pretty good shot . . . well, a fair shot. He could—

Two men emerged from the livery stable, each carrying a shovel. Tom and Joe, to dig a grave . . . **his** grave?

He crossed the street, almost running, and jerked loose the tie-rope. He missed the stirrup with his first try, made it on the second, and was almost crying when he hit the saddle. He wheeled the horse from the hitch rail and left town at a dead run.

His saddle was hot from the sun, but he could **feel** it. The wind was in his face . . . he was free! He was riding, he was living, and there were a lot of other towns, a lot of country.

Brady turned from the window. "He's gone, Else. Malone did it."

"Mason's leaving, too," she added.

The door opened behind them and Stephen Malone stepped in, removing his hat, then the wig and the mustache. "That's one part I never want to play again!"

"Here's your money, son. You earned it."

"Thanks."

"What would you have done, Malone," Cooley asked, "if the Kid had called your hand?"

"Done? Why this—!"

His draw was surprisingly fast, and he fired at Cooley, point-blank. Cooley sprang back, shocked. His hands clutched his abdomen.

His hands came away and he stared at them. No blood. No—!

Malone was smiling.

"Blanks!" Cooley exclaimed. "You faced the Kid with nothing in your gun but blanks!"

"Well, why not? It was all part of the act."

# *Marshal of Canyon Gap*

He rode down from the hills in the morning, a tall, rawboned young man with the quiet confidence of one given to hard work and responsibility. He had a shock of rusty brown hair, gray eyes, and a way of moving in which there was no lost motion.

Sitting in the sunlight on the main street of Canyon Gap, I was sorry to see him come. He was a man who looked like he'd been long on the road. He also looked like trouble aplenty, and I was a man who didn't like trouble at all.

He rode into town on a rawboned buckskin and dismounted at Bacon's hitch rail. All the time he was tying that horse, he was looking up and down the street while seeming to be almighty busy with that knot.

By the time he had his horse tied he knew the location of every man on the street, and every window. I'd not seen Jim Melette before, but he was no tenderfoot, no pilgrim. A man isn't marshal of a cow town for ten years without sizing up the men who come to town, and learning to estimate their capacity for trouble.

He stepped up on the boardwalk, a big man in fringed shotgun chaps and a blue wool shirt, wearing a black flat-brimmed hat. For a moment, his eyes caught me with full attention, and then he turned his back on me and went into the store.

That store didn't worry me so much. What I was thinking about was the saloon. Brad Nolan was over there with Pete Jackson and Led Murry.

Brad was a headstrong, troublemaking man who had a way of bulling about that showed he figured he made mighty big tracks. Trouble was, he'd never done anything to entitle him to that attitude, and he was aching for a chance. Brad was feeling his importance, and for four or five years I'd been watching him put on muscle and arrogance until I knew trouble couldn't be avoided.

Lately he had been swaggering around and I knew he was wondering how far he'd get trying me on, but he'd seen me shoot holes through too many aces and no man wants to buck that kind of shooting.

Pete Jackson was worse because he was a talker. He never knew when to keep his mouth shut, and never considered the results of his loose talk, and such a man can cause more trouble than three Memphis lawyers.

Led Murry was an unknown quantity. He was new in town, and I hadn't made up my mind what to think about Led . . . there was something that happened a short while back that had me wondering if he wasn't the worst of the lot, but I wasn't sure. I just knew he never said much and he had crazy eyes, and that worried me.

Brad Nolan seemed the one inclined to start trouble, but he had seen me toss a playing card in the air, draw, and put a hole in it dead center before it hit the ground. It kept him and a lot of others from starting anything.

It was time I had some tobacco. Not that I didn't have some, but Melette was buying supplies and I figured it might be a good thing to know more about him. Also, he was a fine figure of a man and that Ginnie Bacon was working for her pa this morning.

Jim Melette was looking at the trousers when I came in, and Ginnie, she was looking at him.

Lizzie Porter was there and she was talking to Ginnie like she'd been put up to it. "Who's taking you to the pie supper, Ginnie?"

"I don't know," Ginnie said, looking at Melette. "I'm waiting to be asked."

"What about Brad? Isn't he taking you?"

"Brad? Oh . . . Brad. I don't know yet."

"All I can say is"—Lizzie never said all she could say, but she tried hard enough—"I hope that Ross woman doesn't come." Melette didn't react much but I've watched a good deal of human nature in my time and I could tell he was suddenly on point.

"Oh, she won't come! Who would bring her? Not after the way she was treated last time." Ginnie was watching Melette, who was studying some new boots now. "She's pretty enough if you like that snooty type, too good to talk to anyone . . . and she must be thirty, if she's a day."

Jim Melette went to the counter and took a list from his pocket, and Ginnie gave him one of her dazzling smiles. "What's about this pie supper?" he asked.

"It's tomorrow night." Ginnie was batting her eyes like an owl in a hailstorm and Ginnie was a mighty pretty girl. "We'll all be there. They auction pies, you know, and if you buy a girl's pie you get to sit with her. There's dancing, too. You do dance, don't you?"

"Sometimes . . . I can hold a girl while she dances. Who's this Ross woman you mentioned?"

"Her?" Ginnie wrinkled her nose. "She's nobody. She moved into the house on Cottonwood Hill a few months ago, and the only visitors she has around seem to come of a night, at least there's lots of horse tracks in and out of her gate. Nobody wants her around, but she came to that last social, bold as brass."

That Ginnie . . . she could make a sieve out of

the truth without half trying. Truth was, nobody did want Hanna Ross, nobody but the men. The women looked down their noses at her because she was a stranger who lived alone, but so far as I'd seen none of them had tried to be neighborly.

Thirty years old, Ginnie said, but Hanna Ross couldn't be a day over twenty-four, and was one of the finest-looking girls I'd seen in a coon's age, and believe me, I've seen aplenty.

Ginnie saw me coming to the counter for my tobacco. It was high time because I'd about worn out that saddle, what with turning it and studying it and picking at the stitching. "Oh! Marshal, have you met Mr. Melette?"

He turned around giving me a straight, hard look. "I haven't met the marshal," Melette said, "but I've heard of him."

"Name's McLane," I said. "Folks call me Mac."

"Seems to me I remember you," Melette said. "You've walked the boards of this town quite some time, haven't you, Marshal?"

Inside I stiffened up . . . that there phrase "walked the boards" might have been an accident, but from the smile around his eyes it seemed to me there was something behind it.

"Ten years," I admitted, "and we've had less trouble than most towns. The way I figure is to anticipate trouble and take steps."

"Good idea." Jim Melette gathered his supplies. "What do you do when trouble comes that you can't avoid?"

When he said that I had a chill . . . for ten years that had been my nightmare, that trouble might come that I couldn't sidetrack or outsmart, and I wasn't as young as I used to be.

"Don't ever worry about that," Lizzie said. "Ben McLane had killed fourteen outlaws before he came to Canyon Gap. Many a time I've seen him toss a card in the air and shoot the spots out."

"That's shooting," Melette agreed. "I've only seen one man who could do that. Of course, I was just a youngster then, must have been thirteen, fourteen years ago."

He picked up the rest of his supplies and walked out and I stood there looking at my hole card, and it had suddenly become a mighty small deuce. After all these years, while things shaped up mighty fine, I'd come to believe I was set for life in Canyon Gap. The town liked me and I liked the town, and one way or another, I'd kept the peace. Now it looked like the whole show was going to bust up right in my face.

Walking to the door, I watched Melette stow his stuff in his saddlebags and a sack he had tied behind his saddle. Then he dusted off his hands and started across the street.

A man can only keep the peace by working at it, so I stepped out on the walk. "Melette!" He turned slowly when I spoke his name. "I wouldn't go over there if I were you. There's trouble over there."

Figured first off he'd tell me to mind my own affairs, but instead he walked back to me, and then I was really scared because I thought he'd have something personal to say, and one thing I did not want to do was talk about myself. Not to him.

"All right, McLane, I won't," he said. "Will you tell me where Hanna Ross lives?"

He had called her Hanna, although her first name had not been mentioned inside, so my hunch was right. Trouble **was** coming to Canyon Gap in the person of Jim Melette. He knew more than he was letting on. I pointed the way up the street to her house.

"For a stranger," I said, "you seem to know a lot about folks. Why do you want to see Hanna Ross?"

He was stepping into the saddle. "Why, Mac, I think I used to know her, so I sort've figured I'd stick around for that pie supper and if Hanna Ross will go with me, I'll take her. You keep the peace, Mac!" And he trotted his horse off toward Cottonwood Hill.

Standing there in the street I knew I was scared. For ten years nobody had come to Canyon Gap who knew me, and I'd begun to believe no one ever would. The days of gun battles were about over, tapering off, anyway, and I'd begun to feel that I had it made, as we used to say in the goldfields.

It seemed to me that I was going to get it from two directions unless I was very careful. Ginnie Bacon had been flirtin' around Brad Nolan for the past several months trying to see what kind of trouble she could help him get into. He was spoiling for a fight, and from the way she'd acted toward Jim Melette there in the store, it seemed like she might try to get the two of them to go at it.

The other thing that had me worried was that I knew who'd been leaving all those tracks around Hanna Ross's house . . . it was that crazy-eyed Led Murry. I didn't know what that meant, but I was afraid. Nolan and Murry were some trouble separately, but together they were downright dangerous.

Something like this had happened a time or two before, but I'd been able to break up the dangerous combinations before they realized their strength. Divide and rule, that was my motto, and I made it a point to know about people, and whenever I saw fellers getting together who might cause trouble, I got a girl betwixt 'em, or jealousy about something else, and usually I'd managed to split 'em up.

There's more ways to keep the peace than

with a gun, and I'd proved it in Canyon Gap, where there hadn't been a gunfight in ten years . . . and in the month before I took over there had been three. Nor in all that time had I drawn a gun on a man.

Cottonwood Hill was right up there in plain sight at the edge of town, and from town everybody could see who came or went from the place, so Lizzie Porter saw Jim Melette ride through the gate up there, and she went right back in to tell Ginnie.

No need for me to read the playscript to know Ginnie would get mad . . . she had practically offered herself to Melette for the pie supper, and he had walked away and gone to see Hanna Ross.

Things were bunching up on me.

Ten years it had been, and I'm a man likes a quiet life. When I rode into this town on the stage and saw the snow-capped mountains 'round about, the shaded streets and pine forests on the hills around, and that stream running right through town, I decided this was the place to spend my declining years. The fact that they mistook me for a gunfighter and offered me the marshal's job had provided me with a living.

Now, between Hanna Ross, Ginnie Bacon, the Nolan outfit, and Jim Melette, I could see the whole thing blowing up in my face. It was too late for me to hunt up a new town, and I liked this one. And I never had been able to put by much in the way of money.

Worst of all, suppose Jim Melette told around town what he knew about me?

THEY HAD ten coal-oil lamps with bright reflectors behind them to light the schoolhouse for the pie supper and dance, and they had two fiddlers and a guitar player out there on the floor.

Pete Jackson, Brad Nolan, and Ginnie were there, thick as thieves, the men passing a flask back and forth, Ginnie talking fast and flashing her eyes. Led Murry was there, too, a-settin' against the wall, missing nothing but a-watching everything.

Outside by the hitch rail I waited to fend off trouble, for I could see the storm making up, and I wasn't thinking only of me. I was thinking of the town. There I was when a livery rig came into the yard and Jim Melette got down and helped Hanna Ross to the ground.

"Jim!" My thumb was tucked in my belt, gunfighter fashion. "I want to talk to you!"

Excusing himself, Jim came over to me. "Don't go in there," I said, "as a favor to me. Brad Nolan's in there and he's spoiling for trouble. So's Murry."

"Sorry, Mac," Melette said. "I've nothing against you, but Hanna and I must go in there.

We both figure to live around here the rest of our lives, and we might as well bring matters to a head right now."

"That's one way," I said, "but the wrong way. You two just dig in and hold on and folks will come around. You go in there and you'll make trouble."

"We're going. You don't understand the situation," he said.

"Now, look here!" It was time to be tough. "I—!"

"Mac"—Jim lowered his voice—"don't you pull that act on me. When I was no more than thirteen I saw you on the stage in **Ticket-of-Leave-Man,** and a year later I saw you in **Lady of Lyons**."

"So I've been an actor. That isn't all I've been. Now look!"

From my pocket I took an ace of hearts. "Boy, I want to show you something."

It was time to go into my act, and it was a good act, which had kept more than one tough man from making me trouble.

He stopped me. "Let me show **you** something," Melette said. He took the card from my hand and tossed it into the air. He didn't draw and fire as I had so often, but when the card fell he reached over and grasped my arm. I started to struggle, then let up, knowing it was no use. He knew my secret and he was going to have his say about it. Jim Melette slid two fingers into the cuff of my coat, plucking the hidden card out of its hidden clip.

"After I saw you demonstrate your shooting act in front of the theater one day I figured you for the greatest shot ever, but then a stable boy who used to work on the stage showed me how it was done. You just go out in the hills and shoot holes in fifty cards at three-foot range or whatever's necessary and then just carry them around in a holdout, and when you pick up the tossed up card, palm it and hand over one that's already been shot."

"Nobody around here has ever guessed," I said bitterly. This was what I'd been afraid of for years, and now just when I needed some luck, things were catching up with me.

"What are you going to do, Melette?"

"I'm going to go in there and have it out with Led Murry. If any of the others want a piece of it, that's their lookout."

Have it out with Led Murry. . . . I'd been thinking it was Brad Nolan who was going to be the bigger problem. "You said that I didn't understand—exactly what is it that I don't understand?" I asked.

"Jim and I are married." Hanna Ross had walked over to us. "We've been married for three years."

"We were living near Denver, but I had to go

to Mexico on business. I had an accident in a little mountain village. I was laid up a long time."

"I didn't know what had happened. I thought he was dead." She whispered it, looking off into the night.

They told me their story. In hushed tones, Melette's voice often rough with anger, they recounted how Led Murry had seen Hanna on the street in Denver and begun following her around. He'd asked her if he could come courting, but when she had told him that she was married he refused to leave her alone. He lurked around their house and spied on her at night. When she complained to the constables he would disappear for a while, but sooner or later he was back. All this time Jim Melette was helplessly trying to recuperate south of the border. He tried to send Hanna letters, but was not surprised that none of them were ever received.

Then one night Led Murry broke into Jim and Hanna's house and tried to force himself on her. She fled, and thinking that her husband was dead, she changed back to her maiden name. Finally she found her way to my town, and became the mysterious woman that we all knew as Hanna Ross.

The story had all the elements of a great play, and when Led Murry appeared in our town it was obvious that that play had become a tragedy.

Like a character from a Shakespeare play, he had become a man obsessed.

"After a long time I made it back from Sonora," Jim said, "and the postmaster in Denver helped me find where Hanna had gone. Now that I'm here, I've got to put a stop to this.

"Led's a bad man, McLane. He's an outlaw, but the law never caught up with him but once and he served his time for that. He's a mighty fast man with a gun. Tonight I'm going to see how fast. I'm going to tell him to leave us alone or start shooting."

"No." I spoke sharply. "I'm marshal here, actor or not. Maybe I'm an old fraud, but if you start trouble you'll go to jail. You leave Led Murry to me. He has assaulted a good woman. The next jury he stands in front of will send him away for life."

Melette looked at me like he figured I'd lost my good sense, and I knew there was no sense, good or otherwise, in what I had in mind. When a man has taken a marshal's salary for ten years, he can't hide the first time real trouble shows. My whole life was based on being something I wasn't, but fool that I was, I hoped I wasn't a coward, too.

"You're crazy, McLane. You can't arrest him without shooting."

"Marshal?" Hanna Ross spoke up. "He

knows . . . Led Murry knows that you . . . well, that you did that fake shooting in the Buffalo Bill show. I threatened to go to you when he showed up, and he said you were a fraud!"

"He'll kill you," Jim Melette said. "You leave him to me."

BEFORE HE COULD say more I turned my back on him and walked to the hitch rail where I could be alone.

This was my town. Sure, I'd become marshal because I could play the part, but in the ten years that passed I'd bought my own home, had shade for my porch, and flowers around the garden fence. When I walked along the street folks spoke to me with respect, and passed the time of day.

When first I came to this town I was an old actor, a man past his prime and with nowhere to go but down. For most of my life I'd been dressing in cold, draughty dressing rooms, playing worn-out roles in fourth-rate casts, and all that lay ahead of me was poorer and poorer roles and less and less work. But then I'd come to Canyon Gap.

There had been a time when I'd played with a few of the best, and in the olio between acts I'd do card tricks, juggle eight balls or eight dinner plates, or sing a fair song. The one thing I could still do best was juggle . . . there's a place it pays a man to keep up, keeps his hands fast and his eyes sure. Even a town marshal may someday have to give up and go back to doing what he knows.

When I first came to town, the boy that took my bags to my room saw a Colt pistol in my bag . . . it had fourteen notches on it. That started the story that I was a gunfighter, but it was nothing more than a prop I'd carried when I was with the Bill show.

Whatever I was in the past, I was town marshal now, and I'd been playing the role too long to relinquish it. There was an old adage in the theater that the show must go on. Undoubtedly, that adage was thought up by some leading man who didn't want the understudy to get a chance at his part, but this show had to go on, and I wasn't going to fail the people who had trusted me.

There's something about playing the same role over and over again. After a while a man can come to believe it himself, and over most of those ten years I'd been a good marshal because I'd come to believe I was the part I was playing. Only tonight I could fool myself no longer. I was going up against a man whom I couldn't hope to bluff.

So up the steps I went and into the schoolhouse, and I crossed the room to where Led

Murry was sitting with his back to the wall. And as I was crossing the room I saw one of my problems eliminated.

Jim Melette saw me coming and knew what I was going to do, and he started across the room to stop me. He had taken only two steps when Brad Nolan stepped out in front of him. "Look here, Melette, I—"

Jim Melette hit him. He hit Brad in the belly and then he hit him on the chin, and Brad Nolan went down and he didn't make any show of getting up. What Brad had been looking for all these years he'd gotten in one lump, and it knocked all the muscle out of him.

"Led." I spoke clearly. "Get on your feet. You're under arrest."

He looked at me and he started to smile, but it was a mean smile. Nothing pleasant about it.

"Am I, now? Why, Marshal? Why me?"

"You've assaulted Hanna Ross, a citizen of this town. I'll have nothing of the sort in Canyon Gap. Get on your feet and drop your gun belts!"

He just sat there, smiling. "Marshal," he said, "you're a two-bit fraud. I'm going to show this town just what a fraud you are."

It was dead still in that room. Sweat trickled down my cheeks and I felt sick and empty inside. Why in the world hadn't I stayed outside and let well enough alone?

"After I get through with you, I'll have a talk

with good old Jim and Miss Hanna. But first I'm going to kill you, Marshal."

They were watching, all of them, and they were the people of Canyon Gap, the people of my town. To them I was tall, straight, and indomitable, and though I might be an old man, I was their marshal whom they believed to have killed fourteen men. To myself I was a man who loved peace, who had never drawn a gun in anger, and who had rarely fired one, and who was suddenly called upon to face the results of the role he had created.

My audience, and an audience it was, awaited my reply. Only an instant had passed, and I knew how these things were done, for often I had played roles like this upon the stage. Only to this one there could be but one end. Nonetheless, I owed it to myself, and to the people who had kept me marshal of their town, to play the role out.

"Led Murry," I said coolly, "stand up!"

He stared at me as if he were about to laugh, but there was a sort of astonished respect on his face, too. He stood, and then he went for his gun.

Fear grabbed at my stomach and I heard the smashing sound of a shot. Led Murry took an astonished step forward and fell to the floor, then rolled over on his back. The bullet had gone through his throat and broken his spine.

Then somebody was slapping me on the back

and I looked down and there was a gun in my hand. A gun with fourteen notches filed in the butt, a gun that had fired more blank rounds than live.

There was still the scene. Coolly, I dropped the pistol into my holster and turned my back on Led Murry. Inside I was quivering like jelly. True, we had been only ten feet apart, and it was also true that all my life I'd worked at juggling, sleight of hand . . . I'd had fifty years of practice.

"Marshal!" It was Lizzie Porter. "You were wonderful!"

"He was a danger to the community," I choked. "I deeply regret the necessity."

Inside I was shaking, more scared than I'd ever been in my life, but I was carrying it off . . . I hoped.

It was Jim Melette who forgot himself. "McLane," he protested, "you were on the stage! You're no—!"

"Ah, the stage!" Interrupting him as quickly as I could, I handed him an old quote from the show, when I had appeared onstage as a companion of Buffalo Bill. " 'I was shotgun messenger for the **Butterfield** stage, scouted for George Armstrong Custer, and rode for the Pony Express!' " I squeezed his arm hard and said, "Forget it, Jim. Please. Forget it."

And then I walked out into the night and started for home, my heels hitting the ground too hard, my head bobbing like I was drunk. Right then it hit me, and I was scared, scared like I'd never been in my life. I had no memory of drawing, no memory of firing . . . what if I hadn't been lucky?

No question about it, I was getting too old for this. It was time to retire.

Of course, I could always run for mayor.

# *A Husband for Janey*

He had been walking since an hour before sunup, but now the air had grown warm and he could hear the sound of running water. Sunlight fell through the leaves and dappled the trail with light and shadow, and when he rounded the bend of the path he saw the girl dipping a bucket into a mountain stream.

He was a tall boy, just turned eighteen, and four months from his home on a woods farm in East Texas. He looked at the girl and he swallowed, his Adam's apple bobbing in a throat that seemed unusually long, rising as it did from the wide, too-loose collar of his homespun shirt.

He swallowed again and cleared his throat. The girl looked up, suddenly wide-eyed, and then she straightened, her lips drawing together and one quick hand brushing a strand of dark hair back from her flushed cheek. "Howdy, ma'am," he said, his accent soft with East Texas music. "Sure didn't aim to scare you none."

"It . . . it's all right." Her alarm was fading with her curiosity. "Are you goin' to the gold-fields?"

A measure of pride and manly assurance came into his voice. "I reckon. I aim to git me money to go back home to Texas an' buy a farm."

They faced each other across the stream. The boy swallowed, nervous with the silence. "You . . . your pa washin' gold about here?"

"Yes . . . Well, he was . . . He's gone to the settlement. He's been gone three weeks."

The boy nodded gravely. It had taken him two days to walk up from Angel's Camp, and with that awareness that comes to those who walk the trails he knew her father was not coming back. It was a bad time to be traveling with gold in one's poke.

"You doin' all right?" he asked. "You an' your ma?"

Janey hesitated, rubbing her palms on her apron. She was shy but she didn't want him to go off on his way, for it was lonely with no one about of her own age, and without even neighbors except for Richter. "Ma—she's just back here. Would you like some coffee? We've some fresh."

He crossed the stream on the rounded stones and took her wooden bucket. "Lemme fetch it for you," he said. "It's a big bucket for such a little girl."

She flashed her eyes at him. "I ain't . . . I mean, I'm not so young! I'm sixteen!"

He grinned at her. "You're nigh to it."

MRS. PETERS LOOKED UP from the fire she was tending. She saw the two coming down the trail and her heart seemed to catch with quick realization. And yes, with relief. She carefully noted the boy's serious expression, and when he put the bucket down on the flat rock she saw how his eyes went to Janey's and her quick, flirting glance. This was a strong young man with sloping shoulders and an open, honest look about him.

"Howdy, ma'am." He felt more sure of himself with the older woman. She reminded him of his aunt. "My name is Meadows. Folks back home call me Tandy."

"Glad to know you, Tandy. I'm Mrs. Peters. Jane, get this young man a cup. The coffee's hot." She looked at the boy, liking his clean, boyish face and handsome smile. "Goin' far?"

"To the head of the crick." He slid the pack from his back and placed it on the ground, and beside it his Roper four-shot revolving shotgun. "I figure to stake me a claim."

It was cool and pleasant under the great, arching limbs of the trees. There had been some work done on the bench where the stream curved wide, and the cabin was back under the trees out of the heat. A line had been strung for the washing from its corner to the nearest tree.

He stole a glance at the girl and caught her looking at him. She smiled quickly and looked away, flushing a little. His own face colored and he swallowed.

Em Peters filled the cup Jane brought, and he accepted it gratefully. He had started without breakfast, not liking to take the time to fix a decent meal. Em Peters looked at him thoughtfully. He was a well-mannered boy, and she suddenly knew, desperately, that he must not leave. She must keep him here, for Janey.

It wasn't like back home, where there were lots of boys, nice boys from families one had grown up with, and who would work at honest, respectable work. Out here one never knew what sort of people would be coming around. Dave had been small protection, but where there was a man around—well, it was a good feeling.

Dave should never have come west, of course. It was Roy Bacon who talked him into it, and they had sold their place and started out. The wagon and team used up most of the money, and by the time they arrived in California there was almost nothing left. Dave had been a quiet, serious man who needed a steady job or business in a small town. She knew that now, although she had not tried to dissuade him when he talked of going to California. It was the one big thing in

Dave's life, and fit for it or not, she knew he had loved it. Crossing the plains, he had been happy. Only at the end, when they arrived, had he been frightened.

Em Peters knew with deep sadness that Dave was not coming back. When he had been two days overdue she knew it, for Dave always had been precise about things. Nor was he a man to drink or gamble. The first rush of the gold hunting was over and some of the tougher men who had been unable to find a good claim, or had lacked the energy or persistence to work one, had taken to the trails. Murders were the order of the day even along the creeks, and in the towns it was worse, much worse.

It was not herself for whom she was worried. She would manage—she always had. It was Janey.

Em Peters had seen the speculative eyes of more than one man who came along the trail or paused for a few minutes. Worst of all, there was Richter. She had been afraid of him from the first. Had warned Dave he was not to be trusted, but Dave had waved off her objections because Richter had showed him how to build a rocker, actually helping with the work.

Only two days before, he had come to her. "Ma'am," he said, "I hate to say this here, but I figure somethin' happened to Dave."

"I'm afraid so."

"You two," Richter said, "it ain't safe for you. I figured maybe it'd be better if I moved over here."

Her throat had grown tight, for she could see his eyes following Janey. "We'll be all right," she had said.

He cocked his head. "Maybe," he said, "but that there girl o' yourn, she sets a man's blood to boilin'. If I was you, I'd find her a husband mighty quick."

"Janey has plenty of time." She forced herself to be calm, and not to answer him as sharply as she felt like doing. "And we'll be all right." Her voice stiffened a little. "Men in the goldfields won't allow good women to be molested. I've heard of men being hung just for speaking the wrong thing to a woman."

Richter had heard of it, too, and he did not like the thought. It irritated him that she should mention it. "Oh, sure!" he said. "But you never can tell. Fact is," he said, rubbing his unshaven jaw, "I might marry her myself."

Em Peters had her limits, and this was it. "Why, I'd never hear of such a thing!" she exclaimed. "I would rather see Janey dead than married to you, Carl Richter! You're no man for a girl like Janey!"

Angry blood darkened his cheeks and his eyes grew ugly. "You ain't so high-falutin'," he said angrily. "Gettin' 'long by yourselves ain't goin' to be so easy. You try it, an' see!" He had stomped off angrily, but Em had said nothing to Janey, beyond the suggestion that she avoid him. Janey needed no urging. Richter was nearing fifty, a big, dirty man whose cabin was a boar's nest of unwashed clothing and stale smells.

TANDY LIKED his coffee. He nursed the cup in his hands, taking his time and not wanting to leave. Janey was suddenly very busy, stirring the fire, looking into pots, taking clothes from the line.

Em Peters looked down at Tandy, and then her eyes went down the creek to where it emerged from the shadowing trees into sunshine. The thought that Dave was not coming back waited in the back of her consciousness, waited for the night when she could lie alone and hold her grief tightly to her. There was not time for grief now, and she could not let Janey know that hope was gone. Janey was too young for that. She had no experience with grief, none of the hard-found knowledge that all things change, that nothing remains the same. In time Janey would know, but there was time.

"You . . . you'll be goin' on?" she asked gently. "You have something in mind?"

"Not really, ma'am. Just aimed to find me a bench somewhere an' start workin'. I'm a good worker," he said, looking up at her. "My aunt

Esther always did say I was the strongest boy she knew. For my age, that is," he added modestly.

Em Peters knew no way of approaching it with care. She looked now for the words, hoping they could come, knowing that somehow they had to come. This was a good boy, a boy from a good, simple, hardworking family. He—whatever it was, she forgot, seeing Richter coming up the path.

Richter did not notice Tandy Meadows. He was full of his own thoughts. It was stupid, he decided, to let the woman put him off. Why, there wasn't another man in twenty miles!

"You there!" he said to Em. "Changed your mind about me marryin' Janey? If you ain't, you better! I done made up my mind! No use this here claim standin' idle! No use that there girl runnin' around loose, botherin' men, worryin' me."

They all froze, looking at the big man in astonishment. "Carl Richter." Em Peters's voice was level. "You get out of here! You may go away and don't come back, or the first time the men from the mines come by, I'll set them on you!"

Richter laughed. "Why, that's . . ." His voice broke and trailed off, for the tall young boy was standing there, looking at him calmly. "Who the hell are you?" Richter demanded.

"You-all," Tandy Meadows said, in his soft

East Texas voice, "heard what the lady said. She said you should go."

Richter's eyes went cruel. He had been startled, but then he saw this was only a boy, and a country boy at that. "Shut your trap, pup!" he said. "Beat it. I'll give you what's coming to you 'less you git yourself down the road."

"Ain't figurin' on it," Tandy said quietly. He moved over to stand between Carl Richter and the women.

Richter hesitated. This youngster was bigger than he had thought. He had big hands, and in the lean, youthful body there was a studied negligence that warned him whatever else this boy might be, he had probably done enough fighting around school and the farms to take care of himself. All the boyish shyness was gone now, and Tandy was sure of himself.

"You got no business here," Richter growled. "You git out while the gittin's good. I'm coming back an' you better be out of here. If you ain't," he added, "there'll be a shootin'."

He turned abruptly and walked away, and Tandy looked after him, faint worry in his eyes. But Janey rushed to him at once. "Thank you!" she exclaimed. "I—I can't imagine what got into him." She blushed with embarrassment. "He's talking like a crazy man."

"I reckon." He swallowed, his eyes going to Em. And Em Peters was frightened. What had she drawn this poor boy into? Richter had killed men. She knew that. A man down in town had told Dave about it. Richter had killed several men with a gun. One man he had beaten to death with a neck yoke. He was a bitter, revengeful man.

Tandy picked up his cup. "Any more o' that there coffee, ma'am?" he asked gently.

She gave it to him, then held the pot. "Tandy," she said, "you'd better go. We'll manage all right. I don't want any trouble."

He was still a boy, but there was steel in him. The eyes into which she looked now were cool, but they were eyes strangely mature. "I reckon I'll stay, ma'am. Down where I come from, we don't back water for no man.

"I figure," he added, "I'd better stick aroun' until your own man fetches back with the supplies. Meanwhilst, I can work some on that rocker. Never worked one o' them an' the practice won't do me harm."

He had been working for two hours when Janey came down the path with a pot of coffee and two big sandwiches. She had changed her dress and the one she wore now was freshly smoothed and clean. She looked at him, longing to be pretty in his eyes, and finding that the quick wonder in them was even more than she had hoped.

"Are you getting any color?" she asked. "Pa

said this was one of the best claims along the creek."

"Seems good," he agreed, accepting the coffee and sandwiches. Between bites he looked at her. "You sparkin' anybody?" he asked.

Her chin lifted. "Who wants to know?" He said nothing to that and she glanced at him. "Don't you suppose I know any boys? Don't you suppose they would like me?"

There was not another boy within miles, and Janey Peters had not seen a boy even close to her own age for four months, but he was not going to know **that**.

"Sure. I figure so."

"Well, then. Don't you be sayin' I don't know any boys! I do so!"

He looked at her in complete astonishment. "Why . . ." He was utterly flabbergasted. "I didn't say that—!"

"You did so, Tandy Meadows! You did so!" Tears welled into her eyes and panic tightened in his throat.

"No, ma'am!" he protested desperately. "I never done it! I mean—well, I sure didn't aim to!"

"You needn't think you can come along here an' . . . an' . . . don't call me **ma'am**!"

He got up. "Guess I better get back to work," he said lamely. Women! He thought, who could ever figure them out? No matter what a man said, he was always in the wrong. There was no logic in them.

Janey pouted, occasionally stealing a careful look at Tandy to be sure he was feeling sufficiently miserable. Soon she began to feel miserable herself. She turned a little bit toward him, but he avoided her eyes. She moved her feet on the gravel, and he stole a look at her shoes and ankles. Suddenly aware of her scuffed shoes, she hastily drew her feet under her skirt, flushing with embarrassment.

Tandy had not noticed. He dipped up water with a wooden bucket and let some run into the rocker. Then, holding the bucket with one hand, he began to rock vigorously, letting water trickle over the edge of the bucket. The water and the rocking washed the smaller sizes of gravel through the screen into the apron. The abrupt stops at the end of each stroke jarred the gravel against the sides of the rocker.

Putting down the bucket, he mashed up some chunks of clay and mixed them in water, agitating the rocker as he did so. When no more particles came through the screen, he searched the heavier gravel for any nuggets of a size too large to pass through the mesh. Then he dumped the tailings and filled the rocker once more. Sweat darkened his shirt and trickled down his cheeks. Acutely conscious of Janey's presence, he said nothing. He was sure he had grossly offended her, but suddenly she was bending over the apron. "Oh, you've got some color!" she exclaimed. "A lot!"

He swept the particles together and then blew out the lighter grains of sand. It was not, he decided, a bad bit of work.

Several times Em Peters came to the edge of the bank and looked down toward the bench. There was no more talking now. Tandy was working hard and without any breaks. Janey hovered about him excitedly. Once they found a nugget the size of the end of his finger and she danced with excitement.

When he cleaned the riffles and the apron after two hours of work, he had nearly an ounce and a half of gold to put in the leather sack.

It **was** a good claim. No wonder that Richter was bothering around. Trust him to be thinking of the claim as well as Janey. Although, he decided, beginning to show some intelligence about girls, it would be better not to suggest that to her. At sundown, when he walked wearily back up the path to the cabin, he had two ounces of gold.

Em smiled at him. "My! You've worked hard! How did it go? Did Janey bother you?"

"Naw!" he said. "I didn't even know she was there."

Janey flared. "Oh—oh, you didn't?" She flounced away angrily and began rattling pans.

Tandy stared after her, deeply puzzled. Em put her hand on his shoulder. "That's all right, Tandy," she said. "Girls are like that."

"That's right!" Janey called out angrily. "Take his side!" She burst into tears and walked away toward the edge of the woods.

Tandy stared after her helplessly, and then dried his hands and followed. "Look," he protested. "I didn't—"

"Oh, go away!" She turned half around, not looking at him. "Don't talk to me!"

He looked at the back of her neck where little whorls of hair curled against a whiteness the sun had not reached. He hesitated, tempted to kiss her neck, but the thought made him flush guiltily. Instead, he lifted a tentative hand to her shoulder.

She let it rest there a minute, then jerked her shoulder away. "Don't **touch** me!" she said.

He looked at her, then slowly turned and walked back to the fire where Em smiled kindly and handed him a plate and a cup. He sat down, suddenly conscious of his hunger, and began to eat. He was enjoying the food hugely when he saw Janey come up to the fire, her face streaked with tears. She glared at him. "That's it—**eat**! All you ever think about is **eating**!"

Tandy looked at her in astonishment, his mind filled with protest. Words rose to his lips but were stifled there. He looked at his food, and suddenly his appetite was gone. Disgustedly, he got to his feet. Whoever could figure a girl out, anyway? What was she mad about?

He turned back to Em. "Ma'am," he said, his eyes showing his misery, "I reckon I'm makin' trouble here. Janey, she's some aggravated with me, so I figure you'd best take this here gold. I'll be walkin' along."

"She's not really angry," Em said. "Girls are that way. I expect they always will be. A girl has to fuss a certain amount or she doesn't feel right."

"I don't know about that," he said doubtfully. "Sally, she—"

Janey had turned on him. "So that's it! You've got a—a—" Tears rose to her eyes. "You've got a sweetheart!"

"No such thing!" he protested.

"Well." Her head came up and her eyes flared. "I don't **care**!"

Janey turned away from him, her chin high. He pushed the gold sack into Em Peters's hand and picked up his pack and shotgun and turned away. Em stared after him helplessly, and Janey, hearing his retreating footsteps, turned sharply, pure agony in her eyes. She took an involuntary step after him, then stopped. Tandy Meadows walked into the brush, and they heard him moving away toward the main trail.

Wearily, Em Peters began to scrape the food from the dishes. Neither of them saw Richter until he was close alongside them. "Pulled out, did he? I figured he would."

Em Peters faced him. "You go away, Carl Richter! I don't want you around here, nor any of your kind!"

Richter laughed. "Don't be a fool!" he said. "I'm stayin'. You'll get used to me." He looked around. "Janey, you pour me some of that coffee."

"I'll do no such thing!"

Richter's face turned ugly. With a quick step, he grabbed for her.

"I'd not be doin' that."

All eyes turned toward Tandy Meadows, who had come silently back through the trees.

Carl Richter stood very still, choking with fury. He had thought the boy was gone. By the—! He'd show him. He wheeled and started for his rifle.

"Go ahead." Tandy was calm. "You pick that rifle up. That's what I want."

"I'll kill you!" Richter shouted.

"I reckon not." Tandy Meadows eared back the Roper's hammer.

Not over fifteen yards separated them. Richter considered that and four loads of buckshot in the cylinder of the boy's shotgun and felt a little sick. He backed off warily from the rifle. "I ain't huntin' no trouble!" he said hoarsely.

"Then you start travelin', mister. I see you

along this crick again, an' I'll fill your measly hide with buckshot. You head for Hangtown, you hear me?"

"I got a claim!" Richter protested.

"You get you another one." Tandy Meadows had come from a country where there were few girls but lots of fights. What he lacked in knowledge of the one he more than made up with the other. "You don't get no second chance. Next time I just start a-shootin'."

He stood there, watching Richter start down the trail. He felt a hand rest lightly on his sleeve. Janey said nothing at all, watching the dark figure on the evening trail.

"Did"—the voice was low—"did you like Sally . . . very much?"

"Uh-huh."

"Did . . . do you like her better than me?"

"Not near so much," he said.

She moved against him, her head close to his shoulder. Sally was his sister, but he wasn't going to tell Janey that.

He was beginning to learn about women.

# *Elisha Comes to Red Horse*

There is a new church in the town of Red Horse. A clean white church of board and bat with a stained-glass window, a tall pointed steeple, and a bell that we've been told came all the way from Youngstown, Ohio. Nearby is a comfortable parsonage, a two-story house with a garreted roof, and fancy gingerbread under the eaves.

Just down the hill from the church and across from the tailings of what was once the King James Mine is a carefully kept cemetery of white headstones and neatly fitted crosses. It is surrounded by a spiked iron fence six feet high, and the gate is always fastened with a heavy lock. We open it up only for funerals and when the groundskeeper makes his rounds. Outsiders standing at the barred gate may find that a bit odd . . . but the people of Red Horse wouldn't have it any other way.

Visitors come from as far away as Virginia City to see our church, and on Sundays when we pass the collection, why, quite a few of those strangers ante up with the rest of us. Now Red Horse has seen its times of boom and bust and our history is as rough as any other town in the West, but our new church has certainly become the pride of the county.

And it is all thanks to the man that we called Brother Elisha.

HE WAS six feet five inches tall and he came into town a few years ago riding the afternoon stage. He wore a black broadcloth frock coat and carried a small valise. He stepped down from the stage, swept off his tall black hat, spread his arms, and lifted his eyes to the snowcapped ridges beyond the town. When he had won every eye on the street he said, "I come to bring deliverance, and eternal life!"

And then he crossed the street to the hotel, leaving the sound of his magnificent voice echoing against the false-fronted, unpainted buildings of our street.

In our town we've had our share of the odd ones, and many of the finest and best, but this was something new in Red Horse.

"A sky pilot, Marshal." Ralston spat into the dust. "We got ourselves another durned sky pilot!"

"It's a cinch he's no cattleman," I said, "and he doesn't size up like a drummer."

"We've got a sky pilot," Brace grumbled, "and

one preacher ought to balance off six saloons, so we sure don't need another."

"I say he's a gambler," Brennen argued. "That was just a grandstand play. Red Horse attracts gamblers like manure attracts flies. First time he gets in a game he'll cold deck you in the most sanctified way you ever did see!"

AT DAYBREAK the stranger walked up the mountain. Years ago lightning had struck the base of the ridge, and before rain put out the fire it burned its way up the mountain in a wide avenue. Strangely, nothing had ever again grown on that slope. Truth to tell, we'd had some mighty dry years after that, and nothing much had grown anywhere.

The Utes were superstitious about it. They said the lightning had put a curse on the mountain, but we folks in Red Horse put no faith in that. Or not much.

It was almighty steep to the top of that ridge, and every step the stranger took was in plain sight of the town, but he walked out on that spring morning and strode down the street and up the mountain. Those long legs of his took him up like he was walking a graded road, and when he got to the flat rock atop the butte he turned back toward the town and lifted his arms to the heavens.

"He's prayin'," Ralston said, studying him

through Brennen's glass. "He's sure enough prayin'!"

"I maintain he's a gambler," Brennen insisted. "Why can't he do his praying in church like other folks. Ask the reverend and see what he says."

Right then the reverend came out of the Emporium with a small sack of groceries under his arm, and noting the size of the sack, I felt like ducking into Brennen's Saloon. When prosperity and good weather come to Red Horse, we're inclined to forget our preacher and sort of stave off the doctor bills, too. Only in times of drought or low-grade ore do we attend church regular and support the preacher as we ought.

"What do you make of him, Preacher?" Brace asked.

The reverend squinted his eyes at the tiny figure high upon the hill. "There are many roads to grace," he said, "perhaps he has found his."

"If he's a preacher, why don't he pray in church?" Brennen protested.

"The groves were God's first temples," the reverend quoted. "There's no need to pray in church. A prayer offered up anywhere is heard by the Lord."

Ralston went into the hotel, and we followed him in to see what name the man had used. It was written plain as print: **Brother Elisha, Damascus**.

We stood back and looked at each other. We'd never had anybody in Red Horse from Damascus. We'd never had anybody from farther away than Denver except maybe a drummer who claimed he'd been to St. Louis . . . but we never believed him.

It was nightfall before Brother Elisha came down off the mountain, and he went at once to the hotel. Next day Brace came up to Brennen and me. "You know, I was talking to Sampson. He says he's never even seen Brother Elisha yet."

"What of it?" Brennen says. "I still say he's a gambler."

"If he don't eat at Sampson's"—Brace paused for emphasis—"where does he eat?"

We stared at each other. Most of us had our homes and wives to cook for us, some of the others batched it, but stoppers-by or ones who didn't favor their own cooking, they ate at Sampson's. There just wasn't anywhere else to eat.

"There he goes now," Brennen said, "looking sanctimonious as a dog caught in his own hen coop."

"Now see here!" Ralston protested. "Don't be talking that way, Brennen. After all, we don't know **who** he might be!"

Brother Elisha passed us by like a pay-car passes a tramp, and turning at the corner he started up the mountain. It was a good two miles up that mountain and the man climbed two thousand feet or more, with no switchbacks or twist-arounds, but he walked right up it. I wouldn't say that was a steep climb, but it wasn't exactly a promenade, either.

Brace scratched his jaw. "Maybe the man's broke," he suggested. "We can't let a man of God starve right here amongst us. What would the folks in Virginia City say?"

"Who says he's a man of God?" Brennen was always irreverent. "Just because he wears a black suit and goes up a mountain to pray?"

"It won't do," Brace insisted, "to have it said a preacher starved right here in Red Horse."

"The reverend," I suggested, "might offer some pointers on that."

They ignored me, looking mighty stiff and self-important.

"We could take up a collection," Ralston suggested.

Brother Elisha had sure stirred up a sight of conversation around town, but nobody knew anything because he hadn't said two words to anybody. The boys at the hotel, who have a way of knowing such things, said he hadn't nothing in his valise but two shirts, some underwear, and a Bible.

That night there was rain. It was soft, pleasant spring rain, the kind we call a growing rain, and it broke a two-year dry spell. Whenever we get a rain like that we know that spring has surely come, for they are warm rains and they melt the snow from the mountains and start the seeds germinating again. The snow gone from the ridges is the first thing we notice after such a rain, but next morning it wasn't only the snow, for something else had happened. Up that long-dead hillside where Brother Elisha walked, there was a faint mist of green, like the first sign of growing grass.

Brace came out, then Ralston and some others, and we stood looking up the mountain. No question about it, the grass was growing where no grass had grown in years. We stared up at it with a kind of awe and wondering.

"It's him!" Brace spoke in a low, shocked voice. "Brother Elisha has done this."

"Have you gone off your head?" Brennen demanded irritably. "This is just the first good growing weather we've had since the fire. The last few years there's been little rain and that late, and the ground has been cold right into the summer."

"You believe what you want," Ralston said. "We know what we can see. The Utes knew that hillside was accursed, but now he's walked on it, the curse is lifted. He said he would bring life, and he has."

It was all over town. Several times folks tried to get into talk with Brother Elisha, but he merely lifted a hand as if blessing them and went his way. But each time he came down from the mountain, his cheeks were flushed with joy and his eyes were glazed like he'd been looking into the eternity of heaven.

All this time nothing was heard from Reverend Sanderson, so what he thought about Brother Elisha, nobody knew. Here and there we began to hear talk that he was the new Messiah, but nobody seemed to pay much mind to that talk. Only it made a man right uneasy . . . how was one expected to act toward a Messiah?

In Red Horse we weren't used to distinguished visitors. It was out of the way, back in the hills, off the main roads east and west. Nobody ever came to Red Horse, unless they were coming to Red Horse.

Brennen had stopped talking. One time after he'd said something sarcastic it looked like he might be mobbed, so he kept his mouth shut, and I was just as satisfied, although it didn't seem to me that he'd changed his opinion of Brother Elisha. He always was a stubborn cuss.

Now personally, I didn't cater to this Messiah talk. There was a time or two when I had the sneaking idea that maybe Brennen knew what he was talking about, but I sure enough didn't say it out loud. Most people in Red Horse were kind of proud of Brother Elisha even when he made them uncomfortable. Mostly I'm a man likes a hand of poker now and again, and I'm not shy about a bottle, although not likely to get all liquored up. On the other hand, I rarely miss a Sunday at meeting unless the fishing is awful good, and I contribute. Maybe not as much as I could, but I contribute.

The reverend was an understanding sort of man, but about this here Brother Elisha, I wasn't sure. So I shied away from him on the street, but come Sunday I was in church. Only a half dozen were there. That was the day Brother Elisha held his first meeting.

There must've been three hundred people out there on that green mountainside when Brother Elisha called his flock together. Nobody knew how the word got around, but suddenly everybody was talking about it and most of them went out of curiosity.

By all accounts Brother Elisha turned out to be a Hell-and-damnation preacher with fire and thunder in his voice, and even there in the meeting house while the reverend talked we could hear those mighty tones rolling up against the rock walls of the mountains and sounding in the canyons as Brother Elisha called on the Lord to forgive the sinners on the Great Day coming.

Following Sunday I was in church again, but there was nobody there but old Ansel Greene's widow who mumbled to herself and never knew which side was up . . . except about money. The old woman had it, but hadn't spent enough to fill a coffee can since old Ansel passed on.

Just the two of us were there, and the reverend looked mighty down in the mouth, but nonetheless he got up in the pulpit and looked down at those rows of empty seats and announced a hymn.

Now I am one of these here folks who don't sing. Usually when hymns are sung I hang on to a hymnal with both hands and shape the words and rock my head to the tune, but I don't let any sound come out. But this time there was no chance of that. It was up to me to sing or get off the spot, and I sang. The surprise came when right behind me a rich baritone rolled out, and when I turned to look, it was Brennen.

Unless you knew Brennen this wouldn't mean much. Once an Orangeman, Brennen was an avowed and argumentative atheist. Nothing he liked better than an argument about the Bible, and he knew more about it than most preachers, but he scoffed at it. Since the reverend had been in town his one great desire had been to get Brennen into church, but Brennen just laughed at him, although like all of us he both liked and respected the reverend.

So here was Brennen, giving voice there back of me, and I doubt if the reverend would have been as pleased had the church been packed.

Brennen sang, no nonsense about it, and when the responses were read, he spoke out strong and sure.

At the door the reverend shook hands with him. "It is a pleasure to have you with us, Brother Brennen."

"It's a pleasure to be here, Reverend," Brennen said. "I may not always agree with you, Parson, but you're a good man, a very good man. You can expect me next Sunday, sir."

Walking up the street, Brennen said, "My ideas haven't changed, but Sanderson is a decent man, entitled to a decent attendance at his church, and his congregation should be ashamed. Ashamed, I say!"

Brennen was alone in his saloon next day. Brother Elisha had given an impassioned sermon on the sinfulness of man and the coming of the Great Day, and he scared them all hollow.

You never saw such a changed town. Ralston, who spoke only two languages, American and profane, was suddenly talking like a Baptist minister at a Bible conference and looking so sanctimonious it would fair turn a man's stomach.

Since Brother Elisha started preaching, the two emptiest places in town were the church and the saloon. Nor would I have you thinking wrong of the saloon. In my day in the West, a saloon was a club, a meeting place, a forum, and a source of news all put together. It was the only place men could gather to exchange ideas, do business, or hear the latest news from the outside.

And every day Brother Elisha went up the mountain.

One day when I stopped by the saloon, Brennen was outside watching Brother Elisha through his field glasses.

"Is he prayin'?" I asked.

"You might say. He lifts his arms to the sky, rants around some, then he disappears over the hill. Then he comes back and rants around some more and comes down the hill."

"I suppose he has to rest," I said. "Prayin' like that can use up a sight of energy."

"I suppose so," he said doubtfully. After a moment or two, he asked, "By the way, Marshal, were you ever in Mobeetie?"

By that time most of that great blank space on the mountainside had grown up to grass, and it grew greenest and thickest right where Brother Elisha walked, and that caused more talk.

Not in all this time had Brother Elisha been seen to take on any nourishment, not a bite of anything, nor to drink, except water from the well.

When Sunday came around again the only two in church were Brennen and me, but Brennen was there, all slicked up mighty like a winning gambler, and when the reverend's wife passed the plate, Brennen dropped in a twenty-dollar gold piece. Also, I'd heard he'd had a big package of groceries delivered around to the one-room log parsonage.

The town was talking of nothing but Brother Elisha, and it was getting so a man couldn't breathe the air around there, it was so filled with sanctified hypocrisy. You never saw such a bunch of overnight gospel-shouters.

Now I can't claim to be what you'd call a religious man, yet I've a respect for religion, and when a man lives out his life under the sun and the stars, half the time riding alone over mountains and desert, then he usually has a religion although it may not be the usual variety. Moreover, I had a respect for the reverend.

Brennen had his say about Brother Elisha, but I never did, although there was something about him that didn't quite tally.

Then the miracle happened.

It was a Saturday morning and Ed Colvin was shingling the new livery barn, and in a town the size of Red Horse nobody could get away from the sound of that hammer, not that we cared, or minded the sound. Only it was always with us.

And then suddenly we didn't hear it anymore.

Now it wasn't noontime, and Ed was a working sort of man, as we'd discovered in the two months he'd been in town. It was not likely he'd be quitting so early.

"Gone after lumber," I suggested.

"He told me this morning," Brace said, "that he had enough laid by to last him two days. He was way behind and didn't figure on quitting until lunchtime."

"Wait," I said, "we'll hear it again."

Only when some time passed and we heard nothing we started for the barn. Ed had been working mighty close to the peak of what was an unusually steep roof.

We found him lying on the ground and there was blood on his head and we sent for the doc.

Now Doc McDonald ain't the greatest doctor, but he was all we had aside from the midwife and a squaw up in the hills who knew herbs. The doc was drunk most of the time these days and showing up with plenty of money, so's it had been weeks since he'd been sober.

Doc came over, just weaving a mite, and almost as steady as he usually is when sober. He knelt by Ed Colvin and looked him over. He listened for a heartbeat and he held a mirror over his mouth, and he got up and brushed off his knees. "What's all the rush for? This man is dead!"

We carried him to Doc's place, Doc being the undertaker, too, and we laid him out on the table in his back room. Ed's face was dead white except for the blood, and he stared unblinking until the doc closed his eyes.

We walked back to the saloon feeling low. We'd not known Ed too well, but he was a quiet man and a good worker, and we needed such men around our town. Seemed a shame for him to go when there were others, mentioning no names, who meant less to the town.

That was the way it was until Brother Elisha came down off the mountain. He came with long strides, staring straight before him, his face flushed with happiness that seemed always with him these days. He was abreast of the saloon when he suddenly stopped.

It was the first time he had ever stopped to speak to anyone, aside from his preaching.

"What has happened?" he asked. "I miss the sound of the hammer. The sounds of labor are blessed in the ears of the Lord."

"Colvin fell," Brace said. "He fell from the roof and was killed."

Brother Elisha looked at him out of his great dark eyes and he said, "There is no death. None pass on but for the Glory of the Lord, and I feel this one passed before his time."

"You may think there's no death," Brace said, "but Ed Colvin looks mighty dead to me."

He turned his eyes on Brace. "O, ye of little faith: Take me to him."

When we came into Doc McDonald's the air was foul with liquor, and Brace glared at Doc like he'd committed a blasphemy. Brother Elisha paused briefly, his nose twitching, and then he walked through to the back room where Ed Colvin lay.

We paused at the door, clustered there, not knowing what to expect, but Brother Elisha walked up and bowed his head, placing the palm of his right hand on Colvin's brow, and then he prayed. Never did I know a man who could make a prayer fill a room with sound like Brother Elisha, but there at the last he took Ed by the shoulders and he pulled him into a sitting position and he said, "Edward Colvin, your work upon this earth remains unfinished. For the Glory of the Lord . . . **rise**!"

And I'll be forever damned if Ed Colvin didn't take a long gasping breath and sit right up on that table. He looked mighty confused and Brother Elisha whispered in his ear for a moment and then with a murmur of thanks Ed Colvin got up and walked right out of the place.

We stood there like we'd been petrified, and I don't know what we'd been expecting, but it wasn't this. Brother Elisha said, "The Lord moves in mysterious ways His wonders to perform." And then he left us.

Brace looked at me and I looked at Ralston and when I started to speak my mouth was dry. And just then we heard the sound of a hammer.

When I went outside people were filing into the street and they were looking up at that barn, staring at Ed Colvin, working away as if nothing had happened. When I passed Damon, standing in the bank door, his eyes were wide open and his face white. I spoke to him but he never even heard me or saw me. He was just standing there staring at Colvin.

By nightfall everybody in town was whispering about it, and when Sunday morning came they flocked to hear him preach, their faces shining, their eyes bright as though with fever.

When the reverend stepped into the pulpit, Brennen was the only one there besides me.

Reverend Sanderson looked stricken, and that morning he talked in a low voice, speaking quietly and sincerely but lacking his usual force. "Perhaps," he said as we left, "perhaps it is we who are wrong. The Lord gives the power of miracles to but few."

"There are many kinds of miracles," Brennen replied, "and one miracle is to find a sane, solid man in a town that's running after a red wagon."

As the three of us walked up the street together we heard the great rolling voice of Brother Elisha: "And I say unto you that the gift of life to Brother Colvin was but a sign, for on the morning of the coming Sabbath we shall go hence to the last resting place of your loved ones, and there I shall cause them all to be raised, and they shall live again, and take their places among you as of old!"

You could have dropped a feather. We stood on the street in back of his congregation and we heard what he said, but we didn't believe it, we couldn't believe it.

He was going to bring back the dead.

Brother Elisha, who had brought Ed Colvin back to life, was now going to empty the cemetery, returning to life all those who had passed on . . . and some who had been helped.

"The Great Day has come!" He lifted his long arms and spread them wide, and his sonorous voice rolled against the mountains. "And men shall live again for the Glory of All Highest! Your wives, your mothers, your brothers and fathers, they shall walk beside you again!"

And then he led them into the singing of a hymn and the three of us walked away.

That was the quietest Sunday Red Horse ever knew. Not a whisper, all day long. Folks were scared, they were happy, they were inspired. The townsfolk walked as if under a spell.

Strangely, it was Ed Colvin who said it. Colvin, the man who had gone to the great beyond and returned . . . although he claimed he had no memory of anything after his fall.

Brace was talking about the joy of seeing his

wife again, and Ed said quietly, "You'll also be seeing your mother-in-law."

Brace's mouth opened and closed twice before he could say anything at all, and then he didn't want to talk. He stood there like somebody had exploded a charge of powder under his nose, and then he turned sharply around and walked off.

"I've got more reason than any of you to be thankful," Ed said, his eyes downcast. "But I'm just not sure this is all for the best."

We all glanced at each other. "Think about it." Ed got up, looking kind of embarrassed. "What about you, Ralston? You'll have to go back to work. Do you think your uncle will stand for you loafing and spending the money he worked so hard to get?"

"That's right," I agreed, "you'll have to give it all back."

Ralston got mad. He started to shout that he wouldn't do any such thing, and anyway, if his uncle came back now he would be a changed man, he wouldn't care for money any longer, he—

"You don't believe that," Brennen said. "You know darned well that uncle of yours was the meanest skinflint in this part of the country. Nothing would change him."

Ralston went away from there. Seemed to me he wanted to do some thinking.

When I turned to leave, Brennen said, "Where are you going?"

"Well," I said, "seems to me I'd better oil up my six-shooters. There's three men in that Boot Hill that I put there. Looks like I'll have it to do over."

He laughed. "You aren't falling for this, are you?"

"Colvin sounds mighty lively to me," I said, "and come Sunday morning Brother Elisha has got to put up or shut up."

"You don't believe that their time in the hereafter will have changed those men you killed."

"Brennen," I said, "if I know the Hame brothers, they'll come out of their graves like they went into them. They'll come a-shootin'."

There had been no stage for several days as the trail had been washed out by a flash flood, and the town was quiet and it was scared. Completely cut off from the outside, all folks could do was wait and get more and more frightened as the Great Day approached. At first everybody had been filled with happiness at the thought of the dead coming back, and then suddenly, like Brace and Ralston, everybody was taking another thought.

There was the Widow McCann who had buried three husbands out there, all of them fighters and all of them mean. There were a dozen others with reason to give the matter some thought, and I knew at least two who were packed and waiting for the first stage out of town.

Brace dropped in at the saloon for his first drink since Brother Elisha started to preach. He hadn't shaved and he looked mighty mean. "Why'd he pick on this town?" he burst out. "When folks are dead they should be left alone. Nobody has a right to interfere with nature thataway."

Brennen mopped his bar, saying nothing at all.

Ed Colvin dropped around. "Wish that stage would start running. I want to leave town. Folks treat me like I was some kind of freak."

"Stick around," Brennen said. "Come Sunday the town will be filled with folks like you. A good carpenter will be able to stay busy, so busy he won't care what folks say about him. Take Streeter there. He'll need a new house now that his brother will be wanting his house back."

Streeter slammed his glass on the bar. "All right, damn it!" he shouted angrily, "I'll build my own house!"

Ralston motioned to me and we walked outside. Brace was there, and Streeter joined us. "Look," Ralston whispered, "Brace and me, we've talked it over. Maybe if we were to talk to Brother Elisha . . . maybe he'd call the whole thing off."

"Are you crazy?" I asked.

His eyes grew mean. "You want to try those Hame boys again? Seems to me you came out mighty lucky the last time. How do you know you'll be so lucky again? Those boys were pure-dee poison."

That was gospel truth, but I stood there chewing my cigar a minute and then said, "No chance. He wouldn't listen to us."

Ed Colvin had come up. "A man doing good works," he said, "might be able to use a bit of money. Although I suppose it would take quite a lot."

Brace stood a little straighter but when he turned to Colvin, the carpenter was hurrying off down the street. When I turned around there was Brennen leaning on the doorjamb, and he was smiling.

Friday night when I was making my rounds I saw somebody slipping up the back stairs of the hotel, and for a moment his face was in the light from a window. It was Brace.

Later, I saw Ralston hurrying home from the direction of the hotel, and you'd be surprised at some of the folks I spotted slipping up those back stairs to commune with Brother Elisha. Even Streeter, and even Damon.

Watching Damon come down those back stairs I heard a sound behind me and turned to see Brennen standing there in the dark. "Seems a lot of folks are starting to think this resurrection of the dead isn't an unmixed blessing."

"You know something?" I said thoughtfully. "Nobody has been atop that hill since Brother Elisha started his walks. I think I'll just meander up there and have a look around."

"You've surprised me," Brennen said. "I wouldn't have expected you to be a churchgoing man. You're accustomed to sinful ways."

"Why, now," I said, "when I come into a town to live, I go to church. If the preacher is a man who shouts against things, I never go back. I like a man who's for something.

"Like you know, I've been marshal here and there, but never had much trouble with folks. I leave their politics and religion be. Folks can think the way they want, act the way they please, even to acting the fool. All I ask is they don't make too much noise and don't interfere with other people.

"They call me a peace officer, and I try to keep the peace. If a growed-up man gets himself into a game with a crooked gambler, I don't bother them . . . if he hasn't learned up to then, he may learn, and if he doesn't learn, nothing I tell him will do him any good."

"You think Colvin was really dead?"

"Doc said so."

"Suppose he was hypnotized? Suppose he wasn't really dead at all?"

After Brennen went to bed I saddled up and rode out of town. Circling around the mountain I rode up to where Brother Elisha used to go to pray. Brennen had left me with a thought, and Doc had been drinking a better brand of whiskey lately.

Brace had drawn money from the bank, and so had Ralston, and old Mrs. Greene had been digging out in her hen coop, and knowing about those tin cans she buried there after her husband died kind of sudden, I had an idea what she was digging up.

I made tracks. I had some communicatin' to do and not many hours to do it in.

I spent most of those hours in the saddle. Returning to Red Horse the way I did brought me to a place where the trail forked, and one way led over behind that mountain with the burnt-off slope. When I had my horse out of sight I drew up and waited.

It was just growing gray when a rider came down the mountain trail and stopped at the forks. It was Ed Colvin.

We hadn't anything to talk about right at the moment so I just kept out of sight in the brush and then followed. He seemed like he was going to meet somebody and I had a suspicion it was Brother Elisha. And it was.

"You got it?" Ed Colvin asked.

"Of course. I told you we could fool these yokels. Now let's—"

When I stepped out of the brush I was holding a shotgun. I said, "The way of the transgressor is hard. Give me those saddlebags, Delbert."

Brother Elisha stared at me. "I fear there is some mistake," he said with dignity. "I am Brother Elisha."

"I found those cans and sacks up top of the hill. The ones where you kept your grub and the grass seed you scattered." I stepped in closer.

"You are Delbert Johnson," I added, "and the wires over at Russian Junction say you used to deal a crooked game of faro in Mobeetie. Now give me the saddlebags."

THE REVEREND has a new church now, and a five-room frame parsonage to replace his tiny cabin. The dead of Red Horse sleep peacefully and there is a new iron fence around the cemetery to keep them securely inside. Brennen still keeps his saloon, but he also passes the collection plate of a Sunday, and the results are far better than they used to be.

There was a lot of curiosity as to where the reverend came by the money to do the building, and the good works that followed. Privately, the reverend told Brennen and me about a pair of saddlebags he found inside the parsonage door that Sunday morning. But when anyone else asked him he had an answer ready.

"The ravens have provided," he would say, smiling gently, "as they did for Elijah."

Nobody asked any more questions.

## *The Courting of Griselda*

When it came to Griselda Popley, I was down to bedrock and showing no color.

What I mean is, I wasn't getting anyplace. The only thing I'd learned since leaving the Cumberland in Tennessee was how to work a gold placer claim, but I was doing no better with that than I was with Griselda.

Her pa, Frank Popley, had a claim just a whoop and a holler down canyon from me. He had put down a shaft on a flat bench at the bend of the creek and he was down a ways and making a fair clean-up.

He was scraping rock down there and panning out sixty to seventy dollars a day, and one time he found a crack where the gold had seeped through and filled in a space under a layer of rock, and he cleaned out six hundred dollars in four or five minutes.

It sure does beat all how prosperity makes a man critical of all who are less prosperous. Seems like some folks no sooner get two dollars they can rattle together than they start looking down their noses at folks who only have two bits.

We were right friendly while Popley was sinking his shaft, but as soon as he began bringing up gold he started giving me advice and talking me down to Griselda. From the way he cut up, you'd have thought it was some ability or knowledge of his that put that gold there. I never saw a man get superior so fast.

He was running me down and talking up that Arvie Wilt who had a claim nearby the Popley place, and Arvie was a man I didn't cotton to.

He was two inches taller than my six feet and three, and where I pack one hundred and eighty pounds on that lean a frame, most of it in my chest, shoulders, and arms, Arvie weighed a good fifty pounds more and he swaggered it around as if almighty impressed with himself.

He was a big, easy-smiling man that folks took to right off, and it took them a while to learn he was a man with a streak of meanness in him that was nigh on to downright viciousness. Trouble was, a body never saw that mean streak unless he was in a bind, but when trouble came to him, the meanness came out.

But Arvie was panning out gold, and you'd be surprised how that increased his social standing there on Horse Collar Creek.

Night after night he was over to the Popleys', putting his big feet under their table and being waited on by Griselda. Time to time I was there, too, but they talked gold and how much they weighed out each day while all I was weighing out was gravel.

He was panning a fine show of color and all I had was a .44 pistol gun, a Henry rifle, and my mining tools. And as we all know it's the high card in a man's hand to be holding money when he goes a-courting.

None of us Sacketts ever had much cash money. We were hardworking mountain folk who harvested a lean corn crop off a side-hill farm, and we boys earned what clothes weren't made at home by trapping muskrats or coon. Sometimes we'd get us a bear, and otherwise we'd live on razorback hog meat or venison.

Never will forget the time a black bear treed old Orrin, that brother of mine, and us caught nine miles from home and none of us carrying iron.

You ever tackle a grown bear with a club? Me and Tyrel, we done it. We chunked at him with rocks and sticks, but he paid them no mind. He was bound and determined to have Orrin, and there was Orrin up high in the small branches of that tree like a possum huntin' persimmons.

Chunking did no good, so Tyrel and me cut us each a club and we had at that bear. He was big and he was mean, but while one of us closed in on him from before, the other lambasted him from behind. Time to time we'd stop lambasting that bear to advise Orrin.

Finally that old bear got disgusted and walked off and Orrin came down out of that tree and we went on to the dance at Skunk Hollow School. Orrin did his fiddling that night from a sitting stool because the bear had most of his pants.

Right now I felt like he must have felt then. Every day that Griselda girl went a-walking past my claim paying me no mind but switching her skirts until I was fair sweating on my neck.

Her pa was a hard man. One time I went over there for supper like I had when I'd been welcome, back when neither of us had anything. He would stand up there in his new boots, consulting a new gold watch every minute or two, and talking high and mighty about the virtues of hard work and the application of brains. And all the time that Arvie Wilt was a-setting over there making big eyes at Griselda.

If anything, Arvie had more gold than Popley did and he was mighty welcome at table, but for me the atmosphere was frosting over a mite, and the only reason I dug in and held on was that I'd scraped my pot empty of beans and for two days I'd eaten nothing but those skimpy little wild onions.

Now when it came right down to it, Popley knew I'd worked hard as either of them, but I was showing no color and he wanted a son-in-law who was prosperous, so needing to find fault, he taken issue with me on fighting.

We boys from the high-up hills aren't much on bowing and scraping, but along about fighting time, you'll find us around. Back in the Cumberland I grew up to knuckle-and-skull fighting, and what I hadn't learned there I picked up working west on a keelboat.

Pa, he taught us boys to be honest, to give respect to womenfolk, to avoid trouble when we could, but to stand our ground when it came to a matter of principle, and a time or two I'd stood my ground.

That old six-shooter of mine was a caution. It looked old enough to have worn out three men, but it shot true and worked smooth. My hands are almighty big but I could fetch that pistol faster than you could blink. Not that I made an issue of it because Pa taught us to live peaceable.

Only there was that time down to Elk Creek when a stranger slicked an ace off the bottom, and I taken issue with him.

He had at me with a fourteen-inch blade and my toothpick was home stuck in a tree where I'd left it after skinning out a deer, so I fetched him a clout alongside the skull and took the blade from him. A friend of his hit me from behind with a chair, which I took as unfriendly, and then he fetched out his pistol, so I came up a-shooting.

Seemed like I'd won myself a name as a bad man to trouble, and it saved me some hardship. Folks spoke polite and men seeking disagreement took the other side of the road, only it gave Popley something he could lay a hand to, and he began making slighting remarks about men who got into brawls and cutting scrapes.

Words didn't come easy to me and by the time I'd thought of the right answer I was home in bed, but when Popley talked I felt like I was disgracing Griselda by coming a-courting.

So I went back to my claim shanty and looked into the bean pot again, but it was still empty, and I went a-hunting wild onions.

Nobody could ever say any of us Sacketts fought shy of work, so I dug away at my claim until I was satisfied there was nothing there but barren gravel. Climbing out of that shaft I sat down and looked at my hole card.

There was nothing left but to load up my gear on that spavined mule I had and leave the country. I was out of grub, out of cash money, and out of luck. Only leaving the country meant leaving Griselda, and worst of all, it meant leaving her to Arvie Wilt.

Time or two I've heard folks say there's always better fish in the sea, but not many girls showed me attention. Many a time I sat lonely along the wall, feared to ask a girl to dance because I knew she'd turn me down, and no girl had paid me mind for a long time until Griselda showed up.

She was little, she was pert, and she had quick blue eyes and an uptilted nose and freckles where you didn't mind them. She'd grown into a woman and was feeling it, and there I was, edged out by the likes of Arvie Wilt.

Popley, he stopped by. There I was, a-setting hungry and discouraged, and he came down creek riding that big brown mule and he said, "Tell, I'd take it kindly if you stayed away from the house." He cleared his throat because I had a bleak look to my eye. "Griselda is coming up to marrying time and I don't want her confused. You've got nothing, and Arvie Wilt is a prosperous mining man. Meaning no offense, but you see how it is."

He rode on down to the settlement and there was nothing for me to do but go to picking wild onions. The trouble was, if a man picked all day with both hands he couldn't pick enough wild onions to keep him alive.

It was rough country, above the canyons, but there were scattered trees and high grass plains, with most of the ridges topped with crests of pine. Long about sundown I found some deer feeding in a parklike clearing.

They were feeding, and I was downwind of them, so I straightened up and started walking toward them, taking my time. When I saw their tails start to switch, I stopped.

A deer usually feeds into the wind so he can smell danger, and when his tail starts to wiggle he's going to look up and around, so I stood right still. Deer don't see all too good, so unless a body is moving they see nothing to be afraid of. They looked around and went back to feeding and I moved closer until their tails started again, and then I stopped.

Upshot of it was, I got a good big buck, butchered him, and broiled a steak right on the spot, I was that hungry. Then I loaded the best cuts of meat into the hide and started back, still munching on wild onions.

Down on the creek again the first person I saw was Griselda, and right off she began switching her skirts as she walked to meet me.

"I passed your claim," she said, "but you were not there."

She had little flecks of brown in her blue eyes and she stood uncomfortably close to a man. "No, ma'am, I've give . . . given . . . it up. Your pa is right. That claim isn't up to much."

"Are you coming by tonight?"

"Seems to me I wore out my welcome. No, ma'am, I'm not coming by. However, if you're walking that way, I'll drop off one of these here venison steaks."

Fresh meat was scarce along that creek, and the thought occurred that I might sell what I didn't need, so after leaving a steak with the Popleys, I peddled the rest of it, selling out for twelve dollars cash money, two quarts of beans, a pint of rice, and six pounds of flour.

Setting in my shack that night I wrassled with my problem and an idea that had come to me. Astride that spavined mule I rode down to the settlement and spent my twelve dollars on flour, a mite of sugar, and some other fixings, and back at the cabin I washed out some flour sacks for aprons, and made me one of those chef hats like I'd seen in a newspaper picture. Then I set to making bear-sign.

Least, that's what we called them in the mountains. Most folks on the flatland called them doughnuts, and some mountain folk did, but not around our house. I made up a batch of bear-sign and that good baking smell drifted down along the creek, and it wasn't more than a few minutes later until a wild-eyed miner came running and falling up from the creek, and a dozen more after him.

"Hey! Is that bear-sign we smell? Is them doughnuts?"

"Cost you," I said. "I'm set up for business. Three doughnuts for two bits."

That man set right down and ate two dollars'

worth and by the time he was finished there was a crowd around reaching for them fast as they came out of the Dutch oven.

Folks along that creek lived on skimpy bacon and beans, sometimes some soda biscuits, and real baking was unheard-of. Back to home no woman could make doughnuts fast enough for we Sackett boys who were all good eaters, so we took to making them ourselves. Ma often said nobody could make bear-sign like her son, William Tell Sackett.

By noon I was off to the settlement for more makings, and by nightfall everybody on the creek knew I was in business. Next day I sold a barrel of doughnuts, and by nightfall I had the barrel full again and a washtub also. That washtub was the only one along the creek, and it looked like nobody would get a bath until I'd run out of bear-sign.

You have to understand how tired a man can get of grease and beans to understand how glad they were to taste some honest-to-gosh, down-to-earth doughnuts.

Sun-up and here came Arvie Wilt. Arvie was a big man with a big appetite and he set right down and ran up a bill of four dollars. I was making money.

Arvie sat there eating doughnuts and forgetting all about his claim.

Come noon, Griselda showed up. She came

a-prancing and a-preening it up the road and she stayed around, eating a few doughnuts and talking with me. The more she talked the meaner Arvie got.

"Griselda," he said, "you'd best get along home. You know how your pa feels about you trailing around with just any drifter."

Well, sir, I put down my bowl and wiped the flour off my hands. "Are you aiming that at me?" I asked. "If you are, you just pay me my four dollars and get off down the pike."

He was mean, like I've said, and he did what I hoped he'd do. He balled up a fist and threw it at me. Trouble was, he took so much time getting his fist ready and his feet in position that I knew what he was going to do, so when he flung that punch, I just stepped inside and hit him where he'd been putting those doughnuts.

He gulped and turned green around the jowls and white around the eyes, so I knocked down a hand he stuck at me and belted him again in the same place. Then I caught him by the shirt front before he could fall and backhanded him twice across the mouth for good measure.

Griselda was a-hauling at my arms. "Stop it, you awful man! You hurt him!"

"That ain't surprising, Griselda," I said. "It was what I had in mind."

So I went back to making bear-sign, and after a bit Arvie got up, with Griselda helping, and he wiped the blood off his lips and he said, "I'll get even! I'll get even with you if it's the last thing I do!"

"And it just might be," I said, and watched them walk off together.

There went Griselda. Right out of my life, and with Arvie Wilt, too.

Two days later I was out of business and broke. Two days later I had a barrel of doughnuts I couldn't give away and my private gold rush was over. Worst of all, I'd put all I'd made back into the business and there I was, stuck with it. And it was Arvie Wilt who did it to me.

As soon as he washed the blood off his face he went down to the settlement. He had heard of a woman down there who was a baker, and he fetched her back up the creek. She was a big, round, jolly woman with pink cheeks, and she was a first-rate cook. She settled down to making apple pies three inches thick and fourteen inches across and she sold a cut of a pie for two bits and each pie made just four pieces.

She also baked cakes with high-grade all over them. In mining country rich ore is called high-grade, so miners got to calling the icing on cake high-grade, and there I sat with a barrel full of bear-sign and everybody over to the baker woman's buying cake and pie and such-like.

Then Popley came by with Griselda riding behind him on that brown mule, headed for the baker woman's. "See what a head for business Arvie's got? He'll make a fine husband for Griselda."

Griselda? She didn't even look at me. She passed me up like a pay-car passing a tramp, and I felt so low I could have walked under a snake with a high hat on.

Three days later I was back to wild onions. My grub gave out, I couldn't peddle my flour, and the red ants got into my sugar. All one day I tried sifting red ants out of sugar; as fast as I got them out they got back in until there was more ants than sugar.

So I gave up and went hunting. I hunted for two days and couldn't find a deer, nor anything else but wild onions.

Down to the settlement they had a fandango, a real old-time square dance, and I had seen nothing of the kind since my brother Orrin used to fiddle for them back to home. So I brushed up my clothes and rubbed some deer grease on my boots, and I went to that dance.

Sure enough, Griselda was there, and she was with Arvie Wilt.

Arvie was all slicked out in a black broadcloth suit that fit him a little too soon, and black boots so tight he winced when he put a foot down.

Arvie spotted me and they fetched to a halt

right beside me. "Sackett," Arvie said, "I hear you're scraping bottom again. Now my baker woman needs a helper to rev up her pots and pans, and if you want the job—"

"I don't."

"Just thought I'd ask,"—he grinned maliciously—"seein' you so good at woman's work."

He saw it in my eyes so he grabbed Griselda and they waltzed away, grinning. Thing that hurt, she was grinning, too.

"That Arvie Wilt," somebody said, "there's a man will amount to something. Popley says he has a fine head for business."

"For the amount of work he does," somebody else said, "he sure has a lot of gold. He ain't spent a day in that shaft in a week."

"What do you mean by that?"

"Ask them down to the settlement. He does more gambling than mining, according to some."

That baker woman was there, waltzing around like she was light as a feather, and seeing her made me think of a Welshman I knew. Now you take a genuine Welshman, he can talk a bird right out of a tree . . . I started wondering . . . how would he do with a widow woman who was a fine baker?

That Welshman wasn't far away, and we'd talked often, the year before. He liked a big woman, he said, the jolly kind and who could enjoy making good food. I sat down and wrote him a letter.

Next morning early I met up with Griselda. "You actually marrying that Arvie?"

Her pert little chin came up and her eyes were defiant. "A girl has to think of her future, Tell Sackett! She can't be tying herself to a—a—ne'er-do-well! Mr. Wilt is a serious man. His mine is very successful"—her nose tilted—"and so is the bakery!"

She turned away, then looked back. "And if you expect any girl to like you, you'd better stop eating those onions! They're simply awful!"

And if I stopped eating wild onions, I'd starve to death.

Not that I wasn't half-starved, anyway.

That day I went farther up the creek than ever, and the canyon narrowed to high walls and the creek filled the bottom, wall to wall, and I walked ankle deep in water going through the narrows. And there on a sandy beach were deer tracks, old tracks and fresh tracks, and I decided this was where they came to drink.

So I found a grassy ledge above the pool and alongside an outcropping of rock, and there I settled down to wait for a deer. It was early afternoon and a good bit of time remained to me.

There were pines on the ridge behind me, and the wind sounded fine, humming through their needles. I sat there for a bit, enjoying the shade, and then I reached around and pulled a wild onion from the grass, lifting it up to brush away the sand and gravel clinging to the roots. . . .

IT WAS SUNDOWN when I reached my shanty, but I didn't stop, I rode on into the settlement. The first person I saw was the Welshman. He was smiling from ear to ear, and beside him was the baker woman.

"Married!" he said cheerfully. "Just the woman I've been looking for!"

And off down the street they went, arm in arm.

Only now it didn't matter anymore.

For two days then I was busy as all get-out. I was down to the settlement and back up above the narrows of the canyon, and then I was down again.

Putting my few things into a pack, and putting the saddle on that old mule of mine, I was fixing to leave the claim and shanty for the last time when who should show up but Frank Popley.

He was riding his brown mule with Griselda riding behind him, and they rode up in front of the shack. Griselda slid down off that mule and ran up and threw her arms around me and kissed me right on the lips.

"Oh, Tell! We heard the news! Oh, we're so happy for you! Pa was just saying that he always knew you had the stuff, that you had what it takes!"

Frank Popley looked over at me and beamed. "Can't keep a good man down, boy! You sure can't! Griselda, she always said, 'Pa, Tell is the best of the lot,' an' she was sure enough right!"

Suddenly a boot crunched on gravel, and there was Arvie, looking mighty mean and tough, and he was holding a Walker Colt in his fist, aimed right at me.

Did you ever see a Walker Colt? Only thing it lacks to be a cannon is a set of wheels.

"You ain't a-gonna do it!" Arvie said. "You can't have Griselda!"

"You can have Griselda," I heard myself say, and was astonished to realize that I meant it.

"You're not fooling me! You can't get away with it." And his thumb came forward to cock that pistol.

Like I said, Arvie wasn't too smart or he'd have cocked his gun as he drew it, so I just fetched out my six-shooter and let the hammer slip from under my thumb as it came level.

Deliberately, I held it a little high, and the .44 slug smashed him in the shoulder. It knocked him sidewise and he let go of that big pistol and staggered back two steps and sat down hard.

"You're a mighty disagreeable man, Arvie," I said, "and not much account. When the boys down at the settlement start finding the marks you put on those cards you'll have to leave the country, but I reckon you an' Griselda deserve each other."

She was looking at me with big eyes and pouty lips because she'd heard the news, but I wasn't having any.

"You-all been washing gold along the creek," I said, "but you never stopped to think where those grains of gold started from. Well, I found and staked the mother lode, staked her from Hell to breakfast, and one day's take will be more than you've taken out since you started work. I figure now I'll dig me out a goodly amount of money, then I'll sell my claims and find me some friends that aren't looking at me just to see what I got."

They left there walking down that hill with Arvie astride the mule making pained sounds every time it took a step.

WHEN I HAD PULLED that wild onion up there on that ledge overlooking the deer run, there were bits of gold in the sand that clung to the roots, and when I scraped the dirt away from the base of that outcrop, she was all there . . . wire gold lying in the rock like a jewelry store window.

Folks sometimes ask me why I called it the Wild Onion Mining Company.

# *Booty for a Badman*

When my roan topped out on the ridge, the first thing I saw was that girl. She was far off, but a man riding lonesome country gets so he can pick out anything strange to it, and this girl was standing up straight beside the trail like she was waiting for a stage. Trouble was, nothing but riders or freight wagons used that trail, and seldom.

With fifty pounds of gold riding with me and three days ahead of me, I was skittish of folks. Most times wild country is less trouble than people, no matter how rough the country. And no woman had a right to be standing out there in that empty desert-mountain country.

We Sacketts began carrying rifles as soon as we stood tall enough to keep both ends off the ground.

When I was fourteen I traveled from Cumberland Gap in Tennessee down to the Pine Log Mountains in Georgia, living on cougar meat and branch water, and I killed my own cougars.

Man-grown at fifteen, I hoofed it north and joined up with the Union and fought at Shiloh, and after our outfit was surrendered by a no-account colonel, I was among those exchanged to go north and fight the Sioux in Dakota.

At nineteen I saddled our roan and fetched it for the west to try my hand at gold-panning, but I wasn't making out. Seems like everybody in camp was showing color but me, and I was swallowing my belt notch by notch for lack of eating when those four men came to my fire.

Worst of it was, I couldn't offer them. There I was, booting up for a fresh day with my coffeepot on the fire so's people wouldn't know I hadn't even coffee, but all there was in the pot was water. I dearly wanted to offer them, but I was shamed to admit I was fresh out of coffee—three days out, actually. And so hungry that my stomach thought my throat had been cut.

"Tell," Squires suggested, "you've had no luck with mining, so nobody would suspect you of carrying gold. If you rode out of camp today, folks would take it for granted you had called it deep enough and quit. That way you could carry our gold to Hardyville and nobody the wiser."

The four men facing me had taken out the most dust and, knowing about the Coopers, they were worried men. Three of them were family men and that gold meant schooling for their youngsters and homes for their wives and capital for themselves. They were poor, hard-working men, deserving what they had dug up.

Thing was, how to get it past the Coopers?

"We'll give you one hundred dollars," Hodge said, "if you make it through."

With the best of luck it was a five-day ride, which figured out to twenty dollars a day. With such a grubstake I could take out for California or come back with a grubstake.

My belly was as empty as my prospect hole, and it didn't seem like I had much choice. Coopers or no Coopers, it sized up like the fastest hundred dollars I would ever make. It was Bill Squires done it for me, as we'd talked friendly ever since I staked claim on the creek.

Jim Hodge, Willy Mander and Tom Padgett stood there waiting for me to speak up, and finally I said, "I'll do it, of course, and glad of the chance. Only, I am a stranger, and—"

"Squires swears by you," Padgett interrupted, "and even if we don't know you very well, he's known you and your family. If he says you are honest, that's all there is to it."

"And this is a chance to get you a stake," Squires interrupted. "What can you lose?"

Well, the last two men who rode out of camp with gold were found dead alongside the trail, shot down like you'd shoot a steer; and one of them was Jack Walker, a man I'd known. Neither of them was carrying as much as I'd have.

"Take a pack horse," Squires suggested, "load your gear." He glanced around and lowered his voice. "It seems like somebody here in camp informs the Coopers, but nobody will know about this but us, and all of us have a stake in it."

Later, when the others had gone, Squires said, "Hope you didn't mind my saying I'd known your family. They were willing to trust you if I did, but I wanted them to feel better."

So I packed up and rode off, and in my saddlebags there was fifty pounds of gold, worth around a thousand dollars a pound at the time, and in my pocket I'd a note signed by all four men that I was to have a hundred dollars when the gold was delivered. Never had I seen that much cash money, and since the war I'd not had even ten dollars at one time.

Now, that woman standing down there sized up like trouble aplenty. Pa, he always warned us boys to fight shy of women. "They'll trouble you," Pa said. "Love 'em and leave 'em, that's the way. Don't you get tangled up with no female woman. They got more tricks they can do than a monkey on sixty feet of grapevine."

"Don't believe that, Tell," Ma would say. "You treat women right. You treat a woman like she was your sister, you hear?"

Pa, he would say, "There's two kinds of women, Tell, good and bad, and believe me, a good woman can cause a man more trouble than a bad one. You fight shy of them."

So I fought shy. Of mountain cats and bears, of muskrat and deer, even of horses and cows I knew a sight, but I wasn't up on womenfolk. Orrin now—he was my brother—he was a fiddler and a singer, and fiddlers and singers have a way with women. At home when strange womenfolk showed up, I'd taken to the hills.

Looked to me like I was fair trapped this time, but I wasn't about to turn and run. Any woman waiting in lonesome country was a woman in trouble. Only I begun to sweat. I'd never been close to no lone woman before.

WORST OF IT WAS, there was somebody on my trail. A man like me, riding somewhere, he doesn't only watch the trail ahead, he looks back. Folks get lost because when they start back over a trail they find it looks a sight different facing the other way. When a man travels he should keep sizing up the country, stopping time to time to study his back trail so he recognizes the landmarks.

Looking back, I'd seen dust hanging in the air. And that dust stayed there. It had to be somebody tracking me down, and it could mean it was the Coopers.

Right then I'd much rather have tangled with

the Coopers than faced up to that woman down there, but that no-account roan was taking me right to her.

Worst of it was, she was almighty pretty. There was a mite of sunburn on her cheekbones and nose, but despite that, she was a fine-looking girl.

"How do you do?" You'd of thought we were meeting on the streets of Nashville. "I wonder if you could give me a lift to Hardyville?"

My hatbrim was down over my eyes, and I sized up the country around, but there was no sign of a horse she might have ridden to this point, nor any sign of a cabin or camp.

"Why, I reckon so, ma'am." I got down from the saddle, thinking if trouble came I might have to fetch that big Colt in a hurry. "My pack horse is packing light so I can rig that pack saddle so's you can ride it sidesaddle."

"I would be grateful," she said.

First off, it shaped like a trap. Somebody knowing I had gold might have this woman working with them, for it troubled me to guess how she came here. There were a sight of tracks on the ground, but all seemed to be hers. And then I noticed a thin trail of smoke from behind a rock.

"You have a fire?"

"It was quite cold last night."

When she caught my look, she smiled. "Yes, I

was here all night." She looked directly at me from those big blue eyes. "And the night before."

"It ain't a likely spot."

She carried herself prim, but she was a bright, quick-to-see girl, and I cottoned to her. The clothes she wore were of fine, store-bought goods like some I'd seen folks wear in some of those northern cities I'd seen as a soldier. Where I came from it was homespun, or buckskin.

"I suppose you wonder what I am doing here?"

"Well, now." I couldn't help grinning. "It did come to my mind. Like I said, it ain't a likely spot."

"You shouldn't say 'ain't.' The word is 'isn't.' "

"Thank you, ma'am. I had no schooling, except what ma could give me, and I never learned to talk proper."

"Surely you can read and write?"

"No, ma'am, I surely can't."

"Why, that's awful! Everybody should be able to read. I don't know what I would have done these past months if I could not read. I believe I should have gone insane."

When the saddle was rigged, I helped her up. "Ma'am, I better warn you. There's trouble acoming, so's you'd better have it in mind. It may not be a good thing, me helping you this way. You may get into worse trouble."

We started off, and I looked over my shoulder

at her. "Somebody is following after me. I figure it's them Cooper outlaws."

Worst of it was, I had lost time, and here it was coming up to night, and me with a strange girl on my hands. Pa told me women had devious ways of getting to a man, but I never figured one would set out alongside a lonely trail thataway. Especially one as pretty as she was.

Moreover, she was a lady. A body could see she was quality, and she rode there beside me, chin lifted and proud like she was riding the finest thoroughbred at a county fair, or whatever.

"You running from something, ma'am? Not to be disrespectful, ma'am, but out in the desert thisaway it ain't—isn't—just the place a body would expect to find a lady as pretty as you."

"Thank you." Her chin lifted a mite higher. "Yes, I am running away. I am leaving my husband. He is a thoughtless, inconsiderate brute, and he is an Army officer at Fort Whipple."

"He will be mighty sorry to lose you, ma'am. This here is a lonesome country. I don't carry envy for those soldier boys out here, I surely don't."

"Well! It certainly is not a place to bring an officer's bride. I'll declare! How could he think I could live in such a place? With a dirt floor, and all?"

"What did he say when you left?"

"He doesn't know it yet. I had been to

Ehrenberg, and when we started back, I just couldn't stand the thought, so when no one was looking, I got out of the Army ambulance I was riding in. I am going to catch the steamer at Hardyville and go home."

When I looked to our back trail, no dust hung in the air, and I knew we were in trouble. If it had been soldiers looking for this girl, they would not have stopped so sudden-like, and it looked to me like they had headed us and laid a trap, so I swung up a draw, heading north instead of west, and slow to raise no dust.

It was a sandy wash, but a thin trail skirted the edge, made by deer or such-like and we held to it. When we had been riding for an hour, I saw dust in the air, hanging up there in a fair cloud about where I had come up to this lady. Again I turned at right angles, heading back the way I had come. Off to the north and west there was a square-topped mesa that was only a part of a long, comb-like range.

"We are followed, ma'am," I said, "and those Coopers are mighty thoughtless folks. I got to keep you out of their hands. First off, we'll run. If that doesn't work, we'll talk or we'll fight, leaving it up to them. You hold with me, ma'am."

"They wouldn't bother me," she said. "I am the wife of an Army officer."

"Most Western men are careful of women-folk," I agreed, "but don't set no truck by being an officer's wife. The Coopers murdered two Army officers not a week ago. Murdered them, ma'am. They just don't care a mite who you may be. And a woman like you—they don't often see a woman pretty as you."

She rode up closer to me. "I am afraid I didn't realize."

"No, ma'am, most folks don't," I said.

It was still the best part of two days to Hardyville, and nothing much there when we arrived. It was head of navigation on the Colorado, and last I'd seen there were only three or four buildings there, and about that many folks.

Nobody seemed to know how many Coopers there were, but the guesses ran all the way from five to nine. They were said to be renegades from down in the Cherokee nation and mighty mean.

We held to low ground, keeping off skylines, finding a saddle here and there where we could cross over ridges without topping out where we could be seen. It was darkening by then, with long shadows reaching out, and when we came up the eastern flank of that mesa I'd headed for, we rode in deep shadow.

When we found a way around the butte, we took it, and the western slope was all red from the setting sun, and mighty pretty. The wind blew cool there, but I'd found what I was hunting—a place to hole up for the night.

A man hunting a night camp with somebody trailing him has to have things in mind. He wants a place he can get into and out of without sky-lining himself or showing up plain, and he also wants a place where he can build a fire that cannot be seen, and something to spread out the smoke. And here it was, and by the look of it many an Indian had seen the worth of it before this time.

The falloff from the mesa rim made a steep slope that fell away for maybe five hundred feet. A man could ride a horse down that slope, but it would be sliding half the time on its rump. The wall of the mesa raised up sheer for some three hundred feet, but there at the foot of that cliff and atop the slope was a hollow behind some rocks and brush.

Maybe it was a half-acre of ground with grass in the bottom and some scraggly cedars at one end. We rode down into that hollow, and I reached up and handed down the lady.

"Ma'am, we'll spend the night here. Talk low and don't let any metal strike metal or start any rock sliding."

"Are they that close?"

"I don't rightly know, ma'am, but we should hope for the best and expect the worst. Pa said that was the way to figure."

When the saddles were off, I climbed out on one of those big rock slabs to study the country.

You've got to see country in more than one light to get the lay of it. Shadows tell a lot, and the clear air of early morning or late evening will show up things that are sun-blurred by day. A man scouting country had best size it up of an evening, for shadows will tell him where low ground is, and he can spot the likely passes if only to avoid them.

Pa, who trapped with Bridger and Carson, never lost a chance of teaching us boys how to judge terrain, and the best time was at sundown or sunup with the shadows falling toward you.

When I finished my study, I came down off the rock and cleared a spot of needles and leaves under one of those cedars that sort of arched out toward us. My fire was about the size you could hold in your two hands, for the smaller the fire, the less smoke, and such a fire will heat up just as well if a man wants to cook. And rising up through the branches thataway the smoke would be thinned out so much it could not be seen.

"I'm from Tennessee," I said to her, "and my name is Tell Sackett."

"Oh—I am Christine Mallory, and I was born in Delaware."

"Howdy, Mrs. Mallory. Mostly, the Delawares a man meets out here are Indians. Good trackers and good fighting men."

When I dug out what grub I had, I was ashamed it was so little. It was a mite Squires staked me to before I taken out. The coffee was mostly ground bean and chicory, and all else I had was jerked venison and cold flour.

When the coffee was ready I filled my cup and passed it to her. "Mrs. Mallory, this isn't what you have been used to, but it's all we've got."

She tasted it, and if she hadn't been a lady I think she would have spit, but she swallowed it, and then drank some more. "It's hot," she said, and smiled at me, and I grinned back at her. Truth to tell, that was about all a body could say for it.

"You'd better try some of this jerked venison," I said. "If you hold it in your mouth awhile before you begin to chew, it tastes mighty wholesome. All else I've got is cold flour."

"What?"

"Cold flour—it's a borrowed thing, from the Indians. Only what I have here is white-man style. It's parched corn ground up and mixed with a mite of sugar and cinnamon. You can mix it with water and drink it, and a man can go for miles on it. Mighty nourishing too. Pa was in Montana one time and traveled two weeks on a couple of dry quarts of it."

Last time I got up to scout the country around I caught the gleam of a far-off campfire.

STANDING THERE looking across country and watching the stars come out, I thought of that girl and wondered if I would ever have me a woman like that one, and it wasn't likely. We Sacketts are Welsh, and a proud people, but we never had much in the way of goods. Somehow the Lord's wealth never seemed to gather to us; all we ever had was ourselves and our strength and a will to walk the earth with honesty and pride.

But this girl was running away, and it didn't seem right. She was huddled to the fire, wrapped in one of my blankets when I came down to the fire. Gathering cedar boughs and grass, I made her a bed to one side, but close to the fire.

"The fire smells good," she said.

"That's cedar," I said, "and some creosote brush. Some folks don't like the smell of creosote. Those Spanish men call it **hediondilla,** which means little stinker. Some of the Indians use it for rheumatism."

Nobody said anything for a while, and then I said, "Creosote-brush fires flavor beans—the best ever. You try them sometime, and no beans ever taste the same after."

The fire crackled, and I added a few small, dry sticks and then said, "It ain't right, leaving him thisaway. He's likely worried to death."

She looked across the fire at me, all stiff and perky. "That is none of your business!"

"Mrs. Mallory, when you saddled yourself on

me, you made it my business. Girl who marries a soldier ought to think to live a soldier's life. Strikes me you've no nerve, ma'am, you cut and run because of dirt floors. I'd figure if a girl loved a man it wouldn't make her no mind. You're spoiled, ma'am. You surely are."

She got up, standing real stiff, coming the high and mighty on me. "If you do not want me here, I will go."

"No, you won't. First off, you haven't an idea where you are or which way to go to get there. You'd die of thirst, if that lion didn't get you."

"Lion?"

"Yes, ma'am." I wasn't exactly lying, because somewhere in Arizona there was sure to be a lion prowling. "There's snakes, too, and at night you can't see them until they get stepped on."

She stood there looking unsure of herself, and I kept on with what I had to say. "Woman needs a man out here—needs him bad. But a man needs a woman too. How do you think that man of yours feels now? His wife has shamed him before others, taking on like a girl-baby, running off."

She sat down by the fire, but she looked at me with a chilly expression. "I will thank you to take me to Hardyville. I did not mean to 'saddle' myself on you, as you put it. I will gladly pay you for your trouble."

"Ain't that much money."

"Don't say 'ain't'!" She snapped her eyes at me.

"Thank you, ma'am," I said, "but you better get you some shut-eye. We got to ride fifty miles tomorrow, and I can't be bothered with any tired female. You sit up on that horse tomorrow or I'll dump you in the desert."

"You wouldn't dare!"

"Yes, ma'am, I surely would. And leave you right there, and all your caterwauling wouldn't do you a mite of good. You get some sleep. Come daylight we're taking out of here faster than a scared owl."

Taking up my rifle I went out to scout the country, and setting up there on that rock slab I done my looking and listening. That fire was still aburning, away off yonder, like a star fallen out of the sky.

When I came back, she was lying on the bed I'd made, wrapped in a blanket, already asleep. Seen like that with the firelight on her face she looked like a little girl.

It was way shy of first light when I opened my eyes, and it'd taken me only a minute or two to throw the saddles on those broncs. Then I fixed that pack saddle for her to ride. My outfit was skimpy, so it wasn't much extra weight, carrying her.

When I had coffee going, I stirred her awake

with a touch on the shoulder, and her eyes flared open and she was like to scream when she saw me, not that I'd blame her. In my sock feet I stand six-three, and I run to shoulders and hands, with high cheekbones and a wedge face that sun had made dark as any Indian. With no shave and little sleep I must have looked a frightening thing.

"You better eat a little," I said. "You got five minutes."

We rode out of there with the stars still in the sky, and I was pleasant over seeing no fire over yonder where it had been the night before.

It was just shy of noon, with the sun hot in the sky, when we crossed a low saddle and started out across a plain dotted with Joshua trees—named by the Mormons who thought they looked like Joshua lifting his arms to Heaven.

WE CAME DOWN across that country, and there had been no dust in the sky all morning, but of a sudden four men rode up out of a draw, and it was the Coopers. Their description had been talked around enough.

"Howdy, Coopers! You hunting something?"

They looked at Christine Mallory and then at me. "We're looking for you," one said, "and that gold, but we'll take the lady, too, sort of a bonus-like."

Like I said, when you've quit running, you

can talk or you can fight, and times like this I run long on talk.

"You'll take nothing," I said. "You are talking to Tell Sackett—William Tell Sackett, to be exact, as my pa favored William Tell in his thinking. We Sacketts hail from the Cumberland Gap in Tennessee, and Pa always taught us never to give up nothing without a fight. Specially money or a woman.

"Now," I continued on before they could interrupt, "back to home, folks used to say I wasn't much for fiddling or singing, and my feet was too big for dancing, but along come fighting time, I'd be around.

"Couple of you boys are wearing brass buttons. I figure a forty-four slug would drive one of those buttons so deep into your belly a doc would have to get him a search warrant to find it."

My horse was stepping around kind of uneasy-like, and I was making a show of holding him in.

"Anyway," I said, "this here is General James Whitfield Mallory's wife, and if you so much as lay a hand to her, this territory wouldn't be big enough to hold you. He's the kind to turn out the whole frontier Army just to hunt you."

My horse gave a quick sidestep about then, and when he swung his left side to them, I used the moment to fetch out my gun, and when the roan stopped sidestepping, I had that big Colt looking at them.

Pa, he set me to practicing getting a gun out as soon as the end of my holster quit cutting a furrow in the ground when I walked. Pa said to me, "Son, you ever need that gun, you'll need it in your fist, not in no holster."

They were surprised when they saw that gun staring them down, and this George Cooper was mad clean through. "That ain't going to cut no ice," he said. "We want you, we'll take you."

"One thing about this country," I said, "a man's got a right to his opinion. Case like this here, if you're wrong, you don't get a chance to try it over. Any time you want to give it a try," I said, "you just unlimber and have at it."

Nobody had anything to say, none of those Coopers looking anything but mad right about then, so I kept on, figuring when we were talking we weren't fighting.

"I got me a bet, Coopers; I got me a bet says I can kill three of you before you clear leather—and that last man better make it a quick shot or I'll make it four."

"You talk a good fight," George Cooper said.

"You can call my hand. You got the right. One thing I promise, if I don't kill you dead with my first shots, I'll leave you lay for the buzzards and the sun."

Those Coopers didn't like it much, but my

roan was standing rock still now that I'd quit nudging him with my spur, and at that range a man wasn't likely to miss very often. And it's a fact that nobody wants to die very much.

"If she's Mallory's wife, what's she doing with you?"

"She was headed for Whipple," I said, "and she turned sick, and the doc said she should go back to Ehrenberg. They asked me to take her there. Served with the general during the war," I added. "He knows me well."

"I never heard of no General Mallory," George Cooper said.

"You never heard of **General James Whitfield Mallory**?" By now I believed in him my own self. "He was aide to General Grant! Same class at the Point with Phil Sheridan and Jeb Stuart. Fact is, they are talking of making him governor of the territory just to wipe out outlaws and such.

"Begging the lady's pardon, but he's noted for being a mighty mean man—strict. And smart? He's slicker than a black snake on a wet-clay sidehill. Last thing you want to do is get him riled.

"Lady here was telling me if he is made territorial governor he plans to recruit a special police force from among the Apache. He figures if those Apaches hate white men they might as well turn it to use tracking down outlaws—and he doesn't say anything about them bringing anybody back."

"That's not human!" George Cooper protested.

"That's the general for you. He's that kind." Now that trusty Colt had stayed right there in my fist, and so I said, "Now, we'll ride on."

Motioning her on ahead, I rode after her, but believe me, I sat sidewise in my saddle with that Colt ready for a quick shot. The last I could see they were still a-setting there, arguing.

Most talking I'd done since leaving Tennessee, and the most lying I'd done since who flung the chunk.

WE FETCHED UP to Hardyville about sundown on the second day, and the first person I saw when we rode up to the store was Bill Squires.

"Bill," I said, "the Coopers were a-hunting me. Only way they could have known I had that gold was if you told them. Somebody had to ride out to tell them, and somebody would want to be on hand to divvy up.

"Now," I said, "if you want to call me a liar, I'll take this lady inside and I'll come right back. But you hear this: They didn't get one speck of this gold, and neither are you."

"I panned my share of that gold!" He was looking mighty bleak.

"So you did, but yours wasn't enough; you had to try for all of it. A month or so back Jack Walker left camp and was dry-gulched. I plan to send your gold to his widow and family, and you can save your objections to that until I come out."

So I went inside with Christine Mallory, and there were two or three fresh Army officers right off the boat waiting to go to Fort Whipple.

"My husband is not a general," she said then, "and his name is Robert Mallory."

"I know that, Mrs. Mallory. Your husband is Second Lieutenant Robert Mallory, and he's greener than meadow grass. Month or so back he came out and ordered me to get my horse off the parade ground at Whipple. Mighty stiff-necked he was too.

"Ma'am, you haven't got you a man there, you've got a boy, but a boy sound in wind and limb; and two or three years on the frontier will give you a man you can be proud of. But if you run off now the chances are he will resign his commission and run after you, and you'll have a boy for a husband as long as you live.

"You stay with him, you hear? You ain't much account, either, but give you seasoning and you will be. Fact is, if you'd been a woman back there on that trail I might have been less of the gentleman, but you haven't grown up to a man yet."

She had the prettiest blue eyes you ever saw,

and she looked straight at me. She was mad, but she was honest, and behind those blue eyes she had a grain of sense.

"You may be right," she admitted, "although I'd rather slap your face than agree. After what I have been through these past few days, that dirt floor would look very good indeed."

"Ma'am, when my time comes to marry, I hope I find a woman as pretty as you—and with as much backbone."

Leaving her talking to those officers, I went to the counter with my gold and checked it in with Hardy in the names of those to whom it was credited, to Jim Hodge, Willy Mander, Tom Padgett—and to Mrs. Jack Walker, whose address I supplied.

"And I've got a hundred dollars coming," I said.

Hardy paid it to me, and I put it in my pocket. More money than I'd seen since the coon went up the tree.

Then I went outside like I'd promised, and Bill Squires surprised me. He was sure enough waiting.

He shot at me and missed. I shot at him and didn't.

# *The Defense of Sentinel*

When the morning came, Finn McGraw awakened into a silent world. His eyes opened to the wide and wondering sky where a solitary cloud wandered reluctantly across the endless blue.

At first he did not notice the silence. He had awakened, his mouth tasted like a rain-soaked cathide, he wanted a drink, and he needed a shave. This was not an unusual situation.

He heaved himself to a sitting position, yawned widely, scratching his ribs—and became aware of the silence.

No sound . . . no movement. No rattling of well buckets, no cackling of hens, no slamming of doors. Sentinel was a town of silence.

Slowly, his mind filling with wonder, Finn McGraw climbed to his feet. With fifty wasted years behind him, he had believed the world held no more surprises. But Sentinel was empty.

Sentinel, where for six months Finn McGraw had held the unenvied position of official town drunk. He had been the tramp, the vagabond, the useless, the dirty, dusty, unshaven, whiskey-sodden drunk. He slept in alleys. He slept in barns—wherever he happened to be when he passed out.

Finn McGraw was a man without a home. Without a job. Without a dime. And now he was a man without a town.

What can be more pitiful than a townless town drunk?

Carefully, McGraw got to his feet. The world tipped edgewise and he balanced delicately and managed to maintain his equilibrium. Negotiating the placing of his feet with extreme caution, he succeeded in crossing the wash and stumbling up the bank on the town side. Again, more apprehensively, he listened.

Silence.

No smoke rising from chimneys, no barking dogs, no horses. The street lay empty before him, like a street in a town of ghosts.

Finn McGraw paused and stared at the phenomenon. Had he, like Rip van Winkle, slept for twenty years?

Yet he hesitated, for well he knew the extreme lengths that Western men would go for a good practical joke. The thought came as a relief. That was it, of course, this was a joke. They had all gotten together to play a joke on him.

His footsteps echoed hollowly on the boardwalk. Tentatively, he tried the door of the saloon. It gave inward, and he pushed by the inner, batwing doors and looked around. The odor of stale whiskey mingled with cigar smoke lingered, lonesomely, in the air. Poker chips and cards were scattered on the table, but there was nobody. . . . Nobody at all!

The back bar was lined with bottles. His face brightened. Whiskey! Good whiskey, and his for the taking! At least, if they had deserted him they had left the whiskey behind.

Caution intervened. He walked to the back office and pushed open the door. It creaked on a rusty hinge and gave inward, to emptiness.

"Hey?" His voice found only an echo for company. "Where is everybody?"

No answer. He walked to the door and looked out upon the street. Suddenly the desire for human companionship blossomed into a vast yearning.

He rushed outside. He shouted. His voice rang emptily in the street against the false-fronted buildings. Wildly, he rushed from door to door. The blacksmith shop, the livery stable, the saddle shop, the bootmaker, the general store, the jail—all were empty, deserted.

He was alone.

ALONE! What had **happened**? Where **was** everybody? Saloons full of whiskey, stores filled with food, blankets, clothing. All these things had been left unguarded.

Half-frightened, Finn McGraw made his way to the restaurant. Everything there was as it had been left. A meal half-eaten on the table, dishes unwashed. But the stove was cold.

Aware suddenly of a need for strength that whiskey could not provide, Finn McGraw kindled a fire in the stove. From a huge ham he cut several thick slices. He went out back and rummaged through the nests and found a few scattered eggs. He carried these inside and prepared a meal.

With a good breakfast under his belt, he refilled his coffee cup and rummaged around until he found a box of cigars. He struck a match and lighted a good Havana, pocketing several more. Then he leaned back and began to consider the situation.

Despite the excellent meal and the cigar, he was uneasy. The heavy silence worried him, and he got up and went cautiously to the door. Suppose there was something here, something malign and evil? Suppose— Angrily, he pushed the door open. He was going to stop supposing. For the first time in his life he had a town full of everything, and he was going to make the most of it.

Sauntering carelessly down the empty street to the Elite General Store, he entered and coolly began examining the clothing. He found a hand-me-down gray suit and changed his clothes. He selected new boots and donned them as well as a white cambric shirt, a black string tie, and a new black hat. He pocketed a fine linen handkerchief. Next he lighted another cigar, spat into the brass spittoon, and looked upon life with favor.

On his right as he turned to leave the store was a long rack of rifles, shotguns, and pistols. Thoughtfully, he studied them. In his day—that was thirty years or so ago—he had been a sharpshooter in the Army.

He got down a Winchester '73, an excellent weapon, and loaded it with seventeen bullets. He appropriated a fine pair of Colts, loaded them, and belted them on, filling the loops with cartridges. Taking down a shotgun, he loaded both barrels with buckshot, then he sauntered down to the saloon, rummaged under the bar until he came up with Dennis Magoon's excellent Irish whiskey, and poured three fingers into a glass.

Admiring the brown, beautiful color, the somber amber, as he liked to call it, he studied the sunlight through the glass, then tasted it.

Ah! Now that was something like it! There was a taste of bog in that! He tossed off his drink, then refilled his glass.

The town was his—the whole town—full of whiskey, food, clothing—almost everything a man could want.

But **why**? Where **was** everybody?

Thoughtfully, he walked outside. The silence

held sway. A lonely dust devil danced on the prairie outside of town, and the sun was warm.

At the edge of town he looked out over the prairie toward the mountains. Nothing met his eye save a vast, unbelievable stretch of grassy plain. His eyes dropped to the dust and with a kind of shock he remembered that he could read sign. Here were the tracks of a half-dozen rigs, buckboards, wagons, and carts. From the horse tracks all were headed the same direction—east.

He scowled and, turning thoughtfully, he walked back to the livery barn.

Not a horse remained. Bits of harness were dropped on the ground—a spare saddle. Everything showed evidence of a sudden and hasty departure.

An hour later, having made the rounds, Finn McGraw returned to the saloon. He poured another glass of the Irish, lighted another Havana, but now he had a problem.

The people of the town had not vanished into thin air, they had made a sudden, frightened, panic-stricken rush to get away from the place.

That implied there was, in the town itself, some evil.

Finn McGraw tasted the whiskey and looked over his shoulder uncomfortably. He tiptoed to the door, looked one way, then suddenly the other way.

Nothing unusual met his gaze.

He tasted his whiskey again and then, crawling from the dusty and cobwebbed convolutions of his brain, long befuddled by alcohol, came realization.

INDIANS!

He remembered some talk the night before while he was trying to bum a drink. The Ladder Five ranch had been raided and the hands had been murdered. Victorio was on the warpath, burning, killing, maiming. **Apaches!**

The Fort was east of here! Some message must have come, some word, and the inhabitants had fled like sheep and left him behind.

Like a breath of icy air he realized that he was alone in the town, there was no means of escape, no place to hide. And the Apaches were coming!

Thrusting the bottle of Irish into his pocket, Finn McGraw made a break for the door. Outside, he rushed down to the Elite General Store. This building was of stone, low and squat, and built for defense, as it had been a trading post and stage station before the town grew up around it. Hastily, he took stock.

Moving flour barrels, he rolled them to the door to block it. Atop the barrels he placed sacks, bales, and boxes. He barred the heavy back door, then blocked the windows. In the center of the floor he built a circular parapet of more sacks and barrels for a last defense. He got down an armful of shotguns and proceeded to load ten of them. These he scattered around at various loopholes, with a stack of shells by each.

Then he loaded several rifles. Three Spencer .56's, a Sharps .50, and seven Winchester '73's.

He loaded a dozen of the Colts and opened boxes of ammunition. Then he lighted another Havana and settled down to wait.

The morning was well nigh gone. There was food enough in the store, and the position was a commanding one. The store was thrust out from the line of buildings in such a way that it commanded the approaches of the street in both directions, yet it was long enough so that he could command the rear of the buildings as well, by running to the back.

The more he studied his position the more he wondered why Sentinel inhabitants had left the town undefended. Only blind, unreasoning panic could have caused such a flight.

At noon he prepared himself a meal from what he found in the store, and waited. It was shortly after high sun when the Indians came.

The Apaches might have been scouting the place for hours; Finn had not seen them. Now they came cautiously down the street, creeping hesitantly along.

From a window that commanded the street,

old Finn McGraw waited. On the windowsill he had four shotguns, each with two barrels loaded with buckshot. And he waited. . . .

The Apaches, suspecting a trap, approached cautiously. They peered into empty buildings, flattened their faces against windows, then came on. The looting would follow later. Now the Indians were suspicious, anxious to know if the town was deserted. They crept forward.

Six of them bunched to talk some forty yards away. Beyond them a half dozen more Apaches were scattered in the next twenty yards. Sighting two of his shotguns, Finn McGraw rested a hand on each. The guns were carefully held in place by sacks weighting them down, and he was ready. He squeezed all four triggers at once!

The concussion was terrific! With a frightful roar, the four barrels blasted death into the little groups of Indians, and instantly, McGraw sprang to the next two guns, swung one of them slightly, and fired again.

Then he grabbed up a heavy Spencer and began firing as fast as he could aim, getting off four shots before the street was empty. Empty, but for the dead.

Five Apaches lay stretched in the street. Another, dragging himself with his hands, was attempting to escape.

McGraw lunged to his feet and raced to the back of the building. He caught a glimpse of an

Indian and snapped a quick shot. The Apache dropped, stumbled to his feet, then fell again and lay still.

That was the beginning. All through the long, hot afternoon the battle waged. Finn McGraw drank whiskey and swore. He loaded and reloaded his battery of guns. The air in the store was stifling. The heat increased, the store smells thickened, and over it all hung the acrid smell of gunpowder.

Apaches came to recover their dead and died beside them. Two naked warriors tried to cross the rooftops to his building, and he dropped them both. One lay on the blistering roof, the other rolled off and fell heavily.

Sweat trickled into McGraw's eyes, and his face became swollen from the kick of the guns. From the front of the store he could watch three ways, and a glance down the length of the store allowed him to see a very limited range outside. Occasionally he took a shot from the back window, hoping to keep them guessing.

NIGHT CAME at last, bringing a blessed coolness, and old Finn McGraw relaxed and put aside his guns.

Who can say that he knows the soul of the Indian? Who can say what dark superstitions churn inside his skull? For no Apache will fight at night, since he believes the souls of men killed in darkness must forever wander, homeless and alone. Was it fear that prevented an attack now? Or was it some fear of this strange, many-weaponed man—if man he was—who occupied the dark stone building?

And who can say with what strange expressions they stared at each other as they heard from their fires outside the town the weird thunder of the old piano in the saloon, and the old man's whiskey-bass rolling out the words of "The Wearing of the Green"; "Drill, Ye Tarriers, Drill"; "Come Where My Love Lies Dreaming," and "Shenandoah."

Day came and found Finn McGraw in the store, ready for battle. The old lust for battle that is the birthright of the Irish had risen within him. Never, from the moment he realized that he was alone in a town about to be raided by Apaches, had he given himself a chance for survival. Yet it was the way of the Irish to fight, and the way even of old, whiskey-soaked Finn.

An hour after dawn, a bullet struck him in the side. He spun half-around, fell against the flour barrels and slid to the floor. Blood flowed from the slash, and he caught up a handful of flour and slapped it against the wound. Promptly he fired a shot from the door, an aimless shot, to let them know he was still there. Then he bandaged his wound.

It was a flesh wound, and would have bled

badly but for the flour. Sweat trickled into his eyes, grime and powder smoke streaked his face. But he moved and moved again, and his shotguns and rifles stopped every attempt to approach the building. Even looting was at a minimum, for he controlled most of the entrances, and the Apaches soon found they must dispose of their enemy before they could profit from the town.

Sometime in the afternoon, a bullet knocked him out, cutting a furrow in his scalp, and it was nearing dusk when his eyes opened. His head throbbed with enormous pain, his mouth was dry. He rolled to a sitting position and took a long pull at the Irish, feeling for a shotgun. An Apache was even then fumbling at the door.

He steadied the gun against the corner of a box. His eyes blinked. He squeezed off both barrels and, hit in the belly, the Apache staggered back.

AT HIGH NOON on the fourth day, Major Magruder with a troop of cavalry, rode into the streets of Sentinel. Behind him were sixty men of the town, all armed with rifles.

At the edge of town, Major Magruder lifted a hand. Jake Carter and Dennis Magoon moved up beside him. "I thought you said the town was deserted?"

His extended finger indicated a dead Apache.

Their horses walked slowly forward. Another

Apache sprawled there dead . . . and then they found another.

Before the store four Apaches lay in a tight cluster, another savage was stretched at the side of the walk. Windows of the store were shattered and broken, a great hole had been blasted in the door. At the Major's order, the troops scattered to search the town. Magruder swung down before the store.

"I'd take an oath nobody was left behind," Carter said.

Magruder shoved open the store. The floor inside was littered with blackened cartridge cases and strewn with empty bottles. "No one man could fire that many shells or drink that much whiskey," Magruder said positively.

He stooped, looking at the floor and some flour on the floor. "Blood," he said.

In the saloon they found another empty bottle and an empty box of cigars.

Magoon stared dismally at the empty bottle. He had been keeping count, and all but three of the bottles of his best Irish glory were gone. "Whoever it was," he said sorrowfully, "drank up some of the best whiskey ever brewed."

Carter looked at the piano. Suddenly he grabbed Magoon's arm. "McGraw!" he yelled. " 'Twas Finn McGraw!"

They looked at each other. It couldn't be! And yet—who had seen him? Where was he now?

"Who," Magruder asked, "is McGraw?"

They explained, and the search continued. Bullets had clipped the corners of buildings, bullets had smashed water barrels along the street. Windows were broken, and there were nineteen dead Indians—but no sign of McGraw.

Then a soldier yelled from outside of town, and they went that way and gathered around. Under the edge of a mesquite bush, a shotgun beside him, his new suit torn and blood-stained, they found Finn McGraw.

Beside him lay two empty bottles of the Irish. Another, partly gone, lay near his hand. A rifle was propped in the forks of the bush, and a pistol had fallen from his holster. There was blood on his side and blood on his head and face.

"Dead!" Carter said. "But what a battle!"

Magruder bent over the old man, then he looked up, a faint twinkle breaking the gravity of his face. "Dead, all right," he said. "Dead **drunk**!"

AUTHOR'S NOTE

# The One for the Mohave Kid

> About a mile or so from camp lay Independence Rock, 120 feet high and over 2,000 feet long according to an estimate.* It is covered with the names of travellers. A few miles further along is Devil's Gate, where the Sweetwater passes through a cleft some 30 yards wide and 300 yards long. The rock walls tower several hundred feet, sheer rock. There was grass for our stock. We camped at a bend of the river just after sundown.
>
> From a diary, August 19, 1849

**Twelve years earlier a party of mountain men were camped here: "Immense numbers of buffalo in sight . . . here I am at a beautiful spring, a hot fire of buffalo dung, a set of good, sweet hump-ribs roasting . . . I have forgotten everything but my ribs and my sweetheart."**

*** Above dimensions not accurate, LL**

# *The One for the Mohave Kid*

We had finished our antelope steak and beans, and the coffeepot was back on the stove again, brewing strong, black cowpuncher coffee just like you'd make over a creosote and ironwood fire out on the range.

Red was cleaning his carbine and Doc Lander had tipped back in his chair with a pipe lighted. The stove was cherry red, the woodbox full, and our beds were warming up for the night. It was early autumn, but the nights were already cool. In a holster, hanging from the end of a bunk, was a worn-handled, single-action .44 pistol—and the holster had seen service as well as the gun.

"Whenever," Doc Lander said, "a bad man is born, there is also born a man to take him. For every Billy the Kid there is a Pat Garrett, an' for every Wes Hardin there's a John Selman."

Temple picked up a piece of pinewood and flicking open the stove door, he chucked it in. He followed it with another, and we all sat silent, watching the warm red glow of the flames.

When the door was shut again, Red looked up from his rifle. "An' for every John Selman there's a Scarborough," he said, "an' for every Scarborough, a Logan."

"Exactly," Doc Lander agreed, "an' for every Mohave Kid there's a . . ."

SOME MEN are born to evil, and such a one was the Mohave Kid. Now I'm not saying that environment doesn't have its influence, but some men are born with twisted minds, just as some are born with crooked teeth. The Mohave Kid was born with a streak of viciousness and cruelty that no kindness could eradicate. He had begun to show it when a child, and it developed fast until the Kid had killed his first man.

It was pure, unadulterated murder. No question of fair play, although the Kid was deadly with any kind of a gun. He shot an old Mexican, stole his outfit and three horses which he sold near the border. And the Mohave Kid was fifteen years old when that happened.

By the time he was twenty-two he was wanted in four states and three territories. He had, the records said, killed eleven men. Around the saloons and livery stables they said he had killed twenty-one. Actually, he had killed twenty-nine, for the Kid had killed a few when they didn't know he was in the country, and they had been listed as murders by Indians or travelers.

Of the twenty-nine men he had killed, nine of them had been killed with something like an even break.

But the Mohave Kid was as elusive as he was treacherous. And his mother had been a Holdstock. There were nine families of Holdstocks scattered through Texas, New Mexico, and Arizona, and three times that many who were kinfolk. They were a clannish lot, given to protecting their own, even as bad an apple as the Mohave Kid.

At twenty-two, the Kid was five feet seven inches tall and weighed one hundred and seventy pounds. He had a round, flat face, a bland expression, and heavy-lidded eyes. He did not look alert, but his expression belied the truth, for he was always wary, always keyed for trouble.

He killed for money, for horses, in quarrels, or for pure cruelty, and several of his killings were as senseless as they were ruthless. This very fact contributed much to the fear with which he was regarded, for there was no guessing where he might strike next. People avoided looking at him, avoided even the appearance of talking about him when he was around. Usually, they got out of a place when he came into it, but as unobtrusively as possible.

Aside from the United States marshals or the Texas Rangers in their respective bailiwicks, there was only local law. Little attention was given to arresting men for crimes committed elsewhere, which served as excuse for officers of the law who preferred to avoid the risks of trying to arrest the Mohave Kid.

Ab Kale was an exception. Ab was thirty-three when elected marshal of the cow town of Hinkley, and he owned a little spread of his own three miles out of town. He ran a few cows, raised a few horses, and made his living as marshal. For seven years he was a good one. He kept order, never made needless arrests, and was well liked around town. At thirty-four he married Amie Holdstock, a second cousin to the Mohave Kid.

As the Kid's reputation grew, Kale let it be known throughout the family that he would make no exception of the Kid, and the Kid was to stay away from Hinkley. Some of the clan agreed this was fair enough, and the Kid received word to avoid the town. Others took exception to Kale's refusal to abide by clan law where the Kid was concerned, but those few dwindled rapidly as the Kid's murderous propensities became obvious.

The Holdstock clan began to realize that in the case of the Mohave Kid they had sheltered a viper in their bosom, a wanton killer as dangerous to their well-being as to others. A few doors of the clan were closed against him, excuses were found for not giving him shelter, and the feeling began to permeate the clan that the idea was a good one.

The Mohave Kid had seemed to take no exception to the hints that he avoid making trouble for cousin Kale, yet as the months wore on, he became more sullen and morose, and the memory of Ab Kale preyed upon his mind.

IN THE MEANTIME, no man is marshal of a western cow town without having some trouble. Steady and considerate as Kale was, there had been those with whom he could not reason. He had killed three men.

All were killed in fair, stand-up gunfights, all were shot cleanly and surely, and it was talked around that Kale was some hand with a gun himself. In each case he had allowed an even break and proved faster than the men he killed. All of this the Mohave Kid absorbed, and here and there he heard speculation, never in front of him, that the Mohave Kid was avoiding Hinkley because he wanted no part of Ab Kale.

Tall, well built, and prematurely gray, Kale was a fine-appearing man. His home was small but comfortable, and he had two daughters, one his own child, one a stepdaughter of seventeen whom he loved as his own. He had no son, and this was a matter of regret.

Ab Kale was forty when he had his showdown with the Mohave Kid. But on the day when

Riley McClean dropped off a freight train on the edge of Hinkley, the date of that showdown was still two years away.

If McClean ever told Kale what had happened to him before he crawled out of that empty box-car in Hinkley, Ab never repeated it. Riley was nineteen, six feet tall, and lean as a rail. His clothes were in bad shape, and he was unshaven and badly used up, and somebody had given him a beating. What had happened to the other fellow or fellows, nobody ever knew.

Ab Kale saw McClean leave the train and called out to him. The boy stopped and stood waiting. As Kale walked toward him he saw the lines of hunger in the boy's face, saw the emaciated body, the ragged clothes, the bruises and cuts. He saw a boy who had been roughly used, but there was still courage in his eyes.

"Where you headed for, son?"

Riley McClean shrugged. "This is as good a place as any. I'm hunting a job."

"What do you do?"

"Most anything. It don't make no difference."

Now when a man says that he can do most anything, it is a safe bet he can do nothing, or at least, that he can do nothing well. If a man has a trade, he is proud of it and says so, and usually he will do a passing job of anything else he tackles. Yet Kale reserved his opinion. And it was well that he did.

"Better come over to my office," Kale said. "You'll need to get shaved and washed up."

McClean went along, and somehow, he stayed. Nothing was ever said about leaving by either of them. McClean cleaned up, ate at the marshal's expense, and then slept the clock around. When Kale returned to the office and jail the next morning he found the place swept, mopped, and dusted, and McClean was sitting on the cot in the open cell where he slept, repairing a broken riata.

Obviously new to the West, Riley McClean seemed new to nothing else. He had slim, graceful hands and deft fingers. He cobbled shoes, repaired harnesses, built a chimney for Chalfant's new house, and generally kept busy.

After he had been two weeks in Hinkley, Ab Kale was sitting at his desk one day when Riley McClean entered. Kale opened a drawer and took out a pair of beautifully matched .44 Russians, one of the finest guns Smith & Wesson ever made. They were thrust in new holsters on a new belt studded with cartridges. "If you're going to live out here, you'd better learn to use those," Kale said briefly.

After that the two rode out of town every morning for weeks, and in a narrow canyon on the back of Kale's little ranch, Riley McClean learned how to use a six-shooter.

"Just stand naturally," Kale advised him, "and

let your hand swing naturally to the gun butt. You've probably heard about a so-called gunman's crouch. There is no such thing among gunfighters who know their business. Stand any way that is easy to you. Crouching may make a smaller target of you, but it also puts a man off balance and cramps his movements. Balance is as important to a gunfighter as to a boxer. Stand easy on your feet, let your hand swing back naturally, and take the hammer spur with the inside of the thumb, cocking the gun as it is grasped, the tip of the trigger finger on the trigger."

Kale watched McClean try it. "The most important thing is a good grip. The finger on the trigger helps to align your gun properly, and after you've practiced, you'll see that your gun will line up perfectly with that grip."

He watched McClean keenly and was pleased. The boy had the same ease with a gun he seemed to have with all tools, and his coordination was natural and easy. "You'll find," he added, "in shooting from the hip that you can change your point of aim by a slight movement of your left foot. Practice until you find just the right position for your feet, and then go through the motions until it is second nature."

Finally, he left him alone to practice, tossing him a box of shells occasionally. But no day passed that Riley McClean did not take to the hills for practice.

There are men who are born to skill, whose coordination of hand, foot, and eye is natural and easy, who acquire skills almost as soon as they lift a tool or a weapon, and such a man was Riley McClean. Yet he knew the value of persistence, and he practiced consistently.

It was natural that he knew about the Mohave Kid.

Riley McClean listened and learned. He talked it around and made friends, and he soon began to hear the speculations about the Kid and Ab Kale.

"It'll come," they all said. "It can't miss. Sooner or later him an' Kale will tangle."

As to what would happen then, there was much dispute. Of this talk Kale said nothing. When Riley McClean had been two months in Hinkley, Kale invited him home to dinner for the first time. It was an occasion to be remembered.

The two months had made a change in Riley. The marks of his beating had soon left him, but it had taken these weeks to fill out his frame. He had gained fifteen solid pounds and would gain more, but he was a rugged young man, bronzed and straight, when he walked up the gravel path to the door of the Kale home. And Ruth Kale opened the door for him. She opened the door and she fell in love. And the feeling was mutual.

Ab Kale said nothing, but he smiled behind his white mustache. Later, when they had walked back up to town, Kale said, "Riley, you've been like a son to me. If anything should happen to me, I wish you would see that my family gets along all right."

Riley was startled and worried. "Nothing will happen to you," he protested. "You're a young man yet."

"No," Kale replied seriously, "I'm not. I'm an old man as a cow-town peace officer. I've lasted a long time. Longer than most."

"But you're chain lightning with a gun!" Riley protested.

"I'm fast." Kale said it simply. "And I shoot straight. I know of no man I'd be afraid to meet face to face, although I know some who are faster than I. But they don't always meet you face to face."

And Riley McClean knew that Ab Kale was thinking of the Mohave Kid.

HE REALIZED THEN, for the first time, that the marshal was worried about the Mohave Kid. Worried because he knew the kind of killer the Kid was. Deadly enough face to face, the Kid would be just as likely to shoot from ambush. For the Kid was a killing machine, utterly devoid of moral sense or fair play.

The people of Hinkley knew that Riley McClean had taken to carrying a gun. They looked upon this tolerantly, believing that Riley was merely copying his adopted father. They knew that Kale had been teaching him to shoot, but they had no idea what had happened during those lessons. Nor had Ab Kale realized it until a few days before the payoff.

The two were riding out to look over some cattle, and Kale remarked that it would be nice to have some rabbit stew. "If we see a fat cottontail," he said, "we'll kill it."

A mile farther along, he spotted one. "Rabbit!" he said, and grabbed for his gun.

His hand slapped the walnut butt, and then there was an explosion, and for an instant he thought his own gun had gone off accidentally. And then he saw the smoking .44 in Riley McClean's hand, and the younger man was riding over to pick up the rabbit. The distance had been thirty yards and the rabbit had lost a head.

Ab Kale was startled. He said nothing, however, and they rode on to the ranch, looked over the cattle, and made a deal to buy them. As they started back, Kale commented, "That was a nice shot, Riley. Could you do it again?"

"Yes, sir, I think so."

A few miles farther, another rabbit sprang up. The .44 barked and the rabbit died, half his head and one ear blasted away. The distance was a shade greater than before.

"You've nothing to worry about, Riley," he said quietly, "but never use that gun unless you must, and never draw it unless you mean to kill."

NOTHING MORE was said, but Ab Kale remembered. He was fast. He knew he was fast. He knew that he rated along with the best, and yet his hand had barely slapped the butt before that rabbit died. . . .

The days went by slowly, and Riley McClean spent more and more time at the Kale home. And around town he made friends. He was quiet, friendly, and had a healthy sense of humor. He had progressed from the town handyman to opening a shop as a gunsmith, learning his trade by applying it that way. There was no other gunsmith within two hundred miles in any direction, so business was good.

He was working on the firing pin of a Walker Colt when he heard the door open. He did not look up, just said, "Be with you in a minute. What's your trouble?"

"Same thing you're workin' on I reckon. Busted firin' pin."

Riley McClean looked up into a dark, flat face and flat, black eyes. He thought he had never seen eyes so devoid of expression, never seen a face more brutal on a young man. With a shock of realization he knew he was looking into the eyes of the Mohave Kid.

He got to his feet and picked up the gun the Kid handed him. As he picked it up, he noticed that the Kid had his hand on his other gun. Riley merely glanced at him and then examined the weapon. The repair job was simple, but as he turned the gun in his hand, he thought of how many men it had killed.

"Take a while," he said. "I s'pose you're in a hurry for it?"

"You guessed it. An' be sure it's done right. I'll want to try it before I pay for it."

Riley McClean's eyes chilled a little. There were butterflies in his stomach, but the hackles on the back of his neck were rising. "You'll pay me before you get it," he said quietly. "My work is cash on the barrelhead. The job will be done right." His eyes met the flat black ones. "If you don't like the job, you can bring it back."

For an instant, their eyes held, and then the Kid shrugged, smiling a little. "Fair enough. An' if it doesn't work, I'll be back."

The Mohave Kid turned and walked out to the street, stopping to look both ways. Riley McClean held the gun in his hands and watched him. He felt cold, chilled.

Ab Kale had told the Kid to stay away from Hinkley, and now he must meet him and order him from town. He must do that, or the Kid would know he was afraid, would deliberately stay in town. The very fact that the Mohave Kid had come to Hinkley was proof that he had come hunting trouble, that he had come to call Kale's bluff.

For a minute or two, Riley considered warning the marshal, but that would not help. Kale would hear of it soon enough, and there was always a chance that the Kid would get his gun, change his mind, and leave before Kale did know.

Sitting down, Riley went to work on the gun. The notion of doctoring the gun so it would not fire properly crossed his mind, but there was no use inviting trouble. Running his fingers through his dark rusty hair, he went to work. And as he worked, an idea came to him.

Maybe he could get the Kid out of town to try the gun, and once there, warn him away from Hinkley himself. That would mean a fight, and while he had no idea of being as good as the Kid, he did know he could shoot straight. He might kill the Mohave Kid even if he got killed in the process.

But he did not want to die. He was no hero, Riley McClean told himself. He wanted to live, buy a place of his own, and marry Ruth. In fact, they had talked about it. And there was a chance this would all blow over. The Kid might leave town before Ab Kale heard of his arrival, or something might happen. It is human to hope and human to wish for the unexpected good break—and sometimes you are lucky.

As Riley was finishing work on the gun, Ruth came in. She was frightened. "Riley"—she caught his arm—"the Mohave Kid's in town and Dad is looking for him."

"I know." He stared anxiously out the window. "The Kid left his gun to be repaired. I've just finished it."

"Oh, Riley! Isn't there something we can do?" Her face was white and strained, her eyes large.

He looked down at her, a wave of tenderness sweeping over him. "I don't know, honey," he said gently. "I'm afraid the thing I might do, your father wouldn't like. You see, this is his job. If he doesn't meet the Kid and order him to leave, he will never have the same prestige here again. Everybody knows the Kid came here on purpose."

AB KALE HAD HEARD that the Mohave Kid was in town, and in his own mind he was ready. Seated at his desk he saw with bitter clarity what he had known all along, that sooner or later the Kid would come to town, and then he would have to kill him or leave the country. There could be no other choice where the Kid was concerned.

Yet he had planned well. Riley McClean was a good man, a steady man. He would make a good husband for Ruth, and together they would see that Amie lacked for nothing. As far as that went, Amie was well provided for. He checked his guns and got to his feet. As he did so, he saw a rider go by, racing out of town.

He stopped dead still in the doorway. Why, that rider had been Riley McClean! Where would he be going at that speed, at this hour? Or had he heard the Kid was in town . . . ? Oh, no! The boy wasn't a coward. Ab knew he wasn't a coward.

He straightened his hat and touched his prematurely white mustache. His eyes studied the street. A few loafers in front of the livery stable, a couple more at the general store, a half-dozen horses at the hitch rails. One buckboard. He stepped out on the walk and started slowly up the street. The Mohave Kid would be in the Trail Driver's Saloon.

He walked slowly, with his usual measured step. One of the loafers in front of the store got to his feet and ducked into the saloon. All right, then. The Kid knew he was coming. If he came out in the street to meet him, so much the better.

Ruth came suddenly from Riley's shop and started toward him. He frowned and glanced at her. No sign of the Kid yet. He must get her off the street at once.

"Hello, Dad!" Her face was strained, but she smiled brightly. "What's the hurry?"

"Don't stop me now, Ruth," he said. "I've got business up the street."

"Nothing that won't wait!" she protested. "Come in the store. I want to ask you about something."

"Not now, Ruth." There was still no sign of the Kid. "Not now."

"Oh, come on! If you don't," she warned, "I'll walk right up to the saloon with you."

He looked down at her, sudden panic within him. Although she was not his own daughter, he had always felt that she was. "No!" he said sharply. "You mustn't!"

"Then come with me!" she insisted, grabbing his arm.

Still no sign of the Kid. Well, it would do no harm to wait, and he could at least get Ruth out of harm's way. He turned aside and went into the store with her. She had a new bridle she wanted him to see, and she wanted to know if he thought the bit was right for her mare. Deliberately, she stalled. Once he looked up, thinking he heard riders. Then he replied to her questions. Finally, he got away.

He stepped out into the sunlight, smelling dust in the air. Then he walked slowly across and up the street. As he reached the center of the street, the Mohave Kid came out of the Trail Driver and stepped off the walk, facing him.

Thirty yards separated them. Ab Kale waited, his keen blue eyes steady and cold. He must make this definite, and if the Kid made the slightest move toward a gun, he must kill him. The sun was very warm.

"Kid," he said, "your business in town is finished. We don't want you here. Because of the family connection, I let you know that you weren't welcome. I wanted to avoid a showdown. Now I see you won't accept that, so I'm giving you exactly one hour to leave town. If you are here after that hour, or if you ever come again, I'll kill you!"

The Mohave Kid started to speak, and then he stopped, frozen by a sudden movement.

From behind stores, from doorways, from alleys, stepped a dozen men. All held shotguns or rifles, all directed at the Kid. He stared at them in shocked disbelief. Johnny Holdstock . . . Alec and Dave Holdstock . . . Jim Gray, their cousin . . . Webb Dixon, a brother-in-law . . . and Myron Holdstock, the old bull of the herd.

Ab Kale was petrified. Then he remembered Riley on that racing horse and that today was old Myron's fortieth wedding anniversary, with half the family at the party.

The Mohave Kid stared at them, his face turning gray and then dark with sullen fury.

"You do like the marshal says, Kid." Old

Myron Holdstock's voice rang in the streets. "We've protected ye because you're one of our'n. But you don't start trouble with another of our'n. You git on your hoss an' git. Don't you ever show hide nor hair around here again."

The Mohave Kid's face was a mask of fury. He turned deliberately and walked to his horse. No man could face all those guns, and being of Holdstock blood, he knew what would come if he tried to face them down. They would kill him.

He swung into the saddle, cast one black, bleak look at Ab Kale, and then rode out of town.

Slowly, Kale turned to Holdstock, who had been standing in the door of his shop. "You needn't have done that," he said, "but I'm glad you did. . . ."

THREE DAYS WENT by slowly, and then the rains broke. It began to pour shortly before daybreak and continued to pour. The washes were running bank full by noon, and the street was deserted. Kale left his office early and stepped outside, buttoning his slicker. The street was running with water, and a stream of rain was cutting a ditch under the corner of the office. Getting a shovel from the stable, he began to divert the water.

Up the street at the gun shop, Riley McClean

got to his feet and took off the leather apron in which he worked. He was turning toward the door when it darkened suddenly and he looked up to see the bleak, rain-wet face of the Mohave Kid.

The Kid stared at him. "I've come for my gun," he said.

"That'll be two dollars," Riley said coolly.

"That's a lot, ain't it?"

"It's my price to you."

The Kid's flat eyes stared at him, and his shoulder seemed to hunch. Then from the tail of his eye he caught the movement of the marshal as he started to work with the shovel. Quickly, he forked out two dollars and slapped it on the counter. Then he fed five shells into the gun and stepped to the door. He took two quick steps and vanished.

Surprised, Riley started around the counter after him. But as he reached the end of the counter, he heard the Kid yell, **"Ab!"**

Kale, his slicker buttoned over his gun, looked around at the call. Frozen with surprise, he saw the Mohave Kid standing there, gun in hand. The Kid's flat face was grinning with grim triumph. And then the Kid's gun roared, and Ab Kale took a step backward and fell, face down in the mud.

The Mohave Kid laughed, suddenly, sardonically. He dropped his gun into his holster and started for the horse tied across the street.

He had taken but one step when Riley McClean spoke: **"All right, Kid, here it is!"**

The Mohave Kid whirled sharply to see the gunsmith standing in the doorway. The rain whipping against him, Riley McClean looked at the Kid. "Ab was my friend," he said. "I'm going to marry Ruth."

The Kid reached then, and in one awful, endless moment of realization, he knew what Ab Kale had known for these several months, that Riley McClean was a man born to the gun. Even as the Kid's hand slapped leather, he saw Riley's weapon clearing and coming level. The gun steadied, and for that endless instant the Kid stared into the black muzzle. Then his own iron was clear and swinging up, and Riley's gun was stabbing flame.

The bullets, three of them fired rapidly, smashed the Mohave Kid in and around the heart. He took a step back, his own gun roaring and the bullet plowing mud, and then he went to his knees as Riley walked toward him, his gun poised for another shot. As the Kid died, his brain flared with realization, with knowledge of death, and he fell forward, sprawling on his face in the street. A rivulet, diverted by his body, curved around him, ran briefly red, and then trailed on.

People were gathering, but Riley McClean walked to Ab Kale. As he reached him, the older man stirred slightly.

Dropping to his knees, Riley turned him over. The marshal's eyes flickered open. There was a cut from the hairline on the side of his head in front that ran all along his scalp. The shattered end of the shovel handle told the story. Striking the shovel handle, which had been in front of his heart at the moment of impact, the bullet had glanced upward, knocking him out and ripping a furrow in his scalp.

Ab Kale got slowly to his feet and stared up the muddy street where the crowd clustered about the Mohave Kid.

"You killed him?"

"Had to. I thought he'd killed you."

Ab nodded. "You've got a fast hand. I've known it for months. I hope you'll never have to kill another man."

"I won't," Riley said quietly. "I'm not even going to carry a gun after this."

Ab Kale glanced back up the street. "So he's dead at last. I've carried that burden a long time." He looked up, his face still white with shock. "They'll bury him. Let's go home, son. The women will be worried."

And the two men walked down the street side by side, Ab Kale and his son. . . .

# *A Mule for Santa Fe*

Sell the mules," Hassoldt advised, "you want oxen. Less water for 'em an' their feet flatten out on the prairie country where a mule's dig in. If you get hard up for grub you can always eat an ox."

"If I get that hungry," Scott Miles replied shortly, "I can eat a mule."

Hassoldt was an abrupt man. He turned away now, his irritation plain. "Suit yourself, Miles. But you'll need another mule and I haven't any for sale."

Bitterly, Scott Miles turned away and went out the door. Rain lashed at his face, for outside the building there was neither awning nor board-walk. Head bowed into the rain, he slopped along toward the Carter house where young Bill was waiting.

Hassoldt wanted those mules badly, and no wonder. There would be a big demand for them in a few months, and nobody had mules like those of Scott Miles. They were well-bred and well-fed, strapping big mules with plenty of power. If he could get them west there would be money in them.

Everywhere he went they advised against the mules. On roads they were fine. On rocks they were all right. But out on the prairie?

Pembroke advised against them, too. However, after much argument he had agreed to accept the wagon in his company if Miles had a full team of six mules. Four, Pembroke insisted, were not enough. Not even, he added, if the mules were big as those of Miles's team.

There were half a dozen people in the hotel when he stepped in. Pembroke was there, a big, fine-looking man with a tawny mustache. He was talking to Bidwell, a substantial farmer from Ohio who had been the first to sign for Pembroke's fast wagon train.

Miles looked around and found Billy. He was talking to a pretty woman with dark red hair who sat in a big, leather-bound chair.

Bill saw him at once. "Pa," he said excitedly, "this is Mrs. Hance."

She looked up and he was immediately uneasy. She had blue eyes, not dark eyes like Mary's had been, and there was a friendliness in them that disturbed him. "Bill's been telling me about you, Mr. Miles. Have you found a mule?"

Glad to be on familiar ground, he shook his head. "Hassoldt won't sell. I'm afraid I'm out of luck." He was absurdly conscious of his battered hat, its brim limp with rain, and his unshaven jaws. He wanted to get away from her. Women like this both irritated and disturbed him. She was too neat, too perfectly at ease. He knew what such women were like on the trail, finicky and frightened of bugs and fussing over trifles. Also, and he was frank to admit it to himself, he was a little jealous of Bill's excited interest.

"We'd better go, Bill. Say good-bye to Mrs. Hance."

HE WALKED OUT, red around the ears and conscious that somehow Bill felt he had failed him. It was not necessary for him to have been so abrupt. Just because he looked like a big backwoods farmer was no reason he should act like one.

They lived in the wagon. It was a big new Conestoga, and his tools were all new. He had his plowshare, he'd make the plow when he got there, and he had two rifles and plenty of ammunition. Bill was nine, but already he could shoot, and Scott Miles wanted his son to grow up familiar with weapons. He wanted him to be a good hunter, to use guns with intelligence.

A boy needed two parents, and being an observant man Scott had not failed to notice the wistfulness in Bill's eyes when other children, hurt or imagining a hurt, ran to mother. Bill would never do that with him, he was too proud of being a little man in front of his father. But it wasn't right for the boy.

Farmer Bidwell had a daughter, a pretty, flush-faced girl with corn-silk hair. She had been casting sidelong glances at him ever since their wagon rolled alongside. Tentatively, Scott Miles touched his chin. He had better shave.

He did, and he also trimmed down his mustache. He wore it Spanish style and not like the brush mustaches of Bidwell or so many of the company. He got into a clean shirt then. Bill eyed him critically. "Gettin' all duded up," he said. "You goin' back to see Mrs. Hance?"

"No!" He spoke sharply. "I may go to see Grace Bidwell, later."

"Her?" Bill's contempt was obvious. So obvious that Scott looked at the boy quickly. "She isn't as pretty as Mrs. Hance."

Scott Miles sat down. "Look, Bill," he said, "we're going into a mighty rough country, like I've told you. We won't be in a city. We'll be in the mountains where I'll have to fell trees and trim them for a cabin.

"Now I need a wife, and you need a mother. But just being pretty isn't enough. I've got to have a wife who can cook, who can make her own clothes, if need be. A wife who can take the rough going right with me. I need somebody who can help, not hinder."

Bill nodded, but he remained only half convinced. Scott Miles was shouldering into his coat when Bill spoke again. "Pa"—he was frowning a little—"if we get a new mother, shouldn't it be somebody we like, too?"

Scott Miles stared into the rain, his face grim. Then he dropped his hand to Bill's shoulder. "Yes, son," he said quietly, "it would have to be somebody we like . . . too."

THE RAIN STOPPED, but the sun did not come out. Slopping through the mud, Miles made inquiries about mules. Yes, there was an old hardcase downriver who owned a big black mule. The man's name was Simon Gilbride. Sell him? Not a chance! He wouldn't even talk about it. Nevertheless, Scott Miles saddled his bay mare and rode south. As he started out of town he saw Mrs. Hance on the hotel steps. She waved, and he waved back.

He saw something else, too. Something that filled him with grave disquiet. Hassoldt was standing on the steps talking to three rough-looking men from the river. All wore guns. They turned and looked at him as he passed, and Scott had the uncomfortable feeling they had been talking about him.

Gilbride came to the door when Scott arrived. He was a tall, old man with a cold patrician face and the clothes of a farmer. "Sell my mule? Of course not!" And that was final.

It was dusk before Scott returned to the wagon. He was tired and he sagged in the saddle. It was not so much physical weariness, for he was a big man and unusually strong, but the weariness of defeat. Only a few hours remained and there was only one mule in the country the size of his. Of course, wagons were arriving all the time. If he could keep circulating . . .

He pulled up. There was a fire going and Bill was squatted beside it. He was laughing and eating at the same time, and the girl who was cooking was laughing also. "Good!" he muttered. "Grace has finally got to him. Now things will be easier all around."

Only when she straightened from the fire it was not Grace. It was Mrs. Hance.

She smiled, a little frightened. "Oh! I didn't expect you back so soon. I—I was worried about Bill going without his supper."

The food was good. Had a flavor he didn't know, but mighty good. And Bill was eating as if he hadn't eaten in years. Of course, Bill could digest anything.

"Mr. Miles," she spoke suddenly as if nerved for the effort. "I have a favor to ask. I want to ride in your wagon to Santa Fe."

He blinked. Of all things, this was the least expected. Bill had looked up and Scott could almost feel him listening.

He shook his head. "I am sorry, Mrs. Hance. The answer is no. It is quite impossible."

HE WALKED to the door of the hotel with her, then back to the wagon. Suddenly he decided to check the mules and, nearing them, he was almost positive he saw a shadow move in the darkness near where they were picketed. He waited, his gun ready, but there was no further movement, no sound.

He waited for a long time in silence, seriously worried. Hassoldt wanted mules badly, with a big contract to fill for the government, and he did not impress Miles as a very scrupulous man. In such a place as this there would be thieves, and Hassoldt impressed him as a man likely to stop at nothing to obtain something he wanted.

When he reached the hotel next morning there was no sign of Mrs. Hance. He hesitated, faintly disappointed at not seeing her. Pembroke and Bidwell were together. "Well, Miles." Pembroke was abrupt. "Have you found a mule? I'm sorry, of course, but if you haven't one tomorrow we'll have to make other arrangements."

Wearily Miles walked back to camp, leading the mare. He was walking up to the wagon when the mare whinnied. He looked up. Tied to a wagon wheel was a magnificent sorrel stallion. At least sixteen hands high, it had a white face and three white stockings. After tying the mare, Scott Miles walked admiringly around the stallion. It was one of the finest animals he had ever seen.

Mrs. Hance came out of the trees with Bill. They hung back a little, then walked toward him.

"This," he inquired, "is your horse?"

"You like him?"

"Like him? He's splendid! All my life I've wanted to own just such a horse. Of course," he added quickly, "I could never afford it."

"With your mare it might be very profitable," she assured him quietly. Then she lifted her chin. "Mr. Miles, what would you do for another mule?"

He laughed grimly. "Anything short of murder," he said, "if I got him before tomorrow."

"Even to sharing your wagon with a widow?"

He chuckled. "Even that!"

"Then prepare to have a passenger. I've got a mule!"

He shook his head. "That's impossible. There isn't a mule within miles and miles of here. I've looked."

"I have a mule," she said, "as big as yours. He was sold to me by Simon Gilbride."

Scott Miles sat down, and she explained very quietly. Determined to go to Santa Fe, she had decided the only thing to do was to personally see the old man.

Gilbride, it turned out, had been in her father's

command in Mexico. That, a little pleading, and a little flattery had done the trick. "So," she said, "I have a mule. I have the only mule. So if you go you take me. What do we do?"

Scott Miles got to his feet and bowed politely. "Mrs. Hance, will you do me the honor of allowing me to escort you to Santa Fe?"

She curtsied gravely, then her eyes filled with mischief. "Mr. Miles," she replied formally, "I was hoping you'd ask!"

Pembroke was in the hotel, seated with Bidwell and several others, shaping last details of the trip.

"Count me in." Scott could scarcely keep the triumph from his tone. "I've got my mule!"

As he explained he saw Bidwell's face stiffen. Pembroke frowned slightly, then shook his head. "It won't do, Miles," he said. "The women would never stand for it. We can't have an unmarried couple sharing a wagon. It just won't do."

"Look," he protested, "I—" Argument was fruitless. The answer was a flat no. Disgusted, angry, and desperate, he started back toward the wagon. He was nearing it when he heard a shot, then another. Running, he whipped his pistol from his waistband and broke through the trees to the wagon.

MRS. HANCE STOOD behind the wagon with a smoking rifle. Her face was white. "They got away," she said bitterly, "they've stolen our mules!" She continued icily, "Have you decided to just stand there or are you going to take Admiral and go after them?"

"Admiral?" He was astonished. "They didn't get him? You mean he was tied here?"

"Behind the wagon," she said shortly. "Now take him and get started!"

"He might be killed," he warned

Her lips tightened. "Take him! We're in this together!"

It was morning when he realized he was closing in. Admiral was not merely a beautiful horse, but one with speed and bottom. And one of the men was wounded. He had come upon the place where they bathed and dressed his wound at daylight. He had found fragments of a bloody shirt and fresh boot-tracks.

Two hours later he stopped on the edge of a grove and saw them disappearing into a cluster of piñons a half mile away. They had the mules roped together and they were moving more slowly. The wounded man was riding his mare.

He had no illusions about fair play. They would kill on sight. If he survived he must do the same. Studying the terrain, he saw a long draw off on the right that cut into the plain to the south. If he could get into that draw and beat them to the plain . . .

Admiral went down the bank as if mountain-bred and on the bottom he stepped out into a run. Despite the long night of riding, the big horse had plenty left. He ran and ran powerfully, ran with eagerness.

At the draw's opening, Scott Miles swung down. Grimly, he checked the heavy pistol he carried. Thrusting it into his waistband, he walked along through the scattered greasewood and piñon until he was near the entrance of the larger draw down which they were coming.

The mules came out of the draw with the men behind them. Scott Miles drew his pistol and stepped from the piñons, but as his foot came down a rock rolled and he lost balance. He fell backward, seeing the riders grabbing for their guns. He caught himself on his left hand and fired even as a bullet whisked by his face.

HE ROLLED to one knee and fired again. The second shot did not miss. One man lurched in his saddle and there was blood down the back of his head, and then he fell into the dust, his horse stampeding.

The wounded man had disappeared, but the third man leaped his horse at Scott. There was an instant when Scott saw the flaring nostrils of the horse, saw the man lean wide and point the gun straight at his face. And then Scott fired.

The man's body jolted, seeming to lift from the saddle, and was slammed back as the horse leaped over Miles, one hoof missing him by a hair. The rider hit the sand and rolled over. Taking no chances, Miles fired again.

One man left. Sitting on the sand, half-concealed by brush, Miles reloaded the empty chambers. Then he started through the brush, moving carefully.

The wounded man sat on the ground, holding his one good arm aloft. "Don't shoot!" he begged. "I tossed my gun away."

Scott gathered the guns, then the mules and the horses. He left one horse for the wounded man. "You do what you like, but don't cross my trail again. Not ever."

THE MULES MADE a nice picture ahead of the big Conestoga wagon, and on the seat Scott Miles sat beside his wife. She was not only a very pretty woman, this Laura Hance Miles, but, as he had discovered, a useful one.

He was, he admitted, very much in love, a richer and more exciting love than he had ever experienced. There would always be a place in his heart for Mary, but this woman was one to walk beside a man, not behind him. She had shown it since the first day they were two together, a team, working toward a common end. It was what he had wanted.

There had been a time, he remembered, when he had believed a man could never get close to a woman like this. But that had been a long time ago.

And Bill had been right. It was necessary to like somebody, too.

# *War Party*

We buried Pa on a sidehill out west of camp, buried him high up so his ghost could look down the trail he'd planned to travel.

We piled the grave high with rocks because of the coyotes, and we dug the grave deep, and some of it I dug myself, and Mr. Sampson helped, and some others.

Folks in the wagon train figured Ma would turn back, but they hadn't known Ma so long as I had. Once she set her mind to something she wasn't about to quit.

She was a young woman and pretty, but there was strength in her. She was a lone woman with two children, but she was of no mind to turn back. She'd come through the Little Crow massacre in Minnesota and she knew what trouble was. Yet it was like her that she put it up to me.

"Bud," she said, when we were alone, "we can turn back, but we've nobody there who cares about us, and it's of you and Jeanie that I'm thinking. If we go west you will have to be the man of the house, and you'll have to work hard to make up for Pa."

"We'll go west," I said. A boy those days took it for granted that he had work to do, and the men couldn't do it all. No boy ever thought of himself as only twelve or thirteen or whatever he was, being anxious to prove himself a man, and take a man's place and responsibilities.

Ryerson and his wife were going back. She was a complaining woman and he was a man who was always ailing when there was work to be done. Four or five wagons were turning back, folks with their tails betwixt their legs running for the shelter of towns where their own littleness wouldn't stand out so plain.

When a body crossed the Mississippi and left the settlements behind, something happened to him. The world seemed to bust wide open, and suddenly the horizons spread out and a man wasn't cramped anymore. The pinched-up villages and the narrowness of towns, all that was gone. The horizons simply exploded and rolled back into enormous distance, with nothing around but prairie and sky.

Some folks couldn't stand it. They'd cringe into themselves and start hunting excuses to go back where they came from. This was a big country needing big men and women to live in it, and there was no place out here for the frightened or the mean.

The prairie and sky had a way of trimming folks down to size, or changing them to giants to whom nothing seemed impossible. Men who had cut a wide swath back in the States found themselves nothing out here. They were folks who were used to doing a lot of talking who suddenly found that no one was listening anymore, and things that seemed mighty important back home, like family and money, they amounted to nothing alongside character and courage.

There was John Sampson from our town. He was a man used to being told to do things, used to looking up to wealth and power, but when he crossed the Mississippi he began to lift his head and look around. He squared his shoulders, put more crack to his whip, and began to make his own tracks in the land.

Pa was always strong, an independent man given to reading at night from one of the four or five books we had, to speaking up on matters of principle and to straight shooting with a rifle. Pa had fought the Comanche and lived with the Sioux, but he wasn't strong enough to last more than two days with a Kiowa arrow through his lung. But he died knowing Ma had stood by the rear wheel and shot the Kiowa whose arrow it was.

Right then I knew that neither Indians nor country was going to get the better of Ma.

Shooting that Kiowa was the first time Ma had shot anything but some chicken-killing varmint—which she'd done time to time when Pa was away from home.

Only Ma wouldn't let Jeanie and me call it home. "We came here from Illinois," she said, "but we're going home now."

"But, Ma," I protested, "I thought home was where we came from?"

"Home is where we're going now," Ma said, "and we'll know it when we find it. Now that Pa is gone we'll have to build that home ourselves."

She had a way of saying "home" so it sounded like a rare and wonderful place and kept Jeanie and me looking always at the horizon, just knowing it was over there, waiting for us to see it. She had given us the dream, and even Jeanie, who was only six, she had it too.

She might tell us that home was where we were going, but I knew home was where Ma was, a warm and friendly place with biscuits on the table and fresh-made butter. We wouldn't have a real home until Ma was there and we had a fire going. Only I'd build the fire.

Mr. Buchanan, who was captain of the wagon train, came to us with Tryon Burt, who was guide. "We'll help you," Mr. Buchanan said. "I know you'll be wanting to go back, and—"

"But we are not going back." Ma smiled at

them. "And don't be afraid we'll be a burden. I know you have troubles of your own, and we will manage very well."

Mr. Buchanan looked uncomfortable, like he was trying to think of the right thing to say. "Now, see here," he protested, "we started this trip with a rule. There has to be a man with every wagon."

Ma put her hand on my shoulder. "I have my man. Bud is almost thirteen and accepts responsibility. I could ask for no better man."

Ryerson came up. He was thin, stooped in the shoulder, and whenever he looked at Ma there was a greasy look to his eyes that I didn't like. He was a man who looked dirty even when he'd just washed in the creek. "You come along with me, ma'am," he said. "I'll take good care of you."

"Mr. Ryerson"—Ma looked him right in the eye—"you have a wife who can use better care than she's getting, and I have my son."

"He's nothin' but a boy."

"You are turning back, are you not? My son is going on. I believe that should indicate who is more the man. It is neither size nor age that makes a man, Mr. Ryerson, but something he has inside. My son has it."

Ryerson might have said something unpleasant only Tryon Burt was standing there wishing he would, so he just looked ugly and hustled off.

"I'd like to say you could come," Mr.

Buchanan said, "but the boy couldn't stand up to a man's work."

Ma smiled at him, chin up, the way she had. "I do not believe in gambling, Mr. Buchanan, but I'll wager a good Ballard rifle there isn't a man in camp who could follow a child all day, running when it runs, squatting when it squats, bending when it bends, and wrestling when it wrestles and not be played out long before the child is."

"You may be right, ma'am, but a rule is a rule."

"We are in Indian country, Mr. Buchanan. If you are killed a week from now, I suppose your wife must return to the States?"

"That's different! Nobody could turn back from there!"

"Then," Ma said sweetly, "it seems a rule is only a rule within certain limits, and if I recall correctly no such limit was designated in the articles of travel. Whatever limits there were, Mr. Buchanan, must have been passed sometime before the Indian attack that killed my husband."

"I can drive the wagon, and so can Ma," I said. "For the past two days I've been driving, and nobody said anything until Pa died."

Mr. Buchanan didn't know what to say, but a body could see he didn't like it. Nor did he like a woman who talked up to him the way Ma did.

Tryon Burt spoke up. "Let the boy drive. I've

watched this youngster, and he'll do. He has better judgment than most men in the outfit, and he stands up to his work. If need be, I'll help."

Mr. Buchanan turned around and walked off with his back stiff the way it is when he's mad. Ma looked at Burt, and she said, "Thank you, Mr. Burt. That was nice of you."

Try Burt, he got all red around the gills and took off like somebody had put a bur under his saddle.

Come morning our wagon was the second one ready to take its place in line, with both horses saddled and tied behind the wagon, and me standing beside the off ox.

Any direction a man wanted to look there was nothing but grass and sky, only sometimes there'd be a buffalo wallow or a gopher hole. We made eleven miles the first day after Pa was buried, sixteen the next, then nineteen, thirteen and twenty-one. At no time did the country change. On the sixth day after Pa died I killed a buffalo.

It was a young bull, but a big one, and I spotted him coming up out of a draw and was off my horse and bellied down in the grass before Try Burt realized there was game in sight. That bull came up from the draw and stopped there, staring at the wagon train, which was a half-mile off. Setting a sight behind his left shoulder I took a long breath, took in the trigger slack, then squeezed off my shot so gentle-like the gun jumped in my hands before I was ready for it.

The bull took a step back like something had surprised him, and I jacked another shell into the chamber and was sighting on him again when he went down on his knees and rolled over on his side.

"You got him, Bud!" Burt was more excited than me. "That was shootin'!"

Try got down and showed me how to skin the bull, and lent me a hand. Then we cut out a lot of fresh meat and toted it back to the wagons.

Ma was at the fire when we came up, a wisp of brown hair alongside her cheek and her face flushed from the heat of the fire, looking as pretty as a bay pony.

"Bud killed his first buffalo," Burt told her, looking at Ma like he could eat her with a spoon.

"Why, Bud! That's wonderful!" Her eyes started to dance with a kind of mischief in them, and she said, "Bud, why don't you take a piece of that meat along to Mr. Buchanan and the others?"

With Burt to help, we cut the meat into eighteen pieces and distributed it around the wagons. It wasn't much, but it was the first fresh meat in a couple of weeks.

John Sampson squeezed my shoulder and said, "Seems to me you and your ma are folks to travel with. This outfit needs some hunters."

Each night I staked out that buffalo hide, and each day I worked at curing it before rolling it up to pack on the wagon. Believe you me, I was some proud of that buffalo hide. Biggest thing I'd shot until then was a cottontail rabbit back in Illinois, where we lived when I was born. Try Burt told folks about that shot. "Two hundred yards," he'd say, "right through the heart."

Only it wasn't more than a hundred and fifty yards the way I figured, and Pa used to make me pace off distances, so I'd learn to judge right. But I was nobody to argue with Try Burt telling a story—besides, two hundred yards makes an awful lot better sound than one hundred and fifty.

After supper the menfolks would gather to talk plans. The season was late, and we weren't making the time we ought if we hoped to beat the snow through the passes of the Sierras. When they talked I was there because I was the man of my wagon, but nobody paid me no mind. Mr. Buchanan, he acted like he didn't see me, but John Sampson would not, and Try Burt always smiled at me.

Several spoke up for turning back, but Mr. Buchanan said he knew of an outfit that made it through later than this. One thing was sure. Our wagon wasn't turning back. Like Ma said, home was somewhere ahead of us, and back in the States we'd have no money and nobody to turn to, nor any relatives, anywhere. It was the three of us.

"We're going on," I said at one of these talks. "We don't figure to turn back for anything."

Webb gave me a glance full of contempt. "You'll go where the rest of us go. You an' your ma would play hob gettin' by on your own."

Next day it rained, dawn to dark it fairly poured, and we were lucky to make six miles. Day after that, with the wagon wheels sinking into the prairie and the rain still falling, we camped just two miles from where we started in the morning.

Nobody talked much around the fires, and what was said was apt to be short and irritable. Most of these folks had put all they owned into the outfits they had, and if they turned back now they'd have nothing to live on and nothing left to make a fresh start. Except a few like Mr. Buchanan, who was well off.

"It doesn't have to be California," Ma said once. "What most of us want is land, not gold."

"This here is Indian country," John Sampson said, "and a sight too open for me. I'd like a valley in the hills, with running water close by."

"There will be valleys and meadows," Ma replied, stirring the stew she was making, "and tall trees near running streams, and tall grass growing in the meadows, and there will be game in the forest and on the grassy plains, and places for homes."

"And where will we find all that?" Webb's tone was slighting.

"West," Ma said, "over against the mountains."

"I suppose you've been there?" Webb scoffed.

"No, Mr. Webb, I haven't been there, but I've been told of it. The land is there, and we will have some of it, my children and I, and we will stay through the winter, and in the spring we will plant our crops."

"Easy to say."

"This is Sioux country to the north," Burt said. "We'll be lucky to get through without a fight. There was a war party of thirty or thirty-five passed this way a couple of days ago."

"Sioux?"

"Uh-huh—no women or children along, and I found where some war paint rubbed off on the brush."

"Maybe," Mr. Buchanan suggested, "we'd better turn south a mite."

"It is late in the season," Ma replied, "and the straightest way is the best way now."

"No use to worry," White interrupted; "those Indians went on by. They won't likely know we're around."

"They were riding southeast," Ma said, "and their home is in the north, so when they return they'll be riding northwest. There is no way they can miss our trail."

"Then we'd best turn back," White said.

"Don't look like we'd make it this year, anyway," a woman said; "the season is late."

That started the argument, and some were for turning back and some wanted to push on, and finally White said they should push on, but travel fast.

"Fast?" Webb asked disparagingly. "An Indian can ride in one day the distance we'd travel in four."

That started the wrangling again and Ma continued with her cooking. Sitting there watching her I figured I never did see anybody so graceful or quick on her feet as Ma, and when we used to walk in the woods back home I never knew her to stumble or step on a fallen twig or branch.

The group broke up and returned to their own fires with nothing settled, only there at the end Mr. Buchanan looked to Burt. "Do you know the Sioux?"

"Only the Utes and Shoshonis, and I spent a winter on the Snake with the Nez Percés one time. But I've had no truck with the Sioux. Only they tell me they're bad medicine. Fightin' men from way back and they don't cotton to white folks in their country. If we run into Sioux, we're in trouble."

After Mr. Buchanan had gone Tryon Burt accepted a plate and cup from Ma and settled down to eating. After a while he looked up at her and said, "Beggin' your pardon, ma'am, but it struck me you knew a sight about trackin' for an eastern woman. You'd spotted those Sioux your own self, an' you figured it right that they'd pick up our trail on the way back."

She smiled at him. "It was simply an observation, Mr. Burt. I would believe anyone would notice it. I simply put it into words."

Burt went on eating, but he was mighty thoughtful, and it didn't seem to me he was satisfied with Ma's answer. Ma said finally, "It seems to be raining west of here. Isn't it likely to be snowing in the mountains?"

Burt looked up uneasily. "Not necessarily so, ma'am. It could be raining here and not snowing there, but I'd say there was a chance of snow." He got up and came around the fire to the coffeepot. "What are you gettin' at, ma'am?"

"Some of them are ready to turn back or change their plans. What will you do then?"

He frowned, placing his cup on the grass and starting to fill his pipe. "No idea—might head south for Santa Fe. Why do you ask?"

"Because we're going on," Ma said. "We're going to the mountains, and I am hoping some of the others decide to come with us."

"You'd go alone?" He was amazed.

"If necessary."

We started on at daybreak, but folks were more scary than before, and they kept looking at the great distances stretching away on either side, and muttering. There was an autumn coolness in the air, and we were still short of South Pass by several days with the memory of the Donner party being talked up around us.

There was another kind of talk in the wagons, and some of it I heard. The nightly gatherings around Ma's fire had started talk, and some of it pointed to Tryon Burt, and some were saying other things.

We made seventeen miles that day, and at night Mr. Buchanan didn't come to our fire; and when White stopped by, his wife came and got him. Ma looked at her and smiled, and Mrs. White sniffed and went away beside her husband.

"Mr. Burt"—Ma wasn't one to beat around a bush—"is there talk about me?"

Try Burt got red around the ears and he opened his mouth, but couldn't find the words he wanted. "Maybe—well, maybe I shouldn't eat here all the time. Only—well, ma'am, you're the best cook in camp."

Ma smiled at him. "I hope that isn't the only reason you come to see us, Mr. Burt."

He got redder than ever then and gulped his coffee and took off in a hurry.

Time to time the men had stopped by to help

a little, but next morning nobody came by. We got lined out about as soon as ever, and Ma said to me as we sat on the wagon seat, "Pay no attention, Bud. You've no call to take up anything if you don't notice it. There will always be folks who will talk, and the better you do in the world the more bad things they will say of you. Back there in the settlement you remember how the dogs used to run out and bark at our wagons?"

"Yes, Ma."

"Did the wagons stop?"

"No, Ma."

"Remember that, son. The dogs bark, but the wagons go on their way, and if you're going someplace you haven't time to bother with barking dogs."

We made eighteen miles that day, and the grass was better, but there was a rumble of distant thunder, whimpering and muttering off in the canyons, promising rain.

Webb stopped by, dropped an armful of wood beside the fire, then started off.

"Thank you, Mr. Webb," Ma said, "but aren't you afraid you'll be talked about?"

He looked angry and started to reply something angry, and then he grinned and said, "I reckon I'd be flattered, Mrs. Miles."

Ma said, "No matter what is decided by the rest of them, Mr. Webb, we are going on, but there is no need to go to California for what we want."

Webb took out his pipe and tamped it. He had a dark, devil's face on him with eyebrows like you see on pictures of the devil. I was afraid of Mr. Webb.

"We want land," Ma said, "and there is land around us. In the mountains ahead there will be streams and forests, there will be fish and game, logs for houses and meadows for grazing."

Mr. Buchanan had joined us. "That's fool talk," he declared. "What could anyone do in these hills? You'd be cut off from the world. Left out of it."

"A man wouldn't be so crowded as in California," John Sampson remarked. "I've seen so many go that I've been wondering what they all do there."

"For a woman," Webb replied, ignoring the others, "you've a head on you, ma'am."

"What about the Sioux?" Mr. Buchanan asked dryly.

"We'd not be encroaching on their land. They live to the north," Ma said. She gestured toward the mountains. "There is land to be had just a few days farther on, and that is where our wagon will stop."

A few days! Everybody looked at everybody else. Not months, but days only. Those who stopped then would have enough of their supplies left to help them through the winter, and with what game they could kill—and time for cutting wood and even building cabins before the cold set in.

Oh, there was an argument, such argument as you've never heard, and the upshot of it was that all agreed it was fool talk and the thing to do was keep going. And there was talk I overheard about Ma being no better than she should be, and why was that guide always hanging around her? And all those men? No decent woman— I hurried away.

At break of day our wagons rolled down a long valley with a small stream alongside the trail, and the Indians came over the ridge to the south of us and started our way—tall, fine-looking men with feathers in their hair.

There was barely time for a circle, but I was riding off in front with Tryon Burt, and he said, "A man can always try to talk first, and Injuns like a palaver. You get back to the wagons."

Only I rode along beside him, my rifle over my saddle and ready to hand. My mouth was dry and my heart was beating so's I thought Try could hear it, I was that scared. But behind us the wagons were making their circle, and every second was important.

Their chief was a big man with splendid muscles, and there was a scalp not many days old hanging from his lance. It looked like Ryerson's hair, but Ryerson's wagons should have been miles away to the east by now.

Burt tried them in Shoshoni, but it was the language of their enemies and they merely stared at him, understanding well enough, but of no mind to talk. One young buck kept staring at Burt with a taunt in his eye, daring Burt to make a move; then suddenly the chief spoke, and they all turned their eyes toward the wagons.

There was a rider coming, and it was a woman. It was Ma.

She rode right up beside us, and when she drew up she started to talk, and she was speaking their language. She was talking Sioux. We both knew what it was because those Indians sat up and paid attention. Suddenly she directed a question at the chief.

"Red Horse," he said, in English.

Ma shifted to English. "My husband was blood brother to Gall, the greatest warrior of the Sioux nation. It was my husband who found Gall dying in the brush with a bayonet wound in his chest, who took Gall to his home and treated the wound until it was well."

"Your husband was a medicine man?" Red Horse asked.

"My husband was a warrior," Ma replied

proudly, "but he made war only against strong men, not women or children or the wounded."

She put her hand on my shoulder. "This is my son. As my husband was blood brother to Gall, his son is by blood brotherhood the son of Gall, also."

Red Horse stared at Ma for a long time, and I was getting even more scared. I could feel a drop of sweat start at my collar and crawl slowly down my spine. Red Horse looked at me. "Is this one a fit son for Gall?"

"He is a fit son. He has killed his first buffalo."

Red Horse turned his mount and spoke to the others. One of the young braves shouted angrily at him, and Red Horse replied sharply. Reluctantly, the warrior trailed off after their chief.

"Ma'am," Burt said, "you just about saved our bacon. They were just spoilin' for a fight."

"We should be moving," Ma said.

Mr. Buchanan was waiting for us. "What happened out there? I tried to keep her back, but she's a difficult woman."

"She's worth any three men in the outfit," Burt replied.

That day we made eighteen miles, and by the time the wagons circled there was talk. The fact that Ma had saved them was less important now than other things. It didn't seem right that a decent woman could talk Sioux or mix in the affairs of men.

Nobody came to our fire, but while picking the saddle horses I heard someone say, "Must be part Injun. Else why would they pay attention to a woman?"

"Maybe she's part Injun and leadin' us into a trap."

"Hadn't been for her," Burt said, "you'd all be dead now."

"How do you know what she said to 'em? Who savvies that lingo?"

"I never did trust that woman," Mrs. White said; "too high and mighty. Nor that husband of hers, either, comes to that. Kept to himself too much."

The air was cool after a brief shower when we started in the morning, and no Indians in sight. All day long we moved over grass made fresh by new rain, and all the ridges were pine-clad now, and the growth along the streams heavier. Short of sundown I killed an antelope with a running shot, dropped him mighty neat—and looked up to see an Indian watching from a hill. At the distance I couldn't tell, but it could have been Red Horse.

Time to time I'd passed along the train, but nobody waved or said anything. Webb watched me go by, his face stolid as one of the Sioux, yet I could see there was a deal of talk going on.

"Why are they mad at us?" I asked Burt.

"Folks hate something they don't understand,

or anything seems different. Your ma goes her own way, speaks her mind, and of an evening she doesn't set by and gossip."

He topped out on a rise and drew up to study the country, and me beside him. "You got to figure most of these folks come from small towns where they never knew much aside from their families, their gossip, and their church. It doesn't seem right to them that a decent woman would find time to learn Sioux."

Burt studied the country. "Time was, any stranger was an enemy, and if anybody came around who wasn't one of yours, you killed him. I've seen wolves jump on a wolf that was white or different somehow—seems like folks and animals fear anything that's unusual."

We circled, and I staked out my horses and took the oxen to the herd. By the time Ma had her grub-box lid down, I was fixing at a fire when here come Mr. Buchanan, Mr. and Mrs. White, and some other folks, including that Webb.

"Ma'am"—Mr. Buchanan was mighty abrupt—"we figure we ought to know what you said to those Sioux. We want to know why they turned off just because you went out there."

"Does it matter?"

Mr. Buchanan's face stiffened up. "We think it does. There's some think you might be an Indian your own self."

"And if I am?" Ma was amused. "Just what is it you have in mind, Mr. Buchanan?"

"We don't want no Injuns in this outfit!" Mr. White shouted.

"How does it come you can talk that language?" Mrs. White demanded. "Even Tryon Burt can't talk it."

"I figure maybe you want us to keep goin' because there's a trap up ahead!" White declared.

I never realized folks could be so mean, but there they were facing Ma like they hated her, like those witch-hunters Ma told me about back in Salem. It didn't seem right that Ma, who they didn't like, had saved them from an Indian attack, and the fact that she talked Sioux like any Indian bothered them.

"As it happens," Ma said, "I am not an Indian, athough I should not be ashamed of it if I were. They have many admirable qualities. However, you need worry yourselves no longer, as we part company in the morning. I have no desire to travel further with you—**gentlemen**."

Mr. Buchanan's face got all angry, and he started up to say something mean. Nobody was about to speak rough to Ma with me standing by, so I just picked up that ol' rifle and jacked a shell into the chamber. "Mr. Buchanan, this here's my ma, and she's a lady, so you just be careful what words you use."

"Put down that rifle, you young fool!" he shouted at me.

"Mr. Buchanan, I may be little and may be a fool, but this here rifle doesn't care who pulls its trigger."

He looked like he was going to have a stroke, but he just turned sharp around and walked away, all stiff in the back.

"Ma'am," Webb said, "you've no cause to like me much, but you've shown more brains than that passel o' fools. If you'll be so kind, me and my boy would like to trail along with you."

"I like a man who speaks his mind, Mr. Webb. I would consider it an honor to have your company."

Tryon Burt looked quizzically at Ma. "Why, now, seems to me this is a time for a man to make up his mind, and I'd like to be included along with Webb."

"Mr. Burt," Ma said, "for your own information, I grew up among Sioux children in Minnesota. They were my playmates."

Come daylight our wagon pulled off to one side, pointing northwest at the mountains, and Mr. Buchanan led off to the west. Webb followed Ma's wagon, and I sat watching Mr. Buchanan's eyes get angrier as John Sampson, Neely Stuart, the two Shafter wagons, and Tom Croft all fell in behind us.

Tryon Burt had been talking to Mr.

Buchanan, but he left off and trotted his horse over to where I sat my horse. Mr. Buchanan looked mighty sullen when he saw half his wagon train gone and with it a lot of his importance as captain.

Two days and nearly forty miles farther and we topped out on a rise and paused to let the oxen take a blow. A long valley lay across our route, with mountains beyond it, and tall grass wet with rain, and a flat bench on the mountainside seen through a gray veil of a light shower falling. There was that bench, with the white trunks of aspen on the mountainside beyond it looking like ranks of slim soldiers guarding the bench against the storms.

"Ma," I said.

"All right, Bud," she said quietly, "we've come home."

And I started up the oxen and drove down into the valley where I was to become a man.

# *Ironwood Station*

The riders met where the trails formed a Y with the main road. The man from the north was fat, with a narrow-brimmed hat and round cheeks. He raised a hand in greeting. "Mind if I ride along with you? Gets mighty lonesome, ridin' alone. I ain't seen even a jackrabbit last ten miles, an' a man can say just so much to a horse.

"Figured to make Ironwood Station before sundown. They feed passengers, an' I'm mighty tired of my own cookin'." The fat man bit off a chunk of chewing tobacco and offered the plug to the other man, who shook his head. "Long empty stretch in here," the fat man continued. "Never see nobody 'ceptin' Utes, whom nobody wants to see." The fat man glanced at his companion. "Ain't much for talkin', are you?"

"Not much."

"Well, I'm ready for Dan Burnett's cookin'. That man can sure shake up a nice mess o' vittles. Makes a man's mouth water."

"Somebody north of us," the other rider said. "Somebody who doesn't want to follow a trail."

The fat man glanced at him. "You hear something?"

"I smell dust."

"Could be Utes. This here is Ute country." The fat man was worried. "The Utes have been killin' a lot of folks about here."

"There's three . . . maybe four of them."

"Now, how would you know that?"

"Dust from one horse wouldn't reach this far, but the dust from three or four would."

"My name is Jones," the fat man said. "What did you say your name was?"

"Talon . . . Shawn Talon."

"Odd name. Don't reckon I ever heard that one before."

"You would in County Wicklow. My father was Irish, with an after-coating of Texas."

They rode in silence until they dipped into a hollow, and Talon drew up briefly. "Three riders," Talon said, "on mighty fine horses. See the stride? A long stride and good action, although they've been riding a long time."

"You read a lot from a few tracks."

"Well, they've had to be riding a long time," Talon said, smiling. "This isn't camping country, and where would a man come from to get here?"

Sun glinted on the rifle barrel a split instant

before the bullet whipped past his ear, but the brief warning was enough. Talon slapped the spurs to his horse and was off with a bound, the report of a rifle cutting a slash across the hot still afternoon.

Ahead of him there was a burst of firing, and as the two men, riding neck and neck, came over the rise, they saw three others in a hollow among the rocks defending themselves against an attack by Utes. Glancing back, Talon saw several Indians closing in from behind them. Jumping their horses into the circle of rocks, Talon rolled on his side and began feeding shells into the Winchester. Briefly, he glanced at the other men.

The three strangers were tough, competent-looking men. One, a slim, dark man, had his holster tied down. He was unshaven and he glanced at Talon and grinned. "You showed up on time, mister."

It was very hot. From time to time somebody thought they saw a target and fired, and from time to time the Utes fired back . . . but they were working closer. "Getting set for a rush," Talon said aloud.

"Let 'em come," the man with the tied-down gun said. "The quicker they try it, the quicker this will be over."

Neither of his companions had said anything. One was a short, dark man, the other a burly fellow, huge and bearded. All three looked dirty, and showed evidence of long days in the saddle. Talon noticed that his talkative friend was suddenly very silent.

The rush came suddenly. Talon got in a quick shot with his rifle, and then the man with the tied-down holster was on his feet, his six-gun rolling a cannonade of sound into the hot afternoon. He shot fast and accurately. With his own eyes Talon saw three Indians drop under the gunman's fire before the attack broke. With his rifle Talon nailed another, and saw the gunman bring down the last Indian with a fifty-yard pistol shot.

"That was some shooting," Talon commented.

The man glanced at him briefly. "It's my business," he said.

In the distance, beyond the trail, dust arose. "Thought so," the gunman said. "They're pullin' out."

Talon waited a moment, watching the trail, and then he turned and walked toward his horse, standing with the other horses in the low ground behind the rocks. "Let's ride, Jones."

They mounted up and the three men watched them in silence. The gunman stared at Talon as he swung his horse to ride out. "Something about you," he said. "I've seen you before, somewhere."

"No," Talon said distinctly, "I don't believe so."

"You ridin' west?"

"To Carson City, probably."

"Make it definitely . . . you take my advice and don't stop this side." The gunman grinned. "You might run into more Utes without me to protect you."

Talon said, "You know something? You're in the wrong business."

He loped his horse out of the basin without waiting for a reply, and Jones pulled in alongside him. Jones looked back over his shoulder. "You should be careful," he said. "That was Lute Robeck back there. He's a mighty dangerous man. You see the way he emptied that six-gun?"

"He didn't empty it," Talon said. "He had one shot left."

The desert lay empty and still under the hot morning sun. Heat waves shimmered over the red-brown, sun-baked rocks of the distant mountains, but there was no other movement until a lone dust devil danced out of the greasewood clumps and gained size in the flatland, then died away to nothing.

IN THE BACK ROOM of the stage station at Ironwood, Dan Burnett lay on his back with a broken hip and three broken ribs. It was close and hot in the small bedroom and he gasped painfully with every breath.

Kate Breslin, in the big main room of the station, went to the door for the fiftieth time and stared up the narrow, empty road that went down the flat and curved out of sight around the hill. The road was empty . . . in all that hot, vast, and brassy silence, nothing moved.

Kate Breslin was twice a widow, once by stampede and once by the gun, but at forty-five she was all western, with no idea of ever going elsewhere. She had rolled into Ironwood on the stage bound for Carson and they had found Dan Burnett dragging himself toward the station door with a broken hip . . . he had been kicked by a mule and was in bad shape.

Immediately, she volunteered to remain until a relief man could come and somebody to care for Dan. On impulse, Ruth Starkey had stayed with her. Now, as Ruth could plainly see, Kate was worried, and she was worried about something other than the injured man in the back bedroom.

"Can you handle a gun?" Kate asked suddenly.

"I've shot a rifle, if that's what you mean."

"You may need to. . . ." Kate Breslin looked at her quickly. "You know what he told me? There's seventy thousand dollars in gold on that westbound stage . . . seventy thousand."

"Does anybody know?"

"You darned tootin', somebody knows. Trouble is, they don't know who. Feller worked for the mining company, he suddenly took off, didn't even pick up his wages . . . he lit right out of town. They thought about holding the gold, then decided they would be safer to ship it. That's why Dan is so worried."

"But don't they know about Dan?"

"West they do, but that gold's shipped from east of here . . . and back there they'll think Dan is on his toes. This is one place nobody will expect trouble."

Ruth was standing in the door. "Kate," she said, "two men are coming up the road . . . from the east."

Kate Breslin joined her in the door. Two men riding toward them, both on fine, blooded horses, definitely not the sort of horses ridden by cowhands. One man was short and thickset, the other was a tall man.

"Be careful what you say," Kate said. "You just be careful."

When they rode up it was the tall man who spoke. "Ma'am, we've heard they served the best food along the line at Ironwood, and we're hungry. Could you manage to serve a meal for two?"

"I reckon," Kate said. "Get down and come in."

When they had stabled their horses, the two

men came in and the fat one walked to the bar. "I'd like a whiskey," he said, "I surely would."

"Pour one for him, Ruth." Kate was already rattling dishes in the kitchen. "I'll feed these men so they can get on their way. I expect they're in a hurry to get to Carson."

Talon glanced at her and then at Ruth, momentarily puzzled by the presence of the women. His eyes strayed toward the closed door of the bedroom, but what it was or who was there, Talon had no idea. He sensed that for some reason his presence was not wanted, and he wondered why this was so. He was a sensitive man, aware of changes in the atmosphere, and he was aware of a subtle coldness now.

He had not expected to find women here, and the younger one, the one called Ruth, was extremely pretty . . . but an eastern girl or one who had lately been east. Disturbed, he walked outside and went to the stable, where the mules that pulled the stage over this rough stretch were kept. There were twelve of them, and walking past the stalls, he suddenly glimpsed a gun, half-concealed by the hay on the barn floor.

He picked it up, a worn Remington pistol, but well kept and oiled . . . the man who owned a gun so well kept would not be one to leave it lying carelessly on the dirt floor. Curious, aware of a mystery here, he looked slowly around the long building. The fallen gun was directly behind a stall, and at that point the dirt of the floor was stirred up by boot marks . . . he tried to work out the sign but could make nothing of it, although it looked like a scuffle had taken place. Whatever it was, it had made the owner forget his pistol.

Walking outside, he looked carefully around, and there was little to see. The mules, the barn, the corrals, and several haystacks aside from what hay was in the barn itself. A couple of poles leaned against the side of the house with two coats buttoned around them to make a crude stretcher. So that was it . . . somebody had been hurt.

Strolling across the yard, he stopped to light a cigarette and glanced out of the corner of his eyes at the stretcher. He was close to it now, but he could see no signs of blood, such as would be visible if the man had been shot or injured so that he would bleed.

Jones stepped outside. "Woman in there is Kate Breslin," he said. "Dan's off in the hills rounding up a beef."

"Dan a friend of yours?"

"Sure . . . that is, we talk friendly, and we feel friendly. I don't know Dan the best, but I've stopped by here six, eight times."

"Doesn't make much sense, rounding up a beef when they've plenty of supplies in the station . . . not with the Utes running wild over the country."

"Could be, though." Jones glanced at Talon. "What's wrong? You got something in mind?"

"They're hiding something." Talon jerked his head to indicate the women. "There's something wrong around here." He slid the Remington from his belt. "You ever see this before?"

"Sure. That's Dan's gun. I'd know it anywhere."

"Think he'd be apt to go into the mountains without it? I found it lying in the barn, half-covered with hay."

"Dan's hurt . . . got to be. He was a careful man with a gun, cared for 'em well, and he never left one lyin' around careless."

Kate Breslin appeared in the door, staring at them suspiciously. "You can eat," she said. "I don't want to hold you up any longer'n I have to."

The food was good, the usual beef, beans, and biscuits of the frontier, but potatoes had been added, and beside each plate was a healthy slab of apple pie. Dried apples, Talon reflected, but pie, anyway.

He glanced again at the carefully closed door. Ruth was pouring coffee, and he said, "Burnett should be getting back. What time's the stage due?"

The hands pouring the coffee trembled a little and the girl straightened. "There's plenty of time. Dan will be back, all right."

He took out the gun. "Better give this to him. I found it in the barn."

She picked up the gun quickly, almost snatched it from him, and Talon glimpsed Kate listening in the door to the kitchen. "It's all right . . . he has another."

Talon refilled his cup from the coffeepot and began to build a smoke. Were they worried because they were two women alone? It might be, but he doubted it. Maybe Ruth might worry, although she looked like a girl who could take care of herself, but Kate Breslin wouldn't. She had been in such positions too many times to be daunted by the presence of men, and she would know what to do. So what, then, was wrong?

His thoughts returned suddenly to the gunman on the trail behind them. Odd, when a man came to think of it. "I wonder what became of our friends?" he asked mildly.

Jones looked up from his pie. "On their way, prob'ly."

"They were riding west when we met them."

Jones tore off a slab of bread and began to butter it, ignoring the biscuits. He looked at Talon, his mouth full and chewing, then the chewing slowed and Jones looked thoughtful. "Maybe they turned off," he suggested lamely.

"To where? This is a big, empty country." Talon lit his cigarette. "Remember his advice?

To keep riding for Carson? He sounded like he didn't want us to stop this side of there."

"So?"

"So we've stopped . . . and this might be the place he didn't want us to stop."

"I don't figure it . . . what you gettin' at?"

"These women are scared about something, and this is the loneliest stage stop in the country . . . and back along the trail we meet three very handy men riding horses no cowhand could afford, horses with speed and staying quality."

"You think they were outlaws? I noticed them horses."

"What else?"

Jones stared at him thoughtfully. "Talon," he said carefully, "you ride a mighty fine horse yourself. One with speed and staying quality."

Talon smiled. "That's right," he said quietly.

Ruth collected the dishes. "Do you plan to make Carson tonight? You can do it if you push right along."

"You wouldn't be trying to get rid of us, would you?" Talon smiled at her. "I don't think you women should be here alone with Dan Burnett laid up."

Ruth almost dropped the dishes. She turned sharply, but Kate spoke from the kitchen. "Dan may be laid up, but I'm not. You ride out of here, both of you!"

Jones put his cup down hard and stared at her, his fat jowls quivering. "Now, looka here—!" he started to protest.

"Get! . . . Get goin'!"

Talon picked up the coffeepot and refilled his cup. "Like I said, you're going to need help. Especially with a gold shipment on that coach."

Jones turned to stare at him, astonished. But Kate Breslin walked on into the room, and she had Burnett's Remington in her fist. "You know about that, do you? That means you're what I figured you were. You get goin', mister."

"What else would keep you scared?" Talon asked mildly. "Only that you were afraid of something happening while Dan's laid up."

"We'll handle that . . . **Ride!**"

Suddenly there was a rush of horses in the yard, and Talon said, "Now you'll really need me. Those riders are the worst kind of trouble."

"Don't give me that!" Kate said, but she hesitated, lowering the gun a little.

"There's three men, Kate," Ruth said.

The door opened and the three men from the Indian fight came into the room. The gunman leading them stopped and his expression hardened when he saw Talon and Jones. "You should have kept going," he said. "We told you."

"Tracey, isn't it?" Talon asked the bearded man. "And you," he said to the gunman, "are Lute Robeck."

"That's right." Robeck walked to the bar and picked up a bottle.

"That's two bits a shot," Kate said.

"Shut up." Robeck merely glanced at her.

Kate started to speak, then tightened her lips and was still; her eyes went from face to face and she walked back to the door of the bedroom and stood there, waiting. She knew all about Robeck . . . the man was known to be a gunman, a killer, a rustler, and occasional robber of payrolls at outlying mines. Tracey, too, was a known man. Her eyes went to Talon. Who was he? What was he?

"Well," Robeck said, "you're here, and the stage is due in a couple of hours, so you'll stay, right here, until we're ready for you."

"Lute," Jones said, "you'd better take Talon's gun. I don't know who he is, but he's too smart."

"Let him have it," Robeck said. "It may give me an excuse to kill him."

Talon glanced at Jones. "So you're one of them?"

"Sure." Jones smiled. "I worked for the mining company until they got a good shipment ready. No use pulling holdups when there's no cash coming; we just wait until we know they've got it. Like now."

The dark outlaw who had said nothing loitered in a corner of the room almost beyond Talon's view. There were four of them now, four to one. "Watch that Breslin woman," Jones said. "She's got Burnett's gun."

"Where's Burnett?" Robeck demanded.

"Back of that door. I figure he's hurt. Leastwise that's what Talon here figured out."

Robeck grinned at Talon. "I hope you try for that gun," he said. "I don't like you, much."

Talon lifted his cup and sipped coffee slowly, watching Robeck over the cup's rim.

The outlaw walked to the door, and when Ruth made as if to stop him, he shoved her roughly aside and opened it. He strode to the bedside and looked down at the suffering man. "You lie quiet, Burnett," he said, "and maybe you won't be killed."

"You let me get my hands on a gun," Burnett said, "and I'll not make you any promises!"

Robeck chuckled. "Flat on his back and still full of fight." His eyes went to Ruth. "Food, liquor, a gold shipment, and a girl . . . what more can a man ask?"

"You'd be wise to let her alone."

Robeck turned his head slowly to look at Talon, who had not moved. "Don't push your luck," he said.

Tracey got out a deck of cards and was joined by the dark man, whom he had called Pete. Tracey began to lay out a game of solitaire. Lute Robeck walked to the now open door and leaned against the doorjamb, watching the empty road.

Four to four, Talon thought, only there were two women on his side, and a sick man. And they were all around the room, and even when they did not appear to be, he knew they were watching him. He also knew that he, at least, was to be killed. That was why they had left him his gun. . . . Robeck fancied himself with a gun. He wanted Talon to try it so he could test himself.

An hour went slowly by. Talon wanted to move, but hesitated to give Robeck the chance he might be wanting. The two women had gone quietly to work, cleaning up his table and, at Robeck's order, preparing food for the others. At least one of them watched the women at all times, without making an issue of it.

Talon got out the makings and rolled a smoke. He touched the cigarette paper to his lips and then put the cigarette in his mouth. Robeck watched him with bright interest, but there was a matchbox on the table and Talon took out the match and struck it on the table edge in plain sight.

Robeck chuckled. "Cagey, ain't you?" he said. "Where'd I ever see you before?"

"You never did," Talon said.

Robeck's eyes sharpened. "Maybe. . . . You wanted by the law?"

"No." He turned his head. "Ruth, I'd like some more coffee, if you will."

It was very hot and still. Perspiration stood out on their faces. He had one gun against four, and they were not worried by him. . . . Robeck was actually anticipating trouble. "If you're going to try for that gun," he said, "you'd better have at it. When the stage comes we're going to take it away from you."

"I can wait."

Robeck chuckled, watching Ruth carry the coffee to the table. He got to his feet and walked to the bar to pour a drink. Ruth gave Talon a look then slanted her eyes quickly away in the direction of Robeck. She looked back and gave him a slight little nod. She wanted him to go ahead, she was ready to take her chances.

Robeck's eyes followed the girl. "Now, there's a woman for you. Fire in her, I'll bet." He glanced at the clock on the shelf. "And we've got most of an hour yet. Maybe her and me—"

"Leave her alone."

Robeck turned, his smile gone. Before he could speak, Talon spoke again. "Leave her alone, Robeck. You'll get the gold if you're smart, but leave that girl alone or I'll kill you."

**"What?"** Robeck was on his feet facing Talon. "You'll kill **me**? Get on your feet, tall man, and I'll cut you down! Get up, you hear? **Get up!**"

Talon did not move. He looked at Robeck and smiled. "Don't be in a hurry," he said. "You have some time left."

The moment died. Pete walked to the door, then stepped outside and walked toward the barn. Ruth served the others and watched them eat. Kate Breslin had done nothing since the gun was taken from her but to cook and remain silent. It was very hot, and Talon loafed in his chair, waiting.

A fly buzzed on the window. Pete walked out to the road and looked off into the distance, shading his eyes against the glare. Jones got up and walked to the window and then turned back, and as he came back toward the table he was behind Talon. Suddenly his gun was thrust against Talon's spine. "You may want to play games," he said to Robeck, "I don't. That stage is due any minute." Jones reached down and took Talon's gun, then stepped back away from him, careful not to get within reach of Talon's hands.

"All right." Robeck shrugged. "I just figured maybe he'd like to try it with me." He grinned at Talon. "No guts."

Talon got slowly to his feet and stretched his long arms. Idly, he walked to the bar where Robeck was seated, and poured a drink. Robeck moved back a little, watching Talon cheerfully. "I'll still kill you if you start anything, Talon," Robeck warned. Ruth, tense only a moment before, relaxed, accepted her fate . . . she and Kate were one step further from safety.

IN THE KITCHEN, Kate Breslin had taken an old .31 Colt from her valise, and she slipped it into Ruth's hand. "Only if the chance is just right," she whispered. "Then give it to him."

Pete walked out to the road. "Not much more time, Lute."

"No." Lute glanced around the room. "They don't know the women are here, anyway. They can't know, with the only stage since Burnett was hurt going out the other way. We'll hide them . . . put 'em in Burnett's room."

Tracey got up. "What about Talon?"

Ruth came into the room and crossed to the table where Talon sat. Lute watched her with bright interest, never missing a move. The butt of the little Colt was visible to Talon from under Ruth's apron, but he carefully ignored it. Ruth fussed with the dishes, waiting, and suddenly Robeck began to laugh.

"He's yellow! Yellow! Ruthie, you picked yourself the wrong man!"

Ruth turned away from the table and instantly Robeck motioned to Tracey, who grabbed the girl and shoved her across to Robeck, who jerked the apron from her, and the gun. "You little fool!" He slapped her wickedly across the mouth. "Who do you think you're fooling?" He shoved her back against the counter and slapped her again. Instantly, she lashed out and slapped him, then kicked him on the shins. There was a momentary struggle, and then he shoved the girl from him and slapped her again, thrusting the pistol into his waistband.

Talon stood flat-footed, watching, but making no move away from the table. His expression had not changed as he watched the brief struggle. When it was over he stepped over and helped the girl to her feet. Angrily, Ruth jerked away from him. "Don't touch me, you coward!" she flared.

Robeck laughed.

Pete ran in from the road. "Here she comes!" he said.

Tracey grabbed Ruth and shoved her toward the bedroom door. Robeck stood watching Talon and smiling. "No hurry," he said. "They're bringing it right to us."

Tracey ordered Kate from the kitchen and into the bedroom. "If they make a wrong move," Robeck ordered, "use your gun barrel. And I don't care how hard you hit."

Lute Robeck walked to the door and looked out. The stage was rolling into the yard. "All right." He gestured to Talon. "Walk out there ahead of us and don't say anything or make a wrong move."

Whatever happened now would depend on fast thinking and breaks, and the shotgun guard must do some fast thinking, too. He walked outside with Lute beside him; Jones and Pete moved up behind. Talon angled toward the stage, knowing the men behind him would spread out. If the shotgun guard started shooting, which Robeck well knew, Talon would be the first man killed.

The stage whirled into the yard and came to an abrupt stop in a cloud of dust. The shotgun guard was staring from the door to the waiting men, and as Talon slowly turned he saw a rifle barrel glinting from the bedroom window. . . . Tracey was going to kill the guard.

"Holdup!" Talon yelled, and a Colt Lightning slid from under the arm of his coat.

Robeck swore and swung his gun, blasting fire. His first shot was too quick, Talon's was not. The bullet caught Robeck over the belt buckle and he started back. Talon fired again, then nailed Jones. Pete was already falling and suddenly there was silence broken only by the plunging of the horses and the rattle of harness. They quieted down and Talon got slowly to his feet.

Talon walked over to Robeck and kicked the gun from his hand, but the man was dead.

Tracey was standing in the door, his hands high. "Don't shoot!" he said. "I've quit!"

Ruth came from the door, but the shotgun guard reached Talon first. "Thanks," he said.

"When I didn't see Dan I figured something was wrong."

"I'm sorry," Ruth said, "I just thought—"

"I always carry a spare," he said. "You know, any of us in there could have been killed. Sometimes it's better to reserve judgment . . . when a man's life is on the line, he naturally wants to wait until the time is right."

He walked to the stable for his horse. It was still a long way to Carson.

# *Alkali Basin*

The stage rocked and rolled over the desert road, vainly pursued by a thick cloud of fine white dust. It plunged down a declivity into a dry wash, then swept up the other side and around a hairpin curve at the top, to straighten out on the long dash across the valley.

Price Macomber, vice-president of the Overland Stage Company, was heading west on an inspection tour accompanied by his niece and Pete Judson, the district superintendent. Price, a round man with a round pink face and round rimless spectacles, was holding forth on his pet theme—useless expenditures.

"It has been my experience," he was saying, "that given the slightest excuse each driver and each station operator will come up with a number of items of utterly useless expense, and such items must be eliminated."

He braced himself against the roll of the stage and stared out the window for an instant as if collecting his thoughts. Then his eyes pinned Judson to his seat as a collector pins a butterfly. Judson squirmed, but there was no escape.

"You understand," Macomber continued, "I'm not accusing these men of including items for their own advantage. No doubt at the moment they believe the item essential, yet when viewed logically it usually proves such claims were arrived at without due consideration.

"Take, for example, the ridiculous request of this man Wells, at Alkali Basin. Four times now he has written us demanding we send him blasting powder!

"Now think of that! Blasting powder, of all things! What earthly use would a station agent have for blasting powder? In our reply to his first request, we suggested he submit his reason for wanting it, and he replied that he wished to blast some rocks.

"Were the rocks on the road? No, they were not. They were some seventy yards off the road in the desert. The request was, without doubt, the whimsical notion of an uneducated man at a moment when he was not thinking. By now he no doubt realizes the absurdity of his notion.

"It is such items as this that can be eliminated. And I observed," Macomber added severely, "that you recommended his request be granted. I was surprised, Judson. Needless to say, I was very surprised. We expect better judgment of our district superintendents."

Judson mopped his brow and said nothing. In the past one-hundred-and-ten miles he had learned it was wiser to listen and endure. Price Macomber's voice droned on into the hot, dusty afternoon with no hint of a letup.

The best arguments Judson had offered had been riddled with logic, devastating and inescapable. He would have liked to say that sometimes logic fell short of truth, but lacked the words, and no argument of his could hope to dam the flow of words that poured over the spillway of Price Macomber's lips.

Molly Macomber stared wearily at the desert. Her uncle, so polished, immaculate, and sure of himself, had failed to materialize into the superman he had seemed in Kansas City and St. Louis.

Against the background of the rolling grasslands, she had noticed that his stiff white collar and neat black suit seemed somehow incongruous. Also, among the ragged, stark ridges of the desert, his mouth seemed too prim and precise, his eyes seemed flat and rather foolish. They were like the eyes of a goldfish staring from a bowl at a world it neither understood nor saw clearly.

"Keep the expense down," Macomber was saying, "and the profits will take care of themselves."

Judson stared at the desert and shifted his feet. He felt sorry for Molly, who evidently expected glamour and beauty on this westward trek. He also felt sorry for himself. He took a drink with his stage drivers, and played poker with them. Somehow he had always got results.

He had visited Alkali Basin just once before, and heartily wished he would never have to again. If Wells, keeper of the station there, wanted blasting powder, Judson was for letting him have it. Or anything else, for that matter, including a necklace of silver bells, a Cardinal's hat, or even a steamboat—anything to keep him contented.

In the three months before Wells took over the station at Alkai Basin, no fewer than six station agents had attempted the job.

The first man stuck it ten days. It was a lonely post where he had only to change horses for two stages each day, one going east, and one west. After ten days that agent had come to town on the stage and shook his head decisively. "No!" he said violently. "Not for any price! Not even Price Macomber!"

Four days after the next agent took over, the stage rolled into Alkali Basin and found no horses awaiting it. The horses were gone from the corral, and the agent lay across his adobe doorstep shot three times through the body, mutilated and scalped.

Two more men had tried it, one after the other. The Apaches got the first one of these on his second day, and the other man fought them off for a couple of hours, then went to Mexico with two teams of six horses each, and had not been heard from since.

Blasting powder might be somewhat extreme, but in Judson's private, and oft expressed opinion—to everyone but Macomber—any man who would stick it out for as much as ten days in the white dust and furnace heat of Alkali Basin, was entitled to anything he wanted.

The man called Wells had been on the job for two solid months, and so far, except for the powder, his only request had been for large quantities of ammunition. He sent in a request for more by every stage.

Macomber leaned with the sway of the stage as it swung around a corner of red rock. The movement awakened Molly who had dozed, made sleepy by the motion of the stage and the heat. A thin film of dust had settled on her face, her neck, and her hair. Perspiration, extremely unladylike perspiration, had left streaks on her face.

Her eyes strayed out over the white, dancing heat waves of the basin's awful expanse. The hot sun reflected from it and the earth seemed to shimmer, unreal and somehow ghastly. In the far distance, a column of dust arose and skipped along over the white desolation like some weird and evil spirit. It was the only movement.

The stage reached bottom and paused briefly

in the partial shade while the horses gathered breath for the long, bitter run across the desert bottom, inches deep in alkali.

The pursuing dust cloud caught up with and settled over the stage and the clothing of the occupants. Even Price Macomber's dauntless volubility seemed to hesitate and lose itself in space. He was silent, staring out the window as though totaling a column of figures. Money saved, no doubt.

As the stage stumbled into movement once more, he glanced at Judson. "How much farther to our stop?"

"Forty miles to a decent place. It's no more than ten miles to Alkali Basin. We change horses there, but we'd better get food and water at Green's Creek."

The horses, as though aware of the coming rest, lunged into the harness and charged at the heat waves.

SIX HOURS EARLIER, morning had come to Alkali Basin. The sun, as though worn from its efforts of the previous day, pushed itself wearily over the jagged ridge in the distance and stabbed with white hot lances at the lonely stone building and the corrals.

Wells, his stubble of beard whitened with alkali, stared through one of the small windows with red-rimmed, sleepless eyes. The Apaches were still there. He couldn't see them, but he knew without seeing. They had been there, devilish in their patience, for eighteen hours now. They were out there in front of him, behind that low parapet of rocks.

He was a big, rawboned man, hairy chested, and hard-bitten. His reddish hair was a rumpled, uncombed mass, his shirt was dirty and sweat-stained.

A rough board table occupied the center of the room, and on it was a candle in a bowl, and a lantern. The coals in the fireplace were dead long since and his bunk was a tumbled pile of odorous blankets. Close beside him as he knelt by the window was a wooden bucket. The wood was ingrained with white, and there was a milky film in the bottom. The water looked like skim milk. It was heavy with alkali. It was all he had.

Beside him on the floor, two boxes of shells were broken open. The floor around him was littered with empty shells, and the skin of his right hand was broken by a furrow, raw and bleeding, where a bullet had cut across the back of it.

He squinted his eyes at the desert sun and rolled his quid of chewing in his jaws. Then he spat. No head showed, no hand. Then a shot hit the stone wall near the window and whined away into the dancing heat.

He knew what they were waiting for. Eventually, he would have to sleep, but it was not that. They were waiting for the stage. By only a few minutes they had missed the last of yesterday's stages, and they had no intention of missing the one coming today. Wells believed there were only eight or ten Apaches out there now, but that was plenty. There wouldn't be more than three or four men on the stage, and they would be caught in the open.

From his window he could cover the front approaches to the stone barn beyond the corrals. The horses were in the barn, hence they were reasonably secure. The Indians had rushed him just as he had put them away, and if they had dashed for the house instead of for him, he would have been headed off, killed, scalped and dying by now.

Shooting with his pistol, he had made a break for the house. One bullet made a flesh wound in his side, and he had dropped two Indians. One of them was only wounded, but Wells had finished him off as he crawled for shelter in the rocks.

It was hot and stuffy in the closed-up stage station. Sweat trickled down his face and down his body under the sagging shirt. There was no time after daybreak that Alkali Basin could be described as cool.

Wells was nearing forty and looked all of fifty

when unshaven. None of his years had been easy or comfortable. He had punched cows, driven a stage, placer mined. Nobody had ever called him a pleasant man, and when he smiled, which was rare, his parted lips revealed yellowed and broken teeth. His eyes were black and hard, implacable as the eyes of the Apaches he faced across that seventy yards of alkali and sand.

No one had ever known his real name. When asked, he merely said he came from Wells, so they called him that, and it served its purpose. The Apaches hated, feared, and respected him. They were not concerned about his name.

In the two months of his stay at Alkali Basin, they had attacked him five times. Nine Apaches died in those five attacks. To an Apache, who is supple as a rattler and hard to hit as a hell diver, that meant the stage tender was a warrior of the first order. Several more had been wounded, and two of their ponies killed. It now was a matter of honor that he die.

Wells put a finger in the water bucket and passed it over his cracked lips. He thought he glimpsed a toe against the white of the Alkali behind the end of the wall. Taking careful aim, he squeezed off a shot. A startled yell rewarded him, then a hail of bullets. The storm died as soon as it began.

He crawled to the table and picked up a chunk

of dried beef and cut off a piece. Putting it in his jaws, he went back to the window.

His battered hat lay on the floor. A pair of boots, whitened with alkali, stood in a corner under a stringy yellow slicker. On an extra chair was a cracked enamel washbasin containing some bloody water, a day old.

An hour passed slowly. He stared at the rocks in front of the house. They offered the only shelter available to more than one man at a time within a quarter of a mile. From the sides and back, there was no covered approach as the open alkali plain stretched off as far as the eye could reach in all directions. From the station, a slow rise of ground concealed the hills, miles away.

Almost a mile in front of the stage station lay a series of rocky ridges—foothills of the higher mountains beyond. A tongue of scattered rocks offered occasional concealment to a point some distance in front of the station. From there, to get within killing range, the Apaches had to dodge from rock to rock to get behind the low, natural wall in front of the station. Once there nothing could prevent them from lying entrenched for days and maintaining a sporadic fire on the station.

Water was no problem for them. Among the ridges, less than a mile off, was a good spring of only slightly brackish water. It was much better than that offered by the dug well at the station. Wells had killed one Indian going for water, but they offered only a fleeting, flickering target, visible for no more than a moment.

TIME WAS RUNNING OUT. He knew that when he looked at the water in the bucket—yet he knew there would still be water left when his time was up. That would be when the stage reached the station. If it pulled up between the Indians and himself, they could use the stage as cover from his fire to get closer, while firing on the stage.

They knew as well as he that they had not much longer to wait. That made them careful. A little while longer and then the stage would come rolling up to them. He could, of course, fire a few shots to warn the stage, but it would be in the open and fairly close up before they could hear, unless the wind was right.

Warned, they might get away, but with spent horses, and in that heat, he doubted it. Whether they did or not, he was a gone gosling.

Suddenly, his bloodshot eyes squinted, and then slowly widened with expectant triumph. Several feet behind the rock wall was a lone, flat-faced boulder. Lifting his rifle, Wells took aim at the face of that rock, and fired.

He was rewarded by a startled yell, and he

fired three times, as rapidly as he could squeeze off the shots. One Indian, struck by a ricocheting bullet, lunged to full height, emitting a shrill scream, and Wells triggered his rifle again, to make sure of that one.

The Indian toppled forward over the wall, then hastily was dragged from view.

Wells, chuckling, reloaded his rifle and fired again. An Indian lunged to his feet and raced for the shelter of the rocks toward the ridge, and Wells let him go, content to be rid of him. Then a second Indian left. Wells tried two more shots at the flat rock, then lay quiet, staring with his smarting, red-rimmed eyes at the long, white emptiness of the desert.

An hour dragged slowly by, an hour of unrelenting heat and the endless white glare. A buzzard swung in lazy circles, high overhead. Wells left the muzzle of his rifle leaning against the sill, and put his head against the wall near the window. He dozed, only coming out of it at intervals to stare toward the wall. They might be gone, and they might not. He knew Apaches.

Once he tried a swallow of the thick, alkali water, but it choked him and he was only more thirsty than before. He tried a shot at the rock, but drew no answering fire. Then, after an interval, another shot. Silence, silence and the heat.

It would soon be stage time. He was very

sleepy. He leaned his head against the wall and his lids grew heavy. His head bobbed loosely on his neck. Then he slept.

An instant only. His subconscious jerked him awake, frightened at what might have happened. He fired again, three quick shots.

There was no sound, no movement.

He crawled across the floor and looked from the window facing east. Only the wheelmarks showed, the wheelmarks that reached to the crest of the low rise that obscured his eastern view of the long, alkali basin and the distant hills. He returned to his vantage point and tried another shot.

HE WOULD GET out of this on the next stage after the one coming. She had been right, of course, those eighteen years ago when she picked Ed instead of him. Ed settled into a quiet, easy life, but as for himself, he had lived on, a hard, lonely life along the frontiers. He had the ranch, of course, a cozy little place, and pleasant, but memories of her always drove him away, even after eighteen years.

A long hour dragged away before he heard the stage. It came over the rise and swept down upon the station with its pursuing cloud of dust, then braked to a halt. Wells got to his feet and lounged to the door. His eyes threw a brief glance at the desert and the wall, then he walked out to the stage.

"Howdy, Jim! How was the trip?"

"Hot." Jim climbed down from the stage top. "Where's the hosses?"

"Been sort of busy," Wells said. "I'll get them."

While Jim unhooked the spent team he went down to the stone barn. More asleep than awake he threw the harness on the horses. Jim came down to help him.

"Got the old man aboard," he said. "Macomber."

"Wonder if I'll get that powder?"

"Blazes, no! Judson says all he talks about is cuttin' expenses!"

They led the horses back and noticed that Price Macomber and his niece were out of the stage. Judson was watching them, wearily. Some little thing about the girl's face looked familiar to Wells.

"Any fresh water, my man?" Macomber asked.

"No"—Wells looked around, his eyes bloodshot and hard—"but there's the well."

The name was the same, of course. Wells looked at the girl again. Price Macomber was glaring at him.

"I'd think," Macomber replied testily, "you could at least have some water ready for the passengers!"

Wells looked around, glaring. Then he saw the girl. She was standing helplessly, staring at him. Perspiration had streaked the dust on her face. She was the first woman he had seen in two months.

He straightened from fastening a trace chain, staring at the girl. She paled a little, but watched him, wide-eyed and fascinated.

Macomber noticed his stare and was suddenly angry. "Here!" he demanded. "Get us some water!"

Wells turned his head and looked at Macomber. His black eyes were cold and ugly. "Get it yourself!" he said.

Molly moved away from them and looked off across the alkali. She heard her uncle talking, low-voiced, to Judson. She heard him say, "We'll discharge this man!"

Judson was protesting. "Macomber, don't do it. We can't get anybody else. They are all afraid of this station because of the Apaches!"

"Nonsense! No man is indispensable!"

Molly noticed something bright and gleaming lying on the ground near a bundle of dusty hides and clothing. Curious, she started toward it. Then she stopped sharply, and her breath seemed to leave her. She felt as if she were going to faint. It was not a bunch of old hides and clothing, it was a dead man. A dead Indian.

"Uncle Price!" she cried. She turned and started on a stumbling run for the stage, her eyes great spots of darkness in her dead-white face.

"What's the matter?" Price Macomber wheeled about. "A snake?"

"No," she gasped, one hand on her heart, "it's a dead man! A dead—Indian!"

Price Macomber had heard about dead Indians, but he had never seen any kind of a dead man. He put one arm around his niece and stared at it, alarmed and fascinated.

Wells had not noticed. He was helping Jim carry bundles of food and ammunition into the stage station. When Jim put his armload down, he glanced around, noticing the bright brass of the empty shells. Mentally, he calculated, and then he looked up at Wells, his eyes respectful. "Trouble?" he asked.

"Yeah." Wells peeled the wrapping off a fresh plug of chewing. "Guess I got 'em all run off. I didn't have time to look. They hit me about noon, yesterday."

"That—?" Jim wet his dry lips with his tongue. With chill and unhappy realization he thought of what would have happened had the stage rolled up here with the Indians waiting. Him sitting up there on the box in plain sight, too.

They went outside. Macomber was helping his niece toward the stage. "What's up?" Jim asked, looking at them.

Judson glanced at Wells, seeing for the first

time the mark of sleeplessness, the bullet-burned hand, the blood on his side. "You all right?" he demanded.

"Yeah," Wells replied shortly, "bring that powder?"

"No," Judson said, "Macomber says you don't need it."

MACOMBER WAS scarcely less shaken than his niece. He tried to avoid seeing the dead Indian. From here it was just a brown and patchy-looking hump on the alkali.

Wells walked over to him. "You get me some powder," he said flatly, "or get another man, and get that powder out here by the next stage!"

"See here!" Macomber's poise was shaken, but at this blow to the subject closest to his heart as well as to the respect he believed he deserved, his head came up. "Don't be talking to me like that! I don't see any reason for any powder out here. I told Judson that and I'll tell you now. We can't waste a lot of money on useless expenditure!"

Wells looked at him with hard, bitter eyes. "Those rocks out there"—he gestured at the wall—"need blasting out."

He turned on his heels and started for the corral. Then he stopped on a sudden hunch and looked back. "Say," he said, "are you any relation to Edwin Macomber, of Denver?"

Price was startled. He turned around. "Why, I'm his brother. Why do you ask?"

Wells looked at him for a moment, and then he began to smile. Suddenly, he felt better. He walked on to the corral.

Price Macomber hesitated, staring after him, then he shrugged. Judson beside him, he walked to the wall. It was all nonsense, of course. This wall was completely out of the way, and no earthly excuse would warrant its blasting. He felt better, despite the smile on Wells's face, because this had proved his theory again, that most such unexplained items were the result of the impractical whims of impractical men.

He wanted the appearance of fairness, so he would at least look at the wall, but this was just another of the little details that proved how right he was in his theory. The dead Indian was not explained, but that could wait. He would ask about that when—

Price Macomber glanced across the wall and his face turned green. He backed away, retching violently. When he straightened, he dabbed at his lips with a handkerchief and stared at Judson, eyes bright with horror. There were three dead Indians beyond the wall. Each of them had been hit several times with jagged, ricocheting bullets.

Macomber stumbled a little as he hurried back toward the stage. This was an awful place! He must get out of here. Jim was on the box, holding the lines and waiting. Molly was talking to Wells, showing him something.

Price Macomber got hurriedly into the stage and sat down beside his niece. As they started to roll away, Judson waved to Wells. Macomber did not look back.

When they had gone a little way, he stiffened his face. "Send him that powder, Judson. The wall is an obstruction."

A thought occurred to him, and he turned to his niece. "What were you showing him? What did he say to you?"

She looked around. "I meant to tell you. He said he thought he knew my father and mother, so I showed him that picture of us. This one—"

Judson glanced at the picture as she handed it to her uncle, and could scarcely repress a smile. It was a picture of a prim-faced man who might have been Price Macomber himself. He wore spectacles and stood beside a very fat woman with two chins and a round, moonlike face. A face that once might have been quite pretty. Price Macomber nodded. His brother Ed, a solid, substantial man. He handed the picture back.

"What did he say when he saw the picture?"

She frowned, her eyes puzzled. "Why, he didn't say anything! He just stood there and laughed and laughed!"

★ ★ ★

HIS LOADED RIFLE beside the door, the man called Wells began to sweep up the empty shells. "The ranch will look pretty good after this," he said aloud, "but after all, there are worse things than Apaches!"

## *Stage to Willowspring*

He was a medium-tall man with nice hands and feet, and when he got down from the stage he stood away from the others and lit a small Spanish **cigarro**. Under the brim of the gray hat his features were an even sun-brown, his eyes gray and quiet.

Under a nondescript vest he wore a gray wool shirt, and a dark red bandanna that was worn to exquisite softness. His boots had been freshly heeled, and when he walked it was with the easy step of a woodsman rather than that of a rider. His gun was thrust into a slim, old-fashioned holster almost out of sight behind the edge of his vest.

Koons saw him there when he came out to the stage, and he took a second look, frowning a little. There was a sense of the familiar about the man, although he was sure he had never seen him before.

Avery was standing alongside the stage watching them load the box. Koons was pleased to see Avery. They were carrying a small shipment of gold and he liked to have a steady man riding shotgun.

There were five passengers to ride inside and a sixth riding the top. Everybody along the run knew Peg Fulton. She was sixteen when her parents died and she married a no-account gambler who soon ran off and left her. She had gone to a judge for a divorce, an action much frowned upon. She had since been treated as a fallen woman, although there was no evidence to prove it. Koons regretted his part in what had happened to Peg. He had believed he was too old to marry her but the gambler, who was also his age, had not hesitated. Peg's father had been a dry farmer named Gillis, and she came of good stock.

Bell was a fat, solid little man who had been riding the stages for eight years, a drummer for an arms outfit. Gagnon had a couple of rich claims in Nevada and carried himself with the superior feeling of one who is a success—without realizing his good fortune was compounded of ninety percent luck. The man riding the top was a stranger, an unwashed man with weak eyes and a few sparse hairs trying to become a beard. He carried a Spencer .56 and wore a Navy Colt.

The last passenger came from the stage station, and Koons looked again, surprised at her beauty. She had dark, thick hair and the soft skin of a girl of good family and easy living. Her traveling dress was neat and expensive and she had a way of gathering her skirt when about to get into the stage that told Koons she was a lady.

Bell moved over to Koons. "See the fellow in the gray hat?"

"Who is he?"

"That's Scott Roundy, the Ranger who went into Mexico after Chato."

"Him?" Koons looked again. Curiosity impelled Armodel Chase to pause on the iron step of the stage, listening. "Of course he's not a Ranger anymore, but they say he's killed ten men. Wonder if he knows about Todd Boysee?"

"Likely. Wonder what he's doin' up here? Seems mighty far off his range."

"Boysee will ask him."

Gagnon had been listening, and he said, "He doesn't look so tough to me."

Bell glanced at him irritably. "That's what Chato thought. That Mex killed nine, ten men in gunfights, murdered a dozen more. Roundy followed him to Hermosillo and shot him to death in a cantina."

"I heard the Rurales don't like that sort of thing."

"Huh!" Bell said. "They were so glad to get rid of Chato they looked the other way."

Armodel gathered a skirt again, and suddenly beside her there was a low question—"May I?"—and a hand to help her. She accepted it naturally, without coy hesitation, then glanced at the man. It was Scott Roundy.

He got into the stage and sat opposite her beside Peg Fulton. A whip cracked, the stage jolted, then lunged and they were off, and the dust began to rise behind them. The weather was comfortable, even slightly warm in the direct sun, but after a few minutes the shade had a frosty bite to it that indicated winter was waiting just beyond the horizon. This was a country of rolling hills, sparse grass, and piñon-crested ridges. In the shallow valleys there were scattered oaks.

Peg Fulton's head nodded and after a while fell to Roundy's shoulder. Awakening with a start, she apologized and he said quietly, "That's all right, ma'am. I don't mind."

Armodel looked at him thoughtfully but said nothing. She saw his eyes stray to her several times, and then she dozed a little. It seemed hours later when she awakened to find the stage had come to a stop. Dust climbed into the coach and settled upon their clothes. Koons came to the door. "Might get down a few minutes. One of the mules is a mite sick. Thought I'd let him rest up a little."

Avery walked to a point where he could see over the edge of the arroyo, and with a glance toward him, Roundy moved over to Armodel. "Would you like to have a seat, ma'am? There's a flat rock under the oak."

After she seated herself she saw Peg Fulton looking around helplessly, and she said quickly, "Won't you sit here with me? There's room enough."

Peg thanked her and sat down. Gagnon's eyes flashed irritably and he muttered something to Bell, who ignored it. The passenger with the Spencer had squatted on his heels with his back to the rear wheel of the coach and was smoking.

"Are you traveling far, Mr. Roundy?" The blue-green eyes met his. "I am Armodel Chase, and I am going to Willowspring."

"Not far. . . . I am stopping there also. If I can be of service, please call on me."

Gagnon spoke abruptly. "Ma'am, being new to the West I am afraid you do not know the character of the young woman beside you. I believe I should—"

"And I believe you shouldn't!" The blue-green eyes were dark and cool. "Miss Fulton and I are comfortable here, and I do not believe that a woman's marital misfortune is any reason to withhold one's friendship or civility." Peg bit her lower lip and averted her eyes, but her hand sought out Armodel's and for a moment gave it a tight squeeze.

She caught the faint smile on Scott Roundy's face as Gagnon turned away, his back stiff with offended righteousness.

Later, back on the stage, Armodel studied

Roundy when he was not looking. His was a quiet, thoughtful face, his smile almost shy. It was preposterous that this man could have killed ten men.

Gagnon broke the silence, speaking abruptly to Roundy. "What you figure to do when Boysee braces you?"

"Excuse me, I don't know what you are talking about."

Armodel felt the chill in the Ranger's voice, saw the flicker of irritation there.

"Aw, you heard of Todd Boysee! He's marshal of Willowspring. Killed seventeen or eighteen men. They say he's hell on wheels with a six-gun. He killed Lew Cole."

"Cole's been asking for it for years."

"Maybe he thinks you have, too."

Scott Roundy's voice was cold. "I don't care to continue the conversation, my friend. Todd Boysee's business is his own. I'm sure he won't look for any trouble where there's none to be had."

Gagnon could not resist a final word. "He'll meet the stage." He smiled without warmth. "We'll see then."

Bell opened his eyes. "Nothin' to that talk, Roundy. Boysee's a good man. The men he's killed had it comin'. He's kinda touchy about strangers wearin' guns, though."

The conversation lapsed. Atop the stage they

heard the passenger with the Spencer moving around. The air grew noticeably colder and the wind seemed to be mounting. A gust almost lifted the stage. "A norther," Bell said, "bad place to meet it. All flat country for miles."

Scott Roundy lifted the curtain and peered out. Darkness had fallen, but there was sifting snow in the air, and a scattering of it on the ground.

He sat back in his seat and closed his eyes. It was always the same. Once they knew you were a gunfighter they would not let it alone. Men had been killed in utterly senseless battles created by idle talk, the sadistic urge to see men kill, or the simple curiosity of mild men eager to see champions compete. It was an age-old, timeless curiosity that would live as long as men had the courage for battle. He had heard the endless arguments over what would happen if Hickok shot it out with Ben Thompson, or Wyatt Earp with John Ringo, or Boone May with Seth Bullock. Men compared their respective talents, added up their victories, exaggerated the number they had killed.

It was starting again now. "Charlie Storms," Gagnon was saying, "is one of the fastest men alive. Never saw him beat. I don't think Earp would have a chance with him."

Bell, who heard everything, opened his eyes

again. "Charlie Storms is dead," he said quietly. "Luke Short killed him in Tombstone."

"Short?" Gagnon was contemptuous. "I don't believe it."

"I heard it, too," Peg Fulton said quietly.

Armodel looked again at Scott Roundy. He was leaning back and had his eyes closed, apparently hearing nothing. Yet he was awake. She had seen his eyes open slightly only a minute or two before. How he must feel to hear this talk. Would that man be waiting for him? If so, what would happen? Half frightened, she looked at Roundy. To think that he might soon be dead!

"None of them are as good as they're cracked up to be," Gagnon said, staring at Roundy. "Meet the right man an' they take water mighty fast."

Roundy's eyes opened. "Did you ever face a gun?" he asked mildly.

"No, but—"

"Wait until you do." Roundy closed his eyes and turned his shoulder away from Gagnon.

Through the crack of the curtain he could see the snow was falling fast, but most of it was in the air. For some time now, the stage had slowed to a walk.

Bell was not asleep. Scott Roundy and Todd Boysee. It would be something to see—and something to tell. He knew how avidly men gathered about to hear stories of a famous gun battle. Concannon had seen the fight between Billy Brooks and the four brothers who came to Dodge hunting him. He had been at the restaurant window when Brooks stepped to the door and killed all four of them in the street. It was history now, but Concannon could hold a crowd anytime, just telling of it. Long as he had been in the West, he had known all the great names among gunfighters, but he had never seen a shoot-out between two top men.

This Roundy was cool. He had killed Con Bigelow at Fort Griffin, and Bigelow was ranked with the best. Roundy beat him to the draw and put two slugs into his heart. Bigelow had been a wanted man who laughed at the Rangers and evaded them, until that afternoon when cornered by Scott Roundy.

Roundy hunched into the corner. Irritably, he was thinking of the talk. They never let up. Always after a man.

Todd Boysee . . . no longer a youngster. That meant a cagey and straight-shooting man. But what kind of a man? Was he like Jeff Milton or Jim Gillette, who shot only when absolutely necessary? Or was he a reputation hunter like Old John Selman who had killed more than one man under doubtful, to say the least, circumstances. Some of those hard-bitten old town marshals felt the simplest way to maintain their position was to kill any man who threatened it, even by his presence.

He wanted no trouble, but it would pay to be careful. Once a man had a reputation with a gun there was no rest short of the grave.

The stage rumbled on through the night. During a momentary stop he got blankets out and spread them over the knees of Peg and Armodel. Then he relaxed again in his corner. There was the estate to settle, or he would just ride on through Willowspring. He suddenly knew he did not want to stop. Yet, even if he did not want to, he must. If the idea got around that he had taken water for any man, he would have to kill a half dozen who would want to build reputations at his expense.

He settled down to get some sleep. Outside the snow fell and the wind rocked the stage, moving slowly to keep to the ill-defined trail.

OLD TODD BOYSEE WAS a grim and hard-bitten man. He had found Willowspring a roistering boomtown with two and three killings a night. He had killed four men during his first month on the job, and two later that year. After that there had been little trouble.

Occasionally he laid a pistol barrel over the head of some malcontent who believed he could tree the town, and once he had faced down a mob who intended to lynch a prisoner. Lately, it was becoming difficult. Twice in the past year men had come to town hunting him, one a pink-faced youngster who believed himself a dangerous man, the other a burly loudmouth who believed, and said, that Todd Boysee was too old for his job.

Both of them were buried now, out on Boot Hill. The boy had too much nerve for his skill, and the loudmouth, who might have backed down at the last minute, might also have come back to take a shot from ambush. Todd Boysee had not lived to become fifty-four by taking chances. By the ages of gunmen he was an old man, but his hand was sure, his aim straight.

It was snowing lightly and the wind was blowing when he walked down to the Gold Star. A snow-covered rider was at the bar, pouring a glass of whiskey. He glanced up at Boysee. "Here he is now," he said. "Ask him."

A heavy-set rancher with ill-fitting false teeth turned to Boysee. "Todd," he said, "we was just a-talkin'. Who do you reckon is best man with a gun? Wyatt Earp or Scott Roundy?"

Boysee pulled the end of his white mustache and his cold eyes measured the rancher. He did not like talkative men. "I have no idea," he said coldly.

A thin-legged man with amazingly narrow hips and a long, loose jaw said, "Roundy's comin' up the trail. Jess seen him gettin' on the stage."

The rancher was watching Boysee, his watery blue eyes eager. "Wonder what he's comin' **here** for? He used to be a Ranger, but this ain't Texas."

Boysee ignored them, waiting for the bartender to set up his evening drink. They were loafing, loose-mouthed men who would be better off at home. The rancher had been one of those in the lynch mob he had stopped, and Todd Boysee had not forgotten it. Yet when he found a rustler on his place he ran for help instead of bracing the man then and there.

Yet, what **was** Scott Roundy coming here for? This was far from his usual haunts. It made no kind of sense, and Todd Boysee had made it his business to know about men like Roundy. The man's reputation was good. He had never killed but in performance of his duty, although he was always in the dangerous spots. A couple of times he had not even fired until shot at. A man who did that had a streak of weakness in him. Given a break, men would kill you sooner or later. You had to shoot first, and shoot to kill.

"You still goin' to meet the stage?" Jess asked.

The word "still" angered Boysee. His cold blue eyes flashed. "I'll meet it," he said. He took up the bottle and poured a drink. It was the one drink he permitted himself.

When he closed the door behind him he heard the buzz of excited voices. The fools! What did they know!

Bitterly, he stared into the night and the snow. There should be an easier way to make a living, but how? It was all he knew. He was too old now to punch cows, and who would give him a job? He had no money, only the little house and the garden behind it. Had Mary lived, he might have broken away from this life. She had wanted him to leave it.

What could he do, live on charity? Quitting was not an escape, anyway. The name would follow him, and they would still come hunting him, believing if they killed Todd Boysee it would make them feared. Little did they know.

He had been a buffalo hunter at seventeen, a scout with the Army at nineteen, an express messenger riding shotgun on the stages at twenty. At twenty-five he became a town marshal, and he had followed it since, working a dozen towns before he had settled in Willowspring.

Gifted with natural speed of hand and eye, he had improved by constant practice. For a time he savored the reputation it had given him, and then it had turned to ashes in his mouth after he killed a man he need not have killed. Finally, even that memory grew dim and he killed to live, to survive.

Every cow outfit that came up the trail had at least one man who fancied himself a gunhand. You stopped them or they stopped you. It was too bad, he reflected again, that Mary had not lived. He was fifty-four now, but looked and acted ten years older.

Why was Roundy coming here? What was there for him in Willowspring? It was foolish to think he was coming here to hunt him . . . but was it? Those fools back in the saloon believed it.

He walked down the street, a tall, very straight man. In this town he was the Law. It was all he had left. He never touched a gun except against strangers. Here, all he ever needed to do was to speak, quietly, sternly. He took out his big silver watch. Mary had given it to him for his birthday. He had been pleased. He had always wanted a watch. The wind moaned cold when he stopped at the corner. The sky was a flat black, without stars. It would be bitter cold on the plains tonight.

THE STAGE WAS STOPPED when Armodel opened her eyes. Scott Roundy was gone, although she had not heard him go. Bell was sitting up, wide awake. "What is it?" she asked.

"We're lost. The stage has been circling."

"But how could they get off the trail?"

"No fences, no telegraph posts, just a couple

of wheel tracks, mostly grassed over. We're the second stage since the Indians burned the White Creek Station, last summer."

Outside in the snow, Koons stood beside Avery and Roundy. "If you're sure we passed Three Oaks," Roundy said, "we're south of the Wall."

"Didn't know you knew this country. The Wall's north of the trail, but circlin' wide as we done we'd have hit it."

"So we're south." Roundy was sure. "Bear south some more to North Fork Canyon."

"Don't know the place," Koons said.

"I'll find it." Roundy suggested to Avery, "We go ahead and let Koons line up on us. That would keep us in a straight line."

It had been a long time. The wind moaned along the plains, stirring snow from the grass . . . this place he would not forget, he had never forgotten, no matter how many the years. His name was different, but he was the same.

"And when we get there?"

"A stone cabin and fuel. At least, there was fifteen years ago, and a stone cabin doesn't rot. Anyway, the place is sheltered."

Koons turned. "All right," he said.

The stage lurched into motion and headed south, away from the wind. When they had been proceeding slowly for almost an hour the ground suddenly began to slope away, and after a while

Roundy did not go on ahead but stood and waited, and when Avery came up they guided the coach into the arroyo.

The stage bumped along over frozen earth and occasional rocks, and then a black cliff reared before them, and against the face they could see the rock house. It was barely visible under the overhang.

"Bring the mules inside!" Roundy yelled. "There's a cave back of the house and room enough!"

The first mule balked at the dark opening, but when it finally entered the rest followed. Koons stabled them at a tie-pole in the cave and returned to find a fire going in the house. Roundy was kneeling beside it, and Armodel Chase stood beside him.

Koons stared at Roundy curiously. "Never knowed of this place," he said.

Roundy nodded at the bottom bunk in the tier of two. "I was born in that bed," he said, "in gold rush days."

Armodel stared at him, and looked again at the bunk. Her eyes went around the bare room. There were two tiers of beds, a table, two benches, a chair. There was an iron pot beside the fireplace. Her mind returned to her own comfortable home. Hers no more.

"My mother is buried in the trees across the creek," he said. "She only lived a few days."

Koons brought more fuel and added it, stick by stick, to the fire. "All Injun country then," he said. "Must have been."

"It was during a lull in an attack when I was born," Roundy said. "Wagon broke down up on the trail. The rest of them were gold-hungry and anxious. Only one wagon would stay with us."

Avery brought coffee from the stage and they started getting water hot over the fire. Gagnon was not talking, but Bell was curious. It was like so many tales he had heard, yet he never tired of listening. He probably had heard more Western history in his years of traveling than any man alive, and sometimes he passed the stories on.

"What happened?" Armodel searched the quiet face, thinking of how his mother must have felt, dying here, never knowing if her child would live, never knowing if he would grow up to become a man. Suddenly, she knew that gunfighter or not, his mother would have been proud.

"My father and the people who stayed," he said, "they started Willowspring."

Koons shifted his feet. "Then"—he took his pipe from his mouth, suddenly disturbed—"you must be Clete Ryan's nephew."

"Yes," he said.

Peg Fulton looked across the fire at Koons, and she started to speak, then stopped, looking helpless. Koons got up and walked toward the back of the cave. Peg would know, of course. Peg was a Gillis, and they had lived neighbors to the Ryans. Gillis worked for Clete, time to time, for Dave, too, before Mary got married and Dave went east.

He did not remember Roundy, but he remembered the story. The boy's father had been an Army officer, and he had taken the boy to Fort Brown, Texas. After that they never heard of them again.

The man with the Spencer rifle brought in an armful of fuel from outside and sat down near the fire, keeping back a little, and giving the others room. Despite the cold, the stone cabin was tight and the place was warming up.

Peg moved around and took over the coffee making from Avery. Koons watched her, his eyes angry. This was a good girl. What else could she have done when that gambler left her? People had talked . . . thought the worst of her long ago.

"Warmin' up, Peg," he said suddenly. "Can I take your coat?"

She looked up, surprise changing to a softness and warmth. "Thank you, Alec," she said. "I was warm."

Koons took the coat into the shadows. He was surprised to feel himself blushing. He had not blushed in years. When he came back to the fire,

Gagnon had a faintly knowing smile on his face. Koons felt a sudden murderous fury. **Say something,** he said under his breath. **Make one snide remark and I'll hurt you so badly—!**

The coffee was hot, and Armodel was sitting close beside Scott Roundy. Koons squatted down near Peg Fulton and accepted the cup she handed him. He could hear his mules stomping in the cave. They were eating their oats from the feed bags, and already content. It didn't take much for a mule to be happy . . . or a man either, come to that.

An hour later all were fast asleep except for Alec Koons and Peg. He sat up, tending the fire, and she tossed and turned, finally giving in to wakefulness. He smiled at her shyly, wanting to speak but feeling clumsy and tongue-tied. Finally he cleared his throat and, without looking up from the fire, spoke.

"Peg," he said, "four years ago I came nigh to askin' you, but I figured I was too old for you. I'm older now, but . . . well, so are you.

"Will you marry me?" He looked up at her, finally, seeking out her eyes in the firelight. She reached out her hand and took his and held it tightly.

"Of course, Alec. I wanted you to ask me, but I thought you never saw me like that. I'd be proud to marry you."

She fell asleep not a half hour later, comfortably in his arms.

THE STAGE TO WILLOWSPRING swung into the street at a spanking trot, almost twelve hours late. The wind was down and the sun was out and the little snow was going fast . . . a crowd waited for the stage.

Koons swung his mules up to the stage station and started to get down. Todd Boysee stood off to one side, straight and tall, aloof and lonely in his threadbare black coat.

Koons started to swing down—he wanted to get to Todd first—but something made him look up. The man with the Spencer rifle was sitting unmoved atop the stage. He was half behind Armodel Chase's trunk, and he had his rifle in his hands. He was smiling.

Scott Roundy got down from the stage and handed Armodel to the ground. Roundy felt rather than saw the crowd draw back, and he looked up to see Todd Boysee facing him.

"Roundy!" Boysee's voice was stern. "You huntin' me?"

Scott took a step forward, sensing the old man's feelings. He put up a hand. "No, I—"

Todd Boysee's hand dropped to his gun. Scott distinctly heard his palm slap the walnut butt.

A dull boom slammed against the false-fronted

buildings, and Todd Boysee felt the bullet that would kill him. He took a step back—**Scott Roundy had not drawn!**

Boysee felt a sickness in his stomach. Something had hit him hard in the chest, and the boom was heavy in his ears. Then he saw Scott Roundy was shooting, but not at him. Boysee was on the ground, holding his fire. His eyes found focus.

Over the top of a trunk was the muzzle of a Spencer, and behind it and left of the gun a white spot of brow, eye, and a hat. Todd Boysee fired, and there was a spot over the eye and red on the face. Roundy fired again and then the man with the Spencer rifle humped up and rolled over, falling flat and dead into the dust alongside the stage.

Todd Boysee was down and dying. He was no fool. He had shot enough men and seen enough of them shot. "Who . . . who was it?"

"Johnny Cole," a man from the crowd said. "I guess he come to get you for killin' Lew."

"Boysee." Roundy got his arm under the old man's shoulders. "I **was** huntin' you. You're my uncle. My mother was Mary Ryan's sister."

Todd Boysee was feeling better than he had expected. He always figured to die alone. With Mary's nephew here it was different, somehow. There was a girl beside him. . . . Why, she even looked like Mary. A sight like her, in fact.

His eyes shifted to the girl and his hand gripped her wrist. "You love this boy?" His mind was slipping, he was backing down a dark corridor whose walls he couldn't see. "You stick with him, no matter what. It's all he'll ever have, what you can give him."

Scott Roundy moved back from the walk and stood near Armodel. Todd Boysee had been carried away. The blood was on the boardwalk.

"Where were you goin'?" He turned to look into her eyes.

"Just . . . west."

"Is this far enough?" he asked.

"It has to be. . . . He gave me a job to do."

"I was going to ask you," he said, "only—"

"I know," she said quietly, and she did know. She knew what she had read in the eyes of a lonely old man, and what had been in her heart since the night by the fire. There would be times of gladness and times of sorrow, there would be fear, doubt, and worry . . . but no matter what, they would not be alone, not ever again.

## *Let the Cards Decide*

Where the big drops fell, we had placed a wooden bucket retrieved from a corner of the ancient log shack. The long, earth-floored one-room cabin smelled of wet clothing, wood smoke, and the dampness brought on by unceasing rain. Yet there was fuel enough, and the fire blazed bright on the hearth, slowly dispelling the dampness and bringing an air of warmth and comfort to the cheerless room.

Seven of us were there. Haven, who had driven the stage; Rock Wilson, a mine boss from Hangtown; Henry, the Cherokee Strip outlaw; a slender man with light brown hair, a sallow face, and cold eyes whom I did not at first know; the couple across the room; and myself.

Six men and one woman—a girl.

She might have been eighteen or a year older, and she was one of those girls born to rare beauty. She was slim, yet perfectly shaped, and when she moved it was to unheard music, and when she smiled, it was for you alone, and with each smile she seemed to give you something intimate, something personal. How she had come to be here with this man we all knew. We knew, for he was a man who talked much and talked loud. From the first, I'd felt sorry for her, and admired her for her quiet dignity and poise.

She was to become his wife. She was one of a number of girls and women who had come west to find husbands, although why this girl should have been among them I could not guess. She was a girl born for wealth and comfort, and her every word and movement spoke of breeding and culture. Yet here she was, and somehow she had gotten into the hands of Sam Tallman.

He was a big fellow, wide of shoulder and girth, with big hands and an aggressive manner. Not unhandsome in a bold way, he could appear gentle and thoughtful when it suited him, but it was no part of the man and strictly a pose. He was all the girl was not: rough, unclean, and too frank in his way of talking to strangers of his personal affairs.

That Carol Houston was becoming disillusioned was obvious. That is, if there had been any illusions to start. From time to time she gave him sharp, inquiring glances, the sort one might direct at an obnoxious stranger. And she was increasingly uneasy.

The stage was headed north and was to have dropped several of us here to meet another stage heading west. We were going to be a day late, however, for our coach had overturned three miles back on the muddy trail.

Bruised and shaken, we had righted the stage in the driving rain and had managed to get on as far as the shack. As we could not continue through the night, and this place was at least warm and dry, we made the best of it.

There seemed no end to the rain, and in the few, momentary lulls we could hear the measured fall of drops into the bucket, which would soon be full.

Now in any such place there comes a time when conversation slowly dies. The usual things have been said, the storm discussed and compared to other storms, the accident bewailed, and the duration of our stay surmised. We had exchanged destinations and told of our past lives, and all with no more than the usual amount of lying.

Dutch Henry produced some coffee, and I, ransacking the dismal depths of the farther cabin corners, a pot and cups. So the good, rich smell of coffee permeated the room with its friendly sense of well-being and comfort.

My name, it might be added, is Henry Duval. Born on Martinique, that distant and so lovely island noted for explosive mountains and women. My family had been old, respected, and until it came to me, of some wealth. By profession I had been a gambler.

This was, for a period of nearly a century, the usual profession of a young man of family but no means. Yet from gambling I had turned to the profession of arms, or rather, I had divided my time between them. The riverboats started me on the first, and the revolutions and wars of freedom in Latin America on the second. Now, at thirty-five, I was no longer occupied with either of these, but had succeeded in building a small fortune of my own in handling mining properties.

But let us be honest. During my gambling days I had, on occasion, shall we say, encouraged the odds? An intelligent man with a knowledge of and memory for cards, and some knowledge of people, can usually win, and honestly—when the cards run with him—but of course, one must have the cards. So when they failed to come of themselves, sometimes I did, as I have said, encourage them a bit.

Haven, the stage driver, I knew slightly. He was a solid, dependable man, both honest and fearless. Rock Wilson was of the same order, and both were of the best class of those strong, brave, and often uneducated men who built the West. Both had followed the boom towns—as I once had.

Dutch Henry? You may have heard of him. They hanged him finally, I believe. He was, as I have said, an outlaw. He stole horses, and cattle, and at times robbed banks or stages, but all without malice and without unnecessary shooting. And he was a man of rugged good nature who might steal a hundred today and give it away tomorrow.

The sallow-faced man introduced himself. His accent was that of the deep South. "My given name is John. I once followed the practice of medicine." He coughed into a soiled handkerchief, a deep rattling tubercular cough. "But my ahh . . . condition made that an irony I could no longer endure." He brushed a speck of lint from the frayed cuff of his faded frock coat. "I am now a gentleman of fortune, whatever that may mean."

Henry made the coffee. It had the strong, healthy flavor of cowpuncher coffee, the best for a rainy night. He filled our cups, saving the best for the lady. She smiled quickly, and that rugged gentleman of the dark trails flushed like a schoolboy.

Tallman was talking loudly. "Sure hit the jackpot! All them women, an' me gettin' the best o' the lot! Twenty o' them there was, an' all spoke for! Out in the cold, they said I was, but all right, I told 'em, if there's an extry, I get her! An' this one was extry!"

The future Mrs. Tallman flushed and looked down at her hands.

"How did it happen, Miss Houston?" I asked her. "Why didn't they expect you?"

She looked up, grateful for the chance to explain and to make her position clearer. She was entitled to that respect. "I wasn't one of them—not at first. I was coming west with my father, in the same wagon train, but he died of cholera and something happened to the little money he had. We owed money and I had nothing . . . well, what could I do?"

"Perfectly right," I agreed. "I've known some fine women to come west and make good marriages that way."

Good marriage was an expression I should not have used. Her face changed when I said that, and she looked down at her hands.

"Should o' heard the others howl when they seen what I drawed!" Tallman crowed. "Course, she ain't used to our rough western ways, an' she ain't much on the work, I hear, but she'll learn! You leave that to me!"

Haven shifted angrily on his bench and Rock Wilson's face darkened and his eyes flashed angrily. "You're not married to her yet, you say? I'd be careful if I were you. The lady might change her mind."

Tallman's face grew ugly. His small eyes narrowed and hardness came into his jowls.

"Change her mind? Not likely! You reckon I'd stand for that? I paid off her debts. One o' them young fellers back yonder had some such idea, but I knocked that out of him mighty quick! An' if he'd gone for a gun, I'd o' killed him!" Tallman slapped his six-shooter. "I'm no gunman," he declared, "but I get along!"

This last was said with a truculent stare around the room.

More to get the conversation away from the girl than for any other reason, I suggested poker.

John, the ex-doctor with the sallow cheeks, looked up sharply, and a faint, wry smile hovered about his lips. The others moved in around the table, and the girl moved back. Somehow, over their heads, our eyes met. In hers there was a faint pleading, an almost spoken request to do something . . . anything . . . but to get her out of this. Had we talked an hour she could not have made her wish more clear.

In that instant my resolution was made. As John picked up the cards I placed my palm flat down on the table in the old, international signal that I was a cardsharp. With a slight inclination of my head, I indicated Tallman as the object of my intentions, and saw his agreement.

Tallman played with the same aggressive manner of his talk, and kept a good eye on the cards that were played. We shifted from draw to stud and back again from time to time, and at first Tallman won.

When he had something good you had to pay to stay in the game, and he rode his luck hard. At the same time, he was suspicious and wary. He watched every move closely at first, but as the game progressed he became more and more interested and his vigilance waned. Yet he studied his cards carefully and took a long time in playing.

For me, there were no others in the game but Tallman and John. Once, when I had discarded, I walked to the fire and added a few sticks, then prepared more coffee and put the pot on the fire. Turning my head I saw Carol Houston watching me. From my chair I got my heavy coat and brought it to her. "If you're cold," I whispered.

She smiled gratefully, then looked into the flames.

"I do not wish to intrude on something that is none of my business." I spoke as if to the fire. "It seems that you might be more comfortable if you were free of that man."

She smiled sadly. "Can you doubt it? But he paid bills for me. I owe him money, and I signed an agreement to marry him."

"No one would hold you to such an agreement."

"He would. And I must pay my debts, one

way or another. At the moment I can see no other way out."

"We'll see. Wait, and don't be afraid." Adding another stick to the fire, I returned to the table. Tallman glanced up suspiciously, for he could have heard a murmur, although probably none of the words spoken between us.

It was my deal, and as I gathered the discards my eyes made note of their rank, and swiftly I built a bottom stock, then shuffled the cards while maintaining this stock. I placed the cards in front of Henry for the cut, then I shifted the cut smoothly back and dealt. John gathered his cards, glanced at them, and returned them to the table before him. Tallman studied his own, then fidgeted with his money. I tossed in my ante and we started to build Tallman. We knew he liked to ride hard on a good hand and we gave him his chance. Finally, I dropped out and left it to the doctor. Tallman had a straight, and Doc spread his cards—a full house, queens and tens.

From then on we slowly but carefully took Tallman apart. Haven and Wilson soon became aware of what was happening. Neither John nor I stayed when either of them showed with anything good, but both of us rode Tallman. Haven dropped out of the game first, then Wilson. Henry stayed with us and we occasionally fed him a small pot. From time to time Tallman won, but his winnings were just enough to keep him on edge.

Once I looked up to find Carol's eyes on mine. I smiled a little and she watched me gravely, seriously. Did she guess what was happening here?

"Your bet, Mistah Duval." It was John's soft Georgia voice. I gathered my cards, glanced at them, and raised. Tallman saw me and kicked it up. Henry studied his cards, shrugged, and threw them in.

"Too rich for my blood," he said, smiling.

John kicked it up again, then Tallman raised. He was sweating now. I could see his tongue touch his lips, and the panic in the glance he threw at John when he heard the raise was not simulated. He waited after his raise, watching to see what I would do, and I deliberately let him sweat it out. I was holding three aces and a pair of sixes, and I was sure it wasn't good enough. John had dealt this hand.

My signal to John brought instant response. His hand dropped to the table, and the signal told me he was holding an ace.

Tallman stirred impatiently. Puttering a bit, as if uncertain, I raised twenty dollars. The Southerner threw in his hand and Tallman saw my raise, then felt in his pockets for more money and found none. There was an instant of blank consternation, and then he called. He was holding four queens and a trey when he spread his hand.

Hesitating only momentarily, I put my cards down, bunched together.

"Spread 'em!" John demanded impatiently, and reaching across the table he spread my cards—secretly passing his ace to give me four aces and a six.

Tallman's eyes bulged. He swallowed and his face grew red. He glared at the cards as if staring would change their spots. Then he swore viciously.

Coolly, I gathered in the pot, palming and discarding my extra six as my hand passed the discards. Carefully, I began stacking my coins while John gathered the cards together.

"I'm clean!" Tallman flattened his big hands on the table. He looked around the room. "Who wants to stake me? I'll pay, I'm good for it!"

Nobody replied. Haven was apparently dozing. Rock Wilson was smoking and staring into the fire. Henry yawned and looked at the one window through which we could see. It was faintly gray. It would soon be morning.

From the ceiling a drop gathered and fell with a fat **plop** into the bucket. Nobody spoke, and in the silence we realized for the first time that the rain had almost ceased.

"What's got into you?" Tallman demanded. "You were plenty willin' to take my money! Gimme a chance to get even!"

"No man wants to play agin his own money," Wilson commented mildly.

My winnings were stacked, part of it put away, yet of what remained the entire six hundred dollars had been won from Tallman. "Seems early to end a game," I remarked carelessly. "Have you got any collateral?"

He hesitated. "I've got a—!" He had started to put up his pistol, but changed his mind suddenly. Something inside me tightened when I realized what that might mean.

Tallman stared around, scowling. "I guess I ain't got—" It was time now, if it was ever to be time. Yet as the moment came, I felt curiously on edge myself.

"Doesn't she owe you money?" I indicated Carol Houston. "And that agreement to marry should be worth something."

Even as I said it, I felt like a cad, and yet this was what I had been building toward. Tallman stared at me and his face darkened with angry blood. He started to speak, so I let a string of gold eagles trail through my fingers and their metallic clink arrested him, stopped his voice in his throat. His eyes fell to the gold. His tongue touched his lips.

"Only for collateral," I suggested.

"No!" He sank back in his seat. "I'll be damned if I do!"

"Suit yourself." My shrug was indifference itself. Slowly, I got out my buckskin money bag and began gathering the coins. "You asked for a chance. I gave it to you." I'd played all night for this moment but I was now afraid I'd lost my chance.

Yet the sound of the dropping coins fascinated him. He started to speak, but before he could open his mouth Carol Houston got suddenly to her feet and walked around the table.

"If he won't play for it with you, maybe he will play with me." She looked at Tallman and her smile was lovely to look upon. "Will you, Sam?"

He glared at her. "Sit down! This here's man's business!" His voice was rough. "Anyway, you got no money! No tellin' what you'd be doin' if I hadn't paid off for you!"

Dutch Henry's face tightened and he started to get to his feet. John was suddenly on the edge of his chair, his breath whistling hollowly in his throat, his eyes blazing at the implied insult. "Sir! You are a miserable scoundrel—!"

"Wait!" Carol Houston's voice stopped us.

She turned to John. "Will you lend me six hundred dollars?"

Both Dutch Henry and I reached for our

pockets but she ignored us and accepted the money from the smaller man.

"Now, Sam. One cut of the cards. One hundred dollars against the agreement and my IOUs . . . Have you got the guts to do it?"

He started to growl a threat, but John spoke up. "You could play Duval again if you win." His soft voice drawled, "He gave you quite a thrashing."

Yet as John spoke, his attention, as was mine, was directed at the face of Carol Houston. What happened to our little lady? This behavior did not, somehow, seem to fit.

Tallman hesitated, then shrugged. "Yeah? All right, but I'm warning you." He shook his finger at John. "I'm paying no more of my wife's debts. If she loses, you lose too. Now give me the damn cards."

She handed him the deck and he cut—a queen.

Tallman chuckled. "Reckon I've made myself a hundred," he said. "You ain't got much chance to beat that."

Carol Houston accepted the cards. They spilled through her fingers to the table and we helped her gather them up. She shuffled clumsily, placed the deck on the table, then cut—an ace!

Tallman swore and started to rise.

"Sam, wait!" She put her hand on his arm. He

frowned, but he dropped back into his seat and glared at me.

Carol Houston turned to me, her eyes quietly calculating. The room was very still. A drop of rain gathered on the ceiling and fell into the bucket—again that fat **plop**. The window was almost white now . . . it was day again.

"How much did you win from Sam, Mr. Duval?"

Her face was without expression. "Six hundred dollars," I replied. "Not more than that."

She picked up the cards, trying a clumsy shuffle. "Would you gamble with me for that money?"

John leaned back in his chair, holding a handkerchief to his mouth. Yet even as he coughed his eyes never left the girl. Dutch Henry was leaning forward, frankly puzzled. Neither Wilson nor Haven said anything. This seemed a different girl, not at all the sort of person we had—

"If you wish." My voice strained hard not to betray my surprise. I was beginning to understand that we had all been taken in.

She pushed the entire six hundred dollars she had borrowed from John into the middle of the table. "Cut the cards once for the lot, Mr. Duval?"

I cut and turned the card faceup—the nine of clubs.

She drew the deck together, straightened it,

tapped it lightly with her thumb as she picked it up, and turned—**a king!**

Stunned, and more by the professional manner of the cut than its result, I watched Carol Houston draw the money to her. With careful hands she counted out six hundred dollars and returned it to John. "Thank you," she said, and smiled at him.

His expression a study, John pocketed the money.

Haven, who had left the cabin, now thrust his head back into the door. "All hitched up! We're goin' on! Mount up, folks!"

"Mr. Haven," Carol asked quickly, "isn't there a stage going west soon?"

" 'Bout an hour, if she's on time."

The six hundred she had won from me she pushed over to Sam Tallman. Astonished, he looked at the money, and then at her. "I—is this for me?"

"For you. It is over between us. But I want those IOUs and the marriage contract."

"Now wait a minute!" Tallman roared, lunging up from his chair.

He reached across for her but I stopped him. "That money is more than you deserve, Tallman. I'd take it and get out."

His hand dropped and rested on his pistol butt and his eyes narrowed. "She's goin' with me! I'll be **damned** if I let any of you stop me!"

"No, suh." It was John's soft voice. "You'll just be damned. Unless you go and get on that stage."

Tallman turned truculently toward the slighter man, all his rage suddenly ready to vent itself on this apparently easier target.

Before he could speak, Dutch Henry spoke from the doorway. "You'll leave him alone, Tallman, if you want to live. That's Doc Holliday!"

Tallman brought up short, looking foolish. Doc had not moved, his right hand grasping the lapel of his coat, his gray eyes cold and level. Shocked, Tallman turned and stumbled toward the door.

"Henry Duval, you quit gambling once, did you not?"

She held my eyes. Hers were clear, lovely, grave. "Why . . . yes. It has been years . . . until tonight."

"And you gambled for me. Wasn't that it?"

My ears grew red. "All right, so I'm a fool."

Until that moment I had never known how a woman's face could light up, nor what could be seen in it. "Not a fool," she said gently. "I meant what I said by the fire—up to a point."

We heard the stage rattle away, and then I looked at Carol.

A smile flickered on her lips, and then she picked up the cards from the table. Deliberately, she spread them in a beautiful fan, closed the deck, did a one-hand cut, riffled the deck, then handed them to me. "Cut them," she said.

I cut an ace, then cut the same ace again and again. She picked up the deck, riffled them again, and placing them upon the table, cut a red king.

Picking up the deck I glanced at the ace and king she had cut. "Slick king and a shaved ace," I said. "Tap the deck lightly as you cut and you cut the king every time. But where did you have them?"

"In my purse." She took my hands. "Henry, do you remember Natchez Tom Tennison?"

"Of course. We worked the riverboats together a half dozen times. A good man."

"He was my father, and he taught me what I did tonight. Both things."

"Both things?"

"How to use cards, and always to pay my debts. I didn't want to owe anything to Sam Tallman, not even the money you took from him, and I didn't want to be the girl you won in a poker game."

Dutch Henry, the Cherokee Strip outlaw, slapped his thigh. "Women!" he said. "If they don't beat all!"

It was almost two hours before the westbound stage arrived . . . but somehow it did not seem that long.

## *Duffy's Man*

Duffy's man had been on the job just six days when trouble started.

Duffy, who was older than the gnarled pin-oak by the water hole, knew there would be trouble when he saw Clip Hart riding up to the stable. Duffy had covered a lot of miles in his time, and had forgotten nothing, man or animal, that he had seen in his travels.

Clip Hart had killed a man seven years before in El Paso, and Duffy had seen it happen. Since then there had been other killings in other towns, and three years in the state pen for rustling. From time to time Hart had been investigated in connection with robberies of one kind or another.

Hart was older, heavier, and harder now. He had the coldly watchful eye of a hunted man. There were two men with him and one of them rode across the street to the Pine Saloon and stood alongside his horse, watching the street.

Hart looked at the sign on the livery stable and then at the fat old man in the big chair. "You're Duffy?" Hart measured him as he spoke.

"I'm Duffy." The old man shifted his bulk in the polished chair. "What can I do for you?"

"The use of your stable. I've seven horses coming in tonight. They'll be kept here in your stable, saddled all the time."

Duffy shifted himself in his seat. "None of that here. I'll not want your business. Not here."

"You'll keep them. You don't move very fast, Duffy." Clip Hart struck a match on the seat of his pants and held up the flame. "Your barn can't move at all." He lifted the flame suggestively. "Where's your hostler?"

Duffy turned his head on his fat neck. He was no fool, and he knew Hart was not bluffing. He opened his mouth to call for his hostler, and as he turned his head he saw him there, standing in the door, his hands on his hips.

Duffy's man was tall, lean, and wide-shouldered. His face was still. Sometimes his eyes smiled, rarely his lips. The stubble of beard he had worn when Duffy hired him was gone now, but he wore no hat and he still wore the worn, badly scuffed shoes, unusual foot gear in a country of boots and spurs.

There was a small scar on one cheekbone and sometime long ago his nose had been broken. He was probably twenty-five but he looked older, and the years behind him had probably been rugged years.

Clip Hart stared at him. "There'll be seven

horses brought here tonight. Keep them saddled and ready to go. Understand?"

Duffy's man jerked a thumb at Duffy. "I take my orders from him."

Hart's anger flared. He was a man who could not accept resistance of any kind. It drove him to a killing fury and Duffy knew it, and was worried. "You'll take my orders!" Hart said. "Get back inside!"

Deliberately, the hostler glanced at Duffy and the old man nodded. Duffy's man turned on his heel and went back inside.

"You'll get paid, and plenty," Hart was telling Duffy, "but no arguments, understand?" Then, his tone thick with contempt, he added, "Who in this town could make trouble for us?"

When Hart crossed the street to the saloon, Duffy's man returned to the door. "You goin' to take that?"

"We've no choice. I'm no gunslinger. There's no more than seven men in town right now, all quiet, peaceful men. Anyway, their womenfolks would be scared. We've been expectin' something of the kind for a long time." He looked around. "You're new here. Those men are bad, real bad."

Duffy's man merely looked at him. "Are they?" he asked.

He walked back into the stable and climbed to the loft, forking hay into the mangers, then put corn into seven feed boxes. Walking out he said, "I'll eat now," slipping into his coat as he spoke. He did not look at Duffy. The three horses were still across the street.

There was a sign that said MA'S KITCHEN and when he went inside there were two tables eight feet long with a bench along each side and at each end. Clip Hart was sitting at the end of one table with his back to the wall. Duffy's man sat down alongside the table near the opposite end.

He had been born in the West but left with his mother when he was ten and had grown up in the streets of New York. At fifteen, after two years working on a fishing boat he had shipped out around the Horn. He dealt monte in a Barbary Coast dive, fought a series of bare-knuckle fights, and won them. He had become friendly with Jem Mace and learned a lot about fighting from him, the master boxer of his time. At seventeen he was on a windjammer in the China Sea. Back in New York again he fought several more bareknuckle fights and won each time.

Discontented with his life he found an interest in books and began to study with an eye to bettering himself, although without any definite idea. Running out of money he worked his way West on the railroad and finally, dead broke, he dropped off the stage in Westwater.

Westwater had one restaurant, one saloon, a

livery stable, a blacksmith shop, a crossroads store, and a stage station which doubled as a post office.

Julie came around the table and put a plate before him. He thanked her and watched her fill the cup. She was a slender girl with Irish blue eyes, black hair, and a few freckles. She left him and went around the table, picking up several dirty dishes. It looked like at least three men had left without finishing their meals when Hart came in.

"More coffee!" Hart looked at the girl as he spoke, boldly appraising. When she went to fill his cup he slipped an arm around her waist.

She stepped away so quickly that it jerked Hart off balance and his face turned ugly with anger.

"Put that pot down and come here!" he said.

"Keep your hands to yourself!" Julie flared. "I'll serve you, but I won't be pawed by you!"

Clip started to rise but Duffy's man grabbed the table and shoved hard. The end of the table hit Hart's hip as he was turning to rise, and it caught him off balance. He staggered, the bench behind tripped him. He fell hard, his feet flying up.

Duffy's man stood over him. "Let her alone," he said. "A man in your business can't afford to fool around."

"You're tellin' me my business?" He gathered his feet under him but he was in no position to argue, and something in the face of Duffy's man warned him.

At the same time he realized that what the hostler said was true. He could not afford trouble here and now. He could wait. He got carefully to his feet. "Aw, I was just foolin'!" he said. "No need for her to be so persnickety."

Then as he started to brush himself off, his anger flared again. "You shoved that table!" he exclaimed.

"You catch on fast." Duffy's man spoke calmly, standing there with his hands on his hips, just looking at Hart. The outlaw grew more and more angry. At the same time he felt an impulse to caution. No trouble here and now. That could wait.

Without another word he drew back his bench and sat down. When he had finished eating he threw a half-dollar on the table and went out without so much as a backward glance.

Julie filled his cup again. "He won't forget that."

"I know."

"He'll kill you. He's killed other men."

"Maybe."

Duffy's man finished his meal in silence, ever conscious of her presence. When he got up he dropped two bits on the table to pay for the meal, then went to the door. "You be careful," she warned.

He crossed the street and saw the horses the men had ridden into town were gone. It was dark now, but he could still see Duffy seated in his big old chair.

"Horses come?"

"Not yet." Duffy's chair creaked. "What happened over there?"

"He got fresh with Julie, and I shoved him down with a table. He didn't like it very much."

"He'll kill you."

"I'm not ready to die."

"Take a horse," Duffy advised. "Take that little bay. If you ever get the money you can send it to me. If not, forget it. I like you, son."

"I don't need a horse."

"You won't have a chance."

"You go home, Mr. Duffy, and don't come out tomorrow. Leave this to me. It's my fight."

Duffy's chair creaked as he got up. "The bay's in the box stall if you want it." He paused near the corner of the barn. "Have you got a gun?"

"No, I don't think I'll need one." He was silent, and he was aware that the old man had not moved, but stood there in the shadows.

"The way I see it," he said, "they've got this town treed. They can do as they please. First they will use it as a way station for fresh horses, then they'll take over the town's business, then the people. Men will be killed and women taken."

"Maybe."

"You go home now, Mr. Duffy. You stay out of this."

Duffy's man listened to the slow, retreating steps. Duffy must be nearly eighty. The storekeeper was well past sixty. The tough young men of the town were all gone on a cattle drive. They would be back next year, or maybe they would never come back. The hardships of a cattle drive being what they were. It made no difference now. He was a man who knew what had to be done and he was not accustomed to asking for help.

He sat down in Duffy's chair and waited. There had been a man in a railroad construction camp who was always quoting, and those quotations had a way of sticking in the mind. Duffy's man stirred in the chair, remembering one the fellow had loved to quote. Time and again he had said it.

> They tell us, Sir, that we are weak, unable to cope with so formidable an adversary. But when shall we be stronger? Will it be next week? Will it be next year? Will it be when we are totally disarmed and a guard stationed in every house? Shall we gather strength by

irresolution and inaction? Sir, we are not weak if we make proper use of those means which the God of nature has placed in our power.

The words had a nice sound and he said them aloud, but softly, listening to the smooth sound of them on his lips. He had the Irishman's love of fine sounding words and the Irishman's aptitude for rebellion. He leaned back in the chair and closed his eyes. The fellow in the construction camp who quoted that, he had been better than a book, and all he needed to start him off was a bit of rye whiskey.

It was past midnight when the horses came. Two riders led them up under the trees and then across the street to the stable. One man remained outside in Duffy's chair while the other helped Duffy's man tie them in the stalls. They were all fine, beautifully built animals.

The man was stocky and not very tall. He lifted the lantern to the hostler's face. "New?"

"Drifting."

"You take good care these horses are ready. You do that and you'll have no trouble. You might even find a few extra bucks in your kick when this is over. Do you hear me?"

"I hear you."

The man walked back to the door but did not step out into the light. There was a lantern over the door that was kept burning all night, and it threw a pale glow around the stable door.

Duffy's man watched the glow of their cigarettes and then he went to the harness room. There were several old saddles, odds and ends of harness, and in a corner, behind a dusty slicker there was something else.

It was a Colt revolving shotgun.

He peered out a crack of the door, then put the lantern on the floor between himself and the door. Taking up the shotgun he wiped it free of dust, then he took it apart and went to work on it.

Several times he went to the door to peer out. After almost two hours of work he had the shotgun in firing condition. The cylinder would no longer revolve of itself but could be turned by hand. Duffy's man fed shells into the four chambers. They were old brass shotgun shells, and he had loaded them himself. Then he stood the shotgun back in the corner and hung the slicker over it.

The short, stocky man was in the chair now and the other one was asleep on the hay just inside the door. Duffy's man stopped inside the door. "What time tomorrow?" he asked.

The fellow looked around at him. "Maybe noon. Why?"

"Wonderin' if I should feed them again. They won't run good on a full stomach."

"Say, that's right. Feed 'em now, I s'pose. All right?"

"Yeah."

Duffy's man walked back inside and fed the horses. "They tell us, Sir, that we are weak," he repeated, "but when shall we be stronger?"

He thought it over as he stood there, rubbing the sorrel's neck. "It has a nice sound," he told the horse, "a nice sound."

He walked to the door. "Soon be daylight," he said, "the sky's turning gray."

"Yeah." The stocky man got to his feet and stretched. Duffy's man hit him.

It was a backhand blow with his left fist that caught the stretching outlaw in the solar plexus. Duffy's man stepped around in front of him and with the practiced ease of the skilled boxer he uppercut with the left and crossed a right to the chin. The outlaw never had a chance to know what was happening, and the only sound was a gasp at the backhand to the solar plexus.

Duffy's man pulled him out of sight behind the door. Then he tied his hands and feet and stuffed a dirty rag into his mouth for a gag, tying it there.

Leaning over the sleeping outlaw he very gently lifted the man's hand and slipped a loop over it. His eyes flared open but the hostler grasped his upper arm and flipped him over on his face before he realized what was happening.

Shoving the man's face into the hay and earth,

he dropped on one knee on the man's back and jerked his other wrist over to receive a second loop. Quickly, with a sailor's skill with knots, he drew the wrists together and bound them tight, then tied his feet and gagged him.

They might, he thought, get themselves free just when he was most busy. He dragged them to the center of the barn where there was no loft. It was almost forty feet to the ridgepole. Climbing the ladder to the loft he then mounted a ladder that led to the roof and rigged two ropes over a crosspiece, then went back to the floor.

The outlaws, both conscious now, stared at him, horrified.

"Going to hang you," he said cheerfully, grinning at their agonized expressions. "But not by the necks . . . unless you struggle."

Twenty minutes later he looked up at them with appreciation. More than thirty feet above the hard packed earth of the barn floor he had suspended the two outlaws. Each man had a loose noose around his neck. If they struggled to get free and the knots started to slip they would hang themselves.

"It's up to you," he explained. "You can hang there quietly and when this shindig is over I'll let you down easy. You struggle and you'll both be dead."

He strolled to the door. Smoke was lifting from Ma's Kitchen and Julie was sweeping off the step. He walked across and she glanced up, smiling at him. He saw her eyes go past him to the barn door. The chair was empty.

She got the coffeepot and filled his cup, stealing a glance at his face, which revealed nothing. She had heard the riders come in with the horses, and she knew it meant a bank holdup somewhere near.

The outlaws could run their horses at top speed, switch to fresh horses and be off to the mountains. The fresh horses would assure them of escape, for any posse would have to run their horses hard to try to catch them, and those horses would have been extended to the utmost before reaching Westwater.

Duffy's man ate in silence. When he arose he dropped a quarter on the table. "Better stay inside today," he told Julie, "and tell Ma."

She stopped at the end of the table. "Whatever it is you're planning," she said, "don't do it. You don't know Clip Hart."

"There are Clip Harts wherever one goes. If you start running there's no place to stop. I have it to do or I have to run, and I don't run easy.

"Anyway"—he spoke in a lighter tone, not looking at her—"a man has to stop somewhere and make a start. This seems as good a place as any. A man might even start a ranch of his own."

"That takes money."

"A man who is good with an ax might make

some money cutting ties for that branch line they're about to build. They will need ties," he added, "or they'll have to ship them a long way."

He went out without looking back, but he heard Ma say, "I like that young man."

Julie answered, "He won't live long if he bucks Clip Hart."

At the foot of the steps Duffy's man stopped, thinking. How did one man handle seven men? And how far behind the outlaws would the posse be? How long would it take them to get to Westwater?

Duffy's man considered a half dozen ways of delaying the outlaws and still staying alive. Tying their horses with hard knots? They would cut the ropes. Opening fire as they entered the street? He didn't have shells enough to kill them all if he scored with every shot, and they were too many. He would himself be dead.

There was no way. He had been foolish to begin what he could not end, and he was very glad he had not tried to enlist help in his foolhardy scheme. It had been all too easy to think of doing something, all too easy to say they would never be stronger.

Nonetheless, having started it, it was not in him to quit. What he had begun he would finish, and he would hope to do enough damage in the process that they would come no more to Westwater.

It was natural that he did not consider his own situation. Not that he had not thought of it before, but he had known what his chances were, and now that he had decided to go ahead he simply would have no chance at all. At least, none worth considering.

Finally, he brought the horses out and tied them, according to plan, at the hitch rail. He tied them with slipknots, tying Clip Hart's horse a little closer to the stable and just a little apart from the others. Then he brought the shotgun from the harness room and placed it beside the barn door, but out of sight.

He knew then he had done what he could do, and there was nothing to do but wait. He dropped into Duffy's chair and relaxed.

Word seemed to have gotten around, for no one appeared on the street. The store was open, as was the saloon, but nobody was in either place. Several times Julie came to the door and looked across the street at the young man in the chair by the barn door. Each time he was whittling. Once he even seemed to be asleep.

It was almost eleven o'clock when they heard them coming. They thundered across the bridge just outside of town and came racing around the bend and through the trees. They came at a dead run, piled off their horses and rushed for the fresh horses at the hitch rail. Hart reached his horse and grabbed at the slipknot, and Duffy's man hit him.

There was no warning. Duffy's man had tied that horse within an easy step and his left hook caught Hart on the chin and he went down, spun halfway around, and grabbed for his gun.

Duffy's man slapped away the gun hand and smashed Hart with a big, work-hardened fist. Knocking him back against the rail he proceeded to slug him in the belly, then on the chin with both hands. Hart went down, battered and bleeding. Only then did Duffy's man disarm him.

The other outlaws had leaped for their saddles and no sooner did they hit leather than all hell broke loose. The horses were big, fresh, and full of corn, and they began to pitch madly as if on signal. A girth broke, and then another. Men plunged into the dust, and as they hit, men rushed from the stores and ran among them, clubbing with gun barrels and rifle butts.

Duffy himself was there, moving with surprising agility for one of his age and bulk. Only one man made a break for it. He was near the stable and his cinch did not break. He got his horse turned and as he did so he lifted his pistol and took careful aim at Duffy's man.

The hostler sprang for the shotgun beside the door, knowing he would never reach it in time. Then a rifle shot rang out and as Duffy's man swung around with the shotgun in his hands, he saw the outlaw topple from his saddle into the dust.

He glanced around and saw Julie standing in the door with an old Sharps .50 in her hands, a thin wraith of smoke issuing from the muzzle.

As suddenly as that, it was over. Clip Hart was staggering to his feet, his jaw hanging and obviously broken. There was a deep cut over one eye, and his trigger finger was broken, apparently when he fell or when the gun was slapped from his hand.

One man was dead. Duffy himself had killed him when he stepped from the store. The man Julie had shot had a broken shoulder and an ugly wound where the bullet had ripped the flesh. The others had aching heads and one a broken collarbone.

Herded together in front of the livery stable, they were standing there when the posse arrived, staring at their captors who proved to be four old men, two boys of fourteen, a girl with an apron, and Duffy's man.

"They held up our bank and killed a cashier," the man with the badge told them. "If they'd gotten on those fresh horses they'd have gotten clean away. What happened?"

Duffy had been removing saddles from the horses and now he lifted a saddle blanket and lifted an ugly-looking cocklebur with blood on its stiff spines. "Somebody," he said, "put one of these under each blanket, and then cut the cinches halfway through."

The badge wearer looked at Duffy's man. "You did that?"

"Picked the meanest-looking burrs I could find. What else could I do? I'm no gunfighter!"

The sheriff looked at Hart. "Well, you're some kind of a fighter, and whatever it is, you'll do. Thanks."

Duffy looked at his holster. "Thought we was too old, did you? Well, we got fight left in us yet, ain't we, boys?"

The storekeeper gestured toward the saloon. "I'm standing for the drinks, young or old."

"Have your drink," Duffy's man said. "I'll be along soon."

He looked over at Julie. "As I said, this seemed a good place to stop."

"Are you a good man with an ax?"

"I am. But you know, it gets mighty lonely up there in the mountains. And it would help if I had somebody to cook for me, too."

"Can you cook at all?"

"No, ma'am."

"I can."

He gestured toward the church, half-hidden among the cottonwoods. "The preacher will be home tomorrow. We should make an early start."

"I will be ready." Suddenly, she was embarrassed. She dried her hands on her apron. "You go along and have that drink now."

At the saloon the men lifted their glasses to him. "Not me," he said, "I might never have done it but for something a speaker once said."

He lifted his glass. "We drink to the speaker. To Patrick Henry," he said.

"To Pat Henry," they replied.

# *The Strong Shall Live*

The land was fire beneath and the sky was brass above, but throughout the day's long riding the bound man sat erect in the saddle and cursed them for thieves and cowards. Their blows did not silence him, although the blood from his swollen and cracked lips had dried on his face and neck.

Only John Sutton knew where they rode and only he knew what he planned for Cavagan, and John Sutton sat thin and dry and tall on his long-limbed horse, leading the way.

Nine men in all, tempered to the hard ways of an unforgiving land, men strong in the strengths needed to survive in a land that held no place for the weak or indecisive. Eight men and a prisoner taken after a bitter chase from the pleasant coastal lands to the blazing desert along the Colorado River.

Cavagan had fought on when the others quit. They destroyed his crops, tore down his fences, and burned his home. They killed his hired hand

and tried to kill him. When they burned his home he rebuilt it, and when they shot at him he shot back.

When they ambushed him and left him for dead, he crawled into the rocks like a wounded grizzly, treated his own wounds, and then caught a horse and rode down to Sutton's Ranch and shot out their lights during the victory celebration.

Two of Sutton's men quit in protest, for they admired a game man, and Cavagan was winning sympathy around the country.

Cavagan was a black Irishman from County Sligo. His mother died on the Atlantic crossing and his father was killed by Indians in Tennessee. At sixteen Cavagan fought in the Texas war for independence, trapped in the Rockies for two years, and in the war with Mexico he served with the Texas Rangers and learned the value of a Walker Colt.

At thirty he was a man honed by desert fires and edged by combat with fist, skull, and pistol. Back in County Sligo the name had been O'Cavagan and the family had a reputation won in battle.

Sutton's men surrounded his house a second time thinking to catch him asleep. They fired at the house and waited for him to come out. Cavagan had slept on the steep hillside behind the house and from there he opened fire, shooting a man from his saddle and cutting the lobe from Sutton's ear with a bullet intended to kill.

Now they had him, but he sat straight in the saddle and cursed them. Sutton he cursed but he saved a bit for Beef Hannon, the Sutton foreman.

"You're a big man, Beef," he taunted, "but untie my hands and I'll pound that thick skull of yours until the yellow runs out of your ears."

Their eyes squinted against the white glare and the blistering heat from off the dunes, and they tried to ignore him. Among the sand dunes there was no breeze, only the stifling heaviness of hot, motionless air. Wearily their horses plodded along the edge of a dune where the sand fell steeply off into a deep pit among the dunes. John Sutton drew rein. "Untie his feet," he said.

Juan Velasquez swung down and removed the rawhide thongs from Cavagan's feet, and then stood back, for he knew the manner of man that was Cavagan.

"Get down," Sutton told Cavagan.

Cavagan stared his contempt from the slits where his eyes peered through swollen, blackened flesh, then he swung his leg across the saddle, kicked his boot free of the stirrup, and dropped to the ground.

Sutton regarded him for several minutes, savoring his triumph, then he put the flat of his boot against Cavagan's back and pushed. Cavagan staggered, fought for balance, but the sand crumbled beneath him and he fell, tumbling to the bottom of the hollow among the dunes.

With his hands tied and his body stiff from the beatings he had taken he needed several minutes to get to his feet. When he stood erect he stared up at Sutton. "It is what I would have expected from you," he said.

Sutton's features stiffened, and he grew white around the mouth. "You're said to be a tough man, Cavagan. I've heard it until I'm sick of it, so I've brought you here to see how much is tough and how much is shanty Irish bluff. I am curious to see how tough you will be without food or water. We're leaving you here."

Hannon started to protest. He had himself tried to kill Cavagan, but to leave a man to die in the blazing heat of the desert without food or water and with his hands bound . . . a glance at Sutton's face and the words died on his lips.

"It's sixty miles to water," he managed, at last.

John Sutton turned in his saddle and measured Hannon with a glance, then deliberately he faced front and started away. Reluctantly, the others followed.

Juan Velasquez looked down into the pit at Cavagan. He carried a raw wound in his side from a Cavagan bullet, but that pit was seventy feet deep. Slowly, thinking as he did it, Juan unfastened his canteen and was about to toss it to Cavagan when he caught Sutton's eyes on him.

"Throw it," Sutton suggested, "but if you do you will follow it."

Juan balanced the canteen on his palm, tempted beyond measure. Sixty miles? With the temperature at one hundred and twenty degrees? Reluctantly, he retied the canteen to his saddle horn. Sutton watched him, smiling his thin smile.

"I'll remember that, Juan," Cavagan said. "It was a good thought."

John Sutton turned his square thin shoulders and rode away, the others following. Hannon's shoulders were hunched as if expecting a blow.

When the last of them had disappeared from sight, Cavagan stood alone at the bottom of the sand pit.

This was 1850 and even the Indians avoided the sand hills. There was no law west of Santa Fe or east of the coast mountains. Cavagan had settled on land that Sutton considered his, although he had no legal claim to it. Other would-be settlers had been driven off, but Cavagan would not be driven. To make matters worse he courted the girl Sutton had marked for himself.

Cavagan stood in the bottom of the sand pit, his eyes closed against the glare of the sun on the white sand. He told himself, slowly, harshly, that he would not, he must not die. Aloud he said, **"I shall live! I shall see him die!"**

There was a burning fury within him but a caution born of experience. Shade would come first to the west side of the pit, so with his boot he scraped a small pit in the sand. There, several inches below the surface, it was a little cooler. He sat down, his back to the sun, and waited.

More than seven hours of sunlight remained. To attempt climbing from the pit or even to fight the thongs on his wrists would cause him to perspire profusely and lessen his chances of ultimate survival. From this moment he must be patient, he must think.

Sweat dripped from his chin, his throat was parched and the sun on his back and shoulders was like the heat from a furnace. An hour passed, and then another. When at last he looked up there was an inch of shadow under the western lip of the pit.

He studied the way his wrists were bound. His hands had been tied to the pommel, so they were in front of him. He lifted his wrists to his teeth and began ever so gently to work at the rawhide knots. It took nearly an hour, but by the time his wrists were free the shade had reached the bottom of the pit. He coiled the rawhide and slipped it into his pocket.

The east slope was somewhat less steep, with each step he slid back, but with each he gained a little. Finally he climbed out and stood in the full glare of the setting sun.

He knew where the nearest water hole lay but knew Sutton would have it guarded. His problem was simple. He had to find water, get out of the desert, then find a horse and weapons. He intended to destroy Sutton as he would destroy a rabid wolf.

Shadows stretched out from the mountains. To the north the myriad pinnacles of the Chocolate Mountains crowned themselves with gold from the setting sun. He started to walk.

It was not sixty miles to the nearest water, for Cavagan knew the desert better than Sutton. West of him, but in a direction he dare not chance, lay Sunset Spring. Brackish water, and off the line for him.

Twenty-five miles to the northwest among the pinnacles of the Chocolates were rock tanks that might contain water. A Cahuilla Indian had told him of the natural reservoir, and upon this feeble chance he rested his life.

He walked northwest, his chances a thousand to one. He must walk only in the early hours of the morning and after sundown. During the day he must lie in the shade, if he found any, and wait. To walk in the sun without water was to die.

The sand was heavy and at each step he sank to his ankles. Choosing a distant peak in the Chocolates he pointed himself toward it. When the stars came out he would choose a star above it for a guide. At night landmarks have a way of losing themselves and what was familiar by day becomes strange and unfamiliar in the darkness.

To reach the vicinity of the rock tanks was one thing, to find them quite another. Near such tanks in the Tinajas Altas men had died of thirst within a few feet of water, unaware of its presence. Such tanks were natural receptacles catching the runoff from infrequent rains, and so shaded, that evaporation was slow. As there was no seepage there was no vegetation to indicate the presence of water.

The shadows grew long and only a faint afterglow remained in the sky. On his right and before him lay the valley dividing the dunes from the Chocolate Mountains. Now the air was cool and here and there a star appeared. Desert air is thin and does not retain the heat, hence it soon becomes cool, and in the middle of the night, actually cold. These were the hours Cavagan must use.

If he could not find the tanks, or if there was no water in them, he would die. Cavagan was a man without illusion. His great strength had been sapped by brutal treatment, and he must conserve what strength remained. Locating his peak and a star above it, he walked on. A long time later, descending from the last of the dunes, he took a diagonal course across the valley. Twice he paused to rest, soaking up the coolness. He put a small pebble in his mouth to start the saliva flowing. For a time it helped.

Walking in heavy sand he had made but two miles an hour, but on the valley floor he moved faster. If he reached the **tinajas** and they held water he would have achieved one goal. However, he had no way of carrying water and the next water hole was far. Not that one can place reliance on any desert water hole. Often they were used up or had gone dry.

His battered face throbbed with every step and his head ached. The pinnacles of the Chocolates loomed nearer, but he was not deceived. They were miles away.

An hour before dawn he entered a wash that came down from the Chocolates. He was dead tired, and his feet moved awkwardly. In eleven hours he had probably traveled no more than twenty-three or -four miles and should be near the tanks. He found a ledge that offered shade and stretched out. He was soon asleep.

The heat awakened him. His mouth was dry as parchment and he had difficulty in moving his tongue, which seemed awkward and swollen. A glance at the sun told him it was noon or nearly so. According to the Cahuilla he should be within a few yards of water, certainly within a mile or so. In that maze of cliffs, boulders, rock slabs, and arroyos, cluttered with canelike clumps of ocotillo, he would be fortunate to find anything.

Animals would come to water but many desert creatures lived without it, getting what moisture they needed from succulent plants or cacti. Some insects sought water, and he had noticed bees flying past taking the straight line that usually led to hive or water.

His throat was raw and his mind wandered. Far off, over the desert he had recently crossed, lay a lovely blue lake, shimmering among the heat waves . . . a mirage.

Lying down again he waited for dusk. He was sweating no longer and movement was an effort. He had been almost thirty hours without water and in intense heat.

It was almost dark when he awakened again. Staggering to his feet he started to climb. The coolness refreshed him and gave him new strength. He pushed on, climbing higher. His vision was uncertain and his skull throbbed painfully, but at times he felt an almost delirious gaiety, and then he would scramble up rocks with zest and abandon. Suddenly he sat down. With a shock of piercing clarity he realized he could die.

He rarely thought of dying, although he knew it was expected of him as of all men, yet it was always somebody else who was dying. Suddenly he realized he had no special dispensation against death and he could die now, within the hour.

It was faintly gray in the east when he started again. Amazingly, he found the tanks.

A sheep track directed him. It was a half-sheltered rock tank, but it was dry. Only a faint dusting of sand lay in the bottom.

A few minutes later, and a little higher up, he found a second tank. It was bone-dry.

Soon the sun would rise and the heat would return. Cavagan stared at the empty tanks and tried to swallow, but could not. His throat was raw, and where it was not raw it felt like old rubber. His legs started to tremble, but he refused to sit down. He knew if he sat now he might never get up. There was a queerness in him, a strange lightness as if he no longer possessed weight. Through the semi-delirium induced by heat, thirst, and exhaustion there remained a hard core of resolution, the firmness of a course resolved upon and incomplete. If he quit now John Sutton would have won. If he quit now the desert would have defeated him, and the desert was a friendly place to those who knew how to live with it.

Cunning came to him. To those who knew how to live **with** it, not against it. No man could fight the desert and live. A man must move with it, give with it, live by its rules. He had done that, so what remained?

His eyes peered into the growing light, refusing to focus properly, his thoughts prowling the foggy lowlands of his mind, seeking some forgotten thing.

Think back . . . the rock tanks of the Chocolates. The Chocolates. The Chocolates were a range running parallel to the dunes which the Mexicans called the **algodones**. Bit by bit his thoughts tried to sort out something he knew, but something was missing. Something else the Cahuilla had said. It came to him then like the Indian's voice in his ears. **"If there is no water in the tanks, there is a seep in the canyon."**

Almost due west was the canyon through which ran the old Indian trail . . . maybe five miles.

It was too far. And then he got up without decision and walked away. He walked with his head up, his mind gone off somewhere, walking with a quick, lively step. When he had walked for some distance he fell flat on his face.

A lizard on a rock stared at him, throat throbbing. Something stirred Cavagan's muscles, and he got his hands under him and pushed himself to his knees. Then he got up, weaving a little. It was daylight.

A bee flew past.

He swayed a little, brow puckered, a bee flying straight . . . hive or water or a hive near water? He took a few hesitant steps in the direction the bee had flown, then stopped. After a bit another droned past and he followed, taking a sight on a clump of ocotillo some distance off. He stumbled and fell, scarcely conscious of it until he arose and stared at his palms, lacerated by the sharp gravel.

When he fell again he lay still for what must have been a considerable time, finally becoming aware of a whistling sound. He pushed himself up, listening. The sound reminded him of a cricket, yet was not a cricket. He listened, puzzled yet alerted for some reason he did not understand.

He moved then, and under a clump of greasewood something stirred. He froze, thinking first of a rattler, although the heat was too great for one to be out unless in a well-shaded position. And then his eye caught a movement, and he knew why the sound had alerted him. It was a tiny red-spotted toad.

Long ago he had learned that the red-spotted toad always lived within the vicinity of water and never got far from it.

Awkwardly he got to his feet and looked carefully around. His eyes could not seem to focus properly, yet down the canyon he glimpsed some galleta grass and walked toward it, coming upon the seep quite suddenly.

Dropping to his knees he scooped water in his palm and drank it. A cold trickle down his throat was painful on the raw flesh. With gentle fingers he put water on his lips, bathed his cheeks and face with it, then drank a little more.

Something inside was crying out that he was safe, but he knew he was not. He drank a little more, then crawled into the shade of a rock and lay on his back and slept.

When he awakened he crawled out and drank more and more, his water-starved body soaking up the moisture. He had found water but had no means of carrying it with him, and the canyon of the seep might well become his tomb, his open tomb.

Cavagan got out the rawhide with which his wrists had been bound and rigged a snare for small game. In placing the snare he found some seeds, which he ate. He drank again, then sat down to think his way forward.

From where he now sat there were two possible routes. Northeast toward the Colorado was Red Butte Spring, but it was at least twenty-five miles away and in the wrong direction.

The twelve miles to Chuckawalla Spring began to loom very large, and leaving the water he had found worried him. The Chuckawalla Mountains were a thin blue line on the northern horizon, and even if he reached them the next spring beyond was Corn Springs, just as far away. Yet the longer he waited the more his strength would be drained by lack of food. He had never known such exhaustion, yet he dare not wait.

On the second morning his snare caught a kangaroo rat, which he broiled over a small fire. When he had eaten he got up abruptly, drank some more, glanced at the notch in the Chuckawallas and started walking.

At the end of an hour he rested, then went on at a slower pace. The heat was increasing. In midafternoon he fell on his face and did not get up.

More than an hour must have passed before he became aware of the intense heat and began to crawl like a blind mole, seeking shade. The plants about him were less than a foot high, and he found nothing, finally losing consciousness.

He awakened, shaking with chill. The moon cast a ghostly radiance over the desert, the clustered canes of the ocotillo looking like the headdresses of gigantic Indians. He got to his feet, aware of a stirring in the night. He waited, listening. A faint click of a hoof on stone and then he saw a desert bighorn sheep walk into the wash and then he heard a faint splash. Rising, he walked down to the wash and heard a scurry of movement as the sheep fled. He almost walked into the spring before he saw it. He drank, then drank again.

Late the next afternoon he killed a chuckawalla with a well-thrown stone. He cooked the big lizard and found the meat tender and appetizing. At dusk he started again, crossing a small saddle to the north side of the mountains. It was twelve miles this time, and it was daybreak before he reached Corn Springs. He recognized it by the clump of palms and mesquite in the wash before reaching the spring, some clumps of **baccharis,** clusters of small twigs rising two to three feet. And then he found the spring itself. After drinking he crawled into the shade and was asleep almost at once.

He opened his eyes, aware of wood smoke. Rolling over quickly, he sat up.

An old man squatted near a kettle at a fire near the spring, and on the slope a couple of burros browsed.

"Looks to me like you've had a time of it," the old man commented. "You et anything?"

"Chuckawalla . . . had a kangaroo rat a couple of days ago."

The old man nodded. "Et chuck a time or two . . . ain't as bad as some folks might figger."

Cavagan accepted a bowl of stew and ate slowly, savoring every bite. Finally, placing the half-empty bowl on the ground he sat back. "Don't suppose a man with a pipe would have a cigarette paper?"

"You started that Mex way of smokin'? Ain't for it, m'self. Give me a pipe ever' time." The old man handed him his tobacco pouch and dug into his duffle for a rolled up newspaper. “Don’t tear the readin’ if you can he’p. A body don’t find much readin’ in the desert and sometimes I read through a newspaper five or six times.”

Cavagan wiped his fingers on his pants and rolled a smoke with trembling fingers. Then he put the cigarette down and ate a few more bites before lighting up.

“Come far?”

“Fifty-five, sixty miles.”

“An’ no canteen? You had yourself a time.” The old man said his name was Pearson. He volunteered no more than that. Nor did he ask questions. There were not four white men between the San Jacintos and the Colorado River.

“I’ve got to get to that hot spring this side of the pass, up there by the San Jacintos,” Cavagan said. “I can get a horse from the Cahuillas.”

The old man stirred his fire and moved the coffeepot closer. “You listen to me you won’t go back.”

“You know who I am?”

“Got no idea. Figgered you didn’t get where you was by chance. Six years I been prospectin’ hereabouts an’ I ain’t seen nobody but a Chemehuevi or a Cahuilla in this here country. A man would have himself an outfit, gun, knife, canteen. Strikes me somebody left you out here apurpose.”

"If you could let me have a canteen or a water sack. Maybe a knife."

"How d' you figger to get out of here?"

"West to the Hayfields, then Shaver's Well and the Yuma stage road."

Pearson studied him out of shrewd old eyes. "You ain't no pilgrim. You made it this far on nerve an' savvy, so mayhap you'll go all the way."

He tamped his pipe. "Tell you something. You fight shy of them Hayfields. Seen a couple of gents settin' on that water with rifles. A body could figger they was waitin' for somebody."

The old man helped Cavagan to more stew. He rarely looked directly at Cavagan.

"Are they on the Hayfields or back up the draw?"

Pearson chuckled. "You do know this country. They're on the Hayfields, an' could be they don't know the source of that water. Could be you're figurin' a man might slip around them, get water, and nobody the wiser."

"If a man had a water sack he might get as far as Hidden Spring."

The old man looked up sharply. "Hidden Spring? Never heard of it."

"Southwest of Shaver's . . . maybe three miles. Better water than Shaver's."

"You must be Cavagan."

Cavagan did not reply. He finished the stew, rinsed the bowl, then filled his coffee cup.

"Nobody knows this country like Cavagan. That's what they say. Nobody can ride as far or shoot as straight as Cavagan. They say that, too. They also say Cavagan is dead, left in the **algodones** with his hands tied. Lots of folks set store by Cavagan. Them Californios, they like him."

Cavagan slept the day away, and the night following. Pearson made no move to leave, but loafed about. Several times he cooked, and he watched Cavagan eat.

Cavagan found him studying some Indian writing. "Can't make head nor tail of it," Pearson complained. "If them Cahuillas can, they won't say."

"This was done by the Old Ones," Cavagan said, "the People Who Went Before. I've followed their trails in the mountains and across the desert."

"They left trails?"

"A man can go from here to the Cahuilla village at Martinez. The trail follows the canyon back of the village and goes back of Sheep Mountain. There's a branch comes down back of Indian Wells and another goes to the Indian village at the hot spring at the entrance to San Gorgonio Pass. There's a way over the mountains to the coast, too."

Back beside the fire Cavagan added coffee to what was in the pot, then more water before putting it on the fire. Pearson watched him. "Met a damn fool once who throwed out the grounds . . . throwed away the mother. Never seen the like. Can't make proper coffee until she's two, three days old."

He lit his pipe. "A man like you, he might know a lot about water holes. Worth a lot to a man, knowin' things like that."

"The rock tanks in the Chocolates are dry this year," Cavagan said, "but there's a seep in Salvation Pass." He poked twigs under the coffeepot. "Twenty, twenty-two miles east of Chuckawalla there's a red finger of butte. Maybe a quarter of a mile east of that butte there's a little canyon with a seep of water comin' out of the rock. Good water."

"Place like that could save a man's life," Pearson commented. "Good to know things like that."

"The Cahuillas used the old trails. They know the springs."

Wind was rustling the dry palm leaves when Cavagan crawled out in the early dawn and stirred the coals to life to make coffee.

Pearson shook out his boots, then put on his hat. When he had his boots on he went to the limb where his pants were hung and shook them out. A scorpion about four inches long dropped from a trouser leg and scampered away.

"Last time it was a sidewinder in my boot. A body better shake out his clothes before he puts 'em on."

Pearson slipped suspenders over his shoulders. "Figger you'll hit the trail today. If you rustle through that stuff of mine you'll find you a water sack. Crossin' that ol' sea bottom out there, you'll need it." He hitched his shoulders to settle his suspenders. "Still find shells along that ol' beach."

"Cahuillas say a ship came in here once, a long time ago."

"If they say it," Pearson said, "it did."

Cavagan filled the bag after rinsing it, then dipped it in water from the spring. Evaporation would keep it cool.

Pearson took a long knife from his gear. "Never catered to that one m'self, but a body never knows when he'll need an extry."

Cavagan shouldered the sack and thrust the knife into his belt. "Look me up some time," he said. "Just ask for Cavagan."

Pearson's back was turned, packing gear, when Cavagan spoke. He let him take a dozen steps, and then said, "You get to Los Angeles, you go to the Calle de los Negros. Ask for Jake. He owes me money an' I expect he might have a pistol. Get whatever you need."

JOHN SUTTON SAT at dinner at one end of a long table in his ranch house at Calabasas. The dinner had been enhanced by a turkey killed the day before at a **cienaga** a few miles away. He was restless, but there was no reason for it. Almost a month had gone by. His men had returned to the **algodones** but found no trace of Cavagan. Nor had they expected to. He would have died out on the desert somewhere.

Juan Velasquez saw the rider come up the canyon as he loafed near the gate, standing guard. At the gate the rider dismounted and their eyes met in the gathering dusk. **"Buenos noches, señor,"** Juan said. "I had expected you."

"So?"

"I have an uncle in Sonora, señor. He grows old, and he asks for me."

"**Adíos,** Juan."

**"Adíos, señor."**

Cavagan walked up the steps and into the house where John Sutton sat at dinner.

## *To Make a Stand*

When the snow began to fall, Hurley was thirty-six hours beyond the last cluster of shacks that might be called a town, and the plain around him stretched flat and empty to the horizon.

The sullen clouds sifted sparse snow over the hard brown earth and the short, dust gray grass. The fall of snow thickened and the horizons were blotted out, and Hurley rode in a white and silent world where he was a man alone.

Had he dared, Hurley might have turned back, but death rode behind him, and Hurley was a frightened man, unaccustomed to violence. He had ridden into town and arrived to see a stranger dismounting from a horse stolen from his ranch only a month before.

Following the man into the saloon, Hurley demanded the return of the horse, and the man reached for his gun. In a panic, Hurley grabbed frantically for his own.

His first shot ripped splinters from the floor

and his second struck the thief through the body and within minutes the man was dead.

Clumsily, Hurley reholstered his gun. Shocked by what he had done, he looked blindly around the room like a man suddenly awakened in unfamiliar surroundings. Vaguely, he felt something was expected of him.

"He asked for it," he said then, striving for that hard, confident tone that would convince them he was a man not to be trifled with. Inside he was quivering with shock, and yet through the startled horror with which he looked upon the man he had killed came the realization that he had actually defended himself successfully in a gun battle. The thought filled him with elation and excitement.

Hurley was not a man accustomed to violence. He carried a gun only because it was the custom, and because in the daily round of activity emergencies might arise with wild steers or half-wild horses when a gun was needed, but he had never dreamed of actually killing a man.

From time to time he heard at the store or the post office some talk of gun battles, but that was in another world than his, and he could remember few of the names he had heard and none of the details.

Hurley had come west from Ohio, where he combined his farming with occasional carpentry work. When he first arrived, he drove a freight team for a season. The one time their wagon train was attacked by Indians the attack broke off before he was able to fire a shot. Leaving the freighting, Hurley had bought a few head of cattle and settled on a small stream with a good spring close by, and true to his Ohio upbringing he put in a crop of corn and a few acres of barley, and planted what was the first vegetable garden in that part of the country. He cut hay in the nearby meadow and stacked it for the winter feeding.

He had wanted no trouble, and expected none. He was a sober, hardworking man who had never lifted a hand in violence in his life.

"He asked for it," he repeated.

"Nobody's going to argue that." Pearson was the saloonkeeper, a man Hurley had several times seen but never spoken to. "But what are you going to do about his brothers?"

Pearson looked upon Hurley with cool, measuring eyes that had looked upon many men and assayed their worth. He found nothing special in Hurley, and of the men in the room, he alone had seen Hurley's success had been born of pure panic and unbelievable luck.

The words failed at first to register on Hurley's stunned consciousness, and when they did register he looked around. "Brothers? What brothers?"

"That's Jake Talbot you killed, and Jake has

four brothers, all men mighty big-talking about how tough they are. They're just down the street to Reingold's, and they'll be hunting you."

The momentary elation over his astonishing victory oozed out of him and left Hurley standing empty of all pretense. He looked to Pearson in that moment like a frightened and trapped animal.

"He stole my horse," Hurley protested. "I can prove it."

"Nobody asked for proof. You've got two choices, mister. You can dig in for a fight or you can run."

"I'd better go see the sheriff."

Pearson looked upon him without pity. A man behind a bar cannot afford to take sides. He was an observer, a spectator, and Pearson was not disposed to be otherwise. He viewed all life with complete detachment except as it affected him, personally.

"The sheriff never leaves Springville," he said. "Hereabouts, folks settle their own difficulties."

Hurley walked to the bar and put his hands upon it. Jake Talbot . . . the Talbot brothers. They had an outfit somewhat closer in to town than his, and it seemed that half the stories of shootings and knifings he had heard of centered around them. He could recall no details, only the names and their association with violence.

Four of them . . . how could he be expected to fight four men? He was not a brave man and had never pretended to be one. Fear washed over him and turned his stomach sick. Turning swiftly, he went outside and stood staring down the hundred yards of dusty street into the open prairie. Against the four Talbots he would have no chance. He had worked hard since coming here, but had no friends to go to for help or advice.

If they did not find him in town, they would come at once to his ranch and murder him there. Mounting, Hurley rode west, away from town and away from his ranch.

That had been thirty-six hours ago, and now the snow was falling. Thirty of those hours had been in the saddle, and although the bay gelding was an excellent horse the long miles had sapped his strength and the need for rest was desperate.

Hurley got down from the saddle and looped the reins about his arm as he walked. However little he knew about guns and fighting, he knew a great deal about the weather, and he knew his situation was dangerous. At this time of year such a storm as this might be over within hours, and a bright sun might wipe away the snow as if by a gesture. However, such a storm might last for two or three days and the resulting snow remain for weeks.

Until now his mind had been a blank, with no

thought but to escape, to get away from the danger of tearing, ripping bullets that would spill his life's blood on the ground—and for what?

Hurley had looked upon the dead face of Talbot and had seen himself lying there, knowing better than most how narrow had been the margin. That he had scored with his second shot had been luck of purest variety, for it had been aimed no more than the first.

The snow fell steadily. The trail he followed was no longer visible, but he could feel the frozen ruts with his feet. It was not a narrow trail, but one a hundred yards or more wide where wagons had cut deep ruts into the prairie sod, yet once away from the road the wagons had traveled, the prairie became flat and smooth. The difference he could tell with his feet . . . until the snow became too deep.

Night offered no warning of its coming, for in this white, swirling world of snow there were no advancing shadows, no retreating light, not even, it seemed, a visible darkening. Only suddenly the night was around them and upon them.

A faint stir of wind sent a chill through Hurley. If the wind started now there would be a blizzard, and dressed as he was even his slim chance of survival would be lost. He had never been farther west than the town, and rarely in town in the short time he had been located on the ranch. From overheard conversations in the stores and the livery stable, Hurley knew there was nothing in the direction he was going for several days of riding.

Finally, he stumbled and stumbled again. Wearily, he turned to the horse and, brushing off the saddle, he mounted again. There was no longer any use in trying to follow the trail through the snow for it had become too deep, so he simply gave the gelding its head.

It might have been an hour or even two hours later when the gelding stopped abruptly and awakened him from a doze. He peered through the still falling snow, and at first he saw nothing, but then a gate, and some distance beyond it, a cluster of buildings. Actually, they were not buildings, but merely roofs indicating the sod houses below them.

As he got down from the saddle, his legs were so stiff he almost fell, but he managed to fumble the gate open and get his horse inside, and to fumble the gate shut again. He had farmed and ranched long enough to instinctively close all gates behind him.

The house was built into the side of a low hill where drainage was good, and the door he faced was strongly built. There were two windows, both frosted over, but behind them was a faint glow of light. Hurley lifted his fist and dropped it against the door.

The floor creaked inside and then the door opened, and a tall old man held a rifle in his hand. There was an oil lamp on the table, its wick turned low.

"Can you put me up? I'm lost."

The old man's eyes were cold and measuring. "Can't turn a man away in a storm. Go put your horse up."

The door closed in his face, and Hurley turned away, blinking. There was a dug-out and sod-faced barn not far away and he went to it, kicked back the snow, and forced the door open. It cracked loudly, complaining against the rust and frost in its hinges, and he led the gelding inside and fumbled to light the lantern.

It was a snug barn. The farmer in him appreciated its warmth, the solid construction of the stalls, the strongly made feed bin, and the mangers. He tied the gelding, stripped off saddle and bridle, and then with a handful of hay he wiped the snow and damp from the horse. After he had filled the manger with hay and put a little corn in the feed box, Hurley went to the house.

The single room was square and well built. The plank floor was an unusual feature in a soddy, and it was fitted well. Clothing hung on a row of pegs in the wall, and against the end wall there were four bunks in two tiers, but only one held bedding. There was a glowing kitchen range, and on top of it a teakettle.

The old man was very tall, his wide, thin

shoulders slightly stooped, his face deeply lined under the high cheekbones. The furrows in his cheeks seemed to make him look even more grim and determined. He had started to warm some food.

"No weather to travel." Hurley cupped the coffee the old man offered him in his two hands. "Unexpected storm."

"That's fool talk. This time of year a body can expect any kind of weather."

Hurley pulled a chair up to the table and sat down. The chair sat even on the floor, as did the table; both were well made. There was no arguing with the man's comment, for Hurley knew it to be true. "My name is Hurley," he said.

The old man filled his own cup and glanced over the rim at Hurley. "I'm Benton," he said. "What are you runnin' from?"

Hurley stiffened, half angry. He started to protest, but Benton ignored him.

"No man would be caught this far from the settlements without an outfit unless he was runnin' from something, or somebody."

Hurley did not reply. He accepted the offered stew sullenly. He did not like the implication that he was running away.

"I shot a man back there." He tried to make it sound bigger than it was. He wanted to impress this old man, to get under his hide.

"If he's dead, there's no use to run. If he ain't dead, you better improve your shootin'."

"He was a Talbot . . . with four brothers."

"I know those Talbots," Benton replied. "They're a pack of coyotes."

They ate in silence for several minutes. Hurley stared glumly at his coffee. Benton made it sound petty, like nothing at all. Hurley's killing had made no impression, and the Talbots obviously did not impress him.

"Did you leave anything back there?"

"Yes," Hurley admitted, "I left a good ranch, and a good crop of corn standing, and oats growing. A few head of cattle."

"Where you runnin' to?"

"I never gave it much thought," Hurley admitted. "There were four of them, all rated tough men."

"Were you runnin' when you came out here, too?"

Hurley put down his knife and fork. "Now, see here—!"

Benton never looked up. "A man starts runnin', he doesn't stop. If you run once, you'll run again. Probably you never had as much in your life as you left back there, but you cut out and ran. All right . . . something else happens, you'll run again."

Hurley's features flushed with anger. Who did this old fool think he was? If it hadn't been for the storm he would have taken his horse and ridden on. "There were four of them," he repeated.

"You said that before, and it don't cut no ice. You didn't even meet up with them. Take it from me, you get four men together and one of them has to take the lead, and nobody wants to be that one. I'd rather face four men anytime than one real tough man."

"Easy to talk."

Benton went to the stove for the coffeepot. "You get yourself a shotgun. You go back there and you walk right in on them. You don't give them any chance to talk, you just tell them if they want trouble they've got it and to cut loose their wolf. They'll back down so fast it will make your head swim."

"And if they don't?"

"Then shoot 'em."

Hurley snorted contemptuously. This old man living out here like a hermit . . . what did he know?

"A man who won't fight for what's his ain't much account," Benton said. "You take it from me."

Hurley started to rise from the table. He was mad clear through.

Benton looked up, his hard eyes level and cold. "You set down, Mr. Hurley. Just set down. I ain't about to be scared of no man who can be run clean out of the country by a passel of tin-horns." The old man grinned sardonically. "Anyway, you ain't about to leave a fireside for that storm out there."

Hurley sat down helpless and angry. Benton gathered the dishes and carried them to the sink, then, pouring water into a dishpan from the teakettle, he began washing the dishes.

The warmth of the room, combined with his weariness, made Hurley nod. His head bobbed several times but he struggled to keep his eyes open. It was comfortable to relax after his long battle against the storm, and outside the sod house he could hear the wind blowing, enough to remind him that had he not found shelter he would have been dead by morning.

Benton indicated a drawer in an old-fashioned bureau. "In that drawer there's blankets. You take the other bottom bunk."

Benton was still puttering around when Hurley dropped off to sleep. Hurley's last thought was: "At daybreak . . . when daybreak comes I'll get out of here."

A blast of icy air awakened him and for an instant Hurley lay still, fighting to find himself, to realize where he was. The room was dark, swirling with blown snow, and nothing was familiar. Then it all came back to him, and he scrambled out of bed and slammed the door shut.

"What happened?" he asked into the silence, but the silence remained unbroken. Hurley stood still, listening, and he heard no sound but the wind.

Fumbling for his shirt, he found matches and lit one, then the lamp.

Benton's bunk was empty, but it had been slept in.

Hastily, Hurley got into his pants and boots and picked up his coat and shrugged into it. He strapped on his gun belt and, opening a lantern that stood by the door, he lit it. For an instant, he hesitated.

The Talbots might be out there. They might be . . . but his common sense told him they could not be. They would be holed up somewhere, waiting out the storm.

Opening the door, Hurley stepped out into the darkness. The wind was blowing a gale, and he was almost stifled by a blast of wind that blew his breath right back down his throat. Ducking his head, he stepped into the storm and almost tripped over a body, half buried in swirling snow.

Stooping, Hurley picked up the man and carried him to the door, which he opened with one hand, and stepped inside. Then he returned for the lantern.

The body was that of Benton, and a glance told him the old man's leg was broken.

Stretching him out on the bunk, Hurley covered him with blankets and then went to the fire which had been banked against the long hours of night. Stirring the coals, he added fuel and built a roaring blaze to warm the room. He worked swiftly, knowing warmth would be most important to Benton now. Then he crossed the room to the injured man, slit his trouser leg, and pulled the leg into place. He was binding splints when Benton came out of it and tried to sit up.

"Lie still . . . you've busted your leg."

Benton settled back, his face gray with pain. Hurley turned from him and, searching through a cabinet, found a bottle of whiskey. He poured a slug into a glass and handed it to Benton. "Do you good," he said. "Mighty poor stuff to drink if you're going to stay out in the cold, but once inside it warms you up."

Benton drank the whiskey and handed the glass back to Hurley. He settled back, looking around him. "Last thing I recall," he said, "some noise out at the barn. I started out and slipped on the steps. I felt myself falling . . . that was all."

Hurley explained how he had awakened to find the door open and snow swirling into the room.

Then Benton's remark reached his consciousness. "You say you heard a noise at the barn?"

Benton nodded. "You better go see what's wrong."

The Talbots . . . they could be out there. They knew he would come for his horse, and the barn was warm. They could be out there waiting to shoot him down as he came in out of the morning. Or they might have made the noise on purpose to draw someone to the stable.

"It can wait," Hurley replied sullenly. "The door's shut, I can see that."

He got down the coffee and made a pot. How long he had slept he had no idea, but he was fully awake now. If they were really there.

Benton watched him with sardonic amusement as he made the coffee and brought a cup to the injured man. "Don't know whether them Talbots are out there, or not," he said. "You just got to wait and see, or you've got to go out there and find out. Puts a man in a jim-dandy fix."

"Shut up," Hurley said irritably.

He stood over the stove, feeding sticks into the flames and trying to think it out. Even if the storm let up a man would have no chance afoot, for aside from the distance and the cold his tracks would be laid out plain as print for anyone to follow.

He got down the old man's Spencer and checked the loads. Seven shots. He was a good shot with a rifle, and had hunted rabbits and squirrels back in Ohio. The distance to the barn was no more than sixty or seventy feet, point-blank range.

After a while Hurley put the light out and

stretched out on his bunk. He could hear deep breathing from Benton's bed and decided the old man must be asleep.

Hurley sat up so suddenly he bumped his head on the upper bunk. **What about Benton?**

Somehow, in the excitement of finding the old man with a broken leg, and his worry about the Talbots being in the stable, he had given no thought to Benton.

Hurley could not leave him. He would have to stay on, he would have to stay and face the Talbots whether they were in the stable or not.

He had escaped death in the storm to trap himself here, a sitting duck to be killed whenever they came upon the place, and he had no chance.

He got out of the bunk and walked to the window. The wind had died down, and here and there he could see a break in the clouds. The barn was a low, squat hovel almost buried in snow. No tracks led to or from it, but there need be no tracks now, for it had blown snow long after they would have entered.

Angrily, he stared at the barn. And then he thought of the obvious idea. He had no business here at all. Suppose the old man had fallen when here alone? He would get along, wouldn't he? Suppose no one had been here to carry Benton in out of the snow? He would be dead by now. By bringing him in, Hurley had repaid Benton for whatever shelter he had gotten here. From now on they were quits and he could leave.

Only he could not go.

He picked up the Spencer, then put it down. If somebody was inside, the length of the rifle would be more of a handicap. What he needed was his pistol.

Hurley paused inside the door, taking a deep breath. Why was he going out there? Was he going to get his horse and run?

He was no gunman, he was a farmer, and all he wanted to be was a farmer. Suddenly he knew why he was going out there, and it was very simple. He was going out to feed the stock, just as any farmer would do on any winter morning.

**His** stock?

For the first time he thought of his own stock. The cattle were loose to roam, and they were used to bad weather, and this snow wasn't so deep but what they could scratch through it for grass, and there were several haystacks to which he always let down the bars when he left the ranch. The chance of their coming to the stacks was slight, for usually they stayed well out on the range, but if they did there was feed.

Except for his horses, which were all in stalls, in the barn. He had told Anderson he was going into town, and Anderson would water them if he did not see Hurley return before dark. Anderson was a careful man, and he would realize at once that something had gone wrong, hearing the story as soon as anyone. He would care for the horses.

Standing there in the door, Hurley remembered the house he had built with his own hands, the cattle he owned, the horses, fine stock they were, that he had left behind. Benton was right. He would never have as much again.

Opening the door, he stepped outside into the cold.

The sky was clearing off, and there was a red glow in the east that told him dawn was only minutes away. Facing the barn, Hurley strode toward it. Inside his coat he held his .44, the gun concealed, the hand warmed by contact with his body.

At the barn door he stopped.

There was snow on the door, snow around it. No sign that it had been disturbed since he left it the night before. Unlatching the door he swung it wide, and pulling the .44 from under his coat, he stepped quickly into the barn.

It was, he thought as he took the step, a melodramatic, obvious thing to do. And perfectly foolish, of course, for as he entered the darkness of the barn, he was silhouetted against the snow outside. . . . He moved quickly to one side.

Nothing happened.

From stall to stall he went, and there was no

one there. He put his pistol back in its holster and went about feeding and watering the stock. When he had finished, he came out and closed the door behind him. He stood for a minute in the still, cold air watching his breath, and he remembered how long he had been tortured by doubt, how long he had watched the barn, fearing the Talbots might be there.

Was all fear like that? Was it all, or most of it, just imagination? Was Benton right, after all, and the way to meet fear was head-on?

He walked back to the house. On the steps he paused to stomp the snow from his boots. As he did so the door swept open and Benton stood there with a leveled rifle.

Only the rifle was held steady against the doorjamb, and it was pointed past his head at the ranch yard behind him.

Hurley looked up and saw the grim look on the old man's face, saw the old man had dragged himself from bed to cover him while he fed the stock. But he saw much more. Benton was looking past him and Benton said, "**Hold it!** Hold it right there!"

Hurley knew death then. He knew the Talbots were behind him, and he knew there were four of them, and he knew he was fairly caught.

But he was calm.

That, of all things, was the most astonishing.

There were, he knew in that moment, worse things than death, and there were few things worse than fear itself.

He turned slowly. "It's my fight, Benton," he said. "You get back in bed."

He stepped down off the step. He was scared. He was really scared, and yet somehow it was not as bad as he had expected. He looked at the four shivering men on their horses, and he smiled. "Are you boys looking for me?" he asked.

They hesitated . . . they were cold and shaky from having spent the night in whatever pitiful shelter had been available out on the prairie. And this man had beaten Jake to the draw, and that bullet had gone dead center. It was one thing to chase down a running man, another to face a man who was ready to fight.

"Jake Talbot was riding a horse stolen from me," Hurley spoke loud in the still air. "When I asked him about it he went for his gun. He asked for it and he got it. Now if you boys have anything to say, have at it."

Joe Talbot looked him over more carefully. They had figured they had him on the run, but he did not look scared now. Not none at all.

They could get him; they were four guns to one. Or two if that old man with the rifle declared himself in, but that fool Hurley, he might just get one of them, or even two while they were killing him. They had taken this ride to kill a man, not to be killed themselves, and each one had deep within him the feeling that the first one to pull a gun would be the one to die.

Silence hung in the still, cold air. A horse stamped a hoof impatiently.

"Jake must have bought that horse off a thief," Joe Talbot said, at last. "We don't know anything about it."

It was a retreat, and Hurley was wise enough to recognize it. He took a step nearer to them. "You have that horse back at my place Monday morning," he said, "and we'll call it quits. Understand?"

They did not like it. They knew what was happening to them and they did not like it at all. After this there could be no more tough talk—folks simply wouldn't pay any attention. They were being backed down and they knew it, but no one of them wanted to be the man to die.

"No need for neighbors to fight," Joe Talbot said. "We didn't have the straight of it."

Joe Talbot made a move, finally, but it was to turn his horse toward the gate. And when he turned, the others turned with him.

"Talbot?"

Joe turned his head carefully to look at Hurley. "Stop by Anderson's and ask him to feed my stock, will you? I've got to take care of my friend here. He's got a broken leg."

At the gate one of the Talbots got down from

the saddle and closed the gate carefully, then they rode off, together. It looked like they were not very talkative.

"Hurley?" It was Benton. "Come inside and close the door! You're freezin' the place up! Besides, I want some breakfast."

Hurley stomped his feet again and stepped up in the doorway. He glanced back at the sky. The clouds were blowing off to the north and the sun had already started the icicles dripping. One thing you could say for this country, it didn't take long to clear up.

# *Get Out of Town*

Ma said for me to ride into town and hire a man to help with the cows. More than likely she figured I'd hire Johnny Loftus or Ed Shifrin, but I had no liking for either of them. Johnny used to wink and call Ma "that widder woman" and Ed, he worked no harder than he had to. Man I hired I'd never seen before.

He wasn't much to look at, first off. He was smaller than Johnny Loftus by twenty pound, and Johnny was only a mite more than half of Ed Shifrin, and this stranger was older than either. Fact is, he was pushing forty, but he had a hard, grainy look that made me figure he'd been up the creek and over the mountain.

He wouldn't weigh over a hundred and forty pounds soaking wet, which he wasn't likely to be in this country, and his face was narrow and dark with black eyes that sized you up careful-like before he spoke. He was a-settin' on the platform down to the depot with his saddle and a war bag that looked mighty empty like he was shy of clothes. He was not saying I, yes, or no to anybody when I rode up to town on that buckskin Pa gave me before he was shot down in the street.

Pa let me have the pick of the horses for sale in the town corral, and I taken a fancy to a paint filly with a blaze face.

"Son"—Pa was hunkered down on his heels watching the horses—"that filly wouldn't carry you over the hill. She looks mighty pert, but what a man wants to find in horses or partners is stayin' quality. He wants a horse he can ride all day and all night that will still be with him at sunup.

"Now you take that buckskin. He's tough and he's got savvy. Horse or men, son, pick 'em tough and with savvy. Don't pay no attention to the showy kind. Pick 'em to last. Pick 'em to go all the way."

Well, I taken the buckskin, and Pa was right. Looking at that man setting on the edge of the platform I decided he was the man we wanted. I gave no further thought to Johnny or Ed.

"Mister," I said, "are you rustling work?"

He turned those black eyes on me and studied me right careful. I was pushing fourteen, but I'd been man of the house for nigh three years now. It didn't seem to make no difference to him that I was a wet-eared boy.

"Now I just might be. What work do you have?"

"Ma and me have a little outfit over against the foothills. We figured to roust our cattle out of the canyons and bring 'em down to sell. There's a month of work, maybe more. We'd pay thirty a month and found and if I do say so, Ma is the best cook anywheres around."

He looked at me out of those black, careful eyes and he asked me, "You always hire strangers?"

"No, sir. We usually hire Johnny Loftus or Ed Shifrin or one of the loafers around town, but when I saw you I figured to hire you." The way he looked at me was beginning to worry me some.

"Why me?" he asked.

So I told him what Pa said when we bought the buckskin, and for the first time he smiled. His eyes warmed and his face crinkled up and laugh wrinkles showed at the corners of his eyes where they must have been sleeping all the time. "Your pa was a right smart man, son. I'd be proud to work for you."

We started for the livery stable to get him a horse to ride out to the ranch, and Ed Shifrin was in front of the saloon. He noticed me and then the man who walked beside me.

"Tom," Ed said, "about time your ma started the roundup. You want I should come out?"

Did me good to tell him, the way he'd loafed on the job and come it high and mighty over me. "I done hired me a man, Ed."

Shifrin came down off the walk. "You shouldn't have done that. The Coopers ain't goin' to like a stranger proddin' around among their cows." He turned to the man I hired. "Stranger, you just light a shuck. I'll do the roundin' up."

The man I'd hired didn't seem a mite bothered. "The boy hired me," he said. "If he don't want me he can fire me."

Ed wasn't inclined to be talked up to. "You're a stranger hereabouts or you'd know better. There's been range trouble and the Coopers don't take kindly to strangers among their stock."

"They'll get used to it," he said, and we walked away up the street.

About then I started worrying about what I'd done. We'd tried to avoid trouble. "The Coopers," I told him, "they're the biggest outfit around here. They sort of run things."

"Who runs your place?"

"Well. Me, sort of. Ma and me. Only she leaves it to me, because she says a boy without a father has to learn to manage for himself."

We walked on maybe twenty yards before he said anything, and then he just said, "Seems to me you've had uncommon smart folks, boy."

Old Man Taylor brought out the sorrel for us.

While the stranger was saddling up and I sat there enjoying the warm sunshine and the barn smells of horses and hay and leather, Old Man Taylor came to where I sat the saddle and he asked me low-voiced, "Where'd you find him?"

"Down to the depot. He was rustling work and I was looking for a man."

Old Man Taylor was a man noted for staying out of trouble, yet he had been friendly to Pa. "Boy, you've hired yourself a man. Now you and your ma get set for fireworks."

What he meant I didn't know, nor did it make any kind of sense to me. My hired man came out with the sorrel and he swung into the saddle and we went back down the street. Only he was wearing chaps now and looked more the rider, but somehow he was different from any cowhand I could remember.

We were almost to the end of the street when the sheriff came out of the saloon, followed by Ed Shifrin. He walked into the street and stopped us.

"Tom"—he was abrupt like always—"your ma isn't going to like you hiring this stranger."

"Ma tells me to hire whom I've a mind to. I hired this man and I wouldn't fire any man without he gives me cause."

Sheriff Ben Russell was a hard old man with cold blue eyes and a brusque, unfriendly way about him, but I noticed he cottoned up to the

Coopers. "Boy, this man is just out of prison. You get rid of him."

"I'll not hold it against him. I hired him and if he doesn't stack up, I'll fire him."

My hired hand had sat real quiet up to now. "Sheriff," he said, "you just back up and leave this boy alone. He sizes up like pretty much of a man and it begins to look like he really needs outside help. Seems to me there must be a reason folks want to keep a stranger out of the country."

Sheriff Ben Russell was mad as I'd ever seen him. "You can get yourself right back in jail," he said; "you're headed for it."

My hired man was slow to rile. He looked right back at the sheriff with those cold black eyes and he said, "Sheriff, you don't know who I am or why I was in prison. You recognized this prison-made suit. Before you start shaping up trouble for me, you go tell Pike Cooper to come see me first."

Nobody around our country knew a Cooper called Pike, but it was plain to see the sheriff knew who he meant and was surprised to hear him called so. He said, "Where'd you know Cooper?"

"You tell him. I figure he'll know me."

Seven miles out of town we forded the creek and I showed him with a sweep of the hand. "Our land begins here and runs back into the hills. Our stock has a way of getting into the canyons this time of year."

"Seems plenty of good grass down here."

"This here is deeded land," I told him. "Pa, he always said the day of free range was over, so he bought homesteads from several folks who had proved up, and he filed on land himself. These are all grazing claims, but two of them have good water holes and the stock fattens up mighty well."

When we rode into the ranch yard Ma came to the door, wiping her hands on her apron. She looked at the new rider and I knew she was surprised not to see Ed or Johnny.

The hired man got down from his saddle and removed his hat. Neither Johnny or Ed had ever done that.

"The boy hired me, ma'am, but if you'd rather I'd not stay I'll ride back to town. You see, I've been in prison."

Ma looked at him for a moment, but all she said was, "Tom does the hiring. I feel he should have the responsibility."

"And rightly so, ma'am." He hesitated ever so little. "My name is Riley, ma'am."

Ma said, "Supper's ready. There's a kettle of hot water for washing."

We washed our hands in the tin basin and while he was drying his hands on the towel, Riley said, "You didn't tell me your ma was so pretty."

"I didn't figure there was reason to," I said, kind of stiff.

He took a quick look at me and then he said, "You're right, boy. It's none of my business." Then after a minute he said, "Only it surprised me."

"She was married when she was shy of sixteen," I said.

Supper was a quiet meal. With a stranger at table there were things we didn't feel up to talking about, and you don't ask questions of a man who has been in jail. We made some polite talk about the lack of rain, and how the water on the ranch was permanent, and when he'd finished eating he said, "Mind if I smoke?"

Reckon that was the first time in a while anybody had asked Ma a question like that. Pa, he just took it for granted and other men who came around just lit up and said nothing, but the way Ma acted you'd have thought it was every day. She said, "Please do." It sounded right nice, come to think of it.

"You been getting good returns on your cattle?"

"The calf crop has been poor the last two, three years, but Ed and Johnny said it was because there were so many lions in the mountains. You have to expect to lose some to lions."

"Good range," Riley said, "and plenty of water. I'd say you should make out."

When he had gone to the bunkhouse Ma

started picking up the dishes. "How did you happen to hire him, Tom?"

So I told her about the buckskin and what I thought when I saw this man, and she smiled. "I think you learned your lesson well, Tom. I think he is a good man." And then she added, "He may have been in prison, but he had good upbringing."

Coming from Ma there was not much more she could have said. She set great store by proper upbringing.

A while after, I told her about the talk with Ed Shifrin and Sheriff Russell, and when I came to the part about Riley telling Russell to tell Cooper to come see him, I could see that worried her. Cooper had some tough hands working for him and we didn't want them around.

Year after Pa was killed, some of them tried to court Ma, but she put a stop to that right off.

COME DAYLIGHT just as I was pulling on a boot I heard an ax, and when I looked from behind the curtain I saw it was Riley at the woodpile. Right off I could see he was a hand with an ax, but what surprised me was him doing it at all, because most cowhands resent any but riding work, even digging postholes.

The way it worked out we rode away from the place an hour earlier than I'd ever been able to with Ed or Johnny, and by noon we had hazed seventy head down on the flat, but we were mighty shy of young stuff. Whatever else he was, I'd hired a hand. He was up on Pa's bay gelding and he knew how to sit a cutting horse and handle a rope.

Next three days we worked like all getout. Riley was up early and working late, and I being boss couldn't let him best me, but working with him was like working with Pa, for we shared around and helped each other and I never did see a man learn country faster than he did. Time to time he'd top out on high ground and then he'd set a spell and study the country. Sometimes he'd ask questions. Mostly, he just looked.

Third day we had built us a hatful of fire for coffee and shucked the wrappings off the lunches Ma fixed. "You said your pa was killed. How'd it happen?"

"Ma and me didn't see it. Pa had been to the Coopers' on business and when he got back to town he picked up some dress goods for Ma and a few supplies. He was tying the sack on the saddle when he had a difficulty with a stranger. The stranger shot him."

"Was your pa wearing a gun?"

"Yes, sir. Pa always wore a gun, but not to use on no man. He carried it for varmints or to shoot the horse if he got thrown and his foot caught in the stirrup."

"You hear that stranger's name?"

"Yes, sir. His name was Cad Miller."

That afternoon we ran into Ed Shifrin and Johnny Loftus. First time I'd seen them up thataway except when working for us, but they were coming down the draw just as we put out our fire.

Riley heard them coming before I did, but he looked around at the mountainside like he was expecting somebody else. He looked most careful at the trees and rocks where a man might take cover.

Both of them were armed, but if Riley had a gun I had seen no sign of it. He wore that buckskin jacket that hung even with his belt, but there might have been a gun in his waistband under the jacket. But I didn't think of guns until later.

"You still around?" Shifrin sounded like he was building trouble. "I figured you'd be run out before this."

"I like it here." Riley talked pleasant-like. "Pretty country, nice folks. Not as many cows as a man would expect, but they're fat."

"What d' you mean by that? Not as many cows as you'd expect?"

"Maybe I should have said calves. Not as many calves as a man would expect, but by the time the roundup is over we'll find what happened to the others."

Shifrin looked over at Johnny. "What about the kid?"

Johnny shrugged. "To hell with the kid."

The way they talked back and forth made no sense to me, but it made sense to Riley. "Was I you," Riley said, "I'd be mighty sure Cooper wants it this way. With the kid, and all."

"What d' you mean by that?"

"Why, it just won't work. There's no way you can make it look right. The kid doesn't carry a gun. You boys don't know your business like you should."

"Maybe you know it better?" Johnny sounded mean.

"Why, I do, at that. Did Sheriff Russell tell Pike what I said?"

"Who's Pike?" Shifrin asked suspiciously.

"Why, Pike Cooper. That's what they used to call him in the old days. He ever tell you how he happened to leave Pike County, Missouri? It's quite a story."

Something about the easy way Riley talked was bothering them. They weren't quite so sure of themselves now.

"And while you're at it," Riley added, "you get him to tell you why he left the Nation."

Neither of them seemed to know what to do next. The fact that Riley seemed to know Cooper bothered them, and Johnny was uneasy. He kept looking at me, and I kept looking right back at him, and that seemed to worry him too.

"You boys tell him that. You also tell him not to send boys to do a man's job."

"What's that mean?" Shifrin was sore and he shaped up like a mighty tough man. At least, he always had. Somehow when they came up against Riley they didn't seem either so big or so tough.

"That means you ride out of here now, and you don't stop riding until you get to Pike Cooper. You tell Pike if he wants a job done he'd better come and do it himself."

Well, they didn't know which way was up. They wanted to be tough and they had tried it, but it didn't seem to faze Riley in the least. They had come expecting trouble and now neither one of them wanted to start it and take a chance on being wrong. Or maybe it was the very fact that Riley was taking it so easy. Both of them figured he must have the difference.

"He'll do it!" Johnny replied angrily. "Cooper will want to do this himself. You'll see."

They rode out of there and when Riley had watched them down the slope without comment he said, "We'd best get back to the ranch, Tom. It's early, but we'd better be in when Cooper comes."

"He won't come. Mr. Cooper never goes anywhere unless he feels like it himself."

"He'll come," Riley said, "although he may send Cad Miller first."

When he said that name I stared right at him. "That was the name of the man who killed my father."

"RILEY, what I've seen today, I like. If this comes to a case in court I'd admire to be your lawyer."

"Thank you, but I doubt if it will come to that."

We had a quiet supper. We had come in early from the range, so Riley put in the last hour before sundown tightening a sagging gate. He was a man liked to keep busy.

At supper Riley said to Ma, "Thank you, ma'am. I am proud to work for you."

Ma blushed.

Next morning Ma came to breakfast all prettied up for town. Only thing she said was, "Your father taught you to stand up for what you believe to be right, and to stand by your own people."

There was quite a crowd in town. Word has a way of getting around and folks had a way of being on the street or in the stores when it looked like excitement, and nobody figured to finish their business until it was over.

We left our rig with Old Man Taylor and he leaned over to whisper, "You tell that friend of yours Cad Miller's in town."

Ma heard it and she turned sharp around. "What does he look like, Mr. Taylor?"

Taylor hesitated, shifting his feet nervous-like, not wanting to say, or figuring why Ma wanted to know. But Ma wasn't a woman you could shake off. "I asked a question, Mr. Taylor. I believe you were a friend of my husband's."

"Well, ma'am, I figured so. I figured to be a friend of yours, too."

"And so you are. Now tell me."

So he told her.

It was a warm, still morning. We went down to the hotel, where I waited, and Ma went out to buy some women fixin's like she won't buy with a man along.

All the chairs were taken in front of the hotel, so I leaned against the corner of the building next to the alley. Moment later I heard Riley speak from behind my right shoulder. He was right around the corner of the building in the alley.

"Don't turn around, boy. Is Cooper on the street?"

"Not yet, but Cad Miller is in town."

"Tom," he said, "just so you'll know. I was in prison for killing a man who'd killed my brother. Before that, I was a deputy United States marshal." He hesitated. "I just wanted you to know."

Nobody on the street was talking much. A rig clattered along the street and disappeared. The dust settled. A yellow hound ambled across the street headed toward shade. Ma went walking up the other side of the street and just when I was wondering what she was doing over there the Coopers turned into the upper end of the street. The boys were riding on his flanks and the old man was driving a shining new buckboard.

Cooper pulled up in front of the hotel and got down. His boys were swaggering it, like always, both of them grinning in appreciation of the fun.

Cooper stepped up on the walk and took a cigar from his vest pocket and bit off the end. His hard old eyes glinted at me. "Boy, where's that hired man of yours? I understand he was asking for me."

"He leaves town today," Andy Cooper said loudly, "or he'll be carried out."

Cooper put the cigar in his teeth. He struck a match and lifted it to light the cigar and I heard a boot grate on the walk beside me and knew Riley was there. Cooper dropped the match without lighting his cigar. He just stood there staring past me at Riley.

"Lark!" Cooper almost choked over the name. "I didn't know it was you."

"You remember what I told you when I ran you out of the Nation?"

Cooper wasn't seeing anybody but Riley, the man he had called Lark. He wasn't even aware of anything else. And I was staring at him, because I had never seen a big man scared before.

"I told you if you ever crossed my trail again I'd kill you."

"Don't do it, Lark. I've got a family—two boys. I've got a ranch. I've done well."

"This boy had a father."

"Lark, don't do it."

"This boy's father has been dead three or four years. I figure you've been stealing his cows at least two years before that. Say five hundred head."

Cooper never took his eyes off him, and the two boys acted as if they couldn't believe what was happening.

"You write out a bill of sale for five hundred head and I'll sign it for the boy's mother. Then you write out a check for seven thousand dollars and we'll cross the street and cash it together."

"All right."

"And you'll testify that Cad Miller was told to kill this boy's pa."

"I can't do that. I won't do it."

"Pike," Riley said patiently, "you might beat a court trial, but you know mighty well you ain't going to beat me. Now my gun's around the corner on my saddle. Don't make me go get it."

Cooper looked like a man who was going to be sick. He looked like a school kid caught cheating. I figured whatever he knew about Riley scared him bad enough so he didn't want any argument. And that talk about a gun on the saddle—why, that might be just talk. A man couldn't see what Riley was packing in his waistband.

"All right," Cooper said. His voice was so low you could scarce hear it.

"Pa!" Andy grabbed his arm. "What are you sayin'?"

"Shut up, you young fool! Shut up, I say!"

"Cad Miller's in town," Riley continued; "you get him out here on the street."

"He won't have to." It was Ma's voice.

The crowd moved back and Cad Miller came through with Ma right behind him, and trust Ma to have the difference. She had a double-barreled shotgun, and she wasn't holding that shotgun for fun. One time I'd seen her use it on a mountain lion right in the door yard. She near cut that lion in two.

Sheriff Ben Russell wasn't liking it very much, but there was nothing he could do but take his prisoner. Once Cooper showed yellow, those two boys of his weren't about to make anything of it, and any man who knew our town knew Cooper was through around here after this.

BACK AT HOME I said, "Cooper called you Lark."

"My name is Larkin Riley."

"And you didn't even have a gun!"

"A man has to learn to live without a gun, and against a coward you don't need a gun." He rolled a smoke. "Cooper knew I meant what I said."

"But you'd been in prison yourself."

He sat on the stoop and looked at the backs of his hands. "That was later. Ten or fifteen years ago, what I did would have been the only thing to do. There are laws to handle cases like that, and I had it to learn."

Ma came to the door. "Larkin . . . Tom . . . supper's ready."

We got up and Riley said, "Tom, I think tomorrow we'll work the south range."

"Yes, sir," I said.

# *One for the Pot*

When Laurie reached the water hole at Rustler's Springs she knew she had missed the trail.

Steve had explained about the shortcut across the mountains to Dry Creek Station, and had advised her to take it if anything happened to him. But he had warned her about riding near the Junipers or stopping at Rustler's Springs.

By retracing her trail she might discover the turnoff she had missed, but if she delayed any more it would be long after dark before she reached the stage station.

The logical move was to return to the ranch and make a fresh start at daybreak, as soon as Steve had left the house. Yet if she returned now she might never again muster the nerve to leave him. And she had already been too much trouble to Steve.

While the bay drank of the cool water Laurie slid from the saddle and tried dipping up a drink in the palm of her hand. The swallow of water was unsatisfactory and all she succeeded in doing was getting her face wet and spilling water on her blouse. It was somehow symbolic of all her failures since coming west.

When she got to her feet there was a man standing at the edge of the brush with a rifle cradled in his arms. How long he had been there she had no idea, but suddenly she was keenly aware of the utter loneliness of the spot and that not even Steve knew where she was. And her only weapon was the pistol in her saddlebag.

The man was thin and old with white hair and the coldest eyes she had ever seen looking from a human face. Tiny wrinkles wove a pattern of harsh years across the sun-darkened patina of his skin. It was a narrow face, high in the cheekbones . . . a hawk's face except for the blunted nose. His blue shirt was faded, his jeans worn. Only the narrow-brimmed hat was new.

HE DID NOT SPEAK, merely stared at her and waited.

"I missed the shortcut." She was surprised that she could speak so calmly. "I was going to Dry Creek Station."

His eyes left her face for the carpetbag behind her saddle. It contained only the few belongings she had brought to Red Tanks Ranch and to Steve Bonnet.

"You're Bonnet's woman," he said then. His voice was thin and dry.

Her chin lifted. "His wife."

"Quittin' him?"

Resentment flared. "It's none of your business!"

"Don't blame you for bein' skeered."

"It's not that!" she protested. "It's not that at all!"

His eyes had grown old in the reading of trail sign and the motives of men—and women.

She did not lie. Something other than fear was driving her. He could sense the bitterness in her, the sense of failure, and the hurt.

His head jerked toward the south. "Cabin's over there," he said, "and coffee's on."

Afterward she was to wonder why she followed him. Perhaps it was to show him she was not afraid, or it might have been hesitation to cross that last bridge that would take her from this country and the promise it had held for her.

The cabin was old but neat. There were bunks for several men, empty of bedding save one. The bed was neatly made and the few utensils were clean and hung in place.

Filling two enamel cups he placed one before her. Tasting the coffee she felt envy for the first time. For this had been her greatest failure. At least, it was the failure she was most miserable about. She could not make good coffee, not even good enough to please herself.

It had not taken her long to discover that she

was not cut out to be the wife of a western man, but it was a mistake she could now rectify.

With a little pang she remembered Steve's face when he saw the sore on the gelding's back. A wrinkle carelessly left in her saddle blanket had done that. Then there was the time his spare pistol had gone off in her hand, narrowly missing her foot. He had been furious with her, and she had cried most of the night after he was asleep.

"Surprised you'd take out on your man," the old man said, "didn't figure you for skeered after you throwed down on Big Lew with that shotgun."

She looked up, surprised at his knowledge. "But why should he frighten me? Besides," she added, "the shotgun wasn't loaded."

The cold eyes glinted with what might have been humor. "That'll jolt Lew. You had him right buffaloed."

He pushed the coffeepot back on the fire. "Took nerve. Lew ain't no pilgrim. He's killed hisself a few men."

"He really has?"

"Three, maybe four." He stoked his pipe, glancing out of the corners of his eyes at her face. It was a small, heart-shaped face with large, dark eyes, and her body, while a beautifully shaped woman's body, seemed almost too small, too childlike for this country. Yet his mother had been a small woman, and she had borne ten children in a rugged, frontier community. "If you ain't skeered, why you takin' out?" Then his eyes crinkled at the corners and he said wryly, "But I forgit. That ain't none of my business."

"I'm no good to him." She looked up, her dark eyes wide. "He needs someone who can help. All I do is make trouble for him."

The old man looked thoughtfully at his pipe. Her presence with that shotgun had prevented Big Lew and the Millers from burning the ranch. That had been their purpose in going to Red Tanks.

LITTLE BY LITTLE her story came out. Her father's long illness had absorbed their savings, and after his death she had become a mail-order wife. Steve Bonnet had needed a wife, and when she got off the stage and saw the tall, silent young man with the sun-bronzed face she had felt a queer little quiver of excitement. He needed a wife, she needed a home. It had been simple as that. They had not talked of love.

"In love with him now?"

The question startled her for she had not given it a thought. Suddenly she realized, shocking as it was . . . "Yes," she acknowledged. "I am."

The old man said nothing then, and she watched the shadows of the trees on the ground outside the cabin. She remembered Steve's face when he had come home the night before, the something in his eyes when he saw her. Had it been relief? Pleasure? What?

He refilled her cup. "Will quittin' give you rest? And how will he feel when he comes home tonight?"

She stifled the pang. "He's better off without me."

"Nothin' nice about comin' home to an empty house. You told him you love him?"

"No."

"He told you?"

"No."

"Wrong of him. Knowed a sight of women, here 'n there. Tell 'em you love 'em, pet 'em a mite, do somethin' unexpected nice time to time an' they'll break their necks for you."

The cottonwoods brushed their pale green palms together, rustling in the still, hot afternoon. "I wish I could make coffee like this."

"Not's good as usual." She noticed how the rifle lay where he had placed it, across the corner of the table, pointing a finger at the door. "Helps to have hot coffee when a man gets to home."

He leaned back in his chair and lighted his pipe again. "He know you're gone?"

"No."

"If them Millers come back they could burn him out. And him countin' on you."

"They won't come back."

His reply was a snort of contempt for such ignorance. "This here's a war, ma'am. It's a fight for range . . . and you're the only one your man's got on his side . . . and you quittin'."

"I'm no good to him. I can't do any of the things a wife should do out here."

"You can be home when he gets there. No man likes to stand alone. It's a sight of comfort for a man to know he's fightin' **for** something."

When she remained silent he said quietly, "They figure to have him killed, them Millers do."

"Killed?" She was shocked. "Why, the law . . ."

He looked at her, cold-eyed. "A man carries his law in his holster in this country. Them Millers don't want no part of Steve Bonnet themselves. They hire their killin' done when it's somebody like him. That man of yours"—the old man got to his feet—"is plumb salty."

He was suddenly impatient. "You ain't only a wife. You're a pardner, and you're quittin' when he needs you most."

He started for the door. "No need to go back to Six-shooter Gap. There's a trail back of here that old Stockton used. You stay shut of the Junipers and hold to the trail. It'll take you right to the stage station. You'll hit it near Little Dry."

She did not move. "Will you teach me how to make coffee like that?"

A QUAIL WAS CALLING when she rode into the yard at Red Tanks. Steve was not back, and she hurriedly stripped the saddle from the gelding. Then, remembering what Steve had done, she rubbed the horse down.

An hour later, her second batch of coffee hot and ready, she watched Steve ride into the yard. When she thought how she had nearly failed to be here to greet him she felt a queer little wrench of dismay, and she stood there in the door, seeing him suddenly with new eyes.

This was the man she loved. This man, this tall, narrow-hipped man with the quiet face and the faintly amused eyes. His bronzed hair glinted in the light as he stepped into the door, but there was no amusement in his eyes now. They were shadowed with worry.

"Steve . . . what's wrong?"

He looked at her suddenly, as if detecting a new ring in her voice. And for the first time he shared his troubles with her. Before he had always brushed off her questions, assuring her everything would be all right.

"Heard somethin' today. Old Man Miller has hired a man. A killer."

She caught his arm. "Steve? For you?"

He nodded, closing the door. He took off his hat and started for the wash basin. Then he smelled the coffee and saw the cup freshly poured.

He looked up at her. "Mine?"

She nodded, almost afraid for him to try it. Such a little thing, yet a mark for or against her.

He dropped into the chair and she saw the sudden weariness in his face. He tasted the coffee, then drank.

"A man named Bud Shaw. He's already here."

"You've seen him?"

"Not around here." He was drinking his coffee. "I saw him in El Paso once, when I first came west. He's a known man."

"But he kills for money? They can really hire men to kill someone?"

"This is a hard country, Laurie, and there's a war for range. Men hire out to fight as they join armies of other countries. I don't know as I blame 'em much."

Laurie was indignant. "But to kill for money! Why, that's murder!"

Steve looked up quickly. "Yes, if they dry-gulch a man. Bud Shaw won't do that. He'll meet me somewhere, unexpected-like, and I'll have my chance." He got up. "I shouldn't be telling you this. The country's rough on womenfolks."

He glanced at his empty cup. "Say, how about some more coffee?"

For a long time she lay awake. How like a little boy he looked! In the vague light from the moon she could see his face against the pillow, his hair tousled, his breathing even and steady. Suddenly, on impulse, she touched his cheek. Almost frightened, she drew her hand back quickly, then slid deeper under the coarse blankets and lay there, her eyes wide open, her heart beating fast.

When breakfast was over and he had picked up his rifle, she stopped him suddenly. "Steve . . . teach me to load the shotgun."

He looked around at her and for an instant their eyes held. Suddenly, his cheeks flushed. He turned back and picked up the shotgun, but his eyes avoided hers. Carefully, he showed her how the shotgun functioned, then at the door, he pointed. "See that white rock? If they come here, stop 'em beyond that. If they come closer . . . shoot."

She nodded seriously, and he looked at her again, and suddenly he gripped her shoulder hard. "You'll do, Laurie," he said quietly, his voice shaken, "you'll do."

SHE WAS SITTING where she could see out the door and down the trail when she heard the horse. She got up quickly and put her sewing aside. Heart pounding, she went to the door.

It was a lone man, riding a mouse-gray horse.

A shabby old man, but he wore a neat, narrow-brimmed hat.

He stopped on the edge of the woods and sat his horse there, one hand on the rifle, watching the door. He let his eyes drift slowly over the place, but she had a curious feeling that he was watching her, too, all the time his gaze wandered.

Then he let the horse walk forward and when he stopped he looked at her. "Howdy, ma'am. Mind if I git down?"

"Please do." He swung down, then leaving his horse ground hitched, he walked up to the door. "Passin' by," he said, "and I reckoned I'd try some of that there coffee."

When he was seated she poured a cup, and watched his expression anxiously. He tried it, tasted it again, then nodded. "A mite more coffee, ma'am, and you got it."

He looked around the neat little cabin, then out over the yard. The corrals were new and well built, the cabin was solidly constructed and the stable was no makeshift.

"Seen anything of Big Lew Miller?"

"No." She looked at him suddenly. "Look, did you ever hear of a man named Bud Shaw? He's a killer. A man with a gun for hire."

The old man touched his mustache thoughtfully. "Bud Shaw? The name seems sort of familiar." He looked up at her, his eyes veiled and cold. "A killer, you say? Where did you hear that?"

"Steve told me today. Oh, he said that this man Bud Shaw was different than some, that he'd give a man a chance before he killed him. But I don't think that matters.

"Look"—she leaned toward him—"you know outlaws. If you didn't, you wouldn't be living at Rustler's Springs. At least, Steve says that's a hangout for them. If you know how I can meet Bud Shaw and talk to him, I wish you'd fix it up."

He drank coffee and then rolled a smoke. She watched the slim brown fingers, almost like a woman's. Not one shred of tobacco spilled on the floor. When he had touched his tongue to the cigarette he looked around at her. "What you want to see him for?"

She had a notion of talking to him. No man could be so cruel as to—well, it wasn't right to shoot people, and Steve was a good man, only trying to build a home. That's all. And he wanted children, and . . . she was explaining all this when he interrupted.

"I take it you've changed your mind about runnin' off?"

She flushed. "I—I must have been mad. He does need me. You believe that, don't you? I mean—you think he really does?"

At the last her voice was pleading.

"A man needs a woman. No man is right without one, believe me. And with Steve it's got to be the right woman. He's that kind of man."

"But you said you didn't know him?"

"I don't. Not rightly, I don't. But folks hear things." His voice was suddenly sour. "Lady, Steve Bonnet won't kill easy. Not for Bud Shaw or nobody. Why do you reckon the Millers ain't killed him? There's four Millers. Why ain't they done it?"

He struck a match and lighted his smoke. "The Millers tried it, but there was five of them, then. Your husband killed one Miller and put another in the hospital."

STEVE HAD KILLED a man. Somehow the fact was not so shocking as it might have been a day or two before. Probably that was why he hesitated to condemn even a hired killer.

The old man got to his feet. "I'm driftin', ma'am. See you sometime."

"Wait." She went to the cupboard and hurriedly took down a pan of biscuits. "I just baked these, and some bread. Take them along." She took a brown loaf from the cupboard and put it with the biscuits into a sack. "That is one thing I can do!" Her chin lifted a little. "I can bake bread."

The old man looked at her thoughtfully.

"Thanks, ma'am. I appreciate this. First time anybody has given me anything for a long time."

"And don't forget, you promised to come over and teach me how to make soap."

He actually smiled. "Sure enough, I did at that."

When he was gone she looked down the trail again. And returning to her chair, resumed her work.

It was almost dusk when she saw the rider. For an instant she was sure it was Steve, and then he vanished into the trees. Quickly, she got up, closed the window shutters and got the shotgun. Then she put out the light and waited. It was not yet dark outside and she could see clearly.

A long time later a soft rustle outside the window caused her shotgun to lift. A man rounded into the door and her finger was tightening on her trigger when she recognized Steve.

Frightened, she got to her feet. "Oh, Steve! I might have shot you!"

He glanced at her, his eyes wary. "You're alone?"

"Why—of course! Who would be here?"

He walked to the bedroom and drew back the blanket that curtained the door. When he returned to the kitchen he paused, looking around. "Somebody scouted the place today. A man ridin' a small horse."

She started to explain, then caught herself. If

she told about the friendly old man then she must explain how they had met, and that she had planned to leave Steve. That she could not bring herself to do. Not now.

He was watching her, an odd look in his eyes. Her hesitation had aroused his doubts.

"It must have been a mistake," she said guiltily. "I saw no one."

Her voice trailed off, but she knew she was a poor liar. Steve dropped into a chair and looked at her, frowning a little. To avoid his eyes she hastily began to put food on the table, and then, desperately, tried to open a conversation. Somehow her words trailed off into nothing.

Each time their eyes met, Steve deliberately looked away.

"Steve—what's wrong?"

He did not meet her eyes. He got up. "Nothin'. Just tired, I guess."

At daylight she was up and she got breakfast, her heart tight and cold within her. Steve said nothing, only once when he finished combing his hair and turned away from the glass, their eyes met. His face looked drawn and lonely. Laurie longed to run to him and . . .

"You be careful," he said, sitting down at the table. "Don't let anybody in here. The Millers—they might try anything."

"Have you seen that other man?"

"Shaw?" He shook his head, watching her fill

his cup. "No. He's the one worries me. That was no Miller horse that I tracked. That Shaw—he might try anything. All a man knows is that he'll be where he's least expected."

HE WAITED inside the door for a long time before he went to the stable. He stood there, just studying the place, the trees, the hills. Reluctantly, he stepped out and then moved to the stable, flattened against the wall, then went in.

She waited breathless for him to emerge. When he came out he took a quick look toward the house.

He did not trust her. Laurie knew that now. He believed . . . but what could he believe?

Suddenly, she started out. "Steve!" she ran toward him. "Steve! Don't go!"

He hesitated. "Work to be done. If I hide today, what about tomorrow, and the next day? I can't hide all the time. I got to go on."

The old man came up to the house just before sundown and he was walking, carrying his inevitable rifle. He came up to the door and waited until she saw him.

"Ma'am, I got to talk to you."

"You'd better go away." Laurie's small face was stiff with worry. "Steve saw your tracks. He—doesn't trust me."

"You told him about me? You described me?" he asked quickly.

"No. I told him I had seen no one. He didn't believe me."

"I got to come inside, ma'am. Right away. I got to get out of sight."

She looked at him, saw the queer tightness in the parchmentlike brown skin. She hesitated only a moment, then stepped aside. "You'll help us?"

"I'll help you."

"Against Bud Shaw, too?"

He looked at her. "Yes," he said wryly, "even against him."

Then they heard the horse. A lone horse, and he was coming fast. From somewhere a shot sounded, then a volley. Then another shot.

The old man swore viciously. He started forward, then shrank back.

It was the gelding, and Steve Bonnet was clinging to the saddle horn. He half-fell from the saddle and, with a start of horror, Laurie saw the blood on his shirt and face, blood on his sleeve. He lunged, tripped on the step, and then before she could move to help him, he scrambled into the door. "Laurie!" his voice was hoarse. "The shotgun! They're comin'!"

He grasped the door edge and half-turned, and then he saw the man standing by the table.

Laurie saw a sudden stillness come over his face, a strange coolness. His one good hand, his left, halted above the gun in his waistband. The butt was turned for a right hand draw . . . it was an awkward chance.

"Hello, Bud," he said quietly.

Laurie cried out, a stabbing little cry.

"Hello, Steve."

The man waited, looking at Steve.

"Go ahead," Steve said bitterly. "You've given me my chance. I'm ready."

BUD SHAW LOOKED at him, and nodded gravely. "Sure you are, Steve. I knew that. You'd always be ready." He waited and Laurie could hear the clock tick, and somewhere outside the slow movement of approaching horses with cautious riders.

"You're a lucky man, Steve," Bud said quietly, "you've got a game wife, a fine wife."

Slowly then, with conscious and obvious deliberation he turned and went out the door. He stopped there with his feet wide.

They heard the horses coming on, then heard them stop. Steve stared at Laurie, listening. Then he dropped his hand for the shotgun and lifted it. She could see the blood on his sleeve, reddening his right hand.

"All right, Lew"—it was Bud Shaw speaking—"you can stop right there."

"Never knowed you for a turncoat, Bud," Big Lew spoke carefully.

"I told you I was through," Bud Shaw spoke reasonably, "I told you plain."

"You said nothin' about switchin' sides."

"Well, then. Hear it now. I've switched. If you want to know why, I'll tell you. Two things made me switch. Four yellow bellies that had to hire their killin', and then dry-gulched a lone man. That was only part of it."

They could see him standing there, a slight old man, his shoulders thin under the worn shirt. He had left the rifle inside and stood there with the two sixguns on his belt, facing them.

"The other thing was a little lady who wanted nothin' so much as to make good coffee for her man. I figure the man that little lady could love was too much of a man to be shot down for a pack of coyotes."

Big Lew's voice was harsh. "We won't take that talk, Bud! Not even from you!"

"You'll take it"—the old man's voice was dry with patience and disgust—"you'll take it, and I more than half wish you wouldn't."

He stood there like that in the gathering dusk and watched them ride away. When Laurie moved close to Steve and put her arm around him, she did not know, but she was there when the old man turned back to the door.

"Light the light, Laurie," he said gently, "and let's have a look at that shoulder."

## *Beyond the Chaparral*

Jim Rossiter looked up as the boy came into the room. He smiled, a half-nostalgic smile, for this boy reminded him of himself . . . fifteen, no . . . twenty years ago.

"What is it, Mike?"

The boy's eyes were worried. He hesitated, not wanting to tell what he had to tell, yet knowing with his boyish wisdom that it was better for Rossiter to hear it from him, now.

"Lonnie Parker's back from prison."

Jim Rossiter did not move for a long, long minute. "I see," he said. "Thanks, Mike."

When the boy had gone he got to his feet and walked to the window, watching Mike cross the street. It was not easy to grow up in a western town when one wanted the things Mike Hamlin wanted.

Mike Hamlin did not want to punch cows, to drive a freight wagon or a stage. He did not want to own a ranch or even be the town marshal. Mike was a dreamer, a thinker, a reader. He might be a young Shelley, a potential Calhoun.

He was a boy born to thought, and that in a community where all the premiums were paid to action.

Jim Rossiter knew how it was with Mike, for Jim had been through it, too. He had fought this same battle, and had, after a fashion, won.

He had punched cows, all right. And for a while he had driven a freight wagon. For a time he had been marshal of a trail town, but always with a book in his pocket. First it had been Plutarch—how many times had he read it? Then Plato, Thucydides, Shakespeare, and Shelley. The books had been given to him by a drunken remittance man, and he had passed them along to Mike. A drunken Englishman and Jim Rossiter, bearers of the torch. He smiled wryly at the thought.

But he had won. . . . He had gone east, had become a lawyer, had practiced there. However, memories of the land he left behind were always with him, the wide vistas, the battlements of the mesas, the vast towers of lonely cloud, the fringing pines . . . and the desert that gave so richly of its colors and its spaces.

So he had come back.

A scholar and a thinker in a land of action. A dreamer in a place of violence. He had returned because he loved the land. He stayed because he loved Magda Lane. That love, he had found, was one of the few things that gave his life any meaning.

And now Lonnie Parker was back.

Lonnie, who had given so much to Magda when she needed it, so much of gaiety and laughter. Lonnie Parker, who rode like a devil and fought like a madman. Lonnie, who could dance and laugh and be gay, and who was weak—that was Magda's word.

Rossiter, who was wise in the ways of women, knew that weakness had its appeal. There was a penalty for seeming strong, for those whose pride made it necessary to carry on as best they could although often lonely or unhappy. No one realized—few would take the time to look closely enough. The weak needed help . . . the strong? They needed nothing.

Sometimes it seemed the price of strength was loneliness and unhappiness . . . and the rewards for weakness were love, tenderness, and compassion.

Now Jim Rossiter stared down the dusty street, saw the bleak faces of the old buildings, lined with the wind etchings of years, saw the far plains and hills beyond, and knew the depths of all that loneliness.

Now that Lonnie was back it would spell the end of everything for him. Yet in a sense it would be a relief. Now the threat was over, the suspense would be gone.

He had never known Lonnie Parker. But he had heard of him. "Lonnie?" they would say, smiling a little. "There's no harm in him. Careless, maybe, but he doesn't mean anything by it."

Rossiter looked around the bare country law office. Three years, and he had come to love it, this quiet place, often too quiet, where he practiced law. He walked back to his desk and sat down. He was supposed to call tonight . . . should he?

Lonnie was back, and Magda had once told him herself, "I'm not sure, Jim. Perhaps I love him. I . . . I don't know. I was so alone then, and he understood and he needed me. Maybe that was all it was, but I just don't know."

Jim Rossiter was a tall, quiet man with wide shoulders and narrow hips. He liked people, and he made friends. Returning to the West he had come to this town where he was not known, and had brought a new kind of law with him.

In the past, the law had been an instrument of the big cattleman. The small men could not afford to hire the sort of lawyers who could fight their cases against the big money. Jim Rossiter had taken their cases, and they had paid him, sometimes with cash, sometimes with cattle, sometimes with promises. Occasionally, he lost. More often, he won.

Soon he had cattle of his own, and he ran them on Tom Frisby's place, Frisby being one of the men for whom he had won a case.

Rossiter made enemies, but he also made friends. He rode miles to talk to newcomers; he even took cases out of the county. He was a good listener and his replies were always honest. There had been a mention of him for the legislature when the territory became a state.

He had seen Magda Lane the morning he arrived, and the sight of her had stopped him in the middle of the street.

She had been crossing toward him, a quiet, lovely girl with dark hair and gray-green eyes. She had looked up and seen him there, a tall, young man in a gray suit and black hat. Their eyes met, and Jim Rossiter looked quickly away, then walked on, his mouth dry, his heart pounding.

Even in that small town it was three weeks before they met. Rossiter saw her box handed to a younger girl to smuggle in to the box supper, and had detected the colors of the wrappings. He spent his last four dollars bidding on it, but he won.

They had talked then, and somehow he had found himself telling her of his boyhood, his ambitions, and why he had returned to the West.

Almost a month passed before she told him of Lonnie. It came about easily, a passing mention. Yet he had heard the story before. According to some, Lonnie had held up a stage in a moment of boyish excitement.

"But he didn't mean anything by it," she told him. "He isn't a bad boy."

Later, he was shocked when he discovered that Lonnie had been twenty-seven when he was sent to prison.

But others seemed to agree. Wild, yes . . . but not bad. Not Lonnie. Had a few drinks, maybe, they said. He'd spent most of the money in a poker game.

Only Frisby added a dissenting note. "Maybe he ain't bad," he said testily, "but I had money on that stage. Cost me a season's work so's he could set in that game with George Sprague."

The stolen money, Rossiter learned, had been taken in charge by the stage driver to buy dress goods, household items, and other odds and ends for a dozen of the squatters around Gentry. A boyish prank, some said, but it had cost the losers the few little things they needed most, the things they had saved many nickels and dimes to buy.

Yet, on the evenings when he visited Magda, he thought not at all of Lonnie. He was far away and Magda was here right now. They walked together, rode together. She was a widow—her husband had been killed by Indians after a marriage of only weeks. At a trying time in her life, Lonnie had come along and he had been helpful, considerate.

Now Lonnie was back, and he, Jim Rossiter, was to visit Magda that evening.

★ ★ ★

IT WAS not quite dark when he opened the gate in the white picket fence and started up the walk to the porch. He heard a low murmur of voices, then laughter. He felt his cheeks flush, and for an instant debated turning about. Yet he went on, and his foot was lifted for the first step up the porch when he saw them.

Lonnie was there and Magda was in his arms.

He turned abruptly and started back down the walk. He heard the door open behind, then Magda called, "Jim! Oh, Jim, no!"

He paused at the gate, his face stiff. "Sorry. I didn't mean to interrupt." He heard Lonnie's low chuckle.

She called again but he did not stop. He walked down the street and out of town, clear to the edge of the mesa. He stood there a long time in the darkness.

Leaving the restaurant at noon the next day, he saw Lonnie Parker, George Sprague, and Ed Blick sitting on the bench near the door. They looked up as he passed, and he had his first good look at Lonnie Parker.

He was tall and pink-cheeked, and had an easy smile. His eyes were bland, too innocent, and when he saw Rossiter he grinned insultingly. Lonnie wore two guns, and wore them tied down.

Sprague was a cold, silent man who rarely smiled. Ed Blick boasted of a local reputation as a gunman.

"That's him," Blick said. "That's the gent who's been takin' care of your girl for you, Lon."

"Much obliged," Lonnie called out. He turned to Ed Blick. "I seen him last night. He was just leavin'."

His face burning, Rossiter walked on. Mike Hamlin was waiting for him when he reached the office.

"Jim." He got up quickly. "You said when I was fourteen you'd give me a job. I'm fourteen next week and I'd sure like to earn some money."

Rossiter sat down. This had been his idea, and he had talked to Mike's mother about it. If Mike was going to college he would have to begin to save. "All right, Mike," he said, "get on your horse and ride out to Frisby's. Tell him I sent you. Starting tomorrow morning, you're on the payroll at thirty a month."

Thirty a month was more than any boy in Spring Valley was making. A top hand only drew forty! Mike jumped up, full of excitement. "You'll earn it," Jim told him dryly, "and when you show you can handle it, I'll go up to forty." He grinned suddenly. "Now get at it . . . and save your money!"

During the week that followed he made no effort to see Magda, and carefully stayed clear of the places where she was most likely to be. He avoided mail time at the post office and began to eat more and more at home. Yet he could not close his ears nor his eyes, and there was talk around.

Lonnie was to marry Magda, he heard that twice. He saw them on the street together, heard them laughing. Work was piling up for him and he lost himself in it. And there was trouble around the country. Ed Blick had returned to town from Durango, where he had killed a man.

Lonnie spent most of his time with Sprague and Blick. He had made no effort to rustle a job, but he seemed to have money. Once Jim saw him buying drinks in Kelly's, and he stripped the bills from a large roll.

Rossiter was working late over a brief when Frisby came to his office. He was a solid, hard-working man, but he looked tired now, and he was unshaven.

"Jim," he came to the point at once, "we're losin' cows. Some of yours, some of mine, a few other brands."

During the night Mike Hamlin had heard the sound of hooves. He had gotten out of bed in the bunkhouse and had caught up a horse. There was a smell of dust when he hit the grass country, and at daybreak the boy had found the tracks. At least thirty head had been driven off by four men.

"They drove into the brush east of my place. When we tried to follow, somebody shot at us."

East of the Frisby place was a dense thicket of the black chaparral, a thicket that covered twenty square miles, a thorny, ugly growth of brush through which there were few trails, and none of them used except by wild game or strays. A rider could see no more than a few yards at any time. It was no place to ride with a rifleman waiting for you.

"I'd better get Mike out of there," he said. "I don't want him hurt."

"Don't do it, Jim," Frisby advised. "You'd break his heart. He's might set on provin' himself to you. He sets up night after night with them books, but he figures he's got to earn his money, too. He's makin' a hand, Jim."

Frisby was right, of course. To take the boy off the job would hurt his pride and deprive him of the money he would need if he were going to college. As for the cattle . . . Rossiter walked across the street to the sheriff's office.

George Sprague was standing in front of Kelly's smoking a cigar, and Jim was conscious of the man's sudden attention.

He had never liked Sprague, and never had known him. The man always had money, and he gambled, although he never seemed to win big . . . but he always had cash. He disappeared at intervals and would be gone for several days, sometimes a couple of weeks. His companion on these rides was usually Ed Blick. Now it was also Lonnie Parker.

Sheriff Mulcahy was a solid, serious man. A hard worker, intent on his job. "Third complaint this week," he said. "Folks gettin' hit mighty hard. Got any ideas?"

Rossiter hesitated the merest instant. "No," he said, "not yet."

Stepping out of the sheriff's office, he came face to face with Magda Lane.

"Jim!" Her eyes were serious. "What's happened? You haven't been to see me."

"The last time I called," he said quietly, "you seemed rather preoccupied."

"Jim." She caught his sleeve. "I've wanted to talk to you about that. You made a mistake. You—"

"I think I made my mistake," he said, his voice tightening, "at a box supper. Some time ago." Abruptly he stepped around her and walked on.

A moment later, he was furious with himself. He could have listened . . . maybe there was an explanation. So many things seemed what they were not. Still, what explanation could there be? And it was all over town that she was to marry Lonnie Parker.

Saddling his horse, he rode out of town. The turmoil aroused by seeing her demanded action, and he rode swiftly. He was crossing the plains toward Frisby's when, far and away to the east, beyond the chaparral, he saw a smoke column. He drew up, watching.

The smoke was high and straight. As he watched, the column broke, puffed, then became straight again.

Smoke signals . . . but the days of the Indian outbreaks were over. He turned in his saddle, and from the ridge back of Gentry he saw another signal. Even as he looked, it died out and was gone. Somebody from town was signaling to somebody out there beyond the chaparral.

Taking a sight on that first signal, he started toward it, passing Frisby's road without turning in.

There was only one reason of which he could think for a smoke signal now. Somebody in town would be sending word to their rustlers that the sheriff had been notified, or that he was riding. Probably the former. He, Rossiter reflected, was only a cow town lawyer, and not a man to be feared.

He rode into Yucca Canyon and followed it north, then climbed the steel dust out of it, skirted the mesa, and headed east again. He was high in the chaparral now, where it thinned out and merged with a scattered growth of juniper. Weaving his way through, he was almost to the other side when he came upon the tracks of cattle.

It was a good-sized herd, and it had come out of the chaparral not long before. From droppings he spotted, he judged the herd had been moved not more than four or five hours before.

The country grew increasingly rugged. It was an area into which he had never ventured before, a wild, broken country of canyons and mesas with rare water holes. By sundown he was too far out to turn back. And he had no bedroll with him, no coffee, and worst of all . . . no gun.

Yet to turn back now would be worse than foolish. This was, without doubt, a rustled herd. Time enough to return when he discovered their destination. As there were still some minutes of daylight, he pushed on. On his right was a long tongue of a lava flow, to the left a broken, serrated ridge of rusty rock. Before him, at some distance, lifted the wall of the mountain range, and it seemed the cattle were being driven into a dead end.

Coolness touched his face and the trail dipped down. The desert was gone, and there was a sparse growth of buffalo grass that thickened and grew rich as he moved ahead. The lava flow now towered above his head and the trail dipped down, and rounded a shoulder of the lava. He found himself in a long, shallow valley between the flow and the pine-clad range. And along the bottom grazed more than a hundred head of cattle.

He swung the steel dust quickly right to get the background of the lava for concealment. Then he walked his mount forward until he could see the thin trail of smoke from a starting fire. Concealing his horse, he walked down the slope through the trees.

When he reached a spot near the camp the smoke had ceased, but the fire was blazing cheerfully. A stocky man with a tough, easy manner about him worked around the fire. He wore chaps, a faded red flannel shirt, a battered hat . . . and a gun.

Rossiter turned and started back through the trees. If he cut across country he could have Mulcahy and a posse here shortly after daybreak.

A pound of hooves stopped him and he merged his body with a pine tree and waited, alert for trouble. Through an opening between trees he saw three riders. Two men and a boy.

A boy . . .

With a tight feeling in his chest he turned abruptly about and carefully worked his way back toward the camp. Ed Blick, George Sprague—and Mike Hamlin.

Mike's face was white, but he was game. His hands were lashed to the pommel of his saddle.

The red-shirted man looked up. "What goes on?" He glanced from the boy to Sprague.

"Found him workin' our trail like an Injun."

The man with the red shirt straightened and dropped the skillet. "I don't like this, George. I don't like it a bit."

"What else can we do?"

"We can leave the country."

"For a kid?" Sprague began to build a smoke. "Don't be a fool."

"Lonnie said Frisby went to Rossiter, then Rossiter to the sheriff." Blick was talking. "I don't like it, George."

"You afraid of Rossiter?"

"That lawyer?" Blick's contempt was obvious. "Mulcahy's the one who worries me. He's a bulldog."

"Leave him to me."

Their conclusion had been obvious. Mike Hamlin had found their trail, and now he had seen them. They must leave the country or kill him. And they had just said they would not leave the country.

The red-shirted man had not moved, and Rossiter could see the indecision in his face. Whatever else this man might be, Rossiter could see that he was no murderer. The man did not like any part of it, but apparently could not decide on a course of action.

Rossiter had no gun. . . . He had been a fool to go unarmed, but he had intended only to ride to Frisby's to talk to Mike and look over the situation on the spot. He had never considered hunting the thieves himself, but there came a time when a man had to fork his own broncs.

Whatever they would do would be done at once. There was no time to ride for help. Blick lifted Hamlin from the saddle and put the boy on the ground some distance away. The red-shirted man watched him, his face stiff. Then Blick and Sprague slid the saddles from their horses and led them out to picket. Jim worked his way through the brush until he was close to the fire.

Rossiter knew there was little time and he had to gamble. "You going to let them kill that boy?" he asked quietly.

The man's head came up sharply. "Who's that?"

"I asked if you were going to let them kill that boy?"

He saw Rossiter now. His eyes measured him coolly. "You want them stopped," he said, "you stop them."

"I wasn't expecting trouble. I'm not packing a gun."

It was his life he was chancing as well as Mike's. Yet he believed he knew men, and in this one there was a basic manhood, a remnant of personal pride and integrity. Each man has his code, no matter how far down the scale.

The fellow got to his feet and strolled over to

his war bag. From it he took a battered Colt. "Catch," he said, and walked back to the fire.

Jim Rossiter stepped back into the shadows, gun in hand. He had seen Mike's eyes on him, and in Mike's eyes there had been doubt. Rossiter was a reader of books, a thinker . . . and this was time for violence.

Sprague and Blick came back to the fire and Sprague looked sharply around. "Did I hear you talkin'?"

"To the kid. I asked if he was hungry."

Sprague studied the man for a long minute, suspicion thick upon him. "Don't waste the grub." He started to sit down, then saw the gap in the open war bag. With a quick stride he stepped to the boy and rolled him over, glanced at the rawhide that bound him, then looked around on the ground.

Blick was puzzled but alert. The man in the red shirt stood very still, pale to the lips.

The gambler straightened up and turned slowly. "Bill, where's that other gun of yours?"

"I ain't seen it."

Rossiter smelled the acrid smell of wood smoke. There was the coolness of a low place and damp grass around him. Out on the meadow a quail called.

"You shoved it down in your pack last night. It ain't there now."

"Ain't it?"

Bill knew he was in a corner, but he was not a frightened man. It was two to one, and he did not know whether the man in the shadows would stand by him—or even if he was still present.

"I'm not fooling, Bill. I won't stand for a double-cross."

"And I won't stand for killin' the kid."

Sprague's mind was made up. Ed Blick knew it, and Ed moved left a little. Bill saw that move and knew what it meant. His tongue touched his lips, and his eyes flickered toward the pines.

Rossiter took an easy step forward, bringing him into the half-light. "If you're looking for the gun, Sprague, here it is."

The gun was easy in hand . . . Blick saw something then, and it bothered him. No lawyer ever held a gun like that. He tried to speak, to warn Sprague, but Rossiter was speaking.

"Bill," he said, "untie that boy."

Sprague's lips had thinned down against his teeth. The corners of his mouth pulled down, and the skin on his face looked tight and hard. "Leave him be. I'm not backing up for no cow town lawyer."

"Watch it, George," Blick said. "I don't like this."

"He doesn't dare shoot. One of us will get him."

"Untie the kid, Bill." Rossiter's eyes were on Sprague, a corner of attention for Blick. He sensed that Blick was wiser at this sort of thing than Sprague. Blick was dangerous but he would start nothing. It would be Sprague who would move first.

Bill walked across to Mike and, dropping on his knees, began to untie him.

"Back off, Bill," Sprague warned, "or I'll kill you, too." He crouched a bit, bending his knees ever so slightly. "Get ready, Ed."

"George!" There was sudden panic in Blick's voice. "Don't try—!"

Sprague threw himself left and grabbed for his gun. It was swinging up when Rossiter shot him. Rossiter fired once, the bullet smashing Sprague in the half-parted teeth, and then he swung the gun. He felt Blick's shot burn him, then steadied and fired. Blick backed up two steps and sat down. Then he clasped his stomach as if with cramp and rolled over on his side and lay there, unmoving.

Bill touched his lips with his tongue. "For a lawyer," he said sincerely, "you can shoot."

Rossiter lowered the gun. Mike was sitting up, rubbing his arms. He walked over to where the other man's kit lay on the ground and dropped the pistol onto a blanket. "Much obliged, Bill. Now you'd better saddle up and ride."

"Sure."

Bill turned to go, then stopped. "That gun there. I got it secondhand." He rubbed his palms down his chaps. "I'll need a road stake. You figure it's worth twenty bucks to you?"

Rossiter drew a coin from his pocket and tossed it to Bill. It gleamed gold in the firelight. "It's a bargain, Bill. A good buy."

Bill hesitated, then said quietly, "I never killed no kids, mister."

NOBODY WAS in the street when they rode in at daybreak. There was a rooster crowing and somewhere a water bucket rattled, then a pump squeaked. Rossiter walked his horse up the street, leading two others, the bodies of Sprague and Blick across them.

Mike started to turn his horse toward home, then said, "You never said you could shoot like that, Jim."

"In a lifetime, Mike, a man does many things."

Mulcahy came from the door of his house, hair freshly combed. "Ain't a nice sight before breakfast, Jim." Mulcahy glanced at the two dead men. "You want me to put out a warrant for this Bill character?"

"No evidence," Rossiter replied. "Let him be. The last of them is Lonnie Parker. I want you to let me come along."

"Tomorrow," the sheriff said.

★ ★ ★

IT WAS NOON when he got out of bed. He bathed, shaved, and dressed carefully, not thinking of what was to come. He left Bill's gun on the dresser and went to a chest in the corner and got out a belt, holster, and gun. The gun was a .44 Russian, a Smith & Wesson six-shooter. He checked the loads and the balance, then walked out into the street.

Magda was just leaving her gate. She hesitated, waiting for him. She looked from the gun to his eyes, surprised. "Jim . . . what are you doing?"

He told her quietly of what happened, and of Bill riding away.

"But," she protested, "if they are dead and Bill is gone—"

"There were four rustlers, Magda," he said gently. "I don't know what the other one will do."

She got it then and he saw her face go white. One hand caught the gate and she stared at him. "Jim!" Her voice was a whisper. "Oh, Jim!"

He turned away. "I don't want trouble, Mag. I'm going to try to take care of him for you. After all," he said with grim humor, "he may need a lawyer."

Sheriff Mulcahy was waiting up the street in front of his office. The time had come.

He was gone three steps before she cried out, and then she ran to him, caught his arm.

"Jim Rossiter, you listen to me. You take care of yourself! No matter what happens, Jim! Jim, believe me, there was never anybody else—nobody at all—not after I met you. The night he came to town I . . . I was just so glad to see him, and then you saw us and you wouldn't talk to me. He took too much for granted, but so did you."

His eyes held hers for a long, long minute. Up the street a door slammed, and there were boots on the boardwalk. He smiled, and squeezed her arm. "All right, Mag. I believe you."

He turned then, and felt the sun's heat on his shoulders and felt the dust puff under his boot soles, and he walked away up the street, seeing Lonnie Parker standing there in the open, waiting for them. And he was not worried. He was not worried at all.

# *Home Is the Hunter*

Not even those who knew him best had ever suspected Bill Tanneman of a single human emotion.

He had never drawn a gun but to shoot, and never shot but to kill.

He had slain his first man when a mere fourteen. He had ridden a horse without permission and the owner had gone after him with a whip.

Because of his youth and the fact that the horse's owner was a notorious bully, he was released without punishment, but from that day forward Bill Tanneman was accepted only with reservations.

He quit school and went to herding cattle, and he worked hard. Not then nor at any other time was he ever accused of being lazy. Yet he was keenly sensitive to the attitudes of those around him. He became a quiet, reserved boy who accepted willingly the hardest, loneliest jobs.

His second killing was that of a rustler caught in the act. Three of his outfit, including the foreman, came upon the rustler with a calf down and tied, a heated cinch ring between two sticks.

The rustler dropped the sticks and grabbed his gun, and young Bill, just turned fifteen, shot him where he stood.

"Never seen nothin' to match it," the foreman said later. "That rustler would have got one of us sure."

A month later he killed his third man before a dozen witnesses. The man was a stranger who was beating a horse. Bill, whose kindness to animals was as widely acknowledged as his gun skill, took the club from the stranger and knocked him down. The man got to his feet, gun in hand, and took the first shot. He missed. Bill Tanneman did not miss.

Despite the fact that all three killings had been accepted as self-defense, people began to avoid him. Bill devoted himself to his work, and perhaps in his kindness to animals and their obvious affection for him he found some of that emotional release he could never seem to find with humans.

When riding jobs became scarce, Tanneman took a job as a marshal of a tough cow town and held it for two years. Many times he found himself striding down a dusty street to face thieves and troublemakers of every stripe. Always he found a strange and powerful energy building in him as he went to confront his adversaries. One look at that challenging light in his eyes was enough to back most of them down. Surprisingly enough, he killed not a single man in that time, but as the town was thoroughly pacified by the end of his two years, he found himself out of a job.

At thirty years of age he was six feet three inches tall and weighed two hundred and thirty compact and bone-tough pounds. He had killed eleven men, but rumor reported it at twice the number. He had little money and no future, and all he could expect was a bullet in the back and a lonely grave on Boot Hill.

Kirk Blevin was young, handsome, and had several drinks under his belt. At nineteen he was his father's pride, an easygoing young roughneck who would someday inherit the vast BB holdings in land and cattle. Given to the rough horseplay of the frontier, he saw on this day a man riding toward him who wore a hard, flat-brimmed hat.

The hard hat caught his gleeful attention and a devil of humor leaped into his eyes. His gun leaped and blasted . . . a bullet hole appeared in the rim . . . and Bill Tanneman shot him out of the saddle.

Tanneman's gun held the other riders, shocked by the unexpected action. From the dust at Tanneman's feet Kirk managed a whisper. "Sorry, stranger . . . never meant . . . harm."

The words affected Tanneman oddly. With a

queer pain in his eyes he offered the only explanation of his life. "Figured him for some tinhorn, gunnin' for a reputation."

Milligan, who rode segundo for Old Man Blevin, nodded. "He was a damn fool, but you better make tracks. Seventy men ride for Blevin, an' he loved this kid like nothin' else."

That Tanneman's reason for shooting had been the best would be no help against the sorrow and the wrath of the father. Curiously, Bill Tanneman's regret was occasioned by two things: that Kirk had shown no resentment, and that he had been a much-loved son.

For behind the granite-hard face of the gunfighter was a vast gulf of yearning. He wanted a son.

To see the handsome youngster die in the road had shocked him profoundly, and he was disturbed about the situation in general—he had no wish to fight against the man whose son he had accidentally killed. He thought of trying to speak to the old man, but did not intend to die, and the idea of having to shoot his way out of such a meeting chilled him to the core. The boy had given him no choice, but further tragedy must be avoided at all costs.

He swung swiftly into the hills, and with all the cunning of a rider of the lone trails, he covered the tracks and headed deeper and deeper into the wild vastness of the Guadalupes. He carried food, water, and ample ammunition, for he never started on the trail without going prepared for a long pursuit. When a man has lived by the gun he knows his enemies will be many and ruthless. Yet this time Bill Tanneman fled with an ache in his heart. No matter how justified his shooting, he had killed an innocent if reckless young man—the one bright spot in the life of the old rancher.

For weeks he lost himself in the wilderness, traveling the loneliest trails, living off the land, and only occasionally venturing down to an isolated homestead or mining claim for a brief meal and a moment or two of company.

Finally summer became autumn, and late one afternoon Bill Tanneman made his camp by a yellow-carpeted aspen grove in the shallow valley that split the end of a long ridge. From a rock-rimmed butte that stood like a watchtower at the end of the line of mountains, he scanned the surrounding country. Below him the slope fell away to a wide grass-covered basin several miles across. On the far side, against a low ring of hills, there was a smear of wood smoke and a glint of reflected light that indicated a town. Here and there were a few clusters of farm or ranch buildings. Noting that human habitation was comfortingly close yet reassuringly far away, he retired to his fire and the silence of the valley.

It was past midnight when he heard the walking horse. Swiftly he moved from under his blankets and, pistol in hand, he waited, listening.

The night was cold. Wind stirred down the canyon and rustled softly among the aspen. The stars were bright, and under them the walking horse made the only sound. A weary horse, alone and unguided.

It came nearer, then, seeming to sense his presence, the horse stopped and blew gently through his nostrils. Tanneman got cautiously to his feet. He could see the vague outlines of a man on the horse, a man slumped far forward, and something behind him . . . a child.

"What's wrong, kid?" He walked from the deeper shadows.

"It's my father." The voice trembled. "He's been shot."

Gently, Bill Tanneman lifted the wounded man from the saddle and placed him on the blankets.

He heated water from his canteen, and while the child looked on, he bathed the wound. It was low down and on the left side. From the look of the wound it had been a ricochet, for it was badly torn. Tanneman made a poultice of prickly pear and tied it on, yet even as he worked he knew his efforts were useless. This man had come too far, had lost too much blood.

When at last the wounded man's eyes opened,

they looked at the dancing shadows on the rock wall, then at Tanneman.

"The kid?"

"All right." Tanneman hesitated, then said deliberately, "Anybody you want to notify?"

"I was afraid . . . no, there's nobody. Take care of the kid, will you?"

"What happened?"

The man breathed heavily for several minutes, then seemed to gather strength. "Name's Jack Towne. Squatted on the Centerfire. Big outfit burned me out, shot me up. It was all I had. . . ."

Tanneman built a fire and prepared some stew, and when it was finished he dished some up for the child. He looked again at the dying man's run-down boot heels, the worn and patched jeans, the child's thin body. "I'll get your place back"—his voice was rough—"for the kid."

"Thanks, anyway." The man managed a smile. "Don't try it."

"What was the outfit?"

"Tom Banning's crowd. It was Rud Pickett shot me."

Rud Pickett . . . a money-taking killer. But a dangerous man to meet. And Banning was a tough old hide-hunter turned cattleman, taking everything in sight.

"Your kid will get that ranch. I'm Bill Tanneman."

"Tanneman!" There was alarm in the man's eyes as he glanced from the big gunfighter to the child.

The big man flushed painfully. "Don't worry, he'll be all right." He hesitated, ashamed to make the confession even to a dying man. "I always wanted a kid."

Jack Towne stared at him, and his eyes softened. He started to speak, but the words never came.

Bill Tanneman turned slowly toward the child. "Son, you'd better rest. I—"

"I'm not a son!" The voice was indignant. "I'm a girl!"

Tanneman watched the child with growing dread. What was he going to do? A little girl would take special treatment, but he didn't even know where to start. A boy, now . . . but this was a **girl**. How did one talk to a girl kid? He spoke seldom, and when he did his voice was rough. This was a situation that was going to take some thought.

THOMPSON'S CREEK WAS a town of two hundred and fifty people, two saloons, one rooming house, one restaurant, and a few odds and ends of shops, and at the street's end, a livery stable.

Betty Towne and Bill Tanneman rode to town the next evening. Tanneman remained cautious, as was his nature, but his mind was stubbornly set on the problem of the little girl. Their horses stabled, he brushed his coat and hat while the child gravely combed her hair, then joined him to bathe her hands at the watering trough.

"Let's go eat," he said, when she had dried her hands.

Her little hand slipped confidently into his and Bill Tanneman felt a queer flutter where his heart was, followed by a strange glow. A little more proudly he started up the boardwalk, a huge man in black and a tiny girl with fine blonde hair and blue eyes.

This had been her father's town, and it was near here that he had been shot, driven from the ranch where he had worked to create a home. And in this town were men who would kill Tanneman if they knew why he had come.

The life of Bill Tanneman had left him with few illusions. He knew the power of wealth, knew the number of riders that now rode for Tom Banning, and knew the type of man he was, and the danger that lay in Rud Pickett. Yet Tanneman was a man grown up to danger and trouble, knowing nothing else, and for the first time he was acting with conscious, deliberate purpose.

On the street near the café were tied several horses, all marked with the Banning brand. Tanneman hesitated for a moment, then led the girl toward the door. As they entered the café, he caught the startled glance of a woman who was placing dishes on the table. The glance went from the child to the weather-beaten man with white hair who sat at the end of the table. The man did not look up.

Also in the room there were three cowhands, one other man more difficult to place, and a tall, graceful girl with a neat gray traveling dress and a composed, lovely face.

At the sight of the man at the head of the table, Betty drew back and her fingers tightened convulsively. She looked up at Tanneman with fear in her light blue eyes. Deliberately, Tanneman walked around the table and drew back the two chairs on Banning's right.

The rancher glanced up irritably. "Sorry, that seat's reserved." His glance flickered to the girl and then back to Tanneman, his eyes narrowing. . . .

Ignoring him, Tanneman seated Betty, then drew back the chair nearest the rancher. For an instant their eyes met, and Tom Banning felt a distinct shock. Something within him went still and cold.

Reassured by the presence of Tanneman, Betty began to eat. Soon she was chattering away happily. She looked up into the lovely gray eyes opposite her. "This is my Uncle Bill," she said. "He's taking me home. At least, where we used to live. Our house was burned down." She glanced nervously toward the head of the table, fearful that she had said too much.

Tanneman was stirred by a grim humor. "Don't worry, honey. The men who burned it are going to build you a new house, a much bigger, nicer one. It will belong to you."

One of the cowhands put down his fork and looked up the table. Banning's eyes were on Tanneman, a hard awareness growing in them. The cowhand started to rise.

"You work for Banning?"

"Yeah."

"Then sit down. If you figure on lookin' up Rud Pickett, don't bother. I'll hunt him myself."

Coolly, Tanneman helped himself to some food. "I despise a man," he stated calmly, "who hires his killing done. I despise a man who murders the fathers of children. A man like that is a white-livered scoundrel."

Tom Banning's face went white. He half started to rise, then slid back. "I'm not packin' a gun," he said.

"Your kind doesn't." Tanneman gave him no rest. "You hide behind hired guns. Now you listen to me: I'm here to take up for Jack Towne's daughter. You rebuild that house you burned, you drive his stock back. You get that done right off, or you meet me in the street with your gun. Not your hired men—you, Tom Banning."

He forked a piece of beef and chewed silently

for a minute, and then he looked up. It was obvious that he had everyone in the café's attention. "This here little girl's father was murdered by riders, at Tom Banning's orders. That will be hard to prove, so I don't aim to try. I know it, an' everybody else around here does, too.

"He robbed this little girl of her daddy and her home. I can't give back her father, but I can give back her home."

Tom Banning's face was flushed. The girl was looking at him with horror, and he quailed at the thought of what she must be thinking. In his youth a fire-eater, Banning had come more and more to rely on hired guns, yet this man had called him personally, and in such a way that he could not avoid a meeting. That the stranger had done so deliberately was obvious. And now Tanneman pointed it even more definitely. "Ma'am"—Tanneman glanced up at the older woman—"give that fellow some more coffee." He indicated the cowhand who had started to rise. "He's worked for Banning awhile, I take it, and now he's got him a chance to see who his boss is, whether he's ridin' for a coward or a game man."

The directness of the attack took Banning by surprise, and once the surprise was over, he began to worry. This was no brash youngster, but a mature and dangerous man. If he tried to leave the man might order him to sit down, and then he must submit or risk actual physical combat.

Tanneman turned to the child and began cutting her meat. He talked to her quietly, gently, and the girl across the table was touched by the difference in his voice.

Kate Ryerson, who owned the restaurant, offered to give the child a bed. Slipping from her chair, Betty slipped her arms around him and kissed his rough cheek. "Good night, Uncle Bill."

The tall girl at the table met his eyes and smiled. "You seem to have a way with children."

Bill Tanneman felt himself blushing. "Don't guess I do, ma'am. It's that youngster. She has a way with me."

When the child was gone, the girl with the gray eyes filled her cup. "I think this should be investigated by the United States Marshal, and if these charges are correct Mr. Banning should be charged with murder and theft."

Tom Banning started to speak, then held his peace. For the first time he was really frightened. Guns, even turned against him, were something he understood and against which he could take measures. Explaining his ruthless killings to a jury and being torn apart by a prosecuting attorney was another thing.

When he finished his meal he got up quietly,

but Bill Tanneman ignored him. With his cowhands, Banning walked from the room.

Penelope Gray studied the big, hard-featured man across the table with attention. She remembered with warmth the queer wonderment in his eyes when he looked at the child. Instinctively, she knew this man was lonely for a long time.

"You've never been married?"

"I reckon no woman would want my sort of man."

"I think you're a very good man." She touched her fingers to his sleeve. "A man who would risk his life for the rights of a child who was no kin to him—that's a pretty fine sort of man."

Bill Tanneman remained seated after the girl retired, one thing holding his attention. Skilled at reading men, he had seen that Penny's threat of the law had frightened Banning much more than his own warnings. Asking for pen and paper, he sat down and wrote a letter to Dan Cooper.

It had been long since he had seen Cooper. A sheriff then, Cooper had been pursuing him after a shooting until the sheriff's horse put a foot in a prairie dog hole and broke a leg. It was wild country and the Comanches were riding. Tanneman had turned back, disarmed Cooper, and let him ride double until within a mile of town. Cooper was a judge now, and a power in Territorial politics.

At daybreak, he routed out the storekeeper and bought an express shotgun and fifty rounds for it. He loaded the shotgun and stuffed his pockets with shells. Then he saddled his horse and headed for the Towne place.

It was still early . . . quail called in the mesquite as he rode by at a space-eating canter. He found the Towne place as Kate Ryerson had described it, a flowing spring, a small pool, the weed-grown vegetable garden, and the charred ruins of a cabin.

His fighter's eyes surveyed the terrain. An old buffalo wallow could be a rifle pit . . . that pile of rocks . . . but he must not think in terms of defense, but of attack.

He was tying his horse in the brush behind the spring when he heard approaching hooves. He turned swiftly, his rifle lifting. It was Penny Gray.

His voice was rough when he stepped into the open. "You shouldn't have come. There may be trouble, and this is no place for a woman."

"I think it is, Bill. Banning and his men are coming. Anyway"—a half smile played on her lips—"you need a woman . . . more than you know."

The words caught him where he lived and he turned away angrily. How did women know where to strike? How to hurt? Even when they did not want to hurt.

And then he heard horses, many of them.

Tom Banning and a dozen riders came into the little valley and rode toward them. With something like panic, Bill saw Penny get her rifle from its scabbard. "Stay out of this!" he ordered.

Banning drew up. The presence of the girl disconcerted him. He had never killed a woman, nor did he believe his riders, other than Rud Pickett, would stand for it. Had it just been the two of them, now . . .

"Send that girl back to town!" he demanded angrily. "I'm fightin' men, not women!"

"Then don't fight, Mr. Banning." Penny's voice was serious. "Although it seems that your morals are not so pure as you'd like to let on. You took away everything that little girl had!" She glanced at Tanneman. "I came of my own free will. You do what you have to."

Banning chewed his mustache, and then Tanneman said, "You try any killing here today, Banning, and you'll never live to see it. My first bullet tears your heart out." He raised his rifle and took the slack out of the trigger.

"He may not believe me, Tascosa." Tanneman's eyes flickered briefly to a raw-boned cowhand behind Banning. "Tell him who I am."

Tascosa shifted in his saddle, liking the effect his remark would have. "Boss, this here's Bill Tanneman."

Tom Banning felt the shock of it.

Tanneman . . . the killer. No wonder he had not been worried by Rud Pickett.

Tom Banning sat very still feeling the cold hand of death. Whatever else he loved, he loved living, and this man would kill him. Not all his men, all his power, all his money and cattle could keep that bullet from his heart.

He was whipped and he knew it. He reined around. "Come on, boys."

"Banning!"

He drew up but did not look around. "You've one week to start building a six-room house with two fireplaces, corrals, and a barn. You'd best get busy."

Dust lifted from the trail as they walked their horses away. Defeat hung heavy upon their shoulders.

"You've won."

Tanneman shook his head. "Banning would have gambled if you were not here."

One week . . . He was stalling for his letter to reach Dan Cooper, stalling because he did not want to kill again.

Tanneman was worried by the tall, cool-eyed young woman who rode beside him back to town. What was her interest in this? Who was she, anyway? What was she doing here?

The town knew and the town waited. Rud Pickett was coming in. . . . Banning's hands would get Tanneman. The showdown would be something to see.

Tanneman was used to waiting. Trouble had been his way of life.

On the second day, four Banning riders appeared and entered the saloon. Bill Tanneman followed them in and ordered a drink. The riders felt his presence and knew why he was there. They respected him for it. He was letting them know that if they wanted him, he would not be hard to find.

The fifth day dawned. It was hot, dry, brittle. The heat left a metallic taste in the mouth, and there was no wind. Sweat broke out at the slightest move, yet men remained indoors despite the heat. When they appeared briefly on the street it was to hurry.

At noon, Tom Banning rode into town with fifteen men at his back. They left their horses at the corral and loitered along the streets, smoking idly.

Tanneman heard of their arrival and ordered another cup of coffee. Kate Ryerson brought it to him, and Penny watched him, her lips tight and colorless.

He pushed back his chair. Betty got up quickly. "Where are you going, Uncle Bill? Can I come?"

"Not this time." He touched her hair with his hand. "You stay with Penny."

It was the first time he had used her name, and when he looked up she was smiling at him. He turned quickly away and went out, swearing at himself.

He had to do this job, but he no longer looked forward to it. Once out in the still heat none of his old daring returned, the challenge, the urge to look death in the eye and laugh. How long had it been since he had felt that? That old love of a fight for a fight's sake. What happened to it? To love a fight as he had, one had to accept death, and that was something he found he could no longer do. Bill Tanneman knew what he had to do and he was ready, but he no longer enjoyed it. All he could do was put on a good show.

Every eye saw him, every eye knew. This was Bill Tanneman, almost a living legend. Nobody wanted to be in his shoes now, yet all envied him a little. Each one wished that **he** could step out into a street of enemies with that air, and look as formidable as he looked now.

Tom Banning waited in the saloon. Rud Pickett was beside him. They could have guessed to the instant when Tanneman appeared on the street. And then his shadow darkened the door.

Outside there was movement, the stir of many boots as Banning men converged on the saloon.

Bill Tanneman faced them, faced Banning and Pickett, as they turned from the bar. He was utterly calm, utterly still. Only his eyes moved, alert, watchful. These two men and a dozen more. Would the dozen fight if Banning and his gunman were dead? If they did, Tanneman would surely follow them into the grave. A grim smile tightened across his teeth.

"Here it is, Tom," Tanneman said quietly, "and I see you're hiding behind a hired gun to the last."

Rud Pickett moved out a little from the bar. He was going to draw. He was going to draw now . . . only he didn't. He looked into the cold gray eyes of Bill Tanneman and the seconds ticked by.

"Anytime, Rud."

That was it. Now . . . only he was frozen. He wanted to draw, he intended to draw . . . but he did not draw.

There was a stir at the door and a tall white-mustached man stepped into the room. His voice was sharp. "Stop this right now!"

Sweat broke out on Rud's face. Hesitantly, his eyes wide and on Tanneman's face, he stepped back. He started to turn and saw the contempt on the bartender's face. Banning did not look at him.

The man with the white mustache walked to the bar between Tanneman and Banning. "I'm Judge Dan Cooper," he said. "We'll settle this without guns."

Tom Banning cleared his throat. He was white and shaken. Slowly, Cooper began to explain. The old days were gone. Banning would face a court in the capital. Cooper suggested that if Banning were to do as Tanneman had asked he would recommend some leniency to the court, but like it or not Banning would stand trial for murder. "The sheriff'll have to come down to make the arrest," Cooper said. "You can try to run away if you want, but I figure with all you got you'll try to fight it out in court."

Banning walked from the room. Rud Pickett was on the steps. Banning did not pause. "You're fired," he said, and walked on.

Rud Pickett stared at him, then turned and stumbled off the steps. The sun was not on his shoulders as he walked slowly away up the street. He was not thinking, he was not feeling, he was just walking away.

The bat-wing doors opened and Penny came in. "Bill? You're all right?"

The tension was slowly going out of the big man. "I'm all right. I'm going up to my room, get myself a long night's sleep. I'd . . . I'd like to see you tomorrow, maybe go riding, if you would."

"I'd enjoy that. You just let me know when, Bill." He smiled a tired smile and turned toward the stairs.

Thoughtfully Cooper looked from one to the other. "He's been a lot of things, miss, but he's a good man. I've always known that."

"So do I," she replied seriously. "I knew it when I first saw him with Betty . . . and I knew he was my man."

The next morning the sound of curses and hammering echoed back from the quiet hills. Fifteen tough cowhands were hard at work on Betty Towne's new six-room house.

# *Rustler Roundup*

## CHAPTER 1

Judge Gardner Collins sat in his usual chair on the porch. The morning sunshine was warm and lazy, and it felt good just to be sitting, half awake and half asleep. Yet it was time Doc Finerty came up the street so they could cross over to Mother Boyle's for coffee.

Powis came out of his barbershop and sat down on the step. "Nice morning," he said. Then, glancing up the street and across, he nodded toward the black horse tied at the hitching rail in front of the stage station. "I see Finn Mahone's in town."

The judge nodded. "Rode in about an hour after daybreak. Reckon he's got another package at the stage station."

"What's he getting in those packages?" Powis wondered. "He gets more than anybody around here."

"Books, I reckon. He reads a lot."

Powis nodded. "I guess so." He looked around at the judge and scratched the back of his neck thoughtfully. "Seen anything more of Miss Kastelle?"

"Remy?" The judge let the front legs of his chair down.

"Uh-huh. She was in yesterday asking me if I'd heard if Brewster or McInnis were in town."

"I've lost some myself," Collins said. "Too many. But Pete Miller says he can't find any sign of them, and nobody else seems to."

"You know, Judge," Powis said thoughtfully, "one time two or three years back I cut hair for a trapper. He was passing through on the stage, an' stopped overnight. He told me he trapped in this country twenty years ago. Said there was some of the most beautiful valleys back behind the Highbinders anybody ever saw."

"Back in the Highbinders, was it?" Judge Collins stared thoughtfully at the distant, purple mountains. "That's Finn Mahone's country."

"That's right," Powis said.

Judge Collins looked down the street for Doc Finerty. He scowled to himself, only too aware of what Powis was hinting. The vanishing cattle had to go somewhere. If there were pastures back in the Highbinders, it would be a good place for them to be hidden, and where they could stay hidden for years.

That could only mean Finn Mahone.

When he looked around again, he was pleased

to see Doc Finerty had rounded the corner by the Longhorn Saloon and was cutting across the street toward him. The judge got up and strolled out to meet him and they both turned toward Mother Boyle's.

Doc Finerty was five inches shorter than Judge Gardner Collins's lean six feet one inch. He was square built, but like many short, broad men he was quick moving and was never seen walking slow when by himself. He and the judge had been friends ever since they first met, some fifteen years before.

Finerty was an excellent surgeon and a better doctor than would have been expected in a western town like Laird. In the hit-and-miss manner of the frontier country, he practiced dentistry as well.

Judge Collins had studied law after leaving college, reading in the office of a frontier lawyer in Missouri. Twice, back in Kansas, he had been elected justice of the peace. In Laird his duties were diverse and interesting. He was the local magistrate. He married those interested, registered land titles and brands, and acted as a notary and general legal advisor.

There were five men in Laird who had considerable academic education. Aside from Judge Collins and Doc Finerty there were Pierce Logan, the town's mayor and one of the biggest ranchers; Dean Armstrong, editor and publisher of **The Branding Iron;** and Garfield Otis, who was, to put it less than mildly, a bum.

"I'm worried, Doc," the judge said, over their coffee. "Powis was hinting again that Finn Mahone might be rustling."

"You think he is?"

"No. Do you?"

"I doubt it. Still, you know how it is out here. Anything could be possible. He does have a good deal of money. More than he would be expected to have, taking it easy like he does."

"If it was me," Doc said, "I'd look the other way. I'd look around that bunch up around Sonntag's place."

"They are pretty bad, all right." Judge Collins looked down at his coffee. "Dean was telling me that Byrn Sonntag killed a man over to Rico last week."

"Another?" Doc Finerty asked. "That's three he's killed this year. What was it you heard?"

"Dean didn't get much. He met the stage and Calkins told him. Said the man drew, but Sonntag killed him. Two shots, right through the heart."

"He's bad. Montana Kerr and Banty Hull are little better. Miller says he can't go after them unless they do something he knows about. If you ask me, he doesn't want to."

Finerty finished his cup. "I don't know as I blame him. If he did we'd need another marshal."

The door opened and they both looked up. The man who stepped in was so big he filled the door. His hair was long and hung around his ears, and he wore rugged outdoor clothing that, while used, was reasonably clean and of the best manufacture.

He took off his hat as he entered, and they noted the bullet hole in the flat brim of the gray Stetson. His two guns were worn with their butts reversed for a cross draw, for easier access while riding and to accommodate their long barrels.

"Hi, Doc! How are you, Judge?" He sat down beside them.

"Hello, Finn! That mountain life seems to agree with you!" Doc said. "I'm afraid you'll never give me any business."

Finn Mahone looked around and smiled quizzically. His lean brown face was strong, handsome in a rugged way. His eyes were green. "I came very near cashing in for good." He gestured at the bullet hole. "That happened a few days ago over in the Highbinders."

"I didn't think anybody ever went into that country but you. Who was it?" the judge asked.

"No idea. It wasn't quite my country. I was away over east, north of the Brewster place on the other side of Rawhide."

"Accident?" Finerty asked.

Mahone grinned. "Does it look like it? No, I think I came on someone who didn't want to be seen. I took out. Me, I'm not mad at anybody."

The door slammed open and hard little heels tapped on the floor. "Who owns that black stallion out here?"

"I do," Finn replied. He looked up, and felt the skin tighten around his eyes. He had never seen Remy Kastelle before. He had not even heard of her.

She was tall, and her hair was like dark gold. Her eyes were brown, her skin lightly tanned. Finn Mahone put his coffee cup down slowly and half turned toward her.

He had rarely seen so beautiful a woman, nor one so obviously on a mission.

"I'd like to buy him!" she said. "What's your price?"

Finn Mahone was conscious of some irritation at her impulsiveness. "I have no price," he said, "and the horse is not for sale." A trace of a smile showed at the corners of his mouth.

"Well," she said, "I'll give you five hundred dollars."

"Not for five thousand," he said quietly. "I wouldn't sell that horse any more . . . any more than your father would sell you."

She smiled at that. "He might . . . if the price was right," she said. "It might be a relief to him!"

She brushed on by him and sat down beside Judge Collins.

"Judge," she said, "what do you know about a man named Finn Mahone? Is he a rustler?"

There was a momentary silence, but before the judge could reply, Finn spoke up. "I doubt it, ma'am. He's too lazy. Rustlin' cows is awfully hot work."

"They've been rustling cows at night," Remy declared. "If you were from around here you would know that."

"Yes, ma'am," he said mildly, "I guess I would. Only sometimes they do it with a runnin' iron or a cinch ring. Then they do it by day. They just alter the brands a little with a burn here, an' more there."

Finn Mahone got up. He said, "Ma'am, I reckon if I was going to start hunting rustlers in this country, I'd do it with a pen and ink."

He strolled outside, turning at the door as he put his hat on to look her up and down, very coolly, very impudently. Then he let the door slam after him. Across the room the back door of the restaurant opened as another man entered.

Remy felt her face grow hot. She was suddenly angry. "Well! Who was that?" she demanded.

"That was Finn Mahone," Doc Finerty said gently.

"Oh!" Remy Kastelle's ears reddened.

"Who?" The new voice cut across the room like a pistol shot. Texas Dowd was a tall man, as tall as Mahone or Judge Collins, but lean and wiry. His gray eyes were keen and level, his handlebar mustache dark and neatly twisted. He might have been thirty-five, but was nearer forty-five. He stood just inside the back door.

Stories had it that Texas Dowd was a bad man with a gun. He had been in the Laird River country but two years, and so far as anyone knew his gun had never been out of its holster. The Laird River country was beginning to know what Remy Kastelle and her father had found out, that Texas Dowd knew cattle. He also knew range, and he knew men.

"Finn Mahone," Judge Collins replied, aware that the name had found acute interest. "Know him?"

"Probably not," Dowd said. "He live around here?"

"No, back in the Highbinders. I've never seen his place, myself. They call it Crystal Valley. It's a rough sixty miles from here, out beyond your place." He nodded to Remy.

"Know where the Notch is? That rift in the wall?" Collins continued. "Well, the route to his place lies up that Notch. I've heard it said that no man should travel that trail at night, and no man by day who doesn't know it. It's said to be one of the most beautiful places in the world. Once in a while Mahone gets started talking about it, and he can tell you things . . . but that trail would make your hair stand on end."

"He come down here often?" Dowd asked carefully.

"No. Not often. I've known three months to go by without us seeing him. His place is closer to Rico."

"Name sounded familiar," Dowd said. He looked around at Remy. "Are you ready to go, ma'am?"

"Mr. Dowd," Remy said, her eyes flashing, "I want that black stallion Mahone rides. That's the finest horse I ever saw!"

"Miss Kastelle," Finerty said, "don't get an idea Mahone's any ordinary cowhand or rancher. He's not. If he said he wouldn't sell that horse, he meant it. Money means nothing to him."

Judge Collins glanced at Finerty as the two went out. "Doc, I've got an idea Dowd knows something about Finn Mahone. You notice that look in his eye?"

"Uh-huh." Doc lit a cigar. "Could be, at that. None of us know much about him. He's been here more than a year, too. Gettin' on for two years. And he has a sight of money."

"Now don't you be getting like Powis!" Judge Collins exclaimed. "I like the man. He's quiet, and he minds his own business. He also knows a good thing when he sees it. I don't blame Remy for wanting that horse. There isn't a better one in the country!"

FINN MAHONE strode up the street to the Emporium. "Four boxes of forty-four rimfire," he said.

He watched while Harran got down the shells, but his mind was far away. He was remembering the girl. It had been a long time since he had seen a woman like that. Women of any kind were scarce in this country. For a moment, he stood staring at the shells, then he ordered a few other things, and gathering them up, went out to the black horse. Making a neat pack of them, he lashed them on behind the saddle. Then he turned and started across the street.

He worried there was going to be trouble. He could feel it building up all around him. He knew there were stories being told about him, and there was that hole in his hat. There was little animosity yet, but it would come. If they ever got back into the Highbinders and saw how many cattle he had, all hell would break loose.

Stopping for a moment in the sunlight in front of the Longhorn, he finished his cigarette. "Mahone?"

He turned.

Garfield Otis was a thin man, not tall, with a scholar's face. He had been a teacher once, a graduate of a world-famous university, a writer of intelligent but unread papers on the Battles of Belarius and the struggle for power in France during the Middle Ages. Now he was a hanger-on around barrooms, drunk much of the time, kept alive by a few odd jobs and the charity of friends.

He had no intimates, yet he talked sometimes with Collins or Finerty, and more often with young Dean Armstrong, the editor of **The Branding Iron**. Armstrong had read Poe, and he had read Lowell, and had read Goethe and Heine in the original German. He quickly sensed much of the story behind Otis. He occasionally bought him drinks, often food.

Otis, lonely and tired, also found friendship in the person of Lettie Mason, whose gambling hall was opposite the Town Hall, and Finn Mahone, the strange rider from the Highbinder Hills.

"How are you, Otis?" Finn said, smiling. "Nice morning, isn't it?"

"It is," Otis responded. He passed a trembling hand over his unshaven chin. "Finn, be careful. They are going to make trouble for you."

"Who?" Finn's eyes were intent.

"I was down at Lettie's. Alcorn was there. He's one of those ranchers from out beyond Rawhide. One of the bunch that runs with Sonntag. He said you were a rustler."

"Thanks, Otis." Finn frowned thoughtfully. "I reckoned something like that was comin'. Who was with him?"

"Big man named Leibman. Used to be a sort of a bruiser on the docks in New York. Lettie doesn't take to him."

"She's a good judge of men." Finn hitched up his gun belts. "Reckon I'll trail out of town, Otis. Thanks again."

At Lettie's he might have a run-in with some of the bunch from Rawhide, and he was not a trouble hunter. He knew what he was when aroused, and knew what could happen in this country. Scouting the hills as he always did, he had a very good idea of just what was going on. There was time for one drink, then he was heading out. He turned and walked into the Longhorn.

Red Eason was behind the bar himself this morning. He looked up as Mahone entered, and Finn noticed the change in his eyes.

"Rye," Finn said. He waited, his hands on the bar while the drink was poured. He was conscious of low voices in the back of the saloon and glanced up. Two men were sitting there at one of the card tables. One was a slender man of middle age with a lean, high-boned face. He was unshaven, and his eyes were watchful. The other was a big man, even bigger than Mahone was himself. The man's face was wide and flat, and his nose had been broken.

The big man got up from the table and walked toward him. At that moment the outer door opened and Dean Armstrong came in with Doc Finerty and Judge Collins. They halted as they saw the big man walking toward Mahone.

Armstrong's quick eyes shifted to Banty Hull. The small man was seated in a chair half behind the corner of the bar. If Mahone turned to face the big man who Armstrong knew to be named Leibman, his back would be toward Hull. Dean Armstrong rarely carried a gun, but he was glad he was packing one this morning.

Leibman stopped a few feet away from Mahone. "You Finn Mahone?" he demanded. "From back in the Highbinders?"

Mahone looked up. "That's my name. That's where I live." He saw that the other man had shifted until he was against the wall and Leibman was no longer between them.

"Hear you got a lot of cattle back in them hills," Leibman said. "Hear you been selling stock over to Rico."

"That's right."

"Funny thing, you havin' so many cows an' nobody knowin' about it."

"Not very funny. I don't recall that anybody from Laird has ever been back to see me. It's a pretty rough trail. You haven't been back there, either."

"No, but I been to Rico. I seen some of them cows you sold."

"Nice stock," Mahone said calmly. He knew what was coming, but Leibman wasn't wearing a gun.

"Some funny brands," Leibman said. "Looked like some of them had been altered."

"Leibman," Finn said quietly, "you came over here huntin' trouble. You'd know if you saw any of those cattle that none of them had but one brand. You know nobody else has seen them, so you think you can get away with an accusation and cover it up by trouble with me.

"You want trouble? All right, you've got it. If you say there was an altered brand on any of those cattle, **you're a liar**!"

Leibman sneered. "I ain't wearin' a gun!" he said. "Talk's cheap."

"Not with me, it isn't," Mahone said. "With me talk is right expensive. But I don't aim to mess up Brother Eason's bar, here. Nor do I aim to let your pal Alcorn slug me from behind or take a shot at me.

"So what we're going to do, you and me, is go outside in the street. You don't have a gun, so you can use your hands."

Without further hesitation he turned and walked into the street. "Judge," he said to Collins,

"I'd admire if you'd sort of keep an eye on my back. Here's my guns." He unbuckled his belts and passed them to the judge.

Alcorn and Banty Hull, watched by Doc Finerty and Armstrong, looked uneasily at each other as they moved into the street. Mahone noticed the glance. This wasn't going the way they had planned.

Leibman backed off and pulled off his shirt, displaying a hairy and powerfully muscled chest and shoulders.

Remy Kastelle came out of the Emporium and, noticing the crowd, was starting across the street when Pierce Logan walked up to her.

He was a tall man, perfectly dressed, suave and intelligent. "How do you do, Miss Kastelle!" he said, smiling.

She nodded up the street. "What's going on up there?"

Logan turned quickly, and his face tightened. "Looks like a fight starting," he said. "That's Leibman, but who can be fighting him?"

Then he saw Mahone. "It's that fellow from the Highbinders, Mahone."

"The one they're calling a rustler?" Remy turned quickly. She failed to note the momentary, pleased response to her reference to Mahone as a rustler. Her eyes quickened with interest. "He tricked me. I hope he takes a good beating!"

"He will!" Logan said dryly. "Leibman is a

powerful brute. A rough-and-tumble fighter from the East."

"I'm not so sure." Texas Dowd had walked up behind them. He was looking past them gravely. "I think your man Leibman is in for a whipping."

Logan laughed, but glanced sharply at Dowd. He had never liked the Lazy K foreman. He had always had an unpleasant feeling that the tall, cold cattleman saw too much, and saw it too clearly. There was also a sound to Dowd's voice, something in his way of talking that caught in Logan's mind. Stirred memories of . . . someone.

"Wouldn't want to bet, would you?" Logan asked.

"Yes, I'll bet."

Remy glanced around, surprised and puzzled. "Why, Mr. Dowd! I would never have imagined you to be a gambling man."

"I'm not," Dowd said.

"You think it's a sure thing, then?" Logan asked, incredulously.

"Yes," Dowd replied.

"Well, I think you're wrong for a hundred dollars," Logan said.

"All right." Dowd looked at Remy. "I'll be inside, buying what we need, Miss Remy."

"Aren't you even going to watch it?" Logan demanded.

"No," Dowd said. "I've seen it before." He turned and walked into the store.

"Well!" Logan looked at Remy, astonished. "That foreman of yours is a peculiar man."

"Yes." She looked after Dowd, disturbed. "He sounded like he had known something of Mahone before. Now let's go!"

"You aren't going to watch it?" Pierce Logan was shocked in spite of himself.

"Of course! I wouldn't miss it for the world!"

FINN MAHONE KNEW FIGHTERS of Leibman's type. The man had won many fights. He had expected Mahone to avoid the issue, but Mahone's calm acceptance and his complete lack of excitement were disturbing the bigger man. Mahone pulled off his shirt.

Leibman's face hardened suddenly. If ever he had looked at a trained athlete's body, he was looking at it now. With a faint stir of doubt he realized he was facing no common puncher, no backwoods brawler. Then his confidence came back. He had never been whipped, never . . .

He went in with a rush, half expecting Mahone to be the boxer type who might try to evade him. Finn Mahone had no intention of evading anything. As Leibman rushed, he took one step in and smashed Leibman's lips into pulp with a straight left. Then he ducked and threw a right to the body.

Stopped in his tracks, Leibman's eyes narrowed. He feinted and clubbed Mahone with a ponderous right. Mahone took it and never even wavered, then he leaped in, punching with both hands!

Slugging madly, neither man giving ground, they stood spraddle-legged in the dust punching with all their power. Leibman gave ground first, but it was to draw Finn on, and when Mahone rushed, Leibman caught him with a flying mare and threw him over his back!

Finn hit the ground in a cloud of dust, and as a roar went up from the crowd, he leaped to his feet and smashed Leibman back on his heels with a wicked right to the jaw. Leibman ducked under another punch and tried to throw Mahone with a rolling hip-lock. It failed when Mahone grabbed him and they both tumbled into the dust. Finn was up first, and stepped back, wiping the dust from his lips. Leibman charged, and Finn sidestepped, hooking a left to the bigger man's ear.

Leibman pulled his head down behind his shoulder. Then he rushed, feinted, and hit Mahone with a wicked left that knocked him into the dust. He went in, trying to kick, but Finn caught his foot and twisted, throwing Leibman off balance.

Finn was on his feet then, and the two men came together and began to slug. The big German was tough; he had served his apprenticeship in a hard school. He took a punch to the gut, gasped a long breath, and lunged. Then Finn stepped back and brought up a right uppercut that broke Leibman's nose.

Finn walked in, his left a flashing streak now. It stabbed and cut, ripping Leibman's face to ribbons. Suddenly, Judge Collins realized something that few in the crowd understood. Until now, Mahone had been playing with the big man. What happened after that moment was sheer murder.

The left was a lancet in the shape of a fist. The wicked right smashed again and again into Leibman's body, or clubbed his head. Once Finn caught Leibman by the arm and twisted him sharply, at the same time bringing up a smashing right uppercut. Punch-drunk and swaying, Leibman was a gory, beaten mass of flesh and blood.

Finn looked at him coolly, then measured him with a left and drove a right to the chin that sounded when it hit like an ax hitting a log. Leibman fell, all in one piece.

Without a word or a glance around, Finn walked to his saddle and picked up his shirt. Then he dug into his saddlebags and took out a worn towel. Judge Collins came over to him. "Better put these on first," he said.

Finn glanced at him sharply, then smiled. "I

reckon I had," he said. He mopped himself with the towel, then slid into his shirt. With the guns strapped on his lean hips, he felt better.

His knuckles were skinned despite the hardness of his hands. He looked up at Collins. "Looks like they were figurin' on trouble."

"That's right. There's rumors around, son. You better watch yourself."

"Thanks." Mahone swung into the saddle. As he turned the horse he glanced to the boardwalk and saw the girl watching him. Beside her was a tall, handsome man with powerful shoulders. He smiled grimly, and turned the horse away down the street, walking him slowly.

Texas Dowd appeared at Logan's elbow. Pierce turned and handed him a hundred dollars. "You'd seen him fight before?" he asked.

Dowd shrugged. "Could be. He's fought before."

"Yes," Logan said thoughtfully, "he has." He glanced at Dowd again. "What do you know about him?"

Texas Dowd's face was inscrutable. "That he's a good man to leave alone," he said flatly.

Dowd turned stiffly and strode away. Nettled, Logan stared after him. "Where did you find him?" he asked.

Remy smiled faintly. "He came up over the border when I was away at school. Dad liked the way he played poker. He started working for us, and Dad made him foreman. There was a gunman around who was making trouble. I never really got it straight, but the gunman died. I heard Dad telling one of the hands about it."

Behind them Texas Dowd headed down the street. He made one brief stop at Lettie Mason's gambling hall and emerged tucking a single playing card into his breast pocket. Then he mounted his horse and rode hard down the trail toward the Highbinders. . . .

FINN MAHONE WALKED the black only to the edge of town, then broke the stallion into a canter and rapidly put some miles behind him. Yet no matter how far or fast he rode, he could not leave the girl behind him. He had seen Remy Kastelle, and something about her gave him a lift, sent fire into his veins. Several times he was on the verge of wheeling the horse and heading back.

She was his nearest neighbor, her range running right up to the Rimrock. But beyond the Rimrock nobody ever tried to come. Finn slowed the black to a walk again, scowling as he rode. His holdings were eighty miles from Rawhide where Alcorn and Leibman lived. There was no reason for them jumping him, unless they needed a scapegoat. The talk about rustling was building up, and if they could pin it on him, there were plenty of people who would accept it as gospel.

People were always suspicious of anyone who kept to himself. Nobody knew the Highbinder country like he did. If they had guessed he had nearly five thousand acres of top grassland, there might have been others trying to horn in.

Crystal Valley, watered by Crystal Creek, which flowed into the Laird, was not just one valley, it was three. In the first, where his home was, there were scarcely three hundred acres. In the second there were more than a thousand acres, and in the third, over three thousand. There was always water here, even in the driest weather, and the grass always grew tall. Three times the number of cattle he now had could never have kept it down.

High, rocky walls with very few passes made it impossible for cattle to stray. The passes were okay for a man on foot, or in one or two cases, a man on a mountain horse, but nothing more.

After a while he reined in and looked off across the rolling country toward the Kastelle spread. It was a good ranch, and Remy was making it a better one. She knew cattle, or she had someone with her who did. He smiled bitterly because he knew just who that someone was.

Finn Mahone got down from his horse and rolled and lighted a cigarette. As he faced north, he looked toward the Kastelle ranch with its Lazy K brand. Southwest of him was McInnis and his Spur outfit. The McInnis ranch was small, but well handled, and until lately, prosperous.

East of him was the town of Laird, and south and just a short distance west of Laird, the P Slash L ranch of Pierce Logan.

Northeast of town was Van Brewster's Lazy S, and north of that, the hamlet of Rawhide. Rawhide was a settlement of ranchers, small ranchers such as Banty Hull, Alcorn, Leibman, Ringer Cobb, Ike Hibby, Frank Salter, and Montana Kerr. It was also the hangout of Byrn Sonntag.

He had not been joking when he suggested the best way to look for rustlers was with a pen and ink. There are few brands that cannot be altered, and it was a curious thing that the brands of the small group of cattlemen who centered in Rawhide could be changed very easily into Brewster's Lazy S or McInnis's Spur.

Finn Mahone was a restless man. There was little to do on his range much of the time, so when not reading or working around the place, he rode. And his riding had taken him far eastward along the ridge of the Highbinders, eastward almost as far as Rawhide.

Mounting, Finn turned the stallion toward the dim trail that led toward the Notch. It was a trail not traveled but by himself. A trail no one showed any desire to follow.

Ahead of him a Joshua tree thrust itself up from the plain. It was a lone sentinel, the only one of its kind in many miles. He glanced at it and was about to ride by when something caught his eye. He reined the horse around and rode closer. Thrust into the fiber of the tree was a playing card. A hole had been shot through each corner.

"Well, I'll be damned!" he said. "Texas Dowd. He finally figured out I was here—" His comment to the stallion stopped abruptly, and he replaced the card, looking at it thoughtfully. Then, on a sudden inspiration, he wheeled the stallion and rode off fifty feet or so, then turned the horse again. His hand flashed and a gun was in it. He fired four times as rapidly as he could trigger the gun. Then he turned the horse and rode away.

There were four more holes in the card, just inside the others. A message had been sent, and now the reply given.

THE GREAT WALL of the Rimrock loomed up on his left. It was a sheer, impossible precipice from two to six hundred feet high and running for all of twelve miles. For twenty miles farther there was no way over except on foot. It was wild country across the Rim, and not even Finn Mahone had ever explored it thoroughly.

Straight ahead was the great rift in the wall.

Sheer rock on one side, a steep slope on the other. Down the bottom ran the roaring, brawling Laird River, a tumbling rapids with many falls. The trail to Crystal Valley skirted the stream and the sheer cliff. Eight feet wide, it narrowed to four, and ran on for three miles, never wider than that.

After that it crossed the Laird three times, then disappeared at a long shale bank that offered no sign of a trail. The shale had a tendency to shift and slide at the slightest wrong move. It was that shale bank that defeated ingress to the valley. There was a way across. An outlaw had shown it to Finn, and he'd heard it from an Indian.

By sighting on the white blaze of a tree, and a certain thumblike projection of rock, one could make it across. Beneath the shale at this point there was a shelf of solid rock. A misstep and one was off into loose shale that would start to slide. It slid, steeper and steeper, for three hundred yards, then plunged off, a hundred feet below, into a snarl of lava pits.

Once across the slides, the trail was good for several miles, then wound through a confusion of canyons and washes. At the end one rode through a narrow stone bottleneck into the paradise that was Crystal Valley.

Finn Mahone dismounted at the Rimrock, and led his horse to the edge of the river. While the black was drinking, he let his eyes roam through the trees toward the Notch, then back over the broad miles of the Lazy K.

Remy Kastelle. The name made music in his mind. He remembered the flash of her eyes, her quick, capable walk.

The sun was warm, and he sat down on the bank of the stream and watched the water. Until now he had known peace, and peace was the one thing most to be desired. His cattle grew fat on the grassy valley lands, there were beaver and mink to be trapped, deer to be hunted. Occasionally, a little gold to be panned from corners and bends of the old creek bank. It had been an easy, happy, but lonely life.

It would be that no longer. For months now he had seen the trouble building in Laird Valley. He had listened to the gossip of ranch hands in Rico, the cattle buyers and the bartenders. He had heard stories of Byrn Sonntag, of Montana Kerr, of Ringer Cobb.

Simple ranchers? He had smiled at the idea. No man who knew the Big Bend country would ever suggest that, nor any man who had gone up the trail to Dodge and Hays. They were men whose names had legends built around them, men known for ruthless killing.

Frank Salter was just as bad. Lean and embittered, Salter had ridden with Quantrill's guerrillas, then he had trailed west and south. He had killed a man in Dimmit, another in Eagle Pass. He was nearly fifty now, but a sour, unhappy man with a rankling hatred for everything successful, everything peaceful.

Of them all, Sonntag was the worst. He was smooth, cold-blooded, with nerves like chilled steel. He had, the legends said, killed twenty-seven men.

Looking on from a distance Mahone had the perspective to see the truth. Until lately, there had been no suspicion of rustling. No tracks had been found; there had reportedly been no mysterious disappearances of cattle. The herds had been weeded patiently and with intelligence.

Abraham McInnis suddenly awakened to the realization that the thousand or more cattle he had believed to be in the brakes were not there. The rustlers had carefully worked cattle down on the range so there would always be cattle in sight. They had taken only a few at a time, and they had never taken a cow without its calf, and vice versa.

McInnis had gone to town and met with Brewster, and Van had returned to his own ranch. For three days he covered it as he had not covered it since the last roundup. At the very least, he was missing several hundred head of cattle. The same was true of Collins, the Kastelles, and Pierce Logan.

All of this was known to Finn Mahone. Stories got around in cattle country, and he was a man who listened much and remembered what he heard. Moreover, he could read trail sign like most men could read a newspaper.

He mounted the stallion and started over the trail for Crystal Valley.

PIERCE LOGAN WAS DISTURBED. He was a cool, careful man who rarely made mistakes. He had moved the outlaws into Rawhide, had made sure they all had small holdings, had given them their brands. Then he had engineered, from his office in town and his ranch headquarters, the careful job of cattle theft that had been done. Byrn Sonntag was a man who would listen, and Byrn was a man who could give orders. The stealing had been so carefully done that it had been going on for a year before the first rumbles of suspicion were heard.

Even then, none of that suspicion was directed toward Rawhide. When Rawhide ranchers came to Laird they were quiet and well behaved. In Rawhide they had their own town, their own saloon, and when they felt like a bust, they went, under orders, to Rico.

Logan had understood that sooner or later there would be trouble. He had carefully planned what to do beforehand. He had dropped hints here and there about Finn Mahone, choosing him simply because he lived alone and consequently was a figure of mystery and some suspicion. He had never mentioned Finn's name in connection with rustling. Only a couple of times he had wondered aloud what he found to do all the time, and elsewhere he had commented that whatever he did, it seemed to pay well.

Pierce Logan had seen Mahone but once before, and that time from a distance. He had no animosity toward him, choosing the man cold-bloodedly because he was the best possible suspect.

His plan was simple. When Mahone was either shot, hung for rustling, or run out of the country, the pressure would be off, the ranchers would relax, and his plans could continue for some time before suspicion built up again. If in the process of placing the blame on Mahone he could remove some of the competition from the picture, so much the better. He had a few plans along those lines.

His was not a new idea. It was one he had pondered upon a good deal before he came west to Laird. He had scouted the country with care, and then had trusted the gathering of the men to Sonntag.

Everything had gone exactly as planned. His seeds of suspicion had fallen on fertile soil, and his rustlers had milked the range of over five thousand head of cattle before questions began to be asked. No big bunches had been taken, and he had been careful to leave no bawling cows or calves on the range. The cattle had been shoved down on the open country on the theory that as long as plenty of cattle were in sight, few questions would be asked.

Two things disturbed him now. One of them was the fact that Finn Mahone had proved to be a different type of man than he had believed. He had defeated Leibman easily and thoroughly, and in so doing had become something of a local hero. Moreover, the way he had done it had proved to Logan that he was not any ordinary small-time rancher, to be tricked and deluded. Also, despite himself, he was worried by what Dowd had said.

The unknown is always disturbing. Although he and Dowd had little to do with one another, Texas Dowd had the reputation of being a tough and capable man. The fact that he knew Mahone and had referred to him as dangerous worried Logan. In his foolproof scheme, he might have bagged some game he didn't want.

The second disturbing factor was Texas Dowd himself. Pierce Logan's easy affability, his personality, his money, and his carefully planned influence made no impression on Dowd. Logan knew this, and also knew that Dowd was suspicious of him. He doubted that Dowd had any reason for his suspicion. Yet, any suspicion was a dangerous thing.

Pierce Logan had been careful to see that some

of his own cattle were rustled. He had deliberately planned that. It made no difference to him how they were sold; he got a big share of the money in any event, and it paid to avoid suspicion. Also, he had gone easy on the Lazy K, because Texas Dowd was a restless rider, a man forever watching his grazing land, forever noticing cattle. Also, Pierce Logan was pretty sure he would someday own the Lazy K.

Along with his plans for the Laird Valley, two other things were known only to Pierce Logan. One was that he was himself a fast man with a gun, with nine killings behind him. The second was that he could handle his fists.

He had seen Leibman fight before, and had always been quite sure he could whip him, if need be. Until today he had never seen a man he was not positive he could beat. Finn Mahone was a puzzle. Especially as he noted that Finn had never let himself go with Leibman. He had toyed with him, making a fight of it and obviously enjoying himself. Then suddenly, dramatically, he had cut him down.

Pierce Logan made his second decision that night. Earlier, he had decided that Dowd must be killed. That night he decided that his plans for Finn Mahone must be implemented quickly. Mahone must be used and then removed from the scene, thoroughly.

He got up and put on his wide white hat, then

strolled out on the boardwalk, pausing to light a cigarette. It was a few minutes after sundown, and almost time to go to supper at Ma Boyle's. His gray eyes shifted, and saw the man dismounting behind the livery stable.

Logan finished his smoke, then stepped down off the porch and walked across to the stable. His own gray nickered when it saw him, and he walked in, putting a hand on the horse's flank. Byrn Sonntag was in the next stall.

Speaking softly, under his breath, Logan said, "Watch when Mahone makes his next shipment. Then get some altered brands into them and let me know as soon as it's done."

"Sure," Sonntag said. He passed over a sheaf of bills to Logan. "I already taken my cut," Sonntag said.

Logan felt a sharp annoyance, but stilled it. "Dowd," he said, "looks like trouble. Better have one of the boys take care of it."

Sonntag was quiet for a minute, then he replied, "Yeah, an' it won't be easy. Dowd's hell on wheels with a gun."

Pierce Logan left the barn and walked slowly down the street. He scowled. It was the first time he had ever heard Sonntag hesitate over anything.

BYRN SONNTAG WAS PLEASED beyond measure when he encountered Mexie Roberts in the

Longhorn. He passed him the word, then went on and sat in on a poker game. When the game broke up several hours later he was a winner by some two hundred dollars.

Mexie Roberts joined him on the trail. He was a slight, brown man with a sly face. "You know Texas Dowd?" Sonntag demanded.

**"Sí."** Roberts studied Sonntag.

"Kill him."

"How much?"

Sonntag hesitated. Then he drew out his winnings. "Two hundred," he said, "for a clean job . . . one hundred now."

## CHAPTER 2

The Rimrock that divided the open range of Laird Valley from Mahone's holdings was almost as steep and difficult to scale from the inside. Finn Mahone had often studied the mountains, and knew there was an old, long-unused path that seemed to lead toward the crest. His black stallion was a mountain-bred horse, and he took the trail without hesitation.

The steep mountainside was heavily timbered with pine, mingled with cedar and manzanita. The earth under the trees was buried deep under years and years of pine needles, except where

here and there rock cropped out of the earth: the rough granite fingers of the mountain.

Several times he reined in to let the stallion breathe easier, and while resting the horse, he turned in the saddle to study the land around him. Below him, stretched out like something seen in a dream, were the three links in the Crystal Valley chain, and along the bottom the tumbling silver of Crystal Creek.

His stone cabin, built in a cleft of the mountain, was invisible from here, but he could just see the top of the dead pine that towered above the forest to mark the opening into the trail to Rico. It was a trail rarely used except when he drove his cattle to the railroad siding in the desert town.

Rico was as turbulent as Laird was peaceful, and it was a meeting ground of the cattlemen from Laird, the sheep men from the distant Ruby Hills, and the miners who worked a few claims in the Furbelows. Rico had no charms for Finn Mahone, and he avoided the town and the consequences of trouble there.

His occasional visits to Laird had built friendships. He had come to enjoy his contacts with Judge Collins, Doc Finerty, Dean Armstrong, and Otis.

Big, quiet, and slow to make friends, he had bought drinks for and accepted drinks from these men, and had, at the insistence of Otis, gone around to see Lettie Mason. Her house of entertainment was frowned upon by the respectable, but offered all Laird possessed in the way of theater and gambling. Lettie had heard Mahone was in town and sent Otis to bring him to call.

She was a woman of thirty-four who looked several years younger. She had lived in Richmond, New York, San Francisco, and New Orleans, and had for eight years of her life been married to a man of old but impoverished family who had turned to gambling as a business.

Lettie Mason had met three of the men in Laird before she came west. Two of these were Finn Mahone and Texas Dowd, and the third was Pierce Logan.

Since her arrival she had been in the company of Logan many times, and he had never acknowledged their previous meeting. After some time Lettie became convinced that he had forgotten the one night they met. It was not surprising, since he had been focused on the cards that her husband had been holding and she was introduced by her married name. Dowd was a frequent visitor at the rambling frame house across from the combination city hall and jail, but Mahone had been there only twice.

One other man in Laird knew a little about Lettie Mason. That man was Garfield Otis, who probably knew her better than all the rest. Otis, lonely, usually broke, and always restless, found in her the understanding and warmth he needed.

She fed him at times, gave him drinks more rarely, and confided in him upon all subjects. She was an intelligent, astute woman who knew a good deal about men and even more about business.

Finn Mahone, riding the mountainside above Crystal Valley, could look upon Laird with detachment. Consequently, his perspective was better. In a town where he had no allegiances and few friendships, he could see with clarity the shaping and aligning of forces. He was a man whom life had left keenly sensitive to impending trouble, and as he had seen it develop before, he knew the indications.

Until the fight with Leibman, he had believed he was merely a not-too-innocent bystander. Now he knew he was, whether he liked it or not, a participant. Behind the rising tide of trouble in the Laird basin there appeared to be a shrewd intelligence, the brain of a man or woman who knew what he or she wanted and how to get it.

Understanding nothing of that plan, Mahone could still detect the tightening of strings. Some purpose of the mind behind the trouble demanded that he, Finn Mahone, be marked as a rustler and eliminated.

He was nearing the crest and the trail had leveled off and emerged from the pine forest.

He must have another talk with Lettie. He

knew her of old, and knew she was aware of all that happened around her, that men talked in her presence and she listened well. They had met in New Orleans in one of those sudden contacts deriving from the war. He had found her taking shelter in a doorway during a riot, and escorted her home. She was, he learned, making a success of gambling where her husband had failed. He had died, leaving her with little, but that little was a small amount of cash and a knowledge of gambling houses.

Her husband, who had drawn too slow in an altercation with another gambler, had tried to beat the game on his own. Lettie won a little, and then bought into a gambling house, preferring the house percentage to the risk of a single game. Kindhearted, yet capable and shrewd, she made money swiftly.

Finn reined in suddenly and spoke softly to the stallion. Before him was a little glade among the trees, a hollow where the water from a small stream gathered before trickling off into a rippling brook that eventually reached Crystal Creek. A man was coming out of the trees and walking down to the stream. The man lay down beside the stream and drank. Dismounting, Finn held the big horse motionless and stood behind a tree, watching.

When the man arose, Finn saw that he was an

Indian, no longer young. Two braids fell over his shoulders from under the battered felt hat, and there was a knife and a pistol on his belt.

The Indian looked around slowly, then turned and started back toward the woods. Yet some sense must have warned him he was being watched, for he stopped suddenly and turned to stare back in Finn's direction.

Moving carefully, Finn stepped from behind the tree and mounted his horse. Then he walked the horse down into the glade and toward the Indian.

The fellow stood there quietly, his black eyes steady, watching Finn approach. **"How Kola?"** Finn gave the Sioux greeting because he knew no other. He reined in. "Is your camp close by?"

The Indian gestured toward the trees, then turned and led the way. Sticks had been gathered for a fire, and some blankets were dropped on the ground. Obviously, the Indian had just arrived. Two paint ponies stood under the trees, and the Indian's new rifle, a Winchester, leaned against a tree.

Finn took out his tobacco and tossed it to the Indian. "Traveling far?"

"Much far." The Indian dug an old pipe from his pocket and stoked it with tobacco, then he gestured toward the valley. "Your house?"

"Yes, my house, my cows."

The Indian lit his pipe and smoked without

speaking for several minutes. Finn rolled a cigarette and lighted it, waiting. The Indian nodded toward the valley. "My home . . . once. Long time no home."

"You've come back, huh?" Finn took his cigarette from his lips and looked at the glowing end. "Plenty of beaver here. Why not stay?"

The Indian turned his head to look at him. "Your home now," he suggested.

"Sure," Mahone said. "But there's room enough for both of us. You don't run cattle, I don't trap beaver. You and me, friends, huh?"

The Indian studied the proposition. "Sure," he said, after a while. "Friends." Then he added, "Me Shoshone Charlie."

"My name's Finn Mahone." He grinned at the Indian. "You been to Rawhide . . . the little town?"

"Rawhide no good. Rico no good. Plenty bad white man. Too much shootin'." Charlie nodded. "Already see two white man, ride much along big river. One white man tall, not much meat, bad cut like so." He indicated a point over the eye. "Other white man short, plenty thick. Bay pony."

Frank Salter and Banty Hull. They had been scouting the upper Laird River Canyon. That was on this side of Rico, and beyond the Rimrock from the Laird Valley. It was far off their own range. If they were scouting along there, the chances were they were looking for the route he took to Rico on his cattle drives. He forded the river in the bottom of that canyon.

"Thanks. Those men are plenty bad." Mahone watched the light changing on the mountainside across the Crystal Valley. The Indian knew plenty, and given time, might talk. He had a feeling he had won a friend in the old man.

"I'm headin' back," he said, "after a bit. Suppose you need sugar, tobacco? You come to see me. Plenty of coffee, too. I always have some in the pot, and if I'm not home, you get a cup and have some. Better not go into Rawhide, unless you have to." The Indian watched him as he rode away.

He was restless, knowing things were coming to a head. It disturbed him that Remy thought of him as a rustler. The girl had stirred him more deeply than he liked to admit. Yet, even as he thought of that, he knew it went further. She was so much the sort of person he had always wanted.

If he had read the bullet-marked playing card right, Texas Dowd finally knew he was on the range. The fact that he was riding for her would account for the excellent cattle she had, and the condition of her grass. In his months of riding the Highbinders, he had watched with interest the shifting of the Lazy K cattle. The ground was never grazed too long, and the cattle were moved from place to place with skill instead of allowing them to range freely. They had been shifted to the lowlands during the spring months and then, as hotter weather drew near, moved back where there was shade and greener grass from subirrigated land near the hills.

Dowd would know that Finn Mahone was no rustler, whatever else he might think of him.

Once home, he stabled his horse, gave it a brisk rub-down, and went into the house. After a leisurely supper he brewed an extra pot of coffee, hot and black, and sat down by the lamp. He picked up a book, but found himself thinking instead of the girl with golden hair who had watched his fight from the boardwalk. He recalled the flash of her eyes as he had told her he refused to sell the stallion. He sighed, and settled in to a few hours of reading.

IN THE RAMBLING ADOBE HOUSE on the Lazy K, Remy walked into the spacious, high-ceilinged living room, and sat down. "Dad," she asked suddenly, "have you ever heard of a man named Mahone?"

Frenchy Kastelle sat up in his chair and put his book down. He was a lean, aristocratic man with white hair at his temples and dark, intelligent eyes. He was French mixed with California Spanish, and he had lived on the San Francisco waterfront in exciting and dangerous times. Finally, he had gone into the cattle business in Texas.

His knowledge of cattle was sketchy, but he got into a country where there was free range, and made the most of it. Yet he was just puttering along and breaking even when Texas Dowd rode over the border on a spent horse. The two became friends, and he hired the taciturn Texan as foreman. Few better cattlemen lived, and the ranch prospered, but newcomers began crowding in, and at Dowd's suggestion, they abandoned the ranch and moved westward to the distant Laird River Valley.

The route had been rough, and not unmarked with incident. Texas Dowd had proved himself a fighting man as well as a cattleman.

Frenchy knew how to appreciate a fighting man. Casual and easygoing in bearing, he was a wizard with cards and deadly with a gun. He was, he confessed, a man who loved his leisure. He was willing enough to leave his ranch management to the superior abilities and energies of Remy and Dowd.

He looked at his daughter with interest. For the past two years he had been aware that she was no longer a child, that she was a young lady with a mind of her own. He had looked at first with some disquiet, being entirely foreign to the problem of what to do about a young lady who was blossoming into such extravagant womanhood.

This was the first time she had ever manifested anything more than casual interest in any man, although Frenchy was well aware that Pierce Logan had been taking her to dances in Laird.

"Mahone?" He closed his book and placed it on the table. "Isn't he that chap who lives back in the mountains? Buys a lot of books, I hear."

He studied his daughter shrewdly. "Why this sudden interest?"

"Oh, nothing. Only there was a fight today, and this Mahone fellow whipped that brute Leibman from over at Rawhide. Gave him an awful beating."

"Whipped Leibman?" Kastelle was incredulous. "I'd like to have seen that. Leibman used to fight on the coast, rough-and-tumble fights for a prize. He was a bruiser."

"Dowd won money on Mahone, and from the way he acts I think he knows something about him. He seemed so sure that he would beat Leibman."

"Then why not ask him?" Kastelle suggested.

"I know, Dad," she protested, "but he won't tell me anything. As far as that goes, I don't even know anything about Dowd!"

"Well, it is sometimes best not to ask too much about a man; judge him by his actions . . .

that's a courtesy that I have taken advantage of as much as anyone. Texas Dowd is the best damned cattleman that ever came west of the Mississippi, and that includes Jesse Chisholm, Shanghai Pierce, or any of them! What more do you want?"

"What do you know about him?" Remy demanded. "What did he do before he came to us? He had been shot, but who had done it? Who, in all this world, could make Texas Dowd run?"

Kastelle shrugged and lifted his eyebrows. "A man may run from many things, Remy. He may run from fear of killing as much as fear of death. Fewer run for that reason, but a good man might.

"I've never asked him any questions and he hasn't volunteered anything. However, there are a few things one may deduce. He's been in the army at some time, as one can see by the way he sits a horse and carries his shoulders. He's been in more than one fight, as he is too cool in the face of trouble not to have had experience.

"Moreover, he's been around a lot. He knows New Orleans and Natchez, for instance. He also knows something about St. Louis and Kansas City, and he's hunted buffalo. Also, he knows a good deal about Mexico and speaks Spanish fluently. We know all these things, but what is important is that he is not only our foreman but our friend. He has shown us that, and that is the only thing that has any real meaning."

Remy walked out on the wide flagstone terrace in front of the ranch house. The stars were very bright, and the breeze was cool. Looking off in the distance she could see the dark loom of the Highbinders, jagged along the skyline. She tried to tell herself she was only interested in Mahone because of that magnificent horse, but she knew it was untrue.

She detected a movement near the corrals, and saw Dowd's white shirt. She left the terrace and walked toward him across the hard-packed earth of the yard. "Texas!" she called.

He turned, a lean, broad-shouldered figure, the moonlight silver on his hat. "Howdy, Remy," he said. "Out late, ain't you?"

"Texas," she demanded abruptly, "what do you know about Finn Mahone?" Then hastily, to cover up—"I mean, is he a rustler?"

Texas Dowd drew on his cigarette, and it glowed brightly. "No, ma'am, I don't guess he is. Howsoever, men change. He wouldn't have been once, but he might be now. But offhand, I'd say no. I'd have to be shown proof before I'd believe it."

"Where did you know him?"

"Don't rightly recall saying I did," Dowd said. "Maybe it was just a name that sounded familiar. Maybe he just looked like somebody I used to know."

"Where?" she persisted.

"Remy," Dowd said slowly, "I want to tell you something. You stay clear of Finn Mahone! He's a dangerous man, as dangerous to women in some respects as he is to men! I don't believe there's a man on this range could face him with a gun unless it was Byrn Sonntag."

"Not even you?"

He dropped his cigarette and toed it into the dust. "I don't know, Remy," he said quietly. He drew a long breath. "The hell of it is," he said, sighing bitterly, "I may have to find out."

He turned abruptly and walked away from her toward the bunkhouse. She started to speak, then hesitated, staring after him.

REMY KASTELLE PRACTICALLY LIVED in the saddle. Her white mare, Roxie, loved exploring as much as she did, but in the next few days Remy studiously avoided the wide ranges toward the Highbinders in the west. But, time and again she would find her eyes straying toward the high pinnacle that marked the entrance to the Notch.

Then one day she mounted and turned her horse toward the Rimrock. As she drew closer, her eyes lifted toward the great red wall of the mountain. It was like nothing she had ever seen. In all her riding she had never come this far to the west, although she was aware that Lazy K cattle fed as far as the wall itself.

When she drew near, she turned the mare and

rode along toward the Notch. She was riding in that direction when she saw the bullet-marked card on the Joshua tree. Curiously, she stared at it. This was not the first time she had seen a card with the corners drilled by bullets. Many times she had seen Texas Dowd shoot in just that way. It was the first time she had ever seen the other four bullet holes. She studied the card for a while, then shrugged and rode on. It meant nothing to her.

She rode on, and the sun was warm in her face. She knew she should be turning back, but was determined to see the Notch at close hand. A shoulder of the rock jutted out before her and she rounded it, and the air was suddenly filled with the rushing roar of the Laird River. To her left was a dim trail up through the pines. Scarcely thinking what she was doing she turned the white mare up the trail into the Notch.

Remy told herself she was riding this way because she wanted to see the Notch, and because she was curious about Crystal Valley. Carefully, she kept her mind away from Finn Mahone. The tall rider could mean nothing to her. He was just another small rancher, and a brawler in the bargain.

Yet Dowd's warning, and his obvious respect for Mahone, stuck in her mind. Who was Finn Mahone? What was he?

The trail dipped suddenly and she hesitated.

Only eight feet wide here, and a sheer drop off to her right. The tracks of Mahone's stallion showed plainly. "If he did it, I can!" she told herself, and spoke to the horse. They moved on, and the trail narrowed, almost imperceptibly. Roxie shied nervously at the depth to her right, and Remy bit her lip thoughtfully as she studied the trail. It would be impossible to turn around now. For better or worse, she must keep going.

When the narrow trail finally ended she was nearing the bank of the Laird. She had heard that three crossings must be made, and she hesitated again, looking at the sky. There was going to be little time. The thought of going back over the trail in the dark frightened her.

She forded the Laird and rode up the opposite bank. The side from which she had just come was sheer cliff, towering upward to a height of nearly four hundred feet. The trail was narrow but solid, some fifteen feet above the tumbling Laird.

The country was wild and picturesque. In all her life she had never seen such magnificent heights of sheer rock, nor such roaring beauty as the rushing rapids below her. Tall trees towered against the sky, and when there was a glade or open hillside on her right the grass was green and thick. Entranced by the sheer beauty, she rode on, passing a waterfall that let the Laird go rolling over its brink in a smooth, glassy stream of power, thundering to the stones thirty feet below.

This was the country of which she had heard, the country that was almost unknown to the outside world. She pressed on, forgetful of the dwindling afternoon, and thinking only of the beauty of the landscape. She forded the Laird again, a swift, silent stream this time, and her road came out under great trees, turning the afternoon into a dim twilight as though she rode through a magnificent cathedral of towering columns.

Roxie was as interested as she herself, the mare's ears forward, twitching and curious. They continued, came out in a steep-walled canyon, and forded the stream for the third time. Again it was white water, but slower than below. The trail took her out of the canyon then, and across a valley of some fifty acres, the river, wider and deeper, was backed up behind a natural dam until there was a small lake among the trees. A bird flew up from the water, but she caught only a glimpse and could not identify it.

Then suddenly the trail channeled again and she was in another narrow-mouthed canyon. Great crags leaned over the trail here, and the river was no longer near, but had taken a turn away to the right. Then, riding out of the canyon, she stopped, staring across the first of the dreaded shale banks.

Evening had come, although it was still light, and there was no sound but the soft whisper of the wind in the trees. This was a lonely land, a land where nothing seemed to move, nothing seemed to stir, not even a leaf.

Looking up, she saw the long, steep slide of shale, and looking down, she saw that the shale disappeared in growing darkness below. But when she looked off to the right now, there was no canyon wall, no river. There was only a vast and empty silence, and the somber shadows of twilight lying over a gloomy desert. These were the lava pits, a trackless, lifeless region of blow-holes and jagged rock. It lay below her, something like a hundred feet below.

Roxie shied at the bank, and backed away nervously. There was a route across. That much Remy knew. Yet how it went, or how one knew where to enter, she could not guess. Hopelessness overwhelmed her, and anger, too. Anger at herself for failing now, and for persisting so long.

Fortunately, they would not be worried at home. She often rode to the McInnis ranch, or to Brewster's. Occasionally, she stayed all night. But the thought of staying in this lonely place at night frightened her. She did not want to turn around, yet the slate bank was appalling in its silent uncertainty.

Dismounting, she walked up to it, and stepped in with a tentative foot. Her boot sank, and almost at once the shale began to slide under her feet. She drew back, pale and disturbed.

Roxie pulled back nervously; the mare was obviously afraid and wanted none of it. Standing there, trying to make up her mind, Remy was suddenly startled.

A horseman was riding out of the darkness on the far side, and he rode now up to the edge of the awful drop-off into the lava pits. From across the distance she could hear he was singing, some low, melancholy song.

Remy stood still, her heart caught suddenly by the loneliness of the man, and the low, dreaming voice made the night seem suddenly alive with sadness. Stirred, she stood still, her lips parted as though to call, watching, and listening. It was only when he turned his horse to ride on that she became aware of herself.

She called out, and the man reined in his horse suddenly, and turned, listening. Then she called again. "Hey, over there! How do I get across?"

"What the devil?" It was Mahone. The realization made her eyes widen a little. "Who is it?" he demanded. "What are you doing here?"

"It's Remy Kastelle!" she said. "I started for a look at Crystal Valley! Can you help me over?"

He sat his horse, staring across the way, his face no more than a light spot in the darkness. She could almost imagine him swearing, and then he moved his horse to a new position. "All right," he called, "start toward me. Come straight along until I tell you to stop. How's that mare of yours? Is she skittish?"

"A little," Remy admitted, "but I think she'll be all right."

"Then come on."

Roxie hesitated, put a hoof into the shale, and snorted. Remy spoke soothingly, and the mare quieted. Mahone called again, and the sight of the stallion on the other side of the bank seemed to encourage the white mare. Gingerly, she moved into the slate. It sank sickeningly, then seemed to reach solid footing. Stepping with infinite care, the mare moved on.

When they had gone something over twenty yards, Mahone called to her, and she reined in.

"Now be very careful!" he shouted. "See that tall pine up there? Turn her head and ride that way. Count her steps, and when she has gone thirty steps, stop her again."

Her heart pounding, Remy spoke to the mare, and Roxie moved out, very slowly. This was a climb, and the shale slid around her hooves. Once the mare slipped and seemed about to fall, but scrambled and got her feet under her once more.

When they had gone thirty steps, Mahone called again. When she looked, she saw he had shifted position. "Now ride right to me!" he said.

It was so dark now she could make him out

only by his face and the brightness of some of the studs on the stallion's bridle. She turned again, and after stumbling and sliding for another fifty yards, the mare scrambled onto solid earth and stopped, trembling in every limb.

Remy slid to the ground and her knees melted under her. "I wouldn't do that again," she protested, "for all the money in the world! How do you ever live in such a place?"

Mahone laughed. "I like it!" he said. "Wait until you see Crystal Valley!"

She started to get up and he helped her. The touch of his hand made her start, and she looked up at him in the darkness, just distinguishing the outline of his face. She sensed his nearness and moved back, strangely disturbed. Something about this man did things to her, and she was angered by it.

"But what will we do?" she protested. "Isn't there another slide? Longer than this?"

He grinned and nodded. She saw his white teeth in the darkness. "Yes, there is, but I'll put a rope on your saddle horn for luck and lead the mare by the bridle reins."

"Are you trying to frighten me?" she flared.

"No, not a bit. If you were riding ahead of me, and my horse didn't know the trail, I'd want your rope on my saddle horn. This next slide is a dilly!"

They started on, and he rode rapidly, eager to

get the last of the dim light. The sky was still a little gray. When they reached the edge of the slide it was abysmally dark. He reined in abruptly. "Too dark," he told her. "We'll get off and wait until the moon comes up. It should be over the rim in about an hour. By moonlight we can make it."

He walked over to some trees and tied the two horses loosely. Gathering some sticks, he built a fire. When the dry sticks blazed up, he looked across at her and grinned. "Seems sort of strange. This is the first time a woman's ever crossed that slate bank, unless it was some Indian."

Remy looked at him gravely, then stretched her hands toward the fire. Surprisingly, the evening was quite cool, and the air was damp. Mahone knelt beside the fire and fed dry sticks into it, then looked up at her. "Your name is Kastelle?" he said. "It's an odd name. It has a ring to it, somehow."

"Perhaps you knew my father?" she suggested. "Before we came here we lived in Texas, and before that he was a gambler in San Francisco, what used to be called the Barbary Coast. They called him Frenchy."

He was looking at the fire. "Frenchy Kastelle?" He shook his head thoughtfully. "Seems like I would remember."

"I gathered from what my foreman said today

that you know **him**." Remy leaned back, looking at the fire. "His name is Texas Dowd."

"Did this Dowd say he knew me?"

"No, he didn't, but he won money on your fight. He won a bet from Pierce Logan. Logan was sure Leibman would win."

"This Pierce Logan must know Leibman," Mahone commented. "No man risks his money on a stranger."

It was something she had not considered. Still, Logan got around a good deal, and he might have met the big German. But she was not to be turned from her main interest. "That's why I thought Dowd knew you. He seemed so sure."

"He might know me. In cattle country men get to know others by name lots of times, or maybe you meet in a bar, or in passing."

"Were you ever in Mexico?" It was a shot in the dark, but she noticed that Finn picked up a stick and began poking the fire. Why, she could not have guessed, but suddenly she felt she had touched the nerve of the whole story.

"Mexico? I reckon most every man who lives along the border gets into Mexico. Right pretty country . . . some of it. Fine folks, too."

They were silent for a moment.

"What's it like in there?" Remy indicated the trail toward Crystal Valley.

"Like a little bit of heaven," he said. "Quiet,

peaceful, green . . . the most beautiful spot I ever saw. There's something about living back in these hills that gives a man time to think, to consider. Then, I like to read. Back there I can sit on my porch for hours, or over a fire in the cabin, and read all I like."

"How about your cattle? Don't you ever work them?"

He shrugged, and poked thoughtfully at the fire. "They aren't much trouble," he said. "No other cattle can get to them. I brand the calves while out riding around. Carry a running iron with me all the time. That way the work never gets much behind."

He stood up. "The moon's higher. We'd better go."

Remy knew one thing. She would never forget that night ride across that mile of treacherous shale. It was a ride she would never want to make alone, even by day. Yet she was dozing in her saddle and half asleep when they pulled up at the cabin.

"Go on in," he said. "I'll put up the horses."

She went up the steps and opened the door. It was dark but warm inside. She was struck at once by that warmth. An empty house, empty for hours on a chill night, shouldn't have been warm. She struck a light, and saw the candle on the table. When she lighted it, she turned slowly, half expecting to see someone in the room, but it was empty.

Puzzled, she walked to the fireplace and, with the poker, stirred the coals. They glowed red. Then she saw the coffeepot and, stooping, touched it with her hand. It was warm, almost hot.

She straightened then, and looked around. The room was small, but comfortable, having none of the usual marks of bachelor quarters. Surprisingly, it was neat. The few clothes she saw were hung on pegs, the pots and pans were polished and shining, the dishes on the shelves were neatly stacked, and all was clean. Only one cup stood on the table. In it were a few coffee grounds.

Remy was standing there looking at that cup when Finn came in. He tossed his hat to a peg across the room and it caught. He glanced at the cup, then at her eyes. "We'll warm the coffee up," he said, "and then have something to eat."

She turned and looked at him thoughtfully. "The coffee," she said, and there was a question in her voice, "is warm. Almost hot!"

"Good," he said. She stared at him while he stirred the fire. "We'll eat right away, then."

"Can I help?"

"If you like." He got some plates down and put them on the table.

Why she should be disturbed, she didn't know.

Obviously, there was someone else around. She had understood that Finn Mahone lived alone in the valley. Who was here with him? Where was she now?

Why must it be a woman? Remy didn't know why, but she wondered if it was. There was nothing effeminate about the room, yet it was almost too neat, too perfect. From her experience with cattlemen and cowhands, they usually lived in something that resembled a boar's nest. This was anything but that.

She looked up suddenly to see him watching her with a covert smile. "Would you like to see the rest of the house?" he suggested. She had the feeling that she amused him, and her spine stiffened.

"No, I don't think I'd care to! It isn't at all necessary!"

He grinned and picked up the candle. "Come on," he said.

She hesitated, then followed. She was curious.

The next room was a bedroom with a wide, spacious bed, much resembling an old four-poster. She thought it was, but when she drew nearer she could see it was homemade. On the floor was an Indian rug, and here, too, there were pegs on the walls. There were three pictures.

She started toward them, but he turned away and went into a third room. She followed him, then stopped. Here was a wide, homemade writing desk, and around her the walls were lined with books. The candlelight gleamed on the gold lettering, and she looked at them curiously. How her father would love this room! She could imagine his eyes lighting up at the sight of so many books.

They returned to the other room and he got the coffee and filled two new cups. They ate, almost in silence, but Remy found her eyes straying again and again to that empty cup. If Finn Mahone noticed, he gave no sign.

When they had finished eating, she helped him stack the few dishes. Somewhere not far off a wolf howled, a weird, yapping chorus that sounded like more than a dozen.

She stopped in the act of putting away the last of the food. "It's nice here," she said, "but so quiet. How do you ever stand it . . . alone?"

"I manage." His smile was exasperating. "It is quiet, but I like the stillness."

The problem of the night was before them, but Remy avoided the thought, trying to appear quiet, assured. She should have been frightened or worried. She told herself that would be the maidenly thing. Yet she wasn't. She was curious, and a little disturbed.

Sometimes she saw his eyes on her, calm and amused, and she wondered what he was thinking. No other man had ever upset her so much, nor had she met any other who was so difficult to read. Dowd was older, a simple, quiet man, and if he did not talk about some things, it was something she could understand. Somewhere he had been hurt, deeply hurt.

There was none of that in Finn Mahone. He was simply unreadable.

"You're going to have trouble, you know," she said suddenly.

"Trouble?" He accepted the word, seemed to revolve it in his mind. "I think so. It's been coming for some time. But don't be sure it will only be for me. Before this is over, there will be trouble for all of us."

She looked at him, surprised. "How do you mean?"

He tossed a stick on the fire. "How long has this rustling been going on? They say some five thousand cattle have disappeared. I would say that is about ten percent of what there is on the range around here, yet who has actually **seen** any rustlers?

"Who has seen any cattle being moved? Who has heard of any being shipped? Why were there always cattle on the lower ranges, and none up in the canyons?"

"Why?" Remy watched him, curious and alert.

He looked up at her, and his eyes, she noted, were a strange darkish green. He ran his fingers through his hair. "Why? Because the rustlers have taken cattle slowly, carefully, a few at a time, and when they have taken them they have moved other cattle down from the canyons where they could be seen, so no suspicion would be aroused."

He looked at her with a wry smile. "Five thousand cattle are a lot of cattle! And they are gone. Gone like shadows or a bunch of ghosts. You think that doesn't take planning?"

"You know who is behind it?"

"No. But now that people are accusing me, I aim to find out!"

"We haven't lost many, Dowd says."

Finn nodded. "Want to know why? Because that foreman of yours is a right restless hombre. He keeps moving around. He's up in every canyon and draw on your range. He knows it like the back of his hand. They don't dare take any chances with him. Whoever is behind this rustling doesn't aim to get caught. He means to go on, handling as many cows as he can without suspicion."

"You're a strange man," Remy said suddenly.

He turned his head and looked at her, the firelight dancing and flickering on his cheek. "Why?"

"Oh, living here all alone. Having all those books, and yet fighting like you did down there in the street."

He shrugged. "It's not so strange. Many men who fight also read. As for living alone, it's better that way." His face darkened, and he got to his feet. "It saves trouble. I don't like killing."

"Have you killed so many?" Somehow she didn't believe so. Somehow it didn't seem possible.

"No, but there's one I don't want to kill," he said. "That's one reason I'm back here. That's one reason I'll stay here unless I have to come out."

Remy arose and stood facing him. How tall he was! He stood over her, and looked down, and for an instant their eyes met. She felt hot color rising over her face, and his hands lifted as if to take her by the arms. She stood very still, and her knees were trembling. Suddenly the room seemed to tilt, and she swayed, her eyes wide and dark.

He dropped his hands abruptly and went around the chairs toward the porch. "You sleep in there." He jerked a thumb toward the wide bed. "I'll stay out there with the horses for a while, then sleep in here by the fire."

He was gone. Remy stared after him, her lips parted, her heart beating fast. She knew with an awful lost and empty feeling that if he had taken hold of her at that moment he could have done as he pleased with her. She passed a hand over her brow, and hurried into the other room, closing the door.

## CHAPTER 3

Pierce Logan had made his decision. A long conference with Sonntag and Frank Salter had convinced him that the time had come to make a definite move.

He disliked definite moves, yet had planned for them if it became necessary. His way had always been the careful way, to weed the range of cattle by taking a few here and a few there, until his own wealth grew, and the others were weakened. Then, bit by bit, to take what he wanted.

All in all the Rawhide outfit were making more money than they had ever made, but none of them were content. They wanted a lot of money quick, and they wanted action.

"If they don't git what they want, Pierce," Sonntag said, "they'll begin to drift. I know every man jack of 'em! They don't like none o' this piecin' along."

"Dowd's gettin' suspicious," Salter said. His eyes were cold gray. Pierce Logan had an idea that the old guerrilla didn't like him. "We got t' git rid of Dowd!"

"That's been seen to," Sonntag said. "Any day now."

Pierce Logan had returned to Laird filled with disquiet and anger at his plans deliberately being altered, but it was an anger that slowly seeped away as a plan began to evolve in his mind. A plan whereby he could come out with most of the profits himself. If those fools insisted on starting an out-and-out war, he would appear to be an innocent bystander. His cowhands were men known on the range. None of them were rustlers. Logan had been careful to see to that, and to keep the rustlers off his ranch except when they were getting some of his own cattle. When that happened, he managed to see that his hands were busy elsewhere.

Several of the men who worked for him, like Nick James and Bob Hunter, had ridden for McInnis or Judge Collins. They were known to be capable, trustworthy men. Carefully, Pierce Logan examined his own position. His meetings with Sonntag had always been secret, and there was no way anyone could connect him with the rustling.

Sonntag had done something about Texas Dowd. From what he had said, the foreman of the Lazy K would die very soon. When Dowd was out of the picture, his most formidable enemy would be removed. And in the meanwhile, he had the problem of pinning decisive evidence on Mahone.

So far as anyone knew he had avoided Rawhide. His connection with those ranchers was unknown. In any plans to move against the rustlers, as ranchers the Rawhide group would be included, and so know all the plans made against them. While considered a rough, tough crowd, no suspicion had been directed at them so far.

If anyone suspected them it would be Texas Dowd.

The only other possible joker in the deck would be Finn Mahone. Now, once suspicion was pinned on him, the Rawhide gang could hit the ranches hard, and it could be attributed to Mahone's "gang." Logan meant to sow that thought in the minds of the Laird ranchers: that Mahone had acquired a gang.

He was perfectly aware that Judge Collins, Doc Finerty, and Dean Armstrong did not believe Mahone a rustler. His evidence would have to convince even them.

Once the blame was saddled on the man from the Highbinders, he would turn the Rawhide bunch loose on some wholesale raids that would break McInnis and Brewster, Collins and Kastelle. The raids would still be carefully planned, but no longer would the rustlers take cattle in dribbles, and they would kill anyone who saw them.

The new plan was to clean up while they had Mahone to blame it on. When the big steal was over, when Mahone was shown to be guilty, then killed, and Logan was left in power, he would marry Remy Kastelle and own Laird Valley.

From there, a man might go far. He might, by conniving, be appointed governor of the Territory. He might do a lot of things. A man with money and no scruples could do much, and he meant to see that none remained behind to mark the trail he had taken to wealth.

But in all his speculations and planning he overlooked one man. He did not think of Garfield Otis.

Otis was a drunkard. A man who practically lived on whiskey. He neither intended nor wanted to swear off. He drank because he liked whiskey and because he wanted to forget what he would like to have done, and live in the present. He was always around, and a man who is always around and taken for granted by everyone hears a great deal. If he is a man of intelligence, he learns much more than people give him credit for.

Had Pierce Logan realized it, only one man in the Laird Valley suspected him. That man was Otis.

Texas Dowd smelled something odorous in

the vicinity of Rawhide. He knew men, and if Banty Hull, Montana Kerr, and the rest were peaceful ranchers, then he was the next Emperor of China. He knew all about Sonntag. He did not like Logan, but did not suspect he was the brain behind the rustling.

Neither did Otis. But stumbling along the street one evening, Otis had seen Logan ostentatiously lighting a cigarette in front of his office. Later, he had seen him cross the street and enter the livery stable. Seated on the edge of the walk, he had seen Logan leave the stable, and a moment later a rider headed off across the country. The rider was a big man.

Otis was only mildly curious at the moment. Yet he wondered who the man was. The man had seemed very big, and in the Laird Valley country only five men were of that size. Logan himself, Judge Collins, Finn Mahone, Leibman, and Byrn Sonntag.

Dean Armstrong was bent over the desk when Otis opened the door. He looked up. "Hi, Otis!" he called cheerfully. "Come on back and sit down!"

"Mahone been in town?"

Dean shook his head. "Not that I know of. No, I'm sure he hasn't been back since the fight. He said he would bring me a book he was telling me about, and he never forgets, so I guess he hasn't been in."

Then the man wasn't Finn Mahone.

The idea had never been a practical one, anyway. What would Mahone want with Logan? And meeting him in secret? It wouldn't make sense. It had certainly not been Judge Collins. That left only Leibman and Byrn Sonntag. Otis shoved his hands down in his pockets and watched Armstrong's pen scratching over the paper. "Dean," he asked, "what do you know about Pierce Logan?"

"Logan?" Armstrong put his pen down and leaned his forearms on the desk. Then he shook his head. "Just what everyone knows. He's got one of the best ranches in the valley. Been here about two or three years. He owns the livery stable, and has a partnership in the hotel. I think he has a piece of the Longhorn, too."

Dean picked up his pen again, frowning at the paper. "Why?"

"Oh, just wondering. No reason. Nice-looking man. Do you suppose he'll marry that Kastelle girl?"

"Looks like it." Dean scowled again. Somehow the idea didn't appeal to him. "If he does he'll control over half the range in Laird Valley."

Otis was restless. He got up. "Yes, you're right about that. And if McInnis and Brewster decided to sell out, he would own it all." He turned to go.

"Wait a minute and I'll walk over to the Longhorn with you."

Then Armstrong glanced at Otis. "Have you eaten?"

Garfield Otis hesitated, then he turned and smiled. "Why, no. Come to think of it, I haven't."

"Then let's stop by Ma Boyle's and eat before we have a drink."

They walked out together, and Armstrong locked the door after him. Otis started to speak, and Dean noticed it. "What were you going to say?"

"Nothing. Just thinking what an empire Laird Valley would be if one man owned it. The finest cattle range in the world, all hemmed in by mountains . . . like a world by itself!"

Armstrong was thoughtful. "You know," he said reflectively, "it would be one of the biggest cattle empires in the country. Probably the biggest."

Both men were silent on the way to Ma Boyle's. When they entered, the long table, still loaded with food at one end, was almost empty. Harran, who owned the Emporium, was there, and Doc Finerty. So was Powis.

Armstrong, pleased with himself at getting Otis to eat, sat down alongside Finerty. "How are you, Doc?" he asked. "Been out on the range?"

"Yeah, down to the Mainses' place. She's ailing again." He sawed at his steak, then looked up. "Seen that durned Mexie Roberts down there.

He was coyotin' down the range on that buckskin of his."

Marshal Pete Miller had come in. Miller was a lean, rangy man with a yellow mustache. A good officer in handling drunks and rowdy cowhands, he could do nothing about the rustlers. He overheard Doc's comment.

"Mexie, huh? He's a bad 'un. Nobody ain't never proved nothin' on him, but I always figgered he dry-gulched old Jack Hendry. Remember that?"

"I ought to!" Doc said. "Shot with a fifty-caliber Sharps! Never could rightly figure how that happened. No cover or tracks around there for almost a mile."

"A Sharps'll carry that far," Miller said. "Farther, maybe. Them's a powerful shootin' gun."

"Sure," Doc agreed, "but who could hit a mark at that distance? That big old bullet's dropping **feet,** not just inches. That would take some shooting . . . and he was drilled right through the heart."

"They believed it was a stray bullet, didn't they?" Powis asked. "I remember that's what they decided."

Garfield Otis listened thoughtfully. During the period in question he had lived in Laird, but his memory of the details of Jack Hendry's death was sketchy at best. One factor in the idea interested him, however. He asked a question to which he knew the answer. "What became of Hendry's ranch?"

"Sam, that no-good son of his, sold it," Harran said. "You recall that Sam Hendry? Probably drunk it all up by now. He sold out to Pierce Logan and took off."

"Best thing ever happened to this town!" Powis said. "Logan's really done some good here. That livery stable and hotel never was any good until he bought 'em."

"That's right," Harran agreed. "The town's at least got a hotel a woman can stop in now."

Otis walked to the Longhorn beside Armstrong, and they stood at the bar together and talked of Nathaniel Hawthorne and Walt Whitman. Armstrong returned to his work, and Garfield Otis, fortified by a few extra dollars, proceeded to get very, very drunk.

He had been drunk many times, but when he was drunk he often remembered things he had otherwise forgotten. Perhaps it was the subject of discussion at supper, perhaps it was only the liquor. More likely it was a combination of the two and Otis's worry over Finn Mahone, for out of it all came a memory. At noon the next day, when he awakened in the haymow at the livery barn, he still remembered.

At first he had believed it was a nightmare. He had been drunk that night, too. He had walked out on a grassy slope across the wash that ran along behind the livery stable and the Longhorn. Lying on the grass, he had fallen into a drunken stupor.

Seemingly a long time after, he had opened his eyes and heard a mumble of voices, and then something that sounded like a blow. He had fallen asleep again, and when he awakened once more, he heard the sound of a shovel grating on gravel. Crawling closer, he had seen a big man digging in the earth, and nearby lay something that seemed to be a body.

Frightened, he had stayed where he was until long after the man had moved away. Then he returned to his original bed and slept the night through. It wasn't until afternoon the next day that he remembered, and then he shrugged it off as a dream. The thought returned now, and with it came another.

For the first time, things were dovetailing in his mind. As the pieces began to fit together, realization swept over him, but no course of action seemed plain. His brain was muddled by liquor, and that dulled the knowledge his reason brought him, so he did nothing.

REMY KASTELLE AWAKENED with a start. For an instant she stared around the unfamiliar room, trying to recall where she was and all that had happened.

She bathed and combed her hair, and only then saw the folded paper thrust under the door. She crossed the room and picked it up.

**Had to take a run up to the next valley, be back about eight. There's hot water over the fire, and coffee in the pot.**

When she had dressed, she poured a cup of coffee and went to the door.

She stopped dead still, her heart beating heavily and her eyes wide with wonder.

The stone cabin was on a ledge slightly above the valley, and she looked out across a valley of green, blowing grass toward a great, rust-red cliff scarred with white. It was crested with the deep green of cedars that at one place followed a ledge down across the face of the cliff for several hundred yards. Through the bottom of the valley ran Crystal Creek, silver and lovely under the bright morning sun. In all her life she had seen no place more beautiful than this.

Looking down the rippling green of the grasslands, she saw the enormous stone towers that marked the entrance, a division in the wall that could have been scarcely more than fifty feet wide. From out on the porch, she could look up the valley toward where Crystal Creek cut through another entrance, this one at least two hundred yards across, looking into a still larger valley. Scattered white-face cattle grazed in the bottoms along the stream. Not the rawboned half-fed range cows she knew, but fat, heavy cattle.

As she looked, she saw a horseman come through that upper opening, a big man riding at a fast canter on a black stallion. She watched him, and something stirred deeply within her. So much so that, disturbed, she wrenched her eyes away and walked back into the kitchen. Putting down her cup she went into the bedroom to get her hat. Only then did she see the picture.

There were three, two of them landscapes. It was the third that caught her eyes. It was a portrait of a girl with soft dark eyes and dark hair, her face demure and lovely. Remy walked up to it, and stared thoughtfully.

A sister? No. A wife? A sweetheart?

She looked at the picture first because of curiosity, and then her eyes became calculating, as with true feminine instinct she gauged this woman's beauty against her own. Was this the girl he loved? Was this the reason he preferred to live alone?

Memory of the cup and the warm coffee returned to her. Was he alone?

The sound of the arriving horse jerked her attention from the picture, and hat in hand she walked out to the porch.

"Hi!" Mahone called. "Had some coffee?"

Remy nodded. "If you'll show me the way, I'll start back now."

"Better let me show you the rest of the valley," he suggested. "This is beautiful, but the upper valley is even more so."

"No. I often stay away all night. Father's used to it. But I always head back early. I stay at the Brewsters' occasionally, and sometimes with the McInnis family. Once even at Judge Collins's ranch."

She laughed. "The judge was really nervous. I'm afraid he thought I was compromised and that he might have to marry me!"

Finn looked at her, his eyes curious. "You're right. And I think you'd better be sure somebody knows where you are from now on."

"You think there'll be trouble?"

"Uh-huh." He was deadly serious now. "That valley is going to be on fire from one end to the other in a few weeks. Maybe even a few days. You mark my words."

Remy walked down to the corral while he roped Roxie and saddled her. "You know what they think, don't you?" she said.

"That I'm a rustler?" he asked. "Sure. I know that. But look around . . . why would I rustle? And if I did, how would I get them in here?"

"There isn't any other way?"

"Not from Laird. I've got all the cattle I want. As long as I keep the varmints down there's nothing to worry me here."

"If they accuse you, and try to make trouble, what will you do?" Remy asked as they neared the slate slide again.

He shrugged, and his face was grim. "What can I do? I'll fight if I have to. I never rustled a cow in my life, and I'm not going to take any pushing around."

She looked at Finn thoughtfully. "Texas Dowd doesn't think you're a rustler, but he warned me to stay away from you, that you were dangerous . . . to women."

Finn Mahone's head jerked around, and she could see the flare of anger in his eyes. "Oh, he did, did he? Yes, he would think that."

"Why did he say it?" she asked.

"Ask him," Finn replied bitterly. "He'll tell you. But he's wrong, and if he says that in public, I'll kill him!"

Remy tensed, and her eyes widened. There was something here she didn't understand. "Shall I tell him that, too?"

"Tell him anything you want to!" he snapped. "But tell him he's hunting the wrong man and he's a fool!"

"If there's trouble coming I'd like to think you were on our side," Remy said.

He looked at her cynically. "That cuts both

ways, but Dowd wouldn't stay with you if I was. Dowd wants to kill me, Remy."

"And what about you?"

For a moment, he did not answer, then he said simply, "No, I don't want to kill anybody."

He was silent, leading the way down to the slide. They made it now, by daylight, without mishap, but Remy kept her eyes away from the depths beyond the rim.

"You said," Finn suggested suddenly, "that you wanted me on your side. Who do you think is on the other side?"

They were fording the Laird, and she looked around at him. "I don't know," she protested. "That's what makes the whole situation so bad. Nobody seems to know."

SHE LEFT HIM at the opening of the Notch and rode on toward home. She was well aware what the people of Laird would say if they knew she had spent the night in Crystal Valley. The ranch people who knew her would think little of it, for she came and went on the range as freely as a man. But, in town, those people would be another matter.

She was halfway to the Lazy K ranch when she met Texas Dowd. He was wearing his flat-brimmed black hat and a gray shirt. With him were Stub and Roolin, two of the hands.

"We was lookin' for you, ma'am," Dowd said. "All hell's busted loose!"

"What do you mean?" Remy reined the mare around, frightened at the grimness of their manner.

"Somebody shot Abe McInnis last night. He went off up the valley, with that cowhand named Tony. When they didn't get back, Roolin here, who was up that way waitin' for him, rode up after him with Nick James, that hand of Logan's.

"They found 'em back in a narrow canyon near a brandin' fire. Tony was dead, shot three times through the belly, once in the head. McInnis had been shot twice. Doc says he might live; he's in purty bad shape."

"Who did it? Who could have done it?"

"I don't know who done it," Roolin said suddenly, harshly, "but he took off through the mountains ridin' a black stallion. There was another man or two with him. Abe evidently come up on 'em, an' they went t' shootin'."

"People in Laird's some upset," Dowd said. "Miller's gone out that way to have a look. Abe's got him a lot of friends around."

"I'd like to have a talk with Mahone!" Roolin said. "I got my own ideas about him!"

She started to speak, then hesitated. "Just when did it happen?"

"Near's we can figger it was late yesterday afternoon," Roolin offered. "Could have been evenin', but probably was earlier."

That could have been before she met Mahone

at the slide. Where had he been coming from then? He had offered no explanation. Was there a trail out through one of the narrow canyons that opened up near where she had first seen him? If there was, he could have ridden the distance without trouble.

Brewster was at the ranch when she got there, accompanied by Dowd. Her father had put his book aside and his face was grave. He was a quiet man, but she knew from past experience that when stirred he was hard, bitterly hard, and a man who would fight to the last shell and the last drop of blood.

Van Brewster was a burly man, deep-voiced and hard-bitten. His background was strictly pioneer. He had spent most of his life until now working in the plains country or the mountains, had soldiered, hunted, trapped, and fought Indians and rustlers.

"Abe was my friend!" he was saying as she entered, "and I aim to get the man responsible!"

Dowd drew back to one side of the room and thoughtfully rolled a cigarette. His eyes went from Kastelle to Brewster. He said nothing, invited nothing. A few minutes later, horses were heard in the ranch yard. "That'll be Logan an' Collins," Brewster said. "I told 'em we would meet here."

With them were Harran, the Emporium owner who ran a few cattle on the Collins range, and Dan Taggart, McInnis's foreman. All were grim and hard-faced, and all carried guns. "Miller's comin'," Taggart stated. "He's been on the range all day!"

"Find anything?" Harran asked.

"Some tracks," Taggart said, "mighty big hoss tracks. He thinks they were the tracks o' that stallion o' Mahone's!"

Dowd pushed away from the wall, his thumbs hooked in his belt. "Find 'em close to the body of either man? Or close to the fire?"

"Wal, no," Taggart admitted. "Not right close't. They was under some trees, maybe fifty yards away. The horse could've been tied there, though."

"It could have," Dowd admitted, "or he could have come up there and looked around and rode off, either before then, or later."

"If it was later, why didn't he report it?" Taggart demanded.

"Well," Collins interrupted, "if you recall, he's scarcely been welcomed around Laird. Probably didn't figure it was any of his business! Or maybe he didn't know what was goin' on."

"You defendin' him?" Taggart demanded. "You want t' remember my boss is a-lyin' home durned near dead!"

"I do not want any accusations without proof!" Judge Collins said sharply. "Just because one man's hurt and another's dead, that doesn't make Mahone guilty if he's innocent!"

"Well," Taggart said dryly, "if I see Finn Mahone on that place again, I'm goin' to shoot first and ask questions after!"

Dowd smiled without humor. "Better make sure it's first," he said, "or you won't live long. Finn Mahone's no man to drag iron on unless you intend to kill him."

"You sound like you know him," Brewster suggested.

Footsteps sounded on the porch, and the door opened. Alcorn was standing there, and with him Ike Hibby, Montana Kerr, and Ringer Cobb, all of Rawhide.

"I do," Dowd said, staring at the newcomers. "I know he's a man you hadn't better accuse of rustlin' unless you're ready to fill your hand."

Ringer Cobb was narrow-hipped and wide-shouldered; a build typical of the western rider. His guns were slung low and tied down. He glanced across at Dowd. "If you're talkin' about Mahone," he said casually, "I'll accuse him! All this talk of his bein' fast with a gun doesn't faze me none. I think he's rustlin'. He or his boys."

Judge Collins studied Cobb and pulled at his mustache. "What do you mean . . . his boys?" he asked. "I've understood Mahone played a lone hand."

"So have we all," Harran agreed, "but how do we know?"

That was it, Remy admitted, how did they know? How about that cup on the table, and the still-warm fire? Where had Mahone gone when he rode off that morning?

"How would he get cattle back into that country?" she asked. "Any of you ever tried to go through that Notch?"

"He does it," Cobb said. He looked at the girl, his eyes speculative. "An' for all we know, there may be another route. Nobody ever gets back into that wild country below the Rimrock."

"Nobody but the hombre that killed Tony," Taggart said grimly. "He was in there."

"All this is gettin' us nowhere," Brewster put in. "I've lost stock. It's been taken off my range without me ever guessin' until recent. I can't stand to lose no more."

"I think it's time we organized and did something," Alcorn spoke up.

"What?" Kastelle asked. He had been sitting back, idly shuffling cards and watching their faces as the men talked. His eyes returned several times to Pierce Logan. "What do you think, Logan?"

"I agree," Pierce said. He was immaculate today, perfectly groomed, and now his voice carried with a tone of decision, almost of command. "I think we should hire someone to handle this problem." He paused. "A range detective, and one who is good with a gun."

"That suits me!" Ike Hibby said emphatically. "That suits me right down t' the ground. If Mahone an' his boys are goin' t' work our cows, we got t' take steps!"

"You've said again that he has some men," Collins said. "Does anyone actually know that?"

"I do," Alcorn replied. "I seen him an' three others back in the Highbinders, two, three weeks ago. Strangers," he added.

Harran nodded. "He buys a powerful lot of ammunition. More than one man would use."

"Maybe," Kastelle suggested, smiling a little, "he's heard some of this kind of talk and has been getting ready for trouble."

"It's more than one man would use," Harran insisted.

"What about this range detective?" Brewster asked. "Who could we get?"

"Why not Byrn Sonntag?" Hibby suggested. "He's in the country, and he's not busy runnin' cows like the rest of us."

"Sonntag?" Collins burst out. "Why, the man's a notorious killer!"

"What do you want?" Cobb said. "A preacher?"

"It takes a man like that!" Brewster stated dogmatically. "If he finds a man rustlin', why bother with a trial?"

Pierce Logan said nothing, but inside he was glowing. This couldn't be going better. . . .

"You're bein' quiet, Logan," Brewster said. "What do you think?"

"Well," Logan said, shrugging, "it's up to you boys, but if Miller can't cope with it, then perhaps Sonntag could."

"Mahone's supposed t' be a bad man with a gun," Cobb said, "or so Dowd tells us. Well, Sonntag can handle him."

Kastelle looked up. "By the way," he said, "has anyone ever seen Mahone rustling? Has he been caught with any stolen stock? Has he been seen riding on anybody's range? What evidence is there?"

"Well," Brewster said, uneasily, "not any, rightly, but we know—"

"We know nothing!" Collins said sharply. "Nothing at all! This suspicion stems from a lot of rumors. Nothing more."

"Where there's smoke there's fire!" Alcorn said. "I think Sonntag would be a good bet, myself."

"He could gather evidence," Logan admitted carefully. "We would then know what to do."

"You've not said what you think, ma'am." Taggart looked over at Remy. "Abe sets powerful store by what you think about stock. How do you figger this?"

"I don't believe Finn Mahone is a rustler,"

Remy said. "I think we should have plenty of evidence before we make any accusations. All we know is that we've missed stock and that Mahone keeps to himself."

Logan looked up, surprised. The feeling in Remy's voice aroused him, and he looked at her with new eyes. In the past few months he had taken his time with Remy, feeling he was the only man on the range at whom a girl of her type could look twice. Now, something in her voice made him suddenly alert.

"Well," Brewster said irritably, "what's it to be? Are we goin' to do something or just ride home no better off than when we came?"

"I'm for hirin' Sonntag," Alcorn said seriously.

"Me, too," Cobb said.

"Count me in on that," Ike Hibby said. He lighted his pipe. "I'm only running a few cattle, but I've lost too much stock!"

"Put it to a vote," Logan suggested. "That's the democratic way."

Judge Gardner Collins, Kastelle, Remy, and Texas Dowd voted against it. Alcorn, Hibby, Cobb, Brewster, and Taggart voted for Sonntag.

"How about it, Logan?" Collins said. "Where do you stand?"

"Well," he said with evident reluctance, "if it comes to a vote, I'm with the boys on Sonntag. That looks like action."

"Then it's settled!" Brewster said. He got to his feet. "I'm a-gittin' home."

"Mahone said something to me once," Remy said, in a puzzled tone. "He said the way to look for rustlers was with a pen and ink."

Ike Hibby jerked, and looked around hastily. Ringer Cobb's eyes narrowed, and strayed to Dowd. Texas Dowd was leaning against the wall again, and he looked back at Cobb, his eyes bright with malice.

Hibby shifted his feet. "Reckon I'll be headin' for home," he said. "Got a long ways t' go!"

Brewster picked up his hat and nodded goodbye to everyone. Alcorn and Ike glared at Remy, Alcorn licking his lips. "I don't figure I know what you mean, ma'am. But if anyone is accusin' anyone, it's us against Mahone. Not the other way around."

Slowly, they trooped out.

"Now what did I say?" Remy demanded, looking from her father to Dowd.

The tall Texan walked over and dropped into a chair. "You put your finger on the sore spot," he said grimly. "You blew the lid off the trouble in Laird!"

"Why, how do you mean?" she demanded, wide-eyed.

"Got a pen?" Texas said grimly.

She brought one out, and some paper. He looked up at her. "What's Abe's brand? A Spur, ain't it? Now look, an' I'll draw a Spur. Now what's Ike Hibby's brand? IH joined. Now just you take a look, ma'am . . ."

She looked at the rough drawing.

"You see what I mean? You take Abe's brand, add a mite more to the sides of the Spur to make it look like an I, then put a bar on the end of the Spur to make her look like the outside of the H."

Remy leaned over the table, excitedly. "But then, he could steal the Spur cattle and alter that brand without trouble!"

"Uh-huh, unless we caught him at it. Or unless we found some stock with altered brands. We ain't done either."

"You mean to say you've known this all the time?"

"I been thinkin' about it. But thinking something and havin' evidence ain't the same thing."

"But what about ours? The Lazy K?"

"It's probably made into a Box Diamond, and that's Ringer Cobb's brand. Brewster's Lazy S they change into a Lazy Eight."

"But then, that Rawhide crowd must be the rustlers!" Remy exclaimed.

"Uh-huh," Dowd agreed. "That's what I thought, but what can we prove?

"Something else, too," he added gravely. "Tonight the Rawhide bunch voted their own boss in as a paid, legal killer! Who's goin' to tell him where to stop? Or who he kills? Who will stop him once he's started?"

## CHAPTER 4

Finn Mahone heard of the action of the Cattleman's Association when in Rico. He had made it a duty to visit Rico every so often, always hoping the man he had come west to find would show himself there again.

He had never seen the man for whom he was looking close up. He knew his name, that he had been a riverboat gambler, and that he was a wizard with cards and deadly with a pistol. He knew also that the man carried a derringer in his sleeve and was not above sneak-shooting a man.

Finn Mahone had trailed him from New Orleans to Natchez. All the time, the man had ridden a stolen steel-dust gelding. The man had ridden the big horse all the way to Santa Fe, where he traded it off for another animal. Mahone had bought the steel-dust from the new owner on a hunch and continued on.

Then he heard that a man answering the rough description had killed a man in Rico. But in Rico the trail was lost for good. Eventually, Finn had explored the Crystal Valley and settled down there. He was operating on a hunch that his man was somewhere around. He kept the big gelding, although he could not bring himself to ride it, and the horse grazed his upper pasture even now.

Ed Wheeling was in the Gold Spike Bar when he walked in. Wheeling greeted him with a smile. "How's it, Finn? Got any cattle? That last herd I bought from you was said to be the finest beef in Kansas City!"

"Thanks." Finn ordered a drink. "When do you want some? I reckon I can bring over a few. About a hundred head."

"That all you've got? I'll take them, and top prices anytime you get them over here. What's this I hear about Sonntag being hired as a range detective?"

Mahone looked at him quickly. "Sonntag? That's bad."

"What I thought. The man's a killer. I saw him kill one man here in town only a few weeks ago. The man had an even break, if you can ever call it even when they go against him."

Finn turned his glass in his fingers. "Wheeling, what do you know about this rustling?"

Wheeling glanced right and left, then touched his tongue to his lips. "Nothing, if anybody asks. Me, I don't buy any doubtful beef, but there's others do. I'll tell you this much. There's been some queer-looking brands shipped out of here. Good jobs, but they looked burned over to me."

"Who buys 'em?"

"Well, don't go saying I told you. Jim Hoff bought 'em, but then, he'd buy anything he could get cheap."

"Thanks." He tossed off his drink. "This Sonntag deal is liable to be bad for those folks over to Laird. Sonntag is boss of that Rawhide bunch." He glanced at Wheeling. "They run the Lazy Eight, Box Diamond, and IH connected, if that means anything to you."

"It does," Wheeling replied. "It means plenty!"

Finn left the saloon. What Wheeling had told him only confirmed what he had believed. There was brand altering being done somewhere around. And some, at least, were being sold in Rico. They would move against him now, he had no doubt of that. The employing of Sonntag would give them a free rein. He wondered what the first move would be.

The noose was tightening now. Stopping in at the store he bought three hundred rounds of .44-caliber ammunition. His pistols had been modified to use the same ammunition as his Knight's Patent Winchester, which simplified things in that department.

He was just stowing it in his saddlebags when he saw Dean Armstrong. The newspaperman was coming toward him. "Howdy, Dean!" he said.

Armstrong's face was somber. "Watch yourself, Finn," he said. "I think Sonntag's gunning for you. I know Ringer Cobb is. He made his boast at the Cattleman's meeting that he would accuse you to your face."

"What happened at that meeting?"

"It was ramrodded, in a sense. Judge Collins, Kastelle, Remy, and Dowd voted against Sonntag. But Brewster and Taggart threw in with the Rawhide bunch."

"Taggart?"

"Abe McInnis's foreman. Abe was dry-gulched, wounded badly the same time they killed Tony Welt."

"Hadn't heard about that."

Armstrong looked at him quickly, worriedly. "Finn, they've got you pegged for that job. It happened in one of the canyons in the wild country south of the Rimrock. They found the tracks of a big horse, and some of them say they saw your stallion in there."

"I might have been there," Finn admitted, "but not when any shooting took place."

He dug his toe into the dust. "Remy voted against Sonntag, huh?"

"Yes. In fact, Finn, she spoke right out in the meeting and said she didn't believe you were a rustler."

"What did Dowd say?"

"He was against Sonntag. But on the whole,

he didn't have much to say. I think Texas Dowd believes in killing his own beef."

"You're damned right he does," Mahone said sharply. "That man's got more cold-blooded nerve than any I ever saw!"

"What's between you two, anyway?" Dean demanded, looking curiously at Finn. "I'd think you two would be friends!"

Mahone shrugged. "That's the way things happen. We were friends once, Dean. For a long time. I know that man better than anyone in the world, and he should know me, but he's powerful set in his ways, and once he gets an idea in his head it's hell gettin' it out."

FINN MAHONE HEADED across the plateau in sooty darkness. Dean's information and what he had learned from Wheeling put the problem fairly in his hands. The Rawhide bunch were evidently out to get him. Ringer Cobb had made his boast, and he was the type of man to back it up if he could.

From the beginning there had been an effort to hang the rustling on him. While his living alone would be suspicious to some, Finn had an idea that more than a little planting of ideas had been going on over the range. There was deliberate malice behind it. It was not Dowd's way to stoop to such tactics. Texas Dowd would say nothing. He would wait, patiently, and then one of them would die.

A roving, solitary man all his life, Finn had found but one man he cared to ride the river with. That man was Texas Dowd. They had ridden a lot of rivers, and their two guns had blasted their way out of more than one spot of trouble.

Had there been a chance of talking to Dowd, he would have done it, but there was too much chance the man would shoot on sight. Cold, gray, and quiet, Dowd was a man of chilled steel, the best of friends, but the most bitter of enemies.

One thing was now clear. It was up to him to prove his innocence. It might be a help to ride into town and see Lettie. She always knew what was going on, and was one of the few friends he had. She, and Garfield Otis.

What was it Dean had said about Otis? "Funny about Otis, Finn," he'd said. "He hasn't had a drink in almost a week. Got something on his mind, but he won't talk."

The trail dipped down into the Laird River Canyon, and the sound of rushing water lifted to his ears. Rushing water and the vague dampness that lifted from the trembling river. He should have told Ed Wheeling to say nothing about his bringing the cattle. Ed was a talkative man, and an admirer of those fat white-faced steers of Finn's.

This would be where they would wait for him, here in the canyon. A couple of good riflemen here could stop the passage of any herd of cattle, or of any man.

The cabin on the ledge was very quiet when he rode in. As he swung down from the stallion's back, he remembered the morning Remy Kastelle had stood on the steps waiting for him, and how her hair had shone in the bright morning sun.

The cabin seemed dark and lonely when he went inside, and after he had eaten he sat down to read, but now there was no comfort in his books. He got up and strode outside, all the old restlessness rising within him, that driving urge to be moving on, to be going. He knew what was coming, knew that in what happened there would be heartbreak and sudden death.

Aware of all the tides of western change, Finn Mahone could see behind the rustling in Laird Valley a deep and devious plan. It was unlike any rustling he had seen before. It was no owl-hoot gang suddenly charging out of the night on a wild raid, nor was it some restless cowhands who wanted money for a splurge across the border. This had been a careful, soundless, and trackless weeding of herds. Had it gone on undiscovered, it would have left the range drained of cattle, and the cattlemen broke.

He could see how skillfully the plan had been

engineered. How careful the planning. As he studied what Dean had told him of the Cattleman's meeting, another thought occurred. The vote had been six to four to hire Sonntag. But what if McInnis had been there?

The dour New England Scotsman was not one for plunging into anything recklessly. He would never have accepted the hiring of Sonntag. Especially as Collins and the Kastelles had voted against it. This the leader of the rustlers must have figured. The shooting of McInnis had been deliberately planned and accomplished in cold blood.

Had McInnis been voting, Taggart either would not have been there to vote, or would have followed Abe's lead. Brewster, hotheaded and impulsive as he was, would have been tempered by the McInnis's coolness. Then the vote would have been against hiring Sonntag! At the worst, it would have been a tie, and no action.

That the meeting had been called before the shooting of Abraham McInnis, Mahone knew.

He sat down suddenly and wrote out a short note, a note that showed the vote had McInnis been present. He added, **Show this to the judge.** Then he enclosed it in an envelope, and decided he would send it to the newspaper office by Shoshone Charlie.

Carefully, he oiled his guns and checked his rifle. Then he made up several small packs of food and laid out some ammunition. He was going to be ready for trouble now, for it was coming. He could wait, and they might never get to him, but he preferred to strike first. Also, he had his cattle to deliver.

MEXIE ROBERTS WAS not a man who hurried. Small, dark, and careful, he moved like an Indian in the hills. For several days now he had been studying the Lazy K from various vantage points. He had watched Texas Dowd carefully. Knowing the West as he did, he knew Dowd was a man whom one might never get a chance to shoot at twice. Mexie Roberts prided himself on never having to shoot more than once. His trade was killing, and he knew the tricks of his trade.

Lying on his belly in the dust among the clumps of greasewood, he watched every soul on the Lazy K. Shifting his glass from person to person, he soon began to learn their ways and their habits.

He was not worried about hitting Dowd, once he got him in his sights. The Sharps .50 he carried was a gun he understood like the working of his own right hand.

There was no mercy in Mexie Roberts. Killing was born in him as it is in a weasel or a hawk. He killed, and killed in cold blood. It was his pride that he had never been arrested, never tried, never even accused. Some men had their suspicions, but no man could offer evidence.

He had been given the job of killing Dowd, and there was in the job a measure of personal pride as well as the money. Texas Dowd was to Mexie Roberts what a Bengal tiger is to a big-game hunter. He was the final test. Hunting Dowd was hunting death in its most virulent form.

In a few days now, perhaps a few hours, he would be ready. Then Dowd would die, and when he died, there would be no one near to see where the shot came from, and Mexie Roberts would have his hideaway carefully chosen.

ALL OVER LAIRD VALLEY tides of trouble and danger were rising. Men moved along the streets of Laird with cautious eyes, scanning each newcomer, watching, waiting.

In his office beside the barbershop, Judge Gardner Collins moved a man into the king row and crowned him. Doc Finerty rubbed his jaw and studied the board with thoughtful eyes. Neither man had his mind on the game.

"It was my fault," Collins said. "I should have stopped it. Don't know why I didn't realize how Brewster and Taggart would vote."

Dean Armstrong came in, glanced at the

board, then placed a slip of paper on the checkerboard between them. "Found this under my door this morning," he said. "It's Mahone's handwriting."

| **For** | **Against** |
|---|---|
| Ike Hibby | Collins |
| Ringer Cobb | Kastelle |
| Alcorn | R. Kastelle |
| Taggart | Dowd |
| Logan | |
| Brewster | |

**Had Abe McInnis been there:**

| | |
|---|---|
| Ike Hibby | Collins |
| Ringer Cobb | Kastelle |
| Alcorn | R. Kastelle |
| Logan | Dowd |
| Brewster (?) | McInnis |
| | Taggart (?) |

**Show this to the judge.**

Collins studied it thoughtfully. "I reckon he's got it figured proper," he said. "That would make it at worst a tie vote. Taggart would have gone along with his boss, I know that. Dan's hotheaded, but Abe always sort of calms him down and keeps him thinking straight."

"You see what it implies, don't you?" Dean indicated. "That Abe McInnis was dry-gulched on purpose!"

"Uh-huh," Finerty agreed, "it does. I agree."

"Let's call another meeting," Armstrong suggested, "and vote him out. You've got some stock running with the judge, haven't you, Doc? Enough to vote?"

"It wouldn't do," Collins said. "The Rawhide bunch wouldn't meet. We couldn't get a quorum now. No, he's in, and we might as well make the best of it. What's he been doing, Dean?"

"Riding all over the range so far. That's all."

PIERCE LOGAN SAT in his office. He wore a neatly pressed dark gray suit and a white vest. His white hat lay atop the safe nearby. As he sat, he fingered his mustache thoughtfully.

It had been a long wait, and hard work, but now he was there. Only a few more weeks and he would be in possession of all he had hoped for. They would be shaky, dangerous weeks, but the danger would be of the sort he understood best.

He had come out of the carpetbag riots in New Orleans with money. Enough to come west in obvious prosperity. The little affair near New Orleans, one of those times when the ingrown rapacity of the man had let go like an explosion, had passed over without trouble. Since arriving in Laird he had bided his time. Now he was ready.

He was not worried about Texas Dowd. Sonntag had set something up, and it would be taken care of soon. Sonntag was range detective, and any killings he might commit would have a semblance of legality. There was opposition here in town, he knew. Judge Collins would be against him, but the judge was no longer young. Finerty could not stand against him, and as for Armstrong . . . Logan didn't like Armstrong. At the first hint of trouble from **The Branding Iron,** he would have to have the presses smashed up.

His eyes shifted out the window, and suddenly, he stiffened.

A man was walking slowly along the sandy hillside beyond the livery barn and corrals. He was walking along as though studying the ground. Now and then he would halt, kneel down, and study it carefully, then he would rise and move on. Occasionally he would sift a little dirt through his fingers.

The man was Garfield Otis.

Pierce Logan put a hand to his brow. He was sweating. His heart pounding, he slid a hand in a drawer for a gun. Then drew it back. No, that wasn't the way.

But what could the old fool be looking for?

Why would he be examining that hillside, of all places?

It had been years ago. Certainly, Otis could know nothing. Yet he watched him, and Logan knew for the first time what it meant to fear.

If he was discovered now, he was ruined. Not even the Rawhide bunch could save him. It was only his power and money that held them together, and if the lid blew off this—!

Garfield Otis was wandering back down the wash now. He would be in the saloon in a few minutes. But no, Otis hadn't been drinking lately. And Otis was a friend of Mahone's.

Whatever was done must be done at once, and Logan knew there was only one thing that could be done. He got up and walked out into the street.

FINN MAHONE HAD TAKEN an old game trail east from the entrance to Crystal Valley. It led him down, and across a corner of the lava beds, then into the wild country of the Highbinders north of the Lazy K.

His stallion walked slowly, and Finn kept one hand near his walnut gun butt. The chance of seeing an enemy here was slight, although he had decided against trying the Notch. If anyone were to lie in wait for him, that would be the ideal spot.

The country in which he now rode was country where few horsemen ever went. The hillsides of the Highbinders were too grassless to draw cattle away from the fertile bottoms of the Lazy K range. This was a broken, partly timbered, and very rocky country that offered nothing to any man. Sheep or goats might have lived there; cattle could not.

Yet, when he was almost due north of the Lazy K ranch buildings, he stopped and swung down.

Coming out of the woods and turning into the small trail he followed were the recent tracks of a horse!

Finn loosened his gun in its holster and walked on, leading Fury. On second thought, he turned off the trail and chose a way under the pines, avoiding the dust where his tracks would be seen. When he had gone a little way farther, he smelled smoke.

At first, it was just a faint suggestion, then he got a stronger whiff. Tying the stallion to a low branch, he worked his way cautiously through the brush. He had gone almost a hundred yards when he saw a faint blue haze rising from a hollow among the rocks.

Crawling out on a flat-topped rock that ended in a clump of manzanita, he lay on his belly and stared down into the hollow.

A fire, small and carefully built, burned among

some stones. A coffeepot sat on the stones, being warmed. A buckskin horse was tethered nearby, and not far away, a grulla packhorse.

There was one man, and Finn watched him curiously. The man was small and dark, and at the moment Finn spotted him, he was fastening a long narrow piece of white cloth to a tree trunk. Peering at it, Finn could see that it had a cross printed on it near the top, and then graduated markings running down its length. At the bottom was a weight so that the strip would hang straight down.

When it was fastened, the small man carefully paced off a certain distance and marked the spot, then he picked up his rifle, a Sharps buffalo gun. Finn's brow furrowed.

Puzzled, Mahone watched the man carry his Sharps to the mark on the ground and rest the muzzle in the crotch of a forked stick he carried. Lying prone, the little man carefully aimed at the cloth strip and then proceeded to work the screw-adjustable peep sight that was fitted to the big gun up and down, making minute adjustments until it was lined up with one of the marks on the cloth.

"Well, I'll be forever damned!" Finn Mahone muttered. "That's a new one on me!" The dark man was calibrating his sights for a long shot over a previously measured distance.

When he was satisfied, the man left the rifle

where it was and returned to his fire. He drank coffee, ate a little, and took a hurried look around. Then he put out his fire, scattered it, and carefully wiped out all footprints with a pine bough. For a half hour he worked until every mark of the camp had been obliterated.

Only then did he take his rifle. Mounting the buckskin, which with the packhorse had been led into the trail, he held his rifle with great care, then he moved off, walking the horse.

Finn Mahone got up quietly and walked back to his own horse. Moving carefully, he followed the strange rider. The man's every action gave evidence that he had no intention of riding far, and the only place close to them was the Lazy K ranch!

Who, then, was the killer after? For Finn had no doubts about the man's intentions. Remy? That would serve no purpose. Frenchy Kastelle? Probably not.

Who, of all the men on this range, would be most dangerous to successful rustling? Texas Dowd. Who, on this range, might match guns with Sonntag or Ringer Cobb or Montana Kerr? Only, aside from himself, Texas Dowd. All of which meant that this man intended to kill Dowd.

His conclusion might be mistaken, but Finn could think of no logical alternative.

When they drew near the edge of the timber,

Finn tied the stallion in a concealed position among the trees and, rifle in hand, moved out after the unknown sharpshooter.

The man had tied his horses with a slip knot and had vanished into the brush. Finn started to follow, then hesitated and walked back to the horses. Untying them, he retied the knot, and lashed it hard and fast. The man who rode these horses wasn't going to be getting away in a hurry!

Then, working with infinite care, Finn Mahone worked down along the marksman's trail.

He lost the trail on the edge of the brush. Here the man had moved into a gully, and whether he had gone up or down, Finn could not tell. Yet from where he lay on the side of the bluff Finn had an excellent view of the grassy field between the Lazy K ranch buildings and the position he occupied. The sharpshooter would have to move out into position from here, and get into place to fire on the buildings.

Suddenly, Finn saw the man. He had come out of the gully and was snaking along the ground, keeping low in the grass, still handling his rifle with utmost care. When the man reached the top of a low knoll, his position would be excellent.

Only then did Mahone realize how carefully this had been planned. The way to the knoll was completely covered from observation from anywhere but this bluff. The man could never have been seen from the ranch.

The Sharps rifle, known to kill at distances up to a thousand yards, had occasionally been effective at even greater distances, as Billy Dixon had proved at the Battle of Adobe Wells. It used the most powerful black powder cartridges ever made, and fired up to 550 grains of lead with terrific force and remarkable accuracy.

With the distance deliberately paced off, probably late at night when all were asleep, the unknown marksman would know exactly how much his bullet would drop, and now the finely machined sight was set for precisely that range. One shot would be all he'd get at a target like Dowd, but as Finn correctly surmised, the man had no intention of firing more than one shot.

Mahone lost him, then found him again, and when he next sighted him he was on the crest of the knoll and settling into position. Finn eased his own rifle up, and waited.

There was little movement around the Lazy K. Occasionally someone appeared, then vanished. The man below lay perfectly still. Had Finn not known he was there, he could never have picked him out on the grassy, boulder-strewn knoll.

Then the ranch house door opened, and Finn lifted his head. Remy was walking down to the corrals. A hand led her white mare out, and the girl swung into the saddle and galloped away over the plains, riding west.

Finn's eyes followed her. How beautifully she rode! He had never seen a woman ride with such grace. Angry with himself, he wrenched his eyes away.

A man had come from the ranch house and was walking down to the corral. He wore an old black hat, but even at that distance Finn could recognize the straight carriage, the easy movement of the shoulders. Texas Dowd was a man difficult to forget and easy to pick out.

Mahone's eyes dropped. The man below was waiting for some particular thing, Finn could see that. All men are creatures of habit to some extent, and the marksman had evidently studied Dowd until he knew his every move.

No one else was in sight. The cowhand who led out Remy's horse had vanished, and the ranch lay hot in the glare of the sun. Dowd led out his horse and tied it to a rail of the corral fence. Then he brought out the saddle, and threw it on the horse's back. Dowd was standing with his back squarely to the sharpshooter now, but the man waited. Then, slowly he eased his rifle up and Finn, even at this distance, could almost see the man settling his cheek against the stock ready for his shot.

Finn lifted his rifle and triggered three fast shots at the figure below. Even as he fired, he heard the big rifle boom from the knoll, but his first shot must have come close, for the rifleman threw himself to one side.

Finn got a hasty glimpse of Dowd's horse rearing, but already his eyes were searching the grass below for the killer. The man had vanished as if he had dropped into the earth itself!

Riveting his eyes on the grass, Finn began to search it with infinite care, taking it section by section, but he could see nothing of the man. He suddenly realized this was no place for him. If Dowd was to find him here he would be sure it was Finn who had fired, and the sharpshooter was certainly making his getaway.

Scrambling through the brush, he started back to the horses. Somehow in his rush he took a wrong turn, and though delayed only a minute or two longer than he had expected, he reached the horses just as the marksman appeared. The fellow rushed to the horses and jerked at the slip knot. It stuck, and then Finn said, "All right, turn around and throw up your hands!"

Mexie Roberts wheeled like a cornered rat and his hand flashed for his pistol. Finn's rifle blasted and Roberts staggered back, coughing, his eyes wide and staring. He blinked once, very slowly, then sat down and rolled over, drawing his knees up tightly, and died.

Mahone wheeled and raced for his horse. Then he was in the saddle and heading down range as fast as he could ride. He had no desire to see Dowd now. The Texan would see what had happened from the tracks.

Meanwhile, there was business in town. If Sonntag was there, and looking for him, he could find him. Laird, he felt, was the center of things. Knowing as little as he did about all the people there, Finn had only a few ideas. He intended to learn what he could, and there were two sources on which he could rely: Lettie Mason and Otis.

REMY KASTELLE, riding west, heard the sharp cracking report of the Winchester, followed by the heavy boom of the Sharps, then the Winchester twice again. She wheeled her horse and started back on a dead run. She was just reaching the ranch house when she saw Texas Dowd, gun in hand, leave the ranch at a gallop.

Swinging alongside she disregarded his motions to stay back, and rode on. Suddenly, he seemed to sight something in the grass, and wheeled, riding over to the knoll. He swung down from the horse and picked it up. It was Roberts's Sharps rifle.

He looked up at the girl, then removed his hat. The Sharps had torn a ragged gash in the brim. "Somebody shot at him," Dowd said, "or he'd a had me sure! I heard that first shot and jerked. This came next."

The grass was pressed down where Mexie had

crushed it in his retreat. The route by which he had approached was not the return route. Mexie had been too cagey for that. Yet his return had been a flight, and Dowd followed, riding his horse until he came to the two horses and Roberts's body.

He rolled the man over, and Remy drew back, her face pale. "Who . . . who is it?" she asked.

"I've seen him around. Name of Roberts. Shot twice, right through the heart." He looked up at her. His face was bleak and hard. "Not many men shoot like that!"

Texas stepped over the body and looked at the knot. "No hombre expectin' to leave in a hurry ever tied a horse like that!" he said. "Whoever shot him knew these horses were here. He tied that knot so if he was slow gettin' back, this hombre wouldn't get away!"

Carefully, Dowd went through his pockets. There was some ninety dollars in bills. One, a twenty, was pasted together with a piece of pink paper. Dowd put them in his shirt pocket. Scouting around, he found the bush where the black stallion had been tied. His face stiffened as he looked. Then he lifted his eyes to the girl. "It's him, damn his soul!" he said bitterly.

"Who?"

"Finn Mahone! He seen this hombre catfootin' around the hills. He followed him, an' when he saw what he was up to, he scared him out of there. Then he got back here, an' this hombre tried to shoot it out with him."

"Finn Mahone!" Remy stared at Dowd. "Then he saved your life, Tex!"

"Yeah." Tex stared at the tracks of the big horse. "That's the third time!"

"Tex," Remy said quickly, "what's between you and Mahone?"

Texas Dowd raised his eyes and looked at her. "He murdered my sister," he said coldly.

## CHAPTER 5

Dan Taggart loped his sorrel pony toward the McInnis ranch. At the time Mexie Roberts was lying in wait for his shot at Dowd, Taggart had been inspecting cattle far to the south.

Taggart was a man of nearly forty who looked ten years older. Rarely clean shaven, he was grim, hard, and loyal. He was one of those riders who were the backbone of the cattle business. When he rode, he rode, in the parlance of the cattle country, "for the brand." In other words, his loyalty was not a thing to be taken lightly.

He was a man without imagination. Hard-working, ready to fight if need be, never hesitating at long hours or miserable conditions. Abe

McInnis, who knew a good man when he saw one, had made Taggart foreman. It was the first position of responsibility Dan Taggart had ever held. He took it seriously, and he did more work than any two of his cowhands.

That day he had seen a heifer with a fresh brand. He got a loop on her, and inspected the brand. It was P Slash L, the Logan brand. There was nothing surprising about it, as the cattle of the two ranches grazed the same land in this area, and had done so without question for some time.

Nick James, who had formerly ridden for McInnis, saw Taggart pull down the heifer and rode over. He grinned at the older man. "Figger we're rustlin', Dan?"

"Nope." Taggart released the heifer and got up. "Just havin' a look. That Kastelle girl said somethin' the other day. Bothers me some."

"What was that?" James asked. He rolled a smoke and sat his horse, waiting.

Taggart rolled his quid and spat. "Said somethin' about this here Mahone feller sayin' if we was to hunt rustlers we should do it with a pen an' ink."

Nick looked at Taggart quickly, his eyes shrewd. "Yeah," he said, carefully, "not a bad idea. You got that Spur brand, Dan. Feller could make that over into a lot of things."

"Uh-huh," Taggart agreed. He picked up a bit of dead mesquite root. "Like an IH connected?"

Nick James's face was expressionless. He lighted his smoke. "Yeah," he said again, "you can do purty well with a Lazy K, too."

Taggart looked up. "Nick, I wouldn't say this to many people, but I reckon I got stampeded into doin' somethin' foolish the other night. First time I ever went to one of them Cattleman's meetin's, though." He looked up again. "I voted for Sonntag."

"Heard about it," Nick said gravely. "You seen **The Branding Iron**?"

"No, why?" Taggart looked up at Nick.

The P Slash L cowhand dug into his saddlebag. "Take a look then."

## SONNTAG CHOSEN FOR RANGE INVESTIGATION

By a vote of six to four, the Cattleman's Association voted to appoint Byrn Sonntag as range detective to investigate and deal with rustling activities. Abraham McInnis, popular cattleman of the Spur Ranch, was unable to be present. There has been considerable wonder about how the vote would have gone had McInnis not been confined to his bed due to the mysterious shooting in the canyon below Rimrock. McInnis, seriously wounded in a yet unexplained shooting, is believed by many of his friends to be opposed to any such action as the hiring of a notorious gunman.

Dan Taggart, foreman of the Spur, voted for Sonntag in McInnis's place. Had he voted against Sonntag the question would have been dropped for the time being.

"Looks kind of bad," Taggart admitted. "I wished that girl had spoke up before I voted. Minute she said that, I began seein' pictures in my head of all them brands."

"Yeah," Nick agreed. "Know how you feel."

"Well," Taggart said. "P Slash L's in the clear on that, even if Logan did vote for Sonntag. No brand in the valley can be made into a P Slash L."

"That's right." Nick James glanced off across the prairie. "It's too right."

Taggart looked up, scowling. "Huh? What did you say?"

"Dan," Nick said, "we lost some cows about a month ago. Maybe twenty head. I'd been workin' back in Sage Canyon up until the day before, then Pierce told me to start breakin' a couple of broncs we got."

"What about it?"

"Those broncs could have been broke anytime, Dan."

Dan Taggart got into the saddle and watched Nick James riding away. The more he thought about it, the surer he was that his vote had been a bad thing. He wished that McInnis was conscious so he could talk to him. He was worried, and had no idea what course was best.

Clouds were bunching up over the Highbinders to the north. He dug his slicker out of his saddlebags and rode on with it lying conveniently across the saddle in front of him.

IT WAS already pouring rain when Finn Mahone rode into Laird. On a hunch, he had returned to Crystal Valley and thrown a hackamore on the old steel-dust gelding and brought it with him down into town. If push came to shove in the trouble with Texas Dowd the steel-dust might, just might, get him a fair hearing. In the past his pride had kept him from asking for understanding from the man who once had been his friend. But the situation was now different. He had just saved Dowd's life, and they were both older and wiser. Heavy clouds loomed over the town and rain was falling in sheets. Not knowing what sort of reception he could expect, he avoided the livery stable and rode down a back street until he came to Doc Finerty's. He led the stallion and gelding inside the doctor's barn, rubbed them dry, and got feed from the bin.

Splashing through the gathering pools of rain,

he went to the back door of Lettie's place. Turning the knob, it gave under his hand and he stepped within, loosening the buttons on his slicker to have his guns available. He was standing there, dripping water in the light that reflected from over the stairway, when Lettie came into the hall.

"Finn!" she exclaimed. "Oh, it's good to see you."

She was a small woman, beautifully shaped, and Finn was always surprised to find her in such a business. She wore beautiful but conservative clothing, and always looked smart and attractive. He knew enough of her story to admire her for her determination and her fine independence of spirit. Nor could he blame her for choosing this business, for when left a widow there had been only the choice between running a gambling house or slowly falling into a pauper's life. She had not hesitated to make her decision, heedless of her reputation.

One of those unaccountable movements that swept the tide of drifting mankind into some of the farthest and most unusual backwaters had brought her to Laird.

"It's good to see you again, too, Lettie." He nodded toward the parlor. "Who's in?"

"Nobody, right now. I guess the rain's keeping them home. Finn, what's been happening? I hear Sonntag is gunning for you."

Mahone shrugged. "I haven't seen him. He in town?"

"No, but Ringer Cobb is. Be careful."

"Sure. Is Otis around?"

"No, he isn't. He's wanting to see you, though. He's been acting very strange. Stopped drinking all of a sudden, and seems to have something on his mind. You'd better see him."

"I will. Right now I want to look up Judge Collins." Lightning flashed almost without cessation, and the rain had risen to a thundering roar. "Hombre tried to kill Tex today," he told her. "Slim, wiry, dark fellow."

"Mexie Roberts. He comes and goes, Finn, always by himself."

"Know why he would want to kill Dowd?"

"For money. Roberts never killed anybody unless he got paid. If he tried to kill Texas, somebody was paying him."

Mahone looked down at her. "Who d'you think, Lettie?"

She hesitated, then she looked up quickly. He could see doubt and worry in her eyes. "I don't know, Finn. I would be wrong if I said Sonntag or Salter . . . it feels like someone is playing with everyone like they were puppets!"

"I agree, but that doesn't help me know who it is. Well, I'm going over to see Collins. Armstrong, too."

"Be careful of Cobb!" she warned.

He went out the front door, gathering his slicker about him but not fastening the buttons. At this time of night, Judge Collins might be in the Longhorn, as there was no light at Doc's. Or the judge might be at Ma Boyle's for coffee. At the thought of coffee, Finn suddenly realized he was hungry.

He slopped down the street in the pelting rain, and went on past the lights of the Longhorn. There was loud talk from within, and he hesitated while rain ran down his slicker and dribbled off on the walk. Otis might be in there. Collins, too. On the other hand, Ringer Cobb was almost sure to be. For an instant longer he hesitated, half in mind to go in and end it right then. But when he saw Ringer, if it ended in a fight he might have to get out of town, and he had things he needed to do. He went on down the street.

There was a light burning at **The Branding Iron**. He hesitated, then pushed open the door and walked in. When he had the door closed, he looked around. "Hey, Dean?"

There was no answer. "Dean!" he called again, louder. When there was still no answer, he walked around the high counter toward the trays of type and the desk.

Dean Anderson was lying facedown on the floor, his head bloody. Quickly, Finn bent over him. He was alive. Hurrying to the back door he filled a wash pan from the water bucket, grabbed up the towel that Dean kept hanging there, and hurried back.

Lifting him, he cradled Dean's head on his arm while he put the cold towel on his head. Gently, he sponged away the blood. It was a cut, a very nasty cut.

There was another, higher and in his hair. He sponged that off, too, and then Armstrong began to stir and mutter. "Hold still!" Finn commanded.

When Armstrong's eyes opened, they stared about in confusion. At this moment, without his dignity, he looked strangely young. Then he looked up and saw Mahone.

"Finn!" he said. "Man, I'm glad to see you!"

"What happened?" Mahone demanded.

"Cobb pistol-whipped me. Came in here about six, just after the rain started. Started in half joking about what I'd said in the paper, then he hit me over the eye with a pistol barrel."

"You mean that item about Sonntag?"

Dean shook his head, then gasped and caught it with both hands. "No, the piece I had in today. I put out an extra edition." He looked up. "It's on the table there."

## APPOINTMENT OF SONNTAG A MISTAKE

The appointment of Byrn Sonntag, notorious gunman, to investigate the cattle rustling was a mistake. If the election was to be held again tomorrow, the result would be against him. Since arriving in the Laird Valley country, Sonntag has killed at least three men, and his associates at Rawhide can scarcely be classed as good citizens. There are those on the range who declare it is more than a coincidence that certain brands belonging to Rawhide ranchers are very easily developed from brands already on this range. If Byrn Sonntag is to investigate rustling, it might be a good idea to begin in his own home town.

Finn Mahone looked up, grinning. "Dean," he said, "it took guts to write that, but if I were you, I'd start packing a gun. Your paper gets around. Whoever is behind all this doesn't have a chance of making it work if the news gets outside of Laird Valley."

"That's what I thought, and that's what I wrote!" Dean said firmly. He crawled to his feet and clutched the desk for support. "What good is a newspaper unless it tells the truth and fights for the rights of the people?"

Mahone shrugged. "A lot of them should ask that question of themselves," he said dryly. "I'd better get Doc for you," he said. "You'll need some stitches in that head!"

"He's at Ma Boyle's," Dean said. "Or was starting for there just before Cobb showed up."

"What are you going to do now?" Mahone asked, curiously.

"Do?" Dean demanded. "I'll tell you what I'm going to do! I'm going to print what just happened, call it the cowardly attack it was, and tell who did it and why!"

"Then you'd better pack a gun," Finn advised. "This business is turning bad and I don't like it. I've already killed one man today."

"You have?" Armstrong stared at him. "Who?"

"Fellow named Roberts. He tried to dry-gulch Texas Dowd."

Finn pulled his slicker around him and walked outside. Rain was still pouring down, and the street was dark and empty. The blare of music came from the Longhorn, and he heard shouts there, and once a yell. It sounded like Ringer Cobb.

He pushed open the door and stepped into Mother Boyle's in a gust of wind and water. When he had the door closed, he turned his back to it and stood there, looking at the room, a big, somber figure with his rain-soaked hat, his dark slicker, and his green eyes taking the room in with one measuring glance.

Ma Boyle was standing beside Doc Finerty with a pot of coffee, and Judge Collins had turned as he entered. Nick James was there, the first time Mahone had seen him since the day of the fight. James looked up, quickly and with interest. He had one of those young-old faces, merry and friendly at times, then grave and serious. He was scarcely more than a boy, but had been doing a man's work since he was eleven.

"Doc," Finn said, "better go have a look at Armstrong. Cobb pistol-whipped him."

"I was afraid of that!" Doc said. He got up and reached for his slicker. "Keep some coffee on, Ma!"

Finn sat down at the end of the table, between James and Collins. Collins was concerned. "When Sonntag came in, I knew trouble was coming!"

Finn had hung his slicker and hat near the stove. He dished up some food and poured the coffee. Briefly, and quickly, he outlined the trouble at the Lazy K, and the outcome.

"Roberts is a paid killer." Judge Collins was puzzled. "Doesn't seem like Sonntag would hire any killing done."

"He wouldn't," Mahone said, speaking past half a slice of bread and butter. "Not him."

Nick James stirred his coffee and looked from one to the other. "You ever think maybe something else was behind this?"

Judge Collins turned his head and looked at Nick. This man was shrewd, the Judge knew. James had ridden for him, and for McInnis.

He was one of the best hands in the valley. "What are you thinking, Nick?"

The young puncher shrugged, and gulped a swallow of coffee. "Ain't made up my mind. Some things sure look funny, though."

Finn Mahone put his coffee down carefully. Suddenly he was remembering the tall, powerfully built man who was standing behind Remy that day he fought Leibman. "Any rustlin' out your way?" he asked, casually.

Nick nodded. "A little, here and there. Never when anybody's around." He stirred his coffee again. "I think I'll quit," he said suddenly.

"You can always have a job with me," Collins said. "You were the best hand I had, Nick."

"Or with me," Mahone suggested, looking up.

Their eyes met across the table. "Didn't know you hired any hands," Nick said. "Heard you played it alone."

"I have, but I've got some work ahead and could use help. I'd want a hand that would sling a gun if he had to . . . but not unless he had to."

"I'll get my stuff tomorrow," James agreed. His face tightened. "An' collect my time." Then he glanced at Mahone again. "How do I get there? They tell me a man can't go through the Notch unless he knows the way."

"That's right, and don't try it alone. You get your gear, an' if I don't see you, go up and camp in the Notch. There's good water, and plenty of grass. I'll be along."

The door slammed open then, and wind and rain swept into the room. The newcomer struggled to get the door closed, then turned. It was Ringer Cobb.

Finn knew at once the man had been drinking and was in a killing mood. He was not the type who staggered and floundered when drunk. Liquor brought out all the innate cruelty in the man, and if anything, steadied him and made him colder.

His eyes fastened on Mahone's and a light danced in them, an ugly, dangerous light. "You're Finn Mahone," he said, standing just inside the door, his slicker hanging around him, his hands dangling.

Nick James pushed back gently, out of the way. Finn lifted the coffeepot and calmly filled his cup. "That's right," Mahone replied. "An' you're Ringer Cobb. You're the man who walked into the newspaper office and slapped a defenseless man with a Colt. Makes you a pretty bad boy, doesn't it?" Cobb glared at Mahone, his teeth half bared. "What's the matter?" Mahone said. "Don't you like the sound of the truth?"

"You should be ashamed!" Ma Boyle glared at Cobb.

"I've heard about you." Cobb took a step nearer and tried to change the subject back to the one he had in mind. "Heard you're pretty fast with a gun. That right?"

"I do all right." Finn lifted the cup and sipped a little coffee. "Better sit down and have a cup of coffee. Do you good."

"Huh?" Ringer was puzzled. Then his eyes sharpened. "Scared, huh? Think yuh can talk me out of it."

"No," Mahone replied, and his voice hardened, "I'm just trying to talk you out of Boot Hill, because if you reach for that gun . . . **I'll kill you!**"

Ringer Cobb took a long breath through his nose, and his fingers widened. Finn sat perfectly still, just looking at him, and Cobb's eyes wavered. He looked at Finn, and started to speak, but Mahone seemed to have lost interest, and he remarked to Collins, "Hand me that cup, Judge, and I'll pour this man some coffee." He looked over at Cobb. "If you're not going to shoot me you might as well have some coffee."

He took the cup and filled it. "Better have some of that cake Ma bakes, too, Ringer. She's plenty good."

Ringer Cobb swayed a little, staring around uncertainly. Then he slumped on the bench, and he was trembling with tension. He took the cup, and started to lift it, but some of the coffee slopped over.

Mahone turned back to Nick. "My place is

some of the best range in the world," he said, "most of it subirrigated by water off the Highbinders. Not much erosion in there, an' I don't run enough cattle to keep it fed down. I don't aim to get rich, just to make enough to get along pretty well."

"Sounds all right," Nick said.

None of them seemed to notice Cobb. Several times he started to say something, but Finn Mahone continued to talk, calmly, easily.

Suddenly, Ringer got up, jerking to his feet so hard he tipped over his almost empty cup. Then he wheeled and rammed through the door and was gone. Finn reached across the table and straightened the fallen cup.

Judge Collins looked at Nick James, and James mopped the sweat from his brow. "You backed him down!" Nick said. "Just outnerved him!"

"Better than a shootin', don't you think?"

"Awful close to a shooting, Finn," the judge said. "Awful close."

Finn filled a cup, took the cake, and, holding both under his slicker, went out the door and headed for the print shop.

Nick James looked at Collins. "Judge," he said, "how could anybody ever figger him for a rustler?" Then his eyes widened a little. "Suppose he an' Sonntag . . . ?"

"Don't get anxious, son," the judge said. "I'm sure Finn's good, but you don't want to be out of a job, right? If those two fight, very likely both of them will die!"

DAN TAGGART WAS a slow-thinking man. He sat in the bunkhouse on the Spur and smoked his pipe. The other hands had turned in, but Dan sat there, all through the pounding rain. On his return he had gone in to see Abe, but McInnis was still unconscious, although better. Mrs. McInnis had her sister with her now. Her sister was Mrs. Harran, wife of the storekeeper.

Unable to ask the advice of his boss, the foreman had gone back to the bunkhouse and stayed there except for a few minutes to eat. He was vastly disturbed, afraid he had done wrong, and wanting desperately to repair the damage he had done.

That the fault was not his alone he did not see. Brewster had voted as he had, and so had Logan. When Logan's name came into his mind he remembered Nick's peculiar attitude. What was it Nick said? That they had lost some cows after he had been ordered out of Sage Canyon? That didn't make sense. Would Logan have his own cows rustled? Taggart stirred uneasily, afraid he was out of his depth, but worried and uncertain of what to do.

He glanced around at the sleeping hands, but there was none of them he could turn to, nor who would have been able to give the advice he wanted. Taggart felt the need of advice from a superior, of leadership. His job as foreman was still too new. Only one thing he knew: The voting-in of Sonntag as range detective had been a bad thing. It had put the rustlers in the saddle.

He got up and pulled off his shirt, his pipe still in his mouth. Then he stood for a moment, scratching his stomach. He would ride over to Kastelle's in the morning. Abe McInnis set powerful store by Texas Dowd's opinion, and that of Remy Kastelle.

PIERCE LOGAN WAS SITTING at his desk in a bright, rain-washed world when the door opened and Byrn Sonntag walked in.

He had seen the man fifty times, talked with him nearly as many, and yet the man always did something to him, something he didn't like. There was something in Sonntag's very physical presence, his enormous vitality, the brash, raw health of him, and his deep, somewhat overpowering voice that made Logan feel less than he liked to feel.

Sonntag was in rare form this morning. He stamped into the office and threw his big body into a chair. He tossed his hat to the wide, low windowsill, and stared across at Logan.

He was a big man, weighing all of two hundred and forty pounds, with a leonine head covered with thick, dull red hair. His sleeves were rolled up, and red hair curled on his brawny and powerful forearms.

"Heard the news?" he demanded. His voice was harsh and rang with authority.

Logan looked at him carefully. "What news?"

"Roberts is dead. Somebody killed him when he tried to git Dowd. It wasn't Dowd. Range folks figger it was Finn Mahone. Dowd ain't talkin'. Mahone must've spotted Roberts an' trailed him down. Anyway, he got two slugs through the heart."

Logan scowled. He had been depending on Roberts to do another job for him, too. A job on a man much closer, and eventually more dangerous than Texas Dowd.

"Anything else?"

"Yeah, Cobb went over to that paper an' pistol-whipped Armstrong last night. That was my order. Then he went into the eatin' house, an' Mahone was there."

"Mahone? In town?" Pierce Logan was incredulous. "Where were you?"

"I was busy. I can't be everywhere!" Sonntag growled. "Anyway, Ringer wanted him, an' he went after him."

"Yes?" Logan leaned forward, eagerly.

"An' nothin' happened. Mahone made a fool out of him. Bluffed him out of it. Told him to set down an' have some coffee, an' if he drew a gun he'd kill him. Ringer sat down an' drank the coffee!"

"The devil!" Logan got up angrily. "Only two men blocking this thing and your men muff both of them! I tell you, Sonntag, those men **have** to be out of this!"

"Don't get riled up," Sonntag replied deliberately. "We'll take care of them. Anyway," he added, "it's all in the open now, anyway. That girl of Kastelle's spilled the whole thing. Started people thinkin'. I knowed it was too plain—you could fool 'em only so long as they didn't know there was any rustlin' goin' on."

"Get Dowd and Mahone out of the picture, and I don't care how wild you go," Logan said. "I mean that. You can run off every cow on the range!"

Sonntag sat up and his eyes gleamed suddenly. "Say! That's all right! The boys would like that!" He looked up at Logan who was pacing the floor. "By the way, Mahone was over to Rico. He promised Ed Wheeling a shipment of cattle."

"Good! That's the only good news you've given me! Get some altered brands among them, I don't care whose or how. Nobody will see them over here, anyway. All we want is the story of some funny brands!"

"Fine with me." Sonntag got up to go. "Got

any money? I gave Roberts three hundred out of my own pocket."

Logan hesitated, then drew out a billfold and handed over several bills.

"Better make it four hundred," Sonntag said. "I can use it!"

Pierce Logan looked up, but Sonntag wasn't even looking at him. Logan's eyes were ugly when he counted out the other hundred.

Sonntag was getting too big for his boots, Logan decided. Yet, he needed the man. Only Sonntag could keep the Rawhide bunch in line. Ringer Cobb's failure irritated him, and he got to his feet and paced the length of the office. He would have to do some of these jobs himself.

What had frightened Cobb? The man was reputedly dangerous, and he could sling a gun, but he had backed down cold for Mahone. Roberts was dead. That meant something would have to be done about Dowd immediately. Too bad they couldn't all do their jobs as neatly as he did. He, Pierce Logan, would do the job on Dowd, if necessary.

He turned and walked out of his office and down the street toward the Longhorn. Judge Collins sat on his step, tilted back against the wall. He waved casually at Logan. "Old fool!" Logan muttered. "I'll have all that self-importance out of him in a few days!"

Impatience was driving him, and he realized its danger. Yet inefficiency always irritated him, and he wanted this over and done with.

He saw a roan horse at the hitching rail, and Logan stared at it. What was James doing in town? There was plenty for him to do out on the range.

Logan pushed open the door and strode into the Longhorn. Nick looked up when he came in, and shoved his hat back. "Howdy," he said briefly.

"How are you, James?" Logan said. "Got a message for me?"

"No," James said, "only that I'm quittin'."

"Quitting?" Pierce Logan turned his head to look at Nick again. "Why?"

"No partic'lar reason. I never stay on one job too long. Sort of get off my feed if I do."

"Sorry to lose you." Logan poured a drink from the bottle. "Going to work right away?"

"Uh-huh." Nick's voice was elaborately casual. "For Finn Mahone." Logan put the bottle back on the bar. There might be more in this than was immediately apparent. Nick James was smart. Maybe he was too smart. "I see"—he lifted his drink—"but I didn't know Mahone used any hands?"

"Changed his mind, I guess."

The door pushed open and Texas Dowd walked into the room. With him was Van Brewster. "Where's Sonntag?"

Logan turned. "Haven't seen him. What's the trouble?"

"Plenty!" Dowd's eyes were chill. "Mex Roberts tried to dry-gulch me the other day. When I went through his pockets, I found nearly a hundred dollars. That's a lot of money for a range tramp. One o' the bills was stuck together with pink paper. Brewster here recognized it as one he lost in a poker game to Sonntag."

"Sonntag's the type who does his own killing," Logan suggested. "You're on the wrong track, Dowd."

"I'll make up my mind about that!" Dowd's voice was sharp. "If Sonntag hired Roberts to kill me, he did it on orders. I want to know whose orders!"

Logan almost asked him who he believed had given the orders when he caught himself. If he asked that question Dowd might give the right answer, and if he did, it would mean a shooting. This was neither the time nor the place for that.

"That's an angle I hadn't thought of. Sonntag's out on the range somewhere, and I imagine he'll be in town tonight."

"All right." Dowd turned abruptly. "Then tell him I want to see him. If he's got an explanation, I want it!"

Dowd strode out and Logan poured another drink. He was jumpy. That damned fool

Sonntag! Why did he have to use a marked bill? This whole thing was going to bust wide open, and unless he was mistaken, Sonntag was down at Lettie Mason's right now.

Pierce Logan returned to his office and seated himself at his desk. Abe McInnis was down in bed and in no shape for anything. Van Brewster was a hotheaded fool. Remy Kastelle was a mere girl, and her father a lazy ex-gambler who would rather read books than work. Judge Collins was too old, and Finerty was not a gunfighter. Dean Armstrong could be taken care of at leisure.

It all boiled down to two men, and it always came back to them, to Dowd and Mahone. Dan Taggart, the foreman at the Spur, was rough and ready and a fighter if he ever made up his mind, but that was a process that ran as slow as molasses in January. There were only a few moves left; Logan just had to make those moves pay off.

It was time he rode out to the Lazy K and had a talk with Remy. Once they were married, he could have Dowd discharged, and the man would leave the range—if Sonntag didn't kill him first. The time for waiting had passed, but definitely.

Pierce Logan went to his stable and threw a saddle on his horse. As he rode out of town, he saw a horseman far ahead. It was Nick James, on his way to the Notch.

★ ★ ★

FAR AHEAD of Pierce Logan and already on Lazy K range, Banty Hull, Frank Salter, and Montana Kerr rode side by side. They had their orders from Sonntag, and immediately they moved out. They were after a bunch of Lazy K cattle. At the same time, far to the north and east of them, Ike Hibby, Alcorn, Leibman, and Ringer Cobb were moving down on one of Brewster's small herds. With two hundred head, they started for Rawhide. This was no matter of altering brands, it was an outright, daylight steal.

Montana Kerr saw the rider first, and jerked his head at him. "Who the hell is that?"

Hull rode up a little, peering under his pulled-down hat brim. "Looks like Dan Taggart. Headed for the Lazy K, I reckon."

"He's seen us."

"Yeah." Montana's voice was flat. "I never liked him anyway."

Taggart's route intersected theirs within two miles. He glanced from one to the other, and his heart began to pound. He had never seen Rawhide riders on this range before. Something in their eyes warned him, but Dan Taggart was not the man to back up, and even had he been, he would not have had a chance.

"Howdy, boys." His eyes shifted from one to

the other. Their faces were all grim, hostile. Some sixth sense told him what was coming. "What's up?"

"Your number," Hull said.

"Huh?" Taggart knew he was no match for these men. If he could get some cover, with his rifle, he might . . . but there was no chance of that. It was here and now. "You boys off your range, ain't you?"

"This is all our range," Salter said harshly. "Startin' t'day."

"I reckon other folks'll disagree," Taggart said. "Tex Dowd for instance."

"Dowd!" Salter spat the word. "I reckon I know him. I know him from Missouri, and I'd like t'hang his hide on a fence!"

Taggart shrugged. "Your business," he told them. "You boys go your way, an' I'll go mine. I reckon I'll be ridin' on."

He had his hand in his lap, only inches from his gun, but he knew Montana Kerr, knew the man was a killer, and knew that even leaving the others out, he wouldn't have a chance. He started his horse and rode on. For a moment, he thought he would get away with it. Then Kerr yelled at him.

Dan Taggart turned in his saddle and Kerr's hand flashed with incredible speed. Taggart grabbed for his gun, but two slugs hit him and he went down, hitting the ground in a heap, and dead before he hit it.

All three men emptied their guns into his body. "That'll be a lesson to 'em!" Salter's face was vicious as he spoke. "No use to botch the job like we did on McInnis."

They swung wide and headed around the Lazy K, driving cattle ahead of them.

Behind them Dan Taggart lay sprawled in the thin prairie grass, his shirt darkly stained with blood, and the grass beneath him red. His gun was still in its worn holster.

His horse, after running away when Taggart's body fell from it, watched the three riders trot their horses from the scene of the killing. Curious, and lonely without its master, the cow horse walked back.

Taggart lay on the ground and the horse drew nearer. At the smell of blood, it shied violently, rolling its eyes, but impelled by a curiosity greater than its sense of danger, moved closer. The smell of blood was too much for it, and jerking its head away, it trotted off a little distance.

On the crest of a rise it stopped briefly, looking back. Then, turning away, it trotted toward home, pausing from time to time to crop a mouthful of grass.

## CHAPTER 6

Remy Kastelle sat on the cowhide-covered settee in the great, high-ceilinged living room of the Lazy K ranch house. The room as always was cool and still, and for this very reason she had always loved it. There was something of a cathedral hush in the great room, and the longer she lived in the house, the more she understood why her father had built the room so large.

Kastelle had put his book aside and was idly riffling a deck of cards through his fingers. He had never cared for his onetime profession, and had no longing to return to it. Yet his life had taught him the uncertainty of things if no more, and he felt the necessity of retaining all his old skill.

The silence in the big room was unbroken save for the ripple and snap of the cards. Kastelle shuffled the deck quickly, ran his thumb over the edges, and in a few rapid, easy movements, all apparently part of his shuffling, he had selected the proper cards and run up a couple of good hands.

He in-jogged the top card, took off the bottom and shuffled off, then, locating the break with a finger, he shuffled off again and with a neat throw had his stack on top. Then he cut the deck, shifted the cut back, and dealt the hands, three fives showing up in his imaginary opponent's hand, three jacks in his own.

From time to time he glanced at Remy, but said nothing. Her beauty always came to him with something of a shock. The fact that he had seen her grow from a long-legged, coltish girl, who lived only to ride, into a beautiful woman did nothing to detract from her beauty. Her mother had been lovely, and his own mother had been a beautiful woman, but neither of them could compare to the vivid loveliness that was his daughter.

He had never worried about her. Growing up beside him she had grown up singularly independent, choosing her own way always, and if guided by him, the guiding was so slight that neither of them were ever conscious of it.

Their relationship had always been more than that of father and daughter. They understood each other as people. She knew her father's pride in his appearance, his love of horses, his sensitive response to beauty. She knew what his life had been before he bought the first ranch back in Texas. She had never been ashamed that her father was a professional gambler. She knew what had led to it, and knew how he felt.

The war with Mexico had ended, and Kastelle, a major in the cavalry, had found himself discharged in a foreign country with no prospects except an agile mind and a willingness to embrace the future. He had no possessions other than the horse he rode and the clothes he wore. Gold had recently been discovered in the foothills of the California Sierras, and so like hundreds of other veterans he sold his horse and bought passage on a windjammer headed to San Francisco.

Within months the town was swarming with sailors, treasure seekers, merchants, mining speculators, and revolution plotters from Latin America. Many of them had money. Kastelle, from then on known as Frenchy, became a habitué of the cafés and gambling houses.

A skillful horseman and an excellent shot, he possessed only one other skill. He knew how to handle cards. Swiftly, in the months that followed, he learned more by applying his skill. For a professional gambler he possessed perfect equipment. Cold nerve, an unreadable face, skillful fingers, and a shy, scholarly manner that was deceptive. Best of all, he possessed no gambling instinct. He played cards to win.

A few years before the nation tore itself apart with the war against the Confederate States, Frenchy was briefly married. An outbreak of cholera carried off his young wife, along with thousands of others, and left him with a baby daughter to care for.

With no other attachments in his life, he was

with Remy much of the time. They talked a lot, and he made no attempt to spare her the details of his career. He told her of the men and women he met, sketching them coldly with words as an artist might with a brush. It was not long until all these people lived and breathed for her.

Remy's conception of what was right and wrong, or when men and women were at their best and worst, came entirely from these accounts of her father's. His instinct for people was almost infallible, and she acquired much of it, growing up with a precocious knowledge of the world and the facts of life such as few children ever have.

No matter what her troubles, she always turned to him, and she had never found him lacking in understanding. He rarely reproved her. A suggestion from him, or his unspoken approval or disapproval, was all she needed. Gradually, as she grew older, she came more and more to handle her own problems.

On this day, Kastelle sensed that something was troubling her. Remy was restless, uneasy. Several times he thought he detected tears in her eyes, but he was not certain.

Remy had attracted men to her from the time she was fourteen. She was accustomed to their interest, and she knew how to handle them. The men she met had rarely attracted or interested her. Dowd seemed like an uncle or a friend, and it wasn't until she met Pierce Logan that love and marriage entered her mind.

Tall, handsome, and an interesting conversationalist, he had gone riding with her several times, and she had entertained him at home a bit more. Occasionally, when in town, she had eaten with him at Ma Boyle's. He was exciting and fascinating, but she had never discussed him with her father, nor he with her. Always, she had been a little hesitant about bringing the matter up.

Then had come the morning she walked into Ma Boyle's and asked about the black stallion. She had lifted her eyes and found herself looking at Finn Mahone.

She never forgot that moment. She remembered how imperiously she had swept into the room, her riding crop in her hand, so filled with the picture of that magnificent black stallion that she could think of nothing else.

His calm assurance nettled her, and she was actually pleased when she thought Leibman would whip him. Only Dowd had as much assurance as that, and knowing Dowd's abilities, she had never been put off by his manner.

The fight in the street, the ride across those awful slides, and the night in the cabin, all had served to increase her interest. Carried away by the excitement of the ride across the slate, and by the necessity for getting somewhere, Remy had not fully realized that she was trapped, that she must stay alone in the cabin with him.

She was not too disturbed by it. She carried a .41 derringer that her father had given her, and would not have hesitated to use it. She fully expected to have to warn him away, and then he hadn't even come near her door. She had never decided whether she was pleased or angry about that.

Texas Dowd's disclosure of his reason for hating Mahone shocked her. She wanted to know if the picture of the beautiful woman that she had seen in Finn's bedroom had been Dowd's sister, but his dour and forbidding reaction denied any possibility of further talk.

His statement seemed utterly at variance with every conception she had formed of the character of Finn Mahone. Murder of any kind seemed beyond him, and murder of a woman was unthinkable. Killing, yes. Childhood familiarity with war and sudden death allowed her to accept that. To kill in defense was one thing, however; murder was another. Yet the statement had been made, and there was something in the flat finality of it that had her believing, even while she refused to admit to herself that it was true.

Staring out the door where the shadow of the porch cut a sharp line across the brightness of the morning, Remy tried to analyze her feelings for

Finn, and could find no answer. She was nineteen, a young lady by all the standards of her time, and her own mother had been married well before that age. Yet Remy had had no serious romantic dealings with boys or men. The idea of love, while always in her mind, had never become quite real to her.

Kastelle riffled his cards and waited. Sensitive to all the nuances of Remy's feelings, he knew she was going to talk to him, that she was troubled. It was the first time in almost two years that she had come to him with a problem, and the interval made the silence harder to break.

She picked up a book, then put it down. She got up and crossed to the fireplace and idly toed a stick back off the hearthstone. She looked out the door again, then back to him. "Did Dowd ever tell you about his sister being murdered?"

Kastelle nodded. "Why, yes, he did. It was a long time ago."

"Tell me about it."

He shrugged and put the cards aside. "There is very little I can tell you. Louisiana was in bad shape right then; the whole South was in a turmoil. Carpetbaggers were coming in, the freed slaves were wandering about, uncertain of what to do, and there were renegade soldiers from both armies on the loose.

"Riots and outbreaks were common in New

Orleans, houses were burned on plantations, and there was a lot of looting going on. More than one man decided it was a good chance to get rich, and they weren't all carpetbaggers by a long shot. Renegade southerners were just as bad in many cases.

"Dowd was living with his sister, who was about as old as you are now, on a farm just out of New Orleans. It had belonged to his uncle, and wasn't a large place, at all.

"It was on a bayou, and was quite lovely. He didn't tell me much about it, but it seems there was a friend living there with him, a chap he had met in Mexico right before the war. They had both fought in revolutions down there, and had become friends.

"Dowd went to New Orleans on business, and while he was gone one of those riots broke out, and he was overdue in getting home. When he did get back, his sister had been murdered. From what he said it was pretty ugly.

"He found a button in her hand that had come off a coat this friend was wearing, and the friend was nowhere around. The house had been thoroughly looted. Three men who lived nearby swore they saw the friend riding away on a horse, and he was, they said, bloody as could be.

"Dowd started after his friend, and swore he would kill him on sight. The chase followed clear to Mexico, and Dowd lost him there, was nearly killed by some old enemies, and returned to Texas. That was when I met him."

"He told me the friend was Finn Mahone," she said.

Kastelle looked at her quickly. Her eyes were wide and she was staring out the door.

So that was it! He had noticed how different Remy had been acting of late, and had wondered about it. He recalled, then, how Remy had stood up for Mahone at the Cattleman's meeting.

"I didn't know." Remy had grown up, he realized that with a pang. He had known she would, and had known that when she did, she would fall in love. Now it had to be with this man . . . a murderer.

"You've met Mahone?"

"Yes." Without taking her eyes from the door, she told all that had transpired. He listened attentively, and realized when she had finished that his pipe had gone out. He refilled and lit it.

Kastelle stared at the floor. He never knew what to say at a time like this because there simply wasn't anything he could say. He raised his eyes to look at Remy, and found she was gone. She had walked out of the room and he had not noticed.

He got up and walked to the door. Remy was walking dejectedly toward the corrals. Kastelle shook his head, unaware of any way he could help her except to listen and try to be a strong and stable presence.

Two cowhands were sitting on the steps of the bunkhouse, and one of them had a rifle across his knees. Kastelle walked down to them. They grinned as he came up.

"Howdy!" Jody Carson said. "Dowd told us to stick around today."

Kastelle nodded. He left the ranch business strictly up to the man from Texas. "Is he expecting trouble?"

"Yeah." Carson leaned his elbows on the top step. "Pete was crossin' the Laird trail yesterday an' run into Nick James. Nick's headin' for the Notch. He's goin' to work for Mahone."

"Mahone's hiring hands?"

"Uh-huh. Anyway, Nick said Mahone ran a blazer on Ringer Cobb in Ma Boyle's place an' made him back down. Story's all over town about Roberts tryin' to kill Dowd, too."

"Where's Marshal Miller?"

"Over to the McInnis place, waitin' for Abe to talk, I reckon." He sat up suddenly. "Hey! What's all this?"

They turned, and Kastelle's heart gave a leap. Texas Dowd was coming in with a body across a saddle. His face was hard. He reined in and swung down. "It's Dan Taggart," he said, "killed down on our south range."

Carson and Pete helped him remove the body

from the saddle, and they looked at it. Kastelle's eyes hardened as he looked. He had known and liked Taggart, as these men had. The man was literally riddled with holes.

Dowd's face was grim when he looked up. "This is the beginning," he said. "God knows where it'll end." He looked at Jody. "You an' Pete stick right here. Don't you get off this place on no account. An' watch for that Rawhide bunch!"

Jody Carson had his own opinion of the men from Rawhide. That opinion had been bolstered by what he'd heard from Nick James. His eyes found Dowd's. "Nick told Pete that Taggart was sorry he voted for Sonntag. He wanted to do something about it powerful bad."

"Maybe Sonntag done this?" Pete suggested.

Dowd shook his head. "No, this was more than one man. Sonntag wouldn't have wasted shots, either. I scouted around. There were three men, cutting north toward the Highbinders. Happened several hours ago, I reckon."

Dowd stared at the bloody, shot-up body, and his lips tightened. Yet he was thinking now of Finn. If only Mahone were riding with him! These men . . . they meant well, and they would try, but in the end they were not hard enough, not fast enough. Byrn Sonntag was a bear with lightning in his hands, and he had men like Frank Salter and Montana Kerr riding with him.

Getting that bunch would be a job for men to do, not boys. He stood there, lonely and bitter, remembering the time in Mexico that he and Mahone had been informed by a soldier sent out from town that they must bring themselves to the commandant at once.

They were carrying ten thousand dollars in gold, their payment for fighting. They well knew what would happen to their ten thousand if it ever got in the clutches of that commandant. Mahone had looked up, and he had said in that easy, tough voice of his, "Tell the commandant that Finn Mahone an' Tex Dowd are ridin' down the main street of his town, an' if he wants us, or our gold, tell him to come an' get us!"

And an hour later, after a leisurely meal, they had mounted up and ridden through the little Mexican town . . . and there was not a soul in sight.

Dowd knew he had to kill Mahone. Whenever he thought of that brutal murder, a tide of fierce anger rose within him. Yet somehow, something held him back. It was not only that he had not had the chance to meet Mahone since that time, nor was it that there was no way across the slides. Something in him refused to admit that what had happened had happened.

The dust of the same roads had pounded into their faces, and the powder smoke of the same battles had burned their nostrils. He shook his head, and looked up. He turned then and walked into the bunkhouse.

Resolutely, he put aside all thought of Mahone. There was planning to be done.

He had, as it was a slack time, just four hands on the ranch. With the Negro cook, and Kastelle and himself, there were seven. The cook was a tough man and loyal, but he was as old as Frenchy Kastelle and not in as good shape.

What was coming now was open warfare. He knew without further evidence that this was the beginning. Or rather, Roberts's shot at him had been the beginning. Had Mahone not killed Mexie Roberts, Dowd would be dead now. Abe McInnis was in bed, seriously wounded. Taggart killed. On top of that, if they had killed Dowd the range would have been open to do what they pleased.

He got up and paced the floor. Desperately, he needed someone to side him. This was no longer a lone-wolf job. He couldn't be everywhere, and there was still Sonntag. He was out on the range somewhere, and wherever he was, death would soon follow. Texas Dowd knew without doubt that Sonntag would be gunning for him, and that meant he had to kill Sonntag.

It would settle nothing. Someone else was behind this, someone who had ordered his death.

Mahone?

Dowd shook his head. Finn would do his own killing. Suddenly, he remembered he had two men out on the range. They were riding alone . . . and the killers of Taggart had been headed north!

He lunged from the house and ran for his horse. "Stay here!" he yelled at the men by the bunkhouse. He hit the saddle and was gone.

Frenchy Kastelle walked back into the house. Coolly, he got down from their rack his new Winchester '73 and the Sharps .50. Then he checked their loads and put them within easy reach of his hand. He went into his bedroom and got his .44 and belted it on.

Kastelle snapped to with a start. Remy! Where was **she**? He turned and stepped to the door and saw Jody Carson staring out over the range. "Where's Remy?" he called.

Jody ran around the corner of the bunkhouse and stared at the corral. "Her mare's gone!" he yelled. "She must've headed out."

Kastelle stood an instant in indecision. Carson's face was a picture of worry. "Gosh, Boss! I never give her a thought, we're so used to her comin' an' goin'!"

"I know," he said. He held himself still and tried to think where she could have gone. Perhaps just for a ride, to ride away her own doubts and bitterness. If so, she might have gone in any direction. Kastelle stood there, his mind curiously alert. He tried to think of everything, tried to decide what was best to do. "We would be foolish to look for her," he said finally. "We'll have to wait."

"Well, nobody's goin' to come up to her on that mare. That Roxie can outrun anything on this range, unless it's that black of Mahone's."

"Dowd's out now," Carson said, "an' Bovetas an' Rifenbark are still out there. I reckon Dowd figgered they might run into them Rawhide hands that killed Taggart."

Kastelle sat down on the porch, his Winchester close at his hand. Carson stood for a minute, waiting, then walked back to the bunkhouse. Pete Goodale looked up. "The boss wears those guns like he could use 'em," he said. "Never seen him wear one before."

The day drew along slowly, and the sun reached the meridian, then started its long slide toward the distant Rimrock, a high red bulwark against the green range.

TEXAS DOWD KEPT his horse at a canter to save it, and headed back up range. He saw few cattle, and this area had been covered with them a fortnight ago. His face drew down in hard lines. He had waited too long. He should have gone to

Rawhide and killed Sonntag. If Sonntag was gone, the rest of them would fall apart . . . but again he recalled his belief that behind Sonntag was another, unknown person.

He was almost to the edge of the Highbinders when he heard a faint yell. He reined in his horse and shaded his eyes against the glare of the sun. Someone was waving a hat. He jacked a shell into the chamber of his Winchester and rode ahead, his eyes studying the ground. When he got a little closer, a man got up out of the grass. It was Rifenbark.

"What happened?" Rif's head was bloody and he was limping.

"Three of them Rawhide hands. I seen 'em drivin' some cattle ahead, so I started down range. I was a ways off. Bovetas, he seen 'em before I did, an' he rode down on 'em."

Rifenbark's eyes were bleak. "They never give him a chance. I seen it, an' I also seen I wasn't goin' to do much good agin' three of 'em on a hoss. I hit dirt, an' when they got close enough, I opened up with my rifle.

"Never did no good, though. Never even winged one. They just waved at me an' rode on, then two of 'em circled back, an' one got in this here shot that cut my scalp. I shot again, but didn't get neither one, although I burned 'em up some."

"Where's your horse?"

"Yonder in them trees. I seen him movin' there a minute ago."

Dowd wheeled his horse and started for the trees. He would get Rif mounted, and then they would cut along toward Brewster's. They might come up with the herd again.

FAR AWAY to the east, two separate riders were headed toward Brewster's as toward the apex of a triangle. One of these was Remy Kastelle; the other was Pierce Logan.

Pierce Logan rode rapidly. He was heading for Rawhide, and he had a few plans he wanted to put into execution, and he was looking for a man to replace Mex Roberts. Despite himself, he was worried. He could think of no particular reason why he should be, although he had planned to have Dowd out of the way before things came to a head.

He had chosen Roberts to kill Sonntag when the time came, and now that chance was gone. If Sonntag were to be killed, he must find someone else . . . or do it himself. It might come to that.

A vast impatience lay upon him. Cool planning had been his best hand, but now movement had taken the place of thinking. He knew and approved of what the Rawhide crowd were doing today. Before nightfall, fear would be alive on the range. As long as he had the chance to place the blame on Mahone or his "gang" it would be all right . . . but that was touch and go so far, because they had not had a chance to mix any altered brands into the cattle he was selling.

Pierce Logan had ridden out of town after his meeting with Dowd, and he had stayed the night in a line shack on Brewster's range. He would stay out of sight as much as possible. At all costs, he wished to avoid being forced to show his colors.

He reached the Brewster ranch to find the house in flames and the stock driven off. There was no sign of anyone around the place. Yet he had scarcely ridden into the yard when he heard a low moan. He swung his horse, and his pistol flashed into his hand.

The groan sounded again, and he swung down and walked toward the barn. It had been left standing due to the amount of feed stored there, and some valuable saddles. Logan had been cold-blooded about that. "Might as well keep it, Byrn," he said dryly. "We can use that stuff, and the feed will be good for our horses."

"Logan?" Pierce turned his head to the voice and saw a hand wave feebly from under a pile of sacking. "Help!" The voice was weak.

In two strides he was beside the sacking and jerked it back. Van Brewster, his shirt covered with blood, lay on the barn floor. His lids fluttered and he tried to speak again. Coolly, Logan lifted his pistol. They'd botched the job, but he might as well finish it.

Then he heard a horse's hooves. Wheeling, he saw Remy Kastelle ride into the ranch yard on her white mare. Thrusting his gun into the holster, he called to her. "Come here! Brewster's hurt!"

Remy dismounted and ran to him. He took her elbow and showed her the wounded man. Then, cursing under his breath, he picked up a bucket and went for water while she unfastened the man's rough shirt. Van Brewster was badly wounded, she could see that at a glance. If he lived it would be more luck than anything they could do. If only they had Doc Finerty!

"Logan . . . started . . ." Brewster's mutter faded, then his eyes opened again, ". . . shoot me," he ended.

The words made no sense. Obviously he was delirious, and she thought no more of what he had said. An hour later, with the wounds bathed and bandaged from some supplies she carried in her saddlebags, she stood facing Logan.

"He can't be moved, Pierce." Her voice was worried. "I'm going to stay here with him. Why don't you ride for Doc? That horse of yours will get to him faster than anyone else."

"Leave me with him," Logan suggested. "Your mare is fast, and you'd be safer in town than here."

She hesitated. "No, I'll stay. Ever since this started I've been carrying a few things with me. If he should need help, I could give it to him. I'll be all right."

"Well . . ." He hesitated. She was here, alone. Why not now? In a few days . . . ? Then he told himself not to be a fool. He wanted the Lazy K. He could get a clearer title by marriage, and besides, she would be an asset. There was plenty of time. He told himself that coolly, while he avoided her glance. She was the loveliest girl he had ever seen. Only one had been nearly so beautiful.

"All right, I'll go. Be careful," he advised, "and stay out of sight." This would prevent him from going on to Rawhide, but that could wait. He would appear to be doing more good this way. Finerty would remember it, and Brewster, if he lived. Had Brewster seen him lift that pistol? He doubted it. Mounting, he waved good-bye and started the bay horse at a fast canter.

Remy looked after him, wondering about him again as she often had in these last few days. He sat his horse splendidly. He was a man a woman could be proud of. But . . .

She walked back to the barn and gathered more sacks to make Brewster more comfortable. Time and again she walked to the door, but it would be hours before Logan could return.

* * *

PIERCE LOGAN WAS in no hurry. He was going for Finerty, but he was hoping that Brewster would die before the doctor could reach him to help. Hurrying would only increase the chances for Brewster to live. Still, if he did live he would be ill for a long time, and by that time the whole trouble would be settled, one way or another.

Now that he was away from her, he was glad he had not molested Remy Kastelle. There was something about being alone with a woman like that that always fired him with some strange, burning desire. Yet, he could wait. All this, and her, would soon be his. Only three obstacles remained. Texas Dowd, the plan against Finn Mahone, and Byrn Sonntag.

The Rawhide gunman was his man, but he was too powerful a force for Logan to leave in the field. Sonntag had started changing Logan's policy when the Rawhide boys began their outright theft. Sonntag controlled the men doing the rustling. So Logan had no choice but to go along with it or be sidelined. As soon as the events in the Laird Valley came to a head, Logan and Sonntag were going to have to find out who was boss. Yet it was a simple choice . . . only one would be alive.

NORTH OF HIM the clans were gathering in Rawhide. Byrn Sonntag had been sitting at a table waiting for them. Montana Kerr came in, dusty from his long ride. Briefly, he reported. Sonntag fingered his glass. Dan Taggart was dead. That was good, for the man had fight in him. Bovetas was dead. That was unimportant, but it was another gun eliminated. Brewster was dead, or so the report came in. The Brewster and McInnis operations were out of the fight, and the bulk of their cattle were on the move. There remained only the Lazy K.

Logan was soft on hitting the Kastelle ranch. He had some plan of his own, for he had always told Sonntag to go easy. The reason he gave was the watchfulness of Texas Dowd, but Sonntag suspected it had more to do with the girl. The thought of Dowd irritated Sonntag. The man was good with a gun. But how good?

He knew Dowd slightly. Finn Mahone was still only a name to him, once or twice their trails had crossed, but always at a distance.

Ike Hibby, Ringer Cobb, Banty Hull, and the rest of them had ridden in from the range. The war was on, and the Rawhide riders had struck fast and hard.

He was not worried about Laird. Its citizens would have little effect outside the town. There would be resistance, but a resistance of spirit rather than physical power. Byrn Sonntag had nothing but contempt for resistance of the spirit. Such resistance is of avail only so long as one's enemy is aware of things of the spirit, and aware of public opinion. Sonntag knew that Logan wanted to keep the war bottled up in Laird Valley. Sonntag could see the advantage in that. Yet Pierce Logan disturbed him. Why, he couldn't say.

Logan, he was well aware, was in the clear. At no point was Logan obviously involved. His skirts were clean, and there was nothing for him to worry about if the plan failed. Sometimes Sonntag wondered if he needed Logan. Yet, he had to admit, he was better heeled now than any time in his life, fear of reprisals was almost non-existent, and it looked like his men were riding to complete dominance of the valley.

TEXAS DOWD, sided by Rifenbark, made a wide sweep of the Lazy K range. Mile by mile, bitterness welled up within him. The range had been swept of cattle. Back in the brakes there would be some, of course, but all those in sight had been driven off. Open war had been declared, and the attack was all to the advantage of the enemy.

Distant smoke warned him of fire at Brewster's, so the two rode on. When still some distance away, he recognized Remy's mare and put his horse to a gallop.

Remy ran from the barn to greet him. "It was the Rawhide bunch! If Logan and I hadn't got here—!"

Dowd's interruption was quick. "Logan here? Who got here first, you or him?"

"Why, he did . . . why?"

Dowd's face was expressionless. "Just wondering. This is a long ways from P Slash L range, and a long way from Laird."

"Surely you don't suspect Pierce?" Remy was incredulous.

"I suspect everybody!" Dowd replied shortly. "Hell's broke loose! Taggart's been murdered, an' so's Bovetas!"

Remy's face went white. Dan Taggart she knew well, and Bovie . . . why, he was one of their own boys! Tex went on to tell her about the missing cattle.

While Rif kept watch, Dowd swung down and went inside. Van Brewster was lying on the sacks, breathing hoarsely. His face was wet with sweat and he looked bad. Texas Dowd was familiar with the look of wounded men, and he wouldn't have given a plugged peso for the cattleman's chances.

Without saying anything further to Remy he walked outside. A study of the earth, where it wasn't packed too hard by sun and rain, showed him it was the same lot from Rawhide. The fact that Rawhide was not many miles away made him no happier. They were in no position to defend themselves if attacked. The barn was a flimsy structure, and outnumbered as they might be, there would be almost no chance for them.

That the Kastelle ranch was in the hands of few men was bad. Dowd was a practical fighting man, and he knew such a division of forces was often fatal. Now, when they lacked so much in strength and were encumbered by a dying man, it was infinitely worse. He made his decision quickly.

"Remy," he said, "get on your horse, and you and Rif head for the ranch. I'll stay with Brewster. There's nothing more you or anybody can do until the doctor comes."

Remy shook her head. "No, we'll stay. What if they come back?"

Dowd's face was like ice. "You'll do as I say, Remy. Never since you was a little girl have I given you an order. I'm givin' you one now! Your father's probably worried to death by now. He's alone with just the hands at the ranch, and that's the next place they'll hit. They've wrecked McInnis and Brewster. Believe me, if they tackle the ranch he'll need all the help he can get. You two start back, and don't loaf on the way."

An instant longer she hesitated, but there was a cold logic in what Dowd said. The ranch must not be lost, and their fighting power must be kept intact. "All right, I'll go."

She walked out and swung into the saddle.

Rifenbark hesitated, rubbing his grizzled jaw. "Gosh, Tex, I—"

"Get along," Dowd said. "I'll be all right."

When they had ridden away he stood there in front of the barn. Brewster's house was a heap of charred ruins, still smoking. The barn was a crude building of logs, but most of them were mere poles. It was nothing for defense. Nor was there a good spot around. If he was tackled here . . . well, he would have a damned slim chance. And Brewster could not be moved.

He hunted around until he found Brewster's rifle; luckily, it was in the scabbard on his saddle. With it was an ammunition belt. He brought it back into the barn, and then got some sacks and filled them with sand. These he piled against the wall. There were some grain-filled sacks, and he added them.

Twilight came, and then night. He sat back against the sacks and listened to the hoarse breathing of the wounded man. Outside, little stars of red twinkled and sparked among the black of the dying fire.

Pierce Logan had been here. Why? The thought got into his mind and stuck there. This part of the range held nothing for Logan. He had made no practice of visiting surrounding ranches. There was no reason for his being here, and the thought nettled Dowd. He liked to have a reason for things. He stared into the night, and then let his eyes shift to the ruins of the house.

At that moment he heard the sound of horses' hooves. He sat still, listening.

They were drawing nearer, coming from the direction of Rawhide, and there were a good-sized bunch of them. Texas Dowd got to his feet and walked to the door of the barn. He loosened his six-guns in their holsters and picked up a rifle. His gray eyes worked at the night, striving to see them when they first appeared.

They were talking. He distinguished a voice as the hard, nasal twang of Frank Salter. "You git that Brewster? Was he dead, Al?"

"You was here. Why didn't you look?" Alcorn demanded querulously. "Of course I killed him!"

Texas Dowd had no illusions, nor any compunctions when it came to fighting outlaws and killers. He lifted his rifle, leveled at the voice of Alcorn, and fired.

As though a bolt of lightning had struck among them, riders scattered in every direction, and several of them fired. Dowd saw the flame stab the night, but he was watching his target. Alcorn slid from his horse and fell loosely, heavily into the dust and lay still.

Tex dropped to the ground and lay quiet, listening to the shouting and swearing among the Rawhiders. Then several shots rang out and Dowd heard a bullet strike the log wall. He lay quiet, ignoring it. He had no intention of wasting ammunition on the night air.

He could hear their argument, for their voices carried in the clear, still air. "Like hell Brewster's dead! He got Al!"

"That wasn't him," Montana said. "Brewster might not of been dead, but he was far gone when I last seen him! Somebody else has moved in!"

The voices seemed to be centering around one group of trees, so Dowd lifted his rifle and fired four times, rapid fire. Curses rang out, then silence. He chuckled to himself. "That will make them more careful!" he said.

Texas Dowd settled down behind the sandbags. It was lighter out there, and he could see any movement if an attempt was made to cross the ranch yard. Beside him Brewster stirred, and when Dowd looked down he saw the man's face was gray and his breathing more labored. Van Brewster was going to die.

Dowd whispered to him, "Who shot you, Van?"

He was repeating the question a third time when Brewster's lips stirred. After a moment, the words came. "Bant . . . y Hull, Alcorn . . . an' them."

"I got Alcorn," Dowd told him. "I'll get Hull for you, too."

Brewster's eyes fought their way open and he

caught at Dowd's shirtfront. "Watch . . . Logan. He start . . . ed to shoot me."

Pierce Logan? Dowd's mind accepted the thought and turned it over. Logan, the innocent bystander, the man on the sidelines. Why not him?

OVER IN THE DARK BRUSH, Montana Kerr was growing irritable. "Let's rush the place! Let's dig him out of there, whoever he is!"

"Wait!" Hull suggested. "I have a better plan. We'll try fire!"

## CHAPTER 7

It was Pierce Logan himself, coming for Doc Finerty, who brought the first word of the range war to Laird. As Doc threw a few necessary articles into his saddlebags, Logan gave a brief account of what he wanted them to know. Brewster was badly wounded, perhaps dead, and his ranch house had been burned.

The second bit of news came from Nick James. He was almost at the opposite side of the Lazy K range, heading for the Notch, when he heard the shots fired by the rustlers at Bovetas and Rifenbark. Leaving his packhorse, he turned back, riding warily. So it was that he arrived at the Lazy K just in time to meet Remy as she returned from Brewster's.

Nick James headed for Laird on a fresh horse. His news, added to that brought by Logan, had the town on its ear. The cattle had been driven off the Lazy K and Brewster's spread in one sweep. Bovetas was dead. Taggart was dead. Brewster was wounded. Rifenbark had recognized the Rawhide crowd.

While the streets filled with talking, excited men, Finn Mahone rolled off the bed in the back of Ma Boyle's and pulled on his boots. There were voices in the hall and a sudden pounding on his door. Springing to his feet, gun in hand, he opened it wide. Lettie Mason was standing there.

"Finn!" she cried. "Come quickly! I've just found Otis and he's badly wounded. He's been lying out in the brush where he was left for dead. He wants to see you."

On the way to her place, Lettie told him the news. Finn's mind leaped over the gaps and saw the situation just as it was. Dowd had stayed at Brewster's with the dying man, so he would be there alone. A dangerous position if the rustlers came back. Finn was prepared to find Texas and explain himself. If his plan worked . . . At the thought of riding beside his old comrade again, his heart gave a leap.

Garfield Otis, his face gray and ghastly with

the proximity of death, was fully conscious when they came in. A messenger from Lettie had caught Finerty as he was leaving town. Logan had not been with him, for Pierce had no intention of returning to Brewster's. If Finerty was killed, it would be one more out of the way.

"Don't talk long," Finerty warned, "but it will do him good to get it off his chest, whatever it is!"

Otis put out a hand to stop Finerty from leaving, and then he whispered hoarsely, "Logan shot me . . . he's hand in glove with Sonntag. I've seen him talking with him, more than once. One time I was drunk an' seen . . . Logan kill a . . . man. He's . . . he's . . . buried on the hill back of the liv . . . ery stable. It's Sam . . . Hendry!"

"Hendry?" Finerty grabbed Finn's arm. "Logan must have bought the ranch from Hendry, then stole his money back. We figured Sam went off and blew it in, but he never got away! What do you know about that?"

"Old man Hendry was killed by a dry-gulcher," Lettie suggested. "Probably it was Mex Roberts, so maybe we can guess who hired him?"

"Looks like Logan, all right," Mahone admitted. "I think I'll have a talk with him."

"Finn," Lettie interrupted, "there's something else I'd better tell you. Pierce Logan came from New Orleans. I recognized him and I've heard him talk about it. He used another name then, Cashman . . . I don't remember the first name."

Mahone turned square around. "When did Logan first come into this country? About six months or so before I did?"

"Maybe a little less," Finerty said. He looked from Lettie to Finn. "You know something?"

Finn Mahone ignored the question, his heart racing. Pierce Logan was in town, but what was suddenly more imperative was seeing Texas Dowd. After all these years Finn found himself choosing friendship over vengeance. Now, more than ever, he had to see Dowd. The past could wait!

"Let's go, Doc!" he said. "I'm riding with you. Lettie, you said Nick had come back into town? Tell him to keep an eye on Pierce Logan. Not to get into any fight, just keep watch. I'm coming back for him!"

He saddled the black, grabbed up the gelding, and they headed out.

When they had come most of the way, Finn turned to Finerty. "Doc, I don't like the look of that glow in the sky! You come along as fast as you can."

The black stretched his legs. Finn, crouching forward, kept his attention focused tightly on riding, one hand on the reins, the other gripping the gelding's lead rope as lightly as he dared. He didn't want to lose the horse, especially now, but if it misstepped he would have to let go before he was jerked from the saddle. Finn's eyes were riveted on the glow against the night sky. If they had fired that old pole barn, Dowd would be finished.

After the horses had covered a couple of miles, he slowed them for a breather, and then let them out again. Now he could see the fire, and it was partly the glow from the burned house, and partly the flames from a huge haystack nearby, fired by the rustlers to give them a better shooting light.

Mahone slowed to a canter, and then to a walk. He unlimbered his rifle and moved closer, and when he did, he could see what the outlaws were about.

They had a hayrack piled high with hay, and they were shoving it toward the embattled defender of the barn, obviously planning to set it afire once it was against the pole side of the crude structure. Whether the barn burned or not—and it would—anyone inside would be baked by the awful heat.

Finn watched one of the dark figures moving, and then he lifted his rifle, took careful aim, and fired!

The man screamed and fell over on the ground, and the rustlers, shocked by the sudden attack, broke and ran for cover. Finn got in another shot as they ran, and saw a man stumble.

Dowd must be alive, for a rifle barked from the barn as the attackers fled.

Riding swiftly, Mahone rounded the ranch yard, keeping out of the glow of the fire, and then emptied his Winchester into the grove of trees where the outlaws had gone. Swiftly, and still moving, he reloaded his rifle and checked his six-guns.

Yet even as he moved in for another attack, he heard the gallop of fast-moving horses, and saw the dark band of rustlers sweep off across country. They had abandoned the field for the moment, and were probably headed for an attack upon the Lazy K. Finn rode close, then swung to the ground.

"Tex!" he yelled. "I want to talk, Tex! Peace talk!"

Dowd's voice rang loud over the firelit yard. "I've nothing to say to you, Mahone!"

"Tex, you're a damned, bullheaded fool!" Finn roared back at him. "You got what you thought was evidence and jumped to conclusions. I wasn't anywhere near the plantation when it happened!"

Silence held for several minutes, and then Dowd yelled back. "Is Finerty comin'? Brewster's in a bad way!"

"Be here in a minute. I'm coming in, Tex! You hold your fire!"

Leaving the stallion standing ground-hitched,

Finn walked out into the firelight. With quick, resolute steps he crossed the hard-packed earth toward the barn. Dowd, hatless, his face grimy, was waiting for him.

"The man who killed Honey is in Laird," Finn said, halting, "and I've got some proof."

Dowd's face did not change. Suspicion was still hard in every line of it. "Who?" he demanded.

"Pierce Logan."

"Logan?" Dowd took a step nearer. "What do you mean, Finn? How could that be?"

"I trailed him, Tex. I got home before you did, and I found her. She was still alive then, and she grabbed me. That's how she got that button. She gave me the name of the man, for he had come by the place before. When the riots started and the country was full of fighting and burning, he came back. He went crazy. . . . Well, I trailed him. I lost him, finally, in Rico.

"Now I hear Pierce Logan hit Rico and killed a man there about that time, and then came on over here. Lettie Mason can tell you that he's from New Orleans and the name he was using back then."

"You said Honey knew his name—what was it?"

"Cashman—remember? He was a renegade southerner who tied up with the carpetbaggers and some of the tough crowd around New

Orleans. He lived on the Vickers place a few miles west of you for a while."

Texas Dowd stared at Finn, his bitterness ebbing. This was the one man he had loved like a brother. "How do I know you're not lyin'?"

Finn whistled between pinched fingers. Fury trotted up into the firelight, the steel-dust gelding following. Dowd looked from the horses to Mahone, eyes narrowing.

"What's this?"

"Look closely. That's Vickers's gelding. You chased me quite a ways—did I take two horses?"

"No."

"The only time I ever saw Cashman, it was off across a field, and he'd borrowed that horse to go into town. When he fled, he stole it from Vickers. He left the horse in Santa Fe. I bought him a couple of months later." Finn examined Dowd. "I figured that someday I might get the chance to show him to you."

"I never seen Cashman. Heard of him, though."

"I'm told he's a bad man with a gun, Dowd."

"I'll find out." Dowd's expression was grim. His wind-darkened face was tight and still. Then he turned to Mahone. "Thanks for getting Roberts. He would have killed me sure."

"Ask Lettie, Tex. She can tell you his name, too."

"I'd like to believe all this."

"Then believe it."

Doc Finerty rode up and swung down. Tex wheeled and guided him to Van Brewster. Finn stared after Texas, and then a slow grin swept his face and he followed them until Tex looked up. "Dowd, let's leave Doc and go to Rawhide. Let's burn that rathole around their ears, just you and me."

Texas Dowd held himself thoughtfully for a moment, and then he grinned. "You always were one for raisin' hob," he said. "All right, let's go!"

The two riders covered the distance to Rawhide at a rapid gallop. Byrn Sonntag had ridden out a few minutes after the others had started back into Laird Valley, so except for a few of the followers of the Rawhide crowd, few people were around. As the two horsemen clattered down the street, a shot was fired from a window. Dowd wheeled, putting a bullet through it, and then sprang from his horse and went into the barroom. "Get out!" he said to the fat-faced bartender. "Get out and quick! I'm burnin' this place down!"

"Like hell!" The bartender swung and grabbed for his shotgun, but a bullet smashed his hand into a bloody wreck.

"Get out!" Dowd yelled. "You get the next one in your belly!"

The bartender scuttled for the door, and

Dowd kicked a heap of papers together and broke an oil lamp in them, then dropped a match. Down the street there was shooting, and he rode out to find Finn Mahone standing in the street with his Winchester in his hand. Finn looked up, a dark streak of soot along his jaw, and an angry red burn. "Someone damn near checked me out."

"You get him?"

"Right between the eyes."

The flames inside the saloon were eating at the floor now, and creeping along the bar. The frame buildings, dry as ancient parchment, would go up like tinder in a high wind.

Both men swung into their saddles, and lighting some sacks, raced from door to door, scattering the fire. The wind caught the flames, and in a matter of minutes the outlaw town was one great, roaring, crackling inferno. "That will kill a lot of rats!" Finn yelled above the sound of the flames. "Let's ride out of here!"

Away from the town, Finn glanced at the tall Texan. "It's like old times, Dowd!"

"Sure is." The Texan stared bleakly down the road. "I'm an awful fool, Finn."

"Forget it. How could you know any different? Honey had that button . . . and it was Logan, all right. It checks too close not to be him. My trail petered out in Rico, but I never knew much about Logan, and never paid much attention to him until the day I saw him on the street with Remy Kastelle."

They rode on, heading toward Laird. Neither of them were much worried about the Lazy K. Jody Carson, Rifenbark, and Pete Goodale were there, and aside from them there was the cook and Kastelle himself. As for Remy, she could handle a rifle better than most men.

The two rode on, side by side, looking toward the town of Laird. Texas Dowd eased himself in the saddle. "I want Logan," he said carefully.

"He's yours."

Doc Finerty was standing beside the pole barn when they rode up, and there was already a graying light in the east. "Van's in a bad way, but he's got a chance," Doc said. He glanced from one to the other. "Where you been?"

"We burned Rawhide," Finn said. "Now we're scalp-hunting. Dowd wants Logan."

"Logan! Well, you look out for Sonntag. He's dangerous, Finn. He's the worst of them all."

Mahone gestured at Brewster. "Would he make it to Laird in a buckboard?"

"He might," Doc said dubiously. "I've been studying about it. He would have better care there. Lettie, she'll take him in, and she's a good nurse, the best around here."

Finn got the buckboard from behind the pole barn and they roped a couple of horses and got them hitched. The ride to town was slow and careful, and as daylight came, the buckboard creaked to a stop outside of Lettie Mason's. Finn rounded the stallion and faced down the street. There was no one in sight, for it was barely rising time for the people of Laird. Smoke was beginning to lift from a couple of chimneys.

When Brewster was inside in the care of Lettie, and Doc was sitting over coffee, Finn and Dowd walked outside. "Nick James was to keep an eye on him. Let's walk up to Ma Boyle's."

Laird was quiet in the early morning light, and the dusty street was very still. Somewhere a door slammed, and then a pump began to creak, and afterward they heard a heavy stream of water gushing into a wooden bucket.

The two men walked up the street, then stepped on the boardwalk. Suddenly, Finn saw that the saloon was open. He pushed through the doors. Red Eason looked up, his face growing suddenly still, watchful as he saw who his visitors were.

"Two, and make them both rye," Finn said.

Red poured the drinks and put the bottle on the bar. He glanced from one to the other, and he swallowed. He laid his hands on the bar in plain sight.

"Nice in California, Red," Mahone said suddenly. "You'll enjoy it there."

"Listen," Red Eason said quickly, "I never made any trouble for you fellows. I can't leave.

I . . ." His voice dwindled away as they both looked at him.

"Red"—Finn leaned his forearms on the bar—"I like this town. I feel at home here. Dowd likes it, too. We've some mighty fine folks around here, and we want to see the town clean and keep it a nice place for people to live. Not like that Rawhide. If this place got as bad as Rawhide, we might have to burn it, **too**."

"We don't want to do that," Dowd said gently, "so Finn and me, we sort of decided to weed out the undesirable elements, as they say. We sort of figure you come under that particular handle."

Eason's face was stiff. He was frightened, but there was still fight in him. "You can't get away with it!" His voice was thick. "Pierce won't stand for it!"

"Don't call him that, Red," Finn said. "Call him Cashman. That's what Dowd's going to call him when he sees him. Cashman's the name of a murderer. The murderer of Tex's sister. He killed Sam Hendry, too. Had him drunk and then killed him and buried him out back of the livery stable. Otis saw it."

Both men tossed off their drinks, then turned toward the doors. At the doors, Finn looked back. "It's nice in California, Red. You should be able to get a lot of miles between you and here before sundown . . . if you start now!"

Ma Boyle was bustling about, putting food on

the table and pouring coffee when the two men walked in the door together. Judge Collins looked up, smiling. “How are you, Finn? Hello, Dowd!”

“We brought Brewster to town,” Mahone said. “He may pull through. Logan started to kill him when he found him dying. Remy got there and scared Logan off.”

Powis was at the table, staring at them, his eyes large.

“Logan, was it?” Collins avoided looking at Powis, and although he was disgusted with himself for it, he felt a little glow of satisfaction that Powis was there to hear it, for the man’s abject worship of authority and the power of Pierce Logan had always irritated him.

“Seen the Rawhide bunch?”

“Alcorn’s dead. So is Ike Hibby. They attacked Dowd at Brewster’s place. The rest of them are off on the range, somewhere.”

“You won’t have to worry about Rawhide,” Texas drawled. “It ain’t there anymore.”

The door pushed open suddenly, and Nick James came in. He glanced quickly from Dowd to Mahone. “Finn,” he said quickly, “Pierce Logan’s stayed close to his place all night. He’s getting ready to come out.”

“Thanks.” Mahone glanced over at Texas Dowd. “All right,” he said, “are you going to take him or am I?”

Dowd turned. "I am."

Powis put his cup down. It rattled nervously in his saucer. He pushed back in his chair and cleared his throat. "Well," he said, simulating heartiness, "time I got to work."

"Sit down, Powis." Gardner Collins looked less the judge and more the cowhand and cattleman at that moment. "You stay right here. Dowd will tell Logan he wants him."

Texas turned his eyes toward the barber, and the man's face paled. Finn lifted his cup. "He's a friend of Logan's?"

"Sort of," Collins agreed. "Seems to think he's king."

"Well," Finn said, "times are changing around here." He put his cup down. "Powis, Red Eason is headin' for California and expects to make a lot of distance before sundown. He might like a traveling companion."

The barber stared from one to the other. "But my business!" he protested. "Everything I've got is here!"

Finn Mahone looked at him levelly. "You don't need anything you can't carry. Start traveling."

Nick James had been standing by the window, holding the cup of coffee he had poured. "Logan just came out," he said.

Dowd finished his cup, and got to his feet.

"Ma," he said, "that sure is good coffee." The sound of his boot heels echoed on the floor.

They sat very still, and the slam of the screen door made them all jump a little.

PIERCE LOGAN WAS CROSSING the street to Ma Boyle's when a door slammed, and he looked up. Texas Dowd, tall in his blue jeans and gray shirt, was standing on the step in front of Ma Boyle's. Instantly, Logan was apprehensive, for there was something in Dowd's whole appearance that warned him of trouble.

As he stood there on the step before his office, looking diagonally across the street at Texas Dowd, a peculiar awareness of life came over him. Somehow, he had never seemed to think of the sun's easy warmth, the gray dust in the street, the worn, sun-warped, and wind-battered frame buildings. He had never thought much of the signs along the streets of Laird, their paint cracked and old. Now, he seemed aware of them all, but mostly he was aware of the tall, still figure standing over there, looking up the street at him.

Then, the feeling passed. After all, there was no way his part in all this could be known. He was simply getting jumpy, that was all. He was being foolish. After he had his morning coffee, he would feel better. Why should just the appearance of Dowd startle him so?

"Cashman!"

The voice rang like a great bell in the silent, empty street, and Logan jerked as though stabbed.

"Cashman! Start remembering before I kill you! Start remembering a girl on a plantation in Louisiana! That girl was my sister!"

Pierce Logan stood very still. This alone he had not expected. This past was over. It was gone. That girl . . . Dowd's **sister**? He shook his head suddenly, remembering that awful, bloody afternoon. His lips tightened and a kind of panic came over him, but he stiffened suddenly. That finished it, then. It finished it all, unless he could kill Dowd. His hand flashed for a gun and he drew in a single, sweeping movement, and fired as his gun came level.

His face gray, he crouched in the street, knowing he had missed, and the tall Texan in the gray shirt walked toward him, his long lantern jaw and his face very still, only his cold gray eyes level and hard. In a surge of panic, Logan fired two quick shots. One of them kicked up dust at Dowd's feet, and the other plucked at his sleeve.

Texas Dowd stopped, no more than a dozen feet away, and fired. The sound of his gun was like the roll of a drum, and at each shot, Logan jerked as if struck by a fist. Then, slowly, he sank to the dust, the pistol dribbling from his fingers.

Feeding shells into his gun, Texas Dowd

backed slowly away from the fallen man, then turned and walked back to Ma Boyle's. Judge Gardner Collins cleared his throat as Dowd came in, and Finn Mahone poured a fresh cup of coffee. At no time had he risen from the table. He didn't have to. He knew Dowd.

## CHAPTER 8

Finn Mahone and Texas Dowd reached the Lazy K, riding slowly for the last few miles. Both men rode with rifles ready, uncertain as to whether they would find the ranch safe, or besieged. As they drew near, the two men let a gap widen between them and rode warily up to the ranch. Jody Carson was the first person they saw.

"Howdy," he said, grinning at them. "You two missed the fun."

"We had some our ownselves. What happened here?"

"That Rawhide bunch bit off more'n they could chew. Montana Kerr, Ringer Cobb, Banty Hull, and Leibman rode in here this mornin' about sunup. They were loaded for bear an' looked plumb salty, an' I reckon they was."

"Was?"

"That's what I said." Jody put a hand on Finn's saddle horn. "You know, I never rightly had the boss figured. He lazed around up there to the house, takin' it easy, an' lettin' Texas here an' Remy run the whole shebang, but when we heard the place was liable to be attacked, he r'ared up on his hind legs, strapped on some guns, an' then he told us what was what.

"Well, sir! You should have seen them hard-cases. They rode in here big as life an' tough as all get-out. You could see it stickin' out all over them. They was just a-takin' this here spread over, an' right now. Dowd was gone, an' he was the salty one of the crowd, they reckoned. Well, I reckoned so, too.

"When they rode up they swung down and started for the house, but the boss, he stepped out on the porch. 'Howdy, boys,' he says, big as life an' slick as a whistle, 'lookin' for somethin'?'

" 'Well, I reckon!' Kerr tells him, 'we've come to take over this here place, an' if you don't want no trouble, you stay the hell out of the way!'

" 'But s'posin' I want trouble?' the boss says, an' he says it so nice that they don't take him very serious.

" 'Don't you be foolish,' Kerr says, 'you can come out of this alive if you're smart!'

" 'That's what I was fixin' to tell you,' Kastelle says, 'you boys crawl back in those saddles an' light out of here, an' you can go your way. We'll just make like it never happened,' he says.

"Montana, he still can't figure Frenchy

Kastelle makin' any fuss. Never guessed he was the fightin' type. He starts to say somethin' when Cobb opens his big face. 'Let's get 'em, Monty. Why stand here palaverin'?' Then he went for his gun. . . .

"It was a bad thing to do, Tex. Too bad them boys couldn't have lived long enough to know their mistake. I tell you, we had our orders, an' we were a-layin' there all set with our rifles an' shotguns. There was Pete, Rif, Wash, an' me, with Remy up to the house. Cobb, he reached, but he was a mite slow. The boss shot him so fast I didn't even know what happened. He'd told us aforetime. He says, 'If they ride off, let 'em go. If they fire one shot . . . wipe 'em out!'

"Mister, we wiped 'em! When Cobb went for his gun, the boss drilled him, an' then the whole passel of ours cut loose on 'em an' I don't think they ever knowed what hit 'em. They must have figured we was either gone, or so skeered we wouldn't fight none.

"Pete, he and Rif are out back now, diggin' graves for the lot of them."

"Anybody hurt?"

Jody chuckled. "Nary a one! They never had a chance! Hell, if this don't scare all the outlaws out of Laird Valley, they just ain't the smart folks we figure 'em for."

He looked up at Finn, then at Tex. "What happened to you-all?"

Dowd explained briefly about the fight at the Brewster ranch, the killing of Alcorn and Hibby, and the subsequent raid upon Rawhide and how it had been left in flames. Mahone went on from there to tell about the killing of Pierce Logan, and how Eason and Powis had left town.

Carson chuckled. "Well, now! Ain't that somethin'? This will sure make believers out of those bad hombres! This will be a place to leave alone!" Suddenly, he frowned. "What about Sonntag?"

Mahone shrugged. "Neither Sonntag nor Frank Salter have shown up. Sonntag is plenty bad, and Salter is a fit partner for him. The two of them are poison, and while they may have left the range, I doubt it. They'll stick around."

Finn Mahone's eyes had been straying toward the ranch house. Finally, he shoved his hat back on his head, and his face flushed as he suggested, "I expect I'd better go up and tell Frenchy what happened."

Dowd chuckled. "Sure. You might tell Remy, too!"

As Finn trotted the stallion toward the house, he heard them both laughing at him, and he grinned in spite of himself.

Remy Kastelle came out the door as he mounted the steps. "Finn! Oh, it's you! And Tex is back! What happened?"

Frenchy had come into the doorway behind

her, and Mahone explained the situation as quickly as possible.

It was Remy who repeated the question. "What about Sonntag?"

"Neither he nor Salter have been heard from, but they may show up yet. I've got to get back to my place and move some cattle. Ed Wheeling over at Rico wants to buy some stock from me."

Hours later, on the road back to Crystal Valley, Finn Mahone rode swiftly. Nick James had left that morning and was to meet him at the Notch, and they would go on to the valley together. With James and Shoshone Charlie, he could manage the drive all right. Dowd had offered him a hand, but Mahone refused.

He said nothing to them of his worries, but he had his own ideas about what had become of Byrn Sonntag. The big redheaded gunman was probably in Rico. It would be like him to go there, for he knew the place and they knew him. Jim Hoff, the buyer of stolen cattle, was there; Sonntag would need money and he could sell some of the rustled cattle to Hoff.

THE FOLLOWING DAY, Finn Mahone pushed his own herd of cattle through the upper canyon of the Laird. He had his sale to make, and he had the sense that the last act of the Laird Valley cattle war was going to play itself out in Rico.

Finn knew there would be rustling and robbery in the Laird Valley as long as Byrn Sonntag and Frank Salter were at large. Now that he was no longer being set up to be a scapegoat, the rustlers would have no compunction about taking his cattle along with those of everyone else. Texas Dowd had said little, but Mahone knew that he felt the same.

Nick James rode by. Mopping sweat and dust from his brow, he grinned at Mahone. The white-faced cattle moved briskly ahead, bawling and frisking, occasionally stopping to crop disinterestedly at the sparse desert growth. Soon they were mounting the trail to the plateau on which Rico stood.

The scattered shacks that lay around Rico appeared, and then the stockyards. A couple of hands rode up and helped them to corral the stock. Finn left Shoshone Charlie and Nick James to drown their thirst, and headed for the Gold Spike to see Wheeling.

When the stock buyer saw him, he almost dropped his glass. "Mahone, you'd better be careful. Sonntag is in town selling cattle. If he sees you around, he'll think you've come after him."

"I wouldn't want to disappoint the man," Mahone commented, grimly.

"Well, that Salter is with him, and he's mean as a burro jack and that isn't all! Frenchy Kastelle hit town about noon, rode over from the ranch with his daughter and Texas Dowd. They're trying to figure out where their missing stock got to. Jim Hoff saw them, and I know he's said something to Sonntag."

Finn Mahone thought quickly. Byrn Sonntag would be trying to cash in on Logan's rustling scheme. He and Salter had hundreds, if not thousands, of stolen cattle to sell and that meant the stakes were high enough to kill for. If the Kastelle outfit was in town asking questions, there was a good chance they would run afoul of Sonntag and Salter. No doubt Remy's father was as fast as Carson had assured them, and surely Texas Dowd was as tough as they came, but in a match with a gunman of Sonntag's caliber anyone involved was bound to get hurt.

Mahone turned and walked swiftly to the door. He glanced sharply up and down the street, then pushed outside. Almost the first man he saw was Jim Hoff. The fat, sloppy buyer was coming up the boardwalk toward him, but when he saw Finn, he started to cross the street. "Hoff! Hold on a minute!"

Reluctantly, the man stopped, staring uneasily at Finn. "Where's Sonntag? Tell me, and quick!"

"I don't know," Hoff protested.

Mahone did not wait. He slapped the buyer of stolen stock across the mouth, hard enough to rattle his teeth. "Next time you get a pistol barrel! Where is he?"

"Down to his shack! An' I hope he kills you!"

Hoff pointed farther down the street to a tarpaper cabin half concealed by brush.

Shoshone Charlie had come out of the saloon. "Charlie," Finn said, "keep your eye on this hombre. If he makes a move toward a gun or to communicate with anybody, skin him alive."

The Indian moved nearer Hoff, and the cattle buyer backed away. The Indian might not be young, but he was wiry and tough, and his knife was good steel.

Nick James moved up. "What is it, Boss?"

"Sonntag and me, when I find him!"

Door by door, Finn worked down the street. Sonntag might be at the shack, but he might not be. Mahone also went down the street, only a glance was needed to tell him who was in each place he visited. When he stopped at the stock corrals, and stared down the road, he could see the dark frame shack where Sonntag lived when in Rico. It was an ugly place to approach.

The square little house stood on a mesquite-dotted lot with nothing near it but the crowded corrals and a small stable, not unlike the flimsy structure at the Brewster ranch.

The road approaching it was flat and offered no cover. He could wait until Sonntag started for town, but Finn was in no mood for waiting now. If Kastelle and Remy were in town there was every chance of them getting hurt, for the town was small, and Sonntag was not about to be thwarted at the last minute.

Finn stepped out from the corrals and started down the path, walking fast.

Ed Wheeling walked to the door of the Gold Spike and stared after Mahone, then stepped out on the boardwalk. Slowly, the word had swept the town. Finn Mahone was going after Sonntag and Salter.

Remy was in the general store when she heard it, and she straightened, feeling the blood drain from her face. She turned and started for the door. Her father, seeing her go, was startled by her face. He followed swiftly down the road.

The door of the square house opened, and Byrn Sonntag stepped out.

He had pulled the door closed behind him before he saw Finn Mahone. He squared around, staring at him to make sure he saw aright. Then, stepping carefully, he started toward him.

Neither man spoke.

Seventy feet apart, they halted, as at a signal. Finn Mahone felt a queer leaping excitement within him as he stared across the hot stretch of desert at Byrn Sonntag. Ever since he could recall wearing a gun, he seemed to have been hearing of Sonntag, and always his name had been spoken in awe.

Standing there, his features were frozen and hard now, and his eyes seemed to blaze with a white light.

Sweat trickled down Mahone's cheek. He could smell the sage, and the tarlike smell of creosote bush. The sun was very warm and the air was still. Somewhere, far off, a train whistled.

"Heard you're sellin' cattle, Sonntag."

"Just a few critters, here an' there."

"We may have to skin a few, check the brands."

"No, you're not. I'm goin' to kill you, Mahone."

Finn Mahone drew a deep breath. There was no way around this. "All right, when that train whistles again, Sonntag, you can have it."

They waited, and the silence hung heavy in the desert air. Salter was out there somewhere but Finn knew he couldn't fight both of them, so he put the old guerrilla out of his mind and focused on Sonntag. Sweat trickled down Mahone's brow, and he felt it along his body under his shirt, and then he saw the big gunman drop into a half crouch, his body tense with listening. When the whistle came, both men moved. In a blur of blinding speed, Finn Mahone saw Sonntag's gun sweeping up, saw flame stab toward him, and felt a hammer blow in his stomach, but his own gun was belching fire, and he was walking toward Sonntag, hammering bullets into the big redhead, one after another.

He went to his knees, and sweat came up into his face, and then his face was in the sand, and he looked up, still clutching his guns, then he dug his elbows into the sand, and dragged himself nearer.

Somewhere through the red haze before him he could hear the low bitter cursing of Sonntag, and he fired at the sound. The voice caught, and gagged, and then Finn got his feet under him, and swayed erect only to have his knees crumple under him. In a sitting position, he could see Sonntag down, but the man was not finished. Mahone triggered his gun, but it clicked on an empty chamber.

Sonntag fired, and the bullet plucked at Finn's trouser leg. Finn dug shells from his belt and began to feed them into the chambers of his six-gun. Off to his left there was a rattle of pistol fire and the dull boom of the Spencer that Frank Salter carried. Someone was helping Mahone out.

Sonntag was getting up, his thick shirt heavy with blood, his face half shot away. What enormous vitality forced the man to his feet, Mahone could never imagine, but there he was, big as a barn, seemingly indestructible.

Mahone got to his feet, and twenty feet apart

they stared at each other. Finn brought his gun up slowly.

"You're a good . . . man, Mahone," Sonntag said, "but I'll kill you an' live to spit on your grave!"

His own gun swung up swiftly, and blasted with flame, but the shot went wild, and Finn Mahone fired three times, slowly, methodically.

Sonntag staggered, and started to fall, then pitched over on his face. He squeezed off another shot, but it plowed a furrow in the sand.

It was awfully hot. Finn stared down at the fallen man, and felt his own gun slip from his fingers. He started to stoop to retrieve it, and the next thing he knew was the sound of singing in a low, lovely voice.

His lids fluttered back and he was lying on his back and Remy was bending over him. The singing stopped. "Oh, you're awake? Don't try to talk now, you must rest."

"How long have I been here?"

"A week tomorrow."

"A **week**? What happened to Sonntag?"

"He's dead. . . ."

"And Salter?"

"When you're better you can thank my father."

"I thought Sonntag was going to kill me," Finn said thoughtfully.

"Don't think about it now," Remy advised. "You'll be well soon."

He caught her hand. "I'll be going back to the valley, then. It's never been the same since that morning when you were waiting on the steps for me. I think you should come back, and stay."

"Why not?" Remy wrinkled her nose at him. "That's probably the only way I'll ever get that black stallion!"

He caught her with his good arm and pulled her close. "Wait! That's not the way a wounded man should act!" she protested.

Then their lips met, and she protested no longer.

## *The Moon of the Trees Broken by Snow*

Cold blew the winds along the canyon, moaning in the cedars, whining softly where the sagebrush grew. Their fire was small, and they huddled close, the firelight playing shadow games on the walls, the walls their grandfather's father built when he moved from the pit house atop the mesa to the great arch of the shallow cave.

"We must go," the boy said, "there is no more wood for burning, and the strength is gone from the earth. Our crops are thin, and when the snows have gone, the wild ones will come again, and they will kill us."

"It is so," his mother agreed. "One by one the others fled, and we are not enough to keep open the ditches that water our fields, nor to defend against the wild ones."

"Where will we go?" Small Sister asked.

They avoided looking at each other, their eyes hollow with fear, for they knew not where to go. Drought lay heavy upon the land, and from north, south, east, and west others had come seeking, no place seeming better than another. Was it not better to die here, where they had lived?

The boy was gaunt for each day he hunted farther afield and each day found less to hunt. Small Sister and his mother gathered brush or looted timbers from abandoned dwellings to keep their fires alight.

The Old One stirred and mumbled. "In my sleep I saw them," he muttered, "strange men sitting upon strange beasts."

"He is old," their mother said. "His thoughts wander."

How old he was they did not know. He had come out of the desert and they cared for him. None knew what manner of man he was, but it was said he talked to gods, and they with him.

"Strange men," he said, "with robes that glisten."

"How many men?" The boy asked without curiosity but because he knew that to live, an old one must be listened to and questioned sometimes.

"Three," the Old One said, "no more."

Firelight flickered on the parchment of his ancient face. "Sitting upon beasts," he repeated.

Sitting upon? What manner of beast? And why sit upon them? The boy went to a corner for an old timber. A hundred years ago it had been a tree; then part of a roof; now it was fuel.

They must leave or die, and it was better to die while doing than sitting. There was no corn left in the storage place. Even the rats were gone.

"When the light comes," the boy said, "we will go."

"What of the Old One? His limbs are weak."

"So are we all," the boy said. "Let him walk as far as he may."

"They followed the path," the Old One said, "a path where there was no path. They went where the light was."

On the third day their water was gone, but the boy knew of a seep. At the foot of the rocks he dug into the sand. When the sand grew damp, they held it against their brows, liking its coolness. Water seeped into the hollow, and one by one they drank.

They ate of the corn they carried, but some they must not eat. It would be seed for planting in the new place—if they found it.

During the night snow fell. They filled a water sack made of skin and started on.

With the morning the snow vanished. Here and there a few seeds still clung to the brush. Under an ironwood they rested, picking seed from the ground. They could be parched and eaten or ground into pinole. As they walked they did not cease from looking, and the Old One found many seeds, although his eyes were bad.

"Where do we go?" Small Sister asked.

"We go," the boy replied, but inside he felt cold shivers as when one eats too much of the prickly-pear fruit. He did not know where they went, and he was much afraid.

On the ninth day they ate the last of their corn but for that which must be kept for seed. Twice the boy snared ground squirrels, and three times he killed lizards. One day they stopped at a spring, gathering roots of a kind of wild potato that the people to the south called **iikof**. His mother and the Old One dug them from the flat below the spring.

Day after day they plodded onward, and the cold grew. It snowed again, and this time it did not go away. The Old One lagged farther and farther behind, and each day it took him longer to reach the fire.

The boy did not meet their eyes now, for they looked to him, and he had nothing to promise.

"There was a path of light," the Old One muttered. "They followed the path."

He drew his worn blanket about his thin shoulders. "It is the Moon of the Limbs of Trees Broken by Snow," he whispered, "that was the time."

"What time, Old One?" The boy tried to be patient.

"The time of the path. They followed the path."

"We have seen no path, Old One."

"The path was light. No man had walked where the path lay."

"Why, then, did they follow? Were they fools?"

"They followed the path because they heard and they believed."

"Heard what? Believed in what?"

"I do not know. It came while I slept. I do not know what they believed, only that they believed."

"I believe we are lost," Small Sister said.

The mother looked to the boy. He was the man, although but a small man, and alone. "In the morning we will go on," he said.

The Old One arose. "Come," he said. Wondering, the boy followed.

Out in the night they went, stopping where no firelight was. The Old One lifted his staff. "There!" he said. "There lies the path!"

"I see no path," the boy said, "only a star."

"The star is the path," the Old One said, "if you believe."

It was a bright star, hanging in the southern sky. The boy looked at it, and his lips trembled. He had but twelve summers. Yet he was the man, and he was afraid.

"The star is the path," the Old One said.

"How can one believe in a star?" the boy protested.

"You do not have to believe in the star. They

traveled for a reason. We travel for another. But you can believe in yourself, believe in the good you would do. The men of the star were long ago and not like us. It was only a dream."

The Old One went back to the fire and left the boy alone. They trusted him, and he did not trust himself. They had faith, and he had none. He led them into a wilderness—to what?

He had wandered, hoping. He had found nothing. He had longed, but the longing was empty. He found no place for planting, no food nor fuel.

He looked again. Was not that one star brighter than all the rest? Or did he only believe it so?

The Old One had said, "They followed a star."

He looked at the star. Then stepping back of a tall spear of yucca, he looked across it at the star. Then breaking off another spear, he set it in the sand and lined it up on the star so he would know the direction of the star when dawn came.

To lead them, he must believe. He would believe in the star.

When morning came, they took up their packs. Only the Old One sat withdrawn, unmoving. "It is enough," he said. "I can go no farther."

"You will come. You taught me to have faith; you, too, must have it."

Day followed day, and night followed night. Each night the boy lined up his star with a peak, a tree, or a rock. On three of the days they had no food, and two days were without water. They broke the spines from cactus and sucked on the pulp from the thick leaves.

Small Sister's feet were swollen and the flesh broken. "It is enough," his mother said. "We can go no farther."

They had come to a place where cottonwoods grew. He dug a hole in the streambed and found a little water. They soaked cottonwood leaves and bound them to Small Sister's feet. "In the morning," he said, "we will go on."

"I cannot," Small Sister said.

With dead branches from the cottonwoods he built a fire. They broiled the flesh of a terrapin found on the desert. Little though there was, they shared it.

The boy walked out in the darkness alone. He looked up and the star was there. "All right," he said.

When the light came, he shouldered his pack, and they looked at him. He turned to go, and one by one they followed. The Old One was the last to rise.

Now the land was broken by canyons. There was more cedar, occasionally a piñon. It snowed in the night, and the ground was covered, so they found only those seeds that still hung in their dry pods. They were very few.

Often they waited for the Old One. The walking was harder now, and the boy's heart grew small within him. At last they stopped to rest, and his mother looked at him: "It is no use. I cannot go on."

Small Sister said nothing and the Old One took a long time coming to where they waited.

"Do you stay then?" the boy said. "I will go on."

"If you do not come back?"

"Then you are better without me," he said. "If I can, I will come."

Out of their sight he sat down and put his head in his hands. He had failed them. The Old One's medicine had failed. Yet he knew he must try. Small though he was, he was the man. He walked on, his thoughts no longer clear. Once he fell, and again he caught himself on a rock before falling. He straightened, blinking to clear his vision.

On the sand before him was a track, the track of a deer. He walked on and saw other tracks, those of a raccoon, and the raccoon liked water. Not in two months had he seen the track of an animal. They led away down the canyon.

He went out on the rocks and caught himself abruptly, almost falling over the rim. It was a limestone sink, and it was filled with water. He took up a stone and dropped it, and it hit the pool and sank with a deep, rich, satisfying sound. The well was deep and wide, with a stream running from one side.

He went around the rim and lay down flat to drink of the stream. Something stirred near him, and he looked up quickly.

They were there: his mother, Small Sister, and the Old One. He stood up, very straight, and he said, "This is our place; we will stop here."

The boy killed a deer, and they ate. He wiped his fingers on his buckskin leggings and said, "Those who sat upon the beasts? What did they find, following their star?"

"A cave that smelled of animals where a baby lay on dry grass. The baby's father and mother were there, and some other men wearing skins, who stood by with bowed heads."

"And the shining ones who sat upon the beasts?"

"They knelt before the baby and offered it gifts."

"It is a strange story," the boy said, "and at another time I will listen to it again. Now we must think of planting."

# About Louis L'Amour

**"I think of myself in the oral tradition—as a troubadour, a village tale-teller, the man in the shadows of the campfire. That's the way I'd like to be remembered—as a storyteller. A good storyteller."**

It is doubtful that any author could be as at home in the world re-created in his novels as Louis Dearborn L'Amour. Not only could he physically fill the boots of the rugged characters he wrote about, but he literally "walked the land my characters walk." His personal experiences as well as his lifelong devotion to historical research combined to give Mr. L'Amour the unique knowledge and understanding of people, events, and the challenge of the American frontier that became the hallmarks of his popularity.

Of French-Irish descent, Mr. L'Amour could trace his own family in

North America back to the early 1600s and follow their steady progression westward, "always on the frontier." As a boy growing up in Jamestown, North Dakota, he absorbed all he could about his family's frontier heritage, including the story of his great-grandfather who was scalped by Sioux warriors.

Spurred by an eager curiosity and desire to broaden his horizons, Mr. L'Amour left home at the age of fifteen and enjoyed a wide variety of jobs, including seaman, lumberjack, elephant handler, skinner of dead cattle, and miner, and was an officer in the transportation corps during World War II. During his "yondering" days he also circled the world on a freighter, sailed a dhow on the Red Sea, was shipwrecked in the West Indies and stranded in the Mojave Desert. He won fifty-one of fifty-nine fights as a professional boxer and worked as a journalist and lecturer. He was a voracious reader and collector of rare books. His personal library contained 17,000 volumes.

Mr. L'Amour "wanted to write almost from the time I could talk." After developing a widespread following for his many frontier and adventure stories written for fiction magazines, Mr. L'Amour published his first full-length novel, Hondo, in the United States in 1953. Every one of his more than 120 books is in print; there are more than 270 million copies of his books in print worldwide, making him one of the bestselling authors in modern literary history. His books have been translated into twenty languages, and more than forty-five of his novels and stories have been made into feature films and television movies.

His hardcover bestsellers include The Lonesome Gods, The Walking Drum (his twelfth-century historical novel), Jubal Sackett, Last of the Breed, and The Haunted Mesa. His memoir, Education of a Wandering Man, was a leading bestseller in 1989. Audio dramatizations and adaptations of many L'Amour stories are available on cassette tapes from Bantam Audio Publishing.